Weird Tales™

Weird Tales™

EDITED BY MARVIN KAYE

WITH SARALEE KAYE

BARNES
& NOBLE
BOOKS
NEW YORK

Every effort has been made to acknowledge copyright owners of the stories
in this volume. Any new information pertaining to any tales included should
be forwarded to Marvin Kaye, c/o Nelson Doubleday Books, 245 Park Avenue,
New York, N.Y. 10167.

Thanks to Weird Tales Ltd. for permission to use the *Weird Tales* name, format
and logos, as well as the editorial, "Why *Weird Tales?*" Special thanks to Robert
Weinberg for his assistance.

The jacket painting is based on the story "Skulls in the Stars" by Robert E. Howard,
and is painted by Richard Kriegler.

1996 Barnes & Noble Books

ISBN 0-76070-118-0 *casebound*
ISBN 0-76070-294-2 *paperback*

Printed and bound in the United States of America

MC 9 8 7 6 5 4 3 2 1
MP 9 8 7 6 5 4 3 2 1

OPM

ACKNOWLEDGMENTS

"Mistress Sary" copyright © 1947 by *Weird Tales*. Copyright renewed 1975 by Philip Klass. Published by permission of the author and his agent, Virginia Kidd.

"The Bagheeta" copyright © 1930 by Popular Fiction Publishing Co. Reprinted by permission of Weird Tales Ltd.

"Ghost Hunt" copyright © 1961 by H. Russell Wakefield. Reprinted by permission of Arkham House Publishers, Inc.

"Funeral in the Fog" copyright © 1973 by *Weird Tales*. Reprinted by permission of the author.

"The Damp Man" copyright © 1947 by *Weird Tales*. Reprinted by permission of Weird Tales Ltd.

"Wet Straw" copyright © 1952 by *Weird Tales;* renewed 1980 by Richard Matheson. Reprinted by arrangement with Don Congdon Associates, Inc.

"Mysteries of the Faceless King" copyright © 1987 by Terminus Publishing Co., Inc. Reprinted by arrangement with the author.

"The Sorcerer's Apprentice" copyright © 1949 by *Weird Tales*. Copyright renewed 1977 by Robert Bloch. Reprinted by permission of Kirby McCauley, Ltd.

"Chicken Soup" copyright © 1983 by *Weird Tales*. Reprinted by arrangement with Katherine MacLean.

"He" copyright © 1965 by August Derleth. Reprinted by permission of Arkham House Publishers, Inc.

"The Brotherhood of Blood" copyright © 1932 by Popular Fiction Publishing Co. for *Weird Tales*, May 1932. Reprinted by permission of the author.

"The Weird of Avoosl Wuthoqquan" copyright © 1970 by Carolyn Smith Wakefield. Reprinted by permission of Arkham House Publishers, Inc.

"Men Who Walk Upon the Air" copyright © 1925 by Popular Fiction Publishing Co. for *Weird Tales*, May 1925. Copyright renewed 1953, 1981 by Frank Belknap Long. Reprinted by permission of Kirby McCauley, Ltd.

"The Perfect Host" copyright © 1948 by *Weird Tales*. Copyright renewed 1948 by Theodore Sturgeon. Reprinted by permission of Kirby McCauley, Ltd.

CONTENTS

THE EYRIE

All my life I have been fascinated with imaginative literature and cinema, first as a reader and filmgoer, later as a collector, currently as a fantasy writer, critic and anthologist. When I was a child growing up in a two-story house at the back of my father's radio repair shop in West Philadelphia, two factors shaped my early interest in the bizarre and supernatural. The first was the local motion picture theatre across the street; every Saturday afternoon Hollywood baby-sat me with obligatory rubber-stamped westerns that I very quickly grew bored with and (the good stuff) vintage horror movies like *The House of Frankenstein, Island of Lost Souls, Dracula's Daughter, The Body Snatcher, The Raven, The Lady and the Monster* (the only one that ever gave me nightmares, though the movie didn't scare me—it was the lobby poster, which, ironically, had nothing to do with the actual film plot).

The other determining factor was the frequent presence in our household of a magazine with lurid covers and ominously-titled contents: *Weird Tales.* I don't know who bought it, surely not my mother or siblings. It must have been my father, though I don't recall him ever actually reading a copy—and yet there it was, issue after issue, in our no-nonsense middle class home, a periodical that devoted its pages to stories about ghosts, ghouls, gnomes, murderers, monsters, vampires and mad scientists.

Two issues of "The Unique Magazine" (as it called itself) especially loom in my memory. Before them, I had made several abortive stabs at reading Bram Stoker's *Dracula,* but always got bogged down after the suspenseful conclusion of Chapter Four and never progressed any further. In fact, I never managed to finish reading anything on my own that I started, and it made me feel somehow inadequate. But in March, 1947, and again in September of the same year, I read three *Weird Tales* stories from first word to last and felt proud of the accomplishment. For the record, they were "Mr. George" by August Derleth, a beautifully-wrought ghost story that was the cover story for March and, from September 1947, a grisly neo-gothic, "The Pale Criminal" by C. Hall Thompson and a poignant lycanthropic love story, "Eena", by Manly Banister. (All three are included in this collection.)

As I grew up, I stayed in touch as often as I could with *Weird Tales,* though I seldom could afford the price of a copy. However, I did manage to pick up the September 1954 issue—by that time, it had shrunk from 9¾ inches × 6½ inches to digest size—not realizing it would be the last issue of The Unique Magazine to appear for the next nineteen years, but more about that later—the important thing I want to communicate is that no one but us misfits thought much of *Weird Tales* back then. Nowadays, the academics have caught up with the aficionados and what we always knew has at last become common knowledge: *Weird Tales* was—and hopefully, still will be—the most important periodical devoted to imaginative fiction in the history of American literature. No other serial publication, not even the venerable, excellent *The Magazine of Fantasy and Science Fiction,* has so consistently attracted, nurtured and developed such an impressive stable of genre writers, including, but by no means limited to some of the "stars" of the present volume: Robert Bloch, Anthony Boucher, Ray Bradbury, Fredric Brown, L. Sprague de Camp and Fletcher Pratt, Hugh B. Cave, August Derleth, Harry Houdini, Edward D. Hoch, Robert E. Howard, Tanith Lee, Fritz Leiber, Gaston Leroux, Maurice Level, Frank Belknap Long, H. P. Lovecraft, Richard Matheson, Seabury Quinn, Henry Slesar, Clark Ashton Smith, Jack Snow, Theodore Sturgeon, William Tenn and H. R. Wakefield.

While we're at it, let's name-drop a few of the other significant writers whose bylines have appeared in The Unique Magazine— Robert Aickman, Isaac Asimov, E. F. Benson, Algernon Blackwood, Nelson Bond, Joseph Payne Brennan, Ramsey Campbell, Mary Elizabeth Counselman, Miram Allen de Ford, Nictzin Dyalhis, Edmond Hamilton, Robert Heinlein, Carl Jacobi, David H. Keller, Henry Kuttner, Greye La Spina, Murray Leinster, Brian Lumley, John D. MacDonald, A. Merritt, C. L. Moore, Q. Patrick, H. Beam Piper, Joel Townsley Rogers, Sax Rohmer, Eric Frank Russell, Ray Russell, Margaret St. Clair, Vincent Starrett, William F. Temple, Evangeline Walton, Donald Wandrei, Manly Wade Wellman, Henry S. Whitehead, Tennessee Williams and Jack Williamson. This list is far from complete and does not even take into account the ongoing feature, Weird Tales Reprint, which brought to the readers famous tales by authors whose efforts predated the magazine. (There are six Weird Tales Reprints in this volume, as well as several other early stories collected by Sam Moskowitz in his 1973–74 *Weird Tales* revival issues).

How could *Weird Tales* attract such a steady stream of genre manuscripts from its loyal contributors? Surely not by generous payment—the magazine always had to struggle to stay in business—but by offering an ongoing market for a kind of literature that, though it has always been a significant aspect of world literature, was until comparatively recently decidedly unwelcome in twentieth-century America's fiction periodicals. (Why this was so, though beyond the scope of this article, is a problem I addressed in "Why Are Ghosts Coming Back to Life?", the introduction to *Ghosts,* Doubleday, 1981.) During much of its existence, *Weird Tales* boasted an unusually sympathetic editor, Farnsworth Wright, whose excellent taste and compassionate friendship wooed and held onto so many of that formidable roster of writers listed above. The ongoing policy of *Weird Tales* was authoritatively spelled out in the magazine's thirteenth issue of May/June/July 1924 (Vol. 4, No. 2), which featured an editorial entitled "Why Weird Tales?" (It is reprinted in full as Appendix I of this volume.)

Though this anthology is dedicated to the wonderful fiction that appeared in *Weird Tales,* it should be noted that the magazine was also renowned for the high calibre of its artwork, both interior and exterior. True, the eerie covers often featured semi-nude maidens whose relationship to the magazine's contents was remote, but they were generally well done, especially those drawn by Margaret Brundage. Other important *Weird Tales* artists were Hannes Bok, Lee Brown Coye, Harold DeLay, Bok-influenced Boris Dolgov, Virgil

Finlay, Matt Fox, Frank Kelly Freas, Pete Kuhlhoff, C. Barker Petrie Jr., Hugh Rankin, J. Allen St. John and A. R. Tilburne.

WEIRD TALES—THE MAGAZINE THAT NEVER DIES

The reason so many nudes appeared on the covers was to sell newsstand copies. (No, that's not why I never saw my Dad reading *Weird Tales;* by the 1940s, the emphasis of the artwork was decidedly tipped toward the macabre, rather than the titillative.) *Weird Tales* always had trouble staying alive. During its long, intermittent run from 1923 till the present, it has changed size, staff and physical headquarters; several times, it went out of business . . . only to return from the grave again and again. Here's a rundown of its principal incarnations:

In 1922, Jacob Clark Henneberger, a college man from Lancaster, Pennsylvania, and a partner, John M. Lansinger, formed a company, Rural Publications, Inc., which launched three magazines the following year, *Mystery Stories, Real Detective Tales* and *Weird Tales,* Vol. I, No. 1 of which appeared in March, 1923. It ran 192 pages, was 6 inches × 9 inches in size, cost twenty-five cents and featured two dozen stories, including one by mystery novelist Joel Townsley Rogers and contributions by Otis Adelbert Kline and Farnsworth Wright, both on the magazine's staff. Kline and Wright, a Chicago music critic, assisted editor Edwin Baird. Financial problems with *Weird Tales* developed swiftly, but Henneberger believed in it, sold other of his holdings to Lansinger and obtained all rights to *Weird Tales* for himself.

After a major reorganization and a technical hiatus—Vol. 4, No. 1 never was published—a revamped *Weird Tales* arrived on the newsstands in a special Anniversary Issue dated May/June/July 1924, containing thirty-five stories, two serial episodes, a Weird Crimes article by Seabury Quinn, the above mentioned "Why Weird Tales?" editorial and the department, "Ask Houdini." The issue measured 6½ inches × 9½ inches, sold for fifty cents and remained on sale for three months.

Henneberger offered the editorship of the reorganized periodical to his popular regular author H. P. Lovecraft, but Lovecraft declined. He had just married and his wife preferred remaining in Brooklyn, which sat well with Lovecraft, who hated the cold; accepting the editorship would have meant moving to Chicago. Henneberger next considered his own staff members for the editorship and asked his first reader, Farnsworth Wright, to assume control. Wright did so and more than anyone else turned *Weird Tales* into a great magazine.

Wright (1888–1940), a Californian of urbane tastes with a deep affection for people, contracted sleeping sickness during World War I. His health temporarily improved, but in 1921 the ailment returned in the form of Parkinson's disease, a condition that remained with Wright and worsened throughout his life. Nevertheless, he remained at the helm of *Weird Tales* until 1940 when another reorganization forced him to retire.

During the 1930s, the magazine's size fluctuated slightly and its page count varied from time to time, but all in all held fairly consistent at 128 pages, selling for a quarter. During one financial crisis, *Weird Tales* went bimonthly and in 1939 the cover price actually dropped to fifteen cents. But in late 1938, the publishers decided to retire, and the offices were relocated from Chicago to Rockefeller Center. Wright made the move to New York, but the new owner, a shoe manufacturer who wanted to diversify, decided to cut costs by firing Wright and appointing associate editor Dorothy McIlwraith to the top post. Ms. McIlwraith, also a capable editor, ran *Weird Tales* from May 1940 till September 1954, when it finally went out of business. The last few issues were printed in digest size and some of the contents were never copyrighted.

In 1973, publisher Leo Margulies—having bought the magazine's rights and title some time after it went out of business—resurrected *Weird Tales,* publishing four issues that were poorly distributed. (I found my copies at a newspaper store near the Wilkes-Barre, Pennsylvania, bus terminal; that's the *only* place I ever saw them on sale!) Sam Moskowitz, a distinguished historian-essayist of science-fantasy, edited these issues. Although much of the contents consisted of obscure reprints from sources other than the original magazine, it should be noted that most of Moskowitz's reprints were long unavailable and richly deserved exhumation. (For instance, see F. Marion Crawford's "The Dead Smile," included in the present volume.)

Seven years after the Margulies–Moskowitz revival folded, Zebra Books launched Vol. 48, No. 1 of *Weird Tales* in mass market paperback format. The editor, Lin Carter, put together four excellent issues that resurrected some interesting obscurities by H. P. Lovecraft and Robert E. Howard and also included a good deal of worthwhile new material by such prominent genre writers as Robert Aickman, Ray Bradbury, Tanith Lee, Brian Lumley, and others. Unfortunately, distribution was spotty. (There is an amusing, unconfirmed rumor that the second issue meant for Pennsylvania distribution was literally drop-shipped off a bus at a Keystone State crossroads, never to be seen again.) There were also author payment problems, though reportedly they were eventually amiably resolved by the publisher. The Zebra revival never really caught hold. The last issue printed was dated Summer 1983.

In 1984, yet another *Weird Tales* revival was attempted, the so-called (and infamous) California issues. News items in the trade press announced two different editors, each claiming to be *the* person to whom manuscripts should be submitted. Vol. 49, No. 1, dated Fall 1984, attributed its editorship to Gil Lamont. Its table of contents was distinguished by several fine writers, among them Robert Bloch, Ray Bradbury, Stephen King, Arch Oboler and Henry Slesar ("Speak," included in this volume), though many stories were reprints. Also included was the first installment of a lurid novella by A. E. van Vogt and Brinke Stevens, who was credited on the magazine's masthead as production executive. Subscriptions were solicited and accepted—and the checks cashed—but the magazines never were shipped.

In Winter 1985 a second California issue was published, this time with Mark Monsolo credited as fiction editor. The contents alternated between original stories and reprints, including tales by Robert Bloch, William F. Temple, A. E. van Vogt and others. Curiously, the second installment of the van Vogt–Brinke Stevens thriller, "The Pandora Principle," did not appear, but neither did Stevens' name on the masthead. Again, subscriptions were not filled. Soon afterward, Robert Weinberg, who, with others, now controls the *Weird Tales* title, logo, format, etc., took action and the California issues ended. Some canny dealers who bought up the extant issues sell them at high prices at science-fantasy conventions.

Near the end of 1987, *Weird Tales* came back to life yet again in what is surely the most tasteful and, hopefully, the most successful version since 1954. Terminus Publishing Co., Philadelphia, had its first new issue of The Unique Magazine on display at the October 1987 World Fantasy Convention in Nashville, Tennessee. Subscriptions are now being solicited—*and filled*. (For further details, see Appendix III, page 583.)

My criteria for selecting the contents of this *Weird Tales* anthology have been few and simple:

• I have included at least one story from every above-listed incarnation of the magazine.

• I have tried to include tales representative of as many authors, styles and moods as possible. In this regard, I resolved to use as many of the famous authors generally associated with the magazine as space and budget would permit, but as always, I have selected, whenever possible, less familiar tales over oft-collected warhorses. I have also dipped generously into the works of the more obscure *Weird Tales* writers. In some cases, I have chosen material a bit more "pulpish" than my taste normally would dictate. *Weird Tales,* after all, *was* a pulp magazine and had its share of second-rate filler . . . though sometimes this latter category holds pleasant surprises for patient readers.

• I always like to include weird poetry in my anthologies, but alas, I cannot work up much enthusiasm for the verse that ran in *Weird Tales. Mea culpa.*

• Each author is limited to a single selection.

But you and I have spent far too much time up front with this introduction. Turn the page and enjoy some delicious shivers—the Good Stuff awaits!

Marvin Kaye
New York City
December 1987

Next to Jack Benny, RAY BRADBURY (1920–   ) is surely the most famous celebrity to hail from Waukegan, Illinois. Author of many acclaimed works of fantasy and science fiction (among them *The Martian Chronicles, Fahrenheit 451, The Machineries of Joy, Something Wicked This Way Comes*), Bradbury may well be best remembered for his poignant novel *Dandelion Wine,* which is generally regarded as one of the finest evocations of childhood and lost innocence in American literature. In his early years, Bradbury contributed no fewer than twenty-five eerie stories to *Weird Tales.* (A poem also appeared in the Summer 1983 Zebra Books revival.) Most of them were reprinted in the rare Arkham House collection *Dark Carnival,* and some of them—but far from all—resurfaced in Bradbury's still-in-print collection *The October Country* (Ballantine Books). "Interim" was not included in the latter volume and has rarely been seen since its first *Weird Tales* publication in July 1947.

INTERIM

by Ray Bradbury

The rustle went through the land from one end to the other: and the land was not very large—being bounded on the east and west by poplars, sycamores and great oaks and shrubs, and held on north and south by wrought iron and mortared brick. From one end of this land to the other, shortly before dawn, the rustling traveled. One bird, about to sing, silenced itself, and there was a kind of dim pulsing and a whispering under the earth.

The coffins, each a womb for silent, stiffened contents, each deep, each separate, were being slowly and certainly beat upon. The lids and sides of the deep boxes gave off slow, even, muffled beats.

The earth bore each sound on and on. It started at one dark box and the code beat and beat, passing on to the next box where a new, tired dry hand would repeat the message slowly and tiredly. So it went, until the deep-buried ones all heard and slowly began to understand.

After a time it was like a great heart beating under the earth. The systolic murmuring continued as the sun readied itself beyond the horizon.

The bird upon the tree crooked its bead-eyed head, waiting.

The heart beat on.

"Mrs. Lattimore."

Slowly and painfully the beating spelled out the name.

(She was the one buried up on the north end, under the moss-tree, a year ago, just before the planned birth of her child, remember her? *so* pretty, she was!)

"Mrs. Lattimore."

The heartbeat pounded, dim and far under the compressed sod.

"Have," asked the heartbeat sluggishly. "You," asked the heartbeat tiredly. "Heard," it asked. "What," it asked. "Is happening," it continued. "To her?" it concluded.

The heartbeat paused dramatically. And the thousand cold contents of a thousand deep boxes waited for the answer to the slow, slow, beating question.

The sun hung just beyond the far blue hills. The stars shone coldly.

Then, evenly, quietly, slowly, beat after beat, systolic thudding upon thudding the answer to the question sounded. The land trembled with it, and repeated it, again and again, pounding and pounding away into a shocked and buried silence.

"Mrs. Lattimore."

The pulsing deep under.

"Will have."

Slowly, slowly.

"Her child today."

And then a quick, amazing staccato, as of a thousand hands battering the lids in questioning hysteria:

"What'll it possibly be like? How can this thing be? What will it resemble? Why? Why? Why!"

The pounding faded. The sun rose.

Deep under, as the bird sang, deep under the stone where Mrs Lattimore's name appeared, there was a scrabbling and a twisting and a strange sound from her buried, earthmoist box.

THE HOUSE OF ECSTASY

by Ralph Milne Farley

This actually happened to you. And when I say "you," I mean *you*—now reading these very words. For I know something about you—something deeply personal—something which, however, I am afraid that you have forgotten.

You're puzzled? You don't believe me? Read on, and I'll prove it to you—you'll see that I am right.

To begin with, where were you at eight o'clock on that warm evening of August 4 last summer?

You don't remember? Oh, but I hope you will, my friend. For, as you read on, you will realize the importance of remembering every detail of that eventful night.

The weather was warm and muggy. It made you restless in the house, until finally you went out for a little walk—down to the store at the corner to buy a package of cigarettes—to take the air. Nothing of importance, you thought.

A young fellow stopped you, asked for a light. Undoubtedly you have forgotten this too, for you are so often asked for a light. And in the dusk of that muggy evening there was nothing to stamp this young fellow as any different from hundreds of others.

You gave him a match; and as the match flared up in the darkness, you studied his clean-cut whimsical features. Rather attractive, he seemed to you.

You said to yourself, "Here is a man I'd like to know."

Then you lit your own cigarette, and noticed that the young fellow was studying you. You hoped that he too was favorably impressed by what he saw.

"Rather a warm night," he said in a pleasing voice, as he fell into step beside you.

So the two of you discussed the weather for a few moments, walking aimlessly along.

Having thus broken the ice, the stranger asked, "Are you doing anything this evening?"

Somehow this question put you on your guard. What was his racket, anyway? You glanced sharply at his face, at that moment illumined by a streetlight which the two of you were passing. But what you saw completely reassured you.

"No," you replied. "I'm not doing anything. Why?"

He laughed a bit embarrassedly. "Well, you see, there's a clever seer and mystic who lives just a couple of blocks from here. I was on my way to his house for a séance, when I met you. I'd feel a little less creepy if you'd come along."

It sounded intriguing. But——

"What does he charge?" you asked.

The young man laughed—a pleasant friendly laugh. "No charge at all," he replied. "A *real* mystic doesn't prostitute his weird abilities by making money out of them. Only charlatans do that!"

"Okay," you said, relieved that there was no fee. "I'll try anything once."

"Come on," he invited.

He led you to one of a block of identical three-story brownstone fronts—no one would ever have imagined what it held. A massive butler answered the door. He looked you suspiciously up and down; then stepping aside, he solemnly ushered you and your friend into a small reception room, where a hunchbacked dwarf of indefinable age arose to greet the two of you. His hairless yellow skin was stretched parchment-like over his skull. His eyes were quick-shifting, black and beady. His slit mouth leered, first at your companion and then at you.

"Well?" he asked in a high-pitched querulous voice, shifting his eyes back to your companion.

"Master," the young man replied, bowing stiffly, "here is the person whom you directed me to bring."

"You have done well, my pupil," quavered the dwarf, his hunched shoulders shaking slightly as at some concealed jest. "You may go."

Astonished and indignant, you turned quickly to confront your guide. But a subtle change seemed to have come over him. In the bright light of the reception room he did not look as pleasing as he had looked on the street.

His dark eyes were set at a decided slant. His black brows were thick and tufted. His ears, nose and chin were pointed. And his sleek black hair was brushed up on each side of his forehead into two little peaks, almost like twin horns.

"Why, you said——" you began indignantly.

"What I *said* is of no matter," he replied with a shrug and a nonchalant wave of one slender hand. Turning on his heel, he stalked out of the room.

You wheeled to follow him; but behind you a sharp voice croaked, "Stop!"

Invisible hands seemed to reach out from behind and turn you around, and march you back to the toad-like squatting Master.

He smiled a slitted grin, evidently intended to be ingratiating. "Why should you flee, my dear fellow?" he murmured. "I am about to do you a favor."

"But—but——" you began.

"Silence!" he snapped. His face was stern. His claw-like hands, on the ends of scrawny arms, reached out toward you in a fluttery gesture as he crooned, "Sleep! Sleep! You are in my power. You will do as I command. Sleep! Sleep!"

A delicious languor spread over you; and although your mind remained abnormally clear, all control over your own body gradually slipped from you.

The Master's parchment face relaxed into a friendly grin once more. "You are going to enjoy this," he croaked gleefully, rubbing his taloned hands together. "The ecstasy is going to be all yours. For, alas, my poor crumpled body cannot thrill to the pleasures of the flesh, except vicariously. So I have summoned you here, in the hope that a few crumbs may drop from the table of your enjoyment, for me to pick up."

"Yes, Master." The words came to your lips through no volition of your own.

The little dwarf grinned delightedly, and his hunched shoulders shook with suppressed chuckles. "This is going to be good!" he chortled. "Come. Follow me."

Like a sleepwalker, you followed him out of the little reception room, down the broad hall, up a flight of stairs, and into a large room with softly carpeted floor, and pictures and mirrors on the wall. The only article of furniture was a couch.

On that couch sat a beautiful young girl, clothed in a gown of some filmy blue material. Her skin was a creamy olive shade, her hair blue-black and lustrous, her face piquant and oval, her lips full and inviting and her figure slenderly mature.

But her eyes (so you noted) almost spoiled the picture. They were lusterless and dumb, like those of a stunned animal. You momentarily wondered if your own eyes were not the same. And, when she moved, she moved slowly, swimmingly, as in a slow-motion picture.

"Get up, my little dear," croaked the hunchback, rubbing his hands together and grinning with anticipation.

The girl arose, her sightless sleepwalking eyes on his penetrating ones. "Yes, Master." Her tones were flat and dead, and yet they carried the hint of a bell-like quality.

"Here is your partner, my little dear," he continued, with a leer, waving one skinny talon toward you, as you stood sheepishly, striving to free your paralyzed muscles from his hypnotic spell. "Stand up, my little dear."

"Yes, Master." She rose obediently and faced you.

Somehow, in spite of the dull animal look in her wide eyes, there was something intensely appealing about her. So young. So soft. So virginal. And so alone!

Fascinated, you stared and stared at this vision of loveliness. No longer did you strain to escape, for now your every effort was to break the Master's hypnotic spell, not so as to leap *away*, but rather so as to go *forward*.

As you ran your eyes appraisingly over every line and curve of her perfect figure, the girl mechanically seated herself on the couch, lifted up one shapely leg, crossed her knees, unlatched the slipper, and let it plop to the floor.

Its sudden sound seemed to shock the girl almost into consciousness. Her wide, unseeing eyes narrowed, and her expression became momentarily human—the one touch needed for complete perfection.

But only for a brief instant. Then the Master waved one taloned hand in her direction. "Sleep!" he crooned. "Sleep, my little dear. Sleep."

Her vacant stare returned. She unfastened and took off the other slipper.

The hunchback, grinning fatuously, held up one hand and said, "My little dear, that will be enough for the present." Then, turning to you, "All right, my boy. She is yours."

Released from your paralysis, although still under his spell, you stole slowly, eagerly forward. Your feet seemed planted in shifting sands. Interminable ages elapsed. Would you never reach her?

Behind you the cracked voice of the Master squeaked. "Welcome him, my little dear."

In response to this command, the girl held out her arms to you. A dumb eagerness suffused her piquant oval face. You in turn held out your arms to her with an intense yearning to clasp them tightly around her.

At last, after countless ages it seemed, you almost reached her, your fingertips met hers, just barely brushing them, and a tingling thrill swept through you. With one supreme effort, you leaped forward.

But an invisible hand seemed to clamp itself upon one of your shoulders, pulling you backward. And behind you sounded the croak of the Master, saying, "Bah! You are mere automatons! There is no vicarious pleasure to be had by me from such puppet amours as this!"

Then his invisible hand spun you around to face his toad-like leering features.

"Master!" you implored. "Master!"

His slant eyes narrowed, and his slit mouth broadened into a grin. "I am going to be kind to you," he announced, in his high-pitched, cracked voice. "To the two of you—and to myself. I shall remove my hypnotic spell, and then see if you two cannot react to each other like normal human beings."

He waved one taloned hand imperiously.

"Awake!" he croaked. "It is my command that you both awake."

The invisible hands upon your shoulders relaxed their hold. A shudder passed through you. You lifted up one hand and brushed the cobwebs from your eyes. You drew a deep breath. The sluggish shackles slipped off your mind and soul. You were free. Free!

Wheeling eagerly, you confronted the beautiful, olive-skinned girl. But now she drew away from you—her eyes, no longer dumb, now pools of horror. Her two little hands fluttered up in front of her, as if to ward you off. A dull red flush, commencing at the rounded hollow of her slim young throat, crept slowly up until it suffused her entire face as she cringed back against the couch.

And you—your eagerness to clasp her in your arms now changed to eagerness to protect her. You halted abruptly.

From behind you there came a cackling laugh and the words: "She does not seem to relish you, my friend. Well, I shall leave the two of you alone together for a while, until you and she become better acquainted. *Adios!*"

A door slammed and there was the sound of the turning of a key in the lock.

The girl was now seated on the edge of the couch, with one hand raised to her eyes to blot out the unwelcome sight of you.

But by now you were in complete command of yourself, once more a gentleman. "My dear young lady," you breathed, moving forward, "there's nothing to be afraid of. I want to help you; I want to be your friend. Trust me, and I'll try to get you out of here. That dwarf is a dangerous madman and we've got to forget everything except how to outwit him."

She smiled, and nodded. "I *do* trust you!" she exclaimed, rising and gripping your arm.

Hurriedly you made a circuit of all four walls of the room, carefully inspecting them. It was a room without a single window. There was only one door and that was of solid oak and locked.

"It is no use, Galahad," said the girl, in a rich liquid voice, but with a touch of mocking sadness. "The Master has us safely imprisoned and there's nothing we can do about it. Of course, when he is through with *you*, he will probably let *you* go. But I am to be kept here for good."

"I will come back with the police and raid the place and rescue you," you asserted.

She smiled sadly. "I wonder," she said.

"Why do you wonder?" you asked, surprised. "If that crazy dwarf is fool enough to let me loose, it ought to be a simple matter to come back here and break in."

"I wonder."

"Why do you keep saying, 'I wonder'?"

"Because other men have been brought here to me by the Master and they have promised, just as you are now promising. And yet none of them has ever come back."

"But *I* will."

"I wonder."

"Stop it!" you stormed. "Stop parrotting those words! I'm a gentleman and I keep my word. Besides I—er—I admire you very much," you continued lamely. "I've never seen a girl quite like you. *Of course* I'll come back!"

"The Master is a skilful hypnotist. Before he lets you go, he will hypnotize you into forgetting everything."

"He couldn't make a man forget *you!*"

"Yes, even me. Yet perhaps——"

"Perhaps what?"

"Perhaps—if you were to hold me in your arms——"

Eagerly you clasped her to you and covered her upturned flower-face with kisses until finally your lips met and she returned your passion in one soul-searing embrace.

As you released her, you exultantly exclaimed, "Now let the Master do his worst! I shall never forget that kiss!"

A cackling laugh echoed through the vacant reaches of the room.

Startled, you sprang to your feet; but there was no one in the room. No one except you yourself and the dark-haired, olive-skinned girl.

Again the cackling laugh. It seemed to come from everywhere—from nowhere.

"Where are you, Master?" you cried.

"Aha!" spoke his cracked voice out of the air. "I see that you have learned respect and that you address me by my proper title. And I thank you for a very pleasant evening; I enjoyed that kiss! You too ought to thank *me!*"

"I don't!" you stormed. "Let us out of here or I'll call the police! Where are you, anyway?"

"I am behind one of the mirrors in the wall," he croaked. "It is what is known in the glass trade as an X-ray mirror, that is to say, a transparent one. From *your* side you can see nothing but reflections, whereas from *my* side it is merely a slightly grayed window-pane. And so I have been able to enjoy vicariously your little moment of bliss."

"But your voice?" you asked, incredulous.

"I am talking into a microphone," croaked the invisible dwarf. "There are loudspeakers behind several of the pictures—And now I am coming in to join my two little playmates."

"If you enter this room, I shall wring your neck!" you raged.

"I rather think not," rasped his high-pitched voice, trailing off into nothingness.

You turned and placed one arm comfortingly around the shaken girl.

The key grated in the lock. The door opened. The repulsively leering hunchback came hopping in.

Now was your chance. With cool determination you charged across the room!

But, grinning unconcernedly, he held out one arm in your direction with the flat of his hand toward you. A mighty invisible blow smote you squarely in the chest, flinging you back upon the couch and upon the pathetic little figure there.

Making passes with his hands, the obscene frog-like Master approached you. "Sleep! Sleep!" he murmured. "Sleep, my friend."

Your veins filled with water and you slumped helplessly.

"Get up!" he commanded, not unkindly.

You arose.

"Follow me!"

Like a sleepwalker you followed.

Behind you there sounded the pleading voice of your sweetheart, imploring, "Oh, my lover, be sure and make a note of the number of this house when you leave it and come back and rescue me!"

Love is strong! In spite of the invisible hands which sought to restrain you, you turned and cried, "I will! I promise you!"

Her sweet eyes filled with gladness; then shot a glance toward the

Master, a glance filled with scorn for his thwarted powers, then back to you again, welling with perfect confidence.

"I believe you," she cried happily. "I shall be waiting."

Then you turned and followed the hunchback out of the room. Dazedly you were led to the street door.

On the threshold the Master transfixed you with his penetrating gaze and commanded incisively, "You will now forget all that has happened in this house of ecstasy this evening! Do you hear me? You will forget *all* that has happened! Go down the steps, turn to the right and walk away. When you reach the corner, you will awake. But you will remember nothing. Good-night, my friend, and I thank you for a very pleasant evening."

The door closed behind you.

Ringing in your ears was the insistent command of the wistful girl who had given you her love. "You must not forget! You must not forget."

Already you felt stronger and more free. The spell was beginning to lift. The vision of a piquant oval pleading face was before your eyes.

"I will not forget!" you stalwartly promised as you went down the steps. Then, before you turned to the right as commanded, you took careful note of the house number.

You returned from your walk that evening with a vague idea that something was wrong, a vague realization that you had been out of your house an hour or so longer than you could account for.

You consider yourself to be a man of your word, don't you? And yet you have never returned to the house of ecstasy to rescue that girl, although you solemnly promised her that you would.

I have now told you all that I myself know of the episode. But unfortunately I do not know the address of the house of ecstasy. You need that address. You have to have that address, if you are ever to rescue the girl who loved and trusted you.

Try hard, my friend, try hard.

Can't you remember? You *must* remember!

"The Stolen Body," a fascinating speculation upon the alleged dangers of out-of-body travel, ran in the November 1925 issue of *Weird Tales*. It was the first of three stories that the magazine published by H. G. WELLS (1866–1946), British author of *The War of the Worlds, The Island of Doctor Moreau, The Invisible Man, The Time Machine* and many other imaginative novels and short stories.

THE STOLEN BODY

by H. G. Wells

Mr. Bessel was the senior partner in the firm of Bessel, Hart, and Brown, of St. Paul's Churchyard, and for many years he was well known among those interested in psychical research as a liberal-minded and conscientious investigator. He was an unmarried man, and instead of living in the suburbs, after the fashion of his class, he occupied rooms in the Albany, near Piccadilly. He was particularly interested in the questions of thought transference and of apparitions of the living, and in November, 1896, he commenced a series of experiments in conjunction with Mr. Vincey, of Staple Inn, in order to test the alleged possibility of projecting an apparition of oneself by force of will through space.

Their experiments were conducted in the following manner: At a pre-arranged hour Mr. Bessel shut himself in one of his rooms in the Albany and Mr. Vincey in his sitting-room in Staple Inn, and each then fixed his mind as resolutely as possible on the other. Mr. Bessel had acquired the art of self-hypnotism, and, so far as he could, he attempted first to hypnotise himself and then to project himself as a "phantom of the living" across the intervening space of nearly two miles into Mr. Vincey's apartment. On several evenings this was tried without any satisfactory result, but on the fifth or sixth occasion Mr. Vincey did actually see or imagine he saw an apparition of Mr. Bessel standing in his room. He states that the appearance, although brief, was very vivid and real. He noticed that Mr. Bessel's face was white and his expression anxious, and, moreover, that his hair was disordered. For a moment Mr. Vincey, in spite of his state of expectation, was too surprised to speak or move, and in that moment it seemed to him as though the figure glanced over its shoulder and incontinently vanished.

It had been arranged that an attempt should be made to photograph any phantasm seen, but Mr. Vincey had not the instant presence of mind to snap the camera that lay ready on the table beside him, and when he did so he was too late. Greatly elated, however, even by this partial success, he made a note of the exact time, and at once took a cab to the Albany to inform Mr. Bessel of this result.

He was surprised to find Mr. Bessel's outer door standing open to the night, and the inner apartments lit and in an extraordinary disorder. An empty champagne magnum lay smashed upon the floor; its neck had been broken off against the inkpot on the bureau and lay beside it. An octagonal occasional table, which carried a bronze statuette and a number of choice books, had been rudely overturned, and down the primrose paper of the wall inky fingers had been drawn, as it seemed for the mere pleasure of defilement. One of the delicate chintz curtains had been violently torn from its rings and thrust upon the fire, so that the smell of its smouldering filled the room. Indeed the whole place was disarranged in the strangest fashion. For a few minutes Mr. Vincey, who had entered sure of finding Mr. Bessel in his easy chair awaiting him, could scarcely believe his eyes, and stood staring helplessly at these unanticipated things.

Then, full of a vague sense of calamity, he sought the porter at the entrance lodge. "Where is Mr. Bessel?" he asked. "Do you know that all the furniture is broken in Mr. Bessel's room?" The porter said nothing, but, obeying his gestures, came at once to Mr. Bessel's apartment to see the state of affairs. "This settles it," he said, surveying the lunatic confusion. "I didn't know of this. Mr. Bessel's gone off. He's mad!"

He then proceeded to tell Mr. Vincey that about half an hour previously, that is to say, at about the time of Mr. Bessel's apparition in Mr. Vincey's rooms, the missing gentleman had rushed out of the gates of the Albany into Vigo street, hatless and with disordered hair, and had vanished into the direction of Bond Street. "And as he went past me," said the porter, "he laughed—a sort of gasping laugh, with his mouth open and his eyes glaring—I tell you, sir, he fair scared me!—like this."

According to his imitation it was anything but a pleasant laugh. "He waved his hand, with all his fingers crooked and clawing—like that. And he said, in a sort of fierce whisper, *'Life.'* Just that one word, *'Life!'* "

"Dear me," said Mr. Vincey. "Tut, tut," and "Dear me!" He could think of nothing else to say. He was naturally very much surprised. He turned from the room to the porter and from the porter to the room in the gravest perplexity. Beyond his suggestion that probably Mr. Bessel would come back presently and explain what had happened, their conversation was unable to proceed. "It might be a sudden toothache," said the porter, "a very sudden and violent toothache, jumping on him suddenly-like and driving him wild. I've broken things myself before now in such a case . . ." He thought. "If it was, why should he say *'Life'* to me as he went past?"

Mr. Vincey did not know. Mr. Bessel did not return, and at last Mr. Vincey, having done some more helpless staring, and having addressed a note of brief inquiry and left it in a conspicuous position on the bureau, returned in a very perplexed frame of mind to his own premises in Staple Inn. This affair had given him a shock. He was at a loss to account for Mr. Bessel's conduct on any sane hypothesis. He tried to read, but he could not do so; he went for a short walk, and was so preoccupied that he narrowly escaped a cab at the top of Chancery Lane; and at last—a full hour before his usual time—he went to bed. For a considerable time he could not sleep because of his memory of the silent confusion of Mr. Bessel's apartment, and when at length he did attain an uneasy slumber it was at once disturbed by a very vivid and distressing dream of Mr. Bessel.

He saw Mr. Bessel gesticulating wildly, and with his face white and contorted. And, inexplicably mingled with his appearance, suggested perhaps by his gestures, was an intense fear, an urgency to act. He even believes that he heard the voice of his fellow experimenter calling distressfully to him, though at the time he considered this to be an illusion. The vivid impression remained though Mr. Vincey awoke. For a space he lay awake and trembling in the darkness, possessed with that vague, unaccountable terror of unknown possibilities that comes out of dreams upon even the bravest men. But at last he roused himself, and turned over and went to sleep again, only for the dream to return with enhanced vividness

He awoke with such a strong conviction that Mr. Bessel was in overwhelming distress and need of help that sleep was no longer possible. He was persuaded that his friend had rushed out to some dire calamity. For a time he lay reasoning vainly against this belief, but at last he gave way to it. He arose, against all reason, lit his gas and dressed, and set out through the deserted streets—deserted, save for a noiseless policeman or so and the early news carts—towards Vigo Street to inquire if Mr. Bessel had returned.

But he never got there. As he was going down Long Acre some unaccountable impulse turned him aside out of that street towards Covent Garden, which was just waking to its nocturnal activities. He saw the market in front of him—a queer effect of glowing yellow lights and busy black figures. He became aware of a shouting, and perceived a figure turn the corner by the hotel and run swiftly towards him. He knew at once that it was Mr. Bessel. But it was Mr. Bessel transfigured. He was hatless and dishevelled, his collar was torn open, he grasped a bone-handled walking-cane near the ferrule end, and his mouth was pulled awry. And he ran, with agile strides, very rapidly. Their encounter was the affair of an instant. "Bessel!" cried Vincey.

The running man gave no sign of recognition either of Mr. Vincey or of his own name. Instead, he cut at his friend savagely with the stick, hitting him in the face within an inch of the eye. Mr. Vincey, stunned and astonished, staggered back, lost his footing, and fell heavily on the pavement. It seemed to him that Mr. Bessel leapt over him as he fell. When he looked again Mr. Bessel had vanished, and a policeman and a number of garden porters and salesmen were rushing past towards Long Acre in hot pursuit.

With the assistance of several passersby—for the whole street was speedily alive with running people—Mr. Vincey struggled to his feet. He at once became the centre of a crowd greedy to see his injury. A multitude of voices competed to reassure him of his safety, and then to tell him of the behaviour of the madman, as they regarded Mr. Bessel. He had suddenly appeared in the middle of the market screaming *"Life! Life!"* striking left and right with a bloodstained walking stick, and dancing and shouting with laughter at each successful blow. A lad and two women had broken heads, and he had smashed a man's wrist; a little child had been knocked insensible, and for a time he had driven everyone before him, so furious and resolute had his behaviour been. Then he made a raid upon a coffee stall, hurled its paraffin flare through the window of the post office, and fled laughing, after stunning the foremost of the two policemen who had the pluck to charge him.

Mr. Vincey's first impulse was naturally to join in the pursuit of his friend, in order if possible to save him from the violence of the indignant people. But his action was slow, the blow had half stunned him, and while this was still no more than a resolution came the news, shouted through the crowd, that Mr. Bessel had eluded his pursuers. At first Mr. Vincey could scarcely credit this, but the universality of the report, and presently the dignified return of two futile policemen, convinced him. After some aimless inquiries he returned towards Staple Inn, padding a handkerchief to a now very painful nose.

He was angry and astonished and perplexed. It appeared to him indisputable that Mr. Bessel must have gone violently mad in the midst of his experiment in thought transference, but why that should make him appear with a sad white face in Mr. Vincey's dreams seemed a problem beyond solution. He racked his brains in vain to explain this. It seemed to him at last that not simply Mr. Bessel, but the order of things must be insane. But he could think of nothing to do. He shut himself carefully into his room, lit his fire—it was a gas fire with asbestos bricks—and, fearing fresh dreams if he went to bed, remained bathing his injured face, or holding up books in a vain attempt to read, until dawn. Throughout that vigil he had a curious persuasion that Mr. Bessel was endeavouring to speak to him, but he would not let himself attend to any such belief.

About dawn, his physical fatigue asserted itself, and he went to bed and slept at last in spite of dreaming. He rose late, unrested and anxious and in considerable facial pain. The morning papers had no news of Mr. Bessel's aberration—it had come too late for them. Mr. Vincey's perplexities, to which the fever of his bruise added fresh irritation, became at last intolerable, and, after a fruitless visit to the Albany, he went down to St. Paul's Churchyard to Mr. Hart, Mr. Bessel's partner, and so far as Mr. Vincey knew, his nearest friend.

He was surprised to learn that Mr. Hart, although he knew nothing of the outbreak, had also been disturbed by a vision, the very vision that Mr. Vincey had seen—Mr. Bessel, white and dishevelled, pleading earnestly by his gestures for help. That was his impression of the import of his signs. "I was just going to look him up in the Albany when you arrived," said Mr. Hart. "I was so sure of something being wrong with him."

As the outcome of their consultation, the two gentlemen decided to inquire at Scotland Yard for news of their missing friend. "He is bound to be laid by the heels," said Mr. Hart. "He can't go on at that pace for long." But the police authorities had not laid Mr. Bessel by the heels. They confirmed Mr. Vincey's overnight experiences and added fresh circumstances, some of an even graver character than those he knew—a list of smashed glass along the upper half of Tottenham Court Road, an attack upon a policeman in Hampstead Road, and an atrocious assault upon a woman. All these outrages were committed between half-past twelve and a quarter to two in the morning, and between those hours—and, indeed, from the very moment of Mr. Bessel's first rush from his rooms at half-past nine in the evening—they could trace the deepening violence of his fantastic career. For the last hour, at least from before one, that is, until a quarter to two, he had run amuck through London, eluding with amazing agility every effort to stop or capture him.

But after a quarter to two he had vanished. Up to that hour witnesses were multitudinous. Dozens of people had seen him, fled from him or pursued him, and then things suddenly came to an end. At a quarter to two he had been seen running down the Euston Road towards Baker Street, flourishing a can of burning colza oil and jerking splashes of flame therefrom at the windows of the houses he passed. But none of the policemen on Euston Road beyond the Waxwork Exhibition, nor any of those in the side streets down which he must have passed had he left the Euston Road, had seen anything of him. Abruptly he disappeared. Nothing of his subsequent doings came to light in spite of the keenest inquiry.

Here was a fresh astonishment for Mr. Vincey. He had found considerable comfort in Mr. Hart's conviction: "He is bound to be laid by the heels before long," and in that assurance he had been able to suspend his mental perplexities. But any fresh development seemed destined to add new impossibilities to a pile already heaped beyond the powers of his acceptance. He found himself doubting whether his memory might not have played him some grotesque trick, debating whether any of these things could possibly have happened; and in the afternoon he hunted up Mr. Hart again to share the intolerable weight on his mind. He found Mr. Hart engaged with a well-known private detective, but as that gentleman accomplished nothing in this case, we need not enlarge upon his proceedings.

All that day Mr. Bessel's whereabouts eluded an unceasingly active inquiry, and all that night. And all that day there was a persuasion in the back of Mr. Vincey's mind that Mr. Bessel sought his attention, and all through the night Mr. Bessel with a tear-stained face of anguish pursued him through his dreams. And whenever he saw Mr. Bessel in his dreams he also saw a number of other faces, vague but malignant, that seemed to be pursuing Mr. Bessel.

It was on the following day, Sunday, that Mr. Vincey recalled certain remarkable stories of Mrs. Bullock, the medium, who was then attracting attention for the first time in London. He determined to consult her. She was staying at the house of that well-known inquirer, Dr. Wilson Paget, and Mr. Vincey, although he had never met that gentleman before, repaired to him forthwith with the intention of invoking her help. But scarcely had he mentioned the name of Bessel when Dr. Paget interrupted him. "Last night—just at the end," he said, "we had a communication."

He left the room, and returned with a slate on which were certain words written in handwriting, shaky indeed, but indisputably the handwriting of Mr. Bessel!

"How did you get this?" said Mr. Vincey. "Do you mean?——"

"We got it last night," said Dr. Paget. With numerous interruptions from Mr. Vincey, he proceeded to explain how the writing had been obtained. It appears that in her *séances,* Mrs. Bullock passes into a condition of trance, her eyes rolling up in a strange way under her eyelids, and her body becoming rigid. She then begins to talk very rapidly, usually in voices other than her own. At the same time one or both of her hands may become active, and if slates and pencils are provided they will then write messages simultaneously with and quite independently of the flow of words from her mouth. By many she is considered an even more remarkable medium than the celebrated Mrs. Piper. It was one of these messages, the one written by her left hand, that Mr. Vincey now had before him. It consisted of eight words written disconnectedly "George Bessel . . . trial excav⁎ . . . Baker Street . . . help . . . starvation." Curiously enough, neither Dr. Paget nor the two other inquirers who were present had heard of the disappearance of Mr. Bessel—the news of it appeared only in the evening papers of Saturday—and they had put the message aside with many others of a vague and enigmatical sort that Mrs. Bullock has from time to time delivered.

When Dr. Paget heard Mr. Vincey's story, he gave himself at once with great energy to the pursuit of this clue to the discovery of Mr. Bessel. It would serve no useful purpose here to describe the inquiries of Mr. Vincey and himself; suffice it that the clue was a genuine one, and that Mr. Bessel was actually discovered by its aid.

He was found at the bottom of a detached shaft which had been sunk and abandoned at the commencement of the work for the new electric railway near Baker Street Station. His arm and leg and two ribs were broken. The shaft is protected by a hoarding nearly twenty feet high, and over this, incredible as it seems, Mr. Bessel, a stout, middle-aged gentleman, must have scrambled in order to fall down the shaft. He was saturated in colza oil, and the smashed tin lay beside him, but luckily the flame had been extinguished by his fall. And his madness had passed from him altogether. But he was, of course, terribly enfeebled, and at the sight of his rescuers he gave way to hysterical weeping.

In view of the deplorable state of his flat, he was taken to the house of Dr. Hatton in Upper Baker Street. Here he was subjected to a sedative treatment, and anything that might recall the violent crisis through which he had passed was carefully avoided. But on the second day he volunteered a statement.

Since that occasion Mr. Bessel has several times repeated this statement—to myself among other people—varying the details as the narrator of real experiences always does, but never by any chance contradicting himself in any particular. And the statement he makes is in substance as follows.

In order to understand it clearly it is necessary to go back to his experiments with Mr. Vincey before his remarkable attack. Mr. Bessel's first attempts at self-projection, in his experiments with Mr. Vincey, were, as the reader will remember, unsuccessful. But through all of them he was concentrating all his power and will upon getting out of the body—"willing it with all my might," he says. At last, almost against expectation, came success. And Mr. Bessel asserts that he, being alive, did actually, by an effort of will, leave his body and pass into some place or state outside this world.

The release was, he asserts, instantaneous. "At one moment I was seated in my chair, with my eyes tightly shut, my hands gripping the arms of the chair, doing all I could to concentrate my mind on Vincey, and then I perceived myself outside my body—saw my body near me, but certainly not containing me, with the hands relaxing and the head drooping forward on the breast."

Nothing shakes him in his assurance of that release. He describes in a quiet, matter-of-fact way the new sensation he experienced. He felt he had become impalpable—so much he had expected, but he had not expected to find himself enormously large. So, however, it would seem he became. "I was a great cloud—if I may express it that way—anchored to my body. It appeared to me, at first, as if I had discovered a greater self of which the conscious being in my brain was only a little part. I saw the Albany and Piccadilly and Regent Street and all the rooms and places in the houses, very minute and very bright and distinct, spread out below me like a little city seen from a balloon. Every now and then vague shapes like drifting wreaths of smoke made the vision a little indistinct, but at first I paid little heed to them. The thing that astonished me most, and which astonishes me still, is that I saw quite distinctly the insides of the houses as well as the streets, saw little people dining and talking in the private houses, men and women dining, playing billiards, and drinking in restaurants and hotels, and several places of entertainment crammed with people. It was like watching the affairs of a glass hive."

Such were Mr. Bessel's exact words as I took them down when he told me the story. Quite forgetful of Mr. Vincey, he remained for a space observing these things. Impelled by curiosity, he says, he stooped down, and with the shadowy arm he found himself possessed of attempted to touch a man walking along Vigo Street. But he could not do so, though his finger seemed to pass through the man. Something prevented his doing this, but what it was he finds it hard to describe. He compares the obstacle to a sheet of glass.

"I felt as a kitten may feel," he said, "when it goes for the first time to pat its reflection in a mirror." Again and again, on the occasion when I heard him tell this story, Mr. Bessel returned to that comparison of the sheet of glass. Yet it was not altogether a precise

comparison, because, as the reader will speedily see, there were interruptions of this generally impermeable resistance, means of getting
through the barrier to the material world again. But, naturally, there
is a very great difficulty in expressing these unprecedented impres-
sions in the language of everyday experience.

A thing that impressed him instantly, and which weighed upon
him throughout all this experience, was the stillness of this place—he
was in a world without sound.

At first Mr. Bessel's mental state was an unemotional wonder. His
thought chiefly concerned itself with where he might be. He was out
of the body—out of his material body, at any rate—but that was not
all. He believes, and I for one believe also, that he was somewhere
out of space, as we understand it, altogether. By a strenuous effort of
will he had passed out of his body into a world beyond this world, a
world undreamt of, yet lying so close to it and so strangely situated
with regard to it that all things on this earth are clearly visible both
from without and from within in this other world about us. For a
long time, as it seemed to him, this realisation occupied his mind to
the exclusion of all other matters, and then he recalled the engagement with Mr. Vincey, to which this astonishing experience was,
after all, but a prelude.

He turned his mind to locomotion in this new body in which he
found himself. For a time he was unable to shift himself from his
attachment to his earthly carcass. For a time this new strange cloud
body of his simply swayed, contracted, expanded, coiled, and
writhed with his efforts to free himself, and then quite suddenly the
link that bound him snapped. For a moment everything was hidden
by what appeared to be whirling spheres of dark vapour, and then
through a momentary gap he saw his drooping body collapse limply,
saw his lifeless head drop sideways and found he was driving along
like a huge cloud in a strange place of shadowy clouds that had the
luminous intricacy of London spread like a model below.

But now he was aware that the fluctuating vapour about him was
something more than vapour, and the temerarious excitement of his
first essay was shot with fear. For he perceived, at first indistinctly,
and then suddenly very clearly, that he was surrounded by *faces!*
that each roll and coil of the seeming cloud-stuff was a face. And
such faces! Faces of thin shadow, faces of gaseous tenuity. Faces like
those faces that glare with intolerable strangeness upon the sleeper in

the evil hours of his dreams. Evil, greedy eyes that were full of a covetous curiosity, faces with knit brows and snarling, smiling lips; their vague hands clutched at Mr. Bessel as he passed, and the rest of their bodies was but an elusive streak of trailing darkness. Never a word they said, never a sound from the mouths that seemed to gibber. All about him they pressed in that dreamy silence, passing freely through the dim mistiness that was his body, gathering ever more numerously about him. And the shadowy Mr. Bessel, now suddenly fear-stricken, drove through the silent, active multitude of eyes and clutching hands.

So inhuman were these faces, so malignant their staring eyes, and shadowy, clawing gestures, that it did not occur to Mr. Bessel to attempt intercourse with these drifting creatures. Idiot phantoms, they seemed, children of vain desire, beings unborn and forbidden the boon of being, whose only expressions and gestures told of the envy and craving for life that was their one link with existence.

It says much for his resolution that, amidst the swarming cloud of these noiseless spirits of evil, he could still think of Mr. Vincey. He made a violent effort of will and found himself, he knew not how, stooping towards Staple Inn, saw Vincey sitting attentive and alert in his armchair by the fire.

And clustering also about him, as they clustered ever about all that lives and breathes, was another multitude of these vain voiceless shadows, longing, desiring, seeking some loophole into life.

For a space Mr. Bessel sought ineffectually to attract his friend's attention. He tried to get in front of his eyes, to move the objects in his room, to touch him. But Mr. Vincey remained unaffected, ignorant of the being that was so close to his own. The strange something that Mr. Bessel has compared to a sheet of glass separated them impermeably.

And at last Mr. Bessel did a desperate thing. I have told how that in some strange way he could see not only the outside of a man as we see him, but within. He extended his shadowy hand and thrust his vague black fingers, as it seemed, through the heedless brain.

Then, suddenly, Mr. Vincey started like a man who recalls his attention from wandering thoughts, and it seemed to Mr. Bessel that a little dark-red body situated in the middle of Mr. Vincey's brain swelled and glowed as he did so. Since that experience he has been shown anatomical figures of the brain, and he knows now that this is that useless structure, as doctors call it, the pineal eye. For, strange as it will seem to many, we have, deep in our brains—where it cannot possibly see any earthly light—an eye! At the time this, with the rest of the internal anatomy of the brain, was quite new to him. At the sight of its changed appearance, however, he thrust forth his finger, and, rather fearful still of the consequences, touched this little spot. And instantly Mr. Vincey started, and Mr. Bessel knew that he was seen.

And at that instant it came to Mr. Bessel that evil had happened to his body, and behold! a great wind blew through all that world of shadows and tore him away. So strong was this persuasion that he thought no more of Mr. Vincey, but turned about forthwith, and all the countless faces drove back with him like leaves before a gale. But he returned too late. In an instant he saw the body that he had left inert and collapsed—lying, indeed, like the body of a man just dead —had arisen, had arisen by virtue of some strength and will beyond his own. It stood with staring eyes, stretching its limbs in dubious fashion.

For a moment he watched it in wild dismay, and then he stooped towards it. But the pane of glass had closed against him again, and he was foiled. He beat himself passionately against this, and all about him the spirits of evil grinned and pointed and mocked. He gave way to furious anger. He compares himself to a bird that has fluttered heedlessly into a room and is beating at the window-pane that holds it back from freedom.

And behold! the little body that had once been his was now dancing with delight. He saw it shouting, though he could not hear its shouts; he saw the violence of its movements grow. He watched it fling his cherished furniture about in the mad delight of existence, rend his books apart, smash bottles, drink heedlessly from the jagged fragments, leap and smite in a passionate acceptance of living. He watched these actions in paralyzed astonishment. Then once more he hurled himself against the impassable barrier, and then, with all that crew of mocking ghosts about him, hurried back in dire confusion to Vincey to tell him of the outrage that had come upon him.

But the brain of Vincey was now closed against apparitions, and the disembodied Mr. Bessel pursued him in vain as he hurried out into Holborn to call a cab. Foiled and terror-stricken, Mr. Bessel swept back again, to find his desecrated body whooping in a glorious frenzy down the Burlington Arcade . . .

And now the attentive reader begins to understand Mr. Bessel's interpretation of the first part of this strange story. The being whose frantic rush through London had inflicted so much injury and disaster had indeed Mr. Bessel's body, but it was not Mr. Bessel. It was an evil spirit out of that strange world beyond existence, into which Mr. Bessel had so rashly ventured. For twenty hours it held possession of him, and for all those twenty hours the dispossessed spirit-body of Mr. Bessel was going to and fro in that unheard-of middle world of shadows seeking help in vain.

He spent many hours beating at the minds of Mr. Vincey and of his friend Mr. Hart. Each, as we know, he roused by his efforts. But the language that might convey his situation to these helpers across the gulf he did not know; his feeble fingers groped vainly and powerlessly in their brains. Once, indeed, as we have already told, he was able to turn Mr. Vincey aside from his path so that he encountered the stolen body in its career, but he could not make him understand the thing that had happened: he was unable to draw any help from that encounter . . .

All through those hours, the persuasion was overwhelming in Mr. Bessel's mind that presently his body would be killed by its furious tenant, and he would have to remain in this shadow-land for evermore. So that those long hours were a growing agony of fear. And ever as he hurried to and fro in his ineffectual excitement, innumerable spirits of that world about him mobbed him and confused his mind. And ever an envious applauding multitude poured after their successful fellow as he went upon his glorious career.

For that, it would seem, must be the life of these bodiless things of this world that is the shadow of our world. Ever they watch, coveting a way into a mortal body, in order that they may descend, as furies and frenzies, as violent lusts and mad, strange impulses, rejoicing in the body they have won. For Mr. Bessel was not the only human soul in that place. Witness the fact that he met first one, and afterwards several shadows of men, men like himself, it seemed, who had lost their bodies even it may be as he had lost his, and wandered, despairingly, in that lost world that is neither life nor death. They could not speak because that world is silent, yet he knew them for men because of their dim human bodies, and because of the sadness of their faces.

But how they had come into that world he could not tell, nor where the bodies they had lost might be, whether they still raved about the earth, or whether they were closed for ever in death against return. That they were the spirits of the dead neither he nor I believe. But Dr. Wilson Paget thinks they are the rational souls of men who are lost in madness on the earth.

At last Mr. Bessel chanced upon a place where a little crowd of such disembodied silent creatures was gathered, and thrusting through them he saw below a brightly-lit room, and four or five quiet gentlemen and a woman, a stoutish woman dressed in black bombazine and sitting awkwardly in a chair with her head thrown back. He knew her from her portraits to be Mrs. Bullock, the medium. And he perceived that tracts and structures in her brain glowed and stirred as he had seen the pineal eye in the brain of Mr. Vincey glow. The light was very fitful; sometimes it was a broad illumination, and sometimes merely a faint twilight spot, and it shifted slowly about her brain. She kept on talking and writing with one hand. And Mr. Bessel saw that the crowding shadows of men about him, and a great multitude of the shadow spirits of that shadow land, were all striving and thrusting to touch the lighted regions of her brain. As one gained her brain or another was thrust away, her voice and the writing of her hand changed. So that what she said was disorderly and confused for the most part; now a fragment of one soul's message, and now a fragment of another's, and now she babbled the insane fancies of the spirits of vain desire. Then Mr. Bessel understood that she spoke for the spirit that had touch of her, and he began to struggle very furiously towards her. But he was on the outside of the crowd and at that time he could not reach her, and at last, growing anxious, he went away to find what had happened meanwhile to his body.

For a long time he went to and fro seeking it in vain and fearing that it must have been killed, and then he found it at the bottom of the shaft in Baker Street, writhing furiously and cursing with pain. Its leg and an arm and two ribs had been broken by its fall. Moreover, the evil spirit was angry because his time had been so short and because of the pain—making violent movements and casting his body about.

And at that Mr. Bessel returned with redoubled earnestness to the room where the *séance* was going on, and so soon as he had thrust himself within sight of the place he saw one of the men who stood about the medium looking at his watch as if he meant that the *séance* should presently end. At that a great number of the shadows who had been striving turned away with gestures of despair. But the thought that the *séance* was almost over only made Mr. Bessel the more earnest, and he struggled so stoutly with his will against the others that presently he gained the woman's brain. It chanced that just at that moment it glowed very brightly, and in that instant she wrote the message that Dr. Wilson Paget preserved. And then the other shadows and the cloud of evil spirits about him had thrust Mr. Bessel away from her, and for all the rest of the *séance* he could regain her no more.

So he went back and watched through the long hours at the bottom of the shaft where the evil spirit lay in the stolen body it had maimed, writhing and cursing, and weeping and groaning, and learning the lesson of pain. And towards dawn the thing he had waited for happened; the brain glowed brightly and the evil spirit came out, and Mr. Bessel entered the body he had feared he should never enter again. As he did so, the silence—the brooding silence—ended; he heard the tumult of traffic and the voices of people overhead, and that strange world that is the shadow of our world—the dark and silent shadows of ineffectual desire and the shadows of lost men— vanished clean away.

He lay there for the space of about three hours before he was found. And in spite of the pain and suffering of his wounds, and of the dim damp place in which he lay; in spite of the tears—wrung from him by his physical distress—his heart was full of gladness to know that he was nevertheless back once more in the kindly world of men.

Here is a nasty twist on the old deal-with-the-devil plot by ANTHONY BOUCHER (1911–68), one of the pen names of William Anthony Parker White, whose many literary accomplishments include writing such delightful mystery novels as *The Case of the Baker Street Irregulars* and *Rocket to the Morgue,* as well as several fantasy tales, especially "The Compleat Were-wolf." Boucher founded and coedited *The Magazine of Fantasy and Science Fiction,* perhaps the only other American periodical to rival *Weird Tales* in literary quality and versatility of theme and author. "The Scrawny One," the second of two Boucher tales to appear in The Unique Magazine, was published in May 1949.

THE SCRAWNY ONE

by Anthony Boucher

The old magician had only one arm.

"That is why," he explained, "I now employ the fuse. It is danger-ous to reach any part of your body inside the pentacle when you light the powder. They are hungry, these ones that we call up, and our flesh is to their taste."

John Harker watched the old man lead the fuse from the powder-heaped center of the pentacle to a safe distance from its rim. He watched him lean over and strike a match on the cement floor, watched the sudden flame disquiet the shadows of the deserted ware-house, watched the fuse begin to sputter.

Then John Harker struck. The knife pierced easily through the soft flesh of the old back. His other hand came up to keep the magi-cian from falling across the fuse. He hurled the dying body back, safely away from fuse and pentacle, and thrust it from his mind as his eyes followed the sputtering sparks.

John Harker was unconcerned with fingerprints and clues. After tonight no man could touch him, not even for the most easily proved murder.

He had built to this carefully. Six months of research in the role of a freelance writer, investigating the multitudinous magic cults of

Southern California. A meticulous screening of frauds, fakes and phonies, and finally the discovery of this one-armed man of undeniable powers. The arrangements for this instant of ultimate truth, the calling up of a demon . . .

The hissing boom within the pentacle drowned out the last grating rattle of the old man's voice. John Harker looked at what he had caused to be summoned.

The first word that came to him was *scrawny.* Which is a peculiar word to apply to something not of our flesh, nor shaped in any way conceivable to us; but there was that in what passed for its eyes that told of endless deprivation, insufficiency, hunger.

It spoke, though no sound waves disturbed the stillness of the warehouse. It said, "You called me. I can grant you one wish. Make up your mind."

John Harker smiled. "Are your customers usually so irresolute? I have made up my mind."

The scrawny one's eyes fed on him. "What can you want?" it said, and there was hatred and envy in its soundless words. "What can any *man* want when you have the one thing to be prized above all others . . . *flesh?*"

"How fortunate," Harker observed, "that you are not empowered to call us up. But little though you may believe it, we have our hungers too, and largely because of this so enviable flesh. And my own hungers I am resolved to end now."

"Your wish!" The scrawny one writhed in impatience.

Harker deliberately dawdled, savoring this little moment of power, this curtain-raiser to the ultimate power. "In the opera," he began, "Mephisto, when summoned, proffers Faust first gold, then glory, then power. But that prime idiot the learned Doctor Faust replies, 'I want a treasure that contains them all! . . . I want youth!' " Harker laughed and hummed a snatch of the tripping tune to which Faust expresses his senile desire. "But I know better."

"Your wish!" the scrawny one insisted.

"I know that power and wisdom and strength and honor and glory and blessing can all be summed up, in this most worldly of all possible worlds, in one word: wealth. My wish is simple: You will make me the richest man in the world. From that all else will follow."

The scrawny one made a sign of agreement, while darting hunger glimmered in several of its eyes. Then it added, "You must release me from the pentacle before I can accomplish that."

John Harker hesitated. "I know that you are bound to truth while you are contained there. You swear to me that if I release you you will do no harm to me in soul or body?"

"I swear."

"You swear that if I release you you will, immediately, make me the richest man in the world?"

"I swear. You must cut the pentacle with cold steel."

John Harker nodded and jerked the knife from the dead magician's back. As he extended the bloody knife toward the pentacle there was a flicker of the scrawny shape, and that part of the blade which protruded beyond the rim was licked clean of blood.

The cold steel descended and scraped across the cement floor.

The pentacle was empty and the scrawny one was beside John Harker.

"Now!" he commanded.

But the scrawny one flashed the thought that it had something to do first.

When there was no trace left of the magician's body (and how convenient that was, even when you were unconcerned about damaging evidence), the not quite so scrawny one ceased its intricate vibrations and stood all but motionless beside John Harker

"Are you ready for your wish?" it asked.

John Harker smiled and nodded.

That is, he lowered his chin in assent. A nod is usually concluded by bringing the chin back to its normal position. But his muscles would not obey and his chin remained sunk on his breastbone.

There was trouble with his eyes too. He did not remember closing the lids, but closed they were and obstinately so.

His ears functioned. They brought a sound of music totally unfamiliar to him who had casually prided himself on his knowledge of music. And mingled with the wailing of unknown pipes was the wailing of hundreds of unknown voices. And mingled with the plunking of strings and the thumping of drums was the plunking thump of hundreds of small hard objects, like the rattle of hail close to his ears.

His other senses functioned, too. One told him that he lay suspended on some flat metal surface, that he did not rest in one position, but slowly kept floating higher in the air. And another told him that there was not a fiber of his body that did not ache with a pain so exquisitely refined as to be almost beyond the limits of conscious endurance.

And yet another sense informed him that he was surrounded by a stench of decay, an aura of charnel rot so strong, so intimate, that he could not long resist the conclusion that it rose from his own vile body.

The upward movement had stopped, and he floated in equipoise as the music and the rattle ceased and a shout went up from the hundreds of voices. Now at last his eyes half-opened, and he could see his vast bloated bulk swaying in one pan of a tremendous gold balance, while in the other pan hung his weight in precious stones.

The sight of his wealth gave him a last flash of strength. He was able to move his hand close enough to his eyes for their half-parted slits to watch his little finger slowly detach itself and drop, leaving a ragged stump of corruption. Through the eyes that had once been John Harker's, it read the newspaper story:

RICHEST MAN DYING
Annual gem rite held

RAVENPORE, India (UP).—The Djatoon of Khot, reputedly the wealthiest man in the world, lay dying here today of an obscure disease; but his loyal subjects still performed the traditional annual ceremony in which the Djatoon is presented with his weight in precious stones.

The greatest physicians of three continents profess themselves baffled by the degenerative malignancy which has attacked the wealthy potentate, and express no hopes for his recovery.

The once scrawny one used John Harker's features to shape a satisfied smile. Then it used John Harker's muscles to propel his body and went out into the streets of the city, there to accomplish at its leisure those delightful undertakings which would enable it, in time, quite to forget its starved and scrawny past.

The legend of the apprentice sorcerer who meddles with his master's magic, almost drowns himself, is rescued by his irate boss and then fired is nowadays most often associated with the segment of the Walt Disney film *Fantasia* in which Mickey Mouse performs the titular role to the accompaniment of Paul Dukas' popular tone poem *L'Apprenti Sorcier*. Dukas derived his composition from a long poem by the great German poet-dramatist Johann Wolfgang von Goethe, but the germ of Goethe's plot is still older: a dialogue by LUCIAN OF SAMOSATA (A.D. 117–?). Lucian, a Syrian by birth and later an Antioch lawyer, lived at least until A.D. 192, wrote a large number of satirical sketches, including a dialogue variously translated as "The Lie-Fancier" or "The Pathological Liar." In it, two Athenians stroll together while one of them, Tychiades, tells his friend one tall tale after another, many of which Lucian borrowed from earlier literary sources. But the following anecdote— offered here in the Sir Thomas More translation that was published in the October 1939 issue of *Weird Tales*—is thought to be wholly Lucian's. (For further comment, see Appendix II, page 574. Also note the grim variant on the sorcerer's apprentice tale by Robert Bloch on page 433.)

THE SORCERER'S APPRENTICE

by Lucian
Translated by Sir Thomas More

When a certain Eucrates saw an Egyptian magician named Pancrates do many marvels, he gradually insinuated himself into his friendship until he learned nearly all his secrets. At last the magician persuaded him to leave all his servants in Memphis and accompany him alone, for they would have no lack of servants; and from that time (Eucrates said) thus we lived.

"When we came into an inn, he taking the bolt of the door, or a broom or bar, and clothing it, spoke a charm to it, and to enable it to go, and in all things to resemble a man. The thing going forth, would draw water, provide, and dress our supper, and diligently wait and attend upon us. After his business was done, he pronounced another charm, and turned the broom into a broom again, and the pestle into a pestle. This was an art which, though I labored much, I could not learn of him. For this was a mystery which he denied me, though in all things else he were open.

"One day, hiding myself in a dark corner, I overheard his charm, which was but three syllables. He having appointed the bolt its business, went into the market.

"The next day, he having some other appointment in the market, I taking the pestle and appareling it, in like manner pronounced the syllables, and bid it fetch me some water. When it had brought me a basin full, 'It is enough,' I said, 'fetch no more, but be a pestle again.' But it was so far from obeying me, that it ceased not to fetch water till it had overflowed the room. I, much troubled at the accident, and fearing lest if Pancrates return (as he did) he would be much displeased, took an ax and cut the pestle in two. Then both parts taking several buckets fetched water. And instead of one, I had two servants.

"In the meantime Pancrates came in, and perceiving what had happened, transformed them into wood again, as they were before I uttered the spell. Shortly after he secretly left me, and vanishing went I know not whither."

SKULLS IN THE STARS

by Robert E. Howard

He told how murderers walk the earth
   Beneath the curse of Cain,
With crimson clouds before their eyes
   And flames about their brain:
For blood has left upon their souls
   Its everlasting stain.

                    —*Hood*

There are two roads to Torkertown. One, the shorter and more direct route, leads across a barren upland moor, and the other, which is much longer, winds its tortuous way in and out among the hummocks and quagmires of the swamps, skirting the low hills to the east. It was a dangerous and tedious trail; so Solomon Kane halted in amazement when a breathless youth from the village he had just left, overtook him and implored him for God's sake to take the swamp road.

"The swamp road!" Kane stared at the boy.

He was a tall, gaunt man, was Solomon Kane, his darkly pallid face and deep brooding eyes made more somber by the drab Puritanical garb he affected.

"Yes, sir, 'tis safer," the youngster answered to his surprised exclamation.

"Then the moor road must be haunted by Satan himself, for your townsmen warned me against traversing the other."

"Because of the quagmires, sir, that you might not see in the dark. You had better return to the village and continue your journey in the morning, sir."

"Taking the swamp road?"

"Yes, sir."

Kane shrugged and shook his head. "The moon rises almost as soon as twilight dies. By its light I can reach Torkertown in a few hours, across the moor."

"Sir, you had better not. No one ever goes that way. There are no houses at all upon the moor, while in the swamp there is the house of old Ezra who lives there all alone since his maniac cousin, Gideon, wandered off and died in the swamp and was never found—and old Ezra, though a miser, would not refuse you lodging should you decide to stop until morning. Since you must go, you had better go the swamp road."

Kane eyed the boy piercingly. The lad squirmed and shuffled his feet.

"Since this moor road is so dour to wayfarers," said the Puritan, "why did not the villagers tell me the whole tale, instead of vague mouthings?"

"Men like not to talk of it, sir. We hoped that you would take the swamp road after the men advised you to, but when we watched and saw that you turned not at the forks, they sent me to run after you and beg you to reconsider."

"Name of the Devil!" exclaimed Kane sharply, the unaccustomed oath showing his irritation; "the swamp road and the moor road— what is it that threatens me and why should I go miles out of my way and risk the bogs and mires?"

"Sir," said the boy, dropping his voice and drawing closer, "we be simple villagers who like not to talk of such things lest foul fortune befall us, but the moor road is a way accurst and hath not been traversed by any of the countryside for a year or more. It is death to walk those moors by night, as hath been found by some score of unfortunates. Some foul horror haunts the way and claims men for his victims."

"So? And what is this thing like?"

"No man knows. None has ever seen it and lived, but latefarers have heard terrible laughter far out on the fen and men have heard the horrid shrieks of its victims. Sir, in God's name return to the village, there pass the night, and tomorrow take the swamp trail to Yorkertown."

Far back in Kane's gloomy eyes a scintillant light had begun to glimmer, like a witch's torch glinting under fathoms of cold gray ice. His blood quickened. Adventure! The lure of life-risk and battle! The thrill of breathtaking, touch-and-go drama! Not that Kane recognized his sensations as such. He sincerely considered that he voiced his real feelings when he said, "These things be deeds of some power of evil. The lords of darkness have laid a curse upon the country. A strong man is needed to combat Satan and his might. Therefore I go, who have defied him many a time."

"Sir," the boy began, then closed his mouth as he saw the futility of argument. He only added, "The corpses of the victims are bruised and torn, sir."

He stood there at the crossroads, sighing regretfully as he watched the tall, rangy figure swinging up the road that led toward the moors.

The sun was setting as Kane came over the brow of the low hill which debouched into the upland fen. Huge and bloodred it sank down behind the sullen horizon of the moors, seeming to touch the rank grass with fire; so for a moment the watcher seemed to be gazing out across a sea of blood. Then the dark shadows came gliding from the east, the western blaze faded, and Solomon Kane struck out boldly in the gathering darkness.

The road was dim from disuse but was clearly defined. Kane went swiftly but warily, sword and pistols at hand. Stars blinked out and night winds whispered among the grass like weeping spectres. The moon began to rise, lean and haggard, like a skull among the stars.

Then suddenly Kane stopped short. From somewhere in front of him sounded a strange and eery echo—or something like an echo. Again, this time louder. Kane started forward again. Were his senses deceiving him? No!

Far out there pealed a whisper of frightful laughter. And again, closer this time. No human being ever laughed like that—there was no mirth in it, only hatred and horror and soul-destroying terror.

Kane halted. He was not afraid, but for a second he was almost unnerved. Then stabbing through that awesome laughter, came the sound of a scream that was undoubtedly human. Kane started forward, increasing his gait. He cursed the illusive lights and flickering shadows which veiled the moor in the rising moon and made accurate sight impossible. The laughter continued, growing louder, as did the screams. Then sounded faintly the drum of frantic human feet. Kane broke into a run.

Some human was being hunted to his death out there on the fen, and by what manner of horror God only knew. The sound of the flying feet halted abruptly and the screaming rose unbearably, mingled with other sounds unnamable and hideous. Evidently the man had been overtaken, and Kane, his flesh crawling, visualized some ghastly fiend of the darkness crouching on the back of its victim—crouching and tearing.

Then the noise of a terrible and short struggle came clearly through the abysmal silence of the fen and the footfalls began again, but stumbling and uneven. The screaming continued, but with a gasping gurgle. The sweat stood cold on Kane's forehead and body. This was heaping horror on horror in an intolerable manner.

God, for a moment's clear light! The frightful drama was being enacted within a very short distance of him, to judge by the ease with which the sounds reached him. But this hellish half-light veiled all in shifting shadows, so that the moors appeared a haze of blurred illusions and stunted trees and bushes seemed like giants.

Kane shouted, striving to increase the speed of his advance. The shrieks of the unknown broke into a hideous shrill squealing; again there was the sound of a struggle, and then from the shadows of the tall grass a thing came reeling—a thing that had once been a man—a gore-covered, frightful thing that fell at Kane's feet and writhed and groveled and raised its terrible face to the rising moon and gibbered and yammered and fell down again and died in its own blood.

The moon was up now, and the light was better. Kane bent above the body, which lay stark in its mutilation, and he shuddered—a rare thing for him, who had seen the deeds of the Spanish Inquisition and the witch-finders.

Some wayfarer, he supposed. Then like a hand of ice on his spine he was aware that he was not alone. He looked up, his cold eyes piercing the shadows whence the dead man had staggered. He saw nothing, but he knew—he felt—that other eyes gave back his stare, terrible eyes not of this Earth. He straightened and drew a pistol, waiting. The moonlight spread like a lake of pale blood over the moor and trees and grasses took on their proper sizes.

The shadows melted and Kane *saw!* At first he thought it only a shadow of mist, a wisp of moor fog that swayed in the tall grass before him. He gazed. More illusion, he thought. Then the thing began to take on shape, vague and indistinct. Two hideous eyes flamed at him—eyes which held all the stark horror which has been the heritage of man since the fearful dawn ages—eyes frightful and insane, with an insanity transcending Earthly insanity. The form of the thing was misty and vague, a brainshattering travesty on the human form, like, yet horribly unlike. The grass and bushes beyond showed clearly through it.

Kane felt the blood pound in his temples, yet he was as cold as ice. How such an unstable being as that which wavered before him could harm a man in a physical way was more than he could understand, yet the red horror at his feet gave mute testimony that the fiend could act with terrible material effect.

Of one thing Kane was sure: there would be no hunting of him across the dreary moors, no screaming and fleeing to be dragged down again and again. If he must die he would die in his tracks, his wounds in front.

Now a vague and grisly mouth gaped wide and the demoniac laughter again shrieked out, soul-shaking in its nearness. And in the midst of that threat of doom, Kane deliberately leveled his long pistol and fired. A maniacal yell of rage and mockery answered the report and the thing came at him like a flying sheet of smoke, long shadowy arms stretched to drag him down.

Kane, moving with the dynamic speed of a famished wolf, fired the second pistol with as little effect, snatched his long rapier from its sheath and thrust into the center of the misty attacker. The blade sang as it passed clear through, encountering no solid resistance, and Kane felt icy fingers grip his limbs, bestial talons tear his garments and the skin beneath.

He dropped the useless sword and sought to grapple with his foe. It was like fighting a floating mist, a flying shadow armed with daggerlike claws. His savage blows met empty air, his leanly mighty arms, in whose grasp strong men had died, swept nothingness and clutched emptiness. Naught was solid or real save the flaying, apelike fingers with their crooked talons, and the crazy eyes which burned into the shuddering depths of his soul.

Kane realized that he was in a desperate plight indeed. Already his garments hung in tatters and he bled from a score of deep wounds. But he never flinched, and the thought of flight never entered his mind. He had never fled from a single foe and had the thought occurred to him he would have flushed with shame.

He saw no help for it now, but that his form should lie there beside the fragments of the other victim, but the thought held no terrors for him. His only wish was to give as good an account of himself as possible before the end came and if he could, to inflict some damage on his unearthly foe.

There above the dead man's torn body, man fought with demon under the pale light of the rising moon, with all the advantages with the demon, save one. And that one was enough to overcome all the others. For if abstract hate may bring into material substance a ghostly thing, may not courage, equally abstract, form a concrete weapon to combat that ghost?

Kane fought with his arms and his feet and his hands and he was aware at last that the ghost began to give back before him and the fearful laughter changed to screams of baffled fury. For man's only weapon is courage that flinches not from the gates of Hell itself and against such not even the legions of Hell can stand.

Of this Kane knew nothing; he only knew that the talons which tore and rended him seemed to grow weaker and wavering, that a wild light grew and grew in the horrible eyes. And reeling and gasping, he rushed in, grappled the thing at last and threw it and as they tumbled about on the moor and it writhed and lapped his limbs like a serpent of smoke, his flesh crawled and his hair stood on end, for he began to understand its gibbering.

He did not hear and comprehend as a man hears and comprehends the speech of a man, but the frightful secrets it imparted in whisperings and yammerings and screaming silences sank fingers of ice into his soul, and he *knew*.

2

The hut of old Ezra the miser stood by the road in the midst of the swamp, half screened by the sullen trees which grew about it. The walls were rotting, the roof crumbling, and great pallid and green fungus-monsters clung to it and writhed about the doors and windows, as if seeking to peer within. The trees leaned above it and their gray branches intertwined so that it crouched in the semi-darkness like a monstrous dwarf over whose shoulder ogres leer.

The road which wound down into the swamp, among rotting stumps and rank hummocks and scummy, snake-haunted pools and bogs, crawled past the hut. Many people passed that way these days, but few saw old Ezra, save a glimpse of a yellow face peering throught the fungus-screened windows, itself like an ugly fungus.

Old Ezra the miser partook much of the quality of the swamp, for he was gnarled and bent and sullen; his fingers were like clutching parasitic plants and his locks hung like drab moss above eyes trained to the murk of the swamplands. His eyes were like a dead man's, yet hinted of depths abysmal and loathsome as the dead lakes of the swamplands.

These eyes gleamed now at the man who stood in front of his hut. This man was tall and gaunt and dark, his face was haggard and claw-marked and he was bandaged of arm and leg. Somewhat behind this man stood a number of villagers.

"You are Ezra of the swamp road?"

"Aye, and what want ye of me?"

"Where is your cousin Gideon, the maniac youth who abode with you?"

"Gideon?"

"Aye."

"He wandered away into the swamp and never came back. No doubt he lost his way and was set upon by wolves or died in a quagmire or was struck by an adder."

"How long ago?"

"Over a year."

"Aye. Hark ye, Ezra the miser. Soon after your cousin's disappearance, a countryman, coming home across the moors, was set upon by some unknown fiend and torn to pieces and thereafter it became death to cross those moors. First men of the countryside, then strangers who wandered over the fen fell to the clutches of the thing. Many men have died since the first one.

"Last night I crossed the moors and heard the flight and pursuing of another victim, a stranger who knew not the evil of the moors. Ezra the miser, it was a fearful thing, for the wretch twice broke from the fiend, terribly wounded, and each time the demon caught and dragged him down again. And at last he fell dead at my very feet, done to death in a manner that would freeze the statue of a saint."

The villagers moved restlessly and murmured fearfully to each other and old Ezra's eyes shifted furtively. Yet the somber expression of Solomon Kane never altered and his condor-like stare seemed to transfix the miser.

"Aye, aye!" muttered old Ezra hurriedly; "a bad thing, a bad thing! Yet why do you tell this thing to me?"

"Aye, a sad thing. Harken farther, Ezra. The fiend came out of the shadows and I fought with it over the body of its victim. Aye, how I overcame it, I know not, for the battle was hard and long, but the powers of good and light were on my side, which are mightier than the powers of Hell.

"At the last I was stronger, and it broke from me and fled and I followed to no avail. Yet, before it fled it whispered to me a monstrous truth."

Old Ezra stared, stared wildly, seemed to shrink into himself. "Nay, why tell me this?" he muttered.

"I returned to the village and told my tale," said Kane, "for I knew that now I had the power to rid the moors of its curse forever. Ezra, come with us!"

"Where?" gasped the miser.

"To the rotting oak on the moors."

Ezra reeled as though struck; he screamed incoherently and turned to flee.

On the instant, at Kane's sharp order, two brawny villagers sprang forward and seized the miser. They twisted the dagger from his withered hand and pinioned his arms, shuddering as their fingers encountered his clammy flesh.

Kane motioned them to follow and turning, strode up the trail, followed by the villagers, who found their strength taxed to the utmost in their task of bearing their prisoner along. Through the swamp they went and out, taking a little-used trail which led up over the low hills and out on the moors.

The sun was sliding down the horizon and old Ezra stared at it with bulging eyes—stared as if he could not gaze enough. Far out on the moors reared up the great oak tree like a gibbet, now only a decaying shell. There Solomon Kane halted.

Old Ezra writhed in his captor's grasp and made inarticulate noises.

"Over a year ago," said Solomon Kane, "you, fearing that your insane cousin Gideon would tell men of your cruelties to him, brought him away from the swamp by the very trail by which we came and murdered him here in the night."

Ezra cringed and snarled. "You can not prove this lie!"

Kane spoke a few words to an agile villager. The youth clambered up the rotting bole of the tree and from a crevice, high up, dragged something that fell with a clatter at the feet of the miser. Ezra went limp with a terrible shriek.

The object was a man's skeleton, the skull cleft.

"You—how know you this? You are Satan!" gibbered old Ezra.

Kane folded his arms. "The thing I fought last night told me this thing as we reeled in battle and I followed it to this tree. *For the fiend is Gideon's ghost!*"

Ezra shrieked again and fought savagely.

"You knew," said Kane somberly, "you knew what thing did these deeds. You feared the ghost of the maniac and that is why you chose to leave his body on the fen instead of concealing it in the swamp. For you knew the ghost would haunt the place of his death. He was insane in life and in death he did not know where to find his slayer; else he had come to you in your hut. He hates no man but you, but his crazed spirit can not tell one man from another and he slays all, lest he let his killer escape. Yet he will know you and rest in peace forever after. Hate hath made of his ghost a solid thing that can rend and slay and though he feared you terribly in life, in death he fears you not."

Kane halted. He glanced at the sun.

"All this I had from Gideon's ghost in his yammerings and his whisperings and his shrieking silences. Naught but your death will lay that ghost."

Ezra listened in breathless silence and Kane pronounced the words of his doom.

"A hard thing it is," said Kane somberly, "to sentence a man to death in cold blood and in such a manner as I have in mind, but you must die that others may live—and God knoweth you deserve death.

"You shall not die by noose, bullet or sword, but at the talons of him you slew—for naught else will satiate him."

At these words Ezra's brain shattered, his knees gave way and he fell groveling and screaming for death, begging them to burn him at the stake, to flay him alive. Kane's face was set like death and the villagers, the fear rousing their cruelty, bound the screeching wretch to the oak tree, and one of them bade him make his peace with God. But Ezra made no answer, shrieking in a high shrill voice with unbearable monotony. Then the villager would have struck the miser across the face, but Kane stayed him.

"Let him make his peace with Satan whom he is more like to meet," said the Puritan grimly. "The sun is about to set. Loose his cords so that he may work loose by dark, since it is better to meet death free and unshackled than bound like a sacrifice."

As they turned to leave him, old Ezra yammered and gibbered unhuman sounds and then fell silent, staring at the sun with terrible intensity.

They walked away across the fen, and Kane flung a last look at the grotesque form bound to the tree, seeming in the uncertain light like a great fungus growing to the bole. And suddenly the miser screamed hideously, "Death! Death! There are skulls in the stars!"

"Life was good to him, though he was gnarled and churlish and devil," Kane sighed. "Mayhap God has a place for such souls where fire and sacrifice may cleanse them of their dross as fire cleans the forest of fungus things. Yet my heart is heavy within me."

"Nay, sir," one of the villagers spoke, "you have done but the will of God and good alone shall come of this night's deed."

"Nay," answered Kane heavily, "I know not—I know not."

The sun had gone down and night spread with amazing swiftness, as if great shadows came rushing down from unknown voids to cloak the world with hurrying darkness. Through the thick night came a weird echo and the men halted and looked back the way they had come.

Nothing could be seen. The moor was an ocean of shadows and the tall grass about them bent in long waves before the faint wind, breaking the deathly stillness with breathless murmurings.

Then far away the red disk of the moon rose over the fen and for an instant a grim silhouette was etched blackly against it. A shape came flying across the face of the moon—a bent grotesque thing whose feet seemed scarcely to touch the earth and close behind came a thing like a flying shadow—a nameless, shapeless horror.

A moment the racing twain stood out boldly against the moon, then they merged into one unnamable, formless mass, and vanished in the shadows.

Far across the fen sounded a single shriek of terrible laughter.

One of the first stories I ever read as a boy was "Eena" by MANLY BANISTER (1914–   ) in the September 1947 issue of *Weird Tales*. Though at least one of its characters is a bit stereotypical by today's standards, "Eena" has weathered the years well and still is quite moving. With great compassion, Manly Banister unfolds a tragic tale of a werehuman and the man who fell in love with her.

EENA

by Manly Banister

The she-wolf was silhouetted sharply against the moon-gilded waters of Wolf Lake. Silent as Death in the cover of a rotting log, Joel Cameron sighted along a dully gleaming rifle barrel. He squeezed the trigger.

The gray-tipped wolf leaped high, cavorted grotesquely in midair. The beast threshed in short-lived agony upon the ground and lay still. Joel ejected the cartridge from the smoking chamber.

"Five bucks, and all profit!" he grunted, anticipating the State bounty.

In the act of legging over the log, he stopped and swiftly raised his weapon. His attention had been so intent upon the she-wolf as she slunk from the forest edge, he had not noticed the whelp that followed her. Terrified, the whimpering wolf cub galloped toward the safety of the woods. Joel dropped his rifle and sprinted.

"I'll be darned!" he panted, scooping the wolfling up into his arms. "An albino whelp!"

In this manner, Eena the she-wolfling was introduced to the world and the ways of men.

Joel's cabin was a mile down the lakeshore, hidden in a wooded draw that protected it from wind and weather, and separated from the edge of the lake by a thin screen of timber.

Joel Cameron had been born and raised in the high pine woods. Later fortune, through the medium of a battered typewriter and a skillful ability to weave a fanciful yarn, had led him to life in the city. But each Spring he returned to the cabin he had built in the hills and stayed there until the crispness of early Autumn presaged the coming of snow.

It was an ideal life, one to which Joel's temperament was ideally suited. When editorial favor inclined to the lean side, which it often did, he could depend upon the cabin in the mountains for refuge from the palsied palms of greedy landlords. The state wolf-bounty kept the figurative wolf from his door by inviting the literal one within.

Eena proved to be different from the usual wolfkind. Joel recognized this from the first. Even her albinoism was different. She lacked the red eyes usually associated with the lack of pigmentation. They were gray-hazel, and they gave Joel a weird sense of being somehow human. They were distinctly out of place in the snow-white, lupine visage of the wolflet.

Eena grew rapidly and prodigiously. At one time or another, every homesteader in the valley below passed by to see the albino. Some admired her look of intelligence, the growing strength of her. Some deplored the fact that a wolf so handy for killing should be allowed to live.

Pierre Lebrut, a trapper who had a tumble-down cabin a mile away, rubbed his palms on his greasy overalls and spat toward the caged wolf.

"Cameroon," said he, "I catch her, I keel her, you bat!" He scowled at the white wolf, and Eena's hackles raised in response. "She bad one, all right," Pierre growled. "She breeng bad luck. You see!"

The man went away, and Joel crouched by the chicken-wire fence of Eena's pen. He had got into the practice of talking softly to the animal.

"Kill you? Not you, my beauty!" He chuckled fondly. The half-grown wolf cocked her head at him and stared with unblinking, gray-hazel eyes.

"Sometimes I wonder if you'd let me scratch your ears?" He smiled through the fence. Eena lolled her tongue with a friendly grin. "On the other hand," Joel told her, "I need both my hands to type with! You're an independent she-cuss. Maybe that's why I like you!"

Eena furnished Joel with material for several stories that went over well. As the Summer drifted somnolently past, he regarded her with increasing fondness. By the time Fall came around, Joel considered himself on friendly terms with the wolf, though he never dared venture close enough to touch her.

By this time, too, the curiosity of the countryside was more or less satiated in regard to the albino wolf, and the traffic of visitors had long since returned to normal . . . one every two weeks.

Pete Martin worked the first homestead on the country road that led to Valley Junction. Pete Martin was the valley's pride as a wolf hunter.

"Sent three sons an' a daughter through college on wolf-hides!" he often asserted, referring to the monthly bounty-checks from the State.

"I'll give you fifty bucks fer that wolf-bitch," Pete told Joel. "You'll be winterin' in the city pretty soon, an' you can't take the hellion with you. I want to cross her with some o' my best dogs an' raise me a breed o' good wolf-hunters."

Eena, six months old now and as big as a grown wolf, snoozed in the shade of the kennel Joel had built for her. Joel frowned.

"If I could think of some way to keep her," he told the homesteader, "I'd never part with her. Under the circumstances, I'll take your offer. I'll be driving to the city within three days. I'll bring her by then."

The two men shook hands solemnly on the agreement.

That night, Eena burrowed under the chicken wire fence of her enclosure. Like a silent wraith, she disappeared into the trackless wilds of the pine forest.

Joel drove his battered coupé back to the city, fifty dollars poorer than he might have been.

October winds rustled the waters of Wolf Lake. Deciduous trees turned red and gold and brown. The foothills blazed with Nature's paintpot.

November skies were leaden. The frost giants awakened in the earth. Snow smothered the valley and the hills. Existence in the wild turned bleak and harrowing. On silent pads the wolfpack stole into the haunts of men. They followed the lead of a great white she-wolf, the largest and most cunning wolf ever seen.

The wolves swept down from the hills and lurked in the swirling skirts of the blizzard to strike and kill. They took a costly toll from the livestock that pastured in the valley. The homesteaders cursed the white she-leader of the pack. Joel Cameron's name was anathema on every tongue.

Eena was a year old the following spring. The handful of wolfling Joel Cameron had carried to his cabin a year before was now twice the size of the largest, sturdiest male in her pack. It was to this, and to her wise cunning, that she owed her leadership.

Eena regarded the black wolves lolling around her in the warm sun. These were her kind, yet not her kind. She knew she was different in more ways than size and the color of her pelt. For weeks she had felt a restlessness stirring inside her, an inexplicable thrilling of unknown significance.

Across the lake which glittered like a turquoise jewel in its setting of forest emerald, the sun sparkled upon the snowy mantilla of the mountain that thrust bare, stone shoulders up from a clinging bodice of pine woods.

Memory stirred the mind of the white she-wolf. She was thinking of a cabin hidden in a woodsy draw, hard by the waters of the lake. She remembered a clean-lined young face, a soothing voice that had spoken to her in pleasing, unintelligible syllables. She remembered kindness and something that amounted to friendship with a creature who was called man. Eena whimpered and got up.

The wolves rose with her and ringed around expectantly. A long moment Eena stood poised and silent, dwarfing the members of her pack. A thought, feeling . . . a command . . . went from her to them. The wolves sank back upon their haunches, tongues lolling. Eena turned and trotted alone into the forest.

The white wolf padded silently along sun-barred aisles of the forest. Her path led in an easy circle around the lake. Near sunset, she came unerringly upon the clearing occupied by Joel Cameron's cabin.

She crept into a thicket of elderberry trees and peered expectantly forth. Not toward the cabin, for that with the setting sun was at her back. Her questing glance winged across the darkening blue waters of the lake and fixed upon the glowing summit of the mountain.

Fascinated, Eena watched the fading beauty of it. The sky turned smoky-hued. A star or two glittered diamond-hard. A golden glow paled the sable sky beyond the shoulder of the mountain.

Crouched in the voiceless shadows, Eena held her breath and tingled with suspense. Instinct gave her thrilling warning. She was about to witness the essence of her difference from the wolfkind.

The moon came up full, a pumpkin-yellow disk, and rested its chin upon the mountain to ponder the scene thoughtfully before commencing its climb into the sky . . . And Eena *changed.*

The change shook her with ecstasy.

Bubbling rapture accompanied the smooth flowing of supple muscles, the adjusting of bones in their sockets. An excitement of sensual pleasure engulfed every nerve and sinew. Afterward, she lay for long supine, one arm flung across her eyes to bar the eldritch glare of the moon, panting, trembling with remembered delight.

She sat up at last and thrilled to the shapely beauty of her form. Eena knew she was a woman, and she was content. She did not question how this had come about.

Eena crept down to the water's edge and surveyed her reflection in the dark surface of the lake. A faint breeze stirred the platinum tresses against round, golden shoulders. Her face was eager, full-lipped with flaring brows accenting her gray-hazel eyes. Her body was high of breast and long of leg, and the moonlight caressed her with a touch of mystery and magic.

The cabin was still, high-lighted and shadowed in the moon-brimming canyon. Eena padded around it in a cautious circle. The air was dead, without scent. The man with the kind face and soothing voice was not here.

Puzzled and hurt, Eena turned away. She swam a while in the icy waters of the lake, revelling in the tonic effect of the chill.

Later, she roamed aimlessly, enjoying the easy response of her nerves and muscles. Once, her keen wolf-sense detected a rabbit quaking in a patch of brush. She started it up. As the frightened animal ran out, she sprinted swiftly and seized it in her hands. The rabbit uttered a thin, terrorized shriek and died.

Eena sank her teeth in the rabbit's throat and exulted to the gushing warmth of blood. She sat down upon the needled turf, methodically tore the animal to pieces and ate it.

From time to time in her wandering, Eena responded to her woman's nature and crept down to the lake to admire her reflection.

The night was short . . . too short. Eena's aimless perirgination brought her just before dawn to another cabin. Pierre Lebrut lived here. Eena's sensitive nose caught the trapper's reek strong upon the air. A sluggish memory stirred in her brain. Eena snarled without sound and retreated with the prickling of invisible hackles stirring the length of her spine.

A twig snapped under Eena's foot. Steel piano-wire sang and a bent sapling straightened with a rush. Eena was flung to earth, one foot jerked high in the wire noose of a snare. She threshed in wild panic, clawing and snapping wolf-fashion at the searing pain in her ankle.

Within the musty cabin, Lebrut sat up in his tumbled bunk.

"By gar, she sound like bear in dat trap!"

He slipped into heavy boots—he slept in his pants and undershirt —seized his rifle and hurried outside.

Gray dawn lighted the east, reflected palely into the forest. Lebrut saw the woman caught in his snare, laid down his rifle and hurried to release her.

"Sacre nom d'un loup!" he muttered, slackening the wire to re-move the noose from Eena's threshing ankle. "Lady, you pick fine time an' place for peecneec—an' w'at you do wit' no clo'es on?"

Pierre was excited and his voice shrill. The scent of him was over-powering in Eena's nostrils. She bit him savagely on the calf.

Pierre yelled in sudden fright. He fell heavily on the wolf-girl and she snapped and clawed in renewed terror. The man grunted with anger and fought her, pinioned her arms.

"You wild one, hein?" Eena's body was closed, arched and quiver-ing. Pierre grinned. "Maybe Pierre tame you wit' a kees, hein?"

The sun came up over the shoulder of the mountain and tinged the lake with blood . . . And Eena changed.

It was no sensation of pleasure to return to the wolf. Eena felt the agony of the change in every muscle and nerve. She screamed with the horrid crunching and grinding of bones in her head, lengthening into the lupine muzzle. Albino fur sprouted like a million thorny barbs from her tender skin.

Pierre was still wide-eyed and frozen with horror when the fangs of the agonized wolf ripped the life from his terror-stricken body.

Pete Martin looked grim as he pried open the stiffened fingers of the dead trapper. The wind stirred a tuft of albino fur on the dead man's palm.

"Your albino bitch, Joel," the homesteader said.

Joel bit his lip.

"It's a devil of a thing for a man to come back to, Pete." He looked stolidly down at the dead man. "Poor Pierre! He died hard." Joel brought his glance up to meet the kindly stare of the homesteader. "I know the valley blames me for not killing Eena when she was a pup."

Martin shrugged. "It's too late now for blame, Joel. Maybe I'm to blame for not takin' her with me the day I offered to buy her. I dunno." He scratched his long jaw. "Well, we better see about gettin' Pierre properly planted, I guess."

Joel's expression was darkly stormy. "I feel responsible for the cattle . . . for Pierre." He wondered silently when and where the white wolf would kill again. He tongued dry lips. "I'll track her down and destroy her."

"There's a thousand dollars on her hide, Joel. Every homesteader in the valley chipped in."

"If I bring in her hide," Joel clipped, "it won't cost the homesteaders a cent!"

The homesteader's gray eyes lighted with a friendly gleam.

"Figured you'd look at it like that, Joel. I'll give you what help I can . . ."

Joel spent the following month in the hinterland, returning to his cabin at intervals only to replenish supplies. The wolves were wary. He seldom came upon wolf-sign, and saw no wolves at all. But he heard them. By night their lonesome song rang eerily through the forest and echoed from the mountains.

Joel made final return to his cabin and that night drove his coupé down a moonlit road to the Martin homestead.

"Reckoned you wouldn't find her," the homesteader acknowledged Joel's acquiescence to defeat. "She knows she's hunted an' will always manage to be some place else. She was here night before last with her pack an' got my prize heifer."

Joel made a gesture of despair. "You see what I'm up against? Besides, I'm behind in my work. I came up here to finish a book. The publisher is yelling his head off for it. How can I write a book and hunt wolves, too?"

The homesteader spat a fine stream of tobacco juice. "You go ahead an' write your book, son. You've made your try an' 'twarn't your fault you failed. Some of us are gittin' together in the mornin'. We'll take to the wolf-trail an' stick it out till we git her!"

Joel's heart felt heavy. He still had a fond memory of the white she-wolf he had nursed from babyhood. He remembered her attitude of sage intelligence, her qualities that had made her seem almost human. Then he remembered she had turned killer, and he peered into the moon-shadows as he drove along the county road, half afraid he might spy her lurking there.

He turned down the indistinct ruts that led to his lakeside cabin, and another mile of bumpy going brought him home. The wobbling headlights swept across the cabin front, revealed an open door.

Joel suffered mild panic. Had a bear forced entry? He could imagine the shambles the animal had made of the interior. He sprang out and approached the house cautiously, rifle ready. Everything inside was in order. He lit the mantle of the kerosene lamp, went out and shut off the car lights and reentered the cabin.

Eena lay curled on a bearskin rug in front of the stone fireplace. Her platinum curls glistened silver contrast against the dull gold of her naked skin. She supported her chin with her hands and watched him with wide wary eyes. A patch of full-moon brilliance, brighter than the lamplight, puddled the floor at her feet.

Joel stared. She was a dream come to life. The shock of seeing her there dismayed him.

"Who are you?" he essayed at last.

Eena stirred languidly. Her expression mimicked a wolfish grin. Hot blood surged into Joel's cheeks. He caught up a dressing gown and flung it to her.

"Put it on," he ordered.

Eena sobered, regarded the garment, and swung her level glance back to the man.

"Haven't you ever seen clothes before?" he asked sarcastically. He crossed over and adjusted the robe hastily about her shoulders. "Suppose one of the neighbors came by?"

The possibility was not likely, he knew. He said things simply to cover up his own shock and embarrassment. He sat down heavily in a leather club chair and stared at her. Eena stared back with friendly indifference.

Joel's mind boiled with fantastic questions. The girl remained silent. Only her eyes spoke and their meaning was not quite clear to the beleaguered man.

He gave up trying to draw a word from her. Was she a deaf-mute? Who was she? Why was she here? He recalled stories he had heard of white savages; but those were found only in the wilds of the South American jungle, or in some hidden Shangri-La of Tibet. He tried to place her racial type but was unsuccessful. There was something familiar about the shape and look of her eyes, but what it was eluded him.

He knew only that she was very beautiful, that he wanted her as he had never wanted another human being before. He could not know that Eena was not quite . . . human.

"I can't sit here all night, just looking at you," he said at last. He grinned with wry humor. "It's an idea, though, at that!" He stood up. "Lady, if you will consent to occupy the guest room tonight, the hotel can accommodate you."

Joel held out his hand to help her rise. Eena moved like a flash, shaking off the encumbering dressing gown. She paused at the door and smiled at him. The lamplight made molten gold of her body, a tawny silhouette against the moon-silvered outdoors.

Then she was gone, like a wolf goes, on swift, silent pads.

And with her, the warmth went from the cabin. Joel felt a chill, followed by a helpless feeling of immeasurable loss.

In the cold, gray light of dawn, the cabin shivered to a thunderous knocking. Joel tumbled from bed, threw on a dressing gown and greeted Pete Martin at the door. Martin was backed by half a dozen husky homesteaders.

"Thought I'd let you know we're headin' along the wolf-trail."

Joel grumpily asserted the idea was a fine one, he was glad to know it, and now would they go away and let him sleep?

"We wouldn't have stopped," Martin apologized, "except we wondered about your visitor last night."

Joel's jaw cracked in the middle of a yawn. He swallowed hard and flushed blackly.

"Visitor? What visitor?" he hedged.

The homesteader crooked a finger and Joel followed out upon the porch. Martin pointed out the wolf-tracks that crossed and recrossed the yard.

"Those are the tracks of your white bitch, Joel. She came home last night. Didn't see her, did you?"

Joel closed his eyes. He felt a swimming sensation in his head.

"No. No, I didn't see her." Fantastically, he thought of the visitor he had seen and thought of her body mutilated and torn by sharp wolf-fangs. He shuddered.

The homesteader shrugged. "Keep a look-out for her, Joel. She'll be back again . . . if we don't git her first!"

He gestured to his companions, and they filed off into the forest. Joel stood alone, looking down at the tracks . . . at one track that had gone unnoticed by the others—the single print of a woman's shapely foot.

Joel Cameron was pleased with his own industry. He finished proofreading the final chapter of his book, gathered the manuscript together and wrapped it for shipment. There, it was off his mind.

He took the manuscript down to the village post office, collected a few necessary supplies. Toward sunset, he legged into his car and chugged away up the county road toward home.

Night shadows fell swiftly. The sky turned smoky, then sequinned. The moon came up full over the roof of the forest.

Joel turned into the ruts that meandered through the woods to his cabin. Wobbling headlamps bored a tunnel through the gloom. The night was eerily still throughout the pine woods. Joel slewed the machine around a bumpy turn. The wolf-woman stood starkly illumined in the glare of the headlights.

Joel jammed a foot on the brakes. He scrambled from his seat, calling. Eena flashed into the shadows. After two minutes struggle with the whipping underbrush, Joel gave up and went back to his car.

He was suddenly lonesome and despondent. He ground the coupé through the final furlong and killed the motor in front of the cabin.

Eena sat quietly upon the porch.

Even with the lights off, Joel could see her there. Her form was tawny gold in the moonlight. Her hair was a flashing silver aura enhaloing her laughing face.

Joel started toward her, thought better of it, and sat on the runningboard. Eena was less than ten feet away. Joel said nothing. Eena answered in kind.

After a while, Joel began to talk to her, softly. He mused and wondered aloud, letting his thoughts drift with the association of his words. Eena cocked her head attentively. She appeared to be listening, but he knew that his words held no meaning for her.

What language would serve him? What syllables would convey to her knowledge of the tumultuous beating in his breast her simple presence evoked?

He moved toward her, murmuring softly. He took the firm, golden flesh of her arm in his grasp. Eena looked up into Joel's strong kindly face. Her eyes spoke the thought her tongue could not.

Joel drew her gently to her feet. She swayed, and he caught her to him. Her lips were as tender and responsive as he had dreamed they would be. He took them, hungrily . . .

Eena prowled the forest resentfully. She hated to be hunted. Twice, now, the coming of the full moon had brought her only pangs of frustration. The hunters who swarmed in the woods prevented her going to the man she loved.

The pine woods shimmered in the heat of midsummer. Hunters from all over the state, attracted by the enormous price on Eena's hide, came to blunder among the hills. When they went away, defeated, others came instead of them.

Eena had no rest. She was hounded and harried. By night, the forest twinkled with campfires.

Once, a hunter reckless enough to hunt alone had cornered the she-wolf. Braving the fire of his weapon, Eena attacked and ripped the man to shreds of bloody ruin. The price on Eena's life doubled overnight.

Once, too, she had been trapped by a horde of hunters and their dogs at the lip of a precipice, overlooking Wolf Lake. The she-wolf leaped, and swam to safety through a hail of lead. The rock thereafter was called Wolf Leap and Eena's character became legendary.

The swelling moon nightly presaged the approach of the change. Eena longed for it, longed for the pleasure of her human form, and gladly paid with the pangs of her return to the wolf. All the savage ferocity of her wolf nature rebelled at the restriction the presence of hunters imposed. Then cunning asserted itself.

Joel's cabin lay westward. Eena turned her pointed muzzle into the east. On silent pads she fled through the silver and dross of the moonlit forest. At dawn, she rested.

Facing northward, she took up her way for a number of hours; then she turned into the west.

It was easy running. The way led up steep mountainsides, down precipitous declivities. She swam mountain torrents, crossed ravines on fallen pines. When she hungered, she pulled down a white-tailed deer and gorged on the kill.

In midafternoon, Eena made her way southward. She had completely encircled the hunters that swarmed in the forest.

The white wolf came at last into familiar territory at the west end of the lake. She slackened her pace, although a frantic urge to hurry assailed her. She knew the limitations of her human form, and with moonrise tonight the Change would be visited upon her. She wanted to be close by the cabin when that came to pass.

She had slightly more than an hour to span the miles that yet lay between.

Eena skulked along in the shadowy underbrush, pausing at intervals to scent for danger. She soon paralleled the lakeshore, a hurrying white wraith in the green-gray shadows of the forest. The wind brought a smell of dampness off the lake, a formless breath of stale fishiness. The pines cast long shadows upon the water. The sky darkened in the east.

A rifle cracked. The whistling missile spent itself far out over the lake, and Eena gathered her muscles with the instant response of spring steel and lunged ahead. A man yelled, and dogs began to bark frantically. Eena doubled away from the lake, putting on a fresh burst of speed.

The wind had betrayed her. It had come to her nostrils from the sterile face of the water, while her danger lay on the other hand.

A rifle spat livid flame in the green gloom ahead. Eena leaped, snarling and snapping at the trenchant pain in her shoulder. Spurting blood reddened her muzzle, stained the snowy pelt of her side.

Other rifles cracked all around her. Rifle balls whined nastily through the woods. The yelping of dogs was bedlam.

The white wolf recovered her stride in spite of her searing wound. She ran with desperation and terror hounding her, her goal an idea interlocked with the memory of a kindly face and a soothing voice.

Eena fled for the protection of the one being in all the forest whom she loved, the one man among men who loved her.

Joel Cameron heard the flat racketing of gunfire, the distant shouting and yelping. A strange uneasiness held him motionless, listening. He caught up his rifle and hurried to the door.

The noise swelled louder by the moment. Twilight pressed down upon the forest, swirled into the clearing about the cabin. Joel saw the men, then, flitting silhouettes between the pines, limned against the tarnished silver of the lake. The forest trembled with the belling of the dog-pack.

His ears caught another sound, nearer . . . more terrifying. He heard the swift whisper of racing pads, the sound of a heavy body hurtling through the undergrowth.

The enormous pale form of the wolf leaped from the forest edge, charged relentlessly toward him. A mental gong sounded in the man's clamoring brain. Joel's rifle snapped automatically into the hollow of his shoulder. The report ripped echoes from the hills.

The murderous shock of the ball lifted the white wolf, flung her with bleeding breast back upon her haunches. Gathering the last atom of her strength, Eena lunged and fell kicking at Joe Cameron's feet.

The man sighted carefully for the mercy shot that would send a bullet crashing into Eena's brain. The moon came up full over the shoulder of the mountain, bridged the lake with its golden track, thrust a questing beam through a gap in the pines.

The effulgent glow caressed Eena's wolf-form. Eena died with the ecstasy of the Change soothing the agony of her hurts.

Joel stared, uncomprehending. The rifle fell from his nerveless grasp. Slowly, his knees buckled. He dropped beside the huddled girl-shape, gathered limp, tawny shoulders against his chest and buried his face in the silver cloud of her hair.

He was holding her like that when the hunters burst into the moonlit clearing. He did not look up, even when they went silently away.

MAURICE LEVEL (1875–1928), who, according to the Library of Congress, was really a woman, Jeanne Mareteux-Level, reportedly wrote hundreds of *conte cruelles* for the French periodical *Le Journal.* Most Level stories that have found their way into American anthologies are taken from the scarce book *Tales of Mystery and Horror,* published in 1920 by Robert M. McBride and Co., but *Weird Tales* printed three gruesome Level short stories that are not in the McBride collection. (One of them, "Night and Silence," is included in my anthology *Masterpieces of Terror and the Supernatural.)* Here is the third of Level's *Weird Tales* appearances, "The Look," a chilling glimpse at the darker side of love that was published in March 1933.

THE LOOK

by Maurice Level

The log fire was dying in the grate. About the whole room, lighted by a too heavily shaded lamp, there was something vaguely menacing that chilled my blood the moment I entered it.

My friend came forward. "I am glad to see you, very glad," he said, holding out his hand.

He had aged and altered so that I should hardly have recognized him. Extending his hand in the direction of the fireplace, he said in a low voice, "My friend Janville . . . my wife."

I discerned a very pale face and a slender form that bowed slightly, while a subdued voice, a melancholy, weary voice, murmured, "We are pleased to see you here, *Monsieur.*"

My friend offered me a chair. The white form relapsed into immobility; and silence, a deadened silence through which flitted indefinable thoughts, fell upon us.

I could think of nothing to say. These two had been man and wife for some months. They had been in love for years before they were free to marry. And this was how I found them now!

My friend broke the silence with a hesitating inquiry as to my health, and his thought seemed far from the words that fell from his lips.

"Fine," I replied, and speaking lower, I added, "You are happy?"

"Yes," he muttered.

His wife coughed slightly, and rose.

"Forgive me, *Monsieur*, but I am a little tired. You will excuse me, I am sure. . . . Please do not go."

She crossed the dining-room, presented her forehead to her husband, and left us.

My friend got up and paced the floor with long strides, gnawing his mustache, then, stopping abruptly before me, put his hand on my shoulder.

"I said I was happy. That's a lie!"

I looked at him in mute astonishment.

"No doubt you think I am out of my mind," he continued. "Not yet, but I'm likely to be before long. . . . Don't you feel some sinister influence brooding over this house?"

"Your wife and you appear to be under some cloud, certainly. Some worry, no doubt, the importance of which you exaggerate."

"No! No! No! There's a horror hanging to these walls . . . there's a terror creeping about these floors. Between my wife and me there's the shadow of Crime . . . of Crime!

"As you know, she who today is my wife was for long months my mistress. You know how desperately I loved her . . . or rather you do *not* know . . . no one *can* know . . . I worshipped her, that creature, worshipped her to the point of devotion . . . of frenzy. From the day she came into my life, there was no other life for me. She became a need in my nature, a flaw in my sanity, a vice in my blood.

"I thought of running away with her, of challenging the voice of scandal. But neither of us had any means. I had only my profession to support me. And our being together openly in Paris was not to be thought of . . . so I put aside honor, every moral scruple. To see her more frequently, I obtained an introduction to the husband. I cultivated his acquaintance. I came to be his constant guest, his intimate friend.

"I made that despicable third in a household who, under the shelter of its welcome, steals in cold blood from its master his peace and happiness.

"I spent my holidays with them. He was a great sportsman; while he was out in the woods and fields I passed my time with her.

"One day we two were startled by loud cries. I ran downstairs, and found the terrified servants gathered around the husband.

"Stretched upon a couch, he was fighting for breath with quick, short gasps, as he clutched at a wound in his abdomen.

" 'Ah, *Monsieur,*' faltered the man who carried his game-bag, 'how suddenly it happened! *Monsieur* had just shot a woodcock . . . it fell in the rushes, he ran toward the spot, and all in a moment, I don't know how it happened, but I heard a report—a cry—and I saw *Monsieur* fall forward . . . I brought him here.'

"I cut away the clothes and examined his injuries. The charge had plowed through his side. Blood flowed in jets from a terrible wound extending from above the hip to the thigh.

"Years of training made me regard him solely as a patient. I examined him as if it had been a hospital case. I even gave a sigh of satisfaction as I learned that his injuries were really superficial. The intestines did not appear to be involved, but on the wound's internal surface a small artery was spurting freely.

"Hearing footsteps, I looked up, and saw Her standing in the doorway. A strange and unaccountable agony gripped my heart. It was with a great effort that I said, 'Don't come here. . . . Go away.'

" 'No,' she said, and drew nearer.

"I could not take my eyes from hers—she had fascinated them. My finger still pressing upon the artery, the sufferer full in her view, I watched that look of hers as a man watches a dagger pointed at his throat, a wavering dagger, the gleam of which hypnotizes him.

She drew still nearer, and a cloudy impotence fell upon my will. That look spoke things of terrible import. It seized upon my soul, that look; it spoke—no need of words to make me understand what it asked of me. It said:

" 'You can have me for your own. . . . You can take me and keep me. . . . I shall thrill to no other joy, faint under no other fondness . . . if only you will——'

"Once more I faltered: 'You must not stay here. . . . Go away.'

"But the look spoke again:

" 'Soul without resolution . . . heart that dares not . . . what have you always longed for? . . . Look! . . . Chance changes your dream to reality.'

"The artery pulsed under my finger and, little by little, strive as I would to maintain it, the pressure diminished.'

"She was close to me. She bent above me. Her breath played in my hair; the emanation from her body stole into every fiber of my being, impregnated my hands, my lips—that exhalation of love which was madness to me.

"All conception of time, of danger, of duty, fled from my mind.

"Suddenly the door opened, and a servant appeared with my surgical case. The stupor was dispelled.

" 'Quick! Give it to me!' I shouted rather than called.

"But then . . . I saw that my finger had deserted its post . . . that there was now no pulsation under it . . . that the stricken man's lip was drawn upward into the mocking semblance of a smile . . . and . . . that it was all over.

"Our eyes met. And in that moment a shadow fell between us, a shadow with a mocking smile—the shadow of the dead man. . . .

"I thought at first that this nightmare would fade away. I strove to assure myself that the fatal issue was an accident, unavoidable. But since she became my wife, that shadow is between us, always, everywhere. Neither speaks of it, but it comes between our meeting eyes.

"I—I see once more her eyes, the look, saying, 'Take me. Let us be free.' She—she sees once more my hand, as, by slow degrees, it lets the life of her husband ebb away. And hatred has come, a silent hatred, the hatred of two murderers who are in the bonds of a mutual fear.

"We remain for hours as you have seen us tonight. Words rush up within us, smite asunder the clenched teeth, half open the lips—and we keep silence."

He took a dagger from the table, tried the edge with his finger.

"Cowards . . . both of us!"

He flung the weapon, clanging, to the table, and burying his face in his hands, burst into tears.

"Methought I Heard a Voice," originally titled "When the Night Wind Howls," appeared in the November 1951 issue of *Weird Tales*. It is one of the popular tongue-in-cheek series known as the Gavagan's Bar stories by the late FLETCHER PRATT (1897–1956), novelist and historian, and L. SPRAGUE DE CAMP, (1907–   ), one of the few successful humorists in the science-fantasy genre. Gavagan's Bar, which first opened for business in 1950, shares some family resemblance to Lord Dunsany's Jorkens "club" stories, as well as Arthur C. Clarke's *Tales from the White Hart:* they are establishments where all manner of spirits may be imbibed, discussed and sometimes even experienced . . . but the only thing the patrons truly fear is Closing Time.

METHOUGHT I HEARD A VOICE

by L. Sprague de Camp and Fletcher Pratt

Doc Brenner came in just as Mr. Jeffers was delivering himself explosively.

"Psychiatry, phooey!" he said. "Psychology, phooey! Psychoanalysis, phooey! They're a bunch of witch doctors. All they do is substitute one phony belief for another. It wouldn't do him any good."

"What wouldn't do who any good?" said Doc Brenner. "I will start the evening with a double Manhattan, Mr. Cohan."

"Dr. Bronck here," said the stoop-shouldered and tweedy Professor Thott. "Dr. Bronck, meet Doc Brenner. He's a medical man and may be able to put you onto the person you want."

Brenner shook hands with a tall man who had an alligator-like smile, graying hair worn a little longer than normal, a vest edged with white piping and pince-nez on a black ribbon. "How do you do?" said this individual in a low tone, and glanced apprehensively over his shoulder toward the back of the room where two other customers were playing pinochle at a table. In a still lower tone he said, "I fear this young man is right. I doubt whether a psychiatrist would be the right person for my case."

"What seems to be the trouble?" asked Brenner, downing his double Manhattan and putting the cherry into his mouth.

He addressed Dr. Bronck, but it was Thott who answered. "He has a bad case of zombies."

"Zombies?" said Brenner.

"Zombies!" said Jeffers.

"Only one to a customer," said the bartender, firmly. "I am not forgetting the night that poor young felly, Mr. Murdoch, come in here and I let him have three of them. Him and his dragons!"

"It's all right, Mr. Cohan," said Thott. "As a matter of fact I'll have a Scotch and soda, myself. We weren't ordering, just discussing real zombies—the undead, as they call them in *Dracula.*"

"Is that what they call zombies after, now?" said Mr. Cohan. "Sure, it's a disgraceful thing, putting the name of a corpse to good liquor."

Brenner cleared his throat, and looked at Dr. Bronck. "Do you see them?" he asked.

"No, they see him," said Thott, once more speaking for his acquaintance, and as the latter again looked over his shoulder at the pinochle players. "I suppose I had better tell him about it, Fabian. It might be something that could be cured by a throat operation." Dr. Bronck shuddered; Thott turned to Brenner:

"He's really in a cruel dilemma, since he's a professional lecturer and things have become so bad that he hardly dares raise his voice above a whisper these days. We thought perhaps a psychiatrist"— Jeffers snorted audibly into his beer—"might be able to resolve the problem by reference to something in his past; but it is equally possible that the question is purely medical. We would value your opinion.

"I'm sure you must have heard of Dr. Bronck, even if you haven't met him before. No? That's because you're too exclusively a city mouse, Brenner. You should get out into the heart of America sometime, around among the ladies' clubs, and places adult education is conducted on the basis of attending one lecture a week all winter. You will find Dr. Bronck better known there than Albert Einstein and considerably more intimately. Dr. Bronck is a travel lecturer.

"Especially with regard to Egypt and the Holy Land, a subject on which he is uniquely qualified to speak by reason of having studied for the pastorate of the Dutch Reformed Church. Why didn't you go on with it, Fabian?"

Dr. Bronck whispered something behind his hand to Thott.

"Oh, yes, I remember you telling me now. He felt he could carry a more meaningful message to his audiences, and they would be more interested, if he did it in a secular way. It is his view that when people pay to hear a thing, they will accept it more readily and give it more thought than when it comes to them, so to speak, as a gift. In fact, one might call Dr. Bronck a secular religious teacher. He is very successful at it and has been heard by many thousands; I believe that they have frequently been forced to turn people away from his famous *Breakfast in Bethlehem* and the equally praised *Sailing in the Steps of St. Paul.*

"Both these lectures, like others in Dr. Bronck's repertoire, have been given so many times in the course of the thirty years he has been on the platform that his delivery of them has become practically automatic. It is his custom, I understand, not to alter so much as a word. When he returns from one of his summer trips he works up an entirely new lecture for the delectation of those audiences who have already heard his previous list, but will not willingly forego the privilege of having Dr. Bronck with them again.

"It is thus apparent that the text of what he has to say can in no way be responsible for the extraordinary affliction that has come upon him. Neither can it be his voice alone. Many years ago, at the very outset of his distinguished career, Dr. Bronck underwent a course of instruction at the Della Crusca Institute of Polyrhythmic Vocal Culture to improve both his speaking voice and his knowledge of English. The tonal habits he acquired at that time have changed only so much as advancing years would allow; when he delivers a lecture, it is identical with the last previous reading of the same text, not only in the words used, but as to gestures, intonations and pauses. Do I exaggerate, Fabian?"

Dr. Bronck shook his head, beckoned to Mr. Cohan, and pointed to the glasses. "More libations, good Boniface," he said in a stage whisper.

"It is possible that his voice alone might have a hypnotic effect on certain individuals under the right conditions. It is also possible that the subject matter may in some way combine with the voice, but I am at a loss to account for the—spreading of the contagion.

"However—Dr. Bronck spent his summer in the Holy Land that year, retracing the footsteps of Saul and David. It was something he had done before, but on this occasion he was putting the whole thing onto color film, including the famous cave of the Witch of Endor, for his lecture entitled *Sorcerers and Spiritual Leaders of the Old Testament,* which is so much appreciated throughout the South.

"The lecture is one that he had delivered in previous years without provoking untoward incidents, and then dropped for some time because he had only slides to illustrate it. He revised it somewhat for reappearance on the list, and it made the sensational success that is usual with Dr. Bronck's lectures." (Dr. Bronck smiled his ample, tooth-displaying smile, ducked his head slightly as though acknowledging applause, and said: "Thank you" in a small voice.)

"I do not believe he noticed the change in the reception of this lecture at first, though if he had it is difficult to see how he could have avoided the trouble that later arose. The change came about as gradually as the emergence of a forest fire from a single dropped cigarette, and its origin is as hard to trace as the point where the cigarette was dropped.

"Looking back over it, Dr. Bronck is inclined to believe that the first manifestation which forced itself upon his attention was when he gave *Sorcerers and Spiritual Leaders* in Birmingham. Am I right about it being Birmingham, Fabian? At the end of a lecture it is his custom to have a question period, since a part of his popularity is due to the feeling of personal acquaintanceship he leaves with his audiences. Many people, of course, do not wish to stay for this period, so when the lights are turned on and he says '. . . and so, my friends, we take leave of the Holy Land and return to our workaday world,' there is a certain amount of movement toward the exits. This was true at the Birmingham lecture; but two men in the audience, instead of leaving in the ordinary way by the doors at the back of the hall, marched straight up and out the emergency exit at the side of the speaker's platform.

"At the time Dr. Bronck was extremely busy with his questions and the incident only flicked at his attention as a minor discourtesy which he noted out of the corner of his eye. It was only later, when the matter became more important and he was trying to remember details, that he realized that something odd about the appearance of the pair had registered on his subconscious memory. They were staring straight before them and lifting their feet very high as they walked; and Dr. Bronck recalls the thought flashing across his mind in the fraction of a second that both men must be drunk.

"What is it, Fabian? . . . Oh, yes, he says it is not unusual to prepare for a religious lecture in the South by the liberal ingestion of corn liquor. People seem to feel that it enables them to attain more readily the emotional state desirable for receiving a revelation. Which reminds me, Mr. Cohan, our emotional states require a little bolstering. Will you see to it?

"On that circuit a lecture at Birmingham is usually followed by others at Tuscaloosa, Selma, Montgomery, and Mobile. Dr. Bronck recalls nothing of special interest about the first three, but at Mobile, where the lecture was held in the open air under a tent, the Birmingham incident was repeated—that is, men shouldered out straight past the speaker's platform when the lights came up. Only this time there were four of them instead of two, all walking in the same peculiar dazed manner. Again Dr. Bronck was too busy with his questions to notice the incident except as one makes a mental remark upon a repeated peculiarity. It was not until he had covered Pensacola and Tallahassee and swung up to Waycross, Georgia, that the matter really forced itself upon his attention.

"At Waycross, seven or eight people, men and women alike, nearly half a row, stood up and marched out when the lights came on. They used the normal exit at the rear of the hall this time, but Dr. Bronck was looking directly at them, and he could not miss the fact that the whole group, who had been sitting together, left with the same high step and fixity of vision he had remarked at Birmingham and Mobile.

"After he had finished the usual post-lecture reception at the home of one of the social leaders of Waycross and was in his hotel room, restoring his emotional state, he connected the occurrence with the two previous incidents. As he did so, something struck him with prodigious force. Two of the four men of Mobile had also been present at Waycross, and as nearly as he could recall, the same two were the pair that had pushed past the speaker's platform at Birmingham. Then he remembered also that in all three places he had given the same lecture—*Sorcerers and Spiritual Leaders.* At Selma and Pensacola, where the audience exhibited their admiration of Dr. Bronck in the normal manner, he had given *Breakfast in Bethlehem,* and at

Tuscaloosa, Montgomery and Tallahassee, it was *Sailing in the Steps of St. Paul.*

"You may judge that it was with some trepidation that he approached the next reading of the unfortunate *Sorcerers and Spiritual Leaders* lecture, which was scheduled for Columbia, South Carolina. As soon as he reached the platform and began looking over the audience in the few minutes while being introduced, his fears were justified. The same two men were there, now sitting in the middle of a row of people, all of whom seemed to bear a family resemblance, in that their faces had a curious colorless character. They were pecfectly well-behaved, merely sat there with their hands in their laps, waiting for him to begin; did not even applaud when the chairman finished his introduction and Dr. Bronck stepped to the podium. And when he had finished, they marched out in single file, the whole row of them, moving as though they had been hypnotized or stunned.

"However flattering it is to a lecturer when part of his audience follows him from place to place, it is a somewhat unnerving experience to be a focus of attraction for a growing group of people who look as though they had just come from a graveyard, and who are not really there to listen to the lecture, but to be thrown into a state of ecstatic catalepsy by the lecturer's voice. Not to mention that Dr. Bronck felt his position as a religious teacher might be compromised by such events, which, although not altering the value of his teaching, might be taken in the wrong spirit by the unthinking.

"By the time he reached Asheville and there were twenty of these persons in the audience, Dr. Bronck was more than a little disturbed. It was evident that the people who are normally his hearers had begun to notice the intrusion of these peculiar characters, and were not taking it too well. And it was also apparent that the effect of the lecture on these individuals was impermanent; they reached their period of exaltation after hearing Dr. Bronck for an hour, and then the effect apparently gradually wore off, so that they had to have the dosage renewed. He was thus being pursued about the country by a retinue that was growing embarrassingly.

"Upon consideration, he decided that in a manner which he could by no means explain, the zombie effect was produced by the lecture *Sorcerers and Spiritual Leaders of the Old Testament.* By telegraphing ahead, he managed to persuade his sponsors at Lynchburg, Virginia, to accept *Breakfast in Bethlehem* instead. His special group was present, larger than ever, not having been advised of the change, but he was relieved to see that only one of them—one of the original two from Mobile—left with the typical high step and fixed stare. The rest shambled out, looking at the floor, with their hands in their pockets.

"This particular tour ended at Richmond and Dr. Bronck enjoyed a week of rest before taking a swing through New England and central New York. In the interval he waited on his agents, McPherson and Kantor, and told them firmly that he declined to deliver *Sorcerers and Spiritual Leaders* again. They are notorious slave-drivers—I have been under their management myself—but they were not too averse, as audiences in the northern states require a somewhat more sophisticated and more sentimental approach, and Dr. Bronck's habit of not modifying his lectures was well established.

"He did Connecticut and Rhode Island easily, though at Bristol, where he gave *Characters of the Crusades,* he thought he recognized one of his Southern friends in the audience. At Worcester, however, he was shocked. The lecture was *Sailing in the Steps of St. Paul* and his eye, now attuned to looking for it, caught the zombie effect in at least two of those present. One of them was definitely a person who had attended one of the *Sorcerers and Spiritual Leaders* lectures in the South.

"You will understand that Dr. Bronck has little opportunity to make personal observations of the thousands of people who come to hear him, except as they are unusual in some way. But the Worcester experience was shocking because at that point he realized that his peculiar clientele had not deserted him when he ceased to give *Sorcerers and Spiritual Leaders.* They had merely been following him and accustoming themselves to the accent of his voice until anything he said in any lecture would produce the effect they desired.

"At Albany, he felt himself on safe ground again, having given *Breakfast in Bethlehem,* but at Utica, where he gave *Sailing in the Steps of St. Paul,* there were four who left with the cataleptic march, and by time he reached Binghamton and *Characters in the Crusades,* the number had become eight.

"He managed to finish this tour, which terminated at Buffalo, without having his private audience attract too much attention from the others and, after another brief rest, went out for a trip along the

Pacific Coast, which had no incidents except for the simultaneous exhibition of the zombie effect on almost a third of his audience in Los Angeles. It was fortunately the last lecture of the year; he believed that he had conquered whatever influence was at work—at least on audiences above the Los Angeles level—and happily embarked for Rome, where he spent the summer in working up a new lecture."

(Dr. Bronck abruptly emitted a loud burp and motioned for the refilling of his glass.)

"Yes, Fabian, I know. Mr. Cohan will take care of the matter. In the fall, the first tour arranged for him was through Ohio, Kentucky, and Tennessee. I believe it opened at Columbus, did it not, Fabian? Dr. Bronck had just arrived in the city and was seated in his hotel room, restoring his emotional state, when he received a telephone call. It was a man's voice, with the sugary accent of the deep South; he said that he had heard Dr. Bronck lecture during the previous year, and wished to discuss a theory with him. The theory was that the world had really been created in 1932, complete with records and people whose memories indicated an earlier existence. Now this sort of thing happens rather frequently to lecturers, as good God, I know, and Dr. Bronck put up the standard defense, which was to say that he was engaged with somebody in the room. But the man was persistent, and Dr. Bronck was forced to enter upon explanations. After a minute or two he asked some semi-rhetorical question, ending with "Wouldn't it?" or something like that, and was rather surprised to get no answer. He called "Hello!" two or three times, still without drawing any reply. There was no click of the phone hanging up; just nobody answering at the other end. That night—"

"That night was bloody awful," said Dr. Bronck. "I need a drink when I think of it."

"Indeed, it must have been awful, Fabian. There were at least twenty of the gray-faced people in the audience, and although the lecture was the new one he had made up in Rome, *Children of the Catacombs,* every single one of them got up and went out with the sleepwalker gait. They had apparently been increasing their sensitivity by practicing with transcriptions of Dr. Bronck's voice. Or perhaps, during the summer in Rome, the voice itself had acquired the additional richness and timbre necessary to the easy production of the zombie effect, regardless of the words spoken.

"At Dayton, Dr. Bronck found the numbers of his special audience tragically increased, and at Cincinnati, where he gave *Breakfast in Bethlehem* in an effort to dismiss them for one night at least, he found that they had attuned themselves even to this lecture. He gave but one more public lecture—at Lexington—after which he wired to McPherson and Kantor that he was suffering from a severe nervous breakdown and would have to cancel the rest of the trip. He—"

"That isn't the worst, my friend," said Dr. Bronck, his voice showing evident traces of the improvement in his emotional state. "That isn't the worst at all. They try to telephone me; at all hours of the day and night they try to telephone me. They ash—ask questions —where is the Mount of Gibeon? Wha' line of march did the Israelites take under Joshua? My friends, it is a conspiracy to keep me talking until the wire goes dead. They meet me on the public streets in their cerements of a forgotten world. They are ruining my professhion; they are depriving me of the privilege of carrying joy to many souls in spiritual need. They form associations and besiege my agents with requests that I speak before them—calling themselves the Arcane Adepts of St. Louis, or the Blavatsky Circle of Los Angeles—they offer me fabulous sums to pander to—"

His voice had risen, and as he flung out one arm in an oratorical gesture, "Look!" said Doc Brenner, suddenly, and pointed.

The two pinochle players at the back had dropped their cards. With arms at their sides and heads held back, staring straight before them with unwinking eyes, they were marching toward the door, each foot carefully lifted and placed before the other.

REX DOLPHIN only contributed one story to *Weird Tales* in July 1954, but it is a gem. According to lyricist Alan Jay Lerner and composer Frederick Loewe, there is a charming Scottish town, Brigadoon, that appears only once a century. Dolphin's village of Wychburne is equally hard to find, but that is fortunate; it holds scant charm for the hapless tourist who visits it in "Off the Map."

OFF THE MAP

by Rex Dolphin

Excuse my shivers, but it's good to sit down over a cigarette and recover my wits and talk to someone who can perhaps persuade me that it never happened.

I often knock around about the countryside, looking out unusual and picturesque places, and one of my pleasures in an old English town is to haunt the second-hand bookshops in search of local lore.

See this? Yes, it's an old map—seventeenth century to be exact—and I found it in a musty old shop in a part of the country I'd better not mention. No, this has nothing to do with buried treasure, though to be truthful it does concern some golden guineas; guineas that no one will touch. Give you the chance? Maybe, but there's something you should know first.

Here on the map are three villages. Let's call them Burgholme, Wychburne and Ervington. Burgholme and Ervington you can still find on modern maps; you'll look in vain for Wychburne. Where has it gone, you ask? That's the whole point . . .

As you see, Wychburne lay between the other two villages, but today's large-scale map will show you nothing but wild and waste land, moor, hill and bog. Intrigued by this, I searched encyclopedias and guidebooks old and new, but not a word about Wychburne. There seemed to be a conspiracy of silence wrapped about the place and I began to wonder if it had ever existed except in the old mapmaker's imagination; or, due to the primitive cartographic methods of that day, it had been placed many miles from its true site and now bore a different name.

That disastrous curiosity made me take a train to the nearest town and hike six miles to Burgholme. This place was little more than a hamlet, with no church, chapel or pub. The weather that late summer afternoon was Novemberish, damp with a swirling mist, and the sun giving up his efforts in disgust.

After the long walk the sudden ending of exercise made me chilly, and the need for refreshment was evident. I searched the dismal village for the usual battered and ill-written TEAS sign without which no English village, however small, is complete. There wasn't one in Burgholme.

So it would have to be a cortage. They all looked equally unfriendly. I picked one and knocked at the door.

It was opened by a thin-faced middleaged woman who said: "Well?"

A ragged staring little girl appeared beside her and in the background, a brawny farm laborer.

"Excuse me, but can you provide me with a tea?" I said politely.

She didn't answer. Instead, the man came nearer and said in a pointedly unfriendly manner:

"What are you doing in Burgholme anyway, mister? Nobody ever comes here."

Since I never dress in conventional hiker's kit, perhaps the question was understandable.

"Just hiking," I replied. "And I've got hungry and thirsty."

"Ha!" said the man. And they all looked at me as if I were a being from another world.

"I'll pay you well."

That turned the trick. "All right. Come in."

"Thanks."

It was a silent meal. All attempts at conversation failed. As I ate, they sat and watched every movement of my face and hands; and though to be fair, the food was good and plentiful, it was the most uncomfortable meal I've ever had.

At the end I made one more attempt.

"What is the quickest way to Ervington?"

The inevitable answer: "Why d'you want to go to Ervington, Mister?"

"I'm just walking for pleasure—seeing the countryside. Can't you understand that?"

"No." But he gave me the route to Ervington all the same. It was a roundabout way and entailed going backward to get forward.

"Can't I get there across country, then?" I asked.

"Not if you don't want to get lost."

"Surely there must be some sort of a footpath?" I asked. And then came what I had been leading up to: "After all, long ago there used to be a village—probably in ruins now—between here and Ervington . . ."

A look, queer, as of suppressed horror, came to the faces of the man and woman.

". . . a place called Wychburne . . ."

The woman went dead white. The man made the Sign of the Cross and said in an unnatural voice:

"There are some places it don't do to talk about, mister. Better go."

"What's the matter with Wychburne?" I persisted.

The man got up, stood between me and his family.

"Go," he said, and almost pushed me through the doorway.

As I walked away I saw their terrified faces watching me from behind the curtain.

The air seemed to get grayer and colder as I passed the last few huddled cottages that marked the end of the village—the end that, according to the old map, led past the entrance to the Wychburne road. There was a sound now, that of shuffling and of sticks tapping on the pebbled road.

It came towards me. It came out of the swirling mist, a bent old man making wearily for home. He must have been eighty, to judge by his folded and lined face and deepset rheumy eyes which he turned questingly in my direction. His tattered black coat hung loosely on his body.

I stopped. So did his shuffling.

"Should there be," I said loudly, for I imagined he would certainly be deaf, "be a road leading to Wychburne somewhere along here?"

Dead silence for a few seconds, the silence of utter shock.

Then he dropped his sticks and ran—yes, this old man ran—towards the village. Hoppityhop, like a crippled crow, his coat flapping about him.

My first feeling was to laugh, both at the idea and the spectacle. Then I checked myself. What, other than intense fear, could have given those withered legs wings? What was there about the mere name of Wychburne that inspired terror?

I shrugged my shoulders to myself and persuaded myself that country superstitions—whatever they were in this case—were sheer nonsense. Well clear of the village now, I seemed to be in a deserted land. Getting out my maps, I checked my position. Yes, just around here, perhaps fifty yards along on the left, should be the road or track to Wychburne.

Then the mist closed about me like a blanket dropped over my head. This is where, if I hadn't been dead stupid or hungry with curiosity, I should have turned back to the comparative civilization of Burgholme. Instead, I searched around and found what seemed to be a rough track. I got out my compass, set a course, and went into the fog.

What I had struck I don't know, but I stumbled over rocks, tore my trousers in thorn bushes, sank up to my ankles in squelch, tripped over what the folk in those parts call pot-holes, and fell flat on my face more than once. And all these hazards were invisible. Sweat poured off me from sheer pigheadedness and exhaustion.

How long this lasted I could not judge, but just as I said to myself, "Stop it, you fool, you're all in!" I seemed to come to the end of the difficulties and found beneath my feet a level although still stony track. All my strength flowed back.

Then, from far ahead in the mist, came the thin flowing notes of a fiddle, playing some kind of an old country jig. And, faintly, the ebb and flow of voices raised in revelry, as if Merrie England were here again.

The road led steeply down into the valley, but still nothing could be seen. The sounds of merriment got nearer and nearer, and finally I felt, "I'm here!"

Very gradually the mist cleared and there it was—Wychburne! A compact little village, nestling under the surrounding steep clifflike hills, almost as if a giant had scooped out a spoonful of the earth's surface and dropped the village neatly into the cavity. The houses were grouped around a neat village green on which the fiddlers were playing and a merry crowd dancing. Girls and men, all dressed in the colorful clothes of Restoration days.

There wasn't a thing modern in the place, from the rosecovered timber-and-white cottages to the horse-wagons "parked" in the inn-yard. What could there be about this place to inspire terror? Wychburne was charming!

But what was its secret? Was it a "lost village"—a place that was unknown to outsiders, that had resisted the inroads of modern progress, had become cut off and was so completely self-contained as to be capable of carrying on an independent existence? It was inaccessible enough, and its approaches certainly didn't invite visitors, let alone motor traffic. Surveyors, mapmakers, census takers, county planners—how could all these have overlooked its existence? Yet the fact remained that it didn't exist in present-day records!

The mist—perhaps that explained it. If Wychburne was permanently hidden from view both from land and air, all these things were conceivable.

I moved towards the inn-yard, stood looking at the scene, now close-up, and a strange feeling of timelessness and of not being myself came over me. Everything now was larger than life, overintimate, and as I threaded among the people I saw their faces close to mine, felt the push of their bodies, and the air was full of their rich voices and laughter and snatches of song and music. There was, too, an indefinable odor—a thing one notices only among people of a different race.

Suddenly a face turned towards me and eyes looked straight into mine. It was a heavy countryman's face, but full of dignity and independence, and the wide-brimmed tall feathered hat added to its stature.

"What do ye here, stranger?" the man asked in accents I'd never heard before.

"Traveling," I answered. "What goes on here, a carnival?"

"And whence come ye, stranger?"

"From London."

"From London!" he echoed, and there was a gasp in his voice. Then he shouted to the crowd, "The stranger comes from London!"

The crowd took up the words in a kind of prolonged echo: "From London! From London!"

The words hummed around for some seconds, then the music stopped. The laughter stopped. The voices stopped.

From a window above the inn a low wailing shriek started, gathering strength and building up to a horrible scream that ended abruptly in a choking sob. I looked and saw that it had been uttered by a girl whose beautiful face now expressed final hopelessness.

A hundred faces seemed to turn in my direction, seemingly all accusing me of some awful crime. And indeed there was a feeling of guilt on me, but guilt of just what I didn't know, although I felt I should have knowledge.

The people now seemed to peel away from me, until I was left isolated on the green. The man who had spoken to me had vanished; now he suddenly reappeared at the head of a small group of purposeful-looking men.

They all bore long staves, and the foremost—my man—lunged at me with his, catching me a painful blow under the heart.

"What means this?" I gasped in anger. Fear was to come later.

"Begone, bringer of evil!" he roared.

Then they all set about me with the staves, not one man coming near enough to touch me with his hands. Argument was futile. I turned and ran—ran while I still had brains in my head and whole bones in my legs.

Crash, crash, they hit me with their sticks as they pursued. I stumbled over rocks and tree-roots as I made the rough ascent out of the village in the opposite direction to that from which I had entered. I fell, was beaten all over, rose, ran, fell again—a deadly, killing repetition. In the middle of all this, the mist closed about me again. And still those fiends hounded me. I must have run miles.

I fell for the last time. I was finished. I tried to rise. It was useless. A savage flurry of blows rained on my head. Then—blackout.

When I regained my senses, I was lying flat, face down on the hard rock, soaked to the skin with mist and bruised all over. A few inches from my eyes, lying on the stony ground, was what I took at first to be a much-weathered halfpenny. I reached out for it painfully—I suppose it's a human instinct to pick up a coin however valueless— scraped it and rubbed it clean on my tattered sleeve.

I sat up sharply, my distress forgotten. It was a Charles II golden guinea! And there was another, and another! Five altogether I found, and the remnants of metal buckles, which seemed to argue a whole leather bagful of coins. The others were no doubt scattered around or buried. I told myself I would come back here later and search properly. Meantime, my exhaustion had returned and I had to get to shelter if I wasn't to die of exposure.

There was some sort of a track here and I followed it as best I could. Presently, still with thick mist hiding everything, I felt my feet touch tarmac, and I pushed on, miles it seemed, till a glimmer ahead showed another village. This, I knew, must be Ervington, last of the three villages on the map.

A hanging sign, unreadable in the mist, appeared ahead, and below it the welcome warmth of lights; and soon I heard the friendly undertone of casual inn conversation. I walked in, feeling like a second-hand scarecrow that the crows have defeated.

The conversation stopped. The few customers, all seated, stared at me. The landlord, a shrewd-looking, puckered-faced short man, stopped polishing a glass. His look was enough question.

"Wychburne," I muttered. "What is Wychburne? Can anyone tell me? I've just got back . . ."

The drinkers all stood up, as if drilled, edged their way round me one by one, and dashed out into the road. I gazed after them. When I looked back to the bar, the landlord had laid a double-barrelled shotgun meaningly across it, the snouts in my direction.

"Stay," he rasped. "Don't move an inch nearer my bar."

"Look," I said desperately, "I'm sick of these riddles. Everything that's happened since I arrived in these parts has been inexplicable. Do *you* know the answer?"

He twisted a grin. "I'm no oracle, mister. But though I'm not as dumb as the local population, being a bit of a travelled man and partly educated, I still respect their superstitions. Let's see . . . somehow you heard of Wychburne? You tried to find it? You're a Londoner? You found Wychburne and they drove you out, nearly killing you in the process?"

I answered each question with a nod.

"Yes," he mused, "I suppose it was bound to happen one day."

"You've not quite finished," I pointed out.

"How, mister?"

I fished in my pocket. "Where I fell, I found the remains of a leather bag and these." I held up the gold pieces.

"My God, that as well? *So it isn't just a legend!*" The last words were muttered almost to himself.

He was scared.

"Yes—and now the explanation, man!" I pressed. "What is Wychburne?"

"There's no such place," he said. He lifted the bar-flap, picked up the gun, and grunted: "Go through that door and out into the back-yard, quick!"

In no condition to argue with a shotgun, I obeyed.

"How can you say there's no such place?" I demanded. "After what I've just been through? And what's the meaning of this panto-mime?"

"There was such a place. Not now. Get undressed."

"*What?*"

"Get undressed. Jump into that old butt. Don't argue, man. It's the best I can do for you. Good. Stay there a minute."

He went across the cobbled yard to the back door; returned quickly carrying a can of liquid. He found a long stick, pushed my clothes, still containing the guineas, well away from me as I stood shivering in the empty barrel and poured the fluid over them. It was kerosene, from the oily stench. A match, a sheet of smoky flame, and my clothes were ashes.

What was he going to do to *me?* So far I had believed him—he was by far the most rational being I'd met since arriving in the neighbor-hood—but now, was I dealing with a maniac?

Back into the house he went, coming out this time with a large jug and a long hose which was still attached to something inside the house. He pointed the hose at me . . . Something sprayed out . . .

It was nothing more than water, but almost unbearably hot. "Soap coming over!" he called. "Catch!"

Then he poured the contents of the jug over me into the butt. A very powerful disinfectant, by the smell.

"Now wash!" he ordered. "As thoroughly as you can."

"All right," I spluttered. "You seem to know what you're doing, though it still beats me. Now you tell me all about Wychburne."

"Nearly three hundred years ago," he said slowly, "a traveller set out from London on a horse, carrying all his gold in a leather bag.

He was escaping from something and looking for an isolated country hideout where he could stay till the trouble was over.

"Yes, he found Wychburne. He stayed at the inn there. The first to die was the innkeeper's daughter. They knew he was the cause. They chased him out of the village and beat him to death with the staves. The gold stayed with him. Nobody would touch it.

"In less than a week, there wasn't a life left in Wychburne. The men of Ervington and Burgholme pitched oil, straw, and everything inflammable they could find into Wychburne from the steep hills around it and set fire to the whole village. Then they rolled boulders into it and filled up the little valley with rocks and earth till not a sign of the village remained. That's the story, and it's known to every soul in the two villages—and until today by nobody else."

"But what happened to me?" I cried, shivering.

"That's anybody's guess, mister."

"And what—?" I began, but he'd vanished into the house again.

This time he came back with a rough outfit of clothes, shoes, an old towel, half a bottle of brandy and some sandwiches.

"When you're dressed, get yourself to a doctor, and don't use any transport. You might be all right, but there's no telling."

"You mean I'm to walk?" I gasped.

"Sorry, mister. Yes."

"No chance of staying the night?"

"Ugh. Not likely. You see, these things happened in 1665—the year of the Great Plague."

Don't go, my friend . . . Don't look at me like that . . . for God's sake . . .

FREDRIC BROWN (1906–72), one of my favorite genre authors, produced many novels of mystery, science fiction, humorous fantasy and horror, including *The Fabulous Clipjoint, What Mad Universe, The Lights in the Sky Are Stars, Angels and Spaceships* and "Arena," one of the best "space opera" science fiction adventures ever written. "The Last Train," his third and final *Weird Tales* appearance, was in January 1950.

THE LAST TRAIN

by Fredric Brown

Eliot Haig sat alone at a bar, as he had sat alone at many bars before, and outside it was dusk, a peculiar dusk. Inside the tavern it was dim and shadowy, almost darker than outside. The blue bar mirror heightened the effect; in it Haig seemed to see himself as in dim moonlight from a blue moon. Dimly but clearly he saw himself; not double, despite the several drinks he had had, but single. Very, very single.

And as always when he had been drinking a few hours he thought, maybe this time I'll do it.

The *it* was vague and big; it meant everything. It meant making a big jump from one life to another life that he had so long contemplated. It meant simply walking out on the moderately successful semishyster lawyer named Eliot Haig, walking out on all the petty complications of his life, on the personal involvements, the legal chicanery that was just inside the letter of the law or indetectably outside; it meant cutting the cable of habit that tied him to an existence that had become without meaning or significance or incentive.

The blue reflection depressed him and he felt, more strongly than usual, the need to move, to go somewhere else if only for another drink. He finished the last sip of his highball and slid off the stool to the solid floor. He said, "So long, Joe," and strolled toward the front.

The bartender said, "Must be a big fire somewhere; lookit that sky.

Wonder if it's the lumberyards other side of town." The bartender was leaning to the front window, staring out and up.

Haig looked up after he had gone through the door. The sky was a pinkish gray, as though with the glow of a distant fire. But it covered all of the sky he could see from where he stood, with no clue to the direction of the conflagration.

He strolled south at random. The far whistle of a locomotive came to his ears, reminding him.

Why not, he thought. Why not tonight? The old impulse, ghost of thousands of unsatisfactory evenings, was stronger tonight. He was walking, even now, toward the railway station; but that he had done before, often. Often he had gone so far as to watch trains depart, thinking, as he watched each: I should be on that train. Never actually boarding one.

Half a block from the station, he heard clang of bell and chug of steam and the starting of the train. He'd missed that one, if he'd had the nerve to take it.

And suddenly it came to him that tonight was different, that tonight he'd really make it. Just with the clothes he had on, the money that happened to be in his pocket. Just as he'd always intended; the clean break. Let them report him missing, let them wonder, let someone else straighten the tangled mess his business would suddenly be without him.

Walter Yates was standing in front of the open door of his tavern a few doors from the station. He said, "Hello, Mr. Haig. Beautiful aurora borealis tonight. Best one I've ever seen."

"That what it is?" Haig asked. "I thought it was reflection from a big fire."

Walter shook his head. "Nope. Look north; the sky's kind of shivery up that way. It's the aurora."

Haig turned and looked north, back along the street. The reddish glow in that direction was—yes, "shivery" described it well. It was beautiful, too, but just a little frightening, even when one knew what it was.

He turned back and went past Walter into the tavern, asking, "Got a drink for a thirsty man?"

Later, stirring a highball with the glass rod, he asked, "Walter, when does the next train leave?"

"For where?"

"For anywhere."

Walter glanced up at the clock. "In a few minutes. It's going to highball any second now."

"Too soon; I want to finish this drink. And the next one after that?"

"There's one at ten-fourteen. Maybe that's the last one out tonight. Up to midnight anyway, it is; I close up then, so I don't know."

"Where does it— Wait, don't tell me where it goes. I don't want to know. But I'm going to be on it."

"Without knowing where it goes?"

"Without caring where it goes," corrected Haig. "And look, Walter, I'm serious. I want you to do this for me: if you read in the newspapers that I've disappeared, don't tell anyone I was here tonight, or what I told you. I didn't mean to tell anyone."

Walter nodded sagely. "I can keep my trap shut, Mr. Haig. You've been a good customer. They won't trace you through me."

Haig swayed a little on the stool. His eyes focused on Walter's face, seeing the slight smile. There was a haunting sense of *familiarity* in this conversation. It was as though he had said the same words before, had had the same answer.

Sharply he asked, "Have I told you that before, Walter? How often?"

"Oh, six—eight—maybe ten times. I don't remember."

Haig said, "God," softly. He stared at Walter and Walter's face blurred and separated into two faces and only an effort pulled them back into one face, faintly smiling, ironically tolerant. It had been oftener, he knew now, than ten times. "Walter, am I a lush?"

"I wouldn't call you that, Mr. Haig. You drink a lot, yes, but—"

He didn't want to look at Walter any more.

He stared down into his glass and saw that it was empty. He ordered another, and while Walter was getting it, he stared at himself in the mirror behind the bar. Not a blue mirror here, thank God. It was bad enough to see two images of himself in the plain mirror; the twin images Haig and Haig, only that was now an outworn joke with himself and it was one of the reasons he was going to catch that train. *Going* to, by God, drunk or sober he'd be on that train.

Only that phrase too had a ring of uneasy familiarity.

How many times?

He stared down into a glass a quarter full and the next time it was over half full and Walter was saying, "Maybe it *is* a fire, Mr. Haig, a big fire; that's getting too bright for an aurora. I'm going out a second."

But Haig stayed on the stool and when he looked again, Walter was back behind the bar, fiddling with the radio.

Haig asked, "Is it a fire?"

"Must be. I'm going to get the ten-fifteen newscast and see." The radio blared jazz, a high-riding jittery clarinet over muted brass and restless drums. "Be on in a minute; that's the station."

"Be on in a minute—" He almost fell, getting off the stool. "It's ten-fourteen, then?"

He didn't wait for an answer. The floor seemed tilting a little as he headed for the open door. Only a few doors and through the station. He might make it; he might actually make it. Suddenly it was as though he'd had nothing to drink at all and his mind was crystal clear no matter how his feet might stagger. And trains seldom left on the *exact* second, and Walter might have said "in a minute" meaning three or two or four minutes. There was a chance.

He fell on the steps but got up and went on, losing only seconds. Past the ticket window—he could buy his ticket on the train—and through the back doors to the platform, the gates, and the red tail-light of a train pulling out only yards, but hopeless yards, away. Ten yards, a hundred. Dwindling.

The station agent stood at the edge of the platform looking out after the departing train.

He must have heard Haig's footsteps; over his shoulder he said, "Too bad you missed it. That was the last one."

Haig suddenly saw the funny side of it and began to laugh. It was simply too ridiculous to take seriously, the narrowness of the margin by which he'd missed that train. Besides, there'd be an early one. All he had to do was go back in the station and wait until— He asked, "When's the first one out tomorrow?"

"You don't understand," said the agent.

For the first time he turned and Haig saw his face against the crimson, blazing sky. "You don't understand," he said. "That was *the last train.*"

"Ti Michel," a tale at once both savage and tender, appeared in June 1926, the last of six *Weird Tales* stories by W. J. STAMPER, a little-known author whose area of specialty appears to have been the early history of the island of Haiti.

TI MICHEL

by W. J. Stamper

For two years I had purchased my rum supply from Ti Michel, not only because he gave me better prices than any other of the numerous liquor shops that squat along the waterfront of Port Liberté, but also because there was an air of mystery about the man which I could never quite fathom. In spite of the reputation he had of having been a Caco at one time and of having committed various and bloody crimes, there was about him a gentle and insinuating manner which had won me completely the first time I had visited his shop. He was shorter and blacker than the average Haitian, with a peculiar habit of rubbing his fat hands together rapidly when talking. I do not remember of speaking with him a single time when he failed to rub his hands together and say:

"Ti Michel, *Monsieur,* he is not a bad man."

As I had never dropped the slightest hint that I considered him other than an honest and law-abiding citizen, I was at great loss to understand his reason for repeating this same sentence at our every meeting. I tried to make myself believe it to be a mere mannerism, but there always seemed to be a vague dread or fear in his mind, the reason for which I had not the slightest inkling.

It was late evening of a sultry day when the clouds of mosquitoes swarm up from the marshes to prey upon the inhabitants that I took my jug and sauntered down the squalid street toward the shop of Michel. This was my usual time for going for grog because the fishing craft from outside the reef came in shortly after dark, which meant that Michel's place would be clogged with a type of customer with whom I did not desire to mingle.

He was sitting in a chair outside the door smoking and knocking an occasional mosquito from his fat cheeks when I walked up.

"Ah!" he said suavely between puffs of acrid smoke; "I expected *Monsieur* sooner than this, for it has been three days that he does not come for a jug of Michel's Barbancourt."

He indicated a chair on the other side of the door and invited me to sit down. As soon as I was seated he took his pipe from his mouth, pointed out across the bay with the long stem, and began to speak in a low and reverent voice. The words seemed strangely soft and sentimental for a man who was reputed to have been a member of the murderous Cacos among the wild mountains of Bohouc and Pignon.

"There, *Monsieur*, is the home of Ti Michel. He is not a seller of rum, but a man of the sea. Once I had my own smack, as trim a craft as ever skimmed the bosom of the Caribbean. Many the time I dropped my nets outside yonder reef and whistled through the whole day, crossing the bar at evening with the largest catch of the whole fleet. The *Estrella* was a beauty. I was happy when I held her tiller and felt her leap before the breeze. Now I am useless and must sit here and wait for the boys to come in and buy my liquor. Look, *Monsieur*, look! They're coming in now."

In his excitement he had arisen from his chair. The pipe quivered in his hand and tears stood in his eyes. The reputed murderer was weeping and trembling.

I looked out across the bay where the curling foam rolled over the hidden reef and I saw the fleet moving toward Port Liberté. Out there on the roll of white surf, brightly limned against the red haze of a setting sun, swayed and bellied the gray sails of the tiny fishing boats as they tossed and fought the tide. Then I glanced at the sobbing figure of Michel, something of the mystery of the sea and those swarthy boatmen who wring their living from its heaving depths sweeping over me. The silence was broken by a murmur from Michel.

"Ti Michel, *Monsieur*, he is not a bad man."

"I know you are not a bad man, Michel," I reassured him, as I placed my hands on his shoulders, reminding him that my jug was still empty and darkness was coming on.

I followed him into the long, low building and I noticed that his fat hands were still trembling when he replaced the chimney on the oil lamp. He went slowly through the process of filling my jug from one of the two aged and mossy casks which stood on two square blocks of wood at the end of the room. These casks were of enormous size, holding more than two hundred gallons. He did the very thing I had expected, the very thing I had seen him do scores of times, a thing which had puzzled me ever since I had known him. He filled my demijohn from the left cask. Not once had I seen him draw liquor from the cobwebbed cask on the right, a matter which had caused me much thought and wonderment. My curiosity got the best of me and I questioned him.

"Michel," I asked in as casual a voice as I could command, "why is it you never give me rum from the right cask? Is it not very old and smooth?"

I thought he winced a little at this question, but his answer was forthcoming.

"That rum is for the gendarmes. It is not for my friend, the American. The gendarme is not a smart man, he never asks questions."

Then, as if to explode any theory I might have as to the mystery of Ti Michel and the cobwebbed cask, a uniformed gendarme entered with a jug, which Michel proceeded to fill from the very cask that had occasioned me so much thought.

"This is very excellent rum," said Michel softly, as the jug filled with a liquid the color of a cloudy amber. As the Haitian demijohn is invariably made of glass, I could see very plainly as the liquor mounted to the top, a seething mass of oily beads, evidence of a fine quality of rum.

I bade the old man goodnight and went back to my barracks completely baffled. Why had he never given me liquor from the right cask? Surely it was not poisoned. Before I slept, I hazarded a thousand guesses without arriving at any solution.

It was again mosquito time the next afternoon that a native boy came running breathlessly up the steps and began to tell me something in a rasping patois which I had great difficulty in understanding.

"Michel sick," he said. "He send for *Monsieur, vite, vite!*"

Seizing my hat from the rack, I rushed down the street and into the open door of the shop. I did not see Michel behind the counter, and the oil lamp was still burning, although it was late in the afternoon. The door leading from the bar into the room in the rear, which I judged to be his sleeping quarters was covered with a sort of curtain or portière. This I pushed back, and entered the room. It was an evil-smelling den, dark and musty. One square hole in the adobe wall admitted just enough light to enable me to see the utter poverty of the almost barren room. In a dusky corner, on a native bed consisting of a few boards covered with straw mats and a vile-smelling blanket, lay the huddled form of Ti Michel. I stepped over to him. His face was contorted with pain, the eyes staring with a strange, wild light.

"A little rum, *Monsieur,*" he asked huskily. "I think I am to die very soon and there is much I wish to tell you."

In a moment's time I placed a glass of liquor to his purple lips, and he livened up perceptibly after swallowing it. There was an empty goodsbox in the center of the room. Drawing this close up to the bed where I could hear him more clearly (for his voice had a tone I had heard before, the tone of approaching death) I sat down to listen.

"To begin with, *Monsieur,* Ti Michel is not a bad man. If I have ever done anything of which I should be ashamed, it was not my own fault. I grew up along the waterfront with all the other boys that fish out beyond the reef and come to my place at night for their rum. My fondest wish was to have my own boat, and at the age of twenty, by dint of saving and starving, I had enough money to buy the *Estrella.* Ah, the *Estrella* was a beauty, *Monsieur.* For ten happy years I put out to sea every morning and returned at evening with the biggest catch of the whole fleet. Then, at the age of thirty, I married the woman of my choice and bought a little home near the beach where we lived happily until the dread elephantiasis attacked my legs and rendered me unfit for further life at sea. A daughter had been born to us and she was twelve years of age when I decided that I would have to enter some business to earn a living. I bought this shop and we came here to live.

"Then, *Monsieur,* fate began to take a hand, and no more cruel fate ever pursued mortal than that which struck at me from every side. My wife sickened and passed away. I buried her in the cemetery over on the point and returned to this lonely room. My daugther grew to be very beautiful and she tended the bar when I was away in the hills to buy taffia—that is the white, raw rum, before it is aged. The people began to talk about my trips to the hills. They said I was a member of Norde's band of Cacos among the wild mountains of Pignon, and that I had committed bloody crimes. They were liars, *Monsieur,* just black, black liars. My business began to fail, my customers began to desert me, all except those boys that fish across the reef. They alone believed in me and I love them.

"One day I returned from a trip to the hills and dismounted outside the door, expecting to hear the sweet voice of my loved daughter welcoming me home. Instead there came to my ears a scream of mortal terror. I rushed in and looked through the curtains of this door, and what I saw crazed me with fear and anger. She was struggling in the arms of a burly gendarme, a corporal from the barracks up the street, a great black brute, wearing the uniform of my country. She was very strong and he had thrown her across the bed, his powerful hands at her fair throat, strangling her into submission. I saw her tongue protruding from her lips and heard a choking gurgle in her throat. Red was before my eyes. I leaped behind the counter, and digging into a chest of tools, I found a clawhammer. I dashed through the curtain at a stride and made for the uniformed beast. The hammer rose above my head and I brought it down with all my might on his kinky skull. The crash of bones was like sweet music to my ears. He released his hold and sank across the body of my girl— dead. I rolled his body, like that of a swine, off upon the floor, and with the bedcovers wiped the bloody froth from the crimson mouth of my baby.

"My God, *Monsieur,* I rubbed her cooling body with trembling hands and all the time her great, black eyes stared up at me pleading. I saw the ghastly stare that told me I had come too late. I placed my hand on her full bosom. Her heart was still. Madly I clasped her to my heart and pleaded with her not to leave me. Back and forth across the room I carried her, but she hung limp in my arms. She was dead. I smoothed back her tangled hair, laid her out on this very bed, and closed her dead eyes. Sometimes I have lain here at night, *Monsieur,* and imagined she was sleeping beside me. On those nights I was very happy.

"At length I stooped to examine the brute that had murdered my child. I turned him over, and blood was flowing from his nose and ears. A thick stream was slowly stealing across the floor. There was a hole in the top of his head from which issued a waterish fluid and brains. Fury and madness surged through me. I squatted beside the crimson stream and splashed my hands in it even as a child would play in mud. If *Monsieur* will move that grass rug there just a little, I think he may still see the stains."

"For God's sake, no, Michel!" I said. "Go on."

"After what seemed ages, though in fact it was but a few minutes, my reason began to assert itself and I thought to dispose of the body. I could not make report to the Commandant of Gendarmes, *Monsieur,* for he would have hanged me to the tallest tree in Port Liberté. He would not have believed my story. There was no law in those days before the Americans came to our shores, no justice. The gendarme swaggered up to your counter, bought your rum, and spat in your face as payment. He mistreated your family, and if you reported it to the commandant, you were kicked and clubbed for your trouble. Don't you think Michel would have had a chance for a fair trial if you had been here then, *Monsieur?*"

I nodded and he continued.

"Then a scheme came to my mind, and terrible as it may seem to you, I put it into execution. Life is very sweet and I did not hesitate. I reasoned that if the bodies of my daughter and the gendarme were hidden away and I put out the word that she was missing, the people would think they had eloped, for everyone knew that he frequented my place often and was infatuated with my daughter. I therefore rolled his body under the bed, covered my dead child with a blanket and waited the fall of night.

"I cleansed the hammer and placed it in the chest. A little rum sufficed to clean my hands of bloodstains. I replaced the curtain over there and took my place behind the counter as if nothing had occurred. I sold much rum to the fishermen that night. A few gendarmes came late that evening and I remember hearing two of them talk at a table.

" 'Guess Bousset is in the back room with Michel's daughter,' said one.

"Bousset was the name of the corporal I had killed, *Monsieur.*

"I was very jovial during the whole of the evening and I treated the crowd many times. At length they began to drift away one by one, and when the clock struck the hour of 12 I was alone, standing above the dead with my oil lamp in my hand. Every sound terrified me, for I was afraid the continued absence of Bousset might be noticed and my shop would be the first place they searched. This room was an awful place that night. The light shone with a pale and sickly glimmer as it played on the staring eyes of my dead girl and the boots of the dead gendarme that protruded from beneath the bed.

"I put out the lamp and the ghastly work began. Beneath the small chicken coop behind the house I dug frantically for a long time and finally a shallow grave was finished. Without a cheering word from the old father that reads from a great book when the dead are buried across on the point in the cemetery, I laid my baby sadly in the yellow clay. I think the dirt was damp with my tears when the grave was filled. With a sigh, I replaced the chicken coop and as I did this, the cocks began to crow. I could see the lights from the fishing fleet as they put out to sea. I could hear the fishermen whistling and hallooing to one another amid the bobbing flares. Oh, how I wished I were with them as I had been years before!

"Dawn slowly broadened into day. I took no food, and swallowing a glass of rum, made my way to the barracks of the commandant. This official, somewhat the worse for drink, twisted his long mustache and chuckled when I told him my daughter had been missing since midnight.

"Before he had time to answer me, a sergeant hurried up and saluted.

" 'Sir, I have to report Corporal Bousset as absent over leave since noon yesterday,' he said.

" 'Ah ha!' laughed the commandant gleefully, 'the wench has skedaddled with a deserter. They will be with the Cacos by nightfall. I can hardly imagine Ti Michel as being angry because his daughter has chosen to live with the very people with whom he has so long been associated. She came by her thieving blood honestly, old man. They are both where they belong. To hell with them.' He strode into the barracks, leaving me staring with amazement at the success of my plan.

"I feigned great sorrow and made as if to follow him. A burly sentinel stopped me with a blow in the face and bade me go home lest he split my skull.

"My child and the deserter became the talk of the town and everybody said that no more could have been expected of her because she had Caco blood in her veins. That hurt me, *Monsieur,* but I never answered their slurs. The good fishermen never deserted me and I have been able to live. That has all been three years ago now, and I have been lonely in the death room. I was mighty glad when you came to Port Liberté, *Monsieur*. Do you think Ti Michel a bad man?"

"No," I answered, and I think I was weeping. "Would that we Americans had been here then!"

"Now, *Monsieur*, it is getting late and I think the fishermen will be coming soon. Ti Michel will not be at the bar to serve them."

Suddenly he sat bolt upright in bed and I saw the stare of death in his rolling eyes.

"The cask, *Monsieur*, the right cask!" he gurgled, and sank back among the bedcovers—dead.

I pulled the blanket over his face and stepped softly into the bar, carrying with me the box I had been sitting on. Once beside the cobwebbed cask which had been the source of so much curiosity to me, I almost hesitated to examine it. I mounted the box.

With grim foreboding I lifted the heavy oaken lid. It was mossy and dank and my hands trembled as if I had an ague. I pulled. It creaked and loosened. I dropped it to the floor. I looked and the sight curdled my blood with horror.

There, floating in the liquid that was the color of cloudy amber, was the preserved and gruesome body of Corporal Bousset. It hung suspended, arms half bent, face down. In the top of the head, from which the kinky hair had slipped, was a gaping hole large enough to permit the insertion of a man's thumb, and from this there protruded a whitish and ragged wisp of human brain.

I dropped to the floor, overcome with the ghastly sight, and made for the door. I thought I must smother. I closed the door with a bang that sounded weird and ghostly through the whole house.

As I stepped into the street, the sun was sinking into the bosom of the Caribbean in a haze of red. The mosquitoes were swarming up from the marshes, and out across the white-foamed bar the fishing fleet was coming home. Perhaps many of those dusky boatmen expected to drink at Michel's counter that night.

FRITZ LEIBER, JR. (1910–   ), son of a once-renowned actor of the same name, is one of the Grand Old Men of science-fantasy. Among his prolific output are the semisatiric Fafhrd/Grey Mouser tales of swords and sorcery; *Conjure Wife*, a harrowing thrice-filmed novel of modern-day witchcraft, and eight *Weird Tales* stories, of which perhaps the most obscure is "In the X-Ray," published in July 1949. Perhaps its denouement holds no surprise for the jaded reader, but along the way there is a morbid slant on sibling psychology that—try as one may—is uncomfortably hard to forget.

IN THE X-RAY

by Fritz Leiber, Jr.

"Do the dead come back?" Dr. Ballard repeated the question puzzledly. "What's that got to do with your ankle?' "

"I didn't say that," Nancy Sawyer answered sharply. "I said, 'I tried an ice pack.' You must have misheard me."

"But . . ." Dr. Ballard began. Then, "Of course I must have," he said quickly. "Go on, Miss Sawyer."

The girl hesitated. Her glance strayed to the large gleaming window and the graying sky beyond. She was a young woman with prominent eyes, a narrow chin, strong white teeth, reddish hair and a beautiful doelike figure which included legs long and slim—except for the ankle of the one outstretched stockingless on the chair before her. That was encircled by a hard, white, somewhat irregular swelling.

Dr. Ballard was a man of middle age and size, with strong soft-skinned hands. He looked intelligent and as successful as his sleekly furnished office.

"Well, there isn't much more to it," the girl said finally. "I tried the ice pack, but the swelling wouldn't go down. So Marge made me call you."

"I see. Tell me, Miss Sawyer, hadn't your ankle bothered you before last night?"

"No. I just woke up from a nightmare frightened because something had grabbed my foot, and I reached down and touched my ankle—and there it was."

"Your ankle didn't feel or look any different the day before?"

"No."

"Yet when you woke up the swelling was there?"

"Just as it is now."

"Do you think you might have twisted your foot while you were asleep?"

"No."

"And you don't feel any pain in it now?"

"No, except a feeling of something hard clasped snugly around it and every once in a while squeezing a bit tighter."

"Ever do any sleepwalking?"

"No."

"Any allergies?"

"No."

"Can you think of anything else—anything at all—that might have a bearing on this trouble?"

Again Nancy looked out the window. "I have a twin sister," she said after a moment, in a different voice. "Or rather, I had. She died more than a year ago." She looked back quickly at Dr. Ballard. "But I don't know why I should mention that," she said hurriedly. "It couldn't possibly have any bearing on this. She died of apoplexy."

There was a pause.

"I suppose the X-ray will show what's the matter?" she continued.

The doctor nodded. "We'll have it soon. Miss Snyder's getting it now."

Nancy started to get up, asked, "Is it all right for me to move around?" Dr. Ballard nodded. She went over to the window, limping just a little, and looked down.

"You have a nice view, you can see half the city," she said. "We have the river at our apartment. I think we're higher, though."

"This is the twentieth floor," Dr. Ballard said.

"We're twenty-three," she told him. "I like high buildings. It's a little like being in an airplane. With the river right under our windows I can imagine I'm flying over water."

There was a soft knock at the door. Nancy looked around inquiringly. "The X-ray?" He shook his head. He went to the door and opened it.

"It's your friend Miss Hudson."

"Hi, Marge," Nancy called. "Come on in."

The stocky, sandy-haired girl hung in the doorway. "I'll stay out here," she said. "I thought we could go home together though."

"Darling, how nice of you. But I'll be a bit longer, I'm afraid."

"That's all right. How are you feeling, Nancy?"

"Wonderful, dear. Especially now that your doctor has taken a picture that'll show him what's inside this bump of mine."

"Well, I'll be out here," the other girl said and turned back into the waiting room. She passed a woman in white who came in, shut the door, and handed the doctor a large, brown envelope.

He turned to Nancy. "I'll look at this and be back right away."

"Dr. Myers is on the phone," the nurse told him as they started out. "Wants to know about tonight. Can he come here and drive over with you?"

"How soon can he get here?"

"About half an hour, he says."

"Tell him that will be fine, Miss Snyder."

The door closed behind them. Nancy sat still for perhaps two minutes. Then she jerked, as if at a twinge of pain. She looked at her ankle. Bending over, she clasped her hand around her good ankle and squeezed experimentally. She shuddered.

The door banged open. Dr. Ballard hurried in and immediately began to reexamine the swelling, swiftly exploring each detail of its outlines with gentle fingers, at the same time firing questions.

"Are you absolutely sure, Miss Sawyer, that you hadn't noticed anything of this swelling before last night? Perhaps just some slight change in shape or feeling, or a tendency to favor that ankle, or just a disinclination to look at it? Cast your mind back."

Nancy hesitated uneasily, but when she spoke it was with certainty. "No, I'm absolutely sure."

He shook his head. "Very well. And now, Miss Sawyer, that twin of yours. Was she identical?"

Nancy looked at him. "Why are you interested in that? Doctor, what does the X-ray show?"

"I have a very good reason, which I'll explain to you later. I'll go into details about the X-ray then too. You can set your mind at rest on one point, though, if it's been worrying you. This swelling is in no sense malignant."

"Thank goodness, Doctor."

"But now about the twin."

"You really want to know?"

"I do."

Nancy's manner and voice showed some signs of agitation. "Why, yes," she said, "we were identical. People were always mistaking us for each other. We looked exactly alike, but underneath . . ." Her voice trailed off. There was a change in the atmosphere of the office, a change hard to define. Abruptly she continued, "Dr. Ballard, I'd like to tell you about her, tell you things I've hardly told anyone else. You know, it was she I was dreaming about last night. In fact, I thought it was she who had grabbed me in my nightmare. What's the matter, Dr. Ballard?"

It did seem that Dr. Ballard had changed color, though it was hard to tell in the failing light. What he said, a little jerkily, was, "Nothing, Miss Sawyer. Please go ahead." He leaned forward a little, resting his elbows on the desk, and watched her.

"You know, Dr. Ballard," she began slowly, "most people think that twins are very affectionate. They think stories of twins hating each other are invented by writers looking for morbid plots.

"But in my case the morbid plot happened to be the simple truth. Beth tyrannized over me, hated me and . . . wasn't above expressing her hate in a physical way." She took a deep breath.

"It started when we were little girls. As far back as I can remember, I was always the slave and she was the mistress. And if I didn't carry out her orders faithfully, and sometimes if I did, there was always a slap or a pinch. Not a little-girl pinch. Beth had peculiarly strong fingers. I was very afraid of them.

"There's something terrible, Dr. Ballard, about the way one human being can intimidate another, crush their will power, reduce to mush their ability to fight back. You'd think the victim could escape so easily—look, there are people all around, teachers and friends to confide in, your father and mother—but it's as if you were bound by invisible chains, your mouth shut by an invisible gag. And it grows and grows, like the horrors of a concentration camp. A whole inner world of pain and fright. And yet on the surface—why, there seems to be nothing at all.

"For of course no one else had the faintest idea of what was going on between us. Everyone thought we loved each other very much. Beth especially was always being praised for her 'sunny gaiety.' I was supposed to be a little 'subdued.' Oh, how she used to fuss and coo over me when there were people around. Though even then there would be pinches on the sly—hard ones I never winced at. And more than that, for. . . ."

Nancy broke off. "But I really don't think I should be wasting your time with all these childhood gripes, Dr. Ballard. Especially since I know you have an engagement for this evening."

"That's just an informal dinner with a few old cronies. I have lots of time. Go right ahead. I'm interested."

Nancy paused, frowning a little. "The funny thing is," she continued, "I never understood why Beth hated me. It was as if she were intensely jealous. Yet there was no reason for that. She was the successful one, the one who won the prizes and played the leads in the school shows and got the nicest presents and all the boys. But somehow each success made her worse. I've sometimes thought, Dr. Ballard, that only cruel people can be successful, that success is really a reward for cruelty . . . to someone."

Dr. Ballard knit his brows, might have nodded.

"The only thing I ever read that helped explain it to me," she went on, "was something in psychoanalysis. The idea that each of us has an equal dose of love and hate, and that it's our business to balance them off, to act in such a way that both have expression and yet so that the hate is always under the control of the love.

"But perhaps when the two people are very close together, as it is with twins, the balancing works out differently. Perhaps all the softness and love begins to gather in the one person and all the hardness and hate in the other. And then the hate takes the lead, because it's an emotion of violence and power and action—a concentrated emotion, not misty like love. And it keeps on and on, getting worse all the time, until it's so strong you feel it will never stop, not even with death.

"For it did keep on, Dr. Ballard, and it did get worse." Nancy looked at him closely. "Oh, I know what I've been telling you isn't supposed to be so unusual among children. 'Little barbarians,' people say, quite confident that they'll outgrow it. Quite convinced that wrist-twisting and pinching are things that will automatically stop when children begin to grow up."

Nancy smiled thinly at him. "Well, they don't stop, Dr. Ballard. You know, it's very hard for most people to associate actual cruelty with an adolescent girl, maybe because of the way girls have been glorified in advertising. Yet I could write you a pretty chapter on just that topic. Of course a lot of it that happened in my case was what you'd call mental cruelty. I was shy and Beth had a hundred ways of embarrassing me. And if a boy became interested in me, she'd always take him away."

"I'd hardly have thought she'd have been able to," remarked Dr. Ballard.

"You think I'm good-looking? But I'm only good-looking in an odd way, and in any case it never seemed to count then. It's true, though, that twice there were boys who wouldn't respond to her invitations. Then both times she played a trick that only she could, because we were identical twins. She would pretend to be me—she could always imitate my manner and voice, even my reactions, precisely, though I couldn't possibly have imitated her—and then she would . . . do something that would make the boy drop me cold."

"Do something?"

Nancy looked down. "Oh, insult the boy cruelly, pretending to be me. Or else make some foul, boastful confession, pretending it was mine. If you knew how those boys loathed me afterwards . . .

"But as I said, it wasn't only mental cruelty or indecent tricks. I remember nights when I'd done something to displease her and I'd gone to bed before her and she'd come in and I'd pretend to be asleep and after a while she'd say—oh, I know, Dr. Ballard, it sounds like something a silly little girl would say, but it didn't sound like that then, with my head under the sheet, pressed into the pillow, and her footsteps moving slowly around the bed—she'd say, 'I'm thinking of how to punish you.' And then there'd be a long wait, while I still pretended to be asleep, and then the touch . . . oh, Dr. Ballard, her hands! I was so afraid of her hands! But . . . what is it, Dr. Ballard?"

"Nothing. Go on."

"There's nothing much more to say. Except that Beth's cruelty and my fear went on until a year ago, when she died suddenly—I suppose you'd say tragically—of a blood clot on the brain. I've often wondered since then whether her hatred of me, so long and so cleverly concealed, mightn't have had something to do with it. Apoplexy's what haters die of, isn't it, Doctor?

"I remember leaning over her bed the day she died, lying there paralyzed, with her beautiful face white and stiff as a fish's, one eye bigger than the other. I felt pity for her (You realize, Doctor, don't you, that I always loved her?) but just then her hand flopped a little way across the blanket and touched mine, although they said she was completely paralyzed, and her big eye twitched around a little until it was looking almost at me and her lips moved and I thought I heard her say, 'I'll come back and punish you for this,' and then I felt her fingers moving, just a little, on my skin, as if they were trying to close on my wrist, and I jerked back with a cry.

"Mother was very angry with me for that. She thought I was just a selfish, thoughtless girl, afraid of death and unable to repress my fear even for my dying sister's sake. Of course I could never tell her the real reason. I've never really told that to anyone, except you. And now that I've told you I hardly know why I've done it."

She smiled nervously, quite unhumorously.

"Wasn't there something about a dream you had last night?" Dr. Ballard asked softly.

"Oh, yes!" The listlessness snapped out of her. "I dreamed I was walking in an old graveyard with gnarly gray trees, and overhead the sky was gray and low and threatening, and everything was weird and dreadful. But somehow I was very happy. But then I felt a faint movement under my feet and I looked down at the grave I was passing and I saw the earth falling away into it. Just a little cone-shaped pit at first, with the dark sandy earth sliding down its sides, and a small black hole at the bottom. I knew I must run away quickly, but I couldn't move an inch. Then the pit grew larger and the earth tumbled down its sides in chunks and the black hole grew. And still I was rooted there. I looked at the gravestone beyond and it said 'Elizabeth Sawyer, 1926–48.' Then out of the hole came a hand and arm, only there was just shreds of dark flesh clinging to the bone, and it began to feel around with an awful, snatching swiftness. Then suddenly the earth heaved and opened, and a figure came swiftly hitching itself up out of the hole. And although the flesh was green and shrunken and eaten and the eyes just holes, I recognized Beth—there was still the beautiful reddish hair. And then the ragged hand touched my ankle and instantly closed on it and the other hand came groping upward, higher, higher, and I screamed . . . and then I woke up."

Nancy was leaning forward, her eyes fixed on the doctor. Suddenly her hair seemed to bush out, just a trifle. Perhaps it had "stood on end." At any rate, she said, "Dr. Ballard, I'm frightened."

"I'm sorry if I've made you distress yourself," he said. The words were more reassuring than the tone of voice. He suddenly took her hand in his and for a few moments they sat there silently. Then she smiled and moved a little and said, "It's gone now. I've been very silly. I don't know why I told you all I did about Beth. It couldn't help you with my ankle."

"No, of course not," he said after a moment.

"Why did you ask if she was identical?"

He leaned back. His voice became brisker again. "I'll tell you about that right now—and about what the X-ray shows. I think there's a connection. As you probably know, Miss Sawyer, identical twins look so nearly alike because they come from the same germ cell. Before it starts to develop, it splits in two. Instead of one individual, two develop. That was what happened in the case of you and your sister." He paused. "But," he continued, "sometimes, especially if there's a strong tendency to twin births in the family, the splitting doesn't stop there. One of the two cells splits again. The result—triplets. I believe that also happened in your case."

Nancy looked at him puzzeldly. "But then what happened to the third child?"

"The third sister," he amplified. "There can't be identical boy-and-girl twins or triplets, you know, since sex is determined in the original germ cell. There, Miss Sawyer, we come to my second point. Not all twins develop and are actually born. Some start to develop and then stop."

"What happens to them?"

"Sometimes what there is of them is engulfed in the child that does develop completely—little fragments of a body, bits of this and that, all buried in the flesh of the child that is actually born. I think that happened in your case."

Nancy looked at him oddly. "You mean I have in me bits of another twin sister, a triplet sister, who didn't develop?"

"Exactly."

"And that all this is connected with my ankle?"

"Yes."

"But then how—?"

"Sometimes nothing happens to the engulfed fragments. But sometimes, perhaps many years later, they begin to grow—in a natural way rather than malignantly. There are well-authenticated cases of this happening—as recently as 1890 a Mexican boy in this way 'gave birth' to his own twin brother, completely developed though of course dead. There's nothing nearly as extensive as that in your case, but I'm sure there is a pocket of engulfed materials around your ankle and that it recently started to grow, so gradually that you didn't notice it until the growth became so extensive as to be irritating."

Nancy eyed him closely. "What sort of materials? I mean the engulfed fragments."

He hesitated. "I'm not quite sure," he said. "The X-ray was . . . oh, such things are apt to be odd, though harmless stuff—teeth, hair, nails, you never can tell. We'll know better later."

"Could I see the X-ray?"

He hesitated again. "I'm afraid it wouldn't mean anything to you. Just a lot of shadows."

"Could there be . . . other pockets of fragments?"

"It's not likely. And if there are, it's improbable they'll ever bother you."

There was a pause.

Nancy said, "I don't like it.

"I don't like it," she repeated. "It's as if Beth had come back. Inside me."

"The fragments have no connection with your dead sister," Dr. Ballard assured her. "They're not part of Beth, but of a third sister, if you can call such fragments a person."

"But those fragments only began to grow after Beth died. As if Beth's soul . . . And was it my original cell that split a second time? —or was it Beth's?—so that it was the fragments of half her cell that

I absorbed, so that . . ." She stopped. "I'm afraid I'm being silly again."

He looked at her for a while, then, with the air of someone snapping to attention, quickly nodded.

"But, Doctor," she said, also like someone snatching at practicality, "what's to happen now?"

"Well," he replied, "in order to get rid of this disfigurement to your ankle a relatively minor operation will be necessary. You see, this sort of foreign body can't be reduced in size by heat or X-ray or injections. Surgery is needed, though probably only under local anaesthetic. Could you arrange to enter a hospital tomorrow? Then I could operate the next morning. You'd have to stay about four days."

She thought for a moment, then said, "Yes, I think I could manage that." She looked distastefully at her ankle. "In fact, I'd like to do it as soon as possible."

"Good. We'll ask Miss Snyder to arrange things."

When the nurse entered, she said, "Dr. Myers is outside."

"Tell him I'll be right along," Dr. Ballard said. "And then I'd like you to call Central Hospital. Miss Sawyer will take the reservation we got for Mrs. Phipps and were about to cancel." And they discussed details while Nancy pulled on stocking and shoe.

Nancy said goodbye and started for the waiting room, favoring her bad leg. Dr. Ballard watched her. The nurse opened the door. Beyond, Nancy's friend got up with a smile. There was now, besides her, a dark, oldish man in the waiting room.

As the nurse was about to close the door, Dr. Ballard said, "Miss Sawyer."

She turned. "Yes?"

"If your ankle should start to trouble you tonight—or anything else—please call me."

"Thank you, Doctor, I will."

Dr. Ballard nodded. Then he called to his friend, "Be right with you." The dark, oldish man flapped an arm at him.

The door closed. Dr. Ballard went to his desk, took an X-ray photograph out of its brown envelope, switched on the light, studied the photograph incredulously.

He put it back in its envelope and on the desk. He got his hat and overcoat from the closet. He turned out the light. Then suddenly he went back and got the envelope, stuffed it in his pocket and went out.

The dinner with Dr. Myers and three other old professional friends proved if anything more enjoyable than Dr. Ballard had anticipated. It led to relaxation, gossip, a leisurely evening stroll, a drink together, a few final yarns. At one point Dr. Ballard felt a fleeting impulse to get the X-ray out of his overcoat pocket and show it to them and tell his little yarn about it, but something made him hesitate and he forgot the idea. He felt very easy in his mind as he drove home about midnight. He even hummed a little. This mood was not disturbed until he saw the face of Miss Willis, his resident secretary.

"What is it?" he asked crisply.

"Miss Nancy Sawyer. She. . . ." For once the imperturbable graying blonde seemed to have difficulty speaking.

"Yes?"

"She called up first about an hour and a half ago."

"Her ankle had begun to pain her?"

"She didn't say anything about her ankle. She said she was getting a sore throat."

"What!"

"It seemed unimportant to me, too, though of course I told her I'd inform you when you got in. But she seemed rather frightened, kept complaining of this tightness she felt in her throat . . ."

"Yes? Yes?"

"So I agreed to get in touch with you immediately. She hung up. I called the restaurant, but you'd just left. Then I called Dr. Myers' home, but didn't get any answer. I told the operator to keep trying.

"About a half hour ago Miss Sawyer's friend, a Marge Hudson, called. She said Miss Sawyer had gone to bed and was apparently asleep, but she didn't like the way she was tossing around, as if she were having a particularly bad dream, and especially she didn't like the noises she was making in her throat, as if she were having difficulty breathing. She said she had looked closely at Miss Sawyer's throat as she lay sleeping, and it seemed swollen. I told her I was making every effort to get in touch with you and we left it at that."

"That wasn't all?"

"No," Miss Willis' agitation returned. "Just two minutes before you arrived, the phone rang again. At first the line seemed to be dead. I was about to hang up. Then I began to hear a clicking, gargling sound. Low at first but then it grew louder. Then suddenly it broke free and whooped out in what I think was Miss Sawyer's voice. There were only two words, I think, but I couldn't catch them because they were so loud they stopped the phone. After that, nothing, although I listened and listened and kept saying 'hello' over and over. But Dr. Ballard, that gargling sound! It was as if I were listening to someone being strangled, very slowly, very, very. . . ."

But Dr. Ballard had grabbed up his surgical bag and was racing for his car. He drove rather well for a doctor and, tonight, very fast. He was about three blocks from the river when he heard a siren, ahead of him.

Nancy Sawyer's apartment hotel was at the end of a short street terminated by a high concrete curb and metal fence and, directly below, the river. Now there was a fire engine drawn up to the fence and playing a searchlight down over the edge through the faintly misty air. Dr. Ballard could see a couple of figures in shiny black coats beside the searchlight. As he jumped out of his car he could hear shouts and what sounded like the motor of a launch. He hesitated for a moment, then ran into the hotel.

The lobby was empty. There was no one behind the counter. He ran to the open elevator. It was an automatic. He punched the twenty-three button.

On that floor there was one open door in the short corridor. Marge Hudson met him inside it.

"She jumped?"

The girl nodded. "They're hunting for her body. I've been watching. Come on."

She led him to a dark bedroom. There was a studio couch, its covers disordered, and beside it a phone. River air was pouring in through a large, hinged window, open wide. They went to it and looked down. The circling launch looked like a toy boat. Its searchlight and that from the fire engine roved across the dark water. Shouts and chugging came up faintly.

"How did it happen?" he asked the girl at the window.

"I was watching her as she lay in bed," Marge Hudson answered without looking around. "About twenty minutes after I called your home, she seemed to be getting worse. She had more trouble breathing. I tried to wake her, but couldn't. I went to the kitchen to make an ice pack. It took longer than I'd thought. I heard a noise that at first I didn't connect with Nancy. Then I realized that she was strangling. I rushed back. Just then she screamed out horribly. I heard something fall—I think it was the phone—and footsteps and the window opening. When I came in she was standing on the sill in her nightdress, clawing at her throat. Before I could get to her, she jumped."

"Earlier in the evening she'd complained of a sore throat?"

"Yes. She said, jokingly, that the trouble with her ankle must be spreading to her throat. After she called your home and couldn't get you, she took some aspirin and went to bed."

Dr. Ballard switched on the lamp by the bed. He pulled the brown envelope from his coat pocket, took out the X-ray and held it up against the light.

"You say she screamed at the end," he said in a not very steady voice. "Were there any definite words?"

The girl at the window hesitated. "I'm not sure," she said slowly. "They were suddenly choked off, exactly as if a hand had tightened around her throat. But I think there were two words. 'Hand' and 'Beth.' "

Dr. Ballard's gaze flickered toward the mocking face in the photograph on the chest of drawers, then back to the ghostly black and whites of the one in his hands. His arms were shaking.

"They haven't found her yet," Marge said, still looking down at the river and the circling launch.

Dr. Ballard was staring incredulously at the X-ray, as if by staring he could make what he saw go away. But that was impossible. It was a perfectly defined and unambiguous exposure.

There, in the X-ray's blacks and grays, he could see the bones of Nancy Sawyer's ankle and, tightly clenched around them, deep under skin and flesh, the slender bones of a human hand.

Because of adverse reader reaction, humor rarely raised its shaggy head in *Weird Tales*. One of the most successful examples is also unfortunately the most obscure: "Speak" by HENRY SLESAR (1927–   ) ran in Fall 1984, the first of the two "California issues," which almost rival Vol. 1, No. 1 for scarcity (see The Eyrie, page xx). Slesar, Emmy award-winning former head writer of the long-running TV soap opera "The Edge of Night," has written hundreds of fantasy and science fiction short stories, as well as mysteries and thrillers, one of which, *The Gray Flannel Shroud,* won an Edgar award from the Mystery Writers of America.

SPEAK

by Henry Slesar

"Hello. Phyllis? This is Manny. I'm at the office."

"Wait a minute—"

"No, please, don't interrupt. I gotta do this my way, Phyllis. This one time you should give me the last word. Ha, that's like a joke, the last word. You know what I'm sitting here with? Dr. Pfeiffer's goodnight express, those pills he prescribed me last month for sleeping. I got the whole bottle right here in front of me. Empty."

"Manny—"

"You know why it's empty? On account of they're all inside me, all those nice little white pills pushing against the stomach valves like in the commercial. I wonder if they work fast, fast, fast? I sure hope so—you know me when I make up my mind to do something. This morning, when I got the call from Rodolfo at the Garden, I said to myself, Manny, anybody else in your shoes would kill himself. So why not, I said. Why am I so different from anybody else? I was gonna do it at home, but then I thought, what for? Why should I mess things up for you? Better I should get Pfeiffer's prescription filled at lunch and do it in the office. What could be a more fitting place, this lousy, crummy office?"

"Manny, please listen to me—"

"Maybe you never knew how bad things were with me, maybe I

didn't cry enough. You know what I always told you, Phyllis—show business is no business. I would have been better off going into the florist racket with your brother like your family wanted. But kill me, I had to be a circus type. I couldn't be a regular Joe Shnook making paper boxes or wrapping up posies, not me. I had sawdust in my blood. In this day and age, right? They got Cinerama, they got color television, they got World's Fairs, and what does Manny give them? Freaks and novelties, right? Smart, huh? Some genius, your husband, right?"

"Manny, for Pete's sake—"

"But that wasn't bad enough. I couldn't even do *that* right. All I wanted was something unique, something different, and what do I get? One fake after another. One flop after another. That dumb magician from *Argentina*. That pinheaded cretin. And that bearded lady. Who could forget *him,* that big phony. One after another, ponies, floppolas. Well I'm through. Through with the whole mess—"

"Manny—"

"Yeah, I know, I know. You want to hear what happened to the Siamese twins. That's what finally broke my back, Phyllis, that was the straw. This morning, I get a call from Rodolfo at the Arena. Some wise-guy reporter from the *News* spotted one of the twins in a bar on Third Avenue. Yeah, *one* of the twins. Rodolfo threw me out of the show, of course. He swears I'll never work another circus or carny in the country, and he can do it. No, come to think it, he can't do nothing to me anymore. Nobody can . . ."

"Manny! Please!"

"It's just no use, Phyllis. All these years I kept saying to myself—*one* act'll do it. One big break. One really great novelty. One blockbuster and I'll be right on top. But you know what I think? I wouldn't know a great act if I saw one. I'm a loser, Phyllis. I'm a wrong-guesser. Nothing good ever comes my way, because I got nothing going for me. That's the truth."

"Manny—"

"So long, Phyllis. You've been a good wife to me and I wish I'd treated you better. But take my word for it—you'll be better off without me . . ."

"Manny, will you please *listen?* This *isn't* Phyllis! Phyllis isn't here, she went out to get some groceries. Manny, this is Rex. Your dog. Your *dog.* I don't know what came over me. When I heard the phone ringing, I just *had* to answer. I knocked it off the table with my paw and I started talking. Manny, can you hear me? It's Rex! Manny, say something. Please! Manny, are you there! Rowf! Manny! Manny!"

Crumbling castles in the Black Forest, ruined nobles bent on nefarious doings, hideous entities, bloodstained manuscripts revealing terrible secrets—the stock-in-trade of the "Gothic effect" inherited from the Teutons and filtered through the writings of Horace Walpole, M. G. Lewis, Charles Maturin and Edgar Allan Poe—is an essential portion of the *Weird Tales* cosmos. In "The Pale Criminal" (September 1947), one of four C. HALL THOMPSON stories printed in *Weird Tales,* the mixture is leavened by a soupçon of Freud.

THE PALE CRIMINAL

by C. Hall Thompson

An idea made this pale criminal pale. Adequate was he for the deed when he did it, but the idea of it he could not endure when it was done.
—Friedrich Nietzsche

I confess, in the beginning the case of Simon Conrad did not strike me as singular. On my first visit to the Castle von Zengerstein, I had no suspicion of the secret that lay hidden in the vaults of that Gothic pile that towered on a craggy hillcrest at the Black Forest's edge. I found Luther Markheim, master of Zengerstein, nothing more than a mountainous relic of the decadent line that spawned him; he and his companion, one Doctor Victor Rupert, were mildly concerned over the fate of Simon Conrad, but they feared they could be of little assistance since they had never even seen the gentleman in question. It was all very commonplace. No hint of the festering evil of Zengerstein seeped through the veneer of ordinariness.

But events have taken a strange turn. The Conrad affair is no longer simply a missing persons case; it is a crime whose hideous memory still lurks in the mirror of the tarn that separates the Castle from the deserted village of Zengerstein. Perhaps when you have come to know the facts of the case you will say that I, Ludwig Koch, Inspektor of Police of the town of Donaueschingen, some twenty kilometres to the north, should have guessed at the macabre truth. But I am a simple man. My dealings in the world of crime had been with petty theft and trespassing. Never before had I been drawn into such a web of malignity as shrouded the house of Luther Markheim. I had heard men whisper, on a winter's night in the Hofbrau, of an evil that lingers in shadow, beyond the understanding of normal minds; once, on a visit to Baden, I had seen the Teufels Kanzel on the brink of the Schwarzwald, where, legend has it, the Devil preached to his disciples; to me, it seemed only an altar of scorched stone. The supernatural has always been beyond my ken. But of late, I have undergone a change. Having witnessed the horror of Zengerstein, only an idiot could remain an unbeliever.

The entire truth of the affair has never been disclosed. For years, it has lain in the police archives, at Donaueschingen, buried in the rotting pages of the manuscript of Luther Markheim. Only recently it was decided that in view of work being done by one Sigmund Freud in a new field called psychiatry, it would be advisable to release the story of Zengerstein that these doctors might benefit by study of the quirks of a criminal mind in action. To outward appearances the manuscript does not seem extraordinary; it was written in ink by a precise hand, the story is told with scientific clarity; and, except one turned to the last scrawled lines, except one examined the brownish stains on the final pages and knew them to be the marks of dried blood, one would never guess that these words were written by a man who had been blind for nearly a decade.

THE MARKHEIM MANUSCRIPT

There is so little time. Now, in the night, here in my bedchamber, I should feel safe. I should know that there can be no truth in the unholy phantasms that have come to haunt my every waking moment. The doors are locked. Nothing could penetrate those ponderous panels. Nothing human. Yet, at every whimper of the wind in the grate, I start; the howling of the wolf-hounds gnaws at my nerves. Rain sobs against the casement, lashed by the winds sweeping up from the River Murg. And throughout the stormy night, Koch and his deputies continue to wander the Black Forest, their lanterns bobbing like cat's eyes in outer darkness. Still they search for Simon Conrad. Soon, perhaps, they shall return to Zengerstein to question me again. But it is not Koch I fear. It is that thing no barred portal can ward off; that bloated livid face that floats somewhere in the well of the mirror by the bed; dark beings stir in the pit beyond that glass; and every moment the scabrous visage grows nearer, the blind eyes burn more fiercely. Soon, it will rise from the crypts beneath the castle. I know. There is no escape. Soon, the time will have run out. And then, the slash of the scalpel, the pale face pressed close to mine —and death. The same death that monster brought to Simon Conrad short weeks ago.

It is incredible that things have come to this impasse. Every step of my plan was laid with such care. And now, at the final moment, the whole structure crumbles beneath me. There can be but one answer. Somewhere I have made a mistake; some thread of the web has tangled and snapped. Perhaps, if I retrace every step, there may yet be time for reparation. I must be exceedingly careful. I must not slip again. This is my last chance.

It began nine years ago, in Freiburg, in the winter of 189–. I was a different man then. I was not a ponderous object of pity with a scarred face and sightless eyes; people then did not avoid me and turn to their friends to whisper that a "has-been" always depressed them. In December of 189–, I was one of the most successful men in the city of the Hapsburgs. Mine was a place of honor at the banquet-tables of the Freiherren. My huge bulk then was the impressive figure of a man in the prime of life, well-dressed, imposing, a monument to the scientific genius it embodied; women marvelled at my delicate, sensitive hands—the hands of Herr Doktor Luther Markheim, one of the greatest surgeons in Germany. I was chief of staff at the Spital Hapsburg; the universities of Vienna had honored me with degrees for my work in surgical research. Countless students came to me, inspired, to study the art of the knife; it was among them that I discovered Victor Rupert.

He was not an idiot. An idiot could never have gained my confidence as he did. From the outset, it was obvious that his was the most promising talent in my select class at the Freiburg Universitat. His hands were slim and steady; he used the scalpel with the dexterity of a miniature-painter. No. There was nothing idiotic about Victor Rupert. But he was a weakling and a fool. The only son of a burger who had made a fortune in ale and bestowed on himself a Baron's coronet, from his boyhood Victor was a coddled child; on the death of his parents he came into a considerable estate and continued where his mother and father left off—he coddled himself.

Small, dark-skinned, with huge eyes, he affected florid waistcoats and the softest boots that money could buy. His time was divided between the Hofbrau barmaids and the ladies of the chorus at the Theatre Strauss. The evening invariably ended with some passing companions carrying Victor, dead drunk, to his quarters in the Freiburgstrasse and departing with whatever money they could steal. A fool; a weakling whose brain had lost control of the flesh. I thought I could change him; I thought, in time, I could make him a useful member of the profession. I should have known better. I should have cast him back into drunken oblivion where he belonged. I should have destroyed him before he destroyed me.

I dare not dwell upon the details of the accident; for me every moment of remembering is agony relived. The stench of chemical gas in the laboratory, the horrified look of realization on the face of the student named Lund, the roar of the explosion and hellfire eating into my flesh, slicing across my eyes, Lund's screams slowly dwindling, and at last, merciful darkness. You may find the known facts of the case in the files of any newspaper in Freiburg; they tell me the *Zeitung Leute* bore the headline:

PROMINENT SURGEON BLINDED,
STUDENT KILLED,
IN UNIVERSITY BLAST

It was called a freak accident; the truth never reached the public; no one ever knew that an hour before I had seen Rupert conducting an experiment in that laboratory; no one ever guessed that the "accident" was caused by the negligence of a fool whose mind was still fogged by the burgundy he had swilled the night before.

Rupert was terrified. Exactly how I have never learned—possibly by bribing the orderly—he gained my bedside before the authorities questioned me. He clutched my sleeve; abject terror whined in every breath he drew.

"Before God, Herr Doktor, I'll do whatever you ask! I'll work for you, devote my life to serving you; give you all the money I have in this world. But I beg of you . . . !" A sob broke his words. "On my knees, I beg you, do not tell them it was I . . ."

Anger seethed in the new, obscene, darkness of my brain. My throat felt tight. I freed my arm of his quivering grasp.

"Snivelling swine!" I hissed. "Why? Tell me one reason why I should remain silent!" Laughter tore through my facial bandages. "The priceless fool! He destroys my sight; he ruins the career of a genius! And then he asks my protection!" The laugh shattered on a furious sob. My fingers closed over his wrist; the bones felt thin and brittle; I twisted. "Why? Tell me, Victor; Why?"

I felt his body wince; he whimpered.

"Nein, Herr Doktor! You must understand! They would imprison me! Throw me into a cell; leave me to rot! I . . . I could not endure it; I am a sensitive man . . ."

"Indeed!"

"Lieber Gott, have mercy, mein Herr!" The clammy wrist writhed in my grip. "I promise you! Whatever I have is yours; my money, my life! You must listen to me!"

And in the end, I did.

Do not misunderstand. I did not forgive Rupert. How can you forgive the inane court jester who has destroyed the Castle? No, I listened to Rupert because it was to my advantage to listen. Already I had tasted the first bitter consequences of my blindness; a voice by my bed when they thought I was still unconscious: "Well, that finishes the great Markheim. A pity. But he was getting on in years . . . Perhaps it is as well to go out before your talent deteriorates . . ." This from a medical idiot unfit to be my laboratory assistant! Pity, old acquaintances uneasy in my blind fumbling presence, slow decay surrounded by mocking memories of what I had once been; that was the prospect of life should I remain in Freiburg. I had lived well; now with only the pittance granted by the Spital Hapsburg, I would be buried alive in some dank areaway, three flights up, forgotten, alone. I knew I must escape. Victor Rupert offered the way out. His money would allow me to live comfortably and in seclusion; to hide the ruined tomb of genius that was my body in the solitude of the Castle von Zengerstein.

The Baronial title of Zengerstein was no tinsel honor bought by some grubby burger suddenly grown rich. As early as 1407 the coronet was bestowed upon one General Lothar von Zengerstein of the Army of Ferdinand by the Emperor himself; the title carried with it certain lands some miles south of Donaueschingen, bordering the Black Forest, and dominated by an ancient, brooding Schloss; under the guiding hand of Lothar, a shrewd businessman when not campaigning, the estate and the village that sprang up in the Castle's shadow rapidly became one of the most prosperous in the Lower Schwarzwald region. There was food and comfort for all; the bauer who paid allegiance to Lothar were content. The house of Zengerstein bore sons; like their fathers, they followed the military life; Zengersteinschloss rang with laughter of late revelry and wine. Such was the state of affairs when my grandfather, Bruno, Ninth Baron von Zengerstein, became head of the house.

Bruno was the father of two sons and a daughter, Lizavetta; Lizavetta von Zengerstein was my mother. My earliest recollections center about the mammoth halls of the Castle where I was taken to live when my father, Paul Markheim, a medical student in Vienna, died of consumption shortly after my birth. I recall the towering figures of my grandfather and uncles grouped about the Teutonic hearth, drinking schnapps and laughing boisterously over the success of some past campaign, on the battlefield or in the kitchen of the Inn with the new barmaid. I was in a private school in Berlin when the Franco-Prussian war broke out; vague stirrings of it reached my sheltered world. Baron Bruno and his sons were among the first to reach the front; the younger son was killed by a musket-ball that shattered his brain; Karl, the eldest, died of typhoid in an obscure village in the Midi. Baron von Zengerstein returned a broken man.

The death of his sons destroyed all hope for fulfillment of his one desire; there would never be an heir to carry on the name of Zengerstein. He was an old man, his powers wasted in a profligate youth, and now he entombed himself in the Castle to brood away the final hours of the last of the Zengersteins. Unwholesome legends surround the last days of Bruno von Zengerstein; it is said that in his mad desire to perpetuate his line, he consorted with the powers of darkness; the shelves of his private library were cluttered with volumes of forbidden lore; more than one village girl was terrorized by the cloaked figure that roamed the region of the Castle tarn during the night hours. The bauer grew uneasy; after sundown they clung to their hearthfires behind locked cottage doors. One by one, families packed their belongings and moved on, away from the Schwarzwald, where, if legend does not lie, the souls of Bruno's unborn heirs bayed like hounds to the baleful moon. The village was empty; thatched cottage rooves caved in and rats burrowed in the ruins. Zengersteinschloss fell into disrepair; the priceless tapestries decayed; cobwebs coated the stone walls; cold grates bore charred relics of sacrifices made by the Baron von Zengerstein. The peasants who found his body and buried it in the Castle crypt say that the contorted dead face could only have been that of a madman. My mother was living, at that time, in Berlin; she did not go home for the last rites of the Baron. The strange stories frightened her once; she expressed the desire never to see Zengerstein again; her wish was granted. When she returned to the Castle, she lay in the sightless dark of her coffin. At the age of twenty-nine, I became legal heir to the Baronial lands of Zengerstein.

My homecoming fell far short of that of which I had so often dreamed. I had thought one day to return, triumphant; I had planned again and again the restoration of the State of Zengerstein. And now at last I would return, but the dreams were shattered. I rode to the Castle in the coach of a reluctant driver who feared the lonely road that wound through the hamlet to the gates of Zengerstein. I returned the blind relic of a genius who spoke to none save the companion he called Victor, to pass the lingering years alone and embittered. But at least, I thought, I would find peace in oblivion.

I was wrong. For nine years I pursued the mocking shadow of contentment; nine years tortured by fantasies of what heights my career might have attained but for the weakness of Victor Rupert; nine years of festering blind ambition, during which one idea came to obsess me: I must see again! Together with Victor, I made an exhaustive study of blindness; night after night Victor read aloud from countless ancient volumes; his voice cracked; his eyes ached; I gave him no rest. Every bypath of science and sorcery, every chance of recovery, by miracle or surgery, we explored. And, slowly, in my mind, there began to formulate a rather terrifying theory; bit by bit, fragments of medical knowledge fell into place to weave the weird pattern. It was only a theory; I told myself to be detached, weigh every possibility. There was perhaps one chance in a million that the theory would succeed in practice. Failure might mean death. But I knew I would take that chance, if only I had the materials with which to work—the forbidden human materials. That problem was solved the night Simon Conrad came to Zengerstein.

It is not strange that Conrad lost his way. That evening a bulwark of clouds swept southward along the River Murg; fog crawled through the deserted village lanes and settled like a caul over the tarn outside the gates of Zengerstein. The storm unleashed furiously in the dusk. Winds keened in the catacombs beneath the Castle. Rain lashed at the casements of the library until, with a nervous gesture, Victor closed the velvet portieres. In that storm, Simon Conrad did not have a chance. At best, the roads of the district are few and obscured by the lichen-fingers of the encroaching forest. A single footpath winds on into the flatlands that stretch toward Donaueschingen, but at a certain point in that lane the traveler may easily go astray and find himself lost in the byways of Zengerstein with none of whom to ask the way, no path to take but the rutted passage that climbs the hill to the gates of the Castle itself.

All day, Victor and I had been restless; never ideal companions, penned in too long by the storm, we could scarcely bear each other's presence. Victor haunted the wine cabinet; I lost count of the times the decanter clinked against his glass. I ignored him; my mind busied itself with one thought, the possibilities of the success of my experiment. The library had been long silent, save for the whimpering of the storm.

Then, suddenly, after dark, the wolfhounds that guard the grounds of Zengerstein broke into a howl of attack. Breath hissed between Victor's lips; his light tread crossed the floor to the casement; the portieres were drawn aside. The howling grew louder.

"What is it?" I snapped. "Victor, what's the matter with those infernal beasts?"

"I can't see clearly . . ." Rupert's voice was strained. "There seems to be a light . . . out by the tarn . . . A man carrying a lantern . . ."

"A man . . . ?" I strode to his side, caught his shoulder.

"Yes . . . My shoulder . . . you're hurting me . . . Please, there's no need to be frightened . . . The hounds will rout him . . ."

"Call them off," I cut in sharply.

"What?" Victor whined. "But the man may be a thief . . . a killer . . ."

"You heard me! I want that man unharmed! Call off the dogs!"

He obeyed.

I heard his cry to the animals; the angry baying died away. Victor was still uneasy but he did not question my next command; he ran through the downfall toward the steaming tarn. He was gone some time; he must have had difficulty helping the trespasser to shelter, for, though unharmed, the man who sank into the hearth-chair was badly shaken and terrified. His breath came in sobs; in his grip, the glass of brandy Victor had given him rattled against his teeth. A full five minutes passed before he had grown calm enough to speak or understand what was said to him.

I flatter myself that I handled my first interview with Simon Conrad with consummate art; the circumstances were far from favorable, but, in the minutes that had lapsed since the first baying of the hounds a cunning assurance had laid hold on my mind. Winning Conrad over was ridiculously easy. Victor told me the man's right hand had been scratched by the fangs of Prinz; under my most solicitous directions, Simon Conrad's wound was cared for; he was supplied with dry clothes, steaming coffee and an invitation to spend the night at Zengerstein. I apologized for the necessary precaution of the dogs; with what craft I played upon his sympathies for the idiosyncracies of a blind recluse! As he sighed and sank back in his chair, Simon Conrad brimmed with goodwill and our best wine.

"Jawohl, Herr Doktor, this is quite an adventure I have had! Traveling alone in the Schwarzwald country is not the pastime for a timorous man, I fear . . ."

He laughed with inane good humor; I fancy my response was a trifle false. I was not in a mood for laughter. Alone! I thought. Then, he *is* alone! Excitement dried my throat. Every thread of the pattern fell so neatly into place!

I wearied of his chatter. I writhed under his gauche solicitude for my affliction.

"It must be a lonely world for you. Ja. Me, I do not know what I would do without my eyes. I am a jeweler by trade, you see; the firm of Krondorf in Munich. I have been fortunate, Gott sei dank! My sight has always been perfect . . ."

The mask of polite interest my guest saw gave no hint of the impatience that seethed in my brain. I thought the prattling fool would never be quiet; I thought he would never retire to the bedchamber Victor had prepared for him. But he did.

"Schlafen Sie wohl, Herr Conrad," I called after him.

"Danke . . ."

Two sets of footsteps receded up the stone stairway. I poured myself a drink. Agitation destroyed my usually keen sense of direction; some of the wine spilled. I rose and paced before the hearth until Victor returned. I clutched his arm.

"His eyes!" I hissed. "What were they like, Victor?"

The fragile body drew away from me.

"I do not understand, Herr Doktor. What does all this solicitude for Conrad mean?" The old whine crept into his tone. "You've acted most peculiarly ever since he appeared . . . I . . ."

"The eyes!" I snapped. "The eyes, you idiot!"

"How should I know?" Petulantly, Victor freed his arm. "His eyes are like any others . . . a young man's eyes . . . keen and very blue. I don't see . . ."

I nodded. "Then we need wait no longer . . ."

"Wait? I don't under . . ." The nasal voice withered; Victor swallowed audibly. "The experiment? You don't mean . . . No, you can't . . ."

"But we can—we shall!"

"No!" It was a weak cry of cowardice. "I won't do it . . . It's insane . . . Anyway, it might only fail . . ."

"It can't fail," I said thickly. "I must see again!"

"I won't be involved in this hideous . . ."

"You will!" My fingers caught his lapel, crept upward and closed on his throat. "You'll do as I say or spend the rest of your days rotting in prison. The authorities would still be interested to know who caused the accident at Freiburg, my dear Victor . . ." I thrust him from me. "Think it over," I said levelly. "Think, quickly."

I heard the raw sound of his breathing. His tread approached the wine cabinet; there was the cold clink of bottle and glass. I smiled. After a long minute, Victor said in a soft, beaten voice:

"When?"

It was not easy. I had never done this sort of thing before. I had no grievance against Conrad; but it was his life or mine. If the experiment succeeded, the world would lose an insignificant jeweler but regain a brilliant surgeon. Yes. It was difficult. But anyone must admit, there was no other way. We waited until Conrad slept. I do not know how long Victor crouched by my side in the tower alcove scant feet from Conrad's chamber door. Nocturnal rats skittered and squealed in the shadows; in a lower corridor, the Swiss clock moaned the quarter hour. No sound issued from Conrad's room. With the stealth of a night animal, my hand reached for the latch.

"Quietly!" Victor whimpered. "He may still be awake . . ."

The latch clicked faintly; the door inched inward a crack. A hinge whined; Victor's breath clogged in his throat. We stood quite still. With the sudden changefulness of a regional storm, the rain had abated shortly before midnight; now the moon shimmered in a liquescent sky. Victor touched my arm.

"He's asleep . . ."

"Are you certain . . . ?"

"The moonlight falling across the bed. I can see his face . . ."

I listened more closely; the groan of a snore reached me. I nodded.

"All right," I said. "Now . . ."

It was done very quickly. We were beside the bed and Victor had pinned Conrad's arms to his sides. A gasp ripped from the sleeper's throat. He slept no longer. I felt his neck muscles go taut beneath my searching grasp; I sensed his bulging eyes burning into my face. He managed one desperate "Nein!" and then, deftly, the scalpel in my delicate fingers found the carotid artery. Conrad jolted; his throat gurgled; warm blood bathed my hand. I heard Victor moan at the sight of it. Briefly, Conrad struggled. Then he stopped breathing. The body went rigid, then limp. My hands quivered. It took him longer to die than I had thought it would.

The worst was over. Simon Conrad was no longer a man, only a collection of bones and flesh and dying organisms; a guinea-pig, ripe for experimentation. The laboratory that led off the library had been long in preparation for this moment; even when I had despaired of ever testing my theory, some inner sense of urgency led me to have every instrument in readiness. The only thing I had to fear was the weakness of Victor Rupert, and in this final instant, that fear was dispelled. For, like an actor, nervous until the rise of the curtain, but exquisitely self-assured once on stage, Victor had grown suddenly calm and detached; he was not a weakling now. With the power of my will, the brilliance of my brain to direct his every move, he had become a precise surgical machine; his hands worked over Conrad's head as if they had been my own, responding to each order almost before it was spoken. The operation was a success; in less than an hour, two elliptical blue orbs floated in a jar of physiological saline beside the operating table.

By dawn, we had disposed of the body. The foetid vaults beneath the Castle were perfectly fitted to our needs. Simon Conrad lay in final rest amid the dust of the Barons von Zengerstein. As I climbed the dank stairway to my bedchamber, a thrill of well-being mixed with expectation shot through my weary body. My deliverance was at hand. That day, I slept a more contented sleep than I had known in many years.

Not so with Victor. The tension of that moment of strange scientific achievement past, the weakling lapsed back into the tortured realm of doubt and cowardice. He could not have slept at all; in the evening, when I rose, I found him already in the library. His voice was discordant with strained nerves. He was pouring himself a drink. I went to his side.

"How many have you had?"

"I don't see what business that is of yours!" he snapped. "If I want to drink . . ."

He got no further; I smashed the glass from his fingers. It splintered on the floor.

"I told you to stay sober!"

"But I need it! These trembling hands—I tell you I can't go through with this . . ."

"You must! We've been over the details a thousand times . . ."

"No . . ."

"You will, my dear Victor. Remember the authorities in Freiburg. And one other thing; you are now an accomplice in a premeditated murder . . ." Breath snagged in his throat; I seized his wrist. "I tell you, you *can* do it. Stop being a coward! Your hands are perfect; you worked wonderfully on Conrad last night . . ."

"But you were there to back me up. If I made a mistake . . ."

"There will be no mistakes! Understand, Victor? You dare not make a mistake. You are the one who robbed me of my sight and you are the one who will restore it!"

Despite my insistence, I was not at all certain it was wise to keep Victor from the liquor. Perhaps it would steady his nerves, work his mind to a pitch as coldly surgical as it had been when he worked on Conrad. That night, as I prepared myself for the final step in the experiment, misgiving seized my mind. Perhaps Victor was right; without my will to guide him, once I was under anesthesia, he might falter, he might make a mistake . . .

He stood washing his hands in disinfectant; when he spoke, his tone seemed calm enough. And yet . . . I sighed and shrugged. It was a chance, but it had to be risked. I lay back on the operating table; silent, sure. Victor was at my head. The mask brushed my cheek; the stench of ether swirled in my dark world. I breathed deeply. It did not take long. But as I relinquished the last shred of consciousness, a needle of fear stabbed my brain. Victor's fingers touched my forehead, and, it seemed to me, they trembled . . .

The return to consciousness was slow and painful. There was no sound; only the smell of antiseptic and the tautness of bandages that swathed my head; the skin of my eyesockets ached and stung. My tongue felt thick in the arid hole of my mouth. Something rustled to the right of me.

"Victor . . . ?"

There was no answer; instruments rattled in a sterilizing basin. I pawed the air impatiently.

"Victor, where are you?"

"Here, Herr Doktor . . ." His voice was dry and tight. My groping fingers caught the edge of his tunic.

"Tell me," I croaked. "Quickly, you fool! It was a success? It went well . . . ?"

Victor cleared his throat; his tone turned evasive. "You should be quiet, now, Herr Doktor . . ."

I tightened my grip on his tunic; I drew his face down to mine. His whimpering breath was audible.

"Tell me!" I cried. "You haven't failed. You did not dare to fail! You succeeded! I *will* see again!"

"Yes! Yes! It's all right. I succeeded! Please . . . let me go . . ."

I did. I sank back against the pillows. Relief and weariness flooded my body; after a time, I slept. Once, during the night, I woke to hear the spineless sound of a man sobbing. A bottle and glass clattered, neck-to-mouth. The fool was at it again. I did not interfere. Let him drown in his sotted forgetfulness. He had served his purpose. I was finished with him.

The weeks of convalescence were not as tedious as I had feared; during those last hours of interminable night I was sustained by taut anticipation. I scoffed at Victor's uneasiness. Time and again he sighed at my mocking laughter.

"You must not expect too much, Herr Doktor. We can't be certain . . ."

"Nonsense! You yourself said the operation was a success. I *shall* see! See with the young, perfect eyes of Simon Conrad!"

Victor's pessimism did not touch me. My mind was filled with plans for the resumption of my career; for the rebuilding of the life of the master surgeon, Herr Doktor Luther Markheim. I dreamed of the moment when I should watch the idiots who had supplanted me swallow their loathesome pity for a "blind has-been." My sense of security lasted until three days before the removal of the eye-bandages. Then, quite unexpectedly, a visitor came to Zengerstein.

By his tread and the timbre of his voice, he was a stolid man of perhaps forty-five. He spoke calmly and with respect; his tone was cultured, though with a faint inflection of the bauer. One would not have supposed him to be connected with the police. He said his name was Koch; Inspektor Koch of the Donaueschingen constabulary. Almost imperceptibly, Victor drew a sharp breath. Only a blind man with heightened aural sensitivity could have caught the intensity of that tiny gasp.

"Well, Herr Inspektor," I said quietly. "And what brings the police to Zengerstein . . . ?"

"The need of information," Koch said tonelessly. "We thought perhaps you could help, mein Herr . . ."

"Gladly, but I don't see . . ."

"Perhaps I'd best explain . . . You see, two weeks ago, a man named Conrad, a jeweler from Munich, set out from Donaueschingen on a walking tour of the Schwarzwald region. His wife and several friends chose to stay behind and await his return. He never came back . . ." Koch cleared his throat.

"Victor," I put in. "Perhaps the Inspektor would care for a bit of burgundy . . ."

"Ja . . ." I heard Victor at the cabinet. He brought two glasses. He poured Koch's drink and began to fill my goblet.

"It is wondered," Koch continued, "if perhaps he lost his way . . . and happened onto Zengerstein . . ."

Victor's hand jolted; wine spilled over my fingers.

"Look what you're doing, you idiot!" At that instant, I could have killed him for his treacherous cowardice. I could only cover the slip as quickly as possible, and hope that Koch had not guessed its import.

"I'm afraid, Herr Inspektor, we can be of little assistance . . ." I shook my head, sipping burgundy. "You are the first visitor to Zengerstein in a good many years. No one could have come here without our knowledge. The dogs alone would have frightened him off . . ."

Koch sighed. "I see . . ."

"It is possible the poor devil lost his way in the Forest . . ."

"Ja . . ." The Inspektor rose slowly from his chair. "Ja, that is what we fear . . . Of course, my questioning you was only routine, mein Herr . . ."

"I quite understand." My tone was apologetic. "I should be only too happy to help, if I could . . ."

I did not like the moment of silence that followed; I sensed the shifting of Victor's feet beside my chair, as though he cringed under a steady scrutiny. I liked it even less when Inspektor Koch finally answered me in his flat voice:

"Perhaps you have already, Herr Doktor . . ."

He left; Victor saw him to the door. Sitting alone in the library, I clutched the goblet in both hands; it splintered; needles of pain gashed my palms, and I felt a wet warmth that might have been wine —or blood. That night, in the quiet of my bedchamber, Koch's double-edged words echoed malevolently. And I knew Victor must never make another such mistake as he had made this afternoon; he and the threat of his weakling nature must be wiped out.

This time it was easier. It may be that the second time is always easier. Against Simon Conrad I had harbored no grudge. But loathing for the spineless Victor had festered within me for nearly a decade. Now he had become downright dangerous. Once again, his sotted stupidity threatened to ruin my life. Any scruples I had had in connection with Conrad's murder were entirely lacking as I planned that of Victor Rupert. My hands were steady; my voice calm. I was completely equal to the task that lay before me.

The acquisition of the poison was not difficult; every bottle in the laboratory was so arranged that I, in my blindness, could select from memory; my presence in the laboratory or at the wine cabinet could hardly arouse Victor's suspicion. He had drunk a good deal during the day; the bottle I set on our table at dinner must have seemed as innocent as any other; the poison did not change the color of the wine. I ate little that night; I toyed with my food and waited. Finally it came. He was setting down his glass when it slipped from numbed fingers. A gasp tore from his lungs.

"Doktor! . . . My throat! . . . that wine . . . burning in my chest . . . I . . ."

He broke off, struggling for breath; he must have seen the quiet smile that crossed my lips.

"Nein!" Victor lurched to his feet; his chair crashed backward; china shattered from the table to the stone floor. "Nein!" It was an agonized scream now. "A mistake . . . don't let me die . . . you can't!" His clawed fingers caught at my robe; he whimpered like a dying cur. I thrust him from me; he fell against the cabinet-de-vin; bottles and glasses clattered wildly. "You can't! You must save me . . . I lied . . . You vain fool, I lied . . . Don't you see? . . . If I die . . . If . . ." The words clotted in his seared mouth; a gurgling screech dwindled in the shadowed stillness of Zengerstein. Rupert crumpled in a silent heap.

He was not heavy, but the descent into the crypt seemed endless. Spider-webs brushed my face; a rat slithered across my feet and I stumbled, nearly dropping my hideous burden. The poison had worked quickly; droplets of still-warm blood oozed from Victor's scorched mouth; in the tomb itself a noisome stench choked my nostrils; without benefit of embalming, the remains of Simon Conrad had decomposed rapidly. I lay Victor on the shelf by the side of the maggot-eaten thing he had helped create. I was glad when it was over. I climbed wearily to my chamber and locked myself in. I should have been relieved; the last barrier to the safety of the new life that awaited me had been eliminated. Yet, strangely, I slept ill that night. The howling of the hounds was unbearable. They had been Victor's pets.

I thought the time would never come. The bandages itched intolerably; the waiting had done nothing for my nerves. Early this evening, a fresh storm swept south along the River Murg. Demented winds chanted litanies in the depths of the Schwarzwald. I could hear the voices of men and the baying of hunting dogs rising intermittently above the storm. Inspektor Koch and his deputies were unrelenting in their search for the man whose flesh slowly rotted in the vaults below Zengersteinschloss. I cursed Koch and his infernal curiosity. I soothed myself with the speculation that it was but a matter of hours now; once I had removed the bandages I could leave this damnable place, return to Freiburg and the life in which I belonged. After tonight . . .

The laboratory seemed cold despite the fire in the grate. My hands were coated with sweat. The surgical scissors slipped several times in my trembling fingers. It *will* work, my mind chanted; it *must work!* I unwound the bandages carefully; cotton adhered to the healing flesh of my eyes. Then the last strip of gauze fell away; an instant of darkness and my eyelids flickered. The blackness wavered and at its heart flared a tiny dancing object—the flaming moth of the gaslamp that stood before me! Lieber Gott, I could see!

I celebrated; my triumphant laughter violated the sullen dark Castle. I drank too much wine and ate too heartily. I toasted the impotent ghosts of Conrad and Victor and mocked their shadows that seemed to linger in the dim corners of the library. I was delirious with joy. And why not? Life sprawled before me anew in the wonderful colors of a world I had not seen for nearly a decade. Tomorrow I would quit this house of the dead; tomorrow I would set out for Freiburg. And now, in this last night of farewell, I wandered the halls of Zengerstein drinking in sights I had thought never to know again. The candelabra glinting in errant firelight, the tapestries alive with medieval pageantry, the Gothic arches of the upper corridors, and yes, the chamber that had been my mother's private sitting room —all before me now, just as I remembered them from childhood. Even the needlework my mother's hand had wrought remained as though she had left it there only last evening, incomplete, awaiting her return. How strange, I marvelled, that it has not altered in all these lonely years! How very strange! And my own bedchamber, the same as ever, the canopied bed, the fencing foils and masklike skull-and-crossbones upon the stone wall above the mantlepiece and the full-length mirror by the bed . . . the mirror . . .

Perhaps it was the wine. But as I paused before that mirror, peering into its watery crater, it seemed, for one awful instant, that I saw no reflection of myself. The glass had become a vast threshold on the lip of outer night beyond which lay only steps going down—down to the bowels of earth, through the tombs of Zengerstein. And as I watched, out of those catacombs rose a livid sphere of flesh, shapeless and twisted in a hideous grin. Instinctively, I drew away from that mask, and yet I could not shut from view the pallor of those flaccid jowls, the warped mouth, the hair matted like reptiles on a scabrous skull. The dead-white skin was covered with raw cicatrices, as if some latent putrescence had seeped through the pores; and from scarred pits, sightless eyes glared at me. Breath rasped in my lungs. I reeled away from that hateful reflection, my mind screaming. No, no, it cannot be! And yet I knew beyond a doubt the pale face that scowled from the glass was mine! Terror whirled in my brain; sobbing, I fell across the counterpane to sink almost immediately into a dreamless sleep—a stupor from which I woke—God knows how soon or late!—to find that blasphemous Thing of the mirror's depths bending over me!

It was not real; I lay riveted to the bed by some subconscious paralysis and told myself it was a dream, a hallucination spawned by overwrought nerves and the macabre adventure through which I had gone in the past month. In reality, there could never exist a loathsome monster such as crowded its face close to mine in this horrible instant. Yet even as I denied my sense of sight, a damp hand brushed my chest; fingers closed on my windpipe; the lips bared decayed teeth in a malevolent leer. The form lurched nearer and the free hand rose, very slowly. I stared, unbelieving, at the scalpel grasped in those murderous fingers. And then I knew. This was no childhood nightmare that would wither and die in sobs of waking relief. This was inescapable truth. I knew that in the maniacal visage that bent above my bed, I was seeing *myself*, the pale killer, as my victim had seen me in his moment of final agony; viewing the horror of my soul through the eyes of Simon Conrad, the man I had murdered!

I think I screamed, I tore free of the vise-like talons and crashed blindly to the floor. I stumbled to my feet, clutching the doorway for support. And then I ran. Aimlessly, madly, I ran, winding through the labyrinthian ways of the Castle, whimpering like the fabled child lost in the Forest. I ran until my heart pounded in my ears, my breath jolted from exhausted lungs. In the end, I cowered in some niche in the upper darkness of Zengerstein and waited.

It did not come. I waited like a beaten animal for death and it did not come. The Thing of the mirror gave no pursuit. Behind me, the catacombs of corridor lay silent. Gradually my sobbing quieted; my pulse slowed but remained erratic. Sweat bathed the seamed pallor of my face. Very slowly, I wound my way toward the flickering of the lamp that still burned in my bedchamber; carefully—with what fearful gentleness!—I opened the door . . . Nothing. The room was empty. Plaintively, the storm begged entrance at the casements; outside, the hounds bayed. In the chamber itself, there was no sound save the mocking hiss of the gaslamp.

And it has been thus for the last three hours.

But I am not fooled. I am still as clever as that Thing that lurks in the abyss of the mirror. I know the game it plays with me—a torturing game of cat-and-mouse. It has retreated, now; it would have me hope; it would have me believe it was all a dream, a trick of the imagination. I am not so stupid. There are facts you cannot escape; there are scientific reports of the last image beheld by a dying man remaining indelible in the dead eyes; the last thing Simon Conrad saw was I, the glint of the scalpel in my hand; a murderer come to claim him. So you see why I am not fooled; you see why I am afraid. The mirror is dark now. But in its inscrutable well nameless evil stirs and would come to life—the evil of murder and insanity that claimed Simon Conrad; the pallid horror that, sooner or later, shall rise again from the depths to claim . . .

Wait . . . the liquescence in the mirror shifts . . . the evil writhes like forming ectoplasm . . . You see . . . I was not wrong . . . A rustling . . . the sounds made by the slow approach of ponderous death . . . a blur, now, in the glass . . . Yes! . . . That pale, fat face . . . nearer . . . Dear God . . . the eyes . . . the scarred blind eyes . . . and the scalpel . . . moving . . . upward . . . no . . .

I had come to the conlusion that the case of the disappearance of Simon Conrad was insoluble. I was wet and disgruntled; my men were glad the night was at an end. After hours of wandering the Schwarzwald region, fighting rain and treacherous marshes, we had unearthed nothing. Near dawn, the storm abated; the men returned, stoop-shouldered, to the Inn for dry clothes and warmed schnapps. For a long time, I stood irresolute on the Forest's edge, staring across the lands of Zengerstein to where the ivy-slimed Castle ramparts rose like barricades guarding some ancient secret. I hated the thought of returning to Conrad's wife and friends in Donaueschingen, unable to answer one of their anguished questions.

I am not certain what impulse took me across the village and round the steaming tarn to the gates of Zengerstein; perhaps I merely wanted someone to talk to and the solitary light that still burned in an upper window of the Castle seemed inviting; or, perhaps some inner uncertainty as to the position of Herr Doktor Markheim in this singular affair still nagged me. I do not know. But of one thing I am certain. I did not expect the horrible discovery that awaited me.

The hounds that guarded the estate were chained; I had no difficulty gaining the Castle doors. But there was no answer to the doleful summons of the knocker. The door was not locked. I called out for Markheim; I called for that strange little companion of his named Victor. Nothing. Only solemn reverberations of my own voice. And then I went upstairs.

The light burning in that upper room sent slices of yellow through the portal crevices. I knocked. I tried to break in. In the end, I had to summon four of my men. Even then, the door gave way reluctantly. The bedchamber was in a state of chaos. The mirror by the bed had been smashed to evilly smiling slivers and before it sprawled the corpse of Luther Markheim, the slit in his throat torn wide, the scalpel still in his rigid fingers. A pool of his lifeblood made a scarlet halo about the swollen white mask of his face. On the writing table in one corner, gaslight wavered across the blood-spattered pages of the Markheim manuscript.

Herr Roderick, the coroner from Donaueschingen, is a small man with a cadaverous face and a reputation for being hardheaded and realistic; a man whose profession hovers constantly on the brink of death can hardly be otherwise. He listened to the story of Simon Conrad; he glanced through the manuscript of Luther Markheim and made a minute examination of the body. We followed the corpse down the clammy stairway. It was extremely heavy and took four men to carry it. Gingerly, the men arranged it in the hearse alongside the liquescent decadence that was the remains of Conrad and Victor Rupert. The horses shied in the rain, as though conscious and fearful of the burden they drew slowly down the desolate hillside.

I stayed behind; there was still the routine investigation of the estate to be gotten through for the sake of my official report. Roderick sucked his tobacco-stained teeth and followed me into the gloom of the library. He lit his pipe; a smoke cloud hovered between us as if frozen in the chilled half-light. I sank into a chair and sat staring into the fireless grate. After a time I sighed and riffled the pages of the manuscript that lay in my lap.

"Strange case," I murmured. "Hideously strange . . ."

For a moment Roderick gazed at the tiny bonfire in his pipebowl. Then, quietly, he observed: "Even stranger than you think, my dear Koch . . ."

I looked at him askance; he went on slowly.

"Did you notice anything singular about Markheim's body, Inspektor?"

I shook my head.

"The eyes," Roderick said thoughtfully. "I examined the eyes very closely; there is scar tissue about the sockets, as if an operation had been performed recently . . . But the eyes in Markheim's head were brown . . . and the eyes of a man who had been blind for years!"

I could only stare.

"But Markheim could *see!* He said he could see . . ."

Roderick moved his bony head from side to side.

"Not with those eyes, mein Herr. Nein. Luther Markheim never saw the Castle von Zengerstein; he only thought he saw it; willed himself to see it; what Markheim saw were the reflections of his own memories. The Thing that crept from the mirror, the monster that was himself seen through the eyes of Simon Conrad, existed only in Markheim's ego-warped mind. It was an idea that pursued Markheim into the shadow-valley of madness; the guilty memory of the crime he committed. It was an idea that led him to destruction by the very hand that destroyed Conrad—the hand of Luther Markheim!"

"Still . . ." I frowned. "The manuscript. You read it. Rupert. . . ."

"Rupert!" Roderick interrupted. "Ja. There lies the key to the puzzle, mein freund. I read the manuscript, as you say. I read of Markheim's own fear of Rupert's cowardice; he knew that Rupert was a weakling. But he didn't guess that the weakling had a secret. A secret he was too terrified to disclose after the experiment; a secret he tried to scream out in his dying breath. The weakling, strong, as long as the will of Markheim upheld him, lost his strength as soon as that wavered under anesthetic. Victor Rupert began the transplantation of the eyes, but he never had the nerve to complete it!"

"Fantastic!" I rose abruptly. "My dear Roderick, you've read too much of this new fellow Freud. Why . . . it's absurd. The will isn't that powerful; it could never make a blind man believe he saw; not even a madman . . . Don't be a fool . . ."

The coroner did not argue. He only shrugged and smiled at me through the haze of pipesmoke. His voice was quiet.

"Perhaps we'd better have a drink . . ."

We did; neither of us broached the matter again. After a time he left and I began my inventory of the Castle.

I apologized to Roderick later that day. He was far from being a fool. My final investigation of the house of Zengerstein proved that. In the laboratory of Luther Markheim, on a metal stand near the operating table, I discovered a glass beaker filled with a saline solution of some sort. In the crystal-clear liquid floated two elliptical, shining orbs. The irises seemed to stare up at me, clear and keen and very blue. They were the eyes of a man who smiled in ultimate triumph.

TANITH LEE (1947–   ), a British fantasist of children's and adult literature, has won both the British and World Fantasy awards. Two of her stories appeared in *Weird Tales*— the Zebra Books revival, edited by Lin Carter (see "The Eyrie," page xix–xx). "The Sombrus Tower" comes from the second and reportedly scarcest Zebra issue, dated Spring 1981.

THE SOMBRUS TOWER

by Tanith Lee

Vesontane rode into the Southern Waste. The frigid sunshine became a blue fire reflected in his coal-black armour; the wind unrolled his umber hair.

The fertile lovely land of Krennok was far behind him, and his king's house, and the warrior brotherhood in which he had won his place with spear and sword. Two beautiful women were left behind him also, each wondrous in her own way, pale, and melanine, slender as a flower stalk, lush as a rose. Even his name was, to all effect, left behind him, for in Krennok, most had heard of Vesontane, but here, in the dead country, few men travelled, and less news, and fame died like the grass.

But the five sisters had heard it, those five shadowy witches who had come to Krennok-dol five months ago. They had wailed a prophecy like death, for five men, allegedly all heroes, and certainly among them was Golbrant, reckoned by most the truest of all the king's warriors, the bravest, the most honourable, the best. He had been making music with the gold harp which he lifted like a bird from his shoulder. It had a woman's face, the harp, and when the sisters spoke in the king's hall, among the marble pillar-trees, some had said the woman on the harp wept acidulous green tears, like the sea. Four times the witches had spoken. And then they spoke a name Vesontane knew better than any other, for it was his own.

"Vesontane, Vesontane," they moaned, five reeds sounding as one. "Beware the dark genius of the Sombrus Tower which stands in the desert on the sun's left hand."

Each prophecy they gave sank in the breast like an iron shaft. No man who heard them quite kept his colour. Of the five named, none quite kept his soul. Some part of it seemed blown away. And presently, the five men, too, were blown, like autumn leaves, from the house of the king, from the land of Krennok, away into the wastelands, under the ivory sky. Golbrant rode towards the coast, towards the steel shelves of the sea, the spot where his warning lay in wait for him. But others rode far and wide to shun the warnings that had been given them, to dry hills where the sisters had spoken of a low-lying swamp, into withered forests to avoid the prediction of treeless spaces, to the spreadings of misty low-land lakes to escape the vision of a pointed mountain. But Vesontane, blown like the rest, restless, from the hold of Krennok-dol, sought, as Golbrant did, the scene the women had cursed upon him. The southward land on the left hand of the sun. And on the way, word had reached him, how he was not sure, by a dream, or the voice of a bird calling, that Golbrant had died. It was not without a dreadful irony, for, having hunted his fate along the coast and not found it, Golbrant had turned back towards Krennok, but missed the road, regained the sea, and come on a tall white tower. And in the tower was a blood-haired death—

In the dawn, Vesontane had built a cairn of stones. He had kneeled and prayed for Golbrant's spirit. In the hard rays of the sun, Vesontane took the amber cross from about his neck and laid it under the topmost shard, a thing of sacrifice for the memory of a brother. There was another to avenge Golbrant, and many to pray for him. Vesontane possessed even another cross, of polished slaty corundum. But there is sometimes a need of superfluous show and meaningless gesture. Vesontane had such a need.

Rising from the cairn, he left it alone at the brink of the day, and rode on.

The Southern Waste was the palest brown, the shade of winter acorns. All such lands tended to assume a particular tonal value, and to depart little from it. Here and there a desiccated plant seemed to balance the sky on its prongs. Stacks of nutmeg-tinted rock evolved, floating like enormous ships, their bases lost in a tidal haze of dust.

And it was cold. Primrose clouds let fall a thin dull hail in the west which rattled over the plain. The sun shone bitterly.

On the third night after he had made the cairn, Vesontane dreamed that a girl was watching him. Her face was muffled by her hair, or a veil, but she bent near, and he felt her eyes. All night he dreamed it, dreamed a girl watched him, and when he woke at sunrise, he found it was so.

She stood some paces away, but leaning forward. He had slept armoured here, like a mythical inset, his horse, blue-grey as smoke, tethered nearby, and a fire which had died on the ground between them. The girl had established herself as if to make the fourth corner or ray of a star formed otherwise by fire, horse and man. She was not veiled as in the dream, and her powdery hair was bound about her head. Vesontane returned her look, and saw that, though she was very young, she was ugly. He got to his feet, and bowed his head to her for courtesy. She was a woman, and had come to him alone in the wilderness. It was the habit of the warriors of Krennok-dol to honour women, whatever their station or their face.

"Childlady," Vesontane said to her, "what is it you want of me?"

"Your help," whispered the young and ugly girl.

"Tell me how?"

"A year gone, I wandered by a certain place, and a certain creature seized on me and took me prisoner. Now I languish in that jail it made, and there I'll rot if no brave man can set me free."

Vesontane touched the blue cross at his throat.

"But, childlady, you're frankly here, standing by me in the waste. How also can you be imprisoned elsewhere?"

"Regard what I am," said the girl. "I am youthful but hideous. In reality, I am a woman, and beautiful, but the creature keeps my beauty and my years to itself. These things it imprisons. Only what is left of me is at liberty to wander the plain. Don't abandon me to my anguish."

Vesontane crossed himself, and thereafter he saw the sunlight shining faintly through her. He heard the crunching tread of fate in the dust behind him, but could not turn aside.

"Show me the place where this being imprisons you," he said.

She raised her arm and pointed. The end of her pointing fixed the fifth ray of the star she had made with him, his dead fire and the horse. At her finger's end, on the edge of the horizon, there was a slim tower, the colour of a shadow.

"In God's grace," said Vesontane quietly, "how is it known, or if nameless, speak the title of the plain, as you call it hereabouts."

"Land or tower have no name," she said. "But a creature dwells there and I am its captive. Fight for me, but let me go."

"Go then," he said, and she vanished.

Though nameless, he knew which tower it was that stood before him.

He ate bread and drank wine. He fed the horse and saddled it. He prayed. His face was white, and implacable. He mounted the horse, and rode towards the dark tower on the horizon.

The cold sun climbed, touched the apex and descended. The land flowed, an unrolled carpet of stone, superficially changeable, ultimately changeless. Vesontane saw cliffs march at the corners of his eyes, rising up and sinking down. He saw defiles and chill ravines. At noon, he passed through a wood whose trees were thin as poles, their lower branches lopped to little knobs by a past snow. The leaves on their upper ribs—the boughs curved up there like rib cages of skeleton beasts—were also thin and sallow. It was easy to keep the dim tower in sight between them. Two hours after he had left the sallow wood, he came on another. It held a clear dark pool, at which he allowed the horse to drink. They emerged from the second wood in the last hour of the sun. The tower looked no nearer.

When the sun went out, which truly it seemed to do in the waste, as if pinched suddenly between earth and air, Vesontane dismounted. He prayed, broke his fast and slept.

In the morning, he repeated the process, mounted, rode on.

By noon, the tower looked no nearer.

An acrid wind blew, and it hailed again. The stones struck his armour like spent arrows in battle.

When the hail stopped, he saw, between himself and the distant tower, long-winged birds circling in the sky. Presently he came to a gallows. A man had been hanged there months before and had been eaten by the birds. Pickings were so scarce, they still congregated in the spot, hopefully but without hope. Vesontane glanced at the bones, and they spoke to him.

"Warrior, are you riding to the Tower Sombrus?"

Vesontane reined in the horse, which sidled with fear. Vesontane drew his sword, and held the cross-shaped hilt before him.

"So I believe. Why do you speak to me?"

"Why not? Few pass this way. If you reach the tower, you'll find a part of me there."

"You will tell me," said Vesontane, "that in the tower lie your skin, your flesh and your blood."

"I will."

Vesontane laughed shortly. His hands were numb.

"Tell me, too, how you know the tower's name?"

"I forget," said the bones of the dead man. "Ask my flesh, when you find it."

A bird swooped and flew in Vesontane's face, its beak greedy for his eyes. He slashed with the sword, and the bird fell in two pieces on the ground.

Vesontane rode away. The other birds did not follow him. The bones harped in the wind.

As the sun was setting, he rode through a gully and came out on the shore of a mere. The water was smooth as a mirror but, as if the surface had been breathed on, it reflected nothing. A pavilion stood on the shore by the mere, like an upended flower-bell, of a shade so subtle as to be unrecognisable. The sun gave a last red flash and was gone, and the pavilion opened. A small retinue appeared, who set out chairs and a table and a canopy. Candles were lit into colourless bloom and a woman walked from the pavilion.

She resembled both the women Vesontane had left in Krennok. She had the voluptuous form of Marguin, with whom he lay, and the moon-pale elf face of Liliest, the virgin to whom he made songs. But her headdress, her hair and her gown were a shadow and her eyes were shadow.

"Welcome, warrior," she said. "Dine with me."

He knew the food and the wine would be shadows, too, but he dismounted from the horse and tethered it, and went to her table by the lake.

It was as he had foreseen. Meat and drink, bread and fruit, all ghosts. Even the water in his cup was ghostly, though it had a taste of bruised herbs. They made conversation, but the woman asked him nothing relevant. She said: "How do you find the waste; does it compare favourably with other wastes?" He told her that it did. She spoke of the tedium of sun and moon, passing forever over and over the sky, and he agreed with her that it was hard on them, but worse for the stars, forever fixed. She had one of her shadows bring him a shadowy harp. Vesontane plucked shadows from it. He sang her a song he had fashioned to Liliest, but added words he had spoken in the joy of her bed to Marguin. His voice rang pure and sound across the silences of the night, and he thought of Golbrant, and the woman-faced harp, strummed now only by the currents of the sea.

The woman rose and took Vesontane's hand and led him into the pavilion. Her touch was real, and when he drew her into his arms the rest of her was real and she seemed to burn him with the heat of her blood. A shameful excitement overwhelmed him, for in her he might possess two women together, the timid innocent and the sweetly and profanely knowing. But the tower was shadow, the tower of lust must be a shadow too. At an unbearable instant she stayed him, and whispered in his ear: "I am sealed. Not as a maiden, but worse, more closely. Pierce me? Never, I'll promise you." And when he groaned, she said, "The Sombrus Tower divides. The maiden leaves her maidenhood, the known woman is robbed another way. The tower divides us from ourselves."

Just then the cross about his throat brushed the tip of her breast and she was gone. The whole pavilion lifted up over Vesontane's head. It became an enormous bird and flew away across the mere and he saw its solitary reflection as if in burnished steam.

The crimson moon hung overhead and he perceived the tower, far off, miles away. The pain of his loins seemed to recede as the tower had receded.

With his sword, he wrote in the dust of the shore:

WHY HAVE THEY NAMED YOU SOMBRUS?

The wind blew the letters away.

He kneeled and prayed until he slept. He dreamed he stood by a cairn of stones. He had raped a girl-child and had come to do penance under the scourges of the priests. But there were no priests, only a bird sitting on the cairn, which said to him: "Men name a thing because they fear it, to make it less. The tower has no name. Nor you."

Vesontane woke. The lake had disappeared and he could not, for almost an hour, remember his name.

He rode three further days across the waste, towards the tower occasionally called Sombrus. Always it stood clear before him, and was never obstructed. Where stacks crossed the way, there would be a gap exactly adjacent to the shape of the tower, so that he could see it. When the hail fell, between each stone, the tower stood straight as a long needle. In the darkness he saw it, though it was almost the tone of the dark. But never did it come nearer. Never did he reach it.

By day, there were strange events. He came to a ruin whose chimney smoked, though there was no fire. He beheld a snake changing its skin, but it was the skin which slithered away. At night, stranger. A barge, draped by gauzes, dripping lights, sailed by through the air, and stretching up his sword to the length of his raised arm, he scratched its keel with a rasping noise.

He rode for two more days. He saw a place like a field, but it was a field of skulls, where staked heads had been placed on poles. The skulls did not speak, and he was now so conditioned that he expected them to, listening as he went by.

His food was gone. The horse grubbed dry burned grasses, crisp with morning frost. Now and then, there was a stream, but not all of them were real, or drinkable.

The tower stood always before Vesontane, over slopes, across ravines, beyond rocks, subsidences, dust-bowls. But never did it come nearer. Never did he reach it.

He thought: *Eventually I must break free of the Southern waste, and cross the boundary of some other land. What then? Has it power to persist outside this waste?* He came to know the tedium of the sun and the moon, forced forever to crawl over and over the sky. The whole wilderness was enchanted, tainted by the tower, and he might never reach the limit of it, as he might never reach the tower itself.

One morning, dizzy with hunger, he woke and asked himself what he was doing. He had been warned of a doom, and he had diligently pursued it. But the doom ran from him. He stared towards the slim dark needle on the horizon, no nearer than it had been on the day the ugly child-girl had pointed to it. Was there dishonour in abandoning an enemy who would not stay and give battle? Or in forsaking a quest it was beyond his means to accomplish? Perhaps the answer was before him in the very elusiveness of the phantom. In seeking to confront his fate, he had averted it. His heart lightened, but doubt wailed at his elbow. A quest incomplete was solely that, a vow unkept, a broken thing. And who turned from a fleeing foe had sometimes earned a blade between his shoulders.

Vesontane waited until the sun was three handspans above the rocks, then he set a fire. There were many sides to his nature, and somewhere inside him was a pagan, also. As he had built the cairn for Golbrant, now he built the fire. Every morning and every dusk he had prayed to God, and now he offered to the gods of the waste, cutting a lock of his hair and burning it in the fire, throwing in also a ring of dull gold from his middle finger. With his sword he made a small clean cut in his arm and offered them his blood; he spat, offering the water of his mouth. Lastly, he kneeled again, and performed upon himself the deed supposed a sin since it wasted the procreative force, with a sick and cringing pleasure spilling his seed, shivering, into the pagan fire.

For a while he lay on his side, looking for a sign, either of anger or of absolution, even perhaps of compromise. No sign was vouchsafed him, and at length the fire perished. He thought of the green dol hill, and Krennok's saffron skies, of the fruits and vines, the hunting, of song, of love. He thought of some priest, stern, wise and gentle as a father, the washing away of error, and a white rosebud once seen in Liliest's hair, and Marguin's smooth nails combing his arms.

He saddled the horse and mounted it, and turned its head and his own away from the phantom of the Sombrus Tower, away from the south, towards the north, the border over which he had ridden some seventeen days ago, following death.

Everything at once looked new to him, and he gazed at it, swaying slightly with fatigue and disorientation. The brown earth was studded by glassy pebbles, the rocks veined by quartzes, marbles, carbons. The sky was violently still, choked by cloud which had been immobilised, though somewhere a narrow wind blew, compressed by its passage between tall stones and through mean hollows. Having lowered his eyes, next raised his eyes, he now centered them on the horizon before him with a wild craving for the empty vista which he would see. Continually focusing on the tower had become for him like the continual ache of an unhealing wound.

Above, the sky, below, the waste ground, directly before him, two knife-cut ridges. And framed between them far, far away, the dark tower.

Vesontane gave a cry. It struck the stillness and shattered. He held the horse motionless, and stared at the tower before him. Then, slowly, he turned only his head, and looked back the way he had been travelling.

There, about a hundred paces off over the plain behind him, a rider rode a blue-grey horse southward, towards a distant shadow-coloured tower. His armour was coal-black, the wind unrolled his umber hair. He did not look behind him, as Vesontane was doing, yet suddenly he too cried aloud. He too was Vesontane.

Oh, God deliver me, though I forsook the road of my destiny and am unworthy. Oh God, whose arm is mightier than the gate of hell!

A rider rode into the south towards a distant tower. In the north stood a distant tower. Vesontane had only to ride towards it—

He turned the horse briskly eastward. He drove it to a heavy lumbering gallop. He did not look ahead, nor behind him.

After half an hour, the horse stumbled and he reined it in. Vesontane crossed himself. He prayed. He imagined the pure prayers of Liliest, uttered for his sake, and Marguin's scalding tears. He looked up and saw a distant tower in the east. Looking behind him, he saw three riders; each rode towards a distant tower. One rode south, and one north, and one rode west. While his purpose had been single, he had known tedium and banality, no more. Once his purpose had been split, two purposes, the sorcery of the tower had claimed him. Divided. Divided him from himself. And again. But he did not learn, nor did it matter. He rode this way, and now that. To the points of the compass he rode, quartering, and quartering the quarters. For each digression, his twin appeared at his back, riding opposingly, and when he turned, he saw them. . . .

He shouted after them, and none answered. He looked away from them and a vast shout of many many voices, all his own, stunned the waste. Thereafter he was quiet

Up in the air, as a bird flies, save there are no birds here. Behold the great circle of men, forever riding away from each other towards those slight, far distant towers. Forever riding away, yet drawing no farther from each other than some hundred paces, forever riding, yet drawing no nearer to those distant towers. Yet forever riding, forever riding, forever, forever, away, away, away.

AUGUST DERLETH (1909–71) founded the publishing company Arkham House in Sauk City, Wisconsin, to preserve in hardcover some of the best writing from *Weird Tales,* and he also contributed 114 stories to The Unique Magazine, most of them under his own name, but a few bylined Stephen Grendon. The following haunting (sic) ghost story was credited on its title page in the March 1947 issue to the pseudonymous Grendon, but with the following asterisked disclaimer: "Through a regrettable error, this story is announced on our cover as by August Derleth. Mr. Derleth acted as agent for Mr. Grendon's story, and someone in our office confused the agent's name for the author's. The error was discovered too late to stop printing of the cover." Derleth, who later confessed that Stephen Grendon was the name of the narrator of his own autobiographical novel, *Evening in Spring,* owned up to his pseudonymous tales by collecting them in one volume as *Mr. George and Other Odd Persons.*

MR. GEORGE

by August Derleth

Now that the sunlight of late afternoon slanted across the lawn, Priscilla took the flowers she had gathered and tied a little blue ribbon around them. She attached the note she had written, clutched the bouquet tightly to her, and tiptoed to the door of her room. She opened it. Voices came up the stairs. But *they* were out in back, and would not hear her leaving the house. If they saw her come back, that would make no difference. She closed the door behind her and marched her sturdy five-year-old self down the carpeted stairs to the front door and outside.

The streetcar conductor recognized her. He bent his moustached face above her and asked, "All alone, Miss Priscilla?"

"Yes, sir."

"It's going on for dark, too. Are you off far?"

"Oh no. I'm going to see Mr. George."

He looked unhappy. His smile was pale, thin. He said no more.

The streetcar clanged on its way. Priscilla knew that the conductor would tell her just where to get off, but just the same she counted the blocks—the next but one, where Renshaws lived; the one after that, which was Burtons'; the one of vacant lots; and then at last, after three blocks in which no one she knew lived—seven of them in all—the conductor called in that this was her stop.

"Yes, sir. I know. Thank you," she said.

She smiled at him and got off.

He looked after her, troubled; he shook his head. "And what's to become of her with all those vultures around her?" he asked of the mote-ridden air.

All along the way, Priscilla had been a little apprehensive about the big iron gate; but, since it was not yet six o'clock, it stood open. She passed through the open gate and went directly to Mr. George's place. There was nothing to put the flowers in; so she left them there, right where Mr. George would be sure to see them. She was not quite sure about Mr. George. Of late, many things had puzzled her. She did not understand about Mr. George, nor why he had gone away and left her alone with her mother's cousins, who, she knew with the unerring instinct of a child, did not love her the way Mr. George had loved her, or her mother before him, gone, too.

She pulled out the note and fixed it in such a way that he would be sure to see it. Going away, she looked back several times to see whether he had come; but the flowers lay there undisturbed with the whiteness of the notepaper standing out. The flowers were sweet rocket, forget-me-nots, and roses—old-fashioned flowers, the kind Mr. George liked. But Mr. George did not come; he was not in sight when she got to the gate; so, with one last lingering look, she went out into the street and down to the corner to wait for the streetcar, already beginning to wonder whether *they* had missed her.

But, no, they had not. They were still talking when she slipped into the house, though one of them was in the dining room now, and they were all raising their voices a little—not enough to be audible much beyond the front hall. She stood soundless, listening. Though the two women and the man, their brother, were her mother's cousins, Priscilla thought of them as her aunts and uncle. The women were in the kitchen, and Uncle Laban in the dining-room.

Uncle Laban was saying, "The trouble with you, Virginia, is that you have no sense of refinement, no tact. It's just the money you want, and you don't care how you get it."

"It's just *her* who stands between us. You know it as well as I."

"Now that George is gone," said Laban.

"Yes," said Virginia.

There was a nervous titter from Adelaide.

"I often wonder just what was the relation between them?" resumed Virginia. "Were they lovers?"

"It doesn't matter."

"Oh, it does," put in Addie. "If we could prove perhaps that *she* is his child . . ."

Laban made an impatient clucking sound. "Irrelevant and immaterial. Cissie's will is clear, and it makes no difference whether Priscilla is George's or Henry's or even whether she wasn't Cissie's. The will set forth that George was to stay here in Cissie's house until he wished to go . . ."

"Or died," interposed Virginia.

"Don't be unpleasant," said Laban shortly. "And the house, the grounds, and all the money—"

"Three hundred thousand dollars!" sighed Adelaide.

"—belongs to Priscilla."

"You leave out the most important part," said Virginia. "After Priscilla, we come."

"Say, rather, we are here."

"Oh, yes," said Adelaide bitterly, "as we have always been here. On someone's bounty."

"What do you care about that?" asked Laban pettishly. "We have the run of the house—and almost of her bank account."

"I want it openly, above-board," said Virginia.

"Oh, you are descending to comedy," said Laban. "But I know you're up to something—letting the servants go one by one."

"They were Cissie's—not mine."

"You haven't replaced any of them."

"No. I'll think about that. Have you got that table done?"

"Yes."

"Go and call her."

Priscilla fled noiselessly up the stairs, so that she would be ready when Uncle Laban called.

On the night side of dusk, Canby, who was on his beat, saw something white fluttering beyond the gate. In the course of routine duty he went in to see what it was. He detached the note, flashed his light around to get such details as might be necessary, and in due course turned the note in at precinct headquarters.

The captain read it.

"Dear Mr. George, please come back. We want you to live with us again. We have plenty of room. You just take the streetcar and go straight east. The house is just like you left it, only now more roses are in bloom."

"No signature?"

"None. It was just there on the grave, with some flowers. I left the flowers. Grave of a man named George Newell. Died about a month ago. Fifty-one years old."

"Looks like a kid's printing. Give it to Orlo Ward—that's the kind of thing he wants for *The New Yorker.*"

The old clock in the hall, which had been Grandfather Dedman's, talked all night. Mr. George said that her mother remembered how it talked. It used to say "Cis-sie, Cis-sie, Cis-sie, Go-to sleep-now, Cis-sie!" over and over until she went to sleep. Now Priscilla thought it talked to her in the same way. But Priscilla was not sleepy. She lay listening to all the sounds the old house made. She lay mourning her lot, now that the cook—the last one she liked—had been sent away, and the rest of them in the house disliking her. She could tell by the way they looked at her, by the way they talked to her; and there was the feeling she had. If only Mr. George would come back! Nothing had been the way it had always been after her mother went away since the day Mr. George complained he wasn't feeling well and later called her to his bed and said, "Be a good girl now, Priscilla. And remember, if anything goes wrong, go to Laura."—Laura being something to Mr. George as she had been to her mother. But not, like the Lecketts, blood-relative.

The murmur of voices whispered down the hall.

Virginia Leckett was braiding her hair in her brother's room. Laban was already abed.

"And if something did happen to her, there couldn't be any question about our inheriting, could there?" she was asking.

"That's the tenth time you've asked that, I'll swear," he said.

"Could there?" she insisted.

"How? There aren't any other relatives."

"That's what I thought."

"Anyway, she's as healthy as a cow."

"Oh, things could happen."

"What things?"

"You never can tell, Laban."

"You give me the creeps, Virginia."

"Look at the way George went."

"Well, you can't expect Priscilla to develop heart trouble."

"That's what the doctor *said.*"

"That's what he believed, also."

"That could be seen to. There are things that bring on heart attacks."

"You'd better not talk that way, Virginia."

"No?"

"No!"

"Just the same," she went on, talking more rapidly, "if something happened to Priscilla—just think, three hundred thousand dollars! Laban—think what you could do with your share! And I! Why, I could go to Europe."

"But you never would. Why don't you stop torturing yourself about that money? It's out of your reach."

"Is it?"

"You'd better go to your room."

Virginia's footsteps went down the hall, pausing at the door of Priscilla's room. Don't let her come in, God, asked Priscilla with supreme confidence. Virginia went on down the hall, and the hum of voices came distantly from Adelaide's room. It had been this way many nights since Mr. George went away. Sometimes Priscilla would think that she hated Aunt Virginia the most; but then she would remember mama telling her never to hate anyone because hate hurts the hater more than the hated—or something like that. Just the same, Priscilla did not trust Aunt Virginia. She did not trust Aunt Adelaide or Uncle Laban, either, but she mistrusted Aunt Virginia the most. She could not understand what mama meant when she used to say to Mr. George, "I pity them. They are so narrow, so provincial. When they had money they could have gone to Paris, to Vienna—but no, they had to invest it in shaky stock just to get more, and lost it all. Poor things!"

The clock said, "Pris-sie, Pris-sie, Pris-sie, Go-to sleep-now, Pris-sie."

"I'm not sleepy," said Priscilla into the darkness.

The house settled, groaning and creaking. A faucet dripped some-where, and in the wind outside, a limb of the cedar at the northwest corner of the house rapped from time to time against the wall. The clock went on talking, with its loud *tick-tock, tick-tock, tick-tock.* And outside the streetcars clanged past, ever fewer and fewer of them, as the night deepened. Priscilla lay thinking, dreaming almost, of mama and Mr. George, and of how it had been only a year ago, when they had been where the ocean was, and she had played all day long in the sand, while mama's cough got worse and worse, and Mr. George grew sad and quiet, and the wind blew, it seemed, colder and colder and blew them at last right back here to the house on Elm Street where mama had been born. It seemed a long, long time ago, ever so long. Time seemed to stretch out into endless dimensions on every side of her, and she felt lost, lost from mama and Mr. George, and the sandy beach and all the trains, the strange little coaches of those places far over the ocean, and the ships, and . . .

But now she grew drowsy, and someone came in through the door and bent over her and whispered, "Go to sleep now, Priscilla."

"All right, Mr. George," she said.

In the morning Priscilla, who was up with the sun, took Celine—the oldest of her dolls, and her favorite, for it had come from Arles, bought by mama and Mr. George on a lovely holiday from Paris—and went to play in the teahouse at the end of the garden, sitting in the cool shade of the birch trees leaning over. Long before anyone else in the house was out of bed, Priscilla reached her haven with Celine. She was in the habit of carrying on long conversations with Celine, who was pert and quaint at the same time, looking foreign and strange, and, in the circumstances, not too voluble, always say-ing just the right things.

This morning she was set up in her usual place across from Pris-cilla, and Priscilla arranged the tea things as she talked. Did Celine have a good night's rest, or were her legs crossed under her again? Would Celine like sugar or lemon or both in her tea, or did Celine prefer to drink it in the proper manner, without anything? The birds sang, for the tree-girt garden was a haven in the midst of the city, and seven blocks was a good flying distance to the trees of the cemetery; so they flew back and forth all day long, and made intimate noises in the shrubbery around the teahouse.

Celine made the appropriate answers.

But there was something strange about her this morning and presently Priscilla began to look at her as if with new eyes. It seemed to her that Celine was trying very hard to say something to her—something really original that did not come from Priscilla first. "Take care," she seemed to say. "Watch out."

Priscilla looked around her in momentary alarm, so real did Celine's voice seem. But there was no one there.

"Watch out for whom?" she asked in a whisper.

"For *them!*" said Celine. But what an odd voice for a doll's, thought Priscilla.

Then she looked very covertly around her on all sides of the teahouse. She knew that voice! She did, indeed. It was Mr. George's —and it was just like him to pretend it was Celine's.

She clapped her hands and cried out gaily, "Come out, come out, wherever you are, Mr. George."

No one came.

"Please, Mr. George."

A mourning dove cooed.

"Don't tease me."

No answer.

She looked at Celine, but the doll was as bland as ever. She looked away, over her shoulder.

"Watch out," said Celine in Mr. George's voice.

She whirled, looking this way and that. "I'll find you," she cried out. "I will, I will!" She darted into the bushes, peering this way and that, with such violence that the birds were still, save for a blue jay who sent out warning cries about her intrusion to every part of the garden.

"Whatever is that child doing?" inquired Adelaide from the window.

"What?" asked Virginia, hooking herself into her old-fashioned dress before the mirror.

"Why, running around and around the teahouse. She seems to be looking for something. Or someone."

"Children have imaginary playmates."

"It's crazy, Ginny. Now, I wonder!"

Virginia looked at her. Sometimes that too-large head on that short, thin body produced an idea of merit, from Virginia's point of view. "What is it now, Addie?"

Adelaide looked at her out of narrowed eyes. "Do you suppose it might be possible to have her declared—well, not insane, exactly—but . . ."

"Oh, no, that would never do. There are so many other ways. A slow poison, for instance."

"Don't be crude, Virginia," said Laban from the threshold. "For God's sake, are we going to have breakfast? If you insist on firing the cook, somebody in this household ought to be ready to assume kitchen responsibilities."

"We're coming," said Virginia. "Do see what Priscilla's doing."

Laban crossed to the window and looked out.

After a while he said, "She appears to be holding a conversation."

"Oh, yes, with the doll. I've noticed that," said Virginia.

"No, not with the doll."

"Not? Is she alone?"

"Yes. Her back's to the doll; she's not even looking at it."

Virginia turned. "Adelaide, will you go out and call her in for breakfast?" And, when Adelaide had gone, she said to Laban, "I don't like to be called 'crude', Laban."

He shrugged. He had been thinking about what he might inherit if anything did happen to Priscilla; Virginia had planted seed in fertile ground. "Don't be, then," he said. "What do you suppose people would think if she died like that? After all, the terms of Cissie's will aren't a dead secret. There would be questions. Finally, poison can be traced—even the most obscure poison, which you wouldn't get hold of, anyway."

"If you can think of anything better, why don't you?"

"It would have to be an accident of some kind—or at least, look like one. Only the other day I read something in the *Sun* about an accident which took the lives of two children. Playing in the attic, locking themselves into a trunk. They were suffocated. That could so easily happen, you know. How could anyone prove differently? But poison involves certain chemical and physiological factors which are incapable of being made to tell a story different from the facts."

Adelaide came back, a little breathless. "Imaginary playmates, is it? She says George is out there somewhere, hiding from her. She says he talked to her."

Virginia smiled. "That is putting her innermost wish into a fantasy she can live. It's the height of imagination. What did he say?"

"She didn't tell me."

"Is she in?"

"She's coming."

"We shall see."

Priscilla came in and sat down at the table. It was not set. She waited, looking at the three of them—Uncle Laban, fat, jolly-looking except for his soft, full mouth and his small dark eyes; Aunt Adelaide with her grotesquely fat head, so heavy that it always lolled a little; Aunt Virginia with her thin line of mouth and her hard blue eyes. All were dressed in black—Adelaide in taffeta, Virginia in brocade, Laban in broadcloth. All were now busy in some fashion or other—Laban with the morning paper, Adelaide scurrying about to set the table, Virginia at getting breakfast.

It was hard for Priscilla to sit still, because she was convinced that Mr. George had slipped into the house with her, and was even now concealed somewhere in the room. Her eyes darted inquisitively this way and that; momentarily she expected him to reveal himself. But nothing happened and meanwhile, Adelaide had brought all the dishes and then at last came with Virginia bearing eggs and bacon and toast, and a glass of milk for Priscilla. All sat down, Laban putting his paper aside.

"With whom were you talking in the teahouse, Priscilla?" asked Virginia.

"With Celine," answered Priscilla around her glass of milk, which she had begun to drink.

"Who else?" asked Laban.

No answer.

"I asked you, who else?"

Priscilla shook her head.

"You told me," said Adelaide.

"Mr. George," said Priscilla.

"Indeed! And what did he say?" asked Virginia.

Priscilla shook her head again.

"Answer me."

Priscilla remained silent.

Virginia turned to the others. "You see, it's imagination."

"He came back last night. I asked him to," said Priscilla.

Adelaide tittered. Virginia flashed her a quick, angry glance. Laban hawked and bent to his bacon and eggs.

There were no more questions. Each of them was thinking his own thoughts. Priscilla still hoped secretly for Mr. George to pop up and surprise them all. Adelaide thought of the way in which children played by themselves. Virginia contemplated the three of them alone in the house—*their* house—without Priscilla. Laban thought there was no good in delaying matters; accidents did not wait upon auspicious moments. Besides, the concept of a hundred thousand dollars which might be his to do with as he liked had grown immeasurably and now loomed directly before his mind's eye as a vast mountain of epitomized freedom, opening the world to him as it had never been open before.

Finishing his breakfast, he gazed at Priscilla, who had also finished, and smiled. "Where did George go?" he asked.

She was disarmed. "I think he's hiding."

"I'll bet I know where he's hiding," continued Laban. "Should we go and look?"

"Oh, yes, let's."

Laban pushed his chair away and got up. "Come along, then."

"Excuse me," said Priscilla to the two women.

They went out into the hall, Priscilla clinging to his hand.

"I know just where he would be," said Laban, leading the way to the stairs.

"Upstairs?"

"In the attic. It's dark there."

The dimness of the attic resolved itself for Laban into a giant funnel at the end of which loomed the partly-filled steamer trunk not far from the top of the attic stairs. He began to circle the outer edge of the funnel, moving things and looking behind them. Priscilla darted here and there, but every few moments she stood quite still and asked questioningly of the musty twilight, "Mr. George?"

"We'll find him," said Laban each time, with a nervous heartiness. His hands were clammy, and cold sweat started to his forehead as he drew nearer and nearer to the trunk.

The trunk was large and very heavy; once inside, it would be quite impossible for Priscilla to lift the lid, even if the hasp were not caught. All the darkness of the attic, which was large and reached into the gables of the old house, seemed to converge upon the trunk. Twice Priscilla stopped almost beside it.

"He isn't here," said Priscilla at last.

"I'll bet he is," said Laban. "There's one more place just big enough to hide him. Right there."

He bent and lifted the heavy lid. The trunk was almost as deep as Priscilla was tall, though the things still packed in it diminished its depth a little. He looked at the child from the corners of his eyes; she seemed entranced, standing almost on tiptoe to peer toward the dark maw of the trunk.

"That's too dark for me to see him even if he is there," said Laban. "Maybe he's hidden under the clothes. Crawl in and find him, Pris."

Priscilla took two steps forward and heard someone say, "No, Priscilla."

"Oh!" she exclaimed, clasping her hands. "It's Mr. George!"

"What?" Laban was startled.

"He's here somewhere. I heard him."

Laban gazed at her with amazed wonder at the vividness of her imagination. Then he said, "I'll bet he's hidden under this clothing. Just crawl in and surprise him, Pris."

She shook her head. "Mr. George says not to."

A kind of exasperation was growing in him. He came down to his knees beside the trunk. "See," he said, "I'll prop up the lid." He pushed a heavy book upright between the lid and the trunk. "I'll be right here in case he comes out."

Priscilla shook her head. "You look," she said.

He thought quickly. If she could be persuaded to stand beside him, it would be simple to tip her into the trunk without any kind of rough handling which might later show a bruise on the delicate flesh.

"Come and help me," he said, bending to peer into the darkness.

Priscilla came forward.

Just short of him something stopped her, something like an invisible hand pressing her back. Something tall and dark took shadowy shape beside Laban where he knelt, waiting for her, something that reached down and tore the sustaining book from beneath the trunk-lid, something that pushed the trunk-lid down with weighty impact upon Laban Leckett's neck.

He gave a choking cry, humped up horribly, and collapsed, kicking a little.

"Go away, Priscilla. Go downstairs now."

"Yes, Mr. George."

Priscilla went obediently out of the attic, down the stairs, and back to the teahouse, where she sat and told Celine all about it, very animated.

At the window stood Virginia, looking out with narrowed eyes and a derisive smile on her face. "I knew it," she said over her shoulder to Adelaide. "There never was much man about Laban. He lost his nerve."

On the day after the funeral, Laura Craig came to call. Like the Leckett women, Laura Craig was in her fifties, but she looked considerably younger. She dressed well, having money and knowing how to use it, knowing it was only a means to an end, not an end in itself. She had been a beautiful woman and was still a strikingly handsome one; in appearance there was the difference of day and night between her and her hostesses, Laura being colorful and jeweled as against their almost offensive plainness.

"I was shocked to read about Laban," she said without preamble. "I read it only this morning. I've been up in Connecticut, and I am sorry to have missed the services. However did such a thing happen?"

"The lid of the trunk was very heavy," said Virginia, quick to speak before Adelaide could say anything. "I suppose Laban was careless."

"How dreadful!" exclaimed Laura. "But what was he looking for?"

Virginia shrugged and raised her eyebrows.

"Something of father's, we think," said Adelaide. "That was father's trunk, you know. The last time it was used was when father went to the Exposition in St. Louis."

"It was only by accident that we found him," added Virginia. "We just missed him finally, and went to look for him. He had been dead quite a while. It was awful—the trunk-lid came down with such force that it almost severed his head. We have destroyed the trunk naturally."

"I should think so," said Laura.

The talk drifted politely toward Priscilla, and presently Priscilla herself was walking down to the front gate with Laura Craig, whom she also called "Aunt." The sisters Leckett stood behind the curtains at the windows to make sure that Priscilla did not linger too long with this woman, whom they knew had come primarily to assure herself that the child was all right.

"Let us hope she says nothing of her absurd fancies to *her,*" said Virginia bitterly.

"You forbade her to speak of them again."

"Oh, I know—but children recognize no restrictions. Will she ever forget George Newell? I wonder."

"It won't make any difference, will it?" Adelaide tittered.

"Be still, Adelaide." She sighed. "What *could* have happened up there? Laban was never careless!"

"You know what she said."

"Oh, Addie! A farrago of shadows and George and nonsense! Are you thinking the house is haunted by George? How laughable!"

Adelaide sniffed a little and left the window.

"It can't be denied, however, that Laban's death leaves each of us richer by fifty thousand dollars—after Priscilla, that is."

"How can you say such a thing, Addie!" said Virginia sharply.

Adelaide turned. "How can I say what?"

"What you just said about Laban's death."

"I didn't say anything about Laban's death."

Virginia turned angrily. "Why, Addie! I heard you. Don't try to deny it."

"Are you out of your mind, Ginny? I haven't opened my mouth. What did you imagine you heard now?"

"You said we would each be richer by fifty thousand dollars as a result of Laban's death."

"Why, I never!"

"You did!"

"I did not! That, if anything, is a thought which would occur to you a long time before I would think of it." Thoughtfully, she added, "It's true, though, isn't it?"

Virginia said nothing. Something gnawed persistently at her consciousness; it was the knowledge that if something were to happen to Adelaide before Priscilla died, she, Virginia, would come into three hundred thousand dollars, without the need of sharing it with anyone at all. A little shaken, she forgot about Priscilla and Laura Craig out in the afternoon sun at the gate and came away from the window. She was caught in a mesh of greed and conflicting desires.

The cedar limb tapped against the house once for every five times the old clock in the hall said *tick-tock*. Priscilla counted in the dark and communicated her findings to Celine, whom she had permitted to share her bed that night. She set herself next to counting the times the faucet dripped. But this, she found, was next to impossible, for the drippings were never very certain or clear. And there were other sounds alive in the dark in the old house. The attic shutter was loose; it creaked and banged in the wind. Something rustled down the hall and Priscilla knew it was Aunt Adelaide again; in a few moments their voices made a murmuring sound which joined the voices of the night.

In her sister's room, Adelaide walked nervously beside the bed. "It's no use your telling me it's my imagination, Virginia. I know I saw something. This is the third time, and I never heard that hallucinations come in threes."

"And what was it this time? Try to be coherent, Addie."

"A shadow in the hall, at the head of the stairs."

"If you weren't so vain about your eyes, I think an oculist and a pair of spectacles would lay your shadow."

"I stood still. The shadow moved. It was a man." Her words came faster. "Do you think I *wanted* to see him? Do you? Because if you do, you're crazy! I want to get out of this house. I hate it! I've hated it all my life—since we had to come and live here as Cissie's 'guests'."

"So do I. Just be patient, Addie. It takes time."

"Yes, always waiting!" She turned and bent over Virginia, instinctively lowering her voice. "I've thought of something. You know what Laban said about accidents. I've watched her swing. That's an awfully heavy swing, and when George made it for her he reinforced the oak seat with iron. If she should jump too soon and not get out of the way quickly enough—and if it should catch her somehow . . . I think it could happen."

"Or be made to happen," added Virginia softly. "Think of that now, Addie, instead of absurd hallucinations. And for heaven's sake, don't tell anyone you think you see men on the stairs—you know what people would think!"

Grandfather Dedman's clock said, "Pris-sie, Pris-sie, Pris-sie, Go-to sleep-now, Pris-sie." This time the cedar limb tapped on "sleep." Priscilla snuggled deeper into her bed and turned to Celine.

"Are you sleepy, Celine?" she asked.

Celine obligingly indicated that she was not.

Aunt Adelaide rustled back down the hall to her own room. Priscilla knew that her aunts had things to say to each other they did not want her to hear. She wondered sometimes what it might be they talked about, but she did not mind their ignoring her. No more did she care to have them listen to her conversations with Celine. Or with Mr. George.

She raised up on her elbows and peered into the darkness of the room. Little light came in from outside; the close-pressing trees shut away all but two small rays of the streetlights; one of these struck the opposite wall near the door, the other hit the mirror, where it reflected like a dim opening to a remote world of day.

"Mr. George, are you there?" she whispered into the darkness.

"Yes, Priscilla."

The answer came, it seemed, from all around her and from inside her at the same time. She did not question it.

"Please come where I can see you."

A part of the darkness near the door detached itself and drifted toward her bed; it crossed the light but did not shut it away from the mirror or the door; it left no shadow because it was itself a shadow. It hovered over the bed and settled down to one side of it, sitting there. It was not strange to Priscilla. She was comforted.

"Say goodnight to Mr. George, Celine," she said.

Clad in her negligee, Laura Craig wrote to George Newell's brother in London, the hour being late and everything still, save for the hum of life in the city, the vast subterrene roar, muted by night, the susurration of millions of creatures moving inexorably from birth to death like the sound of earth's turning. She wrote swiftly. The words came easily, for they had been pent up so long . . .

". . . I think there is no question but that Priscilla is George's child. She has his look about her eyes; that was not so noticeable a short time ago, but now it is coming out. And she is constantly obsessed with him. I do not know that that is good. Surely George would not think so if he were still alive, though he was absolutely devoted to her, as you know; so many of us thought that was because of Cissie and her slow dying. What is important, I think, is that some way ought to be found to take Priscilla away from the Lecketts. They are definitely nineteenth century, and they have that kind of repressive way of life which is actually more wicked and evil than sheer wantonness. I mean that they certainly always resented being pitied by Cissie and even her goodness, which they never deserved. They are *not* good for Priscilla, though I found her remarkably self-contained, which is probably because she is left alone so very much. That is not good, either, I think you will agree. She has found time to think up the strangest fancies. For instance, she believes that George is still in the house. She says that George pushed the trunk-lid down on Laban's neck. That is absurd, of course; it is the wildest of fancies —but from all I have heard, the lid did more damage to Laban's neck than it ought to have done, if it fell under its own power. There is something very strange about all this and it will come as no surprise to you to learn that I have begun to wonder a little about George's death, too. After all, his heart wasn't *that* bad. I saw him only three days before he died, and he said then that his condition seemed somewhat improved by sedentary living. I have to admit that my impression of the Lecketts is of the worst—I think they are selfish, greedy, lazy and evil people, who, behind their old-fashioned respectability, are capable of absolutely anything . . ."

The summer deepened, and as it grew more sultry, Priscilla spent still more of her time in the yard. Her routine in the morning was unvaried. She went to the teahouse before breakfast and returned to it afterward. Sometimes she received little notes and presents from Laura Craig, after which she was plagued by questions from Aunt Virginia and Aunt Adelaide. Priscilla could not know that the women were anxious to learn whether she had told Laura Craig anything; Priscilla, failing to understand the real goals of their innocuous questions, did not say. She fenced with them unconsciously, thwarting them. Though she did not understand, she was conscious of a feeling of dislike for her in them; but this did not trouble her; as long as they inflicted no punishment beyond the meanness of their words or actions upon her.

In the afternoon she worked in her own little garden, which the women had allowed her to keep in one corner. And later she retreated to the heavily shaded portion of the walled lawn where the swing hung from the limb of an ancient oak tree. She could swing for hours; from the top of the arc she made, she could look out into the street and once in a while she could see the streetcar going by. Swinging gave her a sense of wild freedom; swinging made her feel that she had escaped the house and the women, that she was back in a world of green trees and sun and sky and birds, like that lovely lost time in Paris and Sorrento and on the beaches in Florida, when they had all three still been together—mama and Mr. George and she. She never tired of pumping with her sturdy little legs until she was high enough to see, and she was glad that no one ever told her to stop. Once in a while, too, Aunt Adelaide had come out to push her, which was even better.

That August afternoon Aunt Adelaide came out again.

"Today I will jump from higher yet," said Priscilla.

She had learned, under Aunt Adelaide's urging, how much fun it was to leap from the careening swing, to fly through the air, as it were, under her own power.

Aunt Adelaide smiled.

It was a day of clouds, with rain impending. The birds were still, and Celine sat sedately forgotten in the teahouse. There was no wind, and the oak leaves drooped with wonderful pungency over that corner of the lawn, shutting out most of the sky, protecting them from the curious eyes of neighbors.

"I will jump from so high," said Priscilla.

"No, that's too high."

"I can do it, Aunt Adelaide."

"No, Priscilla, that is too high. You might break a leg or something. Just think, six feet."

Priscilla was insistent. "I can so jump from that high."

"No," said Aunt Adelaide shortly. "You may jump only from so high."

"But I jumped from that high the last time."

"Just the same, that's high enough."

Adelaide had calculated very carefully. Priscilla jumped in a kind of crouch; then she straightened up and began to run back to get into the swing again. If she were halted at just the right place in that run back, and her attention distracted, the swing would catch her on the back of the head with deadly force. Because Priscilla reminded her of Cissie, whom she had always envied as a girl because of her beauty, so much in contrast to Adelaide's over-sized head, Adelaide hated Priscilla. It seemed to her the most important thing in the world to do something to that lovely little head, because somehow she would be doing something to that even lovelier head which had been Cissie's; obscurely she would achieve a kind of compensation for the abnormality of her own. It was far more important than the money which meant so much to Virginia.

"At least, to begin with, that's high enough," amended Aunt Adelaide.

"I'll jump later, then."

"We shall see. Come, get in."

Priscilla climbed into the swing and Adelaide began to push her slowly, steadily. The swing's arc increased. Now Priscilla could see level with the top of the wall; now she could see over; now she was well up in the hot August air, almost brushing the leaves, taking deep breaths of the oak's perfume each time she came up under the leaves. And the streetcar was coming, *clang-clang* at the corner, and up toward the house; she would see it from both ends of the arc. She always hoped that the conductor would see her, so that she could wave to him; but he never did. The limbs and the leaves were too thick, and he never looked up much from the tracks.

Adelaide stopped pushing her and stepped back a little.

"Stay sitting now," she said.

"I am." said Priscilla.

The swing began to slow down, the arc to diminish. She came down from the leafy sky, she came down out of heaven each time a little more. She came away from a pewee singing up in the oak tree, back toward Aunt Adelaide waiting to catch the swing as soon as she had jumped.

"I'm going to jump now."

"Not yet."

She waited a moment.

"Now, then."

"Not yet."

She waited another of the diminishing arcs.

"Now," she said, and jumped, throwing up her arms like a bird, and like a white bird flying to the ground, coming down in a supple crouch and bounding to her feet.

"Oh, fun!" she cried and turned to run to Aunt Adelaide, who stood with the swing held high over her head.

"Oh, look—a redbird!" cried Aunt Adelaide, pointing toward the wall.

Priscilla stopped and turned quickly.

With all her strength, Adelaide pushed the heavy swing. The curve was right; it would catch Priscilla on the back of the head just past the lowest point of the arc; it would crush and mangle forever that lovely head which was so like Cissie's, that head so lovely in contrast to her own. She took three steps forward, the stimulated cry of horror already rising in her throat . . . and faltered.

The swing stopped short of Priscilla's head.

Caught in a dark, gangling shadow that seemed to depend from the tree, the swing went swiftly up and vanished into the oak. Then it came hurtling down with incredible force, clear of Priscilla, straight at Adelaide. Fear rooted her there directly in its path. The heavy, iron-reinforced board struck her across the temple; she dropped without a sound, while the child still looked in vain for the bird.

Priscilla turned and saw the woman crumpled there.

"Aunt Adelaide!" she cried.

Aunt Virginia came running from the house, crying, "Addie! Addie!"

"Go to your room, Priscilla."

The voice came in the whisper of the oak leaves, where a wind was starting up, it rose out of the shadowed heart of the tree and descended all about her like a cloak, as if to shut away the mangled head and the blood there and the sight of Aunt Virginia like a mad woman coming to her knees beside Adelaide's body.

"All right, Mr. George," said Priscilla.

After Priscilla was in bed, Aunt Virginia came into the room. She came over and sat down beside her on the bed. The undertaker had come and gone a long time ago and some men from a newspaper had been and gone, too.

"Tell me how it happened now, Priscilla."

"I don't know."

"Why are you so stubborn?"

"I don't know. She said to look at the redbird. I tried to see it. I couldn't. When I turned around, she was on the ground."

"What else?"

"Nothing, except that Mr. George told me to go to my room."

"George?"

"Yes."

"Did you see him?"

"No."

"No what?"

"No, Aunt Virginia."

"How do you know it was George?"

"I know."

"How?"

"I heard him." She spoke resentfully, not understanding why Aunt Virginia pressed her so. "Besides, Mr. George talks to me every night before I go to sleep."

Aunt Virginia looked grim and pale. Her lips were twitching a little at one corner and her eyes were narrowed. Her hands were clenched on her knees. Deep within her there was a trembling of fear, an insistent awareness which she pushed back with fierce determination.

"You are a wicked little girl," said Aunt Virginia. "What does he say?"

Priscilla, hurt, shook her head.

"Answer me."

Priscilla said nothing.

"Priscilla!"

No answer.

Baffled and angry, Virginia got up and walked out of the room, turning the light switch at the door.

Priscilla waited until she was sure the woman had gone; then she got up in the darkness and found her doll. She returned to bed with it and tucked Celine in. Then she tiptoed to the door and opened it a little. Aunt Virginia had gone downstairs; a faint scratching sound rose to Priscilla's listening ears. Aunt Virginia was writing something; but of course, she would be writing all about Adelaide. Priscilla closed the door soundlessly and tiptoed back to her bed, crawling in and snuggling close to Celine.

All the intimate sounds of the old house crept into the room, bringing their tranquility. Swinging always made Priscilla tired, and even though she had not been swung as much as usual that afternoon, she was still tired. She drowsed, but she did not sleep. She waited confidently for Mr. George to come.

Having finished her letter, Virginia Leckett put out the lamp and stood for a moment to accustom herself to the darkness. Then she went up the stairs without light. She paused at Priscilla's door.

What was it within? Voices or a voice?

She listened.

"Why don't you ever come where I can see you plainer, Mr. George?"

Virginia heard no answer.

"Do you sleep there by the door, Mr. George?"

No sound.

"All right, Mr. George."

Thereafter, silence.

Noiselessly, Virginia opened the door and looked into the room. The bed was spectral over near the window, and the child dark in it. Darkness filled the room—and yet more dark. Was it an accident of sight that she seemed to see a dark shadow hulking there beside the bed? Yes? Or no? Virginia stared. The intensity of her gaze tricked her; the rays of light from the street seemed to dance; they shone through the shadow beside the bed. Virginia closed her eyes and held her lids down; then she flashed them open. Nothing had changed.

She withdrew, closing the door and standing with her back against it.

In a moment she was sharply, frighteningly aware of menace beyond the door, a potent danger threatening her. It was intangible, but all the more frightening for that intangibility. She started away from the door to stand in the middle of the hall. She took hold of herself, grimly. She was too close to her goal now to be frightened by her imagination. She came back to the door once again, pressing against it with the length of her body. There was something beyond it, something lurking there, waiting. She clenched her hands in a gesture of defiance and moved away to her own room.

There she sat for a long time trying to think what it was that had seized hold of her imagination so vividly, trying to piece together the events of Priscilla's world, thinking always of the insistent fact that, now that Adelaide was gone, she alone would inherit three hundred thousand dollars as soon as Priscilla was gone. That was the world, that was independence, security, freedom for life.

It was late when they came back from the funeral. Virginia had thriftily engaged a car to take them to the cemetery, but not to bring them back. They came back on the streetcar. Laura Craig's presence at the services had vexed Virginia, so that she was unusually short with Priscilla. She recognized that Laura would have liked control over Priscilla; she knew that Laura was genuinely fond of the child and she resented this—not because of any feeling of possession, but simply because she knew that when something happened to Priscilla, Laura Craig would put people up to asking questions. It was a wonder she had not done so about George Newell.

As she stepped into the hall in the late afternoon, Virginia thought she saw someone standing at the foot of the stairs; but at that moment Priscilla darted forward with a little cry, and she followed her with her eyes where she ran for the stairs and up. When she looked back, there was nothing there. Nevertheless, she was troubled by the increasing frequency of what could only be illusions.

She put away her good coat and hat and went out into the kitchen to put together something for the supper table. In the routine of getting a meal she forgot about her illusions and thought only about how long she must wait before she could take care of Priscilla and enter upon that new world of her dreams.

Priscilla came in, divested of her good clothes and plainly attired in a print dress.

"Didn't you see him, Aunt Virginia?" she cried.

"See whom?"

"Mr. George. He was really and truly standing there when we came in."

Virginia prevented herself from striking the child just in time. She stood looking at her coldly for a long time before she could bring herself to speak. "I never want to hear his name again, do you understand?"

"Yes, Aunt Virginia."

"I never want it mentioned in this house again, do you hear?"

"Yes, Aunt Virginia. You don't have to scream."

"I'm not screaming!"

Her voice screamed back at her from the walls, shrill, raucous, unpleasant, until the sound diminished and faded into the kitchen's silence, which lay like a mountain between the child with her curious bright eyes and the angry, frightened woman.

The summer passed and autumn came with rain.

In October, Virginia Leckett could contain herself no longer. Her patience had worn thin. Even the need of showing some superficial concern for Priscilla was becoming increasingly difficult, especially when she thought of how only this child stood between her and the fortune which, by now, she had convinced herself should have been hers all along.

She had evolved a plan for what must be Priscilla's fatal accident. It was not original. She had observed that the child was in the habit of running along the upper hall and down the stairs, despite their steepness. It should be a very simple matter to fix a thin wire across the head of the stairs, half a foot or so from the floor; Priscilla could not possibly avoid tripping over it. The tumble down the stairs might not kill her, but the chances were good that it would.

She waited one night until Priscilla had gone to her room. Then she went quickly to the head of the stairs and fixed the wire around the posts there, and, stepping over it, hastened to the foot of the stairs.

"Priscilla!" she called. "Come down here—quick!"

From where she stood, she could make out the thin wire because a little light struck up toward it from below. It would be invisible to Priscilla.

The door of Priscilla's room opened. "Did you call me, Aunt Virginia?"

"Yes. Come down, quick."

She came running down the hall.

Virginia stood open-mouthed, watching, a kind of bestial eagerness stirring within her.

But at the head of the stairs Priscilla stopped. A kind of shuddering horror chilled Virginia, for she saw a familiar dark shadow holding the child back with one tenuous arm, while with the other it unwound the wire from the posts. Only when it had been pulled away from Priscilla's path was she permitted to go on.

Down she came.

"What's the matter, Aunt Virginia?"

Virginia's tongue was thick. "I told you—to come—quick. What kept you?"

"He did."

"Who?"

"You know who. You said not to mention his name again."

A harsh burst of laughter broke from Virginia's dry lips. She reached down and took the child by the hand.

"Come along," she said. "We'll see."

She went up the stairs, forcing herself, driving herself every step of the way, so that Priscilla walked always a little ahead of her. They went directly to Priscilla's room. Virginia stopped at the threshold.

"There is nobody here but us," she said. "Do you see?"

Priscilla looked around. "He can hide anywhere," she said.

Virginia shook her. "Do you hear me? There is nobody here but us. Say that after me."

"You're hurting me."

"Say it!" said Virginia in a furious voice.

"There is nobody here but us," repeated Priscilla, frightened now.

"There is nobody in this house but us," Virginia went on, her voice rising. "Say it. Go on—say it."

"There is nobody in this house but us," said Priscilla. She took a deep breath and added courageously, "And Mr. George."

In an excess of thwarted rage, Virginia beat Priscilla unmercifully until the child escaped her and ran to hide under the bed. Breathing heavily, Virginia left the room, slamming the door and leaning against it to listen. Only the child's sobbing came into the darkness of the hall.

"Are you ready, Virginia?"

She whirled.

Standing almost near enough to touch her was a dark something that spoke to her in George Newell's voice—a horrible sentient darkness without substance but exuding a malignance great enough to send her pulse high in terror. The malign shadow reached toward her.

She screamed and burst away.

She ran faster than she had ever run before toward the stairs.

Too late, she saw that the wire was back in place. She tripped and hurtled down the stairs like a rag doll, while the shadow paused to unwind the wire once again.

Priscilla, after a few moments of uncertainty, came to the threshold of her room and stood in the open doorway.

"Aunt Virginia?" she asked of the darkness.

"Priscilla."

"Yes, Mr. George."

"Priscilla, go to Laura. Tell her Aunt Virginia fell downstairs and broke her neck. You are going to stay with Laura now."

"Yes, Mr. George. Are you coming, too?"

"No. I'm going away and this time I'll stay. Unless you need me."

"Oh, don't go, Mr. George!"

"Get your things and go to Laura, Priscilla."

Obediently she went back to her room and got Celine out of bed. She put on Celine's hat and then her own. Grandfather Dedman's clock said, "Pris-sie, Pris-sie, Pris-sie, Go-to sleep-now, Pris-sie," and then struck ten somber bongs which rang through the house like a tocsin.

Priscilla went out of the room and down the stairs, walking carefully around Aunt Virginia, expecting that any moment that horrible inert mass might spring up and beat her again. At the front door she turned and looked bravely back into the darkness.

"Goodbye, Mr. George," she said.

She thought there was an answer, but she could not be sure. Perhaps it was just Grandfather Dedman's clock with a last, reproachful "Pris-sie."

She got on the streetcar at the corner.

"Are you alone, Miss Priscilla?" asked the conductor. "At this time of night?"

"Yes, sir."

"Did you run away?"

"Oh no. I've got to go somewhere else." Gravely, she told him the address.

"Why, that's way over on the other side of the city! What can she be thinking of to let you go alone!"

Irate, he clanged a passing taxi to a stop, got out with Priscilla and put her into it, giving the driver explicit directions.

Laura Craig, white-faced, listened to Priscilla, and, having heard, went directly to the telephone. She called the Leckett house.

Priscilla heard the ringing for a long time. But of course, there was no answer. So she knew that Mr. George was gone, too, like all the rest of them.

Five fantasies by WILLIAM HOPE HODGSON (1877–1918) were published in
Weird Tales, four of them in the Leo Margulies–Sam Moskowitz 1973–74
revival issues, including the shivery *what*dunit, ''The Terror of the Water-
Tank'' (Winter 1973). Son of a clergyman, Hodgson was a Briton who spent
his youth as a seaman. Many of his supernatural stories and novels derive
from his fascination with the mysteries of the deep, including *The Boats of
the Glen Carrig* and *The Ghost Pirates,* but he was equally concerned with
writing interdimensional fantasies (such as *The House on the Borderland)*
that are significant precursors of modern science fiction.

THE TERROR
OF THE
WATER-TANK

by William Hope Hodgson

Crowning the heights on the outskirts of a certain town on the east
coast is a large, iron water-tank from which an isolated row of small
villas obtains its supply. The top of this tank has been cemented, and
round it have been placed railings, thus making of it a splendid
"look-out" for any of the townspeople who may choose to promenade upon it. And very popular it was until the strange and terrible
happenings of which I have set out to tell.

Late one evening, a party of three ladies and two gentlemen
climbed the path leading to the tank. They had dined, and it had
been suggested that a promenade upon the tank in the cool of the
evening would be pleasant. Reaching the level, cemented surface,
they were proceeding across it, when one of the ladies stumbled and
almost fell over some object lying near the railings on the town side.

A match having been struck by one of the men, they discovered
that it was the body of a portly old gentleman lying in a contorted
attitude and apparently quite dead. Horrified, the two men drew off

their fair companions to the nearest of the aforementioned houses. Then, in company with a passing policeman, they returned with all haste to the spot.

By the aid of the officer's lantern, they ascertained the gruesome fact that the old gentleman had been strangled. In addition, he was without watch or purse. The policeman was able to identify him as an old, retired mill-owner, living some little distance away at a place named Revenge End.

At this point the little party was joined by a stranger, who introduced himself as Dr. Tointon, adding the information that he lived in one of the villas close at hand, and had run across as soon as he had heard there was something wrong.

Silently, the two men and the policeman gathered round, as with deft, skillful hands the doctor made his short examination.

"He's not been dead more than about half an hour," he said at its completion.

He turned towards the two men.

"Tell me how it happened—all you know?"

They told him the little they knew.

"Extraordinary," said the doctor. "And you saw no one?"

"Not a soul, doctor!"

The medical man turned to the officer.

"We must get him home," he said. "Have you sent for the ambulance?"

"Yes, sir," said the policeman. "I whistled to my mate on the lower beat, and 'e went straight off."

The doctor chatted with the two men, and reminded them that they would have to appear at the inquest.

"It's murder?" asked the younger of them in a low voice.

"Well," said the doctor. "It certainly looks like it."

And then came the ambulance.

At this point, I come into actual contact with the story; for old Mr. Marchmount, the retired mill-owner, was the father of my *fiancée*, and I was at the house when the ambulance arrived with its sad burden.

Dr. Tointon had accompanied it along with the policeman, and under his directions the body was taken upstairs, while I broke the news to my sweetheart.

Before he left, the doctor gave me a rough outline of the story as he knew it. I asked him if he had any theory as to how and why the crime had been committed.

"Well," he said, "the watch and chain are missing, and the purse. And then he has undoubtedly been strangled; though with what, I have been unable to decide."

And that was all he could tell me.

The following day there was a long account in the *Northern Daily Telephone* about the "shocking murder." The column ended, I remember, by remarking that people would do well to beware, as there were evidently some very desperate characters about, and ended that it was believed the police had a clue.

During the afternoon, I myself went up to the tank. There was a large crowd of people standing in the road that runs past at some little distance; but the tank itself was in the hands of the police officer being stationed at the top of the steps leading up to it. On learning my connection with the deceased, he allowed me up to have a look around.

I thanked him, and gave the whole of the tank a pretty thorough scrutiny, even to the extent of pushing my cane down through lockholes in the iron manhole lids, to ascertain whether the tank were full or not, and whether there was room for someone to hide.

On pulling out my stick, I found that the water reached to within a few inches of the lid, and that the lids were securely locked. I at once dismissed a vague theory that had formed in my mind that there might be some possibility of hiding within the tank itself and springing out upon the unwary. It was evidently a common, brutal murder, done for the sake of my prospective father-in-law's purse and gold watch.

One other thing I noticed before I quitted the tank top. It came to me as I was staring over the rail at the surrounding piece of waste land. Yet at the time, I thought little of it, and attached to it no importance whatever. It was that the encircling piece of ground was soft and muddy and quite smooth. Possibly there was a leakage from the tank that accounted for it. Anyhow, that is how it seemed to be.

"There ain't nothin' much to be seen, sir," volunteered the policeman, as I prepared to descend the steps on my way back to the road.

"No," I said. "There seems nothing of which to take hold."

And so I left him, and went on to the doctor's house. Fortunately, he was in, and I at once told him the result of my investigation. Then I asked him whether he thought that the police were really on the track of the criminal.

He shook his head.

"No," he answered. "I was up there this morning having a look round, and since then, I've been thinking. There are one or two points that completely stump me—points that I believe the police have never even stumbled upon."

Yet, though I pressed him, he would say nothing definite.

"Wait!" was all he could tell me.

Yet I had not long to wait before something further happened, something that gave an added note of mystery and terror to the affair.

On the two days following my visit to the doctor, I was kept busy arranging for the funeral of my fiancée's father, and then on the very morning of the funeral came the news of the death of the policeman who had been doing duty on the tank.

From my place in the funeral procession, I caught sight of large local posters announcing the fact in great letters, while the newsboys constantly cried:

"Terror of the Tank—Policeman Strangled."

Yet, until the funeral was over, I could not buy a paper to gather any of the details. When at last I was able, I found that the doctor who had attended him was none other than Tointon, and straightway I went up to his place for such further particulars as he could give.

"You've read the newspaper account?" he asked when I met him.

"Yes," I replied.

"Well, you see," he said, "I was right in saying that the police were off the track. I've been up there this morning, and a lot of trouble I had to be allowed to make a few notes on my own account. Even then it was only through the influence of Inspector Slago with whom I have once or twice done a little investigating. They've two men and a sergeant now on duty to keep people away."

"You've done a bit of detective-work, then?"

"At odd times," he replied.

"And have you come to any conclusion?"

"Not yet."

"Tell me what you know of the actual happening," I said. "The newspaper was not very definite. I'm rather mixed up as to how long it was before they found that the policeman had been killed. Who found him?"

"Well, so far as I have been able to gather from Inspector Slago, it was like this. They detailed one of their men for duty on the tank until two A.M., when he was to be relieved by the next man. At about a minute or so to two, the relief arrived simultaneously with the inspector, who was going his rounds. They met in the road below the tank, and were proceeding up the little side lane towards the passage, when, from the top of the tank, they heard someone cry out suddenly. The cry ended in a sort of gurgle, and they distinctly heard something fall with a heavy thud.

"Instantly, the two of them rushed up the passage, which as you know is fenced in with tall, sharp, iron railings. Even as they ran, they could hear the beat of struggling heels on the cemented top of the tank, and just as the inspector reached the bottom of the steps there came a last groan. The following moment they were at the top. The policeman threw the light of his lantern around. It struck on a huddled heap near by the right-hand railings—something limp and inert. They ran to it, and found that it was the dead body of the officer who had been on duty. A hurried examination showed that he had been strangled.

"The inspector blew his whistle, and soon another of the force arrived on the scene. This man they at once dispatched for me, and in the meantime they conducted a rapid but thorough search, which, however, brought to light nothing. This was the more extraordinary in that the murderer must have been on the tank even as they went up the steps."

"Jove!" I muttered. "He must have been quick."

The doctor nodded.

"Wait a minute," he went on, "I've not finished yet. When I arrived I found that I could do nothing; the poor fellow's neck had been literally crushed. The power used must have been enormous.

" 'Have you found anything?' I asked the inspector.

" 'No,' he said, and proceeded to tell me as much as he knew, ending by saying that the murderer, whoever it was, had got clean away.

" 'But,' I exclaimed, 'he would have to pass you, or else jump the railings. There's no other way.'

" 'That's what he's done,' replied Slago rather testily. 'It's no height.'

" 'Then in that case, inspector,' I answered, 'he's left something by which we may be able to trace him.' "

"You mean the mud round the tank, doctor?" I interrupted.

"Yes," said Doctor Tointon. "So you noticed that, did you? Well, we took the policeman's lamp, and made a thorough search all round the tank—but the whole of the flat surface of mud-covered ground stretched away smooth and unbroken by even a single footprint!"

The doctor stopped dramatically.

"Good God!" I exclaimed, excitedly. "Then how did the fellow get away?"

Doctor Tointon shook his head.

"That is a point, my dear sir, on which I am not yet prepared to speak. And yet I believe I hold a clue."

"What?" I almost shouted.

"Yes," he replied, nodding his head thoughtfully. "Tomorrow I may be able to tell you something."

He rose from his chair.

"Why not now?" I asked, madly curious.

"No," he said, "the thing isn't definite enough yet."

He pulled out his watch.

"You must excuse me now. I have a patient waiting."

I reached for my hat, and he went and opened the door.

"Tomorrow," he said, and nodded reassuringly as he shook hands. "You'll not forget."

"Is it likely?" I replied, and he closed the door after me.

The following morning I received a note from him asking me to defer my visit until night, as he would be away from home during the greater portion of the day. He mentioned 9:30 as a possible time at which I might call—any time between then and 10 P.M. But I was not to be later than that.

Naturally, feeling as curious as I did, I was annoyed at having to wait the whole day. I had intended calling as early as decency would allow. Still, after that note, there was nothing but to wait.

During the morning, I paid a visit to the tank, but was refused permission by the sergeant in charge. There was a large crowd of people in the road below the tank, and in the little side lane that led up to the railed-in passage. These, like myself, had come up with the intention of seeing the exact spot where the tragedies had occurred; but they were not allowed to pass the men in blue.

Feeling somewhat cross at their persistent refusal to allow me upon the tank, I turned up the lane, which presently turns off to the right. Here, finding a gap in the wall, I clambered over, and disregarding a board threatening terrors to trespassers, I walked across the piece of waste land until I came to the wide belt of mud that surrounded the tank. Then, skirting the edge of the marshy ground, I made my way round until I was on the town side of the tank. Below me was a large wall which hid me from those in the road below. Between me and the tank stretched some forty feet of smooth, mud-covered earth. This I proceeded now to examine carefully.

As the doctor had said, there was no sign of any footprint in any part of it. My previous puzzlement grew greater. I think I had been entertaining an idea somewhere at the back of my head that the doctor and the police had made a mistake—perhaps missed seeing the obvious, as is more possible than many think. I turned to go back, and at the same moment, a little stream of water began to flow from a pipe just below the edge of the tank top. It was evidently the "overflow." Undoubtedly the tank was brim full.

How, I asked myself, had the murderer got away without leaving a trace?

I made my way back to the gap, and so into the lane. And then, even as I sprang to the ground, an idea came to me—a possible solution of the mystery.

I hurried off to see Dufirst, the tank-keeper, who I knew lived in a little cottage a few hundred feet distant. I reached the cottage, and knocked. The man himself answered me, and nodded affably.

"What an ugly little beast!" I thought. Aloud, I said: "Look here, Dufirst, I want a few particulars about the tank. I know you can tell me what I want to know better than anyone else."

The affability went out of the man's face. "Wot do yer want to know?" he asked surlily.

"Well," I replied. "I want to know if there is any place about the tank where a man could hide."

The fellow looked at me darkly. "No," he said shortly.

"Sure?" I asked.

"Course I am," was his sullen reply.

"There's another thing I want to know about," I went on. "What's the tank built upon?"

"Bed er cerment," he answered.

"And the sides—how thick are they?"

"About 'arf-inch iron."

"One thing more," I said, pulling half-a-crown from my pocket (whereat I saw his face light up). "What are the inside measurements of the tank?" I passed him over the coin.

He hesitated a moment; then slipped it into his waistcoat-pocket. "Come erlong a minnit. I 'ave ther plan of ther thing upstairs, if yer'll sit 'ere an' wait."

"Right," I replied, and sat down, while he disappeared through a door, and presently I heard him rummaging about overhead.

"What a sulky beast," I thought to myself. Then, as the idea passed through my mind, I caught sight of an old bronze luster jug on the opposite side of the room. It stood on a shelf high up; but in a minute I was across the room and reaching up to it; for I have a craze for such things.

"What a beauty," I muttered, as I seized hold of the handle. "I'll offer him five dollars for it."

I had the thing in my hands now. It was heavy. "The old fool!" thought I. "He's been using it to stow odds and ends in." And with that, I took it across to the window. There, in the light, I glanced inside—and nearly dropped it; for within a few inches of my eyes, reposed the old gold watch and chain that had belonged to my murdered friend. For a moment, I felt dazed. Then I knew.

"The little fiend!" I said. "The vile little murderer!"

I put the jug down on the table, and ran to the door. I opened it and glanced out. There, not thirty paces distant was Inspector Slago in company with a constable. They had just gone past the house, and were evidently going up on to the tank.

I did not shout; to do so would have been to warn the man in the room above. I ran after the inspector and caught him by the sleeve.

"Come here, inspector," I gasped. "I've got the murderer."

He twirled round on his heel. "What?" he almost shouted.

"He's in there," I said. "It's the tank-keeper. He's still got the watch and chain. I found it in a jug."

At that the inspector began to run towards the cottage, followed by myself and the policeman. We ran in through the open door, and I pointed to the jug. The inspector picked it up, and glanced inside.

He turned to me. "Can you identify this?" he asked, speaking in a quick, excited voice.

"Certainly I can," I replied. "Mr. Marchmount was to have been my father-in-law. I can swear to the watch being his."

At that instant there came a sound of footsteps on the stairs and a few seconds later the bearded little tank-keeper came in through an inner door. In his hand he held a roll of paper—evidently the plan of which he had spoken. Then, as his eyes fell on the inspector holding the watch of the murdered man, I saw the fellow's face suddenly pale.

He gave a sort of little gasp, and his eyes flickered round the room to where the jug had stood. Then he glanced at the three of us, took a step backwards, and jumped for the door through which he had entered. But we were too quick for him, and in a minute had him securely handcuffed.

The inspector warned him that whatever he said would be used as evidence; but there was no need, for he spoke not a word.

"How did you come to tumble across this?" asked the inspector, holding up the watch and guard. "What put you on to it?"

I explained and he nodded.

"It's wonderful," he said. "And I'd no more idea than a mouse that it was him," nodding towards the prisoner.

Then they marched him off.

That night, I kept my appointment at the doctor's. He had said that he would be able to say something; but I rather fancied that the boot was going to prove on the other leg. It was I who would be able to tell him a great deal more than "something." I had solved the whole mystery in a single morning's work. I rubbed my hands, and wondered what the doctor would have to say in answer to my news. Yet, though I waited until 10:30, he never turned up, so that I had at last to leave without seeing him.

The next morning, I went over to his house. There his housekeeper met me with a telegram that she had just received from a friend of his away down somewhere on the South coast. It was to say that the doctor had been taken seriously ill, and was at present confined to his bed, and was unconscious.

I returned the telegram and left the house. I was sorry for the doctor; but almost more so that I was not able personally to tell him the news of my success as an amateur detective.

It was many weeks before Dr. Tointon returned, and in the meantime the tank-keeper had stood his trial and been condemned for the murder of Mr. Marchmount. In court he had made an improbable statement that he had found the old gentleman dead, and that he had only removed the watch and purse from the body under a momentary impulse. This, of course, did him no good, and when I met the doctor on the day of his return, it wanted only three days to the hanging.

"By the way, doctor," I said, after a few minutes' conversation, "I suppose you know that I spotted the chap who murdered old Mr Marchmount and the policeman?"

For answer the doctor turned and stared.

"Yes," I said, nodding, "it was the little brute of a tank-keeper. He's to be hanged in three days' time."

"What—" said the doctor, in a startled voice. "Little Dufirst?"

"Yes," I said, yet vaguely damped by his tone.

"Hanged!" returned the doctor. "Why the man's as innocent as you are!"

I stared at him.

"What do you mean?" I asked. "The watch and chain were found in his possession. They proved him guilty in court."

"Good heavens!" said the doctor. "What awful blindness!"

He turned on me. "Why didn't you write and tell me?"

"You were ill—afterwards I thought you'd be sure to have read about it in one of the papers."

"Haven't seen one since I've been ill," he replied sharply. "By George! You've made a pretty muddle of it. Tell me how it happened."

This I did, and he listened intently.

"And in three days he's to be hanged?" he questioned when I had made an end.

I nodded.

He took off his hat and mopped his face and brow.

"It's going to be a job to save him," he said slowly. "Only three days. My God!"

He looked at me, and then abruptly asked a foolish question.

"Have there been any more—murders up there while I've been ill?" He jerked his hand toward the tank.

"No," I replied. "Of course not. How could there be when they've got the chap who did them!"

He shook his head.

"Besides," I went on, "no one ever goes up there now, at least not at night, and that's when the murders were done."

"Quite so, quite so," he agreed, as if what I had said fell in with something that he had in his mind.

He turned to me. "Look here," he said, "come up to my place tonight about ten o'clock, and I think I shall be able to prove to you that the thing which killed Marchmount and the policeman was not —well, it wasn't little Dufirst."

I stared at him.

"Fact," he said.

He turned and started to leave me.

"I'll come," I called out to him.

At the time mentioned, I called at Dr. Tointon's. He opened the door himself and let me in, taking me into his study. Here, to my astonishment, I met Inspector Slago. The inspector wore rather a worried look, and once when Tointon left the room for a minute, he bent over towards me.

"He seems to think," he said in a hoarse whisper, and nodding towards the doorway through which the doctor had gone, "that we've made a silly blunder and hooked the wrong man."

"He'll find he's mistaken," I answered.

The inspector looked doubtful, and seemed on the point of saying something further, when the doctor returned.

"Now then," Dr. Tointon remarked, "we'll get ready. Here," he tossed me a pair of rubbers, "shove those on. You've got rubber heels, inspector?"

"Yes, sir," replied Slago. "Always wear 'em at night."

The doctor went over to a corner, and returned with a double-barreled shotgun which he proceeded to load. This accomplished, he turned to the inspector.

"Got your man outside?"

"Yes, sir," replied Slago.

"Come along, then, the two of you."

We rose and followed him into the dark hall and then out through the front doorway into the silent road. Here we found a plainclothes policeman waiting, leaning up against a wall. At a low whistle from the inspector, he came swiftly across and saluted. Then the doctor turned and led the way towards the tank.

Though the night was distinctly warm, I shuddered. There was a sense of danger in the air that got on one's nerves. I was quite in the dark as to what was going to happen. We reached the lower end of the railed passage. Here the doctor halted us, and began to give directions.

"You have your lantern, inspector?"

"Yes, sir."

"And your man, has he?"

"Yes, sir," replied the man for himself.

"Well, I want you to give yours to my friend for the present."

The man in plainclothes passed me his lantern, and waited further commands.

"Now," said Dr. Tointon, facing me, "I want you and the inspector to take your stand in the left-hand corner of the tank top, and have your lanterns ready, and mind, there must not be a sound, or everything will be spoiled."

He tapped the plainclothes man on the shoulder. "Come along," he said.

Reaching the tank top, we took up positions as he had directed, while he went over with the inspector's man to the far right-hand corner. After a moment, he left the officer, and I could just make out the figure of the latter leaning negligently against the railings.

The doctor came over to us, and sat down between us.

"You've put him just about where our man was when we found him," said the inspector in a whisper.

"Yes," replied Dr. Tointon. "Now, listen, and then there mustn't be another sound. It's a matter of life and death."

His manner and voice were impressive. "When I call out 'ready,' throw the light from your lanterns on the officer as smartly as you can. Understand?"

"Yes," we replied together, and after that no one spoke.

The doctor lay down between us on his stomach, the muzzle of his gun directed a little to the right of where the other man stood. Thus we waited. Half an hour passed—an hour, and a sound of distant bells chimed up to us from the valley; then the silence resumed sway. Twice more the far-off bells told of the passing hours, and I was getting dreadfully cramped with staying in one position.

Then, abruptly, from somewhere across the tank there came a slight, very slight, slurring, crawling sort of noise. A cold shiver took me, and I peered vainly into the darkness till my eyes ached with the effort. Yet I could see nothing. Indistinctly, I could see the lounging figure of the constable. He seemed never to have stirred from his original position.

The strange rubbing, slurring sound continued. Then came a faint clink of iron, as if someone had kicked against the padlock that fastened down the iron trap over the manhole. Yet it could not be the policeman, for he was not near enough. I saw Dr. Tointon raise his head and peer keenly. Then he brought the butt of his gun up to his shoulder.

I got my lantern ready. I was all tingling with fear and expectation. What was going to happen? There came another slight clink, and then, suddenly, the rustling sound ceased.

I listened breathlessly. Across the tank, the hitherto silent policeman stirred almost, it seemed to me, as if someone or something had touched him. The same instant, I saw the muzzle of the doctor's gun go up some six inches. I grasped my lantern firmly, and drew in a deep breath.

"Ready!" shouted the doctor.

I flashed the light from my lantern across the tank simultaneously with the inspector. I have a confused notion of a twining brown thing about the rail a yard to the right of the constable. Then the doctor's gun spoke once—twice, and it dropped out of sight over the edge of the tank. In the same instant the constable slid down off the rail on to the tank top.

"My God!" shouted the inspector, "has it done for him?"

The doctor was already beside the fallen man, busy loosening his clothing.

"He's all right," he replied. "He's only fainted. The strain was too much. He was a plucky devil to stay. That thing was near him for over a minute."

From somewhere below us in the dark there came a thrashing, rustling sound. I went to the side and threw the light from my lantern downwards. It showed me a writhing yellow something, like an eel or a snake, only the thing was flat like a ribbon. It was twining itself into knots. It had no head. That portion of it seemed to have been blown clean away.

"He'll do now," I heard Dr. Tointon say, and the next instant he was standing beside me. He pointed downwards at the horrid thing. "There's the murderer," he said.

It was a few evenings later, and the inspector and I were sitting in the doctor's study.

"Even now, doctor," I said. "I don't see how on earth you got at it."

The inspector nodded a silent agreement.

"Well," replied Dr. Tointon, "after all it was not so very difficult. Had I not been so unfortunately taken ill while away, I should have cleared the matter up a couple of months ago. You see, I had exceptional opportunities for observing things, and in both cases I was very soon on the spot. But all the same, it was not until the second death occurred that I knew that the deed was not due to a human hand. The fact that there were no footprints in the mud proved that conclusively, and having disposed of that hypothesis, my eyes were open to take in details that had hitherto seemed of no moment. For one thing, both men were found dead almost in the same spot, and that spot is just over the overflow pipe."

"It came out of the tank?" I questioned.

"Yes," replied Dr. Tointon. "Then on the railings near where the thing had happened, I found traces of slime; and another matter that no one but myself seems to have been aware of, the collar of the policeman's coat was wet, and so was Mr. Marchmount's. Lastly, the shape of the marks upon the necks, and the tremendous force applied, indicated to me the kind of thing for which I must look. The rest was all a matter of deduction.

"Naturally, all the same, my ideas were somewhat hazy; yet before I saw the brute, I could have told you that it was some form of snake or eel, and I could have made a very good guess at its size. In the course of reasoning the matter out, I had occasion to apply to little Dufirst. From him, I learned that the tank was supposed to be cleaned out annually, but that in reality it had not been seen to for some years."

"What about Dufirst?" I asked.

"Well," said Dr. Tointon dryly, "I understand he is to be granted a free pardon. Of course the little beast stole those things; but I fancy he's had a fair punishment for his sins."

"And the snake, doctor?" I asked. "What was it?"

He shook his head. "I cannot say," he explained. "I have never seen anything just like it. It is one of those abnormalities that occasionally astonish the scientific world. It is a creature that has developed under abnormal conditions, and, unfortunately, it was so shattered by the heavy charges of shot, that the remains tell me but little —its head, as you saw, was entirely shot away."

I nodded. "It's queer—and frightening," I replied. "Makes a chap think a bit."

"Yes," agreed the doctor. "It certainly ought to prove a lesson in cleanliness."

Weird Tales Reprint was a designation begun in 1925. Sometimes it applied to the rerun of a popular story from an earlier issue; other times it permitted editor Farnsworth Wright to resurrect important tales written before the magazine was begun. These latter reprints included many practitioners of *belles lettres,* among them Honoré de Balzac, Charles Baudelaire, Nathaniel Hawthorne, Edgar Allan Poe, Robert Louis Stevenson and GUSTAVE FLAUBERT (1821–80), the nineteenth-century French master who wrote the once-controversial *Madame Bovary.* "La Légende de St. Julien l'Hospitalier," which comprised a third of Flaubert's *Trois Contes* (1877), was the Weird Tales Reprint for April 1928. (For further comment, see Appendix II, page 574.)

THE LEGEND OF ST. JULIAN THE HOSPITALLER

by Gustave Flaubert

1

Julian's father and mother dwelt in a castle built on the slope of a hill, in the heart of the woods.

The towers at its four corners had pointed roofs covered with leaden tiles, and the foundation rested upon solid rocks, which descended abruptly to the bottom of the moat.

In the courtyard, the stone flagging was as immaculate as the floor of a church. Long rainspouts, representing dragons with yawning jaws, directed the water towards the cistern, and on each windowsill of the castle a basil or a heliotrope bush bloomed, in painted flower pots.

A second enclosure, surrounded by a fence, comprised a fruit orchard, a garden decorated with figures wrought in bright-hued flowers, an arbour with several bowers, and a mall for the diversion of the pages. On the other side were the kennel, the stables, the bakery, the winepress and the barns. Around these spread a pasture, also enclosed by a strong hedge.

Peace had reigned so long that the portcullis was never lowered; the moats were filled with water; swallows built their nests in the cracks of the battlements, and as soon as the sun shone too strongly, the archer who all day long paced to and fro on the curtain withdrew to the watchtower and slept soundly.

Inside the castle, the locks on the doors shone brightly; costly tapestries hung in the apartments to keep out the cold; the closets overflowed with linen, the cellar was filled with casks of wine, and the oak chests fairly groaned under the weight of money bags.

In the armoury could be seen, between banners and the heads of wild beasts, weapons of all nations and of all ages, from the sling of the Amalekites and the javelins of the Garamantes, to the broadswords of the Saracens and the coats of mail of the Normans.

The largest spit in the kitchen could hold an ox; the chapel was as gorgeous as a king's oratory. There was even a Roman bath in a secluded part of the castle, though the good lord of the manor refrained from using it, as he deemed it a heathenish practice.

Wrapped always in a cape made of foxskins, he wandered about the castle, rendered justice among his vassals and settled his neighbours' quarrels. In the winter, he gazed dreamily at the falling snow, or had stories read aloud to him. But as soon as the fine weather returned, he would mount his mule and sally forth into the country roads, edged with ripening wheat, to talk with the peasants, to whom he distributed advice. After a number of adventures he took unto himself a wife of high lineage.

She was pale and serious and a trifle haughty. The horns of her headdress touched the top of the doors and the hem of her gown trailed far behind her. She conducted her household like a cloister. Every morning she distributed work to the maids, supervised the making of preserves and unguents, and afterwards passed her time in spinning, or in embroidering altar-cloths. In response to her fervent prayers, God granted her a son!

Then there was great rejoicing; and they gave a feast which lasted three days and four nights, with illuminations and soft music. Chickens as large as sheep and the rarest spices were served; for the entertainment of the guests, a dwarf crept out of a pie; and when the bowls were too few, for the crowd swelled continuously, the wine was drunk from helmets and hunting horns.

The young mother did not appear at the feast. She was quietly resting in bed. One night she awoke and beheld in a moonbeam that crept through the window something that looked like a moving shadow. It was an old man clad in sackcloth who resembled a hermit. A rosary dangled at his side and he carried a beggar's sack on his shoulder. He approached the foot of the bed, and without opening his lips said: "Rejoice, O mother! Thy son shall be a saint."

She would have cried out, but the old man, gliding along the moonbeam, rose through the air and disappeared. The songs of the banqueters grew louder. She could hear angels' voices and her head sank back on the pillow, which was surmounted by the bone of a martyr, framed in precious stones.

The following day, the servants, upon being questioned, declared, to a man, that they had seen no hermit. Then, whether dream or fact this must certainly have been a communication from heaven; but she took care not to speak of it, lest she should be accused of presumption.

The guests departed at daybreak, and Julian's father stood at the castle gate, where he had just bidden farewell to the last one, when a beggar suddenly emerged from the mist and confronted him. He was a gipsy—for he had a braided beard and wore silver bracelets on each arm. His eyes burned and, in an inspired way, he muttered some disconnected words: "Ah! Ah! thy son!—great bloodshed—great glory—happy always—an emperor's family."

Then he stooped to pick up the alms thrown to him, and disappeared in the tall grass.

The lord of the manor looked up and down the road and called as loudly as he could. But no one answered him! The wind only howled and the morning mists were fast dissolving.

He attributed his vision to a dullness of the brain resulting from too much sleep. "If I should speak of it," quoth he, "people would laugh at me." Still, the glory that was to be his son's dazzled him, albeit the meaning of the prophecy was not clear to him, and he even doubted that he had heard it.

The parents kept their secret from each other. But both cherished the child with equal devotion, and as they considered him marked by God, they had great regard for his person. His cradle was lined with the softest feathers, and a lamp representing a dove burned continually over it; three nurses rocked him night and day, and with his pink cheeks and blue eyes, brocaded cloak and embroidered cap, he looked like a little Jesus. He cut all his teeth without even a whimper.

When he was seven years old his mother taught him to sing, and his father lifted him upon a tall horse, to inspire him with courage. The child smiled with delight, and soon became familiar with everything pertaining to chargers. An old and very learned monk taught him the Gospel, the Arabic numerals, the Latin letters, and the art of painting delicate designs on vellum. They worked in the top of a tower, away from all noise and disturbance.

When the lesson was over, they would go down into the garden and study the flowers.

Sometimes a herd of cattle passed through the valley below, in charge of a man in Oriental dress. The lord of the manor, recognising him as a merchant, would despatch a servant after him. The stranger, becoming confident, would stop on his way and after being ushered into the castle hall, would display pieces of velvet and silk, trinkets and strange objects whose use was unknown in those parts. Then, in due time, he would take leave, without having been molested and with a handsome profit.

At other times, a band of pilgrims would knock at the door. Their wet garments would be hung in front of the hearth and after they had been refreshed by food they would relate their travels and discuss the uncertainty of vessels on the high seas, their long journeys across burning sands, the ferocity of the infidels, the caves of Syria, the Manger and the Holy Sepulchre. They made presents to the young heir of beautiful shells, which they carried in their cloaks.

The lord of the manor very often feasted his brothers-at-arms, and over the wine of the old warriors would talk of battles and attacks, of war-machines and of the frightful wounds they had received, so that Julian, who was a listener, would scream with excitement; then his father felt convinced that some day he would be a conqueror. But in the evening, after the Angelus, when he passed through the crowd of beggars who clustered about the church door, he distributed his alms with so much modesty and nobility that his mother fully expected to see him become an archbishop in time.

His seat in the chapel was next to his parents, and no matter how long the services lasted, he remained kneeling on his *prie-dieu,* with folded hands and his velvet cap lying close beside him on the floor.

One day, during mass, he raised his head and beheld a little white mouse crawling out of a hole in the wall. It scrambled to the first altar-step and then, after a few gambols, ran back in the same direction. On the following Sunday, the idea of seeing the mouse again worried him. It returned; and every Sunday after that he watched for it; and it annoyed him so much that he grew to hate it and resolved to do away with it.

So, having closed the door and strewn some crumbs on the steps of the altar, he placed himself in front of the hole with a stick. After a long while a pink snout appeared, and then the whole mouse crept out. He struck it lightly with his stick and stood stunned at the sight of the little, lifeless body. A drop of blood stained the floor. He wiped it away hastily with his sleeve, and picking up the mouse, threw it away, without saying a word about it to anyone.

All sorts of birds pecked at the seeds in the garden. He put some peas in a hollow reed, and when he heard birds chirping in a tree, he would approach cautiously, lift the tube and swell his cheeks; then, when the little creatures dropped about him in multitudes, he could not refrain from laughing and being delighted with his own cleverness.

One morning, as he was returning by way of the curtain, he beheld a fat pigeon sunning itself on the top of the wall. He paused to gaze at it; where he stood the rampart was cracked and a piece of stone was near at hand; he gave his arm a jerk and the well aimed missile struck the bird squarely, sending it straight into the moat below.

He sprang after it, unmindful of the brambles, and ferreted around the bushes with the litheness of a young dog.

The pigeon hung with broken wings in the branches of a privet hedge.

The persistence of its life irritated the boy. He began to strangle it, and its convulsions made his heart beat quicker, and filled him with a wild tumultuous voluptuousness, the last throb of its heart making him feel like fainting.

At supper that night his father declared that at his age a boy should begin to hunt; and he arose and brought forth an old writing book which contained, in questions and answers, everything pertaining to the pastime. In it, a master showed a supposed pupil how to train dogs and falcons, lay traps, recognise a stag by its fumets and a fox or a wolf by footprints. He also taught the best way of discovering their tracks, how to start them, where their refuges are usually to be found, what winds are the most favourable, and further enumerated the various cries and the rules of the quarry.

When Julian was able to recite all these things by heart, his father made up a pack of hounds for him. There were twenty-four greyhounds of Barbary, speedier than gazelles, but liable to get out of temper; seventeen couples of Breton dogs, great barkers, with broad chests and russet coats flecked with white. For wild boar hunting and perilous doublings, there were forty boarhounds as hairy as bears.

The red mastiffs of Tartary, almost as large as donkeys, with broad backs and straight legs, were destined for the pursuit of the wild bull. The black coats of the spaniels shone like satin; the barking of the setters equalled that of the beagles. In a special enclosure were eight growling bloodhounds that tugged at their chains and rolled their eyes, and these dogs leaped at men's throats and were not afraid even of lions.

All ate wheat bread, drank from marble troughs, and had highsounding names.

Perhaps the falconry surpassed the pack; for the master of the castle, by paying great sums of money, had secured Caucasian hawks, Babylonian sakers, German gerfalcons, and pilgrim falcons captured on the cliffs edging the cold seas, in distant lands. They were housed in a thatched shed and were chained to the perch in the order of size. In front of them was a little grass-plot where, from time to time, they were allowed to disport themselves.

Bag-nets, baits, traps and all sorts of snares were manufactured.

Often they would take out pointers who would set almost immediately; then the whippers-in, advancing step by step, would cautiously spread a huge net over their motionless bodies. At the command, the dogs would bark and arouse the quails; and the ladies of the neighbourhood, with their husbands, children and handmaids, would fall upon them and capture them with ease.

At other times they used a drum to start hares; and frequently foxes fell into the ditches prepared for them, while wolves caught their paws in the traps.

But Julian scorned these convenient contrivances; he preferred to hunt away from the crowd, alone with his steed and his falcon. It was almost always a large, snow-white Scythian bird. His leather hood was ornamented with a plume, and on his blue feet were bells; and he perched firmly on his master's arm while they galloped across the plains. Then Julian would suddenly untie his tether and let him fly, and the bold bird would dart through the air like an arrow. One might perceive two spots circle around, unite, and then disappear in the blue heights. Presently the falcon would return with a mutilated bird and perch again on his master's gauntlet with trembling wings.

Julian loved to sound his trumpet and follow his dogs over hills and streams, into the woods; and when the stag began to moan under their teeth, he would kill it deftly, and delight in the fury of the brutes, which would devour the pieces spread out on the warm hide.

On foggy days, he would hide in the marshes to watch for wild geese, otters and wild ducks.

At daybreak, three equerries waited for him at the foot of the steps; and though the old monk leaned out of the dormer window and made signs to him to return, Julian would not look around.

He heeded neither the broiling sun, the rain nor the storm; he drank spring water and ate wild berries, and when he was tired, he lay down under a tree; and he would come home at night covered with earth and blood, with thistles in his hair and smelling of wild beasts. He grew to be like them. And when his mother kissed him, he responded coldly to her caress and seemed to be thinking of deep and serious things.

He killed bears with a knife, bulls with a hatchet, and wild boars with a spear; and once, with nothing but a stick, he defended himself against some wolves, which were gnawing corpses at the foot of a gibbet.

One winter morning he set out before daybreak, with a bow slung across his shoulder and a quiver of arrows attached to the pommel of his saddle. The hoofs of his steed beat the ground with regularity and his two beagles trotted close behind. The wind was blowing hard and icicles clung to his cloak. A part of the horizon cleared, and he beheld some rabbits playing around their burrows. In an instant, the two dogs were upon them, and seizing as many as they could, they broke their backs in the twinkling of an eye.

Soon he came to a forest. A woodcock, paralysed by the cold, perched on a branch, with its head hidden under its wing. Julian with a lunge of his sword, cut off its feet, and without stopping to pick it up, rode away.

Three hours later he found himself on the top of a mountain so high that the sky seemed almost black. In front of him, a long, flat rock hung over a precipice, and at the end, two wild goats stood gazing down into the abyss. As he had no arrows (for he had left his steed behind), he thought he would climb down to where they stood; and with bare feet and bent back he at last reached the first goat and thrust his dagger below its ribs. But the second animal, in its terror, leaped into the precipice. Julian threw himself forward to strike it, but his right foot slipped, and he fell, face downward and with outstretched arms, over the body of the first goat.

After he returned to the plains, he followed a stream bordered by willows. From time to time, some cranes, flying low, passed over his head. He killed them with his whip, never missing a bird. He beheld in the distance the gleam of a lake which appeared to be of lead, and in the middle of it was an animal he had never seen before, a beaver with a black muzzle. Notwithstanding the distance that separated them, an arrow ended its life and Julian only regretted that he was not able to carry the skin home with him.

Then he entered an avenue of tall trees, the tops of which formed a triumphal arch to the entrance of a forest. A deer sprang out of the thicket and a badger crawled out of its hole, a stag appeared in the road, and a peacock spread its fan-shaped tail on the grass—and after he had slain them all, other deer, other stags, other badgers, other peacocks, and jays, blackbirds, foxes, porcupines, polecats and lynxes appeared; in fact, a host of beasts that grew more and more numerous with every step he took. Trembling, and with a look of appeal in their eyes, they gathered around Julian, but he did not stop slaying them; and so intent was he on stretching his bow, drawing his sword and whipping out his knife, that he had little thought for aught else. He knew that he was hunting in some country since an indefinite time, through the very fact of his existence, as everything seemed to occur with the ease one experiences in dreams. But presently an extraordinary sight made him pause.

He beheld a valley shaped like a circus and filled with stags which, huddled together, were warming one another with the vapour of their breaths that mingled with the early mist.

For a few minutes, he almost choked with pleasure at the prospect of so great a carnage. Then he sprang from his horse, rolled up his sleeves, and began to aim.

When the first arrow whizzed through the air, the stags turned their heads simultaneously. They huddled closer, uttered plaintive cries, and a great agitation seized the whole herd. The edge of the valley was too high to admit of flight; and the animals ran around the enclosure in their efforts to escape. Julian aimed, stretched his bow and his arrows fell as fast and thick as raindrops in a shower.

Maddened with terror, the stags fought and reared and climbed on top of one another; their antlers and bodies formed a moving mountain which tumbled to pieces whenever it displaced itself.

Finally the last one expired. Their bodies lay stretched out on the sand with foam gushing from the nostrils and the bowels protruding. The heaving of their bellies grew less and less noticeable and presently all was still.

Night came, and behind the trees, through the branches, the sky appeared like a sheet of blood.

Julian leaned against a tree and gazed with dilated eyes at the enormous slaughter. He was now unable to comprehend how he had accomplished it.

On the opposite side of the valley he suddenly beheld a large stag, with a doe and their fawn. The buck was black and of enormous size; he had a white beard and carried sixteen antlers. His mate was the color of dead leaves, and she browsed upon the grass, while the fawn, clinging to her udder, followed her step by step.

Again the bow was stretched, and instantly the fawn dropped dead, and seeing this, its mother raised her head and uttered a poignant, almost human wail of agony. Exasperated, Julian thrust his knife into her chest, and felled her to the ground.

The great stag had watched everything and suddenly he sprang forward. Julian aimed his last arrow at the beast. It struck him between his antlers and stuck there.

The stag did not appear to notice it; leaping over the bodies, he was coming nearer and nearer with the intention, Julian thought, of charging at him and ripping him open, and he recoiled with inexpressible horror. But presently the huge animal halted, and, with eyes aflame and the solemn air of a patriarch and a judge, repeated thrice, while a bell tolled in the distance:

"Accursed! Accursed! Accursed! some day, ferocious soul, thou wilt murder thy father and thy mother!"

Then he sank on his knees, gently closed his lids and expired.

At first Julian was stunned, and then a sudden lassitude and an immense sadness came over him. Holding his head between his hands, he wept for a long time.

His steed had wandered away; his dogs had forsaken him; the solitude seemed to threaten him with unknown perils. Impelled by a sense of sickening terror, he ran across the fields, and choosing a path at random, found himself almost immediately at the gates of the castle.

That night he could not rest, for, by the flickering light of the hanging lamp, he beheld again the huge black stag. He fought against the obsession of the prediction and kept repeating: "No! No! No! I cannot slay them!" and then he thought: "Still, supposing I desired to?—" and he feared that the devil might inspire him with this desire.

During three months, his distracted mother prayed at his bedside and his father paced the halls of the castle in anguish. He consulted the most celebrated physicians, who prescribed quantities of medicine. Julian's illness, they declared, was due to some injurious wind or to amorous desire. But in reply to their questions, the young man only shook his head. After a time, his strength returned, and he was able to take a walk in the courtyard, supported by his father and the old monk.

But after he had completely recovered, he refused to hunt.

His father, hoping to please him, presented him with a large Saracen sabre.

It was placed on a panoply that hung on a pillar and a ladder was required to reach it. Julian climbed up to it one day, but the heavy weapon slipped from his grasp, and in falling grazed his father and tore his cloak. Julian, believing he had killed him, fell in a swoon.

After that, he carefully avoided weapons. The sight of a naked sword made him grow pale and this weakness caused great distress to his family.

In the end, the old monk ordered him in the name of God, and of his forefathers, once more to indulge in the sports of a nobleman.

The equerries diverted themselves every day with javelins and Julian soon excelled in the practice.

He was able to send a javelin into bottles, to break the teeth of the weathercocks on the castle and to strike doornails at a distance of one hundred feet.

One summer evening, at the hour when dusk renders objects indistinct, he was in the arbour in the garden, and thought he saw two white wings in the background hovering around the espalier. Not for a moment did he doubt that it was a stork and so he threw his javelin at it.

A heart-rending scream pierced the air.

He had struck his mother, whose cap and long streamers remained nailed to the wall.

Julian fled from home and never returned.

2

He joined a horde of adventurers who were passing through the place.

He learned what it was to suffer hunger, thirst, sickness and filth. He grew accustomed to the din of battles and to the sight of dying men. The wind tanned his skin. His limbs became hardened through contact with armour and as he was very strong and brave, temperate and of good counsel, he easily obtained command of a company.

At the outset of a battle, he would electrify his soldiers by a motion of his sword. He would climb the walls of a citadel with a knotted rope, at night, rocked by the storm, while sparks of fire clung to his cuirass and molten lead and boiling tar poured from the battlements.

Often a stone would break his shield. Bridges crowded with men gave way under him. Once, by turning his mace, he rid himself of fourteen horsemen. He defeated all those who came forward to fight him on the field of honour, and more than a score of times it was believed that he had been killed.

However, thanks to Divine protection, he always escaped, for he shielded orphans, widows and aged men. When he caught sight of one of the latter walking ahead of him, he would call to him to show his face, as if he feared that he might kill him by mistake.

All sorts of intrepid men gathered under his leadership, fugitive slaves, peasant rebels and penniless bastards; he then organized an army which increased so much that he became famous and was in great demand.

He succoured in turn the Dauphin of France, the King of England, the Templars of Jerusalem, the General of the Parths, the Negus of Abyssinia and the Emperor of Calicut. He fought against Scandinavians covered with fish-scales, against negroes mounted on red asses and armed with shields made of hippopotamus hide, against gold-coloured Indians who wielded great shining swords above their heads. He conquered the Troglodytes and the cannibals. He travelled through regions so torrid that the heat of the sun would set fire to the hair on one's head; he journeyed through countries so glacial that one's arms would fall from the body and he passed through places where the fogs were so dense that it seemed like being surrounded by phantoms.

Republics in trouble consulted him; when he conferred with ambassadors, he always obtained unexpected concessions. Also, if a monarch behaved badly, he would arrive on the scene and rebuke him. He freed nations. He rescued queens sequestered in towers. It was he and no other that killed the serpent of Milan and the dragon of Oberbirbach.

Now the Emperor of Occitania, having triumphed over the Spanish Mussulmans, had taken the sister of the Caliph of Cordova as a concubine and had had one daughter by her, whom he brought up in the teachings of Christ. But the Caliph, feigning that he wished to become converted, made him a visit and brought with him a numerous escort. He slaughtered the entire garrison and threw the Emperor into a dungeon and treated him with great cruelty in order to obtain possession of his treasures.

Julian went to his assistance, destroyed the army of infidels, laid siege to the city, slew the Caliph, chopped off his head and threw it over the fortifications like a cannonball.

As a reward for so great a service, the Emperor presented him with a large sum of money in baskets; but Julian declined it. Then the Emperor, thinking that the amount was not sufficiently large, offered him three quarters of his fortune and on meeting a second refusal, proposed to share his kingdom with his benefactor. But Julian only thanked him for it and the Emperor felt like weeping with vexation at not being able to show his gratitude, when he suddenly tapped his forehead and whispered a few words in the ear of one of his courtiers; the tapestry curtains parted and a young girl appeared.

Her large black eyes shone like two soft lights. A charming smile parted her lips. Her curls were caught in the jewels of her half-opened bodice, and the grace of her youthful body could be divined under the transparency of her tunic.

She was small and quite plump, but her waist was slender.

Julian was absolutely dazzled, all the more since he had always led a chaste life.

So he married the Emperor's daughter and received at the same time a castle she had inherited from her mother; and when the rejoicings were over, he departed with his bride, after many courtesies had been exchanged on both sides.

The castle was of Moorish design, in white marble, erected on a promontory and surrounded by orange trees.

Terraces of flowers extended to the shell-strewn shores of a beautiful bay. Behind the castle spread a fan-shaped forest. The sky was always blue and the trees were swayed in turn by the ocean breeze and by the winds that blew from the mountains that closed the horizon.

Light entered the apartments through the incrustations of the walls. High, reed-like colums supported the ceiling of the cupolas, decorated in imitation of stalactites.

Fountains played in the spacious halls; the courts were inlaid with mosaic; there were festooned partitions and a great profusion of architectural fancies and everywhere reigned a silence so deep that the swish of a sash or the echo of a sigh could be distinctly heard.

Julian now had renounced war. Surrounded by a peaceful people, he remained idle, receiving every day a throng of subjects who came and knelt before him and kissed his hand in Oriental fashion.

Clad in sumptuous garments, he would gaze out of the window and think of his past exploits and wish that he might again run in the desert in pursuit of ostriches and gazelles, hide among the bamboos to watch for leopards, ride through forests filled with rhinoceroses, climb the most inaccessible peaks in order to have a better aim at the eagles and fight the polar bears on the icebergs of the northern sea.

Sometimes in his dreams, he fancied himself like Adam in the midst of Paradise, surrounded by all the beasts; by merely extending his arm, he was able to kill them; or else they filed past him, in pairs, by order of size, from the lions and the elephants to the ermines and the ducks, as on the day they entered Noah's Ark.

Hidden in the shadow of a cave, he aimed unerring arrows at them; then came others and still others, until he awoke, wild-eyed.

Princes, friends of his, invited him to their meets, but he always refused their invitations, because he thought that by this kind of penance he might possibly avert the threatened misfortune; it seemed to him that the fate of his parents depended on his refusal to slaughter animals. But he suffered because he could not see them, and his other desire was growing well-nigh unbearable.

In order to divert his mind, his wife had dancers and jugglers come to the castle.

She went abroad with him in an open litter; at other times, stretched out on the edge of a boat, they watched for hours the fish disport themselves in the water, which was as clear as the sky. Often she playfully threw flowers at him or nestling at his feet she played melodies on an old mandolin; then, clasping her hands on his shoulder, she would inquire tremulously: "What troubles thee, my dear lord?"

He would not reply, or else he would burst into tears; but at last, one day, he confessed his fearful dread.

His wife scorned the idea and reasoned wisely with him: probably his father and mother were dead; and even if he should ever see them again, through what chance, to what end, would he arrive at this abomination? Therefore his fears were groundless and he should hunt again.

Julian listened to her and smiled, but he could not bring himself to yield to his desire.

One August evening when they were in their bedchamber, she having just retired and he being about to kneel in prayer, he heard the yelping of a fox and light footsteps under the window and he thought he saw things in the dark that looked like animals. The temptation was too strong. He seized his quiver.

His wife appeared astonished.

"I am obeying you," quoth he, "and I shall be back at sunrise."

However, she feared that some calamity would happen. But he reassured her and departed, surprised at her illogical moods.

A short time afterwards, a page came to announce that two

strangers desired, in the absence of the lord of the castle, to see its mistress at once.

Soon a stooping old man and an aged woman entered the room; their coarse garments were covered with dust and each leaned on a stick.

They grew bold enough to say that they brought Julian news of his parents. She leaned out of the bed to listen to them. But after glancing at each other, the old people asked her whether he ever referred to them and if he still loved them.

"Oh! yes!" she said.

Then they exclaimed:

"We are his parents!" and they sat themselves down, for they were very tired.

But there was nothing to show the young wife that her husband was their son.

They proved it by describing to her the birthmarks he had on his body. Then she jumped out of bed, called a page, and ordered that a repast be served to them.

But although they were very hungry, they could scarcely eat and she observed surreptitiously how their lean fingers trembled whenever they lifted their cups.

They asked a hundred questions about their son and she answered each one of them, but she was careful not to refer to the terrible idea that concerned them.

When he failed to return, they had left their château and had wandered for several years, following vague indications but without losing hope.

So much money had been spent at the tolls of the rivers and in inns, to satisfy the rights of princes and the demands of highwaymen, that now their purse was quite empty and they were obliged to beg. But what did it matter, since they were about to clasp again their son in their arms? They lauded his happiness in having such a beautiful wife and did not tire of looking at her and kissing her.

The luxuriousness of the apartment astonished them and the old man, after examining the walls, inquired why they bore the coat-of-arms of the Emperor of Occitania.

"He is my father," she replied.

And he marvelled and remembered the prediction of the gipsy, while his wife meditated upon the words the hermit had spoken to her. The glory of their son was undoubtedly only the dawn of eternal splendours and the old people remained awed while the light from the candelabra on the table fell on them.

In the heyday of youth, both had been extremely handsome. The mother had not lost her hair and bands of snowy whiteness framed her cheeks and the father with his stalwart figure and long beard, looked like a carved image.

Julian's wife prevailed upon them not to wait for him. She put them in her bed and closed the curtains and they both fell asleep. The day broke and outdoors the little birds began to chirp.

Meanwhile, Julian had left the castle grounds and walked nervously through the forest, enjoying the velvety softness of the grass and the balminess of the air.

The shadow of the trees fell on the earth. Here and there the moonlight flecked the glades and Julian feared to advance because he mistook the silvery light for water and the tranquil surface of the pools for grass. A great stillness reigned everywhere and he failed to see any of the beasts that only a moment ago were prowling around the castle. As he walked on, the woods grew thicker and the darkness more impenetrable. Warm winds, filled with enervating perfumes, caressed him; he sank into masses of dead leaves and after a while he leaned against an oak tree to rest and catch his breath.

Suddenly a body blacker than the surrounding darkness sprang from behind the tree. It was a wild boar. Julian did not have time to stretch his bow and he bewailed the fact as if it were some great misfortune. Presently, having left the woods, he beheld a wolf slinking along a hedge.

He aimed an arrow at him. The wolf paused, turned his head and quietly continued on his way. He trotted along, always keeping at the same distance, pausing now and then to look around and resuming his flight as soon as an arrow was aimed in his direction.

In this way Julian traversed an apparently endless plain, then sand-hills, and at last found himself on a plateau that dominated a great stretch of land. Large flat stones were interspersed among crumbling vaults; bones and skeletons covered the ground and here and there some mouldy crosses stood desolate. But presently shapes moved in the darkness of the tombs and from them came panting, wild-eyed hyenas. They approached him and smelled him, grinning hideously and disclosing their gums. He whipped out his sword, but they scattered in every direction and continuing their swift, limping gallop, disappeared in a cloud of dust.

Some time afterwards, in a ravine, he encountered a wild bull with threatening horns, pawing the sand with his hoofs. Julian thrust his lance between his dewlaps. But his weapon snapped as if the beast were made of bronze; then he closed his eyes in anticipation of his death. When he opened them again, the bull had vanished.

Then his soul collapsed with shame. Some supernatural power destroyed his strength and he set out for home through the forest. The woods were a tangle of creeping plants that he had to cut with his sword and while he was thus engaged, a weasel slid between his feet, a panther jumped over his shoulder and a serpent wound itself around an ash tree.

Among its leaves was a monstrous jackdaw that watched Julian intently, and here and there, between the branches, appeared great, fiery sparks as if the sky were raining all its stars upon the forest. But the sparks were the eyes of wildcats, owls, squirrels, monkeys and parrots.

Julian aimed his arrows at them, but the feathered weapons lighted on the leaves of the trees and looked like white butterflies. He threw stones at them but the missiles did not strike and fell to the ground. Then he cursed himself and howled imprecations and in his rage he could have struck himself.

Then all the beasts he had pursued appeared and formed a narrow circle around him. Some sat on their hindquarters, while others stood at full height. And Julian remained among them, transfixed with terror and absolutely unable to move. By a supreme effort of his willpower, he took a step forward; those that perched in the trees opened their wings, those that trod the earth moved their limbs and all accompanied him.

The hyenas strode in front of him, the wolf and the wild boar brought up the rear. On his right, the bull swung its head and on his left the serpent crawled through the grass while the panther, arching its back, advanced with velvety footfalls and long strides. Julian walked as slowly as possible, so as not to irritate them, while in the depth of the bushes he could distinguish porcupines, foxes, vipers, jackals and bears.

He began to run; the brutes followed him. The serpent hissed, the malodorous beasts frothed at the mouth, the wild boar rubbed his tusks against his heels and the wolf scratched the palms of his hands with the hairs of his snout. The monkeys pinched him and made faces, the weasel rolled over his feet. A bear knocked his cap off with its huge paw and the panther disdainfully dropped an arrow it was about to put in its mouth.

Irony seemed to incite their sly actions. As they watched him out of the corners of their eyes, they seemed to meditate a plan of revenge and Julian, who was deafened by the buzzing of the insects, bruised by the wings and tails of the birds, choked by the stench of animal breaths, walked with outstretched arms and closed lids, like a blind man, without even the strength to beg for mercy.

The crowing of a cock vibrated in the air. Other cocks responded; it was day and Julian recognised the top of his palace rising above the orange trees.

Then, on the edge of a field, he beheld some red partridges fluttering around a stubble-field. He unfastened his cloak and threw it over them like a net. When he lifted it, he found only a bird that had been dead a long time and was decaying.

This disappointment irritated him more than all the others. The thirst for carnage stirred afresh within him; animals failing him, he desired to slaughter men.

He climbed the three terraces and opened the door with a blow of his fist, but at the foot of the staircase, the memory of his beloved wife softened his heart. No doubt she was asleep and he would go up and surprise her. Having removed his sandals, he unlocked the door softly and entered.

The stained windows dimmed the pale light of dawn. Julian stumbled over some garments lying on the floor and a little further on he knocked against a table covered with dishes. "She must have eaten," he thought; so he advanced cautiously towards the bed which was concealed by the darkness in the back of the room. When he reached the edge, he leaned over the pillow where the two heads were resting close together and stooped to kiss his wife. His mouth encountered a man's beard.

He fell back, thinking he had become crazed; then he approached the bed again and his searching fingers discovered some hair which seemed to be very long. In order to convince himself that he was mistaken, he once more passed his hand slowly over the pillow. But this time he was sure that it was a beard and that a man was there! a man lying beside his wife!

Flying into an ungovernable passion, he sprang upon them with his drawn dagger, foaming, stamping and howling like a wild beast. After a while he stopped.

The corpses, pierced through the heart, had not even moved. He listened attentively to the two death-rattles, they were almost alike, and as they grew fainter, another voice, coming from far away, seemed to continue them. Uncertain at first, this plaintive voice came nearer and nearer, grew louder and louder and presently he recognised, with a feeling of abject terror, the bellowing of the great black stag.

And as he turned around, he thought he saw the spectre of his wife standing at the threshold with a light in her hand.

The sound of the murder had aroused her. In one glance she understood what had happened and fled in horror, letting the candle drop from her hand. Julian picked it up.

His father and mother lay before him, stretched on their backs with gaping wounds in their breasts; and their faces, the expression of which was full of tender dignity, seemed to hide what might be an eternal secret.

Splashes and blotches of blood were on their white skin, on the bedclothes, on the floor and on an ivory Christ which hung in the alcove. The scarlet reflection of the stained window, which just then was struck by the sun, lighted up the bloody spots and appeared to scatter them around the whole room. Julian walked toward the corpses, repeating to himself and trying to believe that he was mistaken, that it was not possible, that there are often inexplicable likenesses.

At last he bent over to look closely at the old man and he saw, between the half-closed lids, a dead pupil that scorched him like fire. Then he went over to the other side of the bed, where the other corpse lay, but the face was partly hidden by bands of white hair. Julian slipped his finger beneath them and raised the head, holding it at arm's length to study its features, while, with his other hand he lifted the torch. Drops of blood oozed from the mattress and fell one by one upon the floor.

At the close of the day, he appeared before his wife and in a changed voice commanded her first not to answer him, not to approach him, not even to look at him, and to obey, under the penalty of eternal damnation, every one of his orders, which were irrevocable.

The funeral was to be held in accordance with the written instructions he had left on a chair in the death-chamber.

He left her his castle, his vassals, all his worldly goods, without keeping even his clothes or his sandals, which would be found at the top of the stairs.

She had obeyed the will of God in bringing about his crime and accordingly she must pray for his soul, since henceforth he should cease to exist.

The dead were buried sumptuously in the chapel of a monastery which it took three days to reach from the castle. A monk wearing a hood that covered his head followed the procession alone, for nobody dared to speak to him. And during the mass he lay flat on the floor with his face downward and his arms stretched out at his sides.

After the burial, he was seen to take the road leading into the mountains. He looked back several times and finally passed out of sight.

3

He left the country and begged his daily bread on his way.

He stretched out his hand to the horsemen he met in the roads and humbly approached the harvesters in the fields, or else remained motionless in front of the gates of castles, and his face was so sad that he was never turned away.

Obeying a spirit of humility, he related his history to all men and they would flee from him and cross themselves. In villages through which he had passed before, the good people bolted the doors, threatened him and threw stones at him as soon as they recognised him. The more charitable ones placed a bowl on the window-sill and closed the shutters in order to avoid seeing him.

Repelled and shunned by everyone, he avoided his fellow men and nourished himself with roots and plants, stray fruits and shells which he gathered along the shores.

Often, at the bend of a hill, he could perceive a mass of crowded roofs, stone spires, bridges, towers and narrow streets, from which arose a continual murmur of activity.

The desire to mingle with men impelled him to enter the city. But the gross and beastly expression of their faces, the noise of their industries and the indifference of their remarks, chilled his very heart. On holidays, when the cathedral bells rang out at daybreak and filled the people's hearts with gladness, he watched the inhabitants coming out of their dwellings, the dancers in the public squares, the fountains of ale, the damask hangings spread before the houses of princes, and then when night came, he would peer through the windows at the long tables where families gathered and where grandparents held little children on their knees; then sobs would rise in his throat and he would turn away and go back to his haunts.

He gazed with yearning at the colts in the pastures, the birds in their nests, the insects on the flowers; but they all fled from him at his approach and hid or flew away. So he sought solitude. But the wind brought to his ears sounds resembling death rattles; the tears of the dew reminded him of heavier drops and every evening the sun would spread blood in the sky, and every night, in his dreams, he lived over his parricide.

He made himself a hair-cloth lined with iron spikes. On his knees he ascended every hill that was crowned with a chapel. But the unrelenting thought spoiled the splendour of the tabernacles and tortured him in the midst of his penances.

He did not rebel against God, who had inflicted his action, but he despaired at the thought that he had committed it.

He had such a horror of himself that he took all sorts of risks. He rescued paralytics from fire and children from the waves. But the ocean scorned him and the flames spared him. Time did not allay his torment, which became so intolerable that he resolved to die.

One day, while he was stooping over a fountain to judge of its depth, an old man appeared on the other side. He wore a white beard and his appearance was so lamentable that Julian could not keep back his tears. The old man also was weeping. Without recognising him, Julian remembered confusedly a face that resembled his. He uttered a cry, for it was his father who stood before him; and he gave up all thought of taking his own life.

Thus weighted down by his recollections, he travelled through many countries and arrived at a river which was dangerous because of its violence and the slime that covered its shore. Since a long time nobody had ventured to cross it.

The bow of an old boat whose stern was buried in the mud showed among the reeds. Julian, on examining it closely, found a pair of oars and hit upon the idea of devoting his life to the service of his fellow men.

He began by establishing on the bank of the river a sort of road which would enable people to approach the edge of the stream; he broke his nails in his efforts to lift enormous stones which he pressed against the pit of his stomach in order to transport them from one point to another; he slipped in the mud, he sank into it, and several times was on the very brink of death.

Then he took to repairing the boat with débris of vessels and afterwards built himself a hut with putty and trunks of trees.

When it became known that a ferry had been established, passengers flocked to it. They hailed him from the opposite side by waving flags and Julian would jump into the boat and row over. The craft was very heavy and the people loaded it with all sorts of baggage and beasts of burden, who reared with fright, thereby adding greatly to the confusion. He asked nothing for his trouble; some gave him left-over victuals which they took from their sacks or worn-out garments which they could no longer use.

The brutal ones hurled curses at him and when he rebuked them gently they replied with insults and he was content to bless them.

A little table, a stool, a bed made of dead leaves and three earthen bowls were all he possessed. Two holes in the wall served as windows. On one side, as far as the eye could see, stretched barren wastes studded here and there with pools of water and in front of him flowed the greenish waters of the wide river. In the spring, a putrid odour arose from the damp sod. Then fierce gales lifted clouds of dust that blew everywhere, even settling in the water and in one's mouth. A little later swarms of mosquitoes appeared, whose buzzing and stinging continued night and day. After that came frightful frosts which communicated a stone-like rigidity to everything and inspired one with an insane desire for meat. Months passed when Julian never saw a human being. He often closed his lids and endeavored to recall his youth—he beheld the courtyard of a castle, with greyhounds stretched out on a terrace, an armoury filled with valets and under a bower of vines a youth with blond curls sitting between an old man wrapped in furs and a lady with a high cap; presently the corpses rose before him and then he would throw himself face downward on his cot and sob:

"Oh! poor father! poor mother! poor mother!" and would drop into a fitful slumber in which the terrible visions recurred.

One night he thought that someone was calling to him in his sleep. He listened intently, but could hear nothing save the roaring of the waters.

But the same voice repeated: "Julian!"

It proceeded from the opposite shore, a fact which appeared extraordinary to him, considering the breadth of the river.

The voice called a third time: "Julian!"

And the high-pitched tones sounded like the ringing of a churchbell.

Having lighted his lantern, he stepped out of his cabin. A frightful storm raged. The darkness was complete and was illuminated here and there only by the white waves leaping and tumbling.

After a moment's hesitation, he untied the rope. The water presently grew smooth and the boat glided easily to the opposite shore, where a man was waiting.

He was wrapped in a torn piece of linen; his face was like a chalk mask and his eyes were redder than glowing coals. When Julian held up his lantern he noticed that the stranger was covered with hideous sores, but notwithstanding this, there was in his attitude something like the majesty of a king.

As soon as he stepped into the boat, it sank deep into the water, borne downward by his weight; then it rose again and Julian began to row.

With each stroke of the oars, the force of the waves raised the bow of the boat. The water, which was blacker than ink, ran furiously along the sides. It formed abysses and then mountains, over which the boat glided, then it fell into yawning depths where, buffeted by the wind, it whirled around and around.

Julian leaned far forward and, bracing himself with his feet, bent backwards so as to bring his whole strength into play. Hailstones cut his hands, the rain ran down his back, the velocity of the wind suffocated him. He stopped rowing and let the boat drift with the tide. But realising that an important matter was at stake, a command which could not be disregarded, he picked up the oars again and the rattling of the tholes mingled with the clamourings of the storm.

The little lantern burned in front of him. Sometimes birds fluttered past it and obscured the light. But he could distinguish the eyes of the leper who stood at the stern, as motionless as a column.

And the trip lasted a long, long time.

When they reached the hut, Julian closed the door and saw the man sit down on the stool. The species of shroud that was wrapped around him had fallen below his loins, and his shoulders and chest and lean arms were hidden under blotches of scaly pustules. Enormous wrinkles crossed his forehead. Like a skeleton, he had a hole instead of a nose, and from his bluish lips came breath which was fetid and as thick as mist.

"I am hungry," he said.

Julian set before him what he had, a piece of pork and some crusts of coarse bread.

After he had devoured them, the table, the bowl and the handle of the knife bore the same scales that covered his body.

Then he said: "I thirst!"

Julian fetched his jug of water and when he lifted it, he smelled an aroma that dilated his nostrils and filled his heart with gladness. It was wine; what a boon! but the leper stretched out his arm and emptied the jug at one draught.

Then he said: "I am cold!"

Julian ignited a bundle of ferns that lay in the middle of the hut. The leper approached the fire and, resting on his heels, began to warm himself; his whole frame shook and he was failing visibly; his eyes grew dull, his sores began to break and in a faint voice he whispered:

"Thy bed!"

Julian helped him gently to it and even laid the sail of his boat over him to keep him warm.

The leper tossed and moaned. The corners of his mouth were drawn up over his teeth; an accelerated death-rattle shook his chest and with each one of his aspirations, his stomach touched his spine. At last he closed his eyes.

"I feel as if ice were in my bones! Lay thyself beside me!" he commanded. Julian took off his garments and then, as naked as on the day he was born, he got into the bed; against his thigh he could feel the skin of the leper and it was colder than a serpent and as rough as a file.

He tried to encourage the leper, but he only whispered:

"Oh! I am about to die! Come closer to me and warm me! Not with thy hands! No! with thy whole body."

So Julian stretched himself out upon the leper, lay on him, lips to lips, chest to chest.

Then the leper clasped him close and presently his eyes shone like stars; his hair lengthened into sunbeams; the breath of his nostrils had the scent of roses; a cloud of incense rose from the hearth and the waters began to murmur harmoniously; an abundance of bliss, a superhuman joy, filled the soul of the swooning Julian, while he who clasped him to his breast grew and grew until his head and his feet touched the opposite walls of the cabin. The roof flew up in the air, disclosing the heavens, and Julian ascended into infinity face to face with our Lord Jesus Christ, who bore him straight to heaven.

And this is the story of Saint Julian the Hospitaller, as it is given on the stained glass window of a church in my birthplace.

HARRY HOUDINI (1874–1926), born Ehrich Weiss, was probably history's most famous magician and escape artist. He contributed a short-lived column, "Ask Houdini," to *Weird Tales,* as well as three pieces, one of which, "Imprisoned with the Pharaohs," is known to have been ghostwritten by H. P. Lovecraft. But Houdini was a capable writer; he wrote a standard text on fraudulent mediumship as well as a biography of Robert-Houdin, the conjurer from whom he borrowed his own professional name. The following engrossing biographical anecdote would appear to be Houdini's own writing —it rings true; Houdini was passionately dedicated to exposing phony spiritualists.

THE HOAX OF THE SPIRIT LOVER

by Harry Houdini

One of the most remarkable instances of coincidence that ever came under my observation took place some years ago, in Montana, a coincidence so remarkable that if a story or a novel were built around it the incident would be considered so highly improbable that the yarn would be entirely unconvincing.

The incident occurred quite unexpectedly during my attempt to expose a charlatan medium. It made my attempt unnecessary. The medium himself was a victim of the improbable coincidence and his boasted powers of materializing spirits were proved a shabby fraud.

Three men came to my hotel room in——and asked me to aid them in exposing a medium whose powers seemed so miraculous as to admit of no explanation except supernatural aid. One of the three men was a minister of the gospel. All had tried to pick flaws in the medium's powers, and had attended one of his séances without succeeding.

One of the men, a lawyer, declared that he was about convinced of the reality of the medium's pretended spiritualistic powers.

"Were it not that to admit spiritualism opens the door for a wave of superstition and charlatanry," he said, "I would quit right now and acknowledge myself convinced. The three of us attended a séance last night, in the third story of an office building. We locked the door, locked the window, examined the room carefully, examined the medium's portable cabinet, and then the lights were extinguished, and spirit materializations took place. There was no possible chance for the medium to have confederates enter the room, nor is there any explanation of the materializations except that given by the medium."

I smiled, and agreed to do whatever I could to learn what deception the medium was practising in his séances.

"It sounds very convincing," I said. "But there must be some plausible, natural explanation. If, in my study of spiritualistic phenomena, I had accepted defeat every time I was baffled by something that I could not explain, then I would not have got very far with my investigations. Instead of saying that there is no explanation except an acceptance of spiritualism, I have said to myself merely, 'I have not yet found the true explanation.' It may be that I shall absolutely fail to pierce the methods of this charlatan who has tricked you. My failure would not prove that the medium had power to call spirits into materialization. There is no reason we should accept spiritualism, which is contrary to all our natural experiences, unless we have absolute proof of it. Failure to disprove spiritualism is far from being positive proof of the reality of spiritualism. I am as open-minded as anybody else on this subject, but I want positive proof. Mere failure to prove fraud in any given case is not a proof of spiritualism. It is simply an indication that the true explanation of the medium's phenomena has not yet been fathomed."

It was the following night that I was to assist my friends in attempting to show up the medium. The more I pondered the deception played on them, the more inexplicable seemed the materialization. I was certain that the alleged materialization was nothing more nor less than a flesh and blood human being in the employ of the medium. There must be some way of entry to the room. My friends had locked the door and the window. It occurred to me that the medium or his confederate might have had a pass key, or he might have made his way over the transom, or the lock on the window might be broken. I have had too much experience in opening locks to believe very strongly in their power to keep people out of rooms.

We met, late at night, in the third story of an office building, the minister, the lawyer, and myself. The medium and several men and women were already there. The third of the trio who had called on me arrived a little later. He was a grocer or confectioner—I do not remember which. The medium remarked that there were certain psychic influences in the room that worked against any spiritualistic manifestations, and looked pointedly, as he spoke, at the grocer, who was a small man with cold, skeptical gray eyes and rather a determined chin. I had been introduced to the medium as Mr. Kochler, and evidently he did not suspect me.

My eyes traveled around the room. There was but one window, and the door was secured by a Yale lock. It could be opened from inside. Immediately it flashed through my mind that the medium had a confederate in the room, who would open the door and admit the materialization, but the grocer pointed out to me that this could not be done, because there was a light burning in the hall, and this would be visible to those in the room if the door were opened. I answered, rather curtly, that it should be a comparatively easy matter to extinguish the light in the hall, and my friend merely shrugged his shoulders in reply.

There were about a dozen in the room besides the medium when the séance began. Seven of these were women, although the usual proportion of women at a spiritualistic séance is much higher. The medium aroused my suspicions immediately by throwing a double curtain over the window, "to keep out the light," as he explained. The night was dark, and only a very little light could enter the room from outside. One black curtain would be sufficient. When the medium used two, I felt sure that he wished to conceal the entrance of someone through the window after the room should be plunged in darkness. I had examined the window carefully before the curtains were put up, and satisfied myself that there was no means of getting to the window from outside, as there was a drop of two stories to the ground, and no fire escape near, but the action of the medium in arranging a double curtain over the window caused me to revise my theories.

We were required to join hands in a circle around a central table. The lights were put out at the wall switch, and also individually, to prevent any skeptical person in the circle suddenly arising and flashing them on. The grocer, however, at my advice, had brought a strong pocket flashlight, so we were prepared.

The séance was opened by the company singing a hymn. Then there was silence for a space, and more singing, while the medium, tied up in a black bag, went into a trance. The proceedings were directed by a woman who, I think, was a sincere believer in spiritualism, and wanted to make all psychic conditions right for opening spirit communications.

I noticed that the singing was loud enough to deaden any sounds a person might make by entering the room either by the door or through the window, and I knew that if the medium had unlocked the window while he was putting up the drapes, it could be opened very easily without being heard above the noise of the singing. I was uneasy, however, and feared that I was on the wrong track, because I saw no way by which an outsider could gain access to the window, which was too far above ground to be reached by ladder.

Finally the spirit manifestations began. There were table rappings, twanging of mandolins, movements of the speaking trumpet, ghostly touches in the dark—all the old claptrap of spiritualistic séances. Then the messages began, the spirit control being ostensibly an Irishman named Mike, who talked in a thick brogue and cracked numerous jokes, even banging the grocer sharply over the head with the mandolin to cool his skepticism. The medium, during all this excitement, was supposed to be in a deep trance, with his hands made useless by being sealed into the black bag, which in its turn was covered with postage stamps on which everyone present had placed marks by which we should know that the medium had not emerged from the bag. This also is a time-worn device of spiritualistic charlatans. It does not hamper the medium's movements as much as might be expected.

Mike, the spirit control, then asked every person in the circle to think very hard of some departed friend or relative whom they wished to see, for the psychic conditions were right for a materialization. The room was very hot and close, but an almost imperceptible breath of air fanned my cheek, and I knew that the window had been opened. The medium, of course, had unlocked it when he was putting up the curtains.

I moved my chair back, out of the circle, and the grocer, who was on my left, moved in a little to take up part of the space I had occupied. I freed my left hand carefully, and substituted the grocer's hand in the hand of the woman on my left, who must have thought that I sat on her right, still holding her hand. My purpose in leaving the circle was to make an investigation. I wanted a look at that window.

A phosphorescent glow emerging from the cabinet now showed vaguely a human face, whether of man or woman I could not say. But the grocer and lawyer were there to attend to the materialization. It was my purpose to learn how the materialization had gained access to the room. I wormed my way down into the cabinet, and through an opening in the back I reached the window very easily. The double curtain bulged out with a slight breeze, and I knew that *the window was open.*

I poked my head out, and was amazed at what I found. To the left of the window a ladder was hanging from the roof above my head. It was a fireman's extensible hooking ladder, about fifteen feet long, which had been thrust out of the window above, and attached to the top of the building so that the medium's "materialization" could climb down from the window in the third story.

Behind me a scream arose, which I did not take time to investigate. It was a girl's scream, and the name "Marion" was repeated several times.

I tried to push the hooking ladder off from the roof, but I could not dislodge it. The ladder was in two sections, and the lower section, being loose, merely slid upward in its grooves. The upper part of the hooking ladder was securely attached to the roof, and could not be lifted out unless I could raise the rigid upper part of the ladder. So I climbed out, and went up to the window in the story above. Behind me still arose the girl's scream: "Marion! Marion! Oh, God, it's Marion!"

I found the window in the fourth story open. I sat on the sill, lifted the hooking ladder from its position and shoved it in the room. The escape of the medium's materialization was cut off, and my own return by the window was also blocked. I found the door locked from the inside. Evidently the "materialization" wished to make himself secure from intruders while he waited for the singing to tell him that the time had come for him to put out his ladder, attach it to the roof, and descend to take his part in the séance.

I made my way quickly through the corridor and down the stairs to the room of the séance, and found everything in turmoil. I had missed the unmasking of the fraud, but I had prevented the escape of the "spirit." What happened while I was going out of the window and removing the ladder, if told in fiction, would seem like stretching the long arm of coincidence so far that it would break under the strain. That is why I said, at the beginning of this article, that the story would be unconvincing if told by a novelist, because of its improbability.

I had wormed my way into the cabinet and was approaching the window when the grocer flashed his pocket light upon the supposed materialization. A woman's scream split the darkness, and the flashlight was violently knocked from the grocer's hand, but the young woman had thrown her arms around the ghost and was covering his face with kisses, screaming "Marion, Marion! It's you! For God's sake, speak to me, Marion!"

While some tried to find the switch, only to find the lights turned off at the chandelier too, someone probably the medium, was striking the girl's hands with a blackjack, endeavoring to break her hold, and the ghost was muttering in great fright: "Frances, let go of me; you're smothering me, Frances," and fighting to free himself. The combined efforts of the medium and the ghost finally freed him from the girl's hysterical embrace, but the means of escape was cut off by my removing of the ladder. The ghost was a real flesh and blood one, and could not dematerialize into the world of shadows.

The girl, Frances, whose surname I will not mention here, as she is still living, had attended the séance in good faith, and when the spirit control asked everyone present to hold in mind the image of a dear departed one, so that the spirit might be aided in showing itself, she concentrated her thoughts on her fiancé, who had died a little less than a year before.

Out of the cabinet, dimly seen by a phosphorescent glow from the features of the ghost, stepped the materialization. The girl stared, hoping that this was indeed her fiancé, trying to believe, her heart beating between skepticism and faith, when the grocer's flashlight lit up the features distinctly. It was only for an instant, for the flashlight was knocked from the grocer's hand almost immediately, but that instant was enough.

The ghost that had emerged from the cabinet was the man she had been engaged to marry, the man whom she had seen laid away in his coffin and buried in the earth!

Is it any wonder that the poor girl became hysterical? Is it any wonder that she threw her arms about her beloved dead, and sought to hold him in the land of the living? Possessed for the moment of an unnatural strength, she held him tight, screaming her love at him, until the struggles of the ghost and the cruel blackjack of the medium had broken her hold.

The materialization, of course, was a paid employee of the medium. And he really was the girl's fiancé!

It transpired that the man, who lived in Chicago, had a twin brother in Wyoming, who was slowly dying of consumption and had gone west to work on a ranch in hope that the high altitude would help him. Frances knew of the existence of this twin brother, but she had never seen him. Marion, realizing that the end was near for his brother, had himself heavily insured in his brother's name. He sent for the brother, who came to Chicago while Frances was in Montana with relatives. In Chicago Marion changed lodgings to break contact with those who knew him, and he took his brother's name, and gave his own name to his brother. The brother died in a Chicago hospital under the name of Marion, but Marion was speeding west to Wyoming when the end came. Letters from Frances in Montana were found in the pockets of the dead man, and a telegram brought the heartbroken girl back to Chicago to attend the funeral of her fiancé, as she supposed. Marion, by this fraud, was able to collect the insurance on his own death.

The money did him very little good, however, for he squandered it in mining stocks and gambling and other means, and was soon penniless. He then obtained employment as assistant to the charlatan medium, and did materializations for him, with his face smeared with phosphorescent paint that gave a pale, unearthly radiance to his features in the dark, and yet did not light them up enough so that anyone could certainly recognize his face. It was the flashlight of the grocer that accomplished that.

The strangest part of the whole occurrence is that the girl and the man should meet in this strange way. He had not the slightest notion in the world that his fiancée was in that room, while she, of course, believed him dead.

The insurance company prosecuted the man for fraud, but the medium who employed him departed suddenly, and may still be preying, under another name, upon the credulities of those who want to communicate with their beloved dead. He was a clever magician, and under whatever name he perpetrates his fraudulent tricks, he should be very successful. It is much more lucrative to be a charlatan medium than an honest magician, for rich dupes pay well, whereas the amount of money that can be made by parlor magic is relatively small.

The girl, Frances, refused to have anything to do with her fiancé thereafter, for the fraud he practised both on her and on the insurance company killed her love. She went to the hospital, suffering from a nervous collapse, after her hysteria at the séance, but she recovered, and afterward returned to Chicago.

JACK SNOW (1907–1956), in addition to his career in radio which led to an executive position with the National Broadcasting Company, still found time to write two of the best post-L. Frank Baum Oz sequels, *The Magical Mimics of Oz* and *The Shaggy Man of Oz*. His collection of eerie short stories, *Dark Music,* includes his five *Weird Tales* pieces, one of which, "Seed," appeared in the January 1946 issue. (For further comment, see Appendix II, page 575.)

SEED

by Jack Snow

1

The potted plants on the window sill should have given me a clue, but they didn't. After all, they were innocent enough—hardy green vines that added a note of coolness and cheer to the spartanly furnished sanitarium room.

Perhaps I wouldn't have noticed the vines at all, but Myra herself called them to my attention. She had not spoken of them. It was only that occasionally when we were talking, her eyes would wander, almost as though against her will, to the plants. She would stare with peculiar intentness at the vines for a few seconds, and then turn away with an effort. Once I thought I detected a shudder as Myra seemed particularly engrossed in the vines. I meant to ask her if the plants annoyed her and she wished them removed from the room, but at that moment she started a train of conversation that banished the odd little incident from my mind for the time. Upon recalling it later, I decided that Myra's preoccupation with the window plants could have no possible relation to her illness, and if she wished the vines removed, she had only to speak to Nurse Wilkins.

I hadn't known Myra was returning to this country until that evening in middle-May, when, upon entering my home, hot and weary after a stifling hot day filled with the round of calls that are the lot of a doctor in a small suburban town, my good housekeeper handed me a note. It was from Myra, stating simply that she had taken a suite of rooms in a fashionable rest sanitarium in the nearby city, and wished me to call on her that night.

Myra Bradshaw in a rest sanitarium! To say that I was surprised is putting it mildly. Anyone who has read either the Sunday magazine supplements or the scholarly journals of scientific societies will readily recall Myra Bradshaw—beautiful and world-renowned as the famous woman African explorer.

Her exploits were sensational enough to make her a natural subject for the big-circulation, luridly illustrated Sunday magazine sections, while her keenly intelligent monographs on archeology, anthropology and natural history won her acclaim and respect in that comparatively small circle of men and women who subscribe to the reputable journals of geographic and scientific societies.

Myra Bradshaw was a woman of dynamic spirit and energy—a woman who had dared a thousand perils, faced a hundred jungle dangers and had exposed herself to a score of dread tropical diseases —and had never been ill a day in her life! This I long marveled at from a professional standpoint, for it was my interest in archeology and the fact that our families had been friendly for many years that had drawn Myra and me together, not my profession. Indeed, Myra had more than once sniffed that she had as little faith in modern MD's as in African witch doctors!

Nevertheless, I concluded, Myra's latest African trek had proved too much even for her, and she had been forced to retire to the sanitarium for a rest. After a little reflection, I realized this was not too surprising. The years were taking their toll, that was all. Such adventures as Myra indulged in were for the young, and while Myra was by no means old, she was, I mentally calculated, closer to fifty than forty.

The stars were gleaming with tropic brilliance, as I climbed into my car and drove the twenty miles to the city, after receiving Myra's message. In all my sixty odd years I can't recall a summer to equal the oppressive, unhealthful heat of that one which marked the reappearance of Myra Bradshaw in my life. The heat came early in May and remained with unslackened intensity late into September. Nor was it a summer of drought.

Most crops did unusually well, for they were nourished with sunlight of furnace intensity and watered by frequent, sultry, torrential rains that soaked the steaming earth into a jungle-like morass. It was a season of rampant vegetable growth.

That night, the heat was only slightly less than it had been at midday. In the reflected light of the moon, there seemed to be reflected something of the heat of the sun, from whose direct rays this little patch of earth had temporarily turned. The crickets, suffused with the abundance of heat and earthly moistures, filled the night with the din of their scraping. With a shudder I recalled reading somewhere that for every human being on the earth there are twelve million insects. Although the road was lonely, with almost no traffic, the night seemed suddenly crowded.

Nurse Wilkins, whom I knew from previous visits to the sanitarium, showed me the way to Myra's suite. I stopped short inside the doorway, finding it difficult to believe my eyes. Could this be Myra Bradshaw? The Myra Bradshaw I had known had been handsome and splendidly formed, radiating perfect health. The figure on the bed was that of a thin, gaunt woman, wasted and wan.

With an effort I endeavored to conceal the very real shock I suffered. I moved toward the bed, stretching out my hand to clasp Myra's. Yes, it was Myra Bradshaw. Her eyes were unchanged, daring, inquisitive, beautiful, their deep hazel flecked with pure gold. They smiled at me now, and from the pale lips came an invitation to make myself comfortable in a chair near the bed.

Myra and I chatted for the better part of a quarter of an hour, but all the while another part of my mind was busily conjecturing. What had happened to my old friend? What had reduced her to her present pitiably weakened condition? Why had her hand been so icily cold when I had clasped it in greeting? Although the air of the room was constantly, though gently, circulated by several electric fans, and the three large windows were thrown open to the night, the room was stiflingly hot. Yet Myra's hand was cool—cool as—and I recall now with horror and loathing that the homely old simile ran through my mind—cool as a cucumber.

Finally, employing what I fondly believed to be clever conversational strategy, I steered our talk around to Myra and her sudden and wholly unexpected appearance in the sanitarium. Myra laughed, her eyes twinkling with some of their old merriment. "You old faker, you! I know you've been dying to ask me what I'm doing here, and what's wrong with me to put me in a state like this—flat on my back and weak as a cat!"

I admitted I was.

"Well," replied Myra more soberly, "I'm here as a last resort. But I don't want to tell you anything until you have made a complete physical examination. Can you do that in the morning?"

I assured her I could arrange my morning schedule to take care of the examination.

Great as my curiosity was, Myra remained firm in her determination to discuss her condition no further that night. After a few more minutes I realized that any attempt to extract additional information from her was futile, so with a sigh I bade her goodnight, promising to see her at ten the next morning.

As I drove home through the heat of the night, noting the forked prongs of light that darted above the black treetops on the distant horizon, I wondered with mingled curiosity if cooling rain would make sleep enjoyable that night, and what the physical examination of Myra Bradshaw would reveal in the morning. By the time I reached home, it was quite late and the stupor of the heat, combined with the monotony of the night sounds, and the fatigue of the long day, oppressed me with an utter weariness so that I soon sank into a deep and dreamless sleep.

2

"I could've told you, Tom, that there is nothing organically wrong with me, but I knew you wouldn't be satisfied until you had made an examination."

It was shortly after noon the following day, and I had just completed my examination of Myra Bradshaw. Myra was right. I had to admit that my thorough check-up had revealed no trace of any disease, nor could I detect any serious organic impairment. I mopped the perspiration from my brow and sat down beside the bed.

"But Myra," I protested, "there must be something that brought you to your present state. Haven't you any idea—how did it start?"

The woman in the bed smiled at me. "Tom," she said, "if I told you what I suspected is wrong with me, you'd hurry me out of here into the nearest mental hospital. So I'm not going to tell you—not now. I will remain here under your care, and perhaps you will be able to help me. I may be wrong, you know, and I wouldn't want you poking fun at me for the rest of my life, if I told you my suspicions—and then disproved them by recovering!"

I didn't press Myra to tell me what was on her mind. I knew she would confide in me, if she believed her story would be of any aid in treating her. And too, I had some idea how full the jungle is of superstition and I supposed that not even a woman of Myra's fine intelligence could entirely escape being touched by it after spending years in the African wilderness. So I forgot whatever jungle jargon Myra might be harboring in her mind, and concentrated on restoring her health by modern medical science.

The two weeks that followed were ones of continuing intense heat and increasing worry and frustration for me. Nothing that I did helped Myra in the slightest. I visited her daily, and was forced to watch her waste away visibly before my eyes. I consulted with the foremost specialists in America. I investigated, probed and experimented. I formed and ultimately discarded theory after theory. I spent long hours after midnight reading in the sultry night heat of my library, hoping that in my books I would find some clue that would start me on the right trail to solving the riddle of Myra's steadily weakening condition. As the days lengthened into weeks, I was forced to admit I was beaten. In despair I realized that a doctor must first have a disease before he can prescribe treatment. I couldn't find any disease. The only enemy I had to combat was Myra's extreme weakness, which increased progressively and was obviously induced by her apparent inability to derive nourishment from food. I prepared for her every known variety of energy extract, food concentrate and vitamin-mineral compound, but it was of no avail. My patient ate and drank regularly but for all the good the food did her she might have been on a starvation diet. I was forced to the unscientific conclusion that in some weird, inexplicable manner Myra Bradshaw was being robbed of blood as fast as her food was turned into the life-giving fluid.

The case baffled me completely. It was unreal and nightmarish, and combined with the relentless heat, it caused me to endure many sleepless nights, through which I tossed and turned, damp with perspiration and weary with conjecture. In the black of those heavy, sultry nights, my mind flew off on wild tangents, recalling legends of vampires and fantastic blood-sucking creatures of the jungle. This illustrates very well, I believe, just how thin the veneer of modern learning is, and how it can be rendered even more superficial by climate and temperament.

Meanwhile, Myra's condition was growing steadily worse. I could not give up hope of saving her, but my dismay mounted as I was forced to watch her weakness increase. It was early in August when the sweltering heat reached its peak that Myra entered that most dangerous stage in which she lapsed into prolonged comas, regaining semi-consciousness only long enough to take a bit of food. With despair I realized that soon she would lapse into a coma from which there would be no rousing. Death would slip up on her quietly as she slept—and there was nothing I could do. Perhaps intravenous injections would sustain her for a time, but even so her life would soon hang on the hands of the clock.

At a few minutes after eleven o'clock, on the night of August fifteenth, I was in my library studying a recently acquired treatise on rare diseases of the tropics, when my phone rang and Nurse Wilkins, speaking from the sanitarium, informed me that Myra had regained consciousness a few minutes before and was asking for me. Wilkins stated further that my patient seemed to have more strength than she had shown for weeks, and was asking for me with a strange persistency. I told Wilkins to remain with Myra and I would leave immediately for the sanitarium.

I will never forget that drive to the city. The night was black and velvety, and the air seemed to be composed of a heat that possessed actual substance and weight as it pressed down on the smothered earth. Any gleam of stars and moon was blotted from the skies by a black shroud of sultriness.

As I drove down the highway, few cars passed me, and except for the night cries of the insects, I was alone in the night. On either side of the road grew fields of corn and truck gardens of tomatoes, cabbages and other common table vegetables. Never had there been such luxuriant crops. The farmer's only problem was insects, which the heat and moisture favored impartially with the crops.

No doubt it was my own weariness, born of the lateness of the hour, the cumulative enervation of the long weeks of intense heat, and my constant worry over Myra that brought on the extravagant fancy as I drove through the deserted night that the world was intent only on vegetable germination and growth, and that for the time being everything else was of minor importance—swept aside, as it were, from the normal, natural course of life. It was almost as if I could hear the faint crenulation of the leaves as they unfolded, and the rustling and crackling of the stalks and ears as they grew. In the pall of the night there was something repellent, grotesque about the great swollen tomatoes that bulged on the creeping vines, filling the air with their unmistakable vegetable reek.

I shivered in spite of the heat, as my car carried me down the corridor of towering grain. I felt strangely lonely, like an alien being —an outsider in a world of vegetation, where the sole purpose of existence is to grow, grow and grow in the beaming rays of the sun and the secret moistures of the sultry nights.

3

It was a few minutes past midnight when I entered the lobby of the sanitarium and made my way to Myra's suite.

Wilkins, who had been sitting by the bed, arose and quietly greeted me as I entered. A green-shaded bed lamp standing on a table was the room's only illumination. Gently moved by the electric fans, the sultry night air of the room stirred with an almost liquid motion.

The figure on the bed was pathetically wasted. There was almost no resemblance to the handsome Myra Bradshaw who had stirred the imagination of the world with her beauty, bravery and daring. As I gazed at the pale face, the eyes opened and on seeing me they lit up with an animation they had not shown in weeks.

"Come closer, Tom," the bloodless lips whispered. I seated myself on a chair at the side of the bed and bent my head over the still form.

"You sent for me, Myra?" I asked.

"Yes, Tom," replied the thin voice. "I want to tell you my story. It is now or never," she added with a suggestion of the grim, brash humor that had been so much a part of the old Myra Bradshaw's great charm.

"Plenty of time, Myra," I said, patting her emaciated wrist. "You are better now than you've been for days."

"You know that's not true, Tom," the woman replied. "This is only the final flash of light before the darkness. There is very little time left. Let us not waste it. You must hear my story."

"Very well, Myra," I assented. "I'll listen, only don't tire yourself."

"I haven't spoken until now," the woman began, "because I did not believe what must always have been the truth. Tom, you were right when you suspected that the jungle was responsible for my condition; but you were wrong in searching for a disease. It is no malady that afflicts me . . . at least no ordinary malady!" Myra paused briefly and then her pitifully weak voice continued.

"It began less than a year ago. I was in Leopoldville, when I first heard rumors of a strange village of natives deep in the Belgian Congo, who worshipped a flower, periodically sacrificing the fairest maiden of the village to this *fleur de mal.* Theatrical as the story sounded, I knew Africa well enough to suspect that the rumor very probably had a foundation of truth. I determined to be the first white woman to penetrate to this little known village of the interior, as well as the first white woman to set eyes on this jungle flower God. Well, it was the old story. The natives were suspicious of strangers; they had not seen more than half a dozen white men in their lives, and I was the first white woman they had ever seen. They resisted our visit, attacking our bearers. We were forced to wound a few natives to make them behave and to convince them of the effectiveness of our modern arms. Later, of course, we treated and healed their wounds, so really we did them no harm."

Myra paused in her recital, a faraway look in her eyes as she relived for the moment that last weird adventure. Gaining strength to continue, she picked up the thread of her strange story.

"We had no difficulty in locating the temple of the Flower God. It was a bower of unearthly beauty, teeming with such riotous colors and growth as only the jungle can generate. It was nature's own Gothic cathedral with towering walls of infinitely foliated leaves, climbing vines, massive pillars of trees and a green filigree of creepers. Its stained-glass windows were woven of thousands of exotically hued petals.

"I had come, bearing in mind the stories of human sacrifices, fully expecting nothing less than a monster, carnivorous plant—a fly-catcher plant on a gigantic scale. But I was wrong. There was no such plant. Instead, on an altar-like dais of the cathedral blossomed one, small, red flower. At first sight, I was disappointed. It might have been any one of a thousand jungle flowers. But upon approaching it more closely, I perceived that it did not grow from the soil. What it did grow from sent a chill of horror through me. That blossom was supported by a stem that reared from the gaping mouth of a long-dead native girl. Stifling my revulsion, I saw that natural decomposition of the girl's body had never taken place. Her skin hung about her frame like a loose, brown sack that was beginning to fall to shreds. But inside the shell of her skeleton, Tom, I glimpsed the real evil of this devil flower."

Myra paused momentarily, and in her expressive eyes was reflected something of the horror she was recalling.

"That skeleton was filled with an interweaving and interlacing network of tiny green feelers and roots that perfectly and completely duplicated what had once been the arteries, veins and capillaries of the unfortunate girl's body.

"The high priest of this jungle temple sullenly explained to me that the flower blossomed only once each year, producing but one small seed. This seed, when fully ripened, was given in food to the carefully selected sacrifice. A short time later, the victim began to weaken and waste away as the seed germinated, and spread its tiny tentacles, roots and feelers through her circulatory system; each of the thread-like feelers drinking of the victim's life blood, until at last the sacrifice died, and the flower blossomed miraculously from the mouth of the dead girl.

"The priest informed me further that the flower I was observing was about to go to seed, as the plant had absorbed all the blood of the girl's corpse.

"Horrible as the priest's story was, it fascinated me. I determined then and there to carry that fabulous seed back to civilization and put the tale to test by attempting to germinate the seed in a solution of animal blood.

"But the priest was cleverer than I," Myra continued. "During the night, he or one of his servitors must have removed the flower and its seed capsule. I was disappointed, of course, but I wanted no more trouble with these natives, whose enmity I had already earned by violating their sacred flower temple, and the whole idea of the flower and plant was so alien and repellent, that I thereupon dismissed the seed from my thoughts, and decided to head back to the coast immediately.

"We remained only one more day in the village, making observations and gathering additional data on the customs and beliefs of these remote savages. It was that one day, I am now convinced, that cost me my life," Myra concluded solemnly.

"Only one thing could have happened, Tom," she went on, beckoning me to silence, as I started to speak. "There is just no other explanation. That native priest, lusting for vengeance for the violation of his temple, managed in some manner to place the seed in my food. As a result, I am about to die—a modern sacrifice to a primitive jungle Flower God thousands of miles away."

"Nonsense, Myra!" I exclaimed. "Your mind is overwrought with your illness. This is certainly a strange story you have told, but you know as well as I do that what you suggest is incredible."

"Is it, Tom?" Myra seemed to have spent her pitiably small store of strength in her narration, and now that she had finished her words were tired whispers. "Is it incredible, Tom? I wonder. You do not know the jungle as I do."

Myra's eyes closed and she slipped gently into sleep. I took her pulse and found it alarmingly weak. Nurse Wilkins, who had been a fascinated witness to Myra's story, was at my side. "Is there anything I can do, Doctor?"

"No," I replied with a sigh. "There's nothing either of us can do beyond waiting and watching. I think we should both be here, so I will remain for an hour or two."

Wilkins nodded, and with that knack that is a part of a nurse's training, made herself comfortable in a chair, although I knew she had been on duty far beyond the normal span of hours. I settled back into the chair at the side of Myra's bed. Through the open windows drifted the perpetual clamor of the crickets. The window curtains stirred dully in the hot night air.

The torpor of the heat must have caused me to drop off to sleep, for it was more than an hour later when I was aroused by an exclamation from Wilkins. Instinctively I glanced at Myra. She was dead. She had died so gently and quietly as she slept that neither Wilkins nor I had been aware of her passing. Her eyes were rolled back in her head, her mouth slightly opened.

"Ah, well," I commiserated with a pang of real sorrow and regret, "at least she has gone without pain." For that slight consolation, I could be grateful.

I was about to phone to have the body removed, when my attention was drawn by a strange gurgling or rustling sound that issued from the throat of the dead woman. Wilkins heard it, too, for she was staring as fixedly as I.

And then it happened. I shall state it simply with as few words as possible, describing merely what both Nurse Wilkins and I witnessed with no attempt to theorize or elaborate. For when one is describing the impossible—the incredible . . .

As Nurse Wilkins and I stared, petrified, a red abomination that I at first thought was blood, caused perhaps by an internal hemorrhage, spread from the mouth of the dead woman. Then, even while my senses revolted, I was forced to see it for what it really was. It was not blood, but a blood red blossom, unfolding its petals before our very eyes as it reared upward on a pale green stem. In a few short seconds the nightmare flower had completed its deathly growth and was about four inches in width, while the stem supporting it emerged some six inches from the mouth of the corpse. Had my very life depended upon it, I don't believe I would have been able to stir a muscle during those seconds that seemed an eternity. I was as transfixed as any serpent charmed by a Hindu's piping. In that brief blink-of-time all my years of scientific training and learning were blasted to nothingness by the impact of the impossible taking place before my eyes.

It was a noise that broke the spell—the noise caused by steely-nerved Nurse Wilkins collapsing in a heap on the floor. She had fainted dead away. Instantly my mind snapped back into action like a spring suddenly released from tension. Thoughts flew through my head at a furious pace. I knew exactly what must be done. Removing a small pen-knife from my pocket, and fighting down an overwhelming revulsion, I stepped to the bed and forced myself to slip the blade of the knife between the lips of the dead woman, while I severed the stem of the flower in her throat. Then I thrust the clammy blossom into my coat pocket, and gently and tenderly closed the eyes and mouth of what had once been Myra Bradshaw. When I finished, the body appeared a normal corpse.

Nurse Wilkins' eyes were fluttering open. In a moment more I had her resting in a chair, staring blankly at me, and muttering, "What happened, Doctor? I—I must have fainted." A few sips of water refreshed her further, and in a few minutes she was her old self, if a trifle shaken. But she remembered nothing beyond the fact that she had dozed, then had awakened to find Myra Bradshaw dead. All memory of the hideous episode of the flower was wiped from her mind. The defense mechanism of Nurse Wilkins' mind was functioning in a manner that would have delighted an amateur psychoanalyst. The mind of this practical, hard-headed nurse simply couldn't accept what it had been forced to record. So, it had resorted to the mechanism of a fainting spell to reject and blot out the incident. Nurse Wilkins remembered nothing beyond awakening to find Myra Bradshaw had died. Then she fainted—because of the heat and the long months of overwork and extra hours, she stoutly asserted. At any rate, the very next day Nurse Wilkins departed bag and baggage from the sanitarium, grimly determined on a long-delayed and long-needed holiday.

To my relief, I discovered later that Myra Bradshaw had left specific instructions that her body was not to be embalmed. Instead, it was to be consigned, whole and untouched, to the heat of the crematorium. I shuddered to think of the green horror of tiny filaments and delicate lacements the mortician would have found growing through the blood vessels of the corpse.

For by this time I had come to accept Myra Bradshaw's deathbed story in its entirety. Once the incredible had been demonstrated as factual, I found my inborn scientific curiosity reasserting itself. I wanted to know more about this weird flower—this *fleur de mal,* as Myra herself had so rightly termed it. After reporting and recording Myra's death, I hurried through the cloying, humid air of the early morning to my home, my mind busily working all the while, revolving about that curious abomination that lay concealed in my coat pocket.

I determined to carry out an experiment that would prove to me once and for all time, beyond the shadow of the slightest doubt, the final truth or falsity of Myra Bradshaw's story.

4

As soon as I reached home, early as it was in the morning, I went to my laboratory and there carefully prepared a solution of animal blood in a beaker. In it I placed the flower, depositing the beaker in an incubator that would keep the beaker and its contents at blood heat.

That night was five weeks ago. In that time I have replenished the blood in the beaker, keeping the flower supplied with the life-giving fluid it required to remain fresh and blooming. I have made several deductions regarding the blossom. It appears to be an ordinary flower, not unlike the common garden variety of poppy. It possesses no special attributes of motion or action. Unlike the carnivorous fly-trap plants of Africa, it cannot move when excited by foreign stimuli, nor does it sustain itself on flesh. It appears to be an ordinary plant, except that it grows out of a bath of blood, instead of a bed of soil. Also, unlike the fly-trap plant, it is not a tuber, but is a seed-bearing plant. The seed capsule was well formed and had almost reached maturity last week. It was then I noted that the blossom first showed signs of beginning to fade and wilt. This morning, when I examined the flower, I found it almost entirely wilted and apparently lifeless. I determined that tonight I would examine the seed.

Today I could think of little else than the seed, as I went through my routine calls and duties. The late September sun shone with all the heat of August, to which was added the brief fury that accompanies the harvest and brings the final climax of growth to the plant world.

When the day was finally finished, and I had partaken of a light dinner, I retired to my laboratory and flung wide the windows to admit whatever stray breeze there might be. The sun had already set and the horizon was alive with wriggling serpents of heat-lightning, accompanied by a continuous cannonade of thunder, the faint rumble sounding like the approach of a ghostly artillery. Would the coming storm succeed in breaking the relentless grip of the summer's heat? I hoped so fervently. As a doctor, I knew full well the toll this unusual summer had taken in my own small community. Heat prostrations, heart attacks, sunstrokes—all had been far higher than average during these past four months. But now it was late September and the magnitude of the storm that threatened promised real relief from the ghastly heat.

Then I forgot all about the approaching storm, as I turned to the wilted, lifeless flower and the dry seed pod that seemed somehow to epitomize and concentrate in itself all the miserable heat and sultriness of that long summer of torrid sunshine and misty rains. Perhaps it was my subconsciousness linking the origin of the blossom with the jungle-like heat we had endured throughout this strange summer.

Turning from the window, I removed the beaker of blood and the flower from the incubator. The wilted petals dropped away as my hand touched them. The firm, rounded seed capsule was easily detached from the stem. There it lay in the palm of my hand—a small, brownish-red ovule, not more than three-quarters of an inch in length. I cracked the protective shell that enclosed the seed. The fibrous husk fell apart and I discarded it. In my hand lay the seed. Moving to the lamp, I adjusted my spectacles and peered closely at the object in my palm. And then I gasped with shock and amazement. Could I believe my eyes? Did I really see it?—a palely greenish-white image, a miniature human shape, not more than half-an-inch in length, and as delicately and exquisitely formed as a bit of Chinese jade!

The window draperies suddenly whipped aside as a blast of hot air swept into the room. There was a terrific crack of thunder and a brilliant dagger of lightning stabbed its way through the inky black heavens. During the next few minutes the elements stormed their most eloquently. The fury burst with a violence that seemed to shake the very earth. The wind mounted steadily, moaning eerily as it veered around the corners of the house. Great drops of rain were hurled noisily to the earth. It was the prelude of what proved to be an autumnal tempest. But not even the dramatic raging of the storm could distract my attention from the object I held cradled in my palm.

Hastily I shut the window to close out the ravening wind and the pelting rain. Then I seized a powerful magnifying glass and brought it to focus on the faintly chill and clammy bit of vegetable growth in my hand.

It was then that I saw the ultimate, yet horribly logical terror that finally and completely verified Myra Bradshaw's story. As I trained the powerful lens on the seed, there came a blinding flash of lightning, accompanied by an ear-splitting roar of thunder that seemed to explode in the garden just outside my laboratory. My electric lamp went dark, plunging the room in complete blackness. Then came another, more prolonged flash of lightning, and while I stared I saw in that glaring light, more vivid than any noonday sun, that the tiny figure in the palm of my hand was a perfect likeness in every minute detail, to every last delineation of feature—a miniature replica of Myra Bradshaw herself!

While I stared in that weird intensity of illumination, just before the chamber was once more shrouded in blackness, the half inch seed effigy stared back at me, peering up through the thick glass of the lens with blank and soulless eyes that flashed suddenly open revealing hazel depths flecked with gold, while the beautifully formed limbs of the figurine squirmed and threshed about in mindless motion.

SEABURY QUINN (1889–1969) was the most prolific of all *Weird Tales* contributors—fourteen articles and 146 works of fiction. Ninety-three of his stories were adventures of his occult detective, Jules de Grandin. "Masked Ball," one of Quinn's non-de Grandin fictional assays, published in May 1947, is a poignant and delicate romance.

MASKED BALL

by Seabury Quinn

Halfway down the block Holloway came to a halt, a grin of self-derision on his face. "Chump!" he muttered. "If I had a little more sense I'd be a first-class halfwit."

He had been in New Orleans three days, crammed his time with sightseeing and as a climax to his trip had dined at Franchetti's, which was the indirect reason for his present predicament.

If you know New Orleans at all you know you do not merely eat at Franchetti's, you dine there, which is not at all the same thing. He had started with a green turtle soup with clear dry sherry, followed it with oysters Rockefeller washed down with Irroy '93; then filet of pompano with Barr Tramier and breast of guinea hen under glass with Nuits St. George's, and for dessert a bowl of frozen strawberries in half-melted vanilla ice cream with brandy and cointreau poured over them. Dinner had consumed two hours, and by the time he drained his demi-tasse of pungent chicory coffee he was more than merely comfortably fuddled and inclined to let events take their course without assistance from him.

It was the eve of Ash Wednesday and the tide of carnival which had been rising steadily since Twelfth Night had reached full flood. He had considered hiring a domino and mask and going down Canal Street to watch the Parade of Comus, but at the *costumier's* in Conti Street he had allowed himself to be over-persuaded.

"A domino, a simple *masque, M'sieu'?*" the *propriétaire* had asked in shocked, grieved tones. "For *you?* But no. You cannot mean it. It would be unthinkable. Attend me, wait one little minute while I select the *costume juste* for you!"

He was a tiny man, the costumer, all full of bows and gestures, as bustling and officious as a bluebottle-fly. His hair was thin and gray, his little pointed beard and wisp of waxed mustache might have been molded out of burnished pewter, and his small, deep-set eyes were very bright behind the lenses of black-rimmed pince-nez from which trailed a broad black ribbon.

While Holloway waited, he rummaged through a stack of cardboard boxes almost as large as steamer trunks, humming a small tune to himself. Presently he came back smiling broadly, and with something of the air of a magician about to produce a rabbit from a high hat, dragged out his find and held it up for admiration. *"Voilà!"* he exclaimed triumphantly. "Is it not *incroyable?* Is it not made to order for *M'sieu'*— to set his special *type* off as a frame must complement a picture? But yes, of course!"

The costume was by no stretch of imagination to be called "fancy." It consisted of a fringed buckskin shirt worked with wampum and stained baby porcupine quills at neck and cuffs, a pair of buckskin breeches, long buckskin leggings, deeply fringed, and a pair of moccasins on which the beaded design of the jacket had been repeated. To top it off there was a coonskin cap with the hair left on and a wisp of ringed tail swinging from the back. "It is the dress of a *coureur de bois,* not just a modern imitation, but a true, historical antique," the little man explained. "One worn by the so formidable scouts who kept the forest trails open for the government when Louisiana was New France and New Orleans the capital of a great new empire. Yes, certainly."

He stepped back, dragged a full-length mirror forward, and held the buckskin garments out to Holloway. "Put them on, *M'sieu',"* he urged. "Regard yourself in them and say if I have not the flair for costuming a patron in accordance with his character and *physique."*

The costume fitted Holloway as if it had been tailored to his measure, and as he viewed himself in the long mirror he had to admit that it "complemented" him, as the proprietor had declared.

Holloway was long and rangy, six feet in his stockings, loosely jointed, agile, but inclined to be deliberate in his movements. A tennis player since his tenth year, a veteran of three years in the Southwest Pacific, he had not an ounce of surplus flesh on his big frame, though he tipped the scales at an even hundred and eighty. As he surveyed himself in the glass it seemed as if a century and more had been rolled back and he saw one of Governor Kerlerec's Kentucky mercenaries looking back at him. "H'm," he conceded, "it's not half bad, but if I'm to be tricked out as a *coureur de bois* I ought to have some armament—"

"Perfectly, *M'sieu',*" the proprietor was delighted. "Me, I have just what is needed. Oh, yes!" The weapon he produced from an old brass-bound chest was a museum piece, a flintlock rifle with a long octagonal barrel, walnut stock with brass butt plate and a wooden ramrod. Its rear sight was a brass notch, its forward one a small button of silver. With it went two wooden powder flasks, one for the rifle's charge, the other for the finer priming powder and a buckskin bag of bullets.

Holloway slung the rawhide thongs of the ammunition carriers over his shoulders and weighed the gun critically. It was a sweetly balanced piece, some fifty inches long from butt plate to muzzle, and as he laid his cheek against the hollow, carved for it in the dark walnut stock, he realized here was a precision weapon, slower in action and with less striking power than the M-1 he had been used to in the Pacific, but accurate to a hair's width within its rather short range. "Does this go with the suit?" he asked incredulously. "It must be worth—"

"No matter, *M'sieu',*" the costumer broke in. "Me, I do not deal in trash. All my costumes are authentic, all my equipment genuine, I assure you."

Darkness had begun to fall, and purple shadows gathered in the narrow street as he emerged from the costumer's with the long rifle cradled in the bend of his left elbow and a half-mask hiding the upper portion of his face and giving him a comfortable feeling of anonymity. The effects of his excellent dinner were still with him, and somehow he made several wrong turnings and found himself in Basin Street instead of Canal, where already crowds were gathering to watch the gorgeous spectacle of the parade.

Behind him, looking like a giant barrel laid on its side, rose the roof of the Municipal Auditorium, a little to his left were the tall whitewashed walls of the old cemetery, and beyond the iron grille of its gate rose the ornate three-storied tomb of the "Widow Paris," once famous as a voodoo priestess. Behind the tomb, as tightly packed as soldiers marching in close formation, the lime-washed sepulchers of long-dead citizens of New Orleans stood rank on solid rank. "Now, let's see," he murmured. "Rampart Street should be that way; if I walk down it I'll come to Canal, and—"

The sharp, metallic click of a gate latch broke through his unilateral conversation and he looked up just in time to see a girl emerge from the old graveyard. Even at the little distance of the street's width he could not distinguish much of her, for a dark cloak covered her from neck to heels, enveloping her completely as an Arab woman's burnoose, but her walk was graceful as a dancer's movements, a cadenced, sensuous swinging of the hips and breasts that was innate and unconscious as breathing, but none the less provocative, and as she turned her head so unconcernedly that he was sure she was aware of his presence he caught a fleeting glimpse of her face, perfect oval with a small, sharp chin, a small straight nose and hair that curled in a halo of tiny jet-black ringlets round her brow and ears. Then she was gone, her dark cloak blending with the violet shadows till it seemed a part of them.

Holloway had an odd, eerie feeling, a sort of sudden stab of poignant yearning. He had been restless with the restlessness none but the soldier trying desperately to reaccustom himself to civilian life can understand since he had left the separation center. New York, which he had dreamed of with a longing half-painful, half-ecstatic, was somehow disappointing. Life had gone on without him for three years; his old friends had married or formed other interests, and one and all were intent on business. "How are you? Glad to see you! Goodbye, now!" had been the universal formula, and he was terribly lonesome. His old job waited for him, but somehow it seemed to have lost its attraction. "Make up your mind, man; are you coming back, or aren't you?" Wilbur Flacker had asked. "We've got a slue of work in the office—five new accounts came in yesterday and we can use a good copywriter. We want to do the right thing by the returned soldier, of course, but if you don't want the job . . ."

On sudden inspiration he had taken a train for New Orleans. He didn't need to give Flacker a final answer till Monday, in the meantime he might find surcease from restlessness in the gayety of Mardi Gras. So there he was, due to go back tomorrow on the morning train and still as lonesome as a cat in a strange alley, still mentally at sea.

That girl, what had there been about her to attract him so suddenly and powerfully? It couldn't have been love, or even the quick passion of the predatory male. He had no idea whether she were thin or chubby, his glimpse of her face had been only momentary, yet— there it was, as if far down in his subconscious a deep layer of desire had stirred and trembled.

He hesitated for a moment, then set out after her, his long stride eating up the little distance separating them. An immense, inarticulate desire seemed to surge through him, for the moment nothing in the world seemed so important as to speak to this only half-glimpsed girl who had glanced at him so briefly across her cloaked shoulder.

Overtaking her should have been easy, but somehow gathering darkness, unfamiliar streets and perhaps his own eagerness combined to thwart him, so here he was, as much at fault as a hound when the fox takes to a brook, gazing down an empty, shadow-haunted street with no sign of his quarry in sight. "Chump!" he repeated to himself. "Of all the chuckle-headed—"

Plop! Something struck the sidewalk beside him with a soft impact and he looked down to see a white camellia at his feet. "Now, where the devil did that come from—" he began when a light laugh sounded just above him.

The house before which he stood was typical of the older buildings in the *Vieux Carré*— the old French Quarter. Sitting back some eight or ten feet from the sidewalk, it had double porches or "galleries" before it, supported by intricately wrought iron grille work. The lower gallery, at street level, was without railing, but the upper was guarded by a balustrade of quaintly designed iron scroll work. *"Mon fleuron, s'il vous plait, M'sieu'!"* came the command in a soft, high voice— "My flower, if you please!" A girl leaned laughing from the balcony, her slim, bare arm extended toward him and her slender fingers reaching for the flower at his feet.

The pale light of the newly risen moon hung round her like a nimbus, and he recognized her instantly: the lady of the cemetery.

"Oh, hello," he greeted inanely. "I'd been wondering—"

"Ma fleur!" she interrupted imperiously. "Toss it up to me— instantly, if you please!"

He threw the white bloom up, but it fell just short of her questing fingers, and she laughed delightedly as he caught it before it could strike the pavement again. *"Encore!"* she ordered. "Try again, great clumsy one."

Once more he tossed the blossom up, and once again, but each time it eluded her grasp. *"C'est sans profit,"* she told him finally. "You lack the skill or I the length of arm, it seems. Bring her up to me, if you please."

This was more than he had hoped for. "You mean I may come up?"

"But naturally. What is there to fear? Although I have the teeth, I shall perhaps not bite you."

The street door of the house was unlatched and Holloway pushed it back, groped through a narrow, almost lightless hall and up a flight of narrow, winding stairs. She waited for him on the balcony, and close up she was even lovelier than he had realized. Her face was pale, colorless and fine-textured as a magnolia petal, but her lips were brilliant red. Her black hair, worn in a long bob with curls about the brow and neck, was positively gleaming, and he knew instinctively that the ringlets had not been put in with a hot iron. Beneath the haughty arch of slender brows her eyes were dark and soft, he could not say if they were black or pansy-purple, but they were beaming with good humor and the smile upon her crimson lips pushed a small dimple in her cheek.

"Er—ah—" he began ineptly, for suddenly he felt tongue-tied, but she saved the situation.

"Ma fleur, M'sieu'!" she ordered with mock hauteur, as she held out her hand, then, with a sudden, rippling laugh, *"mais non,"* she turned her back to him. "But no. Into your hand it fell; it is that you must set it back into its proper place." She bent her head and pointed to the curl in which she wished the flower set. "Come, *M'sieu',* I wait upon you."

Her hair was almost incredibly soft and fine as it brushed his fingers and his hand trembled as he put the flower in place and took quick stock of her. She made him think of ladies he had seen pictured in old French prints. Her gown was China silk, so heavy that it hung as straight as if it had been weighted at the hem, yet so sheer that it showed the lovely shadow of her figure. It was white, high-waisted, and cut with a low neck line and tiny shoulder-puff sleeves that showed her lovely arms off to perfection. Beneath her bosom was a sash of pale-blue silk that tied at the back underneath her shoulders in a coquettish knot and trailed its fringed ends almost to her dresshem. Her slim, small feet were stockingless and shod with sandals fastened with cross-straps of purple ribbon laced across the instep and high up the ankle. Save for the small gold rings that shone in her ears she wore no ornaments of any kind.

"Good Lord!" he breathed as he set the white flower in place among the gleaming black curls.

"*Comment?*" She looked across her shoulder, arching her brows at him. "What is it that you say?"

"You're lovely!"

"*M'sieu!*" The laugh that rippled from her lips was like the sound of water poured from a tall silver vase. "But it is you who say the pretty things! Poor little Clothilde Deschamps, she is ugly like a frog and scrawny like the plucked pullet, yet you say that she is lovely, her. How can you say such utter flattery? No matter, I delight in it. We shall sit here *tête-à-tête,* and you shall tell me monstrous complimentary lies, and I shall believe them all. Come."

She took his hand and led him to a sofa standing by the wall, dropped down on it and drew him down beside her. "Commence," she ordered arrogantly. "Lie to me *grand comme le bras*— as long as your arm. Tell me I am lovely, me—" She moved a little closer and her soft hair brushed his cheek, its perfume fresh and sweet. Her eyes were wide and soft, and her mouth tender. "You meant it, *Vraiment?*"

Wine could not have raced his blood faster than it was racing with the intoxication of her nearness and the music of her voice. "Lovely!" he whispered, and his heart beat so that he could hardly force the word out.

Her eyelids lowered slowly, as those of one who falls into a gentle sleep might do, and her lips parted like the petals of a flower. "*Embrasse moi!*" she whispered, and put her hands up to his cheeks, drawing his mouth down to hers. Her lips were smooth and soft as the flower petals in her hair, her arms were warm and tender round his neck, the sweetness of her perfumed body pressed against his was like an enervating drug. A humming sounded in his ears; everything went dark around him and a spell of dreamy lassitude crept over him. He was fainting, swooning, dying . . . and he did not care. Nothing mattered. Nothing . . .

Abruptly she pushed him from her and rose to her feet. "We must make haste," she told him almost matter-of-factly. "Await me here while I prepare my *toilette*. I shall be but one little moment, perhaps two or three, no longer."

"Your *toilette?*" he echoed. "Why—"

"*Ah bah,*" she laughed as one might laugh at the inept question of a dull child. "You would not have me put the shame on you by going to the *bal masque* in such clothes as these?" There was a patter of small feet upon the gallery floor, and she was gone.

Holloway rose from the couch and walked to the porch rail. Things were happening so fast he couldn't keep pace with them. He had found her, kissed her, now, it seemed, she was taking him to a masked ball. He looked down on the darkened street. Somehow, it seemed different. The shadows seemed to cluster more thickly, the street lamps burned less brightly and in the changed light the houses lining the curbs seemed less ancient. From somewhere far away, there came the muted throbbing of a drum, not the rhythmic rataplan of a marching cadence, but a dull, persistent thrumming, urgent and impelling; there was insistence and abandon in the hollow booming of the taut parchment. He felt vaguely uncomfortable, recalling stories of the voodoo rites the blacks practiced in the days when Jackson Park was Congo Square.

But the chill vanished and he smiled as from the house there came the sound of singing, a tune that was at once both sad and gay, as if the singer smiled through her tears. He could not distinguish the words, for they were in Creole, but the voice was charming, with the throaty, velvety quality that is the heritage of Latin races.

"*Voilà!*" Once more the pit-pat of her feet sounded and she stood framed in the oblong of the doorway, slim and glowing. Her tightly curling hair had been combed high and tied with a fillet of white silk at the front of which an aigret plume was fastened by a small pearl brooch. In her ears were pearls almost as large as filberts, and round her neck there lay another strand of pearls that made him catch his breath not once but twice—first, because the pearls were almost beyond price, and second, because the neck they rested on was almost the exact color of the pearls. Her gown of heavy white brocaded silk was cut low at the front and back, with little puff-sleeves at the shoulders, tight at the bosom, but flaring sharply from a high-set waist. Across her shoulders draped a scarf of silver tissue which hung down either side like the stole of a cleric. Her narrow feet were shod with satin slippers of pale shell-pink, flat-soled and heelless as a ballerina's shoes, and laced across the instep and about the ankles with narrow ribbons. He felt his heart melt as he looked at her: The dim, misty black hair, the dark eyes like deep pools of shadow in the pale oval of her face, the smiling scarlet mouth—not a flaw in her from small head to tiny feet, her figure fine-drawn as a thoroughbred's, slim, delicate, with dainty wrists and ankles and a neck like the stem of a flower. White and frail as a narcissus, and very beautiful.

"Am I not truly *élegante?*" she demanded as she took her skirts in her hands and dropped him a deep curtsey. I shall not put the shame upon you, brave *coureur de bois?* One moment, while I set my visor on, then let us go." She placed a black half-mask across her face, tying its silk strings behind her head, and put her hand upon his arm, so lightly he could scarcely feel her touch.

He glanced down at her appreciatively. The topmost curl of her coiffeur barely reached his shoulder. "What are you made up as?" he asked. "The Empress Josephine?"

Her eyes came up to his, wide with astonishment, and her lips parted in an indulgent smile for an obviously silly question. "I the Empress of the French? But no, *bon ami,* I am nothing but poor little Clothilde Deschamps who goes out only as herself."

Sudden laughter bubbled up through her smile. "La, la!" she exclaimed. *"C'est drôle, hein?"*

"What's so funny?"

"Me, I have let you hold me in your arms, we have kissed each other; we are going to the *bal masque* together, and I do not even know your name, me! *Ohé,* but it is *scandaleux,* it is infamous, *n'est-ce-pas?"* Her laughter tinkled like a silver bell swung in the wind.

"I'm Horace Holloway," he answered as his chuckle matched her higher, merry laugh. "It is a little unconventional, but—"

"I like your name," she broke in, half gaily, half seriously. "It suits you very well. Horace was a poet, and I think that you are that; the very look of you says so, even if you write no verse your heart is filled with poesy. And hollow-way? A road that holds no traffic, no passengers, *n'est-ce-pas? Bon.* I accept your poetry, my friend, and as for emptiness, cannot you find room in your heart for Clothilde?" As unaffectedly as a child she turned her face up to his and waited for his kiss, eyes closed, lips a little parted.

He kissed her slowly and she put both arms about his neck as she stood on tiptoe and pressed against him. How sweet, he thought, sweeter than the heart of a rose, sweeter than the mists of happiness —far too sweet! For deep within him a small bell seemed ringing, sounding a faint warning tocsin of alarm. Despite the allure of her pale smooth skin, her bright vermilion lips and jet-black hair, despite her sweetness and her unaffected, trustful ardor, there was something vaguely frightening about her, some subtle, secret suggestion of the *femme fatale*, the vampire, the ruin of men's souls and bodies.

She linked her arm in his and laced her fingers in his hands as they resumed their walk. "When did you—when did it happen to you?" she asked suddenly.

He studied the question a long moment. She had a quaint way of expressing herself, with her queer jumble of slow, stilted English and quick, ebullient French. "How do you mean?" he countered.

She seemed to ponder in her turn, then, softly, as if the question were embarrassing, "When did you become—like me—us?"

"Oh!" Understanding flickered through the fog of his perplexity. Even if her words were obscure, the apparent self-consciousness of her hesitant speech gave him his cue. "It must have happened when I first saw you by the old cemetery, my dear."

"Mon Dieu!" Her laugh began as a soft, throaty chuckle and rose to a high silvery tinkle. "But it is you who say the sweet droll things, my Horace! Next you will be telling me that I shot Cupid's dart at you and pierced your heart and laid you low!"

"I think you did," he answered, and in the shadow just outside the disc of light cast by a street lamp they stopped and kissed each other again.

Somehow, the streets seemed different, not changed, exactly, but not quite as he remembered them. The curbside lamp posts seemed farther apart and their lanterns shed less light. The houses, too, seemed smaller, newer, better kept; and here and there he could perceive dimly a sort of shadow hovering over them, as if the faint mirage of larger and more modern buildings poised above them.

His sense of direction was blunted by these odd mutations, but as nearly as he could determine they had come to Orleans Street when his companion guided him around the corner and down the block. Midway between what he thought Bourbon and Royal Streets there stood a plain low building of whitewashed brick that made him think of a warehouse, but through the narrow windows piercing its walls brilliant lights shone.

They crossed the street and mounted the low steps that led to the wide doorway. Inside the place was a kaleidoscope of gaiety. Chandeliers that dripped with scintillating crystal prisms shed the soft, bright glow of candlelight on everything, the walls of paneled precious woods were hung with oil paintings, some depicting landscapes, some pastoral scenes, more showing classic gods and goddesses—or gentlemen and ladies dressed like them—engaged in rather naughty goings-on, while the bright faces of a hundred mirrors echoed and re-echoed the frolicsome scene. Somehow it made him think of the bright prints and paintings of Gros, Gérard, David and Ingres which showed the life of Paris during the Directorate and the First Empire so delightfully.

The dancers circling round the floor of quarter-sawed waxed oak wore almost every sort of costume imaginable. Here a gentleman in the white coat and powdered hair of a French officer of Bourbon days swung past with a frail, lovely lady in hoopskirts in his arms, a little farther off a man in the tight pantaloons and long coat of the Directoire period danced with a girl who wore the neo-classic costume of Napoleon's court, while here and there was to be seen a suit of severe black broadcloth, but with the frilled shirt and stock collar of the early nineteenth century.

"Shall we dance?" asked his companion when he had found a place for his rifle, and placed her left hand in his right while she laid the other on his collar so lightly that it might have been a butterfly taking momentary rest there.

The music was three-quarter time but the dance not quite familiar. The step was quicker than the waltz he knew, and the couples whirled and turned and pirouetted so constantly that he was almost giddy by the time they had completed a circuit of the great ballroom.

"You have money, yes?" she asked as they paused out of breath before the door of a long, brightly-lighted room from which the clatter of roulette wheels and the click of dice sounded.

"A little," he replied, shoved his way through a throng of people grouped about a roulette table and tendered a five dollar bill to the impassive croupier.

"Combien?— how much?" the man asked, and Holloway saw with surprise that he too wore a black half-mask across his face.

"Tout," he replied, "I'll shoot the works," and received a handful of gilded *plaques* about the size of checkers. Half of these he handed to Clothilde, who placed them on a red square marked 23 as the croupier announced in a flat, toneless voice, *"Le jeu est fait, M'sieurs et 'dames. Rien ne va plus—* the play has commenced, no more bets are to be placed"—and spun the wheel.

The people crowding round the table became so still the clatter of the little ball in the wheel was like the rattle of hailstones on a tin roof. Motionless, with parted lips, raised eyebrows and craned necks, they watched the spinning wheel and the little ivory sphere that danced in it.

"Vingt-trois, rouge, M'sieurs, Mesdames," the croupier's bored voice proclaimed as the wheel lost momentum and the ivory pellet spinning in it came to rest. A woman laughed, a high, thin titter of hysteria, and staggered drunkenly from the room. A man rose from his place, looked round him with a sickly smile, and lurched toward the doorway, and half a dozen eager players crowded forward for their places.

"Mon Dieu, mon Dieu, but I have won!" Clothilde cried ecstatically and clapped her hands like a delighted child. "I am rich, me!" Her bet had been two dollars, and the croupier pushed a pile of coin and bills toward her with one hand while with a little wood rake held in the other he gathered in the wagers of the losers.

"Come, let us celebrate, *adoré,"* she cooed, and drew him toward a line of curtained alcoves at the far side of the room. "Champagne it shall be for us, and dozens of those small sweet cakes that I do adore almost as much as I adore you, *mon amoureux. Hola,"* she called to a velvet-coated, black-masked waiter who went hurrying past, "a bottle of champagne, and many, many *petits-fours, mon petit garcon noir,"* and the waiter, a gigantic Negro, grinned appreciation of her pleasantry in calling him "her small black boy."

The champagne frothed and bubbled in their goblets, but to Holloway it seemed to lack substance, as if it were but little more than chilled air he sipped, and the little sugared cakes, delectable to look at, were flat, tasteless and unsubstantial as crumbs of Chinese rice cookies. Clothilde seemed to enjoy them hugely, however, and as she sipped champagne and nibbled small pink-and-white-iced cakes the color rose in her pale cheeks until they glowed a lovely pearly rose, and a new sparkle came into her eyes. "Now, I think we dance some more, *hein?*" she suggested as she rose and stretched a hand to him. "And after that we play some more roulette until he has no more money left. Then we shall drink some more champagne—maybe *aux pêchers*— with peaches in him—and eat some more *petits-fours,* no?"

"Yes!" he assented as he followed her to the ballroom. It was crazy as a hasheesh–eater's dream, a scene straight out of the *Arabian Nights* with overtones of the Left Bank. He knew it couldn't possibly be happening; things like this just didn't happen and women like Clothilde did not exist—but that did not matter. For the first time since his return from the army he was happy, deliriously, feverishly happy. On with the dance—let there be madder music; stronger wine!

The candles in the crystal chandeliers cast golden light on everything; Clothilde's small, slim waist lay sweetly in the circle of his arm. Her laughing eyes looked into his, her lips were parted just a little to show the tips of small white teeth. They whirled about the long room, reached the door of the gaming *salon* and paused for breath, laughing with sheer happiness as only children and lovers know how to do. "Shall we assail the battlements of Fortune once more?" she asked as he released her from his embrace. "We may win more this time, and—oh! *Pardonnez-moi, M'sieu'! Mille pardons!"* As she wheeled she had collided with a young man carrying a silver tray on which were two goblets of champagne, and the spilled wine splashed across the rippling ruffles of his dress shirt.

There was a moment's silence while she waited contritely for his word of forgiveness and Holloway could see the young man's florid face behind his mask go slowly gray, as if the blood drained from it. Deliberately he drew a lace-edged handkerchief from his cuff, blotted his soiled ruffles with it, then turning on Clothilde whispered in a cold voice: *"Cochonnette noire!*—little black pig!"

She cried out as if she had been struck and the blood swept up her throat and cheeks and brow in a quick, outraged blush.

Holloway hit from the hip and felt the man's jaw collapse under the impact. His body curved back under the shock and he sprawled like an upset tailor's dummy, inert and loose-limbed, on the waxed floor.

"But you are marvelous!" Clothilde told him as they entered the game room. "You strike like the ball of the cannon, my Horace." She gave a small ecstatic giggle. "He looked so stupid lying there all sprawled out like a spider, that *sale chameau!*"

Holloway felt his knuckles which still smarted from the force of their collision with the man's jaw. "I wish I hadn't knocked him out with the first swing," he answered. "I'd like to have another go with him."

"Oh, but you will, *bon ami*. Assuredly."

"Think he'll come back for more?"

"He will demand the satisfaction, certainly. He cannot do less in honor."

"I'll be ready to meet him whenever—"

"Be sure to choose the firearms, *chèri*. Do not let them trick you into fighting with the *colchermarde* or *épée*. He is a famous duelist, that one—I know him, me!—and would surely run you through at the first pass—"

"For heaven's sake!" he burst in. "D'ye mean that I'm expected to fight a duel with that little stinker? I'll be hanged if I do. If he wants more of the same I've got it right on ice for him, but a duel—good Lord! People just don't do that sort of thing today."

"Ah, Horace, you would not put shame on me? You would not have them say I came to the *bal masque* with a *poltron* for my protector? They will surely brand you as a coward if you refuse to meet him—*mon Dieu,* I think I see them coming now!"

"Be easy, sweetheart," he soothed, patting the tense fingers which had clasped on his arm. "If I'd get you in wrong by refusing to fight this guy I'll meet him any time and place he wants to name, and shoot the pants off him."

Walking elbow to elbow, two young men were coming toward them. One wore the gold-laced white coat of a French officer of the days of Bourbon ascendancy, the other was in sober black, but scarcely less ornate than his military companion. His shirt of finely tucked linen cambric was trimmed with row on row of lace in which there gleamed studs of green jade set with black pearls, a diamond buckle held the wide black ribbon of his stock, the buttons of his low-cut waistcoat were bright silver.

Both men came to a halt as if obeying a command, struck their heels together and with right hands on their hearts and left behind them jack-knifed forward in a formal bow. *"M'sieu'!"*

Holloway was not to be outdone. Drawing himself up as if to attention he inclined frigidly in what was little more than the suspicion of a bow. "At your services, *Messieurs.*"

The young soldier, who seemed to recognize Holloway as a member of his craft, spoke first. "We have the honor to represent M'sieu' Médard de la Tour, and on his behalf to demand satisfaction for the blow that you have given."

Holloway racked his memory for the proper response. Vaguely, he knew he should have a second. But how to go about securing one? At last: "I have no one to act as second for me, *Messieurs,*" he answered, "but if you will have the kindness to procure me one I shall be happy to put my interests in his hands."

"Très bien." It was the young officer again. "Me, I have nothing else to do; I shall be honored to act as your second, *M'sieu'—*" he paused with raised brows.

"Holloway," the other responded. "Horace Holloway, late of the United States Army." That sounded impressive, especially when he neglected to add he had been Corporal Holloway.

All three exchanged curt, formal bows again, and the civilian left to inform Monsieur de la Tour how things progressed, while the young soldier remained. "I am the Chevalier de Broglie," he announced, "and as a gentleman of France—" he bowed low to Clothilde— "I offer my profound apologies for the affront my *ci-divant* principal offered *Mademoiselle.*"

Clothilde dropped him a deep curtsey, and the young officer turned to Holloway.

"As for the blow you gave, *M'sieu',*" he grinned boyishly, "it was a lovely thing to see, and I can say only *'à merveille*— well done!' I trust that you will be successful on the field of honor as in the ballroom a moment since. Now to business: As the challenged party you have the right to name the time and place of meeting and the weapons to be used. What are your preferences?"

Something about "pistols and coffee for two at daybreak" popped into Holloway's memory. "Why not tomorrow morning at sunrise in St. Anthony's Square?" he hazarded. "I've heard that is a favorite place for—"

"M'sieu', I fear that you forget," de Broglie interrupted coldly. "You know as well as I that this affair must be concluded at once. Your jest is not in the best of taste."

Holloway was amazed at his sudden coolness, but let it pass without comment. "Very well, one time's as good as another. Make it long rifles at forty paces, behind St. Louis Cathedral."

His second bowed and hastened off, and Clothilde looked at him reproachfully. "O, Horace, *adoré,* how could you?" she asked almost tearfully.

"How could I what, dear?"

"Make such a reference to the morning. You know as well as I that with the breaking of the dawn we must—*mon Dieu,* here comes de Broglie now. Be careful, heart of my heart. He is a good shot that one, and may injure you. Be sure to fire first." Impulsively she held out both hands, and he bent above them, kissing each in turn.

Gigantic oak trees, bearded with long garlands of gray Spanish moss, stood solemn, black and silent at the edges of the park, their almost-bare limbs seemed uplifted as if to evoke malignant spirits from the winter sky. From the distance came the moaning of violins as the orchestra in the dance hall played on, but in the square an ominous quiet reigned. Like drifting shadows, members of the company moved on their grim errands of setting the stage for the duel. A gentleman in a long cloak and broad black hat who looked like a conspirator in a melodrama paced off the course; two more set stakes in the short grass where the combatants were to stand; the seconds, conferring in whispers, watched while two others loaded Holloway's long rifle and another like it for his antagonist.

"Messieurs!" The umpire stepped forward with upraised hand. He was a tall, commanding figure in a tight blue uniform piped with gold and scarlet braid and with gold epaulets on his shoulders. The upper portion of his face was obscured by his black mask and the lower half by a wide, curling mustache and a short black beard. He spoke French with the cautious precision of a slight accent. Holloway had the impression he was a Spaniard, but could distinguish little from his unfamiliar uniform. *"Messieurs,* this is a duel between Monsieur Médard de la Tour of Nouvelle Orléans and Monsieur Horace Holloway of the United States Army to avenge a blow given and received. The principals will stand at forty paces from each other, armed with rifles. I shall say, 'Fire—one, two, three, four, five!' and the combatants will discharge their pieces between the

words 'Fire,' and 'Five.' One shot only will be exchanged. Are you ready, gentlemen?"

Young Chevalier de Broglie handed Holloway his rifle with a smile. *"Bon chance, mon ami,"* he whispered. "Aim for the eyeholes in his mask, and just a little low. These rifles have a tendency to elevate their bullets."

With the rifle "ready", Holloway awaited the command. In the moonlight-softened darkness, de la Tour loomed like a spot of darker shadow uncertainly defined against the duskiness of the great oak boles. He had buttoned his coat tightly and tied a black silk handkerchief about his throat, so he was in unrelieved black from head to foot, with no highlight to sight on.

"Clever little devil," Holloway muttered as he weighed the rifle in his hand, "but I don't think it'll get him much." He hadn't earned his expert rifleman's badge for nothing and potting skillfully camouflaged Jap snipers had been an everyday chore for him in the jungle. The buttons on his adversary's coat were silver and shone with a dull luster in the moonlight. The second one on the left side should be almost above his heart. He'd put a slug through it as sure as God made little apples. Killing in war had been impersonal. You shot and were shot at. If the other fellow's bullet had your name on it you were done for, if you had his number on your slug he was. This was different. That grinning little monkey yonder had insulted Clothilde . . . only one shot would be exchanged, eh? All right, if that was how they wanted it . . . he'd killed better men with one shot . . .

The umpire's voice broke through his reverie: *"Attendez, Messieurs.* Fire—one, two—" Bright orange flashes stabbed the darkness and the reports of the rifles were so close that one seemed but the prolongation of the other. Holloway saw a slim arc of silver hurtle through the gloom like a small meteor where his bullet clipped de la Tour's coat button, but de la Tour did not go down. He stood, rifle in hand, and looked at him as if he saw some fearful apparition. Then, slipping down his left arm from the shoulder, he felt the warm ooze of blood and knew he had been hit, though if his wound were light or serious he did not know.

A hum of talk, the sort of frightened whispering that precedes a panic, ran from man to man among the witnesses to the duel.

They looked at the blood seeping through his buckskin shirt with bright, fear-burnished eyes, and one or two raised trembling, frightened hands to point to the stain. *"Sacredieu,"* he heard de Broglie exclaim, "he is one of *them!"*

Slowly, fearfully, they shrank back to the shadows of the oaks as men who see a frightful spectre might give way before it, yet fear to turn and flee, lest it set on them from behind.

"What the devil—" He took a step toward the terror-stricken group, and they shrank from him as if he were plague personified.

There was a rustle in the oleander bushes growing at the park's border and Clothilde came toward him, breathing with quick, jerking gasps, the eyes behind her mask a glaze of sickened fear. "Horace," she spoke thickly through the fear-stiffened lips, "is it truly thou?"

"Of course, dear. And I'm not badly hit. That fellow couldn't shoot fish in a barrel—" He took a step toward her, but she shrank back, hands upraised as if to ward some terror from her.

"Don't—don't come too near!" she begged, and he could see that she was using all her self-control to keep from turning and flying.

"What *is* it?" he demanded. Everyone—his late antagonist, his second, all the men, and now Clothilde, shrank from him as if he were a putrescent corpse. "Tell me, Clothilde—"

"Did not you know—truly?" she asked tremblingly.

"Of course, I don't—"

"You know not who we are?" She seemed to grasp her courage with both hands, holding it by main strength.

"No—"

"We are the dead. Once every year, upon the eve of *mercredi des cendres*— Ash Wednesday—it is permitted us to leave the tomb and come back to the scenes we knew in life in seeming-flesh. Upon this single night in all the year it is permitted that we laugh and love and be as gay as in the days when we were living. Those who loved in life may then renew their sweet communion; those who fought and hated may take up their quarrels if they desire. The city is the same as it was in the days of old, for time moves not for the dead."

He stared at her stupidly, made a move toward her, and she gave way a faltering step. "Forgive me, *chèri,* I would not hurt you, but as the living fear the dead, so we dead fear and shrink from the living. You are terrible to us. So have a little patience with poor frightened Clothilde whose love is greater than her fear—but, *hélas,* not much greater.

"How could I know? When I saw you outside the cemetery in your costume of the ancient days I thought that you were one of us, and though I did not know who you might be, my heart yearned toward you. Then when you passed my house I knew that you had followed me, and I was glad, so I dropped my flower down to you and you came up to me—"

"But—"

"The time is short, *adoré;* I must hasten. Do not interrupt. You will remember that I asked you when it happened as we walked down Royal Street? I meant when were you killed. Me, I was stricken with the plague the year that General Jackson held the city from the British, but you seemed of an earlier day—like one of Governor Kerlerec's Kentucky legionnaires who held the forest pathways for New France. And when you told me that it happened when we met I thought you spoke the lover's jest, and I was so delighted with the pretty compliment that I did not press you for an answer.

"When you accepted de la Tour's challenge I followed to meet you as you came from the *champ d'honneur,* for I well knew that though a sword or bullet could give you great pain, those who are already dead cannot be killed again, so though you might be sorely wounded, there would still be a few minutes in which we could share this new-found love of ours. But when I saw your blood begin to flow, I knew that you were one of *them*— the dreadful living whom we fear so much!"

"But you just said you love me," he broke in. "If that's so, surely—"

"Alas, my heart, within the grave there is no loving. 'Twixt you and me there is a gulf no love can bridge. Not even if you died could you come to me, for—I know not why it is, I know only that it is so —our company is made up of those who died many years ago. Not only life and death, but time as well is set between us like a wall!"

The night was tiring rapidly and in the eastern sky a faint gray streak edged with the palest rose began to show. She came a little nearer, fearfully, but with a loving courage that outfaced her fear, and it seemed to him that suddenly there blew so soft a perfume in the fading dark that he could almost see it take shape. She kept looking at him, her eyes were wide, her lips parted as she breathed faster. Suddenly she snatched the satin mask from her face and flung herself into his arms. "O, Horace, *m'ami, je t'aime, je t'amie—je t'adore!*"

She was sobbing with heart-shattering sobs, fighting hard for breath, but her eyes were bright and steady with mingled adoration and renunciation. *"Un dernier embrassement!—* one last kiss!" she besought in a tearful whisper, and raised her face to his.

He held her to him a long, trembling moment. He could feel her heart beat with quick, light strokes like the ticking of a watch. She gave a little, tortured moan and became limp and yielding in his arms, then twined her hands about his neck, pulling his lips hard against hers and drawing her body against his. *"Adieu,"* she whispered brokenly. *"Adieu, coeur de mon coeur, pour le temps et pour l'éternité!"*

The world about them seemed to have stopped in its course for a long moment by some formula of potent magic, then from a belfry somewhere in the distance a gong sounded; the still air held its echoes till it seemed to quiver and daylight came so quickly that it seemed a gust of wind had blown the dark away.

It was morning. And suddenly his arms were empty.

The train wheels clicked with an insistent monody as compelling as the kettle-drums in Ravel's *Bolero*. Holloway sat in the club car with his glass of bourbon untasted before him as he gazed out at the flat, marshy landscape and the bare trees with their dreary streamers of gray Spanish moss— "like funeral crapes," he thought. Save for the stiffness in his left shoulder where his slight wound pained no longer, he might have been convinced that he had dreamed it all—Clothilde, the masked ball, the duel in the moonlight behind the Cathedral. He was going back to New York, back to work and everyday prosaic sanity. He'd meet his friends again, make new contacts, take life up where he left off when he put on the uniform. He'd find an anodyne for broken dreams in work . . . there would be other women . . . He laughed suddenly, so harshly that the fat man across the aisle put down his copy of the *Times* and stared at him.

Other women—vibrant, living, flesh-and-blood creatures! He knew as he knew that he lived and breathed that, flesh or phantom, lovely dream or sweet reality, Clothilde Deschamps who died in 1814 and lay buried in St. Louis Cemetery was the one and only love of his life, that always while he lived his heart would cleave to her memory as constantly as the tides swing to the moon.

THE WOMAN WITH THE VELVET COLLAR

by Gaston Leroux

"You say that all the tales of Corsican vendettas are just the same old story over again," Gobert, a retired sea captain, remarked to his friend Captain Michel. "Well, you're wrong. I know one story that is so terrible that it makes all the others seem mere child's play. It even sent a chill up my hardened spine."

"Yes?" Michel was skeptical. His was the skepticism of a man who, believing to have known the most thrilling adventures, does not take stock in other men's tales. "Yes," he went on, "another case of a couple of bullets in the back, I suppose. But go ahead, let's hear it. We haven't anything better to do."

With this last shot, he ordered another round of drinks, and the party of old sea-dogs, who gathered every evening in the Café of the Sea at Toulon to spin their yarns, settled themselves to listen.

"First of all," Gobert began, "my story hasn't anything to do with guns. And secondly, you've never heard of a Corsican vendetta like mine unless, of course, you happened to have been at Bonifacio about thirty years ago, as I was. In that case you would have had your fill of the story because the whole town was agog with it."

He looked around inquiringly, but none of the men present had ever touched at Bonifacio during their many voyages.

"Well, I'm not surprised," Gobert went on. "It's not a port of importance, but it is one of the most picturesque towns in Corsica. You've all seen it, probably, on your way to the Orient. A lovely spot with its old fortress, the turreted battlements, and time-stained walls. The fortress juts out over the crags like an eagle's nest . . ."

"Lay off the descriptions and give us the story," the others exclaimed impatiently.

"All right, here it is. I was in command of a small destroyer forming part of the squadron escorting the secretary of the navy on a tour of inspection in Corsica. At that time they were considering the fortification of several ports. In fact, they even thought for a while of turning Porto-Vecchio, which is as large as Brest, into a regular naval base.

"The secretary of the navy went first to Calvi and Bastia, from where we returned to Ajaccio to wait for him while he crossed the island by train, passing by Vizzavona, where he was met with great ceremony by a delegation of bandits who had left the wilds of the interior that very morning to present their respects to him.

"The famous Bella Coscia, himself, commanded the squad that fired the salute. The secretary of the navy was much impressed with his imposing bearing, his rifle whose carved stock had a nick in it for every man he had killed, and his famous knife—the dagger given to him by Edmond About with the request never to leave it in the wound!"

"There you are, the same old stories," Captain Michel interrupted peevishly. "Just a lot of old wives' tales."

"You're right, old chap; these are just stories, but if you'll hold your horses, you'll hear something more important.

"We left Ajaccio and arrived in Bonifacio at night. The larger ships continued to Porto-Vecchio, but I was among those detailed to escort the secretary ashore. It was a gala night, of course. A big dinner was followed by a grand reception at the town hall.

"Bonifacio, situated as it was opposite Magdalena, wanted fortifications and its citizens had turned out in great style to make a good impression. They produced the best of everything they had—flowers, finery, and beautiful women, and you know how beautiful Corsican women can be! At dinner there were some striking beauties and I remarked about it enthusiastically to my neighbor, Pietro Santo, a charming fellow of a frank, good-natured appearance, who was then town clerk.

" 'Wait until you have seen the woman with the velvet collar,' he said seriously in answer to my remark.

" 'Is she more beautiful than these?' I asked with a smile.

" 'Yes,' he replied without smiling, 'yes, she is more beautiful, but it is not the same kind of beauty . . .'

"In the meantime our conversation drifted to the customs of the country. My head was still ringing with all the wild brigand stories I had just been hearing from my comrades, on their return from escorting the secretary to Vizzavona, and their account of the spectacular reception by Bella Coscia had seemed to me like a scene from a musical comedy. I thought it was rather polite on my part to doubt the dangerous character of these outlaws. After all, Corsica was as civilized as certain parts of France itself at that time.

" 'The custom of vendetta,' Santo explained to me after I had spoken, 'continues to be a part of the code of honor here in the same way that dueling is with you. Your revenge accomplished, you automatically find yourself an outlaw. But what can be done about it? It's too bad, of course, but we have to put up with existing facts. I myself am an easy-going man. I was brought up in an antique dealer's shop and I'm sorry to see how savage some of my compatriots still can be when their family honor, as they call it, is in danger.'

" 'You surprise me,' I exclaimed, pointing out to him the jolly, good-natured faces around the banquet table.

"He shook his head. 'Don't trust them,' he warned, and his face grew dark; 'a laugh changes very quickly to a diabolical grin on their lips. All these dark eyes are sparkling with frankness and merriment tonight. Tomorrow they may flash black with thoughts of hate and revenge. And all those slender, delicate hands clasping each other in good fellowship never cease toying with hidden arms.'

" 'I thought those customs had died out in the cities and only existed in the little villages of the interior,' I said.

" 'The first husband of the lady with the velvet collar was mayor of Bonifacio, sir.'

"I did not understand the allusion and was on the verge of asking for an explanation of this somewhat enigmatical remark when I was stopped by a call for silence. The speeches were about to begin. At their conclusion we withdrew to the drawing-room, and it was there that I first saw the woman with the velvet collar. Nor did I need Pietro Santo to point her out to me. There was no mistaking that strange funereal beauty and the velvet ribbon, which circled the base of her neck making a wide, black strip against the whiteness of her skin. This velvet collar was worn very low at the rise of the shoulders and emphasized her long and slender neck. She carried her head very proudly, always holding it in a straight, rigid position. Her face was classic in its beauty but so pale that one would have believed it chiseled in marble had it not been for two flashing eyes of strange brilliancy.

"As she passed through the room they all bowed to her with lowered eyes and I caught a general atmosphere of fear and instinctive recoil which roused my curiosity to full pitch. Her beautiful body was draped in black velvet and as she came forward, slipping in and out of the crowd, with her proud head and tragically pale face, I had the impression of seeing the dignified ghost of some dead and martyred queen. When she had gone, I turned to my new friend and voiced my feelings about this uncanny woman.

" 'There is nothing strange about that,' he answered seriously. *'She was guillotined!'*

"I looked at him in astonishment. 'What do you mean?' I stammered.

"But he could not answer me immediately. The 'woman with the velvet band', having greeted the secretary of the navy, came down the room toward us, stopped and held out her hand to my friend.

" 'Good evening, Pietro Santo,' she said, and I noticed that her head never moved from its rigid position.

"He mumbled something and bowed, and she went on. All the eyes in the room were focused on her and a deep silence had fallen. I noticed then that she was escorted by a handsome, well-built fellow of about thirty. His face had the fine profile often found on old Greek coins. These delicate features are frequently seen among the Corsicans and sometimes give them a family resemblance with the great emperor.

" 'He's her second husband,' Pietro Santo whispered, noticing my gaze.

"The couple disappeared at this moment, and I was conscious of a sigh of relief rising throughout the room, while an old man in a corner crossed himself, muttering a prayer.

" 'They never stay very long,' Pietro Santo explained, 'because they're not on very good terms with the present mayor, Ascoli. Angeluccia—that is her name—has always been proud and ambitious and she wanted her second husband, Giuseppe Girgenti, to be mayor like her first one. But they were defeated at the last elections and I think they always will be because of the guillotine affair.'

"I started and caught my friend by the arm. He smiled.

" 'Oh,' he exclaimed, 'you'd like to know the story . . . I hear the mayor telling it to the secretary this minute; but he doesn't know it as well as I do. . . . You see, Captain, I was a member of the household and *I saw everything even to the bottom of the basket!*'

" 'Have a cigar, Santo?' someone offered. 'You've never smoked any as good as these.'

"Pietro Santo took a cigar and I fumed with impatience while he chatted with the man who had interrupted us. Afterward I suggested he come aboard my ship, for I was determined to know the rest of the story before I left Bonifacio.

" 'And so,' I began with a laugh, as soon as we were installed in my cabin, 'you say that woman was guillotined?'

" 'You do wrong to laugh, sir,' he replied, extremely serious. 'She was guillotined and it happened before the eyes of almost all the people you saw this evening. If you noticed, they all crossed themselves when she came into the room.'

"I stared at him in open-eyed amazement and he went on simply: 'That's why she always wears that velvet band: to hide the scar!'

" 'Mr. Santo, you're making fun of me. I'm going to call on Angeluccia and ask her to take off the band before my eyes. I should like to see that scar.'

"The man shook his head. 'She wouldn't take it off, sir. We all know that if she did her head would fall off!'

"And so saying, he too made the sign of the cross. I studied him by the light of the little swinging lamp. With his curly hair and slight figure, he looked like a timid angel frightened at the sight of the devil. I could not help smiling.

" 'And yet Antonio Macci, Angeluccia's first husband, was the best of men,' he sighed. 'Who would ever suspect such a thing of him? I loved him, sir. He had been very good to me. He was an antique dealer and had brought me up in his shop. He was famous in his line all through Corsica and known to many tourists to whom he sold souvenirs of Napoleon and the imperial family. He manufactured these curios, because the rage for them was such that the authentic pieces had long been sold and there were no more to be had. He made a fortune in this business, and the tourists were quite happy with their purchases, which they were firmly convinced were authentic. Antonio, however, never lost an opportunity to buy any revolutionary articles when the occasion offered. He was able to sell them at a good price to the English and Americans, who never left the island without first paying him a little visit.

" 'From time to time he made short trips to France to renew our stock, and I went with him the last time he went to Toulon. He had read in the papers that there were some very interesting pieces to be sold at auction and he was anxious to acquire them for his shop.

" 'We made a number of purchases that day. We bought a Bastille relief for 425 francs, General Moreau's bed for 215 francs, Mirabeau's death mask for 1,000 francs, a bezel ring with some locks of Louis XVI's hair for 1,200 francs, and last, the famous guillotine which, it seems, Samson, the famous executioner, himself had used. This cost us 921 francs. And we returned home very well pleased with ourselves and our purchases.

" 'We found Angeluccia and her cousin Giuseppe waiting for us on the dock. The deputy mayor and a delegation from the town council were also waiting for us because Antonio, through his successful business, had become one of the most important men in the town and had been elected mayor. He was about forty years old at the time and his wife twenty, but this great difference in age did not keep Angeluccia from loving her husband ardently. Giuseppe, however, who was about her age, obviously adored his cousin. Anyone could see it merely by the manner in which he looked at her. But be that as it may, I must add that I for my part had never seen anything in the behavior of the two to justify the slightest suspicion in the husband. Angeluccia, herself, was too honest and too upright in her actions to give poor Giuseppe any chance to forget her marital duties. And I never believed that he would have had the daring to attempt such an enterprise. He loved Angeluccia. That was all. And my master knew it as well as the rest of us. Perfectly sure of his wife, he used to joke with her sometimes about it.

" 'Angeluccia, who was kind by nature, asked him to spare her poor cousin and not make too much fun of him because Antonio would never find his equal in imitating and redoing furniture of the Empire and Louis XVI. Giuseppe, in fact, was a real artist. Besides, he knew all of Antonio's business secrets, which was probably why the dealer tolerated a workman who looked at his wife with such eloquent eyes.

" 'Giuseppe's forlorn love made him rather melancholy; but Angeluccia was always gay. She had not yet become the funereal beauty you saw today. She laughed often and was affectionate and happy with her husband like any good little wife who has nothing on her conscience.

" 'Our return was well celebrated. Angeluccia had prepared an excellent luncheon and invited a few friends to share it with us. Everyone was anxious to hear of the new and sensational purchases and everyone wanted to see them.

" ' "Does the guillotine still work?" one of the guests asked.

" ' "Would you like to try it?" the master of the house answered with a laugh.

" 'During the meal, Antonio, next to whom I was seated, accidentally dropped his napkin and bent over to pick it up. But I had already seen it slide to the floor and my head was under the table at the same time that his was. I straightened up and returned him his napkin. Then with a hurried excuse I left the room, bewildered.

" 'I stumbled into the shop and sank into a chair. My discovery had momentarily stunned me, but as my wits returned to me my first question was: had Antonio seen? No, my sudden movement and the position of my head under the table must have made that impossible. Besides, the very calmness, with which he had straightened up and received the napkin from me and the quiet way in which he had resumed conversation should have reassured me.

" 'I returned to the dining-room, where the meal was finishing gayly. The deputy mayor, who is the mayor today, was insisting on being shown the guillotine immediately. Antonio, however, answered that he must wait until the instrument of death had been put in working order. "I know my Americans," he added with a laugh; "they won't buy it unless it works perfectly!"

" 'Shortly afterward, the guests took leave of their hosts, and during the rest of the day I could not keep my eyes off Angeluccia, who kissed her husband a hundred times if she kissed him once during the afternoon. It made me shiver to watch her. I did not imagine that such deceit was possible in so young and apparently frank a person.

" 'You see, Captain, when I bent under the table at luncheon I had seen Angeluccia's little foot tightly and amorously pressed between Giuseppe's! Her very movement in releasing her foot had proved the crime to me.

" 'As the days passed, life at the shop went on as usual. A few foreign customers came for the famous guillotine, but the master answered that there were still some necessary repairs and that he would not sell it until it was in perfect working condition. In fact, we were working on it secretly in the basement and had taken it down and put it together several times. It was badly worm-eaten and out of joint and we were trying to balance it properly so that the knife would run smoothly in its grooves. This work revolted me, but it seemed on the contrary to please Antonio.

" 'Angeluccia's birthday and the Pentecost fell on the same date, and as it was customary for the mayor to give a party of some sort on the day of Pentecost, Antonio announced that he had decided to give a costume ball. This would be an excellent opportunity to show his guillotine. No one had seen it yet and it was to be the crowning event of the evening.

" 'Bonifacio is very fond of this sort of amusement, historical reconstructions and pageants, and when Angeluccia heard the plan she flung herself on her husband's neck like a happy child. She herself suggested that she go as Marie Antoinette.

" ' "We'll make it very realistic and guillotine you at the end of the party," Antonio said with a laugh.

" ' "Why not?" Angeluccia answered. "It would be fun."

" 'When the town knew what sort of a party the mayor was planning, everyone wanted to go, and the next fifteen days before Pentecost were filled with preparations. The shop was full from morning to night with people running in and out, asking advice and studying old prints. Antonio was to represent Fouquier-Tinville, the terrible public accuser. Giuseppe was to be Samson, the executioner, and I was to fill the humble rôle of his aid.

" 'The great day arrived. Early in the morning we emptied the shop of all the odds and ends with which it was filled and put up the guillotine. Giuseppe made a knife of cardboard covered with silver paper, so that Angeluccia's desire to play the guillotine scene to the end could be carried out, and we tried the machine several times to make sure it worked.

" 'We danced all afternoon and at night there was a big ball at the town hall. Everyone drank toast after toast enthusiastically to the mayor and his beautiful wife. Angeluccia was dressed in the costume worn by Marie Antoinette during her imprisonment, and this simple dress, well in keeping with the feelings of a poor woman destined to so tragic an end, suited her marvelously. I shall never forget the sight of Angeluccia's beautiful white neck rising proudly from the delicately crossed kerchief, and Giuseppe devoured her with his eyes. Catching the too apparent flame of desire in his look I could not help glancing from time to time at Antonio, who seemed almost wildly gay.

" 'At the end of the dinner, it was he who gave the signal for the start of the horrible play. In a well-prepared speech, he informed the guests that he and some friends of his had planned a little surprise, which consisted in presenting to them the most tragic hours of the revolution; Bonifacio having the great fortune of possessing a guillotine, they were going to make use of it to decapitate Marie Antoinette.

" 'At these words the people laughed and cheered, making a merry ovation to Angeluccia, who rose from her seat and declared that she would know how to die courageously as befitted a queen of France.

" 'A roll of drums suddenly beat in the streets, and we ran to the windows. A miserable cart drawn by a dilapidated horse stood there surrounded by guards and officers of the guillotine all wearing the bonnet of the revolution. A group of horrible knitting-women danced and sang in the streets, calling loudly for the death of the Austrian, dethroned queen of France. One might very easily have imagined himself back in the days of 1793!

" 'We had all taken part in this game without seeing any harm in it, and it wasn't until Angeluccia had stepped into the cart with her hands tied behind her back, and the procession had started to the sinister beat of the funeral drums, that more than one felt a shiver steal up his spine and realized that such a masquerade might well touch upon sacrilege.

" 'The whole scene was horribly effective. Night had fallen, and the flickering light of the torches gave a deathlike beauty to Angeluccia's face. And she played her part well. Holding herself proudly erect, she seemed to be braving the populace with her cold stare, and her face with its changeless severity of expression might well have been carved in stone.

" 'We reached Antonio's house, and there the gay laughs broke out anew. Antonio was already in the shop, where he had seated a chosen group of people who were to watch the mock execution. The mob was thickly packed in, and everyone was in a state of extreme excitement at finally seeing the famous guillotine at such close range. My master asked for silence and began by making a little speech on the good points of his instrument of death. He mentioned all the noble necks which, he claimed, had rested on the headboards, and he ended by exhibiting the real knife which he had bought at the same time.

" ' "I had the paper knife up there made so that you could see just how the thing worked," he explained; then, turning to Giuseppe, "Are you ready, Samson?"

" 'Samson replied that he was ready.

" ' "Bring forth the Austrian," Antonio ordered in a deep voice.

" 'Giuseppe and I placed Marie Antoinette-Angeluccia on the plank, and Antonio himself lowered the board that held her head in position.

" 'The laughter in the room suddenly ceased and an uneasy feeling swept over the crowd. The sight of the lovely body stretched out on the plank brought to the minds of even the hardened men present the memory of all the unfortunates who had really lain there to die. The joke had been carried too far. The merriment was revived for the moment, however, by the sight of Angeluccia's amused face as she looked here and there at the guests while her husband finished his lecture on the machine, showing the basket which received the body and that into which the head fell.

" 'But suddenly, as we watched Angeluccia an awful change came over her face. Wild terror was written there. Her eyes had widened horribly and her mouth half opened as though to let out a cry which stuck in her throat.

" 'Giuseppe was at the back and had seen nothing of this; but I, who was at the side, was struck with a nameless fear as the others had been. We were looking at the sight of one who really *knew* she was going to be decapitated. The laughter had died out and some of the people even shrank back as though struck by an invincible terror.

" 'As for me, I came closer, for I suddenly noticed that Angeluccia's horror-stricken eyes were staring at something in the bottom of the basket which was to receive the head. I looked into this basket, which Antonio had opened only a moment before, and I too read what Angeluccia had read—I too read the little placard fastened to the bottom:

> Pray to the Virgin Mary, Angeluccia, wife of Antonio, mistress of Giuseppe, for you are about to die!

" 'I uttered a hollow cry and turned like a madman to stop Giuseppe, who, at a motion from Antonio, had seized the rope. Alas! I was too late. The knife fell, and what followed was horrible, too horrible for words. The unfortunate woman let out a scream, a scream which ended in an abrupt gurgle—a scream which will echo in my ears to my dying day—and then her blood spouted out over the audience, which let out sickening cries and made a desperate fight for the door. I fainted.'

"Here Pietro Santo stopped and grew so pale at the memory of the awful scene that I feared he was going to be ill again. I restored some of his strength with a glass of old grappa.

" 'But in spite of all that,' I said to him, 'Angeluccia was not killed. I saw her myself and she certainly was alive.'

"He sighed and lifted his head.

" 'Are you sure she really is alive?' he asked. 'There isn't a soul in Bonifacio who passes her in the street without crossing himself. Seeing her never look to the right nor to the left, always holding her head rigid, they firmly believe that her head is held to her neck by some supernatural miracle. That is how the legend of the velvet collar grew. Besides, she looks like a ghost, and when she shakes hands with me, the touch of her icy skin makes me tremble.

" 'Yes, I know it's childish, but the whole affair was such a strange one that you must excuse the fantastic tales which our peasant folk have created. The truth of the matter is, I suppose, that Antonio planned his blow badly, that the machine was too old and did not work properly, and that Angeluccia's head was pushed too far through the opening, in such a way that the knife struck her at the rise of the shoulders. This is not the first time that such an accident has occurred with the guillotine. We have heard of cases where it took five tries to cut the head off. Giuseppe was the only one present when the doctor, whom he himself had fetched, saw her, and he says the wound was quite large. Everybody ran away at the time, and Antonio himself disappeared. You can see how all this helped form the legend that grew up overnight. Even those who were present at the time claim that they saw Angeluccia's head actually drop into the basket!

" 'Naturally, when Angeluccia reappeared some weeks later with her velvet ribbon, imaginations ran riot. And even when I look at her, there are times when I am hypnotized by her neck and wouldn't dare under any circumstances untie her velvet band!'

" 'And what happened to Antonio?'

" 'He is dead, or at least so they say. At any rate, his decease has been legally published since Giuseppe and Angeluccia are married. They found his body half eaten by crabs on the beach near the grottoes. The corpse was completely disfigured, but they found papers on it and the clothes were his. He probably ran away, believing Angeluccia dead, and threw himself over the cliff. He had prepared his revenge well, silently and cunningly as they do here, but I am still amazed at the skill with which he hid his feelings from the day that he first got an inkling of the truth of the relations between Angeluccia and her cousin.

" 'The police have the duplicate knife that he made so that it would look like Giuseppe's. It is in Ajaccio.' "

"Your story isn't bad," Captain Michel conceded generously to Gobert. "It has an element of horror in it."

"It's not finished yet," Gobert explained, asking for another few minutes of silence. "Let me go on and you will see that it really is horrible. I didn't know the end myself until some time later on a second voyage to Bonifacio, and it was good old Pietro Santo who related the concluding details to me.

"Imagine my extreme amazement when on asking him news of the woman with the velvet collar, he answered me in perfect seriousness: 'Captain, the legend was right after all. Angeluccia died on the day that the velvet collar was touched!'

" 'What!' I cried. 'But who undid the collar?'

" *'I did. And her head fell off!'*

"While I stared at Pietro Santo, wondering if he had lost his mind, he explained to me that after I had left Bonifacio a doubt had spread through the town as to the truth of Antonio s supposed death. It seemed that Ascoli, the mayor, was responsible for this and claimed to know what he was talking about. He was convinced that he had met Antonio one day when he was out hunting. The man had been almost naked, living like a wild beast, and when Ascoli tried to speak to him he ran away.

"It was during this time that the elections for mayor came up again and Giuseppe was Ascoli's rival for the post. During the entire campaign, Ascoli declared that Giuseppe was the accomplice of a bigamous woman and therefore unworthy of the position. His rage knew no bounds when he was defeated and he resolved to hunt Antonio out. It took him several months to do so, but he finally accomplished his purpose. Antonio, who for ten years had never spoken to a soul, learned that his wife was not dead as he had supposed but was living happily with Giuseppe in the very house in which he had been mayor and had believed himself loved by her.

" 'What happened then,' Pietro Santo went on in a hollow voice, 'is beyond conception, and would make even the demons in hell shrink in horror. Good Lord, if I live to be a thousand . . . But to cut it short, sir, the story can be told in a few words.

" 'One evening, a soft, clear evening like this, I was returning from an expedition to the grottoes, where I had escorted some friends, and was seated in the little boat taking us back to port when, in passing the cliffs, I heard a chant that made my blood run cold. It was the song which is always sung here by those who have some mortal affront to avenge. I lifted my head. A man stood like a statue on the edge of the rocks which served as a sort of pedestal to him. Although he was dressed in rags, he shouldered his gun proudly, and suddenly, as the last rays of the sun caught his face and brought it into full relief, I uttered one cry: "Antonio!"

" 'It was he! It was he! Oh, I was sure it was he! His fatal song and exalted air convinced me that he had not returned to these parts, after playing dead for ten years, without nursing some abominable purpose.

" 'Fortunately, I could reach town quicker by boat than he could on foot. There would be time to warn Giuseppe and Angeluccia. I threw myself on the oars and reached the dock in a few minutes. The first person I met was Giuseppe himself, who was on his way home from the town hall. I thanked heaven I had arrived in time and called out to him to hurry, that a terrible misfortune was about to fall, that I had seen Antonio—Antonio himself—alive, and that he was on his way to town.

" 'While questioning me he fell into step beside me and we both ran for his house at full speed and arrived there panting.

" ' "Angeluccia! Angeluccia!" we called, flinging open the door.

" 'No answer.

" ' "God help us if she's gone for a walk," Giuseppe groaned desperately.

" 'We went upstairs, still calling her, and he went into one room while I entered another. And it was there that I found her. She was seated by the window in a large armchair, her head resting against the cushion, and she seemed to be sleeping. As she was always extremely pale, the pallor of her beautiful face did not surprise me although it might have struck another.

" ' "Come," I cried to Giuseppe; "she is here."

" 'In the meantime I had come closer, surprised that she did not awake. I touched her . . . I touched the velvet band, which came loose in my hands, *and her head rolled off!*

" 'I fled with my heart pounding wildly from shock and fright, but on my way I slipped and fell in a horrible pool of blood, which I had not noticed on entering because of the shadows which darkened the room. I picked myself up with a yell and left the house madly. People ran from me in the streets as one runs from a wild beast.

" 'During the next few days I came near to going insane. Fortunately I completely recovered my senses, well enough, in fact, to be the present mayor of Bonifacio. As you probably understand by now, sir, I had seen Antonio *as he was returning from the deed!* It was easy enough to figure the whole thing out then. He had entered the house, found Angeluccia alone and killed her with a stab in the heart. Then, his mind haunted by what Ascoli had told him, he completed the work which he had commenced so clumsily ten years before. More certain of his Corsican dagger than of the mock-historical instrument which had failed him before, he decapitated her and, without shrinking from the atrocity of the deed, replaced her head on her shoulders and tied it in position with the velvet ribbon!

" 'And now,' concluded Pietro Santo, 'if you want news of Giuseppe you will have to go into the wilds for it. Two days after the murder, he disappeared into the mountains with a gun over his shoulder and Angeluccia's head, which he had embalmed himself, in a sack around his waist. Giuseppe, Ascoli and Antonio have never been seen since, but they have probably met in the approved fashion and killed each other in some hidden corner of the woods.

" 'That, sir, is the only way in which the custom of vendetta will be done away with in this country: when everybody is dead!' "

"Mistress Sary," a shivery voodoo fantasy, marks the sole *Weird Tales* appearance (May 1947), of WILLIAM TENN. (1920–   ), pseudonym of Professor Philip Klass, of The Pennsylvania State University. Tenn/Klass is best known for his incisively satirical science fiction, much of which may be found in the paperback volumes *The Human Angle, The Seven Sexes, Time in Advance, The Square Root of Man* and *The Wooden Star.*

MISTRESS SARY

by William Tenn

This evening, as I was about to enter my home, I saw two little girls bouncing a ball solemnly on the pavement to the rhythm of a very old little girls' chant. My lips must have gone gray as the sudden pressure of my set jaws numbed all feeling, blood pounded in my right temple; and I knew that whatever might happen, I couldn't take another step until they had finished.

> *"One, two, three alary—*
> *I spy Mistress Sary*
> *Sitting on a bumble-ary,*
> *Just like a little fairy!"*

As the girl finished the last smug note, I came to life. I unlocked the door of my house and locked it behind me hurriedly. I switched on the lights in the foyer, the kitchen, the library. And then, for long forgotten minutes, I paced the floor until my breathing slowed and the horrible memory cowered back into the crevice of the years.

That verse! I don't hate children—no matter what my friends say, I don't hate children—but why do they have to sing that stupid little song? Whenever I'm around . . . As if the unspeakably vicious creatures know what it does to me . . .

Sarietta Hawn came to live with Mrs. Clayton when her father died in the West Indies. Her mother had been Mrs. Clayton's only sister, and her father, a British colonial administrator, had no known relatives. It was only natural that the child should be sent across the Caribbean to join my landlady's establishment in Nanville. It was natural, too, that she should be enrolled in the Nanville Grade School where I taught arithmetic and science to the accompaniment of Miss Drury's English, history and geography.

"That Hawn child is impossible, unbelievable!" Miss Drury stormed into my classroom at the morning recess. "She's a freak, an impudent, ugly little freak!"

I waited for the echoes to die down in the empty classroom and considered Miss Drury's dowdy Victorian figure with amusement. Her heavily corseted bosom heaved and the thick skirts and petticoats slapped against her ankles as she walked feverishly in front of my desk. I leaned back and braced my arms against my head.

"Now you better be careful. I've been very busy for the past two weeks with a new term and all, and I haven't had a chance to take a good look at Sarietta. Mrs. Clayton doesn't have any children of her own, though, and since the girl arrived on Thursday the woman has been falling all over her with affection. She won't stand for punishing Sarietta like—well, like you did Joey Richards last week. Neither will the school board for that matter."

Miss Drury tossed her head angrily. "When you've been teaching as long as I have, young man, you'll learn that sparing the rod just does not work with stubborn brats like Joey Richards. He'll grow up to be the same kind of no-account drunk as his father if I don't give him a taste of birch whenever he gets uppity."

"All right. Just remember that several members of the school board are beginning to watch you very closely. Now what's this about Sarietta Hawn being a freak? She's an albino, as I recall; lack of pigmentation is due to a chance factor of heredity, not at all freakish, and is experienced by thousands of people who lead normal happy lives."

"Heredity!" A contemptuous sniff. "More of that new nonsense. She's a freak, I tell you, as nasty a little devil as Satan ever made. When I asked her to tell the class about her home in the West Indies, she stood up and squeaked, 'That is a book closed to fools and simpletons.' Well! If the recess bell hadn't rung at that moment, I tell you I'd have laced into her right then and there."

She glanced down at her watch pendant. "Recess almost over.

You'd better have the bell system checked, Mr. Flynn: I think it rang a minute too early this morning. And don't allow that Hawn child to give you any sass."

"None of the children ever do." I grinned as the door slammed behind her.

A moment later there was laughter and chatter as the room filled with eight-year-olds.

I began my lesson on long division with a covert glance at the last row. Sarietta Hawn sat stiffly there, her hands neatly clasped on the desk. Against the mahogany veneer of the classroom furniture, her long, ashen pigtails and absolutely white skin seemed to acquire a yellowish tinge. Her eyes were slightly yellow, too, great colorless irises under semi-transparent lids that never blinked while I looked at her.

She *was* an ugly child. Her mouth was far too generous for beauty; her ears stood out almost at right angles to her head and the long tip of her nose had an odd curve down and in to her upper lip. She wore a snow-white frock of severe cut that added illogical years to her thin body.

When I finished the arithmetic lesson, I walked up to the lonely little figure in the rear. "Wouldn't you like to sit a little closer to my desk?" I asked in as gentle a voice as I could. "You'd find it easier to see the blackboard."

She rose and dropped a swift curtsey. "I thank you very much, sir, but the sunlight at the front of the classroom hurts my eyes. There is always more comfort for me in darkness and in shade." The barest, awkward flash of a grateful smile.

I nodded, feeling uncomfortable at her formal, correct sentences.

During the science lesson, I felt her eyes upon me wherever I moved. I found myself fumbling at the equipment under that unwinking scrutiny, and the children, sensing the cause, began to whisper and crane their necks to the back of the room.

A case of mounted butterflies slid out of my hands. I stopped to pick it up. Suddenly a great gasp rippled over the room, coming simultaneously from thirty little throats.

"Look! She's doing it again!" I straightened.

Sarietta Hawn hadn't moved from her strange, stiff position. But her hair was a rich chestnut now; her eyes were blue; her cheeks and lips bore a delicate rose tint.

My fingers dug into the unyielding surface of my desk. Impossible! Yet could light and shade play such fantastic tricks? But—impossible!

Even as I gaped, unconscious of my pedagogical dignity, the child seemed to blush and a shadow over her straighten. I went back to cocoons and *Lepidoptera* with a quavering voice.

A moment later, I noticed that her face and hair were of purest white once more. I wasn't interested in explanations, however; neither was the class. The lesson was ruined.

"She did exactly the same thing in my class," Miss Drury exclaimed at lunch. "Exactly the same thing! Only it seemed to me that she was a dark brunette with velvet black hair and snapping black eyes. It was just after she'd called me a fool—the nerve of that snip! —and I was reaching for the birch rod, when she seemed to go all dark and swarthy. I'd have made her change to red though, I can tell you, if that bell hadn't rung a minute too early."

"Maybe," I said. "But with that sort of delicate coloring any change in lighting would play wild tricks with your vision. I'm not so sure now that I saw it after all. Sarietta Hawn is no chameleon."

The old teacher tightened her lips until they were a pale, pink line cutting across her wrinkled face. She shook her head and leaned across the crumb-bespattered table. "No chameleon. A witch. I know! And the Bible commands us to destroy witches, to burn them out of life."

My laugh echoed uncomfortably around the dirty school basement which was our lunchroom. "You can't believe that! An eight-year-old girl—"

"All the more reason to catch her before she grows up and does real harm. I tell you, Mr. Flynn, I know! One of my ancestors burned thirty witches in New England during the trials. My family has a special sense for the creatures. There can be no peace between us!"

The other children shared an awed agreement with Miss Drury. They began calling the albino child "Mistress Sary." Sarietta, on the other hand, seemed to relish the nickname. When Joey Richards tore into a group of children who were following her down the street and shouting the song, she stopped him.

"Leave them alone, Joseph," she warned him in her curious adult phraseology. "They are quite correct: I *am* just like a little fairy."

And Joey turned his freckled, puzzled face and unclenched his fists and walked slowly back to her side. He worshiped her. Possibly because the two of them were outcasts in that juvenile community, possibly because they were both orphans—his eternally soused father was slightly worse than no parent at all—they were always together. I'd find him squatting at her feet in the humid twilight when I came out on the boarding house porch for my nightcap of fresh air. She would pause in mid-sentence, one tiny forefinger still poised sharply. Both of them would sit in absolute silence until I left the porch.

Joey liked me a little. Thus I was one of the few privileged to hear of Mistress Sary's earlier life. I turned one evening when I was out for a stroll to see Joey trotting behind me. He had just left the porch.

"Gee," he sighed. "Stogolo sure taught Mistress Sary a lot. I wish that guy was around to take care of Old Dreary. He'd teach her all right, all right."

"Stogolo?"

"Sure. He was the witch-doctor who put the devil-birth curse on Sary's mother before Sary was born 'cause she had him put in jail. Then when Sary's mother died giving birth, Sary's father started drinking, she says, worse'n my pop. Only she found Stogolo and made friends with him. They mixed blood and swore peace on the grave of Sary's mother. And he taught her voodoo an' the devil-birth curse an' how to make love charms from hog liver an'—"

"I'm surprised at you, Joey," I interrupted. "Taking in that silly superstition! A boy who does as well as you in science! Mistress Sary —Sarietta grew up in a primitive community where people didn't know any better. But you do!"

He scuffed the weeds at the edge of the sidewalk with a swinging foot. "Yeah," he said in a low voice. "Yeah. I'm sorry I mentioned it, Mr. Flynn."

Then he was off, a lithe streak in white blouse and corduroy knickers, tearing along the sidewalk to his home. I regretted my interruption, then, since Joey was rarely confidential and Sarietta spoke only when spoken to, even with her aunt.

I've regretted it much, *much* more ever since.

The weather grew surprisingly warmer. "I declare," Miss Drury told me one morning, "I've never seen a winter like this in my life. Indian summers and heat waves are one thing, but to go on this way day after day without any sign of a break, Land sake's!"

"Scientists say the entire earth is developing a warmer climate. Of course, it's almost imperceptible right now, but the Gulf Stream—"

"The Gulf Stream," she ridiculed. She wore the same starched and heavy clothes as always and the heat was reducing her short temper to a blazing point. "The Gulf Stream! Ever since that Hawn brat came to live in Nanville the world's been turning turtle. My chalk is always breaking, my desk drawers get stuck, the erasers fall apart—the little witch is trying to put a spell on me!"

"Now look here." I stopped and faced her with my back to the school building. "This has gone far enough. If you do have to believe in witchcraft, keep it out of your relations with the children. They're here to absorb knowledge, not the hysterical imaginings of a—of a—"

"Of a sour old maid. Yes, go ahead, say it," she snarled. "I know you think it, Mr. Flynn. You fawn all over her so she leaves you be. But I know what I know and so does that evil little thing you call Sarietta Hawn. It's war between us, and the all-embracing battle between good and evil will never be over until one or the other of us is dead!" She turned in a spiral of skirts and swept up the path into the schoolhouse.

I began to fear for her sanity then. I had not yet learned to fear for mine.

That was the day my arithmetic class entered slowly, quietly as if a bubble of silence enveloped them. The moment the door shut behind the last pupil, the bubble broke and whispers splattered all over the room.

"Where's Sarietta Hawn?" I asked. "And Joey Richards," I amended, unable to find him either.

Louise Bell rose, her starched pink dress curving in front of her scrawny body. "They've been naughty. Miss Drury caught Joey cutting a lock of hair off her head and she started to whip him. Then Mistress Sary stood up and said she wasn't to touch him because he was under the pro-tec-tion. So Miss Drury sent us all out and now I bet she's going to whip them both. She's real mad!"

I started for the back door rapidly. Abruptly a scream began. Sarietta's voice. I tore down the corridor. The scream rose to a high treble, wavered for a second. Then stopped.

As I jolted open the door of Miss Drury's classroom, I was prepared for anything, including murder. I was not prepared for what I saw. I stood, my hand grasping the door knob, absorbing the tense tableau.

Joey Richards was backed against the blackboard, squeezing a long tendril of brownish hair in his sweaty right palm. Mistress Sary stood in front of Miss Drury, her head bent to expose a brutal red welt on the back of her chalky neck. And Miss Drury was looking stupidly at a fragment of birch in her hand; the rest of the rod lay in scattered pieces at her feet.

The children saw me and came to life. Mistress Sary straightened and with set lips moved toward the door. Joey Richards leaned forward. He rubbed the lock of hair against the back of the teacher's dress, she completely oblivious to him. When he joined the girl at the door, I saw that the hair glistened with the perspiration picked up from Miss Drury's blouse.

At a slight nod from Mistress Sary, the boy passed the lock of hair over to her. She placed it very carefully in the pocket of her frock.

Then, without a single word, they both skipped around me on their way to join the rest of the class.

Evidently they were unharmed, at least seriously.

I walked over to Miss Drury. She was trembling violently and talking to herself. She never removed her eyes from the fragment of birch.

"It just flew to pieces. Flew to pieces! I was—when it flew to pieces!"

Placing an arm about her waist, I guided the spinster to a chair. She sat down and continued mumbling.

"Once—I just struck her once. I was raising my arm for another blow—the birch was over my head—when it flew to pieces. Joey was off in a corner—he couldn't have done it—the birch just flew to pieces." She stared at the piece of wood in her hand and rocked her body back and forth slowly, like one mourning a great loss.

I had a class. I got her a glass of water, notified the janitor to take care of her and hurried back.

Somebody in a childish spirit of ridicule or meanness had scrawled a large verse across the blackboard in my room:

"One, two, three alary—
I spy Mistress Sary

> Sitting on a bumble-ary,
> Just like a little fairy!"

I turned angrily to the class. I noticed a change in seating arrangements. Joey Richards' desk was empty.

He had taken his place with Mistress Sary in the long, deep shadows at the back of the room.

To my breathless relief, Mistress Sary didn't mention the incident. As always she was silent at the supper table, her eyes fixed rigidly on her plate. She excused herself the moment the meal was over and slipped away. Mrs. Clayton was evidently too bustling and talkative to have heard of it. There would be no repercussions from that quarter.

After supper I walked over to the old-fashioned gabled house where Miss Drury lived with her relatives. Lakes of perspiration formed on my body and I found it all but impossible to concentrate. Every leaf on every tree hung motionless in the humid, breezeless night.

The old teacher was feeling much better. But she refused to drop the matter; to do, as I suggested, her best to reestablish amity. She rocked herself back and forth in great scoops of the colonial rocking-chair and shook her head violently.

"No, no, *no!* I won't make friends with that imp of darkness: sooner shake hands with Beelzebub himself. She hates me now worse than ever because—don't you see—I forced her to declare herself. I've made her expose her witchery. Now—now I must grapple with her and overthrow her and Him who is her mentor. I must think, I must—only it's so devilishly hot. So very hot! My mind—my mind doesn't seem to work right." She wiped her forehead with the heavy cashmere shawl.

As I strolled back, I fumbled unhappily for a solution. Something would break soon at this rate; then the school board would be down upon us with an investigation and the school would go to pot. I tried to go over the possibilities calmly but my clothes stuck to my body and breathing was almost drudgery.

Our porch was deserted. I saw movement in the garden and hurried over. Two shadows resolved into Mistress Sary and Joey Richards. They stared up as if waiting for me to declare myself.

She was squatting on the ground and holding a doll in her hands. A small wax doll with brownish hair planted in her head that was caught in a stern bun just like the bun Miss Drury affected. A stiff little doll with a dirty piece of muslin for a dress cut in the same long, severe pattern as all of Miss Drury's clothes. A carefully executed caricature in wax.

"Don't you think that's a bit silly," I managed to ask at last. "Miss Drury is sufficiently upset and sorry for what she did for you to play upon her superstitions in this horrible way. I'm sure if you try hard enough, we can all be friends."

They rose, Sarietta clutching the doll to her breast. "It is not silly, Mr. Flynn. That bad woman must be taught a lesson. A terrible lesson she will never forget. Excuse my abruptness, sir, but I have much work to do this night."

And then she was gone, a rustling patch of whiteness that slipped up the stairs and disappeared into the sleeping house.

I turned to the boy

"Joey, you're a pretty smart fellow. Man to man now—"

"Excuse me, Mr. Flynn." He started for the gate. "I—I got to go home." I heard the rhythmic pad of his sneakers on the sidewalk grow faint and dissolve in the distance. I had evidently lost his allegiance.

Sleep came hard that night. I tossed on entangling sheets, dozed, came awake and dozed again.

About midnight, I woke shuddering. I punched the pillow and was about to attempt unconsciousness once more when my ears caught a faint note of sound. I recognized it. That was what had reached into my dreams and tugged my eyes open to fear. I sat upright.

Sarietta's voice!

She was singing a song, a rapid song with unrecognizable words. Higher and higher up the scale it went and faster and faster as if there were some eerie deadline she had to meet. At last, when it seemed that she would shrill beyond the limits of human audibility, she paused. Then, on a note so high that my ear drums ached, came a drawn-out, flowing "Kurunoo O Stogoloooo!"

Silence.

Two hours later, I managed to fall asleep again.

The sun burning redly through my eyelids wakened me. I dressed, feeling oddly listless and apathetic. I wasn't hungry and, for the first morning of my life, went without breakfast.

The heat came up from the sidewalk and drenched my face and hands. My feet felt the burning concrete through the soles of my shoes. Even the shade of the school building was an unnoticeable relief.

Miss Drury's appetite was gone too. She left her carefully wrapped lettuce sandwiches untouched on the basement table. She supported her head on her thin hands and stared at me out of red-rimmed eyes.

"It's so hot!" she whispered. "I can hardly stand it. Why everyone feels so sorry for that Hawn brat, I can't understand. Just because I made her sit in the sunlight. I've been suffering from this heat a thousand times more than she."

"You . . . . made—Sarietta . . . sit—in—"

"Of course I did! She's no privileged character. Always in the back of the room where it's cool and comfortable. I made her change her desk so that she's right near the large window, where the sunlight streams in. And she feels it too, let me tell you. Only—ever since, I've been feeling worse. As if I'm falling apart. I didn't have a wink of sleep last night—those terrible, terrible dreams: great hands pulling and mauling me, knives pricking my face and my hands—"

"But the child can't stand sunlight! She's an albino."

"Albino, fiddlesticks! She's a witch. She'll be making wax dolls next. Joey Richards didn't try to cut my hair for a joke. He had orders to— Ooh!" She doubled in her chair. "Those cramps!"

I waited until the attack subsided and watched her sweaty, haggard face. "Funny that you should mention wax dolls. You have the girl so convinced that she's a witch that she's actually making them. Believe it or not, last night, after I left you—"

She had jumped to her feet and was rigid attention. One arm supporting her body against a steam pipe, she stood staring at me.

"She made a wax doll. Of me?"

"Well, you know how a child is. It was her idea of what you looked like. A little crude in design, but a good piece of workmanship. Personally, I think her talent merits encouragement."

Miss Drury hadn't heard me. "Cramps!" she mused. "And I thought they were cramps! She's been sticking pins into me! The little — I've got to— But I must be careful. Yet fast. Fast."

I got to my feet and tried to put my hand on her shoulder across the luncheon table. "Now pull yourself together. Surely this is going altogether too far."

She leaped away and stood near the stairs talking rapidly to herself. "I can't use a stick or a club—she controls them. But my hands —if I can get my hands on her and choke fast enough, she can't stop me. But I mustn't give her a chance," she almost sobbed, *"I mustn't give her a chance!"*

Then she had leaped up the stairs in a sudden, determined rush.

I swept the table out of my way and bolted after her.

Most of the children were eating their lunches along the long board fence at the end of the school yard. But they had stopped now and were watching something with frightened fascination. Sandwiches hung suspended in front of open mouths. I followed the direction of their stares.

Miss Drury was slipping along the side of the building like an upright skirted panther. She staggered now and then and held on to a wall. Some two feet in front of her, Sarietta Hawn and Joey Richards sat in the shade. They were looking intently at a wax doll in a muslin dress that had been set on the cement just outside the fringe of coolness. It lay on its back in the direct sunlight and, even at that distance, I could see it was melting.

"Hi," I shouted. "Miss Drury! Be sensible!" I ran for them.

At my cry, both children looked up startled. Miss Drury launched herself forward and fell, rather than leaped, on the little girl. Joey Richards grabbed the doll and rolled out of the way toward me. I tripped over him and hit the ground with a bone-breaking wallop. As I turned in mid-air, I caught a fast glimpse of Miss Drury's right hand flailing over the girl. Sarietta had huddled into a pathetic little bundle under the teacher's body.

I sat up facing Joey. Behind me the children were screaming as I had never heard them scream before.

Joey was squeezing the doll with both hands. As I watched, not daring to remove my eyes, the wax—already softened by the sunlight —lost its shape and came through the cracks in his tight freckled fingers. It dripped through the muslin dress and fell in blobs on the school yard cement.

Over and above the yells of the children, Miss Drury's voice rose to a mind-cracking scream and went on and on and on.

Joey looked over my shoulder with rolling eyes. But he kept on squeezing the doll and I kept my eyes on it desperately, prayerfully, while the screaming went on all about me and the immense sun pushed the perspiration steadily down my face. As the wax oozed through his fingers, he began singing suddenly in a breathless, hysterical cackle. Louder and louder grew his voice until it seemed to dominate the world.

> *"One, two, three alary—*
> *I spy Mistress Sary*
> *Sitting on a bumble-ary,*
> *Just like a little fairy!"*

And Miss Drury screamed and the children yelled and Joey sang, but I kept my eyes on the little wax doll. *I kept my eyes on the little wax doll drooling through the cracks of Joey Richard's strained little fingers. I kept my eyes on the doll . . .*

Most tales of Irish writer BRAM STOKER (1847–1912) that are included in fantasy anthologies come from his posthumous collection *Dracula's Guest and Other Stories; Weird Tales* reprinted six of that volume's nine stories. "The Judge's House" was included in *Weird Tales'* March 1935 issue. In addition to *Dracula,* Stoker wrote many other novels of mystery and terror, including *Jewel of the Seven Stars, The Lady of the Shroud* and *The Lair of the White Worm.*

THE JUDGE'S HOUSE

by Bram Stoker

When the time for his examination drew near, Malcolm Malcolmson made up his mind to go somewhere to read by himself. He feared the attractions of the seaside and also he feared completely rural isolation for of old he knew its charms, and so he determined to find some unpretentious little town where there would be nothing to distract him. He refrained from asking suggestions from any of his friends, for he argued that each would recommend some place of which he had knowledge, and where he had already acquaintances. As Malcolmson wished to avoid friends, he had no wish to encumber himself with the attention of friends' friends, and so he determined to look out for a place for himself. He packed a portmanteau with some clothes and all the books he required, and then took ticket for the first name on the local timetable which he did not know.

When at the end of three hours' journey he alighted at Benchurch, he felt satisfied that he had so far obliterated his tracks as to be sure of having a peaceful opportunity of pursuing his studies. He went straight to the one inn which the sleepy little place contained, and put up for the night. Benchurch was a market town, and once in three weeks was crowded to excess, but for the remainder of the twenty-one days it was as attractive as a desert. Malcolmson looked around the day after his arrival to try to find quarters more isolated than even so quiet an inn as "The Good Traveller" afforded. There was only one place which took his fancy, and it certainly satisfied his wildest ideas regarding quiet; in fact, quiet was not the proper word to apply to it—desolation was the only term conveying any suitable idea of its isolation. It was an old rambling heavy-built house of the Jacobean style with heavy gables and windows, unusually small, and set higher than was customary in such houses, and was surrounded with a high brick wall massively built. Indeed, on examination, it looked more like a fortified house than an ordinary dwelling. But all these things pleased Malcolmson. "Here," he thought, "is the very spot I have been looking for, and if I can only get opportunity of using it I shall be happy." His joy was increased when he realised beyond doubt that it was not at present inhabited.

From the post office he got the name of the agent, who was rarely surprised at the application to rent a part of the old house. Mr. Cranford, the local lawyer and agent, was a genial old gentleman, and frankly confessed his delight at anyone being willing to live in the house.

"To tell you the truth," said he, "I should be only too happy, on behalf of the owners, to let anyone have the house rent free for a term of years if only to accustom the people here to see it inhabited. It has been so long empty that some kind of absurd prejudice has grown up about it, and this can be best put down by its occupation— if only," he added with a sly glance at Malcolmson, "by a scholar like yourself, who wants its quiet for a time."

Malcolmson thought it needless to ask the agent about the "absurd prejudice"; he knew he would get more information, if he should require it, on that subject from other quarters. He paid his three months' rent, got a receipt, and the name of an old woman who would probably undertake to "do" for him, and came away with the keys in his pocket. He then went to the landlady of the inn, who was a cheerful and most kindly person, and asked her advice as to such stores and provisions as he would be likely to require. She threw up her hands in amazement when he told her where he was going to settle himself.

"Not in the Judge's House!" she said, and grew pale as she spoke. He explained the locality of the house, saying that he did not know its name. When he had finished she answered:

"Aye, sure enough—sure enough the very place! It is the Judge's House sure enough." He asked her to tell him about the place, why so called, and what there was against it. She told him that it was so called locally because it had been many years before—how long she could not say, as she was herself from another part of the country, but she thought it must have been a hundred years or more—the abode of a judge who was held in great terror on account of his harsh sentences and his hostility to prisoners at Assizes. As to what there was against the house itself she could not tell. She had often asked, but no one could inform her; but there was a general feeling that there was *something,* and for her own part she would not take all the money in Drinkwater's Bank and stay in the house an hour by herself. Then she apologised to Malcolmson for her disturbing talk.

"It is too bad of me, sir, and you—and a young gentleman, too—if you will pardon me saying it, going to live there all alone. If you were my boy—and you'll excuse me for saying it—you wouldn't sleep there a night, not if I had to go there myself and pull the big alarm bell that's on the roof!" The good creature was so manifestly in earnest, and was so kindly in her intentions, that Malcolmson, although amused, was touched. He told her kindly how much he appreciated her interest in him, and added:

"But my dear Mrs. Witham, indeed you need not be concerned about me! A man who is reading for the Mathematical Tripos has too much to think of to be disturbed by any of these mysterious 'somethings,' and his work is of too exact and prosaic a kind to allow of his having any corner in his mind for mysteries of any kind. Harmonical Progression, Permutations and Combinations, and Elliptic Functions have sufficient mysteries for me!" Mrs. Witham kindly undertook to see after his commissions, and he went himself to look for the old woman who had been recommended to him. When he returned to the Judge's House with her, after an interval of a couple of hours, he found Mrs. Witham herself waiting with several men and boys carrying parcels, and an upholsterer's man with a bed in a cart, for she said, though tables and chairs might be all very well, a bed that hadn't been aired for mayhap fifty years was not proper for young bones to lie on. She was evidently curious to see the inside of the house; and though manifestly so afraid of the 'somethings' that at the slightest sound she clutched on to Malcolmson, whom she never left for a moment, went over the whole place.

After his examination of the house, Malcolmson decided to take up his abode in the great dining-room, which was big enough to serve for all his requirements; and Mrs. Witham, with the aid of the charwoman, Mrs. Dempster, proceeded to arrange matters. When the hampers were brought in and unpacked, Malcolmson saw that with much kind forethought she had sent from her own kitchen sufficient provisions to last for a few days. Before going she expressed all sorts of kind wishes; and at the door turned and said:

"And perhaps, sir, as the room is big and draughty it might be well to have one of those big screens put round your bed at night—though, truth to tell, I would die myself if I were to be so shut in with all kinds of—of 'things,' that put their heads round the sides, or over the top, and look on me!" The image which she had called up was too much for her nerves, and she fled incontinently.

Mrs. Dempster sniffed in a superior manner as the landlady disappeared, and remarked that for her own part she wasn't afraid of all the bogies in the kingdom.

"I'll tell you what it is, sir," she said; "bogies is all kinds and sorts of things—except bogies! Rats and mice, and beetles; and creaky doors, and loose slates, and broken panes, and stiff drawer handles, that stay out when you pull them and then fall down in the middle of the night. Look at the wainscot of the room! It is old—hundreds of years old! Do you think there's no rats and beetles there! And do you imagine, sir, that you won't see none of them! Rats is bogies, I tell you, and bogies is rats; and don't you get to think anything else!"

"Mrs. Dempster," said Malcolmson gravely, making her a polite bow, "you know more than a Senior Wrangler! And let me say that as a mark of esteem for your indubitable soundness of head and heart, I shall, when I go, give you possession of this house, and let you stay here by yourself for the last two months of my tenancy, for four weeks will serve my purpose."

"Thank you kindly, sir!" she answered, "but I couldn't sleep away from home a night. I am in Greenhow's Charity, and if I slept a night away from my rooms I should lose all I have got to live on. The rules is very strict; and there's too many watching for a vacancy for me to run any risks in the matter. Only for that, sir, I'd gladly come here and attend on you altogether during your stay."

"My good woman," said Malcolmson hastily, "I have come here on purpose to obtain solitude; and believe me that I am grateful to the late Greenhow for having so organised his admirable charity—whatever it is—that I am perforce denied the opportunity of suffering from such a form of temptation! Saint Anthony himself could not be more rigid on the point!"

The old woman laughed harshly. "Ah, you young gentlemen," she said, "you don't fear for naught; and belike you'll get all the solitude you want here." She set to work with her cleaning; and by nightfall, when Malcolmson returned from his walk—he always had one of his books to study as he walked—he found the room swept and tidied, a fire burning in the old hearth, the lamp lit, and the table spread for supper with Mrs. Witham's excellent fare. "This is comfort, indeed," he said, as he rubbed his hands.

When he had finished his supper, and lifted the tray to the other end of the great oak dining table, he got out his books again, put fresh wood on the fire, trimmed his lamp, and set himself down to a spell of real hard work. He went on without pause till about eleven o'clock, when he knocked off for a bit to fix his fire and lamp and to make himself a cup of tea. He had always been a teadrinker and during his college life had sat late at work and had taken tea late. The rest was a great luxury to him and he enjoyed it with a sense of delicious, voluptuous ease. The renewed fire leaped and sparkled and threw quaint shadows through the great old room; and as he sipped his hot tea he revelled in the sense of isolation from his kind. Then it was that he began to notice for the first time what a noise the rats were making.

"Surely," he thought, "they cannot have been at it all the time I was reading. Had they been, I must have noticed it!" Presently, when the noise increased, he satisfied himself that it was really new. It was evident that at first the rats had been frightened at the presence of a stranger and the light of fire and lamp; but that as the time went on they had grown bolder and were now disporting themselves as was their wont.

How busy they were! and hark to the strange noises! Up and down behind the old wainscot over the ceiling and under the floor they raced and gnawed and scratched! Malcolmson smiled to himself as he recalled to mind the saying of Mrs. Dempster, "Bogies is rats, and rats is bogies!" The tea began to have its effect of intellectual and nervous stimulus, he saw with joy another long spell of work to be done before the night was past, and in the sense of security which it gave him, he allowed himself the luxury of a good look round the room. He took his lamp in one hand and went all around, wondering that so quaint and beautiful an old house had been so long neglected. The carving of the oak on the panels of the wainscot was fine, and on and round the doors and windows it was beautiful and of rare merit. There were some old pictures on the walls, but they were coated so thick with dust and dirt that he could not distinguish any detail of them though he held his lamp as high as he could over his head. Here and there as he went round he saw some crack or hole blocked for a moment by the face of a rat with its bright eyes glittering in the light, but in an instant it was gone and a squeak and a scamper followed.

The thing that most struck him, however, was the rope of the great alarm bell on the roof, which hung down in a corner of the room on the right-hand side of the fireplace. He pulled up close to the hearth a great high-backed carved oak chair and sat down to his last cup of tea. When this was done he made up the fire and went back to his work, sitting at the corner of the table, having the fire to his left. For a while the rats disturbed him somewhat with their perpetual scampering but he got accustomed to the noise as one does to the ticking of a clock or to the roar of moving water and he became so immersed in his work that everything in the world, except the problem which he was trying to solve, passed away from him.

He suddenly looked up, his problem was still unsolved, and there was in the air that sense of the hour before the dawn which is so dread to doubtful life. The noise of the rats had ceased. Indeed it seemed to him that it must have ceased but lately and that it was the sudden cessation which had disturbed him. The fire had fallen low, but still it threw out a deep red glow. As he looked he started in spite of his *sang froid*.

There on the great high-backed carved oak chair by the right side of the fireplace sat an enormous rat steadily glaring at him with baleful eyes. He made a motion to it as though to hunt it away but it did not stir. Then he made the motion of throwing something. Still it did not stir, but showed its great white teeth angrily, and its cruel eyes shone in the lamplight with an added vindictiveness.

Malcolmson felt amazed, and seizing the poker from the hearth ran at it to kill it. Before, however, he could strike it, the rat, with a squeak that sounded like the concentration of hate, jumped upon the floor, and, running up the rope of the alarm bell, disappeared in the darkness beyond the range of the green-shaded lamp. Instantly, strange to say, the noisy scampering of the rats in the wainscot began again.

By this time Malcolmson's mind was quite off the problem; and as a shrill cock-crow outside told him of the approach of morning, he went to bed and to sleep.

He slept so sound that he was not even waked by Mrs. Dempster coming in to make up his room. It was only when she had tidied up the place and got his breakfast ready and tapped on the screen which closed in his bed that he woke. He was a little tired still after his night's hard work, but a strong cup of tea soon freshened him up, and, taking his book, he went out for his morning walk, bringing with him a few sandwiches lest he should not care to return till dinner time. He found a quiet walk between high elms some way outside the town and here he spent the greater part of the day studying his Laplace. On his return he looked in to see Mrs. Witham and to thank her for her kindness. When she saw him coming through the diamond-paned bay-window of her sanctum she came out to meet him and asked him in. She looked at him searchingly and shook her head as she said:

"You must not overdo it, sir. You are paler this morning than you should be. Too late hours and too hard work on the brain isn't good for any man! But tell me, sir, how did you pass the night? Well, I hope? But, my heart! sir, I was glad when Mrs. Dempster told me this morning that you were all right and sleeping sound when she went in."

"Oh, I was all right," he answered, smiling, "the 'somethings' didn't worry me, as yet. Only the rats; and they had a circus, I tell you, all over the place. There was one wicked looking old devil that sat up on my own chair by the fire and wouldn't go till I took the poker to him, and then he ran up the rope of the alarm bell and got to somewhere up the wall or the ceiling—I couldn't see where, it was so dark."

"Mercy on us," said Mrs. Witham, "an old devil, and sitting on a chair by the fireside! Take care, sir! take care! There's many a true word spoken in jest."

"How do you mean? 'Pon my word I don't understand."

"An old devil! The old devil, perhaps. There! sir, you needn't laugh," for Malcolmson had broken into a hearty peal. "You young folks thinks it easy to laugh at things that makes older ones shudder.

Never mind, sir! never mind! Please God, you'll laugh all the time. It's what I wish you myself!" and the good lady beamed all over in sympathy with his enjoyment, her fears gone for a moment.

"Oh, forgive me!" said Malcolmson presently. "Don't think me rude; but the idea was too much for me—that the old devil himself was on the chair last night!" And at the thought he laughed again. Then he went home to dinner.

This evening the scampering of the rats began earlier; indeed it had been going on before his arrival, and only ceased whilst his presence by its freshness disturbed them. After dinner he sat by the fire for a while and had a smoke; and then, having cleared his table, began to work as before. Tonight the rats disturbed him more than they had done on the previous night. How they scampered up and down and under and over! How they squeaked and scratched and gnawed! How they, getting bolder by degrees, came to the mouths of their holes and to the chinks and cracks and crannies in the wainscoting till their eyes shone like tiny lamps as the firelight rose and fell. But to him, now doubtless accustomed to them, their eyes were not wicked; only their playfulness touched him. Sometimes the boldest of them made sallies out on the floor or along the mouldings of the wainscot. Now and again as they disturbed him Malcolmson made a sound to frighten them, smiting the table with his hand or giving a fierce "Hsh, hsh," so that they fled straightway to their holes.

And so the early part of the night wore on; and despite the noise Malcolmson got more and more immersed in his work.

All at once he stopped, as on the previous night, being overcome by a sudden sense of silence. There was not the faintest sound of gnaw, or scratch, or squeak. The silence was as of the grave. He remembered the odd occurrence of the previous night and instinctively he looked at the chair standing close by the fireside. And then a very odd sensation thrilled through him.

There, on the great high-backed carved oak chair beside the fireplace, sat the same enormous rat, steadily glaring at him with baleful eyes.

Instinctively he took the nearest thing to his hand, a book of logarithms, and flung it at it. The book was badly aimed and the rat did not stir, so again the poker performance of the previous night was repeated; and again the rat, being closely pursued, fled up the rope of the alarm bell. Strangely too, the departure of this rat was instantly followed by the renewal of the noise made by the general rat community. On this occasion, as on the previous one, Malcolmson could not see at what part of the room the rat disappeared, for the green shade of his lamp left the upper part of the room in darkness, and the fire had burned low.

On looking at his watch he found it was close on midnight; and, not sorry for the *divertissement,* he made up his fire and made himself his nightly pot of tea. He had got through a good spell of work and thought himself entitled to a cigarette, and so he sat on the great carved oak chair before the fire and enjoyed it. Whilst smoking he began to think that he would like to know where the rat disappeared to, for he had certain ideas for the morrow not entirely disconnected with a rat-trap. Accordingly he lit another lamp and placed it so that it would shine well into the right-hand corner of the wall by the fireplace. Then he got all the books he had with him and placed them handy to throw at the vermin. Finally he lifted the rope of the alarm bell and placed the end of it on the table, fixing the extreme end under the lamp. As he handled it he could not help noticing how pliable it was, especially for so strong a rope, and one not in use. "You could hang a man with it," he thought to himself. When his preparations were made he looked around, and said complacently:

"There now, my friend, I think we shall learn something of you this time!" He began his work again, and though as before somewhat disturbed at first by the noise of the rats, soon lost himself in his propositions and problems.

Again he was called to his immediate surroundings suddenly. This time it might not have been the sudden silence only which took his attention; there was a slight movement of the rope and the lamp moved. Without stirring, he looked to see if his pile of books was within range and then cast his eye along the rope. As he looked, he saw the great rat drop from the rope on the oak armchair and sit there glaring at him. He raised a book in his right hand, and taking careful aim, flung it at the rat. The latter, with a quick movement, sprang aside and dodged the missile. He then took another book, and a third, and flung them one after another at the rat, but each time unsuccessfully. At last, as he stood with a book poised in his hand to throw, the rat squeaked and seemed afraid. This made Malcolmson more than ever eager to strike, and the book flew and struck the rat a resounding blow. It gave a terrified squeak, and turning on its pursuer a look of terrible malevolence, ran up the chair-back and made a great jump to the rope of the alarm bell and ran up it like lightning. The lamp rocked under the sudden strain, but it was a heavy one and did not topple over. Malcolmson kept his eyes on the rat, and saw it by the light of the second lamp leap to a moulding of the wainscot and disappear through a hole in one of the great pictures which hung on the wall, obscured and invisible through its coating of dirt and dust.

"I shall look up my friend's habitation in the morning," said the student, as he went over to collect his books. "The third picture from the fireplace; I shall not forget." He picked up the books one by one, commenting on them as he lifted them. *"Conic Sections* he does not mind, nor *Cycloidal Oscillations,* nor the *Principia,* nor *Quarternions,* nor *Thermodynamics.* Now for the book that fetched him!" Malcolmson took it up and looked at it. As he did so he started, and a sudden pallor overspread his face. He looked round uneasily and shivered slightly, as he murmured to himself:

"The Bible my mother gave me! What an odd coincidence." He sat down to work again and the rats in the wainscot renewed their gambols. They did not disturb him, however; somehow their presence gave him a sense of companionship. But he could not attend to his work, and after striving to master the subject on which he was engaged gave it up in despair, and went to bed as the first streak of dawn stole in through the eastern window.

He slept heavily but uneasily, and dreamed much; and when Mrs. Dempster woke him late in the morning he seemed ill at ease and for a few minutes did not seem to realise exactly where he was. His first request rather surprised the servant.

"Mrs. Dempster, when I am out today I wish you would get the steps and dust or wash those pictures—specially that one the third from the fireplace—I want to see what they are."

Late in the afternoon, Malcolmson worked at his books in the shaded walk and the cheerfulness of the previous day came back to him as the day wore on and he found that his reading was progressing well. He had worked out to a satisfactory conclusion all the problems which had as yet baffled him, and it was in a state of jubilation that he paid a visit to Mrs. Witham at "The Good Traveller." He found a stranger in the cosy sitting-room with the landlady, who was introduced to him as Dr. Thornhill. She was not quite at ease, and this, combined with the Doctor's plunging at once into a series of questions, made Malcolmson come to the conclusion that his presence was not an accident, so without preliminary he said:

"Dr. Thornhill, I shall with pleasure answer you any question you may choose to ask me if you will answer me one question first."

The Doctor seemed surprised, but he smiled and answered at once. "Done! What is it?"

"Did Mrs. Witham ask you to come here and see me and advise me?"

Dr. Thornhill for a moment was taken aback, and Mrs. Witham got fiery red and turned away; but the Doctor was a frank and ready man, and he answered at once and openly:

"She did; but she didn't intend you to know it. I suppose it was my clumsy haste that made you suspect. She told me that she did not like the idea of your being in that house all by yourself, and that she thought you took too much strong tea. In fact, she wants me to advise you if possible to give up the tea and the very late hours. I was a keen student in my time, so I suppose I may take the liberty of a college man, and without offence, advise you not quite as a stranger."

Malcolmson with a bright smile held out his hand. "Shake! as they say in America," he said. "I must thank you for your kindness and Mrs. Witham too, and your kindness deserves a return on my part. I promise to take no more strong tea—no tea at all till you let me— and I shall go to bed tonight at one o'clock at latest. Will that do?"

"Capital," said the Doctor. "Now tell us all that you noticed in the old house." And so Malcolmson then and there told in minute detail all that had happened in the last two nights. He was interrupted every now and then by some exclamation from Mrs. Witham, till finally when he told of the episode of the Bible the landlady's pent-up emotions found vent in a shriek; and it was not till a stiff glass of brandy and water had been administered that she grew composed again. Dr. Thornhill listened with a face of growing gravity, and when the narrative was complete and Mrs. Witham had been restored he asked:

"The rat always went up the rope of the alarm bell?"

"Always."

"I suppose you know," said the Doctor after a pause, "what the rope is?"

"No!"

"It is," said the Doctor slowly, "the very rope which the hangman used for all the victims of the Judge's judicial rancour!" Here he was interrupted by another scream from Mrs. Witham and steps had to be taken for her recovery. Malcolmson, having looked at his watch and found that it was close to his dinner hour, had gone home before her complete recovery.

When Mrs. Witham was herself again she almost assailed the Doctor with angry questions as to what he meant by putting such horrible ideas into the poor young man's mind. "He has quite enough there already to upset him," she added. Dr. Thornhill replied:

"My dear madam, I had a distinct purpose in it! I wanted to draw his attention to the bell rope, and to fix it there. It may be that he is in a highly overwrought state and has been studying too much, although I am bound to say that he seems as sound and healthy a young man, mentally and bodily, as ever I saw—but then the rats— and that suggestion of the devil." The Doctor shook his head and went on: "I would have offered to go and stay the first night with him but that I felt sure it would have been a cause of offence. He may get in the night some strange fright of hallucination, and if he does I want him to pull that rope. All alone as he is it will give us warning and we may reach him in time to be of service. I shall be sitting up pretty late tonight and shall keep my ears open. Do not be alarmed if Benchurch gets a surprise before morning."

"Oh, Doctor, what do you mean? What do you mean?"

"I mean this; that possibly—nay, more probably—we shall hear the great alarm bell from the Judge's House tonight," and the Doctor made about as effective an exit as could be thought of.

When Malcolmson arrived home he found that it was a little after his usual time and Mrs. Dempster had gone away—the rules of Greenhow's Charity were not to be neglected. He was glad to see that the place was bright and tidy with a cheerful fire and a well-trimmed lamp. The evening was colder than might have been expected in April and a heavy wind was blowing with such rapidly increasing strength that there was every promise of a storm during the night. For a few minutes after his entrance, the noise of the rats ceased, but so soon as they became accustomed to his presence they began again. He was glad to hear them, for he felt once more the feeling of companionship in their noise, and his mind ran back to the strange fact that they only ceased to manifest themselves when that other—the great rat with the baleful eyes—came upon the scene. The reading-lamp only was lit and its green shade kept the ceiling and the upper part of the room in darkness, so that the cheerful light from the hearth spreading over the floor and shining on the white cloth laid over the end of the table was warm and cheery. Malcolmson sat down to his dinner with a good appetite and a buoyant spirit. After his dinner and a cigarette he sat steadily down to work, determined not to let anything disturb him, for he remembered his promise to the Doctor and made up his mind to make the best of the time at his disposal.

For an hour or so he worked all right, and then his thoughts began to wander from his books. The actual circumstances around him, the calls on his physical attention, and his nervous susceptibility were not to be denied. By this time the wind had become a gale, and the gale a storm. The old house, solid though it was, seemed to shake to its foundations, and the storm roared and raged through its many chimneys and its queer old gables, producing strange, unearthly sounds in the empty rooms and corridors. Even the great alarm bell on the roof must have felt the force of the wind, for the rope rose and fell slightly, as though the bell were moved a little from time to time, and the limber rope fell on the oak floor with a hard and hollow sound.

As Malcolmson listened to it he bethought himself of the Doctor's words, "It is the rope which the hangman used for the victims of the Judge's judicial rancour," and he went over to the corner of the fireplace and took it in his hand to look at it. There seemed a sort of deadly interest in it, and as he stood there, he lost himself for a moment in speculaton as to who these victims were, and the grim wish of the Judge to have such a ghastly relic ever under his eyes. As he stood there, the swaying of the bell on the roof still lifted the rope now and again; but presently there came a new sensation—a sort of tremor in the rope, as though something were moving along it.

Looking up instinctively Malcolmson saw the great rat coming slowly down towards him, glaring at him steadily. He dropped the rope and started back with a muttered curse, and the rat turning ran up the rope again and disappeared, and at the same instant Malcolmson became conscious that the noise of the rats, which had ceased for a while, began again.

All this set him thinking, and it occurred to him that he had not investigated the lair of the rat or looked at the pictures, as he had intended. He lit the other lamp without the shade, and, holding it up, went and stood opposite the third picture from the fireplace on the right-hand side where he had seen the rat disappear on the previous night.

At the first glance he started back so suddenly that he almost dropped the lamp, and a deadly pallor overspread his face. His knees shook, and heavy drops of sweat came on his forehead and he trembled like an aspen. But he was young and plucky and pulled himself together, and after the pause of a few seconds stepped forward again, raised the lamp and examined the picture which had been dusted and washed and now stood out clearly.

It was of a judge dressed in his robes of scarlet and ermine. His face was strong and merciless, evil, crafty, and vindictive, with a sensual mouth, hooked nose of ruddy colour, and shaped like the beak of a bird of prey. The rest of the face was of a cadaverous colour. The eyes were of peculiar brilliance and with a terribly malignant expression. As he looked at them, Malcolmson grew cold, for he saw there the very counterpart of the eyes of the great rat. The lamp almost fell from his hand; he saw the rat with its baleful eyes peering out through the hole in the corner of the picture, and noted the sudden cessation of the noise of the other rats. However, he pulled himself together, and went on with his examination of the picture.

The Judge was seated in a great high-backed carved oak chair, on the right-hand side of a great stone fireplace where, in the corner, a rope hung down from the ceiling, its end lying coiled on the floor. With a feeling of something like horror, Malcolmson recognised the scene of the room as it stood and gazed around him in an awestruck manner as though he expected to find some strange presence behind him. Then he looked over to the corner of the fireplace—and with a loud cry he let the lamp fall from his hand.

There in the Judge's armchair with the rope hanging behind sat the rat with the Judge's baleful eyes, now intensified and with a fiendish leer. Save for the howling of the storm without there was silence.

The fallen lamp recalled Malcolmson to himself. Fortunately it was of metal, and so the oil was not spilt. However, the practical need of attending to it settled at once his nervous apprehensions. When he had turned it out, he wiped his brow and thought for a moment.

"This will not do," he said to himself. "If I go on like this I shall become a crazy fool. This must stop! I promised the Doctor I would not take tea. Faith, he was pretty right! My nerves must have been getting into a queer state. Funny I did not notice it. I never felt better in my life. However, it is all right now, and I shall not be such a fool again."

Then he mixed himself a good stiff glass of brandy and water and resolutely sat down to his work.

It was nearly an hour when he looked up from his book, disturbed by the sudden stillness. Without, the wind howled and roared louder than ever and the rain drove in sheets against the windows, beating like hail on the glass; but within there was no sound whatever save the echo of the wind as it roared in the great chimney and now and then a hiss as a few raindrops found their way down the chimney in a lull of the storm. The fire had fallen low and had ceased to flame, though it threw out a red glow. Malcolmson listened attentively, and presently heard a thin, squeaking noise, very faint. It came from the corner of the room where the rope hung down, and he thought it was the creaking of the rope on the floor as the swaying of the bell raised and lowered it. Looking up, however, he saw in the dim light the great rat clinging to the rope and gnawing it. The rope was already nearly gnawed through—he could see the lighter colour where the strands were laid bare. As he looked the job was completed, and the severed end of the rope fell clattering on the oaken floor, whilst for an instant the great rat remained like a knob or tassel at the end of the rope, which now began to sway to and fro. Malcolmson felt for a moment another pang of terror as he thought that now the possibility of calling the outer world to his assistance was cut off, but an intense anger took its place, and seizing the book he was reading he hurled it at the rat. The blow was well aimed, but before the missile could reach it the rat dropped off and struck the floor with a soft thud. Malcolmson instantly rushed over towards it, but it darted away and disappeared in the darkness of the shadows of the room. Malcolmson felt that his work was over for the night, and determined then and there to vary the monotony of the proceedings by a hunt for the rat and took off the green shade of the lamp so as to insure a wider spreading light. As he did so, the gloom of the upper part of the room was relieved, and in the new flood of light, great by comparison with the previous darkness, the pictures on the wall stood out boldly. From where he stood, Malcolmson saw right opposite to him the third picture on the wall from the right of the fireplace. He rubbed his eyes in surprise, and then a great fear began to come upon him.

In the centre of the picture was a great irregular patch of brown canvas, as fresh as when it was stretched on the frame. The background was as before, with chair and chimney-corner and rope, but the figure of the Judge had disappeared.

Malcolmson, almost in a chill of horror, turned slowly round, and then he began to shake and tremble like a man in a palsy. His strength seemed to have left him, and he was incapable of action or movement, hardly even of thought. He could only see and hear.

There, on the great high-backed carved oak chair, sat the Judge in his robes of scarlet and ermine, with his baleful eyes glaring vindictively, and a smile of triumph on the resolute, cruel mouth, as he lifted with his hands a *black cap*. Malcolmson felt as if the blood were running from his heart, as one does in moments of prolonged suspense. There was a singing in his ears. Without, he could hear the roar and howl of the tempest, and through it, swept on the storm, came the striking of midnight by the great chimes in the market place. He stood for a space of time that seemed to him endless, still as a statue and with wide-open, horror-struck eyes, breathless. As the clock struck, so the smile of triumph on the Judge's face intensified, and at the last stroke of midnight he placed the black cap on his head.

Slowly and deliberately the Judge rose from his chair and picked up the piece of rope of the alarm bell which lay on the floor, drew it through his hands as if he enjoyed its touch, and then deliberately began to knot one end of it, fashioning it into a noose. This he tightened and tested with his foot, pulling hard at it till he was satisfied and then making a running noose of it, which he held in his hand. Then he began to move along the table on the opposite side to Malcolmson, keeping his eyes on him until he had passed him, when with a quick movement he stood in front of the door. Malcolmson then began to feel that he was trapped, and tried to think of what he should do. There was some fascination in the Judge's eyes, which he never took off him, and he had, perforce, to look. He saw the Judge approach—still keeping between him and the door—and raise the noose and throw it towards him as if to entangle him. With a great effort he made a quick movement to one side, and saw the rope fall beside him, and heard it strike the oaken floor. Again the Judge raised the noose and tried to ensnare him, ever keeping his baleful eyes fixed on him, and each time by a mighty effort the student just managed to evade it. So this went on for many times, the Judge seeming never discouraged nor discomposed at failure, but playing as a cat does with a mouse. At last in despair, which had reached its climax, Malcolmson cast a quick glance round him. The lamp seemed to have blazed up, and there was a fairly good light in the room. At the many rat-holes and in the chinks and crannies of the wainscot he saw the rats' eyes; and this aspect, that was purely physical, gave him a gleam of comfort. He looked around and saw that the rope of the great alarm bell was laden with rats. Every inch of it was covered with them, and more and more were pouring through the small circular hole in the ceiling whence it emerged, so that with their weight the bell was beginning to sway.

Hark! it swayed till the clapper touched the bell. The sound was but a tiny one, but the bell was only beginning to sway, and it would increase.

At the sound the Judge, who had been keeping his eyes fixed on Malcolmson, looked up, and a scowl of diabolical anger overspread his face. His eyes fairly glowed like hot coals and he stamped his foot with a sound that seemed to make the house shake. A dreadful peal of thunder broke overhead as he raised the rope again, whilst the rats kept running up and down the rope as though working against time. This time, instead of throwing it, he drew close to his victim and held open the noose as he approached. As he came closer there seemed something paralysing in his very presence and Malcolmson stood rigid as a corpse. He felt the Judge's icy fingers touch his throat as he adjusted the rope. The noose tightened—tightened. Then the Judge, taking the rigid form of the student in his arms, carried him over and placed him standing in the oak chair, and stepping up beside him, put his hand up and caught the end of the swaying rope of the alarm bell. As he raised his hand the rats fled squeaking, and disappeared through the hole in the ceiling. Taking the end of the noose which was round Malcolmson's neck he tied it to the hanging bell-rope and then descending, pulled away the chair.

When the alarm bell of the Judge's House began to sound, a crowd soon assembled. Lights and torches of various kinds appeared and soon a silent crowd was hurrying to the spot. They knocked loudly at the door, but there was no reply. Then they burst in the door and poured into the great dining-room, the Doctor at the head.

There at the end of the rope of the great alarm bell hung the body of the student, and on the face of the Judge in the picture was a malignant smile.

VAL LEWTON (1904–1951) born Vladimir Ivan Leventon, was a native of Yalta who distinguished himself in America as the low-budget producer of some of the finest horror films of the 1940s, including *Bedlam, Isle of the Dead, The Body Snatcher* (whose final scene is surely one of the fantasy cinema's most harrowing episodes), *The Leopard Man, I Walked with a Zombie* and the classic *The Cat People* and its sequel, *Curse of the Cat People.* Lewton was an author before he was a producer, but "The Bagheeta" was the only story he sold to *Weird Tales* (July 1930). Thematically, it is certainly allied to his lycanthropic movies, but ultimately it bears a curious connection to certain stories that Farnsworth Wright occasionally featured in *Weird Tales.* (For further comment, see Notes on Flaubert's "The Legend of St. Julian the Hospitaller" on page 574.)

THE BAGHEETA

by Val Lewton

The church bells of Ghizikhan pealed out slow, lazy music to mark the end of the morning prayer. Kolya turned his head idly to look at the village. From his vantage-point in the open porch of the armorer's shop where he was engaged in polishing the swords and other weapons which his uncle had chosen to place on display that day, Kolya could see the entire length of Ghizikhan's single street. It was early and the long shadows of the Caucasian peaks fell like dark, irregular bars across the valley. Only through the gap between Mount Elbruz and the volcanic peak of Silibal came sunlight, falling squarely upon the village. In this pleasant light, the folk of Ghizikhan went about their early morning tasks. At the well, the maidens jostled one another, giggling as they drew up water. Kolya's eyes, although he had just grown to manhood, avoided this group, but turned with interest upon the shepherds who were having a last, long draft at the inn door before going on to relieve the men who had guarded the flocks through the night hours.

It was a sight that Kolya could see any time, and, yawning, he turned back to the task in hand, the scouring of a new sword blade with water and white sand. Diligently he worked the scouring-cloth back and forth, his long, fair hair falling down over his forehead as he bent to the task. Of a sudden a cry went up at the other end of the village, and Kolya's head was upflung as if by magic.

Two men were running toward the inn. Between them they carried a shapeless bundle. Kolya could only catch the colors of the object—red and white. As they ran they cried out: "A Bagheeta! A Bagheeta! We have seen her!"

Kolya identified the burden which they carried between them. It was a sheep, torn to death by a panther. Dropping the scouring-cloth, Kolya ran to where a knot of men had gathered about the two shepherds. He forced his way toward the center of the crowd until he could hear the words of one of the men: "——black as wood from a fire, bigger than any natural leopard—a monster, I tell you! Varla and I came upon her at her meal. With my own eyes I saw her—you can measure for yourselves —from here to here," the shepherd indicated a huge, bloody rent in the flank of the slain sheep, "she took one mouthful. A real Bagheeta—I swear it!"

The men around him crowded closer to see the evidence. It was true; an enormous mouth had made those long gashes in the carcass.

The *hetman* of Ghizikhan, pulling at his virgin beard, questioned the shepherd: "Fool, what did you do? Did you let the beast escape so that it may enjoy such a feast as this from our table whenever he wills it?"

The shepherd protested: "It was a real Bagheeta, I tell you, Hetman! What could we do? Varla shot at her, but you know that no bullet can harm a Bagheeta—not even a silver bullet. She just snarled at us and walked away."

"Walked away?" the hetman's tones were dubious.

"Yes, Hetman, I have said it so: walked away, just turned and walked away. She knew we couldn't hurt her. Both Varla and I are married men, you know!"

"Aye, Hetman, I believe them." It was Davil who spoke, Davil the old minstrel, who in his youth had killed a Bagheeta. "This Bagheeta must be the same leopard we hunted all these last three days. If it had been a real leopard, its skin would have been drying on the walls of your house by now, Hetman, but only a pure youth who can resist her blandishments can kill a Bagheeta. You must select a pure youth to hunt down this were-beast—a real St. Vladimir, pure of heart as a virgin."

"Nonsense! These are old wives' tales, falser than your rimes, Davil," Rifkhas the huntsman, whose very garments smelled always of the forest, spoke out heatedly. "What is this beast, you say—a black leopard? To the east, beyond Elbruz, they are as common as black crows are in our land! It was the hard winter and the heavy snows which have driven them here. One good shot from my old rifle and your Bagheeta will be deader than the sheep he's killed. Do not forget, Davil, that I too have killed one of these black kittens, and with a rifle and a lead ball—I saw no signs of magic or sorcery.

"I have grown sick of these old lies which send our young men frightened into the forest. Believe me, it is safer in the forest than before the coffeepots in the *khan*. King God has made man lord above the beasts and they all fear him."

But by now the women of Ghizikhan had swarmed to the scene of the excitement, and their loud outcries drowned out the old huntsman's logic. Shrill voices explained the myth to those too young to know the significance of a black leopard among the spotted ones.

It is a were-beast, they said, half leopard and half woman, the reincarnation of a virgin who has died from wrongs inflicted upon her by sinful men, and who comes again to the world so that she may prey upon the flocks of the sinful. Only a pure youth, one who has lain clean and alone, can hope to slay the mystic beast. He must ride out against the Bagheeta with only a sword at his side and a prayer to King God upon his lips. The Bagheeta, so the women said, will change at his coming into a beautiful woman and attempt to coerce him into an embrace. If she is successful, if the youth kisses her, his life is forfeited. Changing again into a black leopard, the Bagheeta will tear him limb from limb. But, if he remain steadfast in his purity, then surely will he slay the beast.

Kolya listened eagerly. It was not the first time he had heard the legend. When they had done talking, he looked again at the dead sheep. The bloody, mangled flesh, bearing clear marks of the enormous fangs which had rent it so hideously, sent little shivers up his spine. He had often heard Davil sing his song of the slaying of the Bagheeta, and standing in the warm sunlight, Kolya grew cold thinking on the dark forest and the dark beast, only its golden eyes visible in the night. He could see vividly the heavy, crushing paws, the curving claws, the red and rending mouth.

Suddenly the hetman's voice rang clearly above the chatter of the women: "Who among the *Jighitti*— the good, brave horsemen of our village—is pure of heart and free of sin? Let him stand forward, sword in his right hand!"

A silence fell upon the villagers, and all eyes were turned, first to the face of one youth and then to the face of another. All upon whom the eyes of the villagers fell turned blood-red and averted their faces.

The hetman grew impatient. He began to call the young men by name: "Rustumsal? What! And you but sixteen! Fie upon the women of Ghizikhan! Valodja? Shame! Badyr? Shamyl? Vanar?"

All shook their heads.

Then Kolya, his heart pounding with excitement, stepped forward. In his right hand he held his sword, a silent declaration of his intention. Behind him he could hear his mother shrilling: "Hetman, he is too young! It is but yesterday that he rode in the *Jigitovka*. Only two days has he worked as a man among men."

The hetman paid no attention to her.

Bending forward so that he might look into Kolya's eyes, he asked: "How old are you?"

Kolya answered sturdily: "Sixteen."

"And you have never laid yourself down beside a woman, nor lusted after her with your eyes?"

"No," said Kolya.

The hetman doffed his karakul *chapka* and with it still clasped in his hand, pointed to Kolya. A shout went up. Kolya, nephew of the armorer, had been chosen to hunt down the Bagheeta.

An hour later the men of the village, accoutered as if for war or holiday, rode out from Ghizikhan in a long cavalcade. Kolya, dressed in his best *kaftan* of Burgundy-colored silk, a sleek black chapka set jauntily on his head, and wreaths of flowers about his horse's neck, rode at their head. At his side hung the best sword from his uncle's shop. The Silver Maid, his uncle called it, and for no price would he sell it, neither to prince nor commoner, saying always: "Only by the grace of King God was I able to forge such a sword. One can not sell God's gifts for gold."

Beside Kolya rode the hetman, and behind them the two old enemies, Davil the minstrel and Rifkhas the huntsman, wrangling as they rode.

"I have lived in the woods my whole life," the huntsman was saying, "and not one, but many of these Bagheetas have I seen killed with bullets. The Russians pay well for their black skins."

Davil silenced his arguments with a burst of song:

> *"I ride beneath the silver stars,*
> *   All in my war array;*
> *I ride beneath the silver stars*
> *   To break Bagheeta's sway.*

> *"The stars are bright and bright am I*
> *   Clad in my war array.*
> *The land about does gloomy lie,*
> *   And black Bagheeta's way.*

> *"I ride with flowers in my hair*
> *   And grim sword at my side,*
> *Among the youths I am most fair*
> *   And in war foremost ride.*

> *"To me unknown a maiden's wiles:*
> *   For see, my heart is pure.*
> *God looks upon my head and smiles:*
> *   For see, my heart is pure."*

"Blah!" said Rifkhas, spurring his horse a bit so as to catch up with Kolya and leave Davil to ride by himself, singing the song which he had composed many years ago in celebration of his own victory over a Bagheeta.

Kolya heard the song behind him go on and on as they rode forward to where the shepherds had seen the leopard.

> *"Unfeared by me the Deva's call,*
> *   The war's grim chance of death,*
> *But here soft footsteps thud and fall,*
> *   And quickly comes my breath."*

The lad shuddered. He could well imagine the sinuous body of the beast, black as the night it walked through, creeping through the tree trunks in the forest. How dark the forest would be after the moon had gone down! Kolya's horse quivered. It was as if his master's agitation had been conveyed to her too, and that she also knew of the trial ahead of them.

Davil's song went on:

> "Of death alone I have no fear,
>   Nor yet of sword hurt deep,
> But now a silent move I hear,
>   From darkness gold eyes peep.
>
> "My brave horse trembles in his fear,
>   And tighter grows my rein.
> Somewhere from night two gold eyes peer,
>   And mark his frightened pain."

A restive horse in the darkness of the midnight forest; a silent and unseen foe, waiting to leap from ambush, to strike one down with huge paws, to rend one with enormous teeth; Kolya could almost smell the fetid, hot breath which was to issue from the gaping jaws. Yet all this must be true; had not the minstrel killed just such a beast in his youth? Was not this the very song inspired by the feat? Kolya gazed nervously into the green depths of the forest, crowding in upon the trail. Somewhere in its fastnesses was the Bagheeta, crouched, waiting, confident in its supernatural powers.

Rifkhas' voice was speaking to his ear: "I'm sorry that they're not letting you carry a gun, lad. You could wait for the Bagheeta by the water hole. He must drink after his kill. Didst ever note how the cats go to the water butt when they have eaten a rat in the granary? These leopards, black or spotted, are but big cats; they too must drink after they eat. You could shoot the beast easily if the light were good. But these fools, full of old wives' tales, they make it difficult for you. When the good King God has given us gunpowder, what sense is there to send you into the forest with but a sword in your hand? Likewise, when God gives mankind a full moon to hunt by, why in the name of the Seven Peris must they make you wait until the moon has set before you go a-hunting? Why? Because old women like

Davil are frightened of the dark, and they would have you be frightened also. Have no fear! There is no beast nor were-beast that will not run from a man. Have no fear, Kolya. I, who have been a huntsman for thirty years, tell you that."

From behind them came the voice of the other old man. He had changed his tune. It was no longer slow, measured and fearsome, the words filled with dread. It came forth exultantly, as if he had just conquered fear. He sang:

> "But now I tremble once again,
>   For here a fair maid comes.
> I tremble with no thought of pain
>   For here a fair maid comes.

> "Her lips are scarlet pomegranates,
>   Her cheeks like Kavkas' snows,
> Her eyes are tense as one who waits
>   For sounds of ringing blows.

> "Her speech is all of lovely things
>   That are in other climes,
> Of butterflies with silver wings
>   And bells with silken chimes.

> "She lifteth up her laughing mouth
>   And I bend down my own."

Davil's voice fell. Deep and fearsome it pounded against Kolya's ears:

> "What is this chill wind from the south?
>   This noise of bone on bone?"

Kolya's heart skipped a beat. What if he were to have no warning? What if he were to be so entranced by the Bagheeta's charms that he were to kiss her?

Davil's chant answered the question for him:

> "I fear, I fear and gaze at her
>   Who looks with such a mien;

I fear, I fear and strain from her
Whose yellow eyes are keen.

"Out sword: Out sword! Bagheeta's eyes
Look now into your own.
Out sword! Out sword! He only dies
Who must the kiss atone.

"With tooth and claw Bagheeta flies
Straight at my armored throat,
And now so close his yellow eyes
That I have falsely smote——"

Kolya's imagination conjured up the gleaming eyes, the hot breath of the beast, its claws sinking into his shoulder. He could feel the sense of helplessness as he was torn from the saddle—the weight of the giant cat upon his body.

Rifkhas' cranky voice, speaking in the calming tones of prose, allayed his fears.

"I'd like to have your chance at this beastie, Kolya," Rifkhas was saying. "One black pelt like that would supply me with wine and caresses for an entire year—aye, even an old fellow like myself could buy the soft arms of women with the price of such a pelt. It's a rare chance you have. If only these fools would let you go on foot. You can't hunt leopards on horseback. Why, the sound of your horse's hoofs will echo for miles about. Get off your horse and creep to the water hole, being careful to see that he doesn't get the wind of you; that's the only way you'll get close enough to Master Bagheeta to kill him with a sword.

"Mind what I tell you, Kolya, and forget all these old women who'd tell you that a leopard can change into a woman just because it happens to be black instead of spotted. Mind what I tell you, Kolya, and with the money you get for the pelt you can set up an armorer's shop of your own."

Behind him, Kolya could hear Davil still singing, describing his own encounter with the dread and mystic beast long, long ago. The fierce half-joy of the conflict and the anguish of those long-healed wounds were in the voice of the old minstrel as he sang:

> *"Deep, deep I strike, again, again;*
> *Deep do his talons rend.*
> *I am oblivious of my pain*
> *And fast my blows descend.*
>
> *"With horrid shriek he falls aback,*
> *And now my sword is free.*
> *Again he leapeth to attack,*
> *But now my sword is free.*
>
> *"Halfway in air the leaping beast,*
> *The cleaving sword, have met;*
> *Now may the herdsmen joyful feast,*
> *For sword and beast have met!"*

"Stop!" The hetman's command cut short both Davil's song and the movement of the cavalcade. The men grouped themselves about the leader as he explained to them how they could best aid Kolya in his adventure. They had arrived at the copse where the Bagheeta had been seen, he told them, and they would now surround the place in such a way as to turn back the Bagheeta if he, sensing Kolya's innocence, were to attempt an escape. None of the men, he warned them, must dare to engage the creature. This was safe only for Kolya, who was pure of heart.

With the point of his spear the hetman drew a rough map in the sand showing the copse and the hollow between two steep cliffs in which it was situated. To each man he designated a certain post at which to watch. He told them that if the Bagheeta approached their positions they must raise up their swords with the crosslike hilts uppermost and loudly sing the hymn of Saint Ivan. Thus and thus only could they turn the were-beast back.

At a word from their leader the men galloped off, shouting, to their positions. Only Davil and Rifkhas remained with Kolya and the hetman to wait for the coming of night and the dark of the moon.

It was still late afternoon and, although a pale slice of luminous white moon already rode high in the heavens—sure indication that it would set early—Kolya and the men with him still had a long while to wait before he could ride forth in search of the Bagheeta. Davil was all for passing the time in prayer and the singing of songs, but Rifkhas brought forth an earthen jug of wine and a pack of greasy playing-cards. Soon the three grown men were hard at it, playing one game of cards after another.

Kolya was left to his own devices. He fussed with his horse, watering it at the brook and removing the bridle so that it could graze at will. This took only a short time, and then Kolya was again left with nothing to occupy him but his own fears of the night's trial.

He turned his attention to the copse before him. It was dark with the shadows of the larch and fir trees growing on either side of the brook. This stream had, in the course of the centuries, cut itself a hard bed through the solid rock. Its either bank was precipitous. No animal, Kolya thought to himself, could drink from the stream unless somewhere there was a cleft in the rocky banks. If he were to follow Rifkhas' advice he would have to find such a spot where the leopard could come to drink and there await the Bagheeta's coming.

"But there will be little need to find the Bagheeta," he reasoned. "She will come creeping upon me and, when she divines that I am pure of heart and have no knowledge of women, then she will turn herself into a maiden, and so lure me to my death."

On whispering feet, darkness came stealing into the little glen in which they had halted. The beech leaves, quivering in the evening wind, lisped a plaintive song of nervous fear to Kolya's heart. The same breeze, straying through the pine boughs, struck deep soughing chords. Then, as the sun finally set, plunging the land into intense darkness, the evening noises quieted. Robbed of light by which to continue their card game, the three older men sat quietly. Even the horses ceased their trampling and champing in the place where they had been tethered. A cloud was over the slim, silver moon, shaped ominously, Kolya imagined, like a Persian dagger.

Some current of the upper air swept the cloud from before the moon's face. The hetman, looking up, remarked that the moon would set in another hour.

Kolya walked to where he had tied his horse. He saddled the animal carefully, glad to crowd fear out of his mind with activity. Putting his knee sharply against his mount's belly, Kolya jerked the girth tight. Then he bridled the horse, feeling with anxious fingers in the darkness to see that the check strap was properly set. When he had done all this, he led the beast to where the hetman, Davil and

Rifkhas sat about a tiny fire that they had kindled, more for light than for warmth.

The hetman lectured him: "Pray earnestly, Kolya. Ask forgiveness for your sins. This is a creature of deep sin that you go to fight. Only through sin may it vanquish you. It will tempt you in many ways, but you must resist evil. The sign of the cross and the prayers of our people are most potent against magic. Keep your lips clean from its lips, and your heart clean from the evil it will try to teach you. Only in this way may you hope for victory."

Davil spoke to him: "Have no fear, Kolya. If your heart is pure, and you resist the blandishments of the Bagheeta—beautiful as she may become—then surely King God will send strength to your sword. I can see you now, riding back to us in the morning with the slain were-beast over your saddle bow——"

Rifkhas cut him short: "I can see you too, Kolya! But I can see what a fool you will look if you follow the advice of this impotent old rimester. There is but one way to hunt—whether you hunt leopards or were-leopards, it makes no difference—and that way is to go stealthily—and not on horseback with a clanking sword at your side. Do what I have told you to do and you will not fail to find the Bagheeta: go to the water hole and wait—else you will not see hair nor hide of the creature all the long night through."

The crescent moon edged down below the horizon.

"It is time, Kolya," said the hetman. "May King God bless you, pure of heart."

Kolya mounted, and wheeling his horse, rode toward the forest at a foot pace.

"Mind what I have told you," Rifkhas shouted after him.

As the first slender saplings of the wood brushed against him, Kolya could hear Davil singing:

> "I ride beneath the silver stars,
>   All in my war array.
> I ride beneath the silver stars
>   To break Bagheeta's sway."

His sword swung reassuringly at Kolya's side. From behind him the second verse of Davil's song came floating to his ears.

"The land about does gloomy lie,
And black Bagheeta's way."

The distance muffled the other words of Davil's ballad. But Kolya could remember them. They sang through his mind as the wood grew denser and denser about him. He had often heard them before. Some verses brought him courage. He recalled:

"I ride with flowers in my hair,
And grim sword at my side,
Among the youths I am most fair,
And in war foremost ride.

"To me unknown a maiden's wiles:
For see; my heart is pure.
God looks upon my head and smiles:
For see; my heart is pure."

Other verses brought him dread:

"King God, look on my woeful plight:
Pity and give me aid.
Hang out the moon to give me light
And guide my palsied blade."

The trees rustled in the light night currents. Each falling leaf, each snapping twig, brought sharp ice to the skin of Kolya's back. Clumps of deeper darkness—some fallen tree or jagged stump—denser than the overflowing night, caused Kolya to tighten his reins and grip fast the hilt of his sword. Out of earshot of the hetman and the others, Kolya drew his sword slowly from its sheath. The weight of the weapon, its fine balance, brought no comfort to his disturbed mind. The empty sheath banged now and again against his leg, making him wince at each contact. It would be just so softly, and with just such lack of warning, that the Bagheeta would spring upon him from the dark thickets at either side of the path.

Slowly, drawing rein again and again so that he might strain his ears for some sound of his mystic foe, Kolya traversed the wood. Now so frightened was he by the menacing stillness of the forest that he would have preferred to return to the men; but fear of the taunts which he knew to be the lot of a coward forced him on.

Again he rode through the wood. Again he peered right and left for some sign of the beast, fearful always of seeing golden eyes glow at him from the pitch blackness of the night. Every rustle of the wind, every mouse that scampered on its way, flooded his heart with fear, and filled his eyes with the lithe, black bulk of the Bagheeta, stalking toward him on noiseless paws. With all his heart he wished that the beast would materialize, stand before him, allow him opportunities to slash and thrust and ward. Anything, even deep wounds, would be better than this dreadful uncertainty, this darkness haunted by the dark form of the were-beast.

Near to the place where he had entered the forest, Kolya turned his horse about and rode through again. This time a greater fear crept into his heart. What if the were-cat were to take advantage of its magical powers? It had done so with Davil. He remembered how he had gone, while still a student at the riding-school, to the village well to wash the blood from his face after a spill, and of how Mailka, the daughter of Davil, had placed her arm about his shoulder, so that with the corner of her apron she might wipe the blood from his forehead. He remembered now with a sense of horrible fear how he had longed to crush her to him, how some strange wellspring in his blood had forced him, against his own will, closer to her. It was only the passing of Brotam, the shepherd, which had prevented him from folding Mailka to his heart. And Mailka was not beautiful, nor willing for embraces. How then would he resist the Bagheeta, beautiful and inviting? He was sick with fear. His stomach was like a pit of empty blackness, as black as the night, as black as the Bagheeta.

It was with relief that he reached the opposite end of the woods and remembered that so far he had not come upon the Bagheeta. Somehow this thought gave food and drink to his fainting heart. If the Bagheeta were so strong, if these tales of supernatural power were true, why then did it not appear and make away with him? It must be, he thought to himself, an ordinary, spotted leopard which had frightened the shepherds in the morning. With this in mind, Kolya began to make plans to find and kill the beast.

"Thrice have I ridden through the wood on this side of the stream," he deliberated; "then it is reasonable that the Bagheeta, if it is such a creature, is on the other side of the stream. I will go there."

Where the stream narrowed a bit, Kolya jumped his horse across, landing with a thud on the firm bank of the opposite side.

Twice he rode through the woods on this side of the stream, making, at intervals, little sorties through the forest as far as the cliffs which bound the copse on either side. He could find no trace of the Bagheeta.

Intent upon the hunt now, Kolya had lost all fear. "It must be," he reasoned, "just as Rifkhas told me, that I must hunt the beast on foot, waiting for him at the water hole."

With this plan in mind, Kolya rode directly along the bank of the creek. The high walls of the creek bed, Kolya clearly saw, would prevent even a creature as agile as a leopard from going to the water's edge for a drink. Then, of a sudden, his horse shied back. Before him, Kolya could see where a slide on each side of the creek had made a sloping pathway to the water. Dismounting, he inspected the place. Hoof marks and paw prints were indubitable proof that the place was in use by all the animals of the vicinity. Kolya led his horse a little way from the bank and tethered it stoutly to an oak sapling.

He divested himself of his kaftan and sword belt, pulled his dagger from its sheath and stuck it through the waistband of his breeches. Then, sword in hand, he returned quietly to the water hole. Carefully he stole down halfway to the water and then, flattening his back against the wall of the cut, prepared to wait.

Even as he settled himself in a comfortable position, the falling of a pebble attracted his attention to the other bank of the stream. He could distinguish nothing. The water was as dark as the night. But from the water came a lapping sound. Something was drinking there at the edge of the creek. Kolya strained his eyes. He could see nothing. But as he continued to stare into the darkness he caught a gleam of eyes, yellow, round and burning as the burnished brass of the altar rail. Again Kolya heard the sound of water being lapped up by the rough tongue of the animal. The round, golden eyes were hidden as the creature drank.

Lifting his left hand to his mouth, Kolya ran his tongue across the palm and across the back of his fingers. Lifting it cautiously above his head he held it, palm forward, toward the Bagheeta. The palm of his hand felt colder than the back; the wind was blowing toward him. There was no danger of the Bagheeta taking his scent. But there was the danger that the Bagheeta might go back by the way he had come, without passing Kolya's ambush.

Slowly, ever so slowly, Kolya bent and picked up a large stone. With all his strength he threw it into the bushes on the other bank of the stream, then braced himself to cleave down his sword with all his might. The stone landed on the farther bank with a crash. Gold eyes turned up and with a shriek the Bagheeta flung herself across the stream and began to climb past Kolya.

With bated breath he waited until the powerful haunches had lifted the creature until its eyes were on a level with his own. For one moment the beast stared straight into his eyes; then Kolya's sword plunged down, slashing the black leopard's shoulder. The Bagheeta shrieked piercingly and fell back a few feet. Again Kolya struck at it, but the beast, snarling, rolled free. Kolya gathered himself and lunged forward with the point as if toward a human opponent. A great feeling of satisfaction flooded his heart as he felt the blade sink deep into the thick neck of the Bagheeta. There was a choking sound, the quick pant and insuck of painful breathing, and then silence. The Bagheeta was dead.

"It was so easy. It was so easy!" Kolya repeated the phrase again and again in wonderment.

Dawn was breaking. Thin, gray light began to filter into the wood. Mists and vapors like gray wraiths whirled without rime or reason between the tree trunks. Stiff-legged, body and tail relaxed, with blood flowing over the sandstone on which it lay, Kolya could see the Bagheeta. The heavy jaws gaped wide open, and the boy could see clearly the long, thick fangs of the beast. Its paws were thrust out stiffly, the claws, cruel as Tartar scimitars, still unsheathed.

Kolya laughed a bit hysterically. It had been so easy, it had been so easy to kill this fearsome thing of dreadful aspect and terrible strength. Two cuts and a single thrust of his sharp sword had killed the Bagheeta. Tough sinews, tearing fangs and rending jaws had been subdued by the steel of his sword. There had been no magic trial of virtue and morals. Davil was a liar, and Rifkhas a true man.

Kolya sank down upon a stone to rest himself, his eyes still drawn to the inert body of the leopard.

"How they will laugh at Davil when I tell them what a liar he is!" Kolya thought to himself. "How fat and respected he has grown on

that one lie these many years! That song of his—with its beautiful
maiden and terrible struggle—why, every child in Ghizikhan knows
it by heart, and even the hetman believes it. What a lie!"

But then doubts began to steal into Kolya's mind. He thought
deeply: "If this is untrue, if a Bagheeta is but a black leopard, no
more dangerous than a spotted one, why then even the story about
Lake Erivan having been created by the tears of God as he wept for
the crucifixion of his only Son might be untrue. And the story of
Saint Ilya the Archer and his arrows of fire, giving courage to the
pure of heart in perilous places, might also be a lie. Even God might
be a lie!"

But the gray dawn was ghostly. The trees moved mysteriously in
the light winds and the half-light of the morning, and the mountain
towered dimly toward the sky. Who knew what dread creatures
stalked abroad in the mist? The trees might fall in upon him, the
mountains topple to crush him! Kolya put the unreality of God
quickly from his mind. A ray of light touched the peak of Silibal and
it shone, rose-colored and white, against the blue sky of the morning.

Birds began to twitter in the bushes. A deer came to the water hole
to drink, but, upthrusting her muzzle at the scent of the slain leopard, trotted off otherwheres.

"How they will laugh when I tell them what a liar Davil has been
these many years!"

Stretching himself, Kolya rose, smiling, and prepared to return to
where he knew the hetman and the *jigits* of the village awaited him.

He donned his kaftan and sword belt, replaced his dagger in its
sheath, and started to cleanse his bloody sword with a wisp of grass.
As he started on this task, a thought struck him. No, he must let the
sword remain bloody—proof of the conflict. He laid it down in the
grass carefully. Then, wondering at the weight and size of the animal, Kolya dragged the Bagheeta to where he had tethered his horse.
The mare plunged and curvetted at the sight of the dead animal and
at the smell of its coagulating blood. When he had secured the body
to the high cantle with thongs, Kolya picked up his bloody sword,
untethered the horse and mounted into the saddle deliberately.

As the horse nervously threaded its way under the double burden
of victor and vanquished, Kolya rode slowly out of the wood with
the reins held tight in his left hand. His mind was busy. A thought
had come to him. For years Rifkhas had said that a Bagheeta was

but a black leopard among the spotted ones. The people of the village had only laughed at him. Davil, the liar, they loved and respected. Rif'khas they thought a strange man, a little mad from having lived so long alone in the woods.

"Even if they believed me," Kolya was thinking, "they would laugh at Davil only for a day, and then what? Then no one would fear the Bagheeta any more. And so no longer," Kolya reasoned, "would I be honored as a man who had slain a Bagheeta."

He said to himself: "Surely there must be some reason for this lie. Others have invented it so that they might appear brave and good in the eyes of the village."

And Mailka, Mailka would certainly never give herself to one who had betrayed her father's secret. How warm and softly firm her arm had felt against his shoulder that day she had washed his wounds by the well.

"I will do as Davil has done." Kolya spoke decisively. "I shall tell them that I first saw the Bagheeta as a beautiful maiden, bathing at the water hole, her body surrounded by a white light. That she called me by name and spoke to me courteously—and that, enchanted by her beauty, I had forgotten all warning and bent to kiss her. Then I shall say that an arrow of fire sprang through the sky. Knowing it for the sign of Ilya the Archer, I will say that I took warning from this and, springing away from the maiden, drew my sword. So fast that I could not even see the change, the Bagheeta transformed herself again into a leopard and sprang at me. I shall tell them that we fought for an hour and then, just as I was ready to drop my sword from weariness, a great strength surged through me and I killed the beast. Even as Davil has done, so will I do."

At a sharp trot Kolya rode through the outskirts of the wood. Before him, cooking their breakfasts around little fires. were the men of Ghizikhan. With a great shout of triumph, Kolya struck heels to his horse and charged toward them. The men raised their voices in a hail of welcome which sounded thin and shrill among the mountains.

Kolya began to shout the words of Davil's song as he rode toward them:

> "Halfway in air the leaping beast,
> The cleaving sword, have met.

Now may the herdsmen joyful feast,
For sword and beast have met.

"I rode beneath the silver stars.
And broke Bagheeta's sway———"

Kolya lifted his bloody sword high in the air, the cross of the hilt extended toward heaven, as if giving the victory to God. The men doffed their sheepskin caps and knelt in prayer at this proof of King God's all-powerful goodness.

"Blah!" said Rifkhas the huntsman, as he knelt with the rest.

"Ghost Hunt" (March 1938) is the first of six fantasies by H. RUSSELL WAKE-FIELD (1888–1965) to appear in *Weird Tales*. Wakefield was a Briton whose supernatural tales mostly appeared between 1928 and 1935 in the following collections: *Imagine a Man in a Box, Ghost Stories, A Ghostly Company, Hearken to the Evidence* and *They Return at Evening.*

GHOST HUNT

by H. R. Wakefield

Well, listeners, this is Tony Weldon speaking. Here we are on the third of our series of Ghost Hunts. Let's hope it will be more success-ful than the other two. All our preparations have been made and now it is up to the spooks. My colleague tonight is Professor Mignon of Paris. He is the most celebrated investigator of psychic phenom-ena in the world and I am very proud to be his collaborator.

We are in a medium-sized, three-story Georgian house not far from London. We have chosen it for this reason: it has a truly terrible history. Since it was built, there are records of no less than 30 sui-cides in or from it and there may well have been more. There have been eight since 1893. Its builder and first occupant was a prosperous city merchant and a very bad hat, it appears: glutton, wine bibber and other undesirable things, including a very bad husband. His wife stood his cruelties and infidelities as long as she could and then hanged herself in the powder closet belonging to the biggest bedroom on the second floor, so initiating a horrible sequence.

I used the expression "suicides in and from it," because while some have shot themselves and some hanged themselves, no less than nine have done a very strange thing. They have risen from their beds during the night and flung themselves to death in the river which runs past the bottom of the garden some hundred yards away. The last one was actually seen to do so at dawn on an autumn morning. He was seen running headlong and heard to be shouting as though to companions running by his side. The owner tells me people simply will not live in the house and the agents will no longer keep it on their books. He will not live in it himself, for very good reasons, he declares. He will not tell us what those reasons are; he wishes us to have an absolutely open mind on the subject, as it were. And he declares that if the professor's verdict is unfavorable, he will pull down the house and rebuild it. One can understand that, for it seems to merit the label, "Death Trap."

Well, that is sufficient introduction. I think I have convinced you it certainly merits investigation, but we cannot guarantee to deliver the goods or the ghosts, which have an awkward habit of taking a night off on these occasions.

And now to business—imagine me seated at a fine satinwood table, not quite in the middle of a big reception room on the ground floor. The rest of the furniture is shrouded in white protective covers. The walls are light oak panels. The electric light in the house has been switched off, so all the illumination I have is a not very powerful electric lamp. I shall remain here with a mike while the professor roams the house in search of what he may find. He will not have a mike, as it distracts him and he has a habit, so he says, of talking to himself while he conducts these investigations. He will return to me as soon as he has anything to report. Is that all clear? Well, then, here is the professor to say a few words to you before he sets forth on his tour of discovery. I may say he speaks English far better than I do. Professor Mignon—

Ladies and gentlemen, this is Professor Mignon. This house is without doubt, how shall I say, impregnated with evil. It affects one profoundly. It is bad, bad, bad! It is soaked in evil and reeking from its wicked past. It must be pulled down, I assure you. I do not think it affects my friend, Mr. Weldon, in the same way, but he is not psychic, not mediumistic, as I am. Now shall we see ghosts, spirits? Ah, that I cannot say! But they are here and they are evil; that is sure. I can feel their presence. There is, maybe, danger. I shall soon know. And now I shall start off with just one electric torch to show me the way. Presently I will come back and tell you what I have seen, or if not seen, felt and perhaps suffered. But remember, though we can summon spirits from the vasty deep, will they come when we call for them? We shall see.

Well, listeners, I'm sure if anyone can, it's the professor. You must have found those few words far more impressive than anything I said. That was an expert speaking on what he knows. Personally, alone here in this big, silent room, they didn't have a very reassuring effect on me. In fact, he wasn't quite correct when he said this place didn't affect me at all. I don't find it a very cheerful spot, by any means. You can be sure of that. I may not be psychic, but I've certainly got a sort of feeling it doesn't want us here, resents us, and would like to see the back of us. *Or else!* I felt that way as soon as I entered the front door. One sort of had to wade through the hostility. I'm not kidding or trying to raise your hopes.

It's very quiet here, listeners. I'm having a look around the room. This lamp casts some queer shadows. There is an odd one near the wall by the door, but I realize now it must be one cast by a big Adams bookcase. I know that's what it is because I peeped under the dust cover when I first came in. It's a very fine piece. It's queer to think of you all listening to me. I shouldn't really mind if I had some of you for company. The owner of the house told us we should probably hear rats and mice in the wainscoting. Well, I can certainly hear them now. Pretty hefty rats, from the sound of them—even you can almost hear them, I should think.

Well, what else is there to tell you about? Nothing very much, except that there's a bat in the room. I think it must be a bat and not a bird. I haven't actually seen it, only its shadow as it flew past the wall just now and then it fanned past my face. I don't know much about bats, but I thought they went to bed in the winter. This one must suffer from insomnia. Ah, there it is again—it actually touched me as it passed.

Now I can hear the professor moving about in the room above. I don't suppose you can—have a try. Now listen carefully—

Hello! Did you hear that? He must have knocked over a chair or something—a heavy chair, from the sound of it. I wonder if he's having any luck. Ah, there's that bat again—it seems to like me. Each time it just touches my face with its wings as it passes. They're smelly things, bats—I don't think they wash often enough. This one smells kind of rotten.

I wonder what the professor knocked over—I can see a small stain forming on the ceiling. Perhaps a flower bowl or something. Hello! Did you hear that sharp crack? I think you must have. The oak paneling stretching, I suppose, but it was almost ear-splitting in here. Something ran across my foot then—a rat, perhaps. I've always loathed rats. Most people do, of course.

That stain on the ceiling has grown quite a lot. I think I'll just go to the door and shout to the professor to make sure he's all right. You'll hear me shout and his answer, I expect—

Professor!— Professor!—

Well, he didn't answer. I believe he's a little bit deaf. But he's sure to be all right. I won't try again just yet, as I know he likes to be undisturbed on these occasions. I'll sit down again for a minute or two. I'm afraid this is rather dull for you, listeners. I'm not finding it so, but then of course— There, I heard him cough. Did you hear that cough, listeners—a sort of very throaty double cough? It seemed to come from— I wonder if he's crept down and is having a little fun with me, because I tell you, listeners, this place is beginning to get on my nerves just a wee little bit, just a bit. I wouldn't live in it for a pension, a very large pension— Get away, you brute! That bat— faugh! It stinks.

Now listen carefully—can you hear those rats? Having a game of Rugger, from the sound of them. I really shall be quite glad to get out of here. I can quite imagine people doing themselves in in this house. Saying to themselves, after all, it isn't much of a life when you think of it—figure it out, is it? Just work and worry and getting old and seeing your friends die. Let's end it all in the river!

I'm not being very cheerful, am I? It's this darned house. Those other two places we investigated didn't worry me a bit, but this— I wonder what the professor's doing, besides coughing. I can't quite make that cough out because—get away, you brute! That bat'll be the death of me! Death of me! Death of me!

I'm glad I've got you to talk to, listeners, but I wish you could answer back. I'm beginning to dislike the sound of my own voice. After a time, if you've been talking in a room alone, you get fanciful. Have you ever noticed that? You sort of think you can hear someone talking back—

There!— No, of course you couldn't have heard it, because it wasn't there, of course. Just in my head. Just subjective, that's the word. That's the word. Very odd. That *was* me laughing, of course. I'm saying "of course" a lot. Of course I am. Well, listeners, I'm afraid this is awfully dull for you. Not for me, though, not for me! No ghosts so far, unless the professor is having better luck—

There! You must have heard that! What a crack that paneling makes! Well, you must have heard that, listeners—better than nothing! Ha, ha! Professor! Professor! Phew, what an echo!

Now, listeners, I'm going to stop talking for a moment. I don't suppose you'll mind. Let's see if we can hear anything—

Did you hear it? I'm not exactly sure what it was. Not sure. I wonder if you heard it? Not exactly, but the house shook a little and the windows rattled. I don't think we'll do that again. I'll go on talking. I wonder how long one could endure the atmosphere of this place. It certainly is inclined to get one down.

Gosh, that stain has grown—the one on the ceiling. It's actually started to drip. I mean form bubbles—they'll start dropping soon. Colored bubbles, apparently. I wonder if the professor is okay? I mean he might have shut himself up in a powder closet or something, and the powder closets in this house aren't particularly—well, you never know, do you?

Now I should have said that shadow had moved. No, I suppose I put the lamp down in a slightly different position. Shadows do make odd patterns, you must have noticed that. This one might be a body lying on its face with its arms stretched out. Cheerful, aren't I? An aunt of mine gassed herself, as a matter of fact—well, I don't know why I told you that. Not quite in the script.

Professor! Professor! Where is that old fuzzy-whiskers? I shall certainly advise the owner to have this place pulled down. Emphatically. Then where'll *you* go! I must go upstairs in a minute or two and see what's happened to the professor. Well, I was telling you about auntie—

D'you know, listeners, I really believe I'd go completely crackers if I stayed here much longer—more or less, anyway, and quite soon, quite soon, quite soon. Absolutely stark, staring! It wears you down. That's exactly it, it wears you down. I can quite understand—well, I won't say all that again. I'm afraid this is all awfully dull for you, listeners. I should switch it off if I were you—

I *should!* What's on the other program? I mean it—switch off! There, what did I tell you—that stain's started to drip drops, drip drops, drip drops, drip drops! I'll go and catch one on my hand—

Good God!

Professor! Professor! Professor! Now up those stairs! Which room would it be? Left or right? Left, right, left, right—left has it. In we go—

Well, gentlemen, good evening! What have you done with the professor? I know he's dead—see his blood on my hand? What have you done with him? Make way, please, gentlemen. What have you done with him? D'you want me to sing it—tra-la-la—

Switch off, you fools!

Well, if this isn't too darned funny—ha, ha, ha, ha! Hear me laughing, listeners—

Switch off, you fools!

That can't be him lying there—he hadn't a *red* beard! Don't crowd round me, gentlemen. Don't crowd me, I tell you!

What do you want me to do? You want me to go to the river, don't you? Ha, ha! Now? Will you come with me? Come on, then! To the river! To the river!

FUNERAL IN THE FOG

by Edward D. Hoch

At times Simon Ark was a difficult person to find. He might just as easily be halfway around the world in Egypt or Poland or India as in the little 10th Street apartment he sometimes used. So I wasn't really surprised when my secretary was unable to locate him for me on that misty November morning. I wasn't even surprised when the day ended with her still shaking her head over the telephone.

A day passed, two days, and then Simon Ark returned to New York. He didn't phone the office, but turned up at my home in Westchester on the evening of his return, shaking the rain from the great black coat he always wore when autumn came.

"Simon! My secretary's been trying to reach you everywhere!" I motioned him into the living room where Shelly was catching up on her reading. "Simon Ark's here, honey," I announced.

My wife was always happy to see Simon, perhaps because he had helped to bring us together. But she was a bit frightened of him at times too, as people often were.

"Hello, Simon," she said, rising to greet him. "It's good to see you again."

"You grow younger with every visit," he told Shelly.

She blushed nicely, perhaps considering him something of an expert on the subject of age. "Can I get you fellows something to drink?"

Simon Ark nodded and settled his big frame into a chair. "Anything will do—a little wine, perhaps."

"Just where have you been?" I asked him. "Egypt again?"

"No, only California this time. It's hardly the same, though they do have some interesting Ra cults springing up near Los Angeles." He smiled slightly at some memory. "The weather out there makes it difficult to return to New York. But why were you trying to reach me?"

"It's about your book on Satanism," I began as Shelly reappeared with the drinks. "We received an interesting letter about it last week."

"After all this time!" Simon marveled. "Surely it must be eight years since you published my little study."

"Books on Satanism and witchcraft are big these days. It's one of our stronger backlist items. Of course we always get the usual number of crank letters, and I know you do too, but this one seems more interesting than most. It's from a man upstate who claims the Devil is threatening to kill him."

"Very possible," Simon admitted with a slight frown, "although Satan usually works in a more indirect manner. What is this man's name?"

"Jason Bloomer is what he calls himself."

He nodded as if the name meant something to him. "Oh, yes. He's written a few little pamphlets which he publishes himself. Full of half forgotten incantations and the like. I fear he's a bit obsessed with the subject of Satan."

This seemed an odd criticism for someone as obsessed as Simon to offer, but I let it pass. "Do you think it's worth running up there? He might have an interesting story, at least. He's in Putnam County, across the river from West Point. We could drive it in an hour or so."

"We could drive up on Saturday if you'd like," Simon said, smiling. "Perhaps Shelly would like to come with us."

I glanced at her and she nodded. "It might be fun, if you'll promise there'll be no murders."

"I never promise that," Simon said quietly. He was no longer smiling.

Saturday dawned with a light drizzle of misty November rain. It was a terrible day for a drive up the Hudson, but Simon seemed anxious to go, and after a week of puttering around the house, Shelly was eager too. So, at ten o'clock, we were on our way up the Taconic State Parkway with wheels splashing through shallow puddles. Presently we turned off the Parkway and drove past the gate of a little cemetery shrouded in mist. We continued down the road for about a mile, until we came to an old two-story house surrounded by fields overgrown with brush. Perhaps once it had been a farm, long ago. In the yard a little wooden sign bore the single word *Bloomer.*

"This is the place," I said. "You want to wait for us, Shelly?"

"Never! And miss meeting this Jason Bloomer?" Simon had told us a bit about him on the trip up, about his occasional writings and his interest in Satanism.

We went up the walk, all three of us, and I pressed the bell. After a moment, the door was opened by a tall, slim man with a bald head and gray-streaked beard.

"I'm from Neptune Books," I began, extending my card. "You wrote us recently."

"And this would be the famous Simon Ark," he said, ignoring Shelly and me to turn his attention to Simon. "I'm honored. You must come in."

The living room was in casual disarray, like so many bachelor quarters, but there was a touch of the bizarre in exotic hand-carved masks that hung from the walls. There was a small totem pole, too, and an incongruous model of an oil derrick. The crowded bookshelves, which both Simon and I inspected, held well-thumbed copies of witchcraft books by Montague Summers, Willy Ley's *Exotic Zoology, The Golden Bough,* Charles Fort, Aleister Crowley and even an ancient bound volume of the *Journal of the Royal Asiatic Society* for 1837.

Jason Bloomer made a slight bow. "You honor my house."

Simon extended his hand. "I am pleased to meet you, Mr.

Bloomer. Writings such as yours always interest me, and your letter to my friend here was of special interest."

Jason Bloomer nodded. "Your book was good. When I began to receive these threats, you were the first person I thought to turn to. One does not ring up the police to say that Satan is threatening his life." He stroked his beard as he talked, and Shelly and I could only watch from the sidelines.

"But you think I can help?"

"Certainly," Bloomer insisted. "In your book, you state that the devil once appeared to the Duchess of Gloucester while she and the astrologer Bolingbroke were in the midst of bewitching Henry VI to death. That is the sort of knowledge very few men share."

Simon Ark shrugged it off. "The scene is depicted in a painting by Fuseli. My only special knowledge comes in knowing that the scene is a true one."

"Exactly! And your special knowledge can protect me!"

I cleared my throat. "If you want protection from a murder threat, Mr. Bloomer, wouldn't it be easier to hire a private detective?"

He turned on me, eyes blazing. "I could not hire a private detective to protect me from a man—or devil—who can strangle a person without even touching them!"

That was all he needed to hook Simon. I saw the sudden flicker of interest in his eyes. "Really? And the police did nothing?"

"There were no police. It happened on an island halfway around the world—on Java, to be exact. I saw it happen."

"And that's why he wants to kill you?"

"That and other reasons which needn't concern you. But mainly, it's because I saw him murder this girl without ever laying a finger on her."

"And how long has he been threatening your life?"

"For a month now, ever since he discovered where I was living."

Beneath the beard and the deep, searching eyes, he was a man afraid. I knew it, and Simon knew it too. "My experience has been that true murderers do not give their victims that much warning."

"He—he wants something from me."

"Suppose you tell me the whole story," Simon urged. "That's the only way I can help you."

And the bearded man sank back in his chair and began to talk.

"I suppose it really started about six years ago in Vietnam. It was during the early days of the American troop buildup, and with war staring us in the face a good many people like me left the country. I'd been there for several months, studying the modes of devil-worship among the tribesmen back in the hills, but now I knew it was time to get out fast.

"I heard of a small private plane that was flying two passengers south to Java, one of the islands of Indonesia, and I bargained for a seat on the plane. That was when I met Rolf Dagon. I was attracted to the man immediately, for two reasons. His name—Dagon—was that of a fish god of the Philistines. He was, in addition, perhaps the strangest-looking man I had ever seen. Tall, very tall, thinner than me, but with great powerful hands. I could easily imagine him strangling someone, but not, certainly, the girl he was traveling with. Her name was Li Chow and she was obviously Dagon's mistress.

"We landed on Java at Jogjakarta, a fairly large city near the south coast of the island. They were still having trouble with Communists, and I was a bit timid about being left on my own. So I stuck pretty close to Dagon and Li Chow. He claimed to be French, left over after his country's collapse in Indo-China, but that seemed unlikely to me. I was more willing to believe him a soldier of fortune or a mercenary of some sort. Finally, one night over drinks in a little side street bar, he told me what he was really after. The Japanese had occupied Java during World War II—it was about as far south as they ever got— and he had learned from a Japanese veteran that when the war suddenly ended they'd been forced to leave nearly a million dollars in gold on the island, wealth originally intended for certain island rulers further along.

"Well, Dagon claimed to know the location of this twenty-year-old horde of gold, and the three of us set out for the place. It was said to be in a little valley near the town of Baturetno, deep in the southern jungle.

"It was a strange country, with half-covered patches of volcanic ash and trees that twisted their limbs to the sky while sending off snake-like roots from their branches. We traveled that last part mainly by foot, until at last we reached the place Dagon sought. There was a little hill, a low, grassy mound that stretched upward some thirty feet. It was a hard climb, especially for the little Chinese girl, but finally we reached the top and stood looking down into a circular valley, like a bowl, some 300 yards across.

"We found the remains of the Japanese camp along the crest of the hill, and we settled there ourselves. The camp itself was deserted, of course, but down in the lowest point of the valley, in a singularly barren area, we could see two skeletons.

"We inspected them as one would a skeleton in a museum or doctor's office. There is nothing really horrible about a pile of bleached bones, you know. A body with skin still attached is much more horrible than a bare skeleton. There was no sign of violence to the bones, no clue as to how they'd died.

"The next morning I detected a growing tension between Dagon and Li Chow. When he was away, exploring the floor of the valley by himself, the little Chinese girl spoke to me. She said he was a devil and that he planned to kill us both as soon as he found the gold. She showed me a knife she carried to defend herself, but I doubted it would be much protection against Dagon. He was a full head taller and had a good eighty pounds on her.

"They argued again that afternoon and he took her for a walk in the valley. I watched them through binoculars from the crest of the hill because I feared what he might do to her. But even with me watching, he still did it. They were walking together in the valley, near where we'd found the skeletons, when suddenly she started to gasp for breath, as if some invisible hands were choking the life from her.

"I looked for a cord or wire of some sort, but there was nothing. After a moment she collapsed to the ground and seemed to lose consciousness. Rolf Dagon merely stood there watching, unharmed himself. After another moment, he began waving his arms slowly in the air above her, like some ancient high priest summoning the powers of darkness. In that instant I remembered what Li Chow had said about him being a devil.

"Presently, after he'd stood watching her in the act of dying, he bent and lifted her body in his arms. He brought her back to the crest of the hill where I waited, and said that she'd simply died. I looked her over very closely, but there was not a mark on her body. She'd simply stopped breathing, as if some giant hand had strangled her without leaving a trace. Naturally I suspected poison, but all three of us had eaten the same packaged food. I even wondered if he'd killed her with a poison gas of some sort, but when I walked carefully through the valley myself I found no traces of it.

"After that, I was anxious to leave. We abandoned our search for the Japanese gold and made our way back to the airport at Jogjakarta. We obtained passage on a commercial airliner to Australia, but at the last minute I slipped away from Dagon and flew to Hong Kong instead. I was taking no chances ending up the way Li Chow did."

We'd sat there listening to his story, while the skies outside began to brighten. I don't think either Shelly or I believed a word of it. But now, as he finished talking, I saw that Simon Ark was deeply intent on the man's story.

"And now," he asked, "Rolf Dagon has reappeared?"

"Exactly. The threats began about a month ago. Letters at first, and then telephone calls."

"Do you have any of the letters?"

Bloomer shook his head. "I threw them away."

"If he's telephoned, you must have some idea of his whereabouts."

"Not really, except that he's getting closer. That's why I wrote to Neptune Books to contact you. I knew if anyone could save me, Simon Ark could."

Simon nodded, thought for a moment, and then asked, "Tell me, sir, how tall are you?"

"Me? Why, I'm just six feet."

"And you described Rolf Dagon as being quite tall. Just how tall?"

"Oh, he must be six-four or five."

Simon seemed satisfied, but he had one more question. "You said he was a head taller than the girl, but since she was small and Chinese, she might have been only about five feet in height. Correct?"

"Yes, I suppose he was more than a head taller."

"As much as sixteen or seventeen inches?"

"That's possible. Why?"

Simon Ark let his breath out slowly. "I believe I can help you, even though you have lied about a very important point in your story."

"I—"

Simon waved a hand. "I will return tomorrow. Perhaps then you will be ready with the truth, Mr. Bloomer."

He would say no more, and we left Jason Bloomer standing in the doorway as we departed. Though the weather had cleared, there was a decided November chill to the air.

I started driving back the way we had come, and Shelly said, "What a strange man! Do you really believe any of that story, Simon?"

"That is the problem," he answered, turning up the collar of his black topcoat. "What to believe and what not to believe. He lies in part, but does he lie entirely? Are we simply the victims of some quite elaborate hoax, or are we up against an evil genius who really threatens Bloomer's life?"

Shelly snorted and took out a cigarette. "Well, I for one don't believe a word of it! There's no reason why we should! How could this Rolf Dagon kill that Chinese girl without touching her or leaving a mark, while Bloomer was watching? And more important, why should he kill her? Just because they had a little argument? It just doesn't make sense."

I joined in then. "But if it's not true, why should Bloomer get us all the way out here just to tell us a crazy story?"

"It may be true," Simon said. "There is one explanation that would fit the facts, provided we assume a single lie on Mr. Bloomer's part."

I turned back onto the parkway and headed for home. "So what do we do now?"

"Would you be willing to bring me up here again tomorrow, when our friend has had time to consider his story and make a slight correction in it?"

"Only if you stop being so mysterious, Simon. What lie did Bloomer tell? What fact would make it all clear?"

"All right," Simon said with a smile. "I won't keep you in the dark. Consider—why did they abandon their search for the gold after the death of the girl? If Dagon killed her, why did he do so? And most important, when Bloomer saw her dying, why didn't he run down the hill and try to save her?"

"I give up," Shelly said. "Why?"

"Because, my friends, Bloomer left out one little fact. They found the gold."

We were silent for a moment, taking that in, and then Shelly said, "You can't be sure of that."

"I can be sure. They found the gold, and Dagon killed the girl to keep from splitting with her."

"Why didn't he kill Bloomer, too?" I asked him.

"Because I think our Mr. Bloomer made good use of the time while Dagon was killing the girl. I think he stayed at the top of the hill so he could do something with the gold—hide it, or dispose of it in some way. When Dagon returned, Bloomer had him just where he wanted him. He must have promised Dagon his share only when they were safely out of that place. Dagon had to agree, but when they reached the airport, Bloomer doublecrossed him. He flew off with the gold, or the secret of it. Dagon has been searching for him all these years. Bloomer won't show us his messages because they mention the gold."

"All right," I granted. "It fits the facts as we know them, but it still doesn't explain this Satan business, or how Dagon killed the girl."

"That, my friend, has to do with the height of the people involved."

"You mean Dagon used a method of murder that would kill only short people?"

"Exactly."

"Then Jason Bloomer is safe. He's six feet tall." I couldn't help being a bit sarcastic.

"Jason Bloomer is not safe," Simon said quietly. "I only hope he is at least safe until tomorrow."

On Sunday morning, Simon and I drove back up the Hudson to the graying house where Jason Bloomer had lived in hiding for all these years. Shelly had not joined us this time. She said that one day of weirdos like Bloomer was all she could stomach at a time. So we went alone, driving over the familiar road through little wind-gathered piles of damp leaves. It was trying hard to be a sunny day, but there was a mist in the air that wouldn't quite give up, casting a sort of haze over everything in sight.

The house seemed deserted when we reached it, and I was beginning to think that the whole thing had been some product of our imaginations. But then Simon tried the door and it opened inward. The main floor was unchanged from our visit of the previous day, except that now a pen and paper lay on a little writing desk in one corner. Jason Bloomer had started to write a letter, or at least a message of some sort.

Rolf—It will do you no good to come here and threaten me. The gold will never be found. If you kill me, I will take it with me to the grave. To settle our accounts once and for all, I offer you a fair share of

The message stopped there, as if Bloomer had been interrupted at that point. "Bloomer!" I shouted. "Bloomer! Are you home?"

"Come on," Simon said. "Quickly!"

We went through the house, every room of it, but there was no sign of Jason Bloomer. There was only more evidence of his strange way of life, the paraphernalia of mysticism, the accessories of the Satanic. Then, from the second floor bedroom, I happened to spot something out the window.

"Simon! There, across the field, near the woods!"

There were two men, walking. One was certainly Jason Bloomer, and the other was taller—slim and straight and somehow evil. There could be no doubt as to his identity.

"Come on," Simon breathed. We were down the stairs and out of the house in a moment, running across the open field toward the spot where we'd seen the two men. It was a good two hundred yards away, and once on the ground the gently rolling terrain effectively shielded the two figures from our eyes.

But then, topping a small rise, we saw Jason Bloomer once again. He was stretched out on the ground, arms outflung as if to ward off the beat of some giant wings. There was no one else in sight. The tall figure with whom he'd been walking had vanished into the nearby woods.

"He's dead, Simon," I said, moving closer.

Simon bent to feel for a pulse and then rose, nodding. "Dead. And no marks on his body."

I remembered the story Bloomer had told us. "Just like the Chinese girl. My God, Simon; maybe Rolf Dagon really is the devil!"

Jason Bloomer was buried two days later, on a foggy Tuesday morning when even the heavens seemed to be in mourning. Simon and I had spent most of Monday searching the old house, but there was no gold hidden in it anywhere. There was also no evidence of a safe deposit box or any other hiding place large enough to hold a small fortune in gold. All we found was the name of an undertaker with whom Bloomer had made arrangements for his burial, as well as the name of a married sister in New York, whom we notified of his death.

The funeral procession was a skimpy one, moving from the undertaking parlor to the little tree-lined cemetery we'd observed on our first visit. Behind a uniformed motorcycle escort, there was only the hearse and three cars—one for the hired pallbearers, one for the sister and her husband and one for Simon and me. Bloomer had no neighbors close enough or interested enough to journey to the cemetery on that foggy morning.

"What do you think, Simon?" I asked as we kept pace with the cars ahead. "Does Rolf Dagon really exist, or did Bloomer make the whole thing up?"

"Oh, he exists, my friend. I spent all day Saturday checking that out. He's a former French mercenary who was indeed in Vietnam six years ago. His description fits what Bloomer told us, too."

"And the Chinese girl?"

"I have no reason to doubt Bloomer's story."

"Then how did Dagon kill her? And how did he kill Bloomer?"

"The medical examiner says that Jason Bloomer died of something as simple as a heart attack."

"Do you believe that, Simon?"

"It seems likely."

"But we saw him with Dagon!" I insisted.

"It could be that Jason Bloomer read too many books on Satanism for his own good," Simon said. Ahead, the motorcycle escort had turned into the cemetery gate, and the little line of mourners followed along. The fog was thicker here, all but obscuring the road at times. When at last the handful of cars halted, Simon did not immediately leave our vehicle. Instead, he sat watching the pallbearers as they unloaded the coffin.

"You seem disappointed," I observed, hearing the sigh escape his lips.

"I am."

"About the funeral?"

"About the height of the pallbearers. They are quite average."

"You expected Dagon to show up here?"

Simon got out of the car without answering and started up the little hill to the side of the freshly-dug grave. I saw that a gravestone was already in place, with the family name *Bloomer*. The funeral director guided the coffin into place while the dead man's sister and her husband stood to one side. Back on the winding road, the motorcycle driver sat astride his machine, smoking a cigarette.

A minister of some uncertain faith appeared to say a few words and then the group scattered to move off through the mist to their cars. It had been as simple as that. Later, sometime, the gravediggers would appear to complete the job.

"Ready to go, Simon?" I asked.

"In a moment, my friend."

He waited until the others had departed, their cars swallowed up by fog, and then he acted. "Quickly! Into the grave!"

"Simon! Have you gone mad?"

"We only have a few minutes. Hand me that shovel and use the other one yourself."

"But—"

Moving with more agility than I would have dreamed possible, Simon dropped into the open grave, edging past the waiting coffin. I had no choice but to follow. He drove the shovel down, digging a bit in one spot and then moving to another. Above and around us, all seemed muffled in fog.

"Simon, could you tell me what we're looking for?"

"The gold, my friend. Remember Bloomer's unfinished note to Dagon? He said he'd take the gold to the grave with him, and I think he meant it literally. He'd made funeral arrangements and even ordered the tombstone for this plot in advance. I think—"

He paused, staring up at the great marble block with the word *Bloomer* on its face. "What now, Simon?"

"Help me out of here, quickly!"

"I thought you said the gold was in here."

"He wouldn't have buried it in the earth, where any incautious gravedigger might have found it. Much more likely it's hidden in this gravestone."

We tugged and pulled at it, but nothing moved. Then, as we were about to give up, something happened. The upper block edged away from its base and we saw that the base was hollow. There was a metal box visible inside.

"My God, Simon, I think you're right!"

But he was clutching my arm. He had heard something, some

sound which had not yet reached my fog-muffled ears. "Quiet! He's coming back!"

"Who?"

"Rolf Dagon, unless I'm mistaken."

"But how could he come back when he wasn't even here, Simon? There was no one at the funeral taller than six feet."

And then I heard it. A low, gradually rising sound that at first I couldn't identify. Simon turned to face the fog-laden road, gripping the shovel in his hands.

Suddenly a motorcycle broke through the curtain of mist, heading straight for us. I recognized the uniformed man who'd escorted the funeral procession, only now he seemed different. In a blur of movement almost too fast to follow, I saw the gun in his right hand. Simon shoved me to one side as the shot tore between us into the marble gravestone, then hurled his shovel at the motorcycle's wheels as it tore past us up the hill.

His aim was good. Out of control, with one hand still gripping his pistol, the rider tumbled off his machine as it crashed into a nearby headstone. Before he could rise, Simon and I were on him, disarming him, pinning him to the damp earth.

"That's all, Dagon," Simon said.

The tall, thin man under us cursed and tried to roll over. I kicked away his gun and held him fast.

Later, back home over drinks, Shelly said, "But Simon—I still don't understand how you knew Dagon was the motorcycle rider."

Simon Ark took a sip of his wine and replied, "He was the only one there who never stood up, never got off his cycle. If Dagon was at the funeral, as I believed him to be, the motorcycle escort was the only one who could have been tall enough."

"How did you know he'd be at the funeral?"

"If Bloomer really had hidden the gold in or around his grave, I knew Dagon would want to find it. The most likely time was at the funeral, rather than searching through the cemetery at a later date. I imagine he bribed the real motorcycle rider to take his place. Then, after the funeral, he came back for the gold and tried to kill us."

"And the Chinese girl?" Shelly asked. "What about her?"

"That part was simple, really, once I concluded the story was true. You remember Bloomer's mention of volcanic ash? That was the key to it, that and his description of the valley. It was round, remember

—like a bowl. Isn't it obvious that the valley was really the long-dead crater of an extinct volcano?"

"Even so," I argued, "it certainly didn't erupt, Simon?"

"No," he agreed, "it didn't erupt. It simply gave off quantities of carbon dioxide gas from time to time. The gas, passing through fissures in the floor of the inactive volcano, accounted for the skeleton of the Japanese soldier. And it killed the Chinese girl, Li Chow."

"Wait a minute," I objected. "Since when is carbon dioxide gas poisonous? I always thought carbon monoxide was the deadly one."

"And why didn't Dagon die too?" Shelly added.

"Because the carbon dioxide built up only in the valley's low points, displacing the vital oxygen. The soldier and Li Chow simply suffocated for lack of air. She was led to the low spot deliberately, and drowned in a sea of carbon dioxide as surely as she might have drowned in the ocean. Her killer, being a head taller, was able to keep his nose above the deadly layer and breathe fresh air."

"I find that hard to believe," Shelly said.

Simon Ark shrugged. "It is true, nevertheless. There is a cave in Italy where a layer of carbon dioxide near the floor makes it fatal to dogs and other small animals, but humans of average height can walk through without feeling a thing."

Shelly still shook her head. "And you mean to tell me that Dagon killed the girl and then killed Bloomer, all for the gold you two found hidden in the tombstone?"

Simon sipped his wine and smiled. "Ah, dear Shelly, I fear I have misled you. There was no gold in the tombstone—only an empty metal box. And Rolf Dagon killed no one, though he came close with us. It was Jason Bloomer who killed the Chinese girl, and Jason Bloomer who would have killed Dagon if fate had not intervened."

I'd heard some of it on the ride down, but I could see that Simon's words were a shock to my wife. "Bloomer? But how could you know that?"

"The key to Bloomer's supposed belief in Dagon's Satanic powers was the death of the girl, which seemed a complete mystery to him. And yet on his bookshelves we saw well-thumbed copies of *Willy Ley's Exotic Zoology* and the *Journal of the Royal Asiatic Society* for 1837—both of which carry detailed accounts of such deadly valleys on Java. Certainly Bloomer knew what really killed the girl, and thus his whole fear of Dagon was a skillful bit of acting."

"But you say he killed Li Chow."

"Quite right. His story had it that Dagon stood over the fallen girl waving his arms. It conjures up quite a Satanic picture, but hardly one in keeping with the facts. If Li Chow was drowning in a sea of carbon dioxide, the last thing her killer would do would be to wave his hands in the air and disperse the deadly layer. If he lied about that, he lied about Dagon killing her. Remember, Bloomer was also a foot taller than the girl. He could have lured her to her death as easily as the taller man."

"And the gold?"

"Could we really believe that Bloomer stole the gold and hid it from Dagon, smuggling it back to America? It was much easier to believe the gold never existed, that it was merely a ploy to lure Dagon to his destruction. Bloomer walked with him in that field, awaiting our arrival. He planned to wait till we were on the scene, and then appear to kill Dagon in self-defense, before witnesses."

"And if we hadn't come?" I asked Simon Ark.

"Then he would have used his graveyard scheme—luring Dagon to the hiding place in the tombstone and then killing him, probably burying his body right there."

"But *why?*" Shelly asked.

"Dagon told us a little of that after we disarmed him. He was a soldier of fortune with whom Bloomer fell in. There was money involved and some talk of Japanese gold, but none ever appeared. Something else did appear, though—evidence of oil deposits. Remember the somewhat incongruous little oil derrick in Bloomer's study? In any event, Bloomer felt he had to kill Dagon and the girl so any oil discovery would be all his. He succeeded with Li Chow. But it was Dagon who escaped from him, rather than the other way around. So the long charade began, to lure Dagon back here to his death. Dagon, for his part, was enough of a mercenary to be attracted by the possibility of gold. Bloomer told him about the gravestone before he died, or hinted at it, and Dagon took part in the funeral to observe it close up. When he returned and saw us, he tried to kill us, thinking we'd been paid by Bloomer to finish him."

"And Bloomer?"

"A simple heart attack in a field, as the medical examiner ruled it. The pressure, the anticipation of killing Dagon, was too much for him. Dagon told me Bloomer actually had the gun out when the seizure hit him. Dagon took the gun himself and ran into the woods."

"Then all this Satanism business was just a ruse to get you up there as a witness, Simon?"

But Simon Ark merely shrugged and reached for his wine glass. He might have been a kindly uncle instructing Shelly and me on the proper care of our garden. "That, my friend, we will not ever know. Perhaps, in his twisted mind, Jason Bloomer had truly become Rolf Dagon, the man he intended to kill. Perhaps, in that final moment with the gun, facing the supreme evil which was really himself, all the Satanic trappings became too real for him. Perhaps that is why his heart gave out—because the evil he had to destroy was the evil within himself."

According to *Weird Tales* historian Robert Weinberg, ALLISON V. HARDING was the pseudonym of a distaff New York City attorney, now deceased. From 1943 to 1951, she sold thirty-six stories to the magazine, most of them dismissed by latter-day critics as second-rate filler. But in spite of its somewhat "pulpish" style, "The Damp Man," published in July 1947, is a page-turning nightmare that introduces one of the most compellingly original villains in all fantasy literature. (For further comment, see Appendix II, page 575.)

THE DAMP MAN

by Allison V. Harding

George Pelgrim sat with exaggerated boredom on the uncomfortable wood benches of the amphitheatre. The sign above the several rows proclaimed that this was the section reserved for the press, but George, as his sprawled long legs and discontented manner indicated, was neither impressed by the sign nor the spectacle going on beneath him in the pool where the Women's State Swimming Championships were being held.

Despite his comparatively young years, Pelgrim had covered a newspaper reporter's average quota of big stories, including those of the sports variety. This was a comedown. More than that, it was an out-and-out indignity, and for at least the tenth time that day, Pelgrim reviewed the disadvantages of working for a big short-handed metropolitan daily with the inevitable shuffling of assignments to its younger members that shorthandedness dictated. Still, covering something like a girls' swimming meet, and a relatively obscure one at that, was going too far. He'd taken a lot from McBrien, his editor, but this was . . .

Five similar forms splashed mightily below him, and one in a red cap finally forged ahead and touched the pool's end. The p.a. system then announced that the 100-yard free style winner was Miss Linda Mallory. Second was Miss Mary Ciphers, the former title-holder in this event.

George yawned. Thank God it was the last event. He slouched out of the stands, passing by the public relations table to pick up a press sheet with Events, Winners and Times. Now a few words from the new 100-yard champion and he'd be through this day's work. He took his time getting to the clubhouse and then he flashed his press pass at the doorway that proclaimed, "No Visitors —Contestants' Entrance." He nodded to a timer he recognized as someone he'd seen several times before at track meets—Oh happy days!—then he buttonholed one of the ribboned committeemen.

"I'd like to see that girl who won the 100-yard. Just a few words." He looked down at his sheet. "Mallory?"

"Ah yes, Miss Mallory," said the committeeman, filled with be-nice-to-the-press resolutions. "A fine swimmer!"

He beckoned the newspaperman to follow him and went down a corridor stopping before a door, knocking on it and then sticking his head in to murmur a few words. Then he turned back.

"Go right in."

Pelgrim went in. Linda Mallory was standing just inside. Pelgrim got the impression of well-built blondeness. She was dressed in street clothes now.

"I'm Pelgrim of the *Gazette,*" he mumbled. "I'd just like a few words, Miss Mallory. Is this the first district championship you've won? How old are you?"

He shot forth a few other questions. Get - it - over - with - as - soon - as - possible Pelgrim. Then for the first time he really looked at her. She was very pretty, if you like the big healthy athletic type. But there was something else. One shapely arm was holding onto the dressing table as though she needed its support. George's eyes narrowed. This was a strange way for a newly crowned champion to act. She ought to be pleased. Instead, Linda Mallory was terrified.

There was an awkward silence and then the girl managed the ghost of a smile.

"I'm sorry," she said and squared her shoulders. "I'm twenty and this is the first time I've won a county championship. It's very nice." Her voice trailed off and she didn't look as though she thought there was anything nice about it.

"Okay, thanks, Miss Mallory."

George's puzzlement at the girl's anxiety was being submerged by his indignation at having this assignment. He turned on his heel.

"Wait a minute, please!" She touched his arm imperatively. "Did you see anyone outside in the hall or coming through the clubhouse? A large man, fat, that is, in a dark suit with . . . with . . . ?"

George frowned. "Didn't notice. Say, are you all right, Miss Mallory? I mean, are you sick or anything?"

She shook her head. "No, no, I'm all right. I just wondered if you'd seen this person. I'm afraid I haven't been much good at being interviewed."

"I've got enough," replied Pelgrim and he stepped to the door. "About this friend of yours, I wouldn't worry, though. He'll find you."

"Yes," said Linda Mallory, "I guess he will!"

The best part of the day for Pelgrim started twenty minutes later when he ran into Al Holden entirely unexpectedly. He filed his story hurriedly and left the telegrapher's office arm in arm with Al. There were many "You old son-of-a-gun. Haven't seen you since . . ." He and his former pal repaired to the nearest bistro, and within a few minutes all thoughts of Linda Mallory had gone from Pelgrim's consciousness. He had enough presence of mind come six-twenty-five, though, to slap Holden on the back.

"It's been great, Al, but I've got to run. That old buzzard boss of mine has probably got three or four other jobs for his errand boys tonight!"

He made the 6:45 train to the city and settled into an empty seat, pleasantly mellowed by the five or six drinks and the realization that he had a three-quarters of an hour ride before he reached town, with the possibilities therein contained for a little nap.

He was dreaming gently of riding a huge rubber sea serpent in Central Park Lake when the sea serpent reached up a suddenly grown tentacle and began to shake him. He did what he could, but the sea serpent was persistent. George woke up and looked into Linda Mallory's startled face. It was her hand on his arm.

"Mr. Pelgrim, I'm so sorry. I saw you and sat down here in the seat next to you. I . . . I'm scared, Mr. Pelgrim. He's on this train."

Still only half awake, the only thing the reporter could think of was the sea serpent, and where Linda Mallory came in with the sea serpent was more than he could figure out. He straightened against the car seat with the self-conscious air of someone who is silently saying that of course he wasn't really asleep. He looked at the girl's agitated face and then took her hand because it seemed the thing to do. It was a nice hand, cool, or maybe that was because he'd had those drinks with Al Holden. Or maybe it was because she was so frightened.

"Now listen," he spoke in the heavy paternal manner of someone of his years to another person not too many years younger. "What's this all about?"

He remembered her as someone so self-possessed and confident that afternoon in her blue bathing suit with the red cap. Now she was, well, almost pathetic. Pelgrim was good at listening. He listened. He nodded at the right times and looked straight ahead, hoping his breath wasn't still one hundred percent alcoholic. After all, you don't meet an old friend like Al Holden every day. And that was a good excuse to top off a few.

Linda Mallory's story was straightforward and well-expressed, he analyzed. The telling of it seemed to help her. Anyway, she was less agitated at the finish. She was from the West. From the earliest she could remember, she told Pelgrim, she'd just had an aunt in the world and an ability to swim faster than other kids in school. Her home town had first sent her east to compete in a small meet and she'd won. There were the usual offers then to compete in other meets.

In the meantime, she'd gotten a modest job in an office in town—she could type—and everything seemed fine until one day she'd meet him. It was just recently. She'd competed in a meet and had been walking to the clubhouse when this man loomed up in front of her. He said something, she wasn't quite sure now, like "You are to be mine," or some such strange statement. He held his arms out to her, maybe beseechingly, maybe threateningly, she wasn't sure. She dodged his advances and brushed on by hurriedly, but he was outside when she left the dressing quarters.

He followed her to the bus the swimmers took back to town. She boarded it, heaving a sigh of relief as his gross figure faded in the distance when they got under way. Then miraculously he turned up one morning not many days later, sitting in the lobby of her hotel. He followed her through the streets. He'd been outside her office when she left at five-thirty.

Once she called a policeman, but when the officer turned to look in the direction she indicated, there was no one. He was clever, this big man.

Pelgrim thought to himself, Well, why not? There are plenty of these cranks around. You don't need to work on a newspaper to realize that and she's a cute kid. She *was.*

Aloud he asked, "You think you saw him this afternoon out at the meet and you think he's on this train?"

She nodded. "I know he is, Mr. Pelgrim."

"Well, we'll look into that, and in the meantime, cut out the Mister Pelgrim business. A lot of people have worse names for me but let's compromise and you call me George. Just what does this man look like?"

Linda shuddered. "He's . . . he's awful! I don't know how to describe him exactly except that he's very big and fat and he always has on a dark suit like a chauffeur's suit but it isn't really. But you know that dark material. And his face is lumpy and kind of swollen. And his eyes scare me, too. I tell you, Mr. Pel—George—that time I came downstairs in my hotel and saw him sitting there, those eyes looked at me over a newspaper he'd been reading. It made me feel all . . ." She shuddered again.

"You sit tight," George advised. "I'm going to see if I can spot him."

"He's back of us," Linda Mallory indicated. "I saw him get on the end of the train."

George got up and tried to look formidable. Maybe walking would clear the last "Great-to-see-you-Al-Holden" cobwebs out of his brain. He smiled and pointed towards the back.

"He went this way?"

Linda smiled back. "Look, is this the right thing to do? I mean, don't get into any trouble on account of me."

"I'm interested. I want to see this fascinated fan of yours for myself."

He left her sitting there looking after him. There were one, two, three, four cars behind theirs. The reporter walked slowly down the aisle, hands thrust deep in his pockets, looking casually from side to side. The usual assortment of flower-dress ladies, candy-eating children, men with their papers. A couple of long-stouts with papers. In the last car one had on a brown suit, the other had on sort of a gray and darkish sort of suit. He was buried in his paper, too. Looked pretty big from the shoulders.

The train slowed for a suburban station and stopped. George stood on the back platform with his eyes on the big fellow's back, undecided. Then he started up the aisle retracing his steps. When he came abreast of the suspect, he bobbed his head down.

"Pardon me," he thumbed at an item in the paper.

The fellow's face came out the other side of the tabloid.

"Friend of mine," murmured George apologetically.

The stranger's face was belligerent. It was also long, thin and horsey. It looked as though it were backed up by a good wallop. George smilingly backed away. It wasn't the man. The train started up again. Maybe he'd missed the guy the first time, or maybe he'd gotten off. George got back to his car and rehearsed a small speech. It was an excuse to hold her nice, capable hand again. He'd say, "There's nothing to worry about. Believe me, I fingerprinted all the guys back there. There's nobody answering your three-state alarm on the train."

But there was no speech because Linda Mallory was gone. And she wasn't on the train. George assured himself of that by looking through the forward cars. He fumed the rest of the way into town.

Three days later Pelgrim's desk phone jangled. It was Linda. Despite himself, he'd wondered about her even though with proper reportorial cynicism he told himself the whole business was probably screwy.

"Well, why the vanishing act?"

She apologized fervently. "But I had to. Just after you'd gone up the aisle out of the car, he appeared. I couldn't stand it. I got off at the next stop."

George um-hummed.

"Could I talk to you sometime?"

George with studied effort answered slowly. "Well, I guess so. Where are you?"

Linda Mallory gave the name of a hotel.

"I'll come up this evening," he said and hung up.

As he sat at his desk, the reporter realized he wasn't at all sure about Linda Mallory, about a lot of things concerning her. He admitted to himself reluctantly though that he was sure of one thing. He was glad to hear from her.

That night he arrived in the lobby of her building at the appointed time. It was a women's hotel and the downstairs was filled with potted palms and waiting males. She was there standing by the desk, and he thought mentally that the simple blue dress became her. She certainly didn't *look* like someone suffering from hallucinations.

He liked the way she stuck her hand out when she saw him and her smile—he'd liked that before.

"Let's sit over here," she motioned towards an off-the-floor alcove where there were a couple of chairs. He followed.

She looked at him intently. "If I were you, I'd probably think I was crazy."

He smiled. "My sentiments almost exactly," Pelgrim replied.

"I really don't have any right to get you into this and you've been very kind."

"Into what?" he persisted. "After all, if you don't mind my saying so, and if you do, I'll still say it, aren't you getting a little over-wrought about the attentions of a fan of yours?"

"He's been here," she went on, ignoring his question. "I think he got off just as I did at that station. I got a bus, but he followed me."

"Look, if this thing is bothering you so much," George suggested, "why not get the police in on it? I mean, really, a man sitting in your hotel lobby, following you to your job, shadowing you home from work. You've got a perfect right to—"

"He's clever," she said, and the fear look came back into her eyes. "I told you before, once in the street I spoke to an officer. He seems to anticipate . . . I mean he was just gone when the policeman looked. Last night, George, I worked late. When I came out, I didn't see him. I didn't look for him very hard. I guess I thought that he'd have gotten tired waiting for me. I went to a restaurant a couple of blocks away from here, and when I came out it was pitch dark. I was walking, not thinking of anything, you understand, not expecting to hear anything when I heard his steps behind me. You can't miss the sound. It's the sort of noise wet crepe rubber makes.

"I guess I lost my head. I ran the rest of the way here. Then I stood just inside the door and looked outside. I didn't see him again."

Pelgrim thought that over for a minute.

"Tell you, what you need is to get out of here for a little while. Stop thinking about it. Let's go to a show or something."

She brightened. "That'd be swell."

"All right, I'll wait right here and you go upstairs and get your coat."

He saw her disappear into the shining maw of the elevator. Then his eyes wandered over the people in the lobby. His spot was advantageous. From his side alcove he could see without himself being noticed. Harmless enough looking, everybody was.

His mind running over the things Linda Mallory had told him turned a sudden flip-flop, landing in a new position. This man, this follower she complained of and seemed so frightened of. It was strange no one else ever noticed him. He himself, for instance, or the policeman Linda admitted having spoken to one day on the street. There were all these episodes, these macabre details of some ungainly creature trailing her through the streets and everywhere, and yet no one apparently but Linda Mallory ever saw the man.

George had the average college-educated young man's rudimentary knowledge of psychology. How many times in the lay press had he read of things like a persecution complex—persons thinking other people are plotting against them, following them, whispering about them, etc.? Linda, in spite of her small job and her occasional swimming contests, was essentially very much alone here in the city, and he knew nothing about her background, really. It was an uncomfortable thought, one that shouldered its way into his mind rather than was welcomed there, but newspaper work demands objectivity, and this conclusion was at least a possible one, based on the facts as he knew them.

He could admit to himself that Linda Mallory was attractive, straightforward and nice. There was a simplicity about her that pleased him, and yet fear had been the most dominant chord in her make-up, a fixed fear about one thing that she hadn't been able to demonstrate for anyone else.

Unhappy at his own thoughts, George got up and ambled towards the front door. It was hot in here. He pushed through the portal, coming out on the street. There was one small bulb set in the middle of the awning that ran out to the curb. George stepped out of its depressingly feeble circle of light, fumbling for a cigarette in his jacket pocket. As he did so, he collided with someone.

The reporter mumbled, "Sorry," and the other figure moved away from him towards the door of the hotel. George turned. He gaped. The retreating figure was that of a very large fat man, his ungainly body fitted into a rumpled dark cloth suit. Pelgrim flicked his cigarette into the street and followed.

Inside, he saw the other man walking purposefully toward the alcove which George, himself, had just quit a moment or so ago. George took a few tentative steps in that direction. The man picked out the chair George had been sitting in and lowered himself heavily into it. Pelgrim had a glimpse of a fleshy dead-white face, and then an evening paper ascended in front of the waistcoat and head like a protective barrier.

George changed his mind, turned around and headed towards the desk. It was placed near the elevators and he would see her the moment she got down. He waited, tapping nervously on the counter. From this point he couldn't quite see into the corner of the alcove where the man sat.

Finally the metal door of the lift opened and Linda came out. He was at her side in an instant and ferried her across the floor towards the door. He said something, something trivial about what movie do you think we ought to see? or some such, and he purposely walked on the alcove side.

As George pushed her through the door, he flashed a quick glance to one side. The big man in the dark suit was still sitting there, the paper still in front of him, but it had lowered just a trifle, just enough to show a pair of eyes. And the eyes were on them . . .

They decided on a movie nearby. As they walked, George said to himself, Now you mustn't look back. You'll make her nervous, and yet look back was what he wanted to do more than anything else and still he couldn't be sure. There were other large men in dark suits who sat around reading papers. Pelgrim tried listening, but have you ever attempted to pick out a particular set of footsteps on a street in a crowded city?

When they got under the lighted theatre marquee, he was able to crane his neck. He spotted no one in the square of yellow light or on its outskirts. They went in and sat halfway down on the right side. The double feature was a whodunit and a comedy. Linda laughed at the slapstick and George was pleased.

It meant she was forgetting herself some, enjoying herself.

He murmured to her, "I've got to call into the office. Be back in just a sec."

It was a half-truth. The phone to his paper was not imperative, but Pelgrim did want to do a reconnaisance. The movie audience had thinned out even more, and with his back to the screen and the reflected light shining on the empty seats, it was easy for him to see the large, bulking figure sitting eight rows behind them. His emotions were half and half as he thumbed a nickel into the dial phone. He was annoyed and angry and there was also a sort of creepy feeling up his back and neck because he had thought all sorts of things about Linda in the beginning. Maybe she was pulling a fake or throwing a psycho at him and all the time there was a guy and he did just what she said he did.

He got the paper. "Hello, is Jim Crosier there?"

He was told Crosier had left half an hour earlier. He had reasons of his own for wanting to speak to the veteran newspaperman, but if he wasn't there—that was that.

George hurried back down the aisle and then he slowed as he neared it. For directly back of Linda, now, the big man was sitting. He'd moved up in the couple of moments Pelgrim had been away. George moved down beside her. She was smiling at something on the screen, oblivious of anything else around her. He'd have to handle this skillfully.

"Look," he said, "I'm sorry, but it looks as though we ought to head out. We must be almost up to where we came in."

He hated to take the kid away from this thing. She seemed to be enjoying it, but she nodded, good sport that she was. He pushed her hurriedly down the row and maneuvered her up the aisle so she wouldn't notice.

"I'm sorry," Linda Mallory apologized when they got outside. "You shouldn't have spent so much time with me tonight, should you?"

He sighed in mock tragedy and tried to make his tones light, "They'll probably have me back filling inkwells in the morning!"

They stopped at an all-night eatery, and over a cup of coffee George made a decision. The whole thing was queer and mysterious enough without adding unnecessarily to those factors. The diner clock said that it was after twelve.

The streets were deserted as they walked from out of the oblong of light thrown down by the eatery's windows. A soft spring fog had crept in from the sea, muffling the sound of occasional midnight traffic, swathing the lonely streetlamps in ghostly halos and cutting visibility to not many yards.

They walked between rows of brick-fronted houses, houses that were lonely and ghostly as though they had never known human habitation, and their steps echoed soddenly from the pavements.

It was in the middle of one dingy block that George felt Linda's fingers tighten on his arm. Her hearing had been perhaps keener than his, but when the dying sound of a distant el train was completely gone, he knew too that there were footsteps behind them. He looked at Linda Mallory. Her red mouth was partly open as though there were a question which she feared to ask.

He put his fingers over his hand. "What's the matter?"

He smiled even though he knew; they both knew. They walked on, and as though by mutual consent their steps were faster, but there seemed no end to this long black block. And the sounds behind them were more clearly defined. Perhaps because their senses were keyed so high and sent so completely backward towards the one focus point, or perhaps because the steps were actually nearer, gaining on them.

You know how it is when you were a child, a child somewhere in the darkness of night or in the darkness of an old house or in the darkness of your own imagination, the mad irresistible urge that sweeps over you suddenly, so suddenly to flee with all the strength of your being, to run, to hide.

There is some of that in all of us at certain times. It touched George briefly, a touch of darkness and fog, the run-and-hide urge, and he felt it in Linda too and her frightened look at him said so. With the other emotions and the thinking that was going on in his head, there was still room for pity for her. She'd had this unpleasant thing to fight with before and before. He was new to it, and the newness must be worth something, he resolved.

"Take it easy," he murmured to her.

She worked a little grin. "I just know I'd be sprinting by now if I were alone," Linda admitted.

In the tunnel of darkness ahead, there beckoned the wan yellow beacon of a street light. The single bulb glowed weakly in the sticky atmosphere. They marched toward it, and marched was the word, for George kept their paces even. It was a matter of morale, he knew instinctively; that if they once broke stride, they would run helter-skelter, an absurd mad spectacle of two very frightened people who should know better, plummeting down the lonely thoroughfare until they would trip and hurt themselves or come suddenly upon a greater brightness and busyness of the city and suddenly feel ashamed.

Pelgrim was no fool. He thought he had calculated their situation and their chances. No casual bad man, no mugger or stick-up artist wastes his time tracking one person night after night. A big-city hold-up is as impersonal as an auto accident. It is completely indiscriminate. If you happen to be on such-and-such a street at such-and-such a time, you will feel a gun in your ribs or a billy on your skull, you or you or anyone else.

No, the lure here was the girl, and what he did not know about her could be his undoing, their undoing, and this disquieting thought made George stare at Linda again, so suddenly that she felt it and looked back. He felt ashamed of himself for any suspicions he might have had. This girl was honest. She'd told him what she knew. There was nothing contrived that she was a party to. A kidnaping was absurd and seemed out of the question. There were easier ways. This long surveillance, for instance. Why would that be necessary? And not Linda Mallory, a girl who made a tiny salary and was, at the most, only a promising swimmer of small local accomplishment.

This left another field, a category as dark and dank and misty as the night. This large man was one of those myriads of persons who tramp through the city and country on some small, strange purpose of their own. Small to us but large to them. The not wholly normal people. The twisted. The insane.

George wished he had a gun or a club or anything. They reached the oasis of light and he told her quickly, "You stand on the other side of it. Do you know the way to your hotel from here?"

She nodded.

"Sure?"

She nodded again.

"Just stand there. Don't say anything. Don't do anything, but if I tell you to run, run as fast as you can and keep running until you get where there are some more people or you see a policeman or you reach your hotel. Don't stop for anything else, you understand?"

She nodded for the third time. "But what about you?"

"I'm going to try and find out about this guy. Linda, there must be some explanation to this."

He hoped it sounded good the way he put it.

"Maybe he thinks you're his long-lost daughter or something."

The steps were much nearer now and Pelgrim could see what she meant about wet crepe-rubber soles, almost a sloshing sound on the damp pavements. Linda backed away from him into the shadows on the other side of the circle of luminance. Satisfied, the reporter turned and faced the way they'd come. He took a few steps into the darkness, turned his head to look once more where Linda was. Good. From here, even knowing she was there, he could hardly make out her figure, and he waited.

The sounds seemed an endless number of heartbeats, of deep anticipatory breaths and then out of the blackness loomed up a greater blackness. It was the large man, looking even larger than George had remembered him, looking of the night itself with his dark suit and midnight fedora.

The steps stopped. The man stopped not a pace away from Pelgrim. The light shone on his lumpy, whitish face. The thin street-lamp light and shadows made more grotesqueness of the ungainly figure and the pads of flesh that were hands and jowls.

George stepped nearer quickly. Attack was his only plan.

"You following someone, Bud?"

Closer, he was appalled by the repulsiveness of the man. The eyes were one color black. They had no depth, no expression. They were simply round disks like the button gimlets of a cod exhibited in the window of a fish store. There was something else about the man that came over George, suddenly freezing him with a horror that was hard to control. He looked . . . he looked like someone George remembered years ago, a bloated body grappling irons had pulled out of the river one cold night onto a police-launch deck.

The skin looked like this, the puffiness, the blue-whiteness, the eyes expressionless with death. You don't see a thing like that often. But dead men don't speak. This one said, "Where is she?" and there was a flash of something unreadable in the dark ugly eyes.

The voice was deep with a resonant barrel-like quality. The words were spoken slowly.

"Where's who?" shot back Pelgrim.

"The girl."

"What do you want with her? You've got a hell of a nerve, Mister . . ."

The big fellow's eyes stopped their peripatetic course and fixed themselves over the reporter's shoulder. Without looking, Pelgrim knew Linda had been spotted. He sensed the big body before him gathering itself and he dove forward just as the other man lunged.

As George drove his fists, he yelled, "Run, Linda, run!"

And above the sound of that message's echo in the lonely street, he heard her heels clicking away furiously. His fists pounded into the spongy monstrous hulk, and then a heavy fat hand smacked into the side of his neck making his senses reel. George almost went down but clung to a thick flaying arm. The large man reached forward. A shoulder caught him and George went to his knees grabbing a leg.

The big man grunted.

George saw the kick coming too late. It landed between his eyes and then the blackness of the street and the dark bulk of his opponent were swallowed up into an even greater blackness.

The next thing George knew, he felt the pressure of an arm under his head. He blinked at the flashlight in his eyes as a voice was saying, "There now, buddy, you're coming around."

He struggled to raise himself, and the light of the flashlight glanced off shiny policeman buttons. Another cop held the torch, and behind them was the white dome of a police radio car. George finally made it to his feet. There was a lump on his forehead and his senses were still faint with more fog than the night air. He gave his name and address mechanically to the inquiring policeman, showing his press card.

"You don't know who this guy was?" queried one of the uniforms.

"Nope." No use telling the full story now. The important thing was to find out whether Linda had made it okay to her building.

"Will you give me a lift?" He designated the street where she lived.

They piled him in behind them and drove him to his destination. Almost before he got out of the police car, Linda came through the door and greeted him.

She was shaking.

"George, I was scared stiff!"

"C'mon, let's get back inside," Pelgrim said.

"George, your head . . ."

"Never mind that." He steered her towards the alcove. "Any sign of him here?"

She shook her head sideways. "What happened? Those police and that head of yours!"

He told her quickly what had happened.

"You shouldn't have made me leave you," she criticized.

"You would have been a fine lot of help. No, this baby's a tough one, Linda. Now listen. I want you to go up to your room and I want you to stay there. No matter what happens, stay there! He can't get upstairs in this building. I'll phone you in the morning. Okay?"

She agreed.

"This time Buster has overstepped himself. We'll get that guy, Linda, don't worry."

"What . . . who is he?" she asked. "I mean, what's it all about, George?"

The fear look he hated to see was there again but he couldn't blame her.

"There's something else I want to ask you, George."

"Yeah?"

"When you fought with him just now, did he grab hold of you at any time, or did you touch him?"

Pelgrim smiled wryly and motioned to his forehead.

"A pretty good grab, don't you think?"

"I mean . . ." she persisted, "there's something about that man that's not right. I told you the time at the swimming meet, he took hold of my arms and then I had to push him away. It was, well, it was almost as though he'd been in *swimming*. Did you notice anything strange like that?"

George laughed raucously. "You think the bird is dead! Someone come back from a watery grave! Your Uncle Egbert who sailed before the mast and died on the Spanish Main!"

"Don't laugh," she protested. "It's just that I . . ."

"He's flesh and blood, Linda. There's nothing dead about him."

"I didn't quite mean that."

"Well, stop meaning or thinking anything," the reporter ordered.

"Go upstairs to your room and get some sleep. Forget it. I know that's pap advice but it's best. I'll call you in the morning. All right?"

They both rose. She squeezed his hand. "And thank you so much. This is my affair and my trouble and yet you've made it yours. I don't know what I'd have done without you. Probably gone completely batty."

"Forget it." He was embarrassed. "Call you in the morning."

He saw her to the elevator and only when the doors clanged shut behind her did he head for the hotel entrance. Pelgrim still felt a bit shaky, so he hailed a taxi. As they drew into the avenue, George spotted something out the side window. As they flashed by, he saw the unmistakable familiar bulk leaning casually against a mailbox, face turned towards the hotel facade. George tapped on the partition.

"Cabby, wait up a minute! I want to go back."

"Can't make a U-turn here, mister," the driver complained. "Against the law."

The next best thing was to describe a square around the block. By the time the mailbox landmark came in sight again though, the large man was gone. George settled back in the cab satisfied there was nothing more he could do this night.

Home in his apartment he wrung a towel out in cold water and put it around his head. It helped the throbbing, made him think better. That little thing Linda had spoken of, what she'd noticed about this man. He'd noticed it, too. The strange abnormal wetness of those beefy hamlike hands. Perhaps there were physical diseases that caused these things, he wouldn't know, and perhaps with them there was some sort of mental derangement that went as companion symptoms. All these things he could and would find out. In the meantime, he was going to shuffle the deck and make the Queen of Hearts disappear.

His alarm knocked the sleep out of him at seven-thirty. Within half an hour with a shower and a coffee-and-eggs breakfast out of the way, he was on the phone to Linda Mallory.

"Number One," he enumerated pedantically, "I want you to pack up, Linda. Buster knows where you are. We're going to fix that. Number Two, phone that place where you work and tell them you're terribly sorry you're not coming back."

He forced both points home over her mild protests.

"Do anything you want around there, but don't leave the hotel. Understand?"

She did. He hung up and left for the office, surprising the newspaper staff considerably from copy boy to junior reporters by his early arrival.

He went into the office he shared with Jim Crosier and slammed the door. It was too early for the other man to be there, but George made good use of his time. By ten o'clock he'd located a place on the other side of town where he could get a room for Linda. It was in a respectable neighborhood not far from a subway. By ten-thirty he'd fixed it up with Mort Hoge, the Sunday feature editor, to take Linda on as a typist in that department.

Crosier came in then and Pelgrim went to town.

"So you're the number one crime reporter in the county." It was a joke between them and Crosier liked it that way. Actually, the older man did know the subject. He was an expert on the history of violence, on court procedure and the legal aspects.

George outlined his experiences with Linda Mallory. At the end, the other reporter smiled.

"You stuck on the girl?"

Pelgrim huffed and puffed.

"I see you are," Jim answered his own question. "And you haven't been drinking too much lately, have you?"

"Say now, wait a minute. If you think I got this kick in the head . . ."

"Probably fell off a bar stool. Listen, George. The young lady evidently has other admirers besides you. This fat man is one of them. You know what they say about our present civilization and competition. You'll just have to accept it, kid. What's that? No, son, it's a tough point legally to get a man arrested because you say he's been following someone. About your drunken brawl with him last night . . ." Crosier guffawed, ". . . I don't know."

George choked down an angry retort as the other reporter turned to his typewriter. And yet hadn't he, himself, been skeptical in the beginning? No, he guessed he'd have to handle it himself without court orders or the Police Department or Crosier.

There was one little thing, though, that would help. He'd get a gun. That was only feasible.

He left the office at noon and took a taxi up to Linda's hotel. He buzzed her on the house phone, told her to come downstairs with her luggage. She was with him inside of ten minutes and he was quieting her protests.

"Now don't worry. I've got another place for you."

No, she wasn't to leave the new address as a forwarding one. After a moment they decided that she could refer any messages or mail to the swimming club she belonged to.

The taxi they took drove an eccentric course until George, peering out of the back window, was satisfied there was no pursuit. Their destination was an old five-story brownstone house. The landlady was a Mrs. Brumley, a plump oldish woman, the widow of a former *Gazette* reporter. She bestowed a motherly greeting on them both.

"It's good to see you," she said to Pelgrim. "And I've got the third floor rear for the young lady."

George saw Linda up the creaking carpeted stairs. Hers was a big airy room looking out over back yards.

"Like it?"

"I think it's grand," Linda replied.

"Okay now, you get settled and then tomorrow you arrive down at my newspaper office at nine sharp." He gave her the address. "Don't expect to see me," George warned, "but they're expecting you in Department D."

He went downstairs and spoke to Mrs. Brumley for a moment before he left. He explained that Miss Mallory had had the unwanted attentions of a man forced upon her for some time and that that was the reason for the hurry-up change of address. Mrs. Brumley was to see that she was disturbed by no strangers here, especially—and George described the large man carefully.

The telephone cut into Pelgrim's sleep the next morning. One half-opened eye focused on the clock beside the receiver. He pulled the instrument from its cradle, grouchily, noting that it was before eight. He made the noise that is a sleepy man's hello, and then her words cut into him deeper than the phone bell.

It was Linda and she was frightened, very frightened. George Pelgrim's eyes were open wide now.

"Hey, wait a minute. Hold on," he checked her. "What was that again?"

"It's in the paper," she repeated. "Peggy Greene, she lived next door to me at the hotel! I've mentioned her to you, George. Well, maybe I haven't."

"Well, what about—?"

"She's dead, I'm trying to tell you! They found her in the night!"

"That's tough," he sympathized, "awfully tough. I know it's an awful shock, but I don't get—"

"George, it's the same business, I'm sure! Listen to me. Peggy was almost my size. Yesterday when I was packing up, she asked to borrow my blue suit. I loaned it to her. She wanted to wear it last night. Don't you *see,* George? She's blonde like me, too. *He* thought it was me!"

The reporter thought for a moment.

"Get your breakfast there and wait for me. I'll pick you up," he ordered and hung up.

Thirty minutes later in a taxi he read the early edition *Gazette.* The crime rated a four-column headline. She'd been choked, police thought, some time around midnight "in a lonely section not a dozen blocks from her hotel—." It made George wonder if it was the same "lonely section" where he and Linda had had their experience earlier. "The cause of death was strangulation. From marks on the throat the victim had been killed by choking." "—no trace of the assailant although police feel certain that it was a man."

There was a picture of Peggy Greene. She was blonde, older than Linda and well built and large of frame. In the dark with her light hair and in the swimmer's dress, she could easily have been mistaken for the other girl. And she had been; there was the epitaph.

Mrs. Brumley was bustling with solicitude and "poor child." Linda was holding back the tears with an effort. George tried patting her shoulder. It seemed inadequate. He finally persuaded the girl to come with him down to the *Gazette* office.

"You don't want to sit around here all day going over and over this thing," he pointed at the paper on the table.

But they went over it going downtown. George forced an optimism he didn't feel.

"We can give the cops a steer on this thing," he opinionated. He tried to avoid saying, Obviously the big guy was after you.

But Linda Mallory got it. She turned to him.

"He's crazy, isn't he, George? Completely crazy. Some sort of strange perverted maniac."

"I don't know. I don't know what he is."

No matter what is the trouble with the rest of the world or with your own world, it helps to be in a big, impersonal office with a lot of people. You are caught up in the bustle and the activity. It is an intangible. It is *esprit de corps* and the power of suggestion, and no matter what your trouble, you feel better.

Linda did. Two hours after she was introduced to Department D, she was sitting there doing routine typing, listening to the gum-chewing redhead on the left of her complaining about her boy friend and laughing despite herself at the wisecracks of one of the office boys who kept popping in.

There was the other thing inside of her, the shock and the fear and the regret at losing a friend—perhaps she hadn't known the Greene girl long. Maybe it was only a month or so but still—but the feeling was deeper within her now.

George looked in two or three times that morning, noticed and was pleased. He had their lunches sent upstairs, and afterward he took her around, showing her some of the printing presses and the composition rooms.

Later that day she called her swimming club. She told them, as George had instructed, simply that she had to move and that she'd come in within a week. They, in turn, passed on the information that there were a couple of letters for her and a persistent caller, a man who kept asking about her whereabouts.

"We've got him guessing." That evening George saw her straight home in a cab.

At the end of the week she persuaded him to let her go to the swimming club. He got some mid-afternoon time off for both of them.

"After all," she argued, "I'm supposed to be a swimmer. I have to practice once in a while."

There was a pool in the basement of the building. Linda glanced at her mail and then at George. He guessed what was coming. There was a leathery-faced, mannish-looking woman who had been fussing over her by the desk. He caught snatches like, "Neglecting your practice, my dear, and after such a promising beginning."

Linda said, "George, I ought to do a little practicing in the pool.

It's perfectly all right here. You can stay or go, as you want. Isn't that okay?"

"I'll stay," he replied curtly.

The tank was in the basement level, a small twenty-yard pool, green-sided, white-tiled bottom. There were a few benches running down one side. On the other were two corridors, one leading to the stairs from above and the other leading to the dressing and shower rooms. He sat down on one of the benches and stretched his long frame.

The water was very clear and completely quiescent. He supposed later in the afternoon and the evening other girls came here. But now it was very lonely, and the yellow dome lights blinked down solemnly on him.

In a moment Linda came out in her bathing suit. The leathery-faced woman who had been introduced to George as the Association's swimming coach came and stood by the side of the pool and called down instructions as the girl swam up and down the tank, first slowly and then faster.

"You're rolling a little too much, dear. That's it."

George, less the perfectionist than old Leather Face, marveled at Linda's powerful, long strokes.

"That's fine," the coach clapped her hands. "Now you do a few dozen pool lengths."

The coach then beckoned to Pelgrim.

"There's something I'd like to speak to you about," she said in a low voice. "Not here. Come up to my office a moment."

George looked doubtfully back at Linda in the pool. She waved gaily to him. He followed the older woman up the stairs. She led him into a small, dingy office and closed the door. The walls were covered with photographs of girl swimmers.

"My girls," old Leather Face intoned proudly, "and you know, I really think Linda Mallory could be one of the best, but she hasn't been practicing enough. Oh my no, not nearly enough."

The woman fluttered on talking about Linda and swimming, and around the edges of several other subjects. Finally the reporter asked, "And what was it you wanted to speak to me about?"

The swimming coach reddened. Her hands waved in the air. Why, she's positively embarrassed, George realized.

"I think I'd better be getting back to the pool."

"No, no," she cried and laid a claw-like hand on his arm. She tried for a smile and fluttered some more. "You see, Linda should devote her entire time to swimming. She could really, well, I think she could really become very good. It's a great opportunity." The woman went on.

He agreed. "But I really think I ought to go back."

She protested feebly again. The transparent stall of the thing suddenly hit Pelgrim. He yanked at the door and started down the stairs to the basement two at a time.

He heard the woman following some steps behind.

The pool was empty, and its emptiness caught at his throat. He'd been upstairs how long? Ten, fifteen minutes, maybe a little longer. He turned to old Leather Face, raging.

"Where's her room! Where's Linda Mallory's dressing room?"

She beckoned down the other corridor. "It's really all right. Now don't get so excited, young man."

He pounded down the corridor.

"That one," she indicated to the left.

Everywhere else the dressing room doors were open showing emptiness, nothing but utter emptiness. Without knocking he flung open the one closed door. It, too, was completely empty. The older woman stood in the door behind him outside.

"Really, it's all right," she protested. "You're becoming much too excited."

"What's all right!" George yelled.

"She's with the gentleman," the coach insisted. "She's all right."

The story poured out. This man who had phoned so often for Linda, and the time he'd come, admitting whimsically that as a suitor he was losing out to someone else. Would they . . . would they let him know the next time she came, phone him immediately?

"He gave me his number," Leather Face proclaimed, "and forced, positively forced a fifty-dollar bill on me." The memory of it still embarrassed her. "He was very persistent."

"What did he look like?" Pelgrim cried.

"Well, not what you'd really call attractive. No, really not at all. He was very large, big, almost fat, yes, fat. A large white face with very dark eyes, but he was very courteous to me."

George could see her remembering the fifty-dollar bill.

"And you think Linda left here with him of her own accord?"

"Why, of course. He was her fiancé, sort of. At least that's what I gathered."

"That's what you gathered!" George sneered, and he heard the strange sound of his own voice rising. "Just look in here a minute."

The woman came forward peering into the chamber, eyes bulging as though she expected to find a corpse.

"Her clothes!" Pelgrim thundered. "Her dress, all her things are here. You think she vanished, left this building of her own accord just in a bathing suit?"

The woman shook her head, amazement spreading across her face.

"Certainly he wouldn't risk taking her upstairs and out front that way. Is there a back entrance? Quick!"

The woman nodded and beckoned out the way they'd come. George found it. The way led to an alley beside the building. It too was empty, but outside lying beside the brick wall was her bright-red bathing cap, a rubber seam split at one place as though it had been torn off. He picked it up, and without another word to the startled older woman still dogging his trail, he got into a cab and told the driver, "Take me to the nearest police station."

Sergeant Murphy was very helpful in that imperturbable, unconstructive way that police officials have in the face of any catastrophe. George gave a complete description of Linda, and as best he could, a complete description of the big man. The only factor that caused the vestiges of life to light small fires for a moment in that sergeant's face was mention that the abductee was abducted in a bathing suit.

"In a bathing suit, you say now!" That was Sergeant Murphy's sole contribution.

George left for home. He poured himself a stiff drink and another, then he remembered to phone the office and told them to transfer any calls to his apartment. George turned on the radio. He called the precinct. There was no news. He'd never before been a floor-pacer. But now he paced. It was doubly hard because it was his own fault for leaving her there.

That stupid fool of a woman mouthing on about the gentleman giving her a fifty-dollar bill! Not to know the name of the person he was seeking. Except that fifty-dollar bills don't grow on trees could mean he was rich, must mean he was well off.

At one-fifteen a.m. in the morning (George knew the time exactly because he'd just listened to the news on the radio), the knocking came at his door. The knocking was insistent, hysterical.

Pelgrim opened the door, expecting anything. The anything was Linda. She fell into his arms. Her knees gave way and she sagged to the floor. There was an old, tattered long coat around her and an ugly bruise on her cheekbone. She mumbled something to him about a taxi driver downstairs and she got out of the long coat. George got it.

"Will you be all right for a minute?"

She nodded but sat there on the floor where she'd collapsed. Her face was gray, her eyes circled with fatigue. He made sure the catch was on the door and felt it lock from the outside.

The cab driver was waiting skeptically and getting increasingly nervous.

"Hadn't ought to do it, mister. Hadn't of excepting your wife is so pretty." He accepted his long coat back gratefully.

George paid him the fare and a five-dollar tip, upon which the cabby grew loquacious.

"Ought to take better care of your wife, mister, beautiful girl like that. Masquerade party, she says to me. Some masquerade party, I says to myself! Going around the city in a bathing suit! It's none of my business, but if you ask me, mister!"

George left the driver still talking and hurried back into the building. In a moment he'd let himself back into his apartment. Her eyes were large with fear and glazed with shock. He pulled her over to his bed and hoisted her onto it. Then he called a doctor friend of his, a man who didn't mind being disturbed at this hour and wouldn't ask too many questions.

Linda said little. She was plainly exhausted. Dr. Allen, when he came, confirmed that.

"I've given her something to make her sleep." He punched his friend playfully on the shoulder. "What're you up to, George, my boy, and what's the swimming-suit stunt? After mermaids now?"

"She's all right?" Pelgrim was in no mood for jokes.

"She's okay. A good sleep will do it. She's got a nasty bruise on her cheekbone there. I'd hate to see whatever she bumped into."

After Allen left, George tiptoed in and saw that Linda was sleeping. He shut the door quietly and then curled up on the living-room sofa.

She slept late, and before he heard the first stirrings from her room, he'd already put together some breakfast and phoned the office saying she wouldn't be in and he'd be late. When he took coffee and toast in to her, he was pleased at how much better she looked, although the cheekbone was still ugly.

She had a hearty, "Hi, what goes here!" for him.

"You mean you don't remember?" he came back.

She didn't shake her head but she looked doubtful, just this side of shaking her head. Then she clenched her hands together tightly.

"Yes," her voice was low. "Yes, I do remember. I remember all of it, George, and I don't want to."

He didn't like the look on her face and he chattered quickly about something else and got some coffee into her. He told her to stay put, not to answer the door or even the telephone unless it rang in a simple code he explained to her. Then he went out.

The Civil Administration offices of the city were not unfamiliar to him. He'd been there before on stories. Once there'd been a conference in the mayor's chambers. Another time, when the Commissioner of Police had been sworn in. The Commissioner, George remembered, was a tall man with the erect carriage of the military and a bristly gray mustache, a rather fine-looking man.

Waiting in the anteroom, George rehearsed in his mind what he was going to say. It was unusual, of course, to take a complaint to the Commissioner, but he felt under the circumstances it was justifiable. He wasn't at all averse to cashing in on a public officials's desire to please representatives of the press. A good press often elects public officials and sympathetic reporting is a good press. Anybody from the lowest ward-heeler on up knows this.

He would state it simply, "Mister Commissioner, I realize this is rather an extraordinary case, but this acquaintance of mine" —and he would outline the situation, ending up with a description of the big man. The Commissioner would listen politely, and at the very least, there would be some sort of alarm or alert posted to pick up this character at least for questioning.

George waited. And then the door to the Commissioner's office opened. The Commissioner himself walked out. But George's eyes were not for his erect bearing and the neatly trimmed gray mustache. Instead they were caught and fascinated by the Commissioner's companion. The hugeness, the dark, rumpled suit . . .

The two men shook hands fervently and then the dark-suited monster lumbered past Pelgrim as though he hadn't seen him, and out of the offices.

The Commissioner beckoned to the stunned reporter, frowning as he did so. The frown stayed put when they sat down inside. George's mouth was dry. His throat was tight. Words wouldn't come. Nothing came. Instead, the Commissioner spoke from out of the frown.

"Now, Mister Pelgrim. You are Pelgrim of the *Gazette,* of course?"

George managed to nod. The Commissioner went on:

"Ah, yes, of course I remember you. Please don't tell me you've come here to make a complaint!"

George was immobile. The Commissioner waved one hand.

"We all make mistakes. Of course, I don't want to embarrass you with a recital of what you know only too well, for the fact remains that Mr. Remsdorf—er, you just saw him leaving—er—has just made a complaint against you! He told me just now that going by your conduct of the last few months, you would probably be following him here!" The Commissioner made another wave in the air with his hand.

"He did say you might probably lodge a complaint against him." The Commissioner smiled as though this last contingency was so utterly ridiculous that no other facial reaction could satisfy it.

"There's a girl, I know," the Commissioner continued.

George started to speak but the official motioned him to silence.

"I know, I know how these misunderstandings come up. But I would suggest under the circumstances that you back out of this situation gracefully. I, of course, don't like to take any action on behalf of the city or the Police Department against you or speak to your employer."

"Who is he?" George finally got out.

The Commissioner looked surprised. "You don't know? That's Lother Remsdorf, Jr!"

The name went around in Pelgrim's mind and then the lights came on. Lother Remsdorf, Sr., had been the brilliant experimentalist and multi-millionaire who owned the huge place up on Grandview Avenue, some plantations in the South, coal ore, timber and vast real-estate holdings. Remsdorf, Jr., could buy and sell Commissioners of Police.

"What does he charge me with?" George asked, tight-lipped.

"Now, now, Mister Pelgrim. This can all be done with a minimum of dramatics and without any great loss to yourself. There are, you know" —with what he meant to be a witty smile— "other girls in the world. Just leave Mr. Remsdorf's fiancée alone! I make myself clear, I hope."

The next few days were tortuous. Linda regained her physical strength and slowly the shock of her experiences with Remsdorf passed. George learned about it bit by bit, not wanting to force her. How the big man appeared from nowhere soon after George went upstairs with the swimming coach. He grabbed her before she could escape into the pool again and forced her out the back way.

They'd driven for a long time in his long, black, expensive limousine, chauffeured by some sort of liveried South American, she thought.

He told her a strange tale about himself and about her and where, like a crossword puzzle, their two destinies fitted together. He'd said quite candidly, she recalled the story to Pelgrim, that he wasn't the same as other men.

She'd listened to him with growing horror as he'd talked, not wanting to accept what he said, her eyes fascinatedly watching the drops of moisture on the backs of his huge, fleshly hands, and she remembered that when he touched her, his hands were wet as though *he* had been in swimming and not she.

The prosaic, matter-of-fact way he presented what he averred was the scientific truth about himself made the revelations even more horrible. Linda sat huddled in the corner of his huge sedan, stunned, speechless.

Finally he drove to the family town house on Grandview Avenue. He helped her inside. Helped was hardly the word, for his giant hand closed over her forearm and she sensed that he would have wrenched it out of the socket before he would have let her escape. And where could she go? The impossibility of fleeing down a city street in a bathing suit!

He talked to her in the large house, as silent and imperturbable as its servants who came and went with drinks and food which she assiduously avoided touching. He drank, she noticed, huge quantities of liquids, beakers of milk, glasses and glasses of water and assorted liqueurs.

Finally, it was some time later that night, he sat dozing and looking water-logged before her, surrounded by empty glasses. She gathered her strength and ran off down the corridors of the old monstrous house. She heard him come awake, the sound of a bell being rung, undoubtedly to summon the servants, and then his huge flapping weight coming after her in pursuit.

Thankfully, she found a door, and just as his nightmare shape rounded a corner behind her, she burst into the street, unmindful of her appearance. It was then she found a taxi, and brokenly told her story. It was any story then, that she'd been at a masquerade, and she gave George's address.

Pelgrim listened, half disbelieving some of the time but the terror was a valid thing stamped on her face, as real as the bruise where the big man struck her when he dragged her struggling from the pool.

The days became weeks, and the weeks with their uneventfulness gratefully lent themselves to a growing feeling of security. Linda sensed it and thrived on it. The color came back into her pretty face. She continued on at Mrs. Brumley's and their routine was simple.

George picked her up every morning in a cab and they went to the *Gazette*. They went home again together at night, and in all that time they never once saw Remsdorf. In the first few days of that period of time, George found out what he could about Lother Remsdorf, Sr. and Jr. The father had been a brilliant scientist. No less an authority than Carrel called him "decades ahead of his time."

He had the brilliant analytical incisive and curious mind of the born experimentalist, plus the family heredity of vast wealth which allowed him to delve where he would, independent of the politics that surround the monetary grants from scientific and medical institutions.

There were no limits, some experts felt, to the anthropological, biological and protoplasmic advances Remsdorf might have been able to make when the catastrophic explosion destroyed his mountain laboratory. Most of his equipment and all of his notes were obliterated, and no trace of Remsdorf, Sr., was ever found by searching parties who came to the lofty eyrie to search among the blackened ruins.

There was a son, though, to carry on the name—Lother Remsdorf, Jr. Although his interests were not, seemingly, concerned with science, he had supposedly a brilliant mind, and as direct and only heir was one of the three wealthiest men in the country. A man in his position could purchase almost anything he wished from property to human lives to do with, to distort or destroy, as he willed.

Pelgrim felt a vast futility in those first few days, but as time passed and Linda grew more cheerful, he, too, had hopes that they had seen the last of the big man. With the months came early winter, and that past spring and summer seemed like some half-forgotten evil story laid in the distant past.

Linda's work at the paper went on, but one day she came to George, her eyes bright. It was the Southern Indoor Swimming Meet, the last of the season. She wanted to compete.

"I know I've neglected my practice," she admitted, "but I'd like to try. George, that awful business is behind us now. Don't you think it's all right?"

He said he thought so, but somehow the association with swimming bothered him. He wangled the assignment from his editor, and a week later they were on the train, Linda's entry acceptance in her handbag.

The trip to the southern city was an overnight hop. George saw Linda safely into her lower berth. Her upper was occupied by an elderly woman going to visit her son, while George had an upper across the aisle.

His desire for a cigarette before turning in took the reporter to the rear of the train. The observation car was empty at this hour except for a porter counting up tips. Pelgrim pushed open the door onto the observation platform and fumbled his way in the darkness to a seat. He cupped his hands over a match to light his cigarette. He inhaled deeply and then blew the smoke out into the currents of air that rushed past.

It was quiet as a railroad car can be with its rhythmical clicking of wheels, quiet enough so that when a voice said, "Good evening, Mr. Pelgrim," George jumped as though at a revolver shot.

He turned his head and just made out the shape of someone sitting on the opposite rail of the platform. The tones and the shape were all too familiar. George let out air suddenly and a gasp that sounded like, "You!" The revolver he'd gotten the license for several months ago was back inside in his suitcase.

"Please don't say anything as prosaic as that I'm following you," the big man chuckled, "or I shall have to suggest to the authorities that quite the reverse is true. How is Miss Mallory?"

"She's—she *was* all right," George said angrily, rising to his feet. He stood at the entrance door looking down at Lother Remsdorf. "I don't care who you are! I'm going to get rid of you, do you understand?"

But this heated denunciation only caused the big man to chuckle more.

"I mean to have her, Mr. Pelgrim, in spite of all your efforts. You see, she and I, our destinies are together to start a new race. Ah, but there I go. You wouldn't understand." His voice took on a brittle hardness. "She'll be mine or she will not be at all! As for your worries about who I am, well, let that be subordinate, Mr. Pelgrim. I would suggest you worry about *what* I am!"

George left the platform raging at the sound of laughter behind him. He got into his berth and lay there the rest of the night while the clicking wheels counted off the miles and the hours, and he thought and wondered and thought some more, always ending up at an impasse.

The next morning he transferred the revolver from his suitcase into his pocket. He'd planned to say nothing about Lother Remsdorf to Linda, but getting off the train, she spotted the big man alighting two cars down. The hugeness, the bulk, the dark rumpled suit, these characteristics were not to be mistaken. Nor were they lost on the girl. She lunged against Pelgrim.

"Dear God," she almost cried, "aren't we ever to be free of him? He's turned up again, George! What can we do?"

He tried to quiet her, to soothe her. Their hotel was a small one, and George made sure there was no Remsdorf registered there.

The next evening at the Indoor Championships, though, the big man was seated prominently in a front-poolside seat. George wondered at Linda's courage. From his perch in the press row, he could see her strained face, her eyes drawn almost as though hypnotized to the dark bulk sitting, watching her implacably.

In the finals her start was poor as though she were preoccupied with something else and hardly heard the gun. She swam courageously and splendidly, making up most of the lost ground. It was Remsdorf and Remsdorf alone that cost her first place. As it was, she came in second a foot or so behind the leader.

Later in her hotel, the girl came close to hysteria. The medal presentations were scheduled for the next day.

"We've got to get out of here, George," Linda insisted. "I'm so terribly afraid of him."

He agreed. They packed hurriedly and left by a back way. The small southern town was filled with visitors attracted by the aquatic show. In spite of the chill air, a carnival spirit pervaded the streets. George found a cab and pushed Linda inside, directing the driver to the station.

The first time he turned around and looked out the back window, there was nothing suspicious. The second time he thought they were being followed. When they pulled into the railroad terminal, he was sure. He threw a bill at the driver, grabbed their luggage and hustled the girl into the waiting room. A last glance showed another cab trundling down the street towards the station.

The ticket agent blinked at him sleepily. "Now, don't be so excited, young man. The next express for the North doesn't come through here for better than two hours yet. Can't understand why you Yankees are so goldarn anxious to get back up to that blighted country!"

The other cab stopped in the driveway. George pushed Linda out the door that led to the platform. The tracks gleamed coldly under the occasional electric bulbs. They hurried up the platform a way, and then Pelgrim, looking back, saw the oblong of light when the station door opened. Still, they couldn't be seen by someone coming out of the lighted waiting room.

"We'll cut across the tracks," he muttered. "It's the only way."

It was flight now, blind hysterical flight to get away. Months long the pursuit had lasted, its tempo increasing. He helped Linda as her heels caught in the ballast underneath the ties. Four tracks, eight rails they stumbled across, and then there were bushes and shrubs, thankfully on the other side.

"You know where we're going?" she asked.

"I'm not sure, but I remembered when we came here there was an airfield not far from the station."

They pushed on through the wooded area. Almost at the same time that they saw the circular beacon in the sky ahead of them, they both detected the sounds of pursuit, heavy, methodical tramping, unmistakably the sounds of a big person following them.

"Go on!" George panted to Linda, and the scene was faintly reminiscent of that other time months earlier in the city. "Go on, you can make it. I'll follow."

He wanted to keep both bags, but she insisted on taking one. She was gone then into the darkness. Her lips brushed his cheek. She murmured, "I don't want to leave you," and he ordered her roughly away, "I'm running this for better or worse." She saw the revolver in his hand and she understood.

The minutes passed, more time than he'd dared to hope for. She was well away by now, nearly to the municipal airport, he thought. And then out of the shrubbery loomed Lother Remsdorf, the clothes on his huge bull-like body more rumpled than ever, hands hanging at his sides, his black hat clamped tight on his head.

He came forward slowly, and what light there was reflected from the stars and the sky glanced off the dull barrel of Pelgrim's revolver.

"Now will you leave us alone?" the reporter snarled between clenched teeth. "Will you go back the way you've come and never bother us again?"

The laughter started then inside the big man, deep inside, and it grew to a gurgling sound to hear. The giant hands were raised and the first menacing step forward was taken when George fired.

He was aiming squarely at the gigantic middle, and at the range of only several paces, he couldn't have missed. Remsdorf lurched on towards him and the slobbering sound of his laughter seemed to beat down on the reporter. George fired again and again, but the monster kept coming.

Two more shots, and then with one chamber left, Pelgrim raised his revolver, pointed it squarely at the hideous white swollen face looming before him. He pulled the trigger and saw the course of the bullet in the man's face. Remsdorf shook his head then and stopped, but Pelgrim was as though rooted to the spot, fascinated.

The big man was still grinning, and one hand came up and touched his cheek. The hole there was apparent, but what was oozing out, slowly, thickly, almost like honey, was not blood. It could not be blood for it was not red. It was a neutral-colored liquid, strange and terrible to see as it was inexplainable. An almost whitish, thick serum-like substance.

"You've water in you, not blood," the reporter screamed involuntarily. "You're not human. . . ."

Almost imperceptibly the gigantic head nodded, as though in mute, mirthful agreement . . .

George turned and ran then. Ran as fast as he could, as long as he could. There was somewhere in the back of his consciousness the youngster-thought that this could not be and that he would wake up and find it was dream-stuff, but he had enough presence of mind to shove the empty revolver in his coat pocket as he came onto the municipal airport field.

She was beckoning to him and they got on a flight to the North. He couldn't speak for gasping, but they sat huddled together while the plane filled. The minutes ticked away and Linda kept murmuring, her head against his shoulder, Why didn't they leave, why didn't they leave? He held her head there because he was too tired to do anything else and because he didn't want her to see who had just gotten into the plane, their plane . . . grinning still . . . A man with six bullets in him. A man? ·

They flew into the night and into the dawn, and all the time George could feel, without looking, those eyes on them from the rear. Linda slept against his shoulder fitfully and he brushed her golden hair gently over her eyes.

The flight ended at a Northern airport and the two disembarked groggily with little fight left in them. Remsdorf was close behind.

It was one of those vagaries of Fate that made George look towards the Canadian plane warming up in the next runway. On the spur of the moment he bought two tickets, and in fifteen minutes they were flying north again, but no more alone, no more unpursued than they had been before.

George had a relative in this certain Canadian town, towards which they headed, an uncle of some influence locally but who could not be expected to contribute to their problem concretely. It was only the impulse to keep going that had driven Pelgrim on. Linda was too cold and too tired to care any longer.

It was beginning to snow when they landed in the northern Canadian airport. George got Linda into a hack. The faithful Remsdorf was close behind in another. They got out at his uncle's address, leaning together for support. The snow was heavier and the wind was freezing.

George looked for his uncle's name on the doorbells. There was nothing. Frantically he pushed "Superintendent." Remsdorf's trailing cab stopped outside, and the big man got out across the street. George hoped he froze in his rumpled dark suit, got sick, dropped dead, anything.

The superintendent shoved a bleary face around the door jamb.

"He's not here any more. He's moved. He's ten blocks or so up the street."

He scribbled an address for Pelgrim and handed it to him. The two started out again, heads bent against the storm. The snow had all but stopped as the mercury tumbled even lower, but the going was bad and the wind ferocious. Linda's teeth chattered as they trudged on, endlessly it seemed.

The final half of the way led through a small park, deserted in this weather. The big man was still behind them, George saw when he craned his head, but there was something newly strange.

"What is it?" Linda's fingers dug into Pelgrim's arm.

"It's all right," George reassured. "Let's just keep going," but his head was still craned backward.

The big man was walking staggeringly, stiffly. He seemed to be trying as hard as before to keep up with them, but his steps were clumsy even for him.

They had almost reached the other side of the park when George saw Remsdorf stagger and put his great hands out to clutch at a bench. He eased himself stiffly into it like a very old, old man with rheumatism.

George turned his head away and there was the address ahead. Soon they were inside out of the bitter weather and his uncle, small, gray as ever, was clucking over them like a mother hen. Linda was put to bed immediately in the guest room with a hot-water bottle and a pint of spiked hot tea.

George talked with his uncle for a while, grateful that the older man didn't press him.

"I know you newspaper fellows," his relative wagged, "always up to some kind of scalawag, looking for stories. Son, you ought to turn in now. You look pretty tuckered."

George assured him he would but said no, certainly he wouldn't take the older man's bed. He'd sleep outside here.

By midnight the house was quiet. George tiptoed to the front closet and took out a greatcoat. Then as silently he let himself out the front door.

The night was bright with snow and clear with the zero temperature. He made his way into the barren and deserted park. He walked down the path they'd taken earlier until he came to the desolate bench set by the way. There was Remsdorf, no longer grinning, sitting fixedly. The reporter's thoughts went back to the water-substance that had flowed from the monster's wound where red blood should have been.

George came closer and his eyes bulged. It was too much, it was incredible, but Remsdorf's head under the black slouch hat, seemed a snowball, his hands were stiff claws of ice. Disbelieving, George took the revolver from his pocket, and with its barrel struck gently against one of the outstretched fingers. The tip broke off as easily as if this thing were a candy figure.

For Remsdorf was not of this world. He was frozen. He was dead. He was an ice man and no more!

THE LOST CLUB

by Arthur Machen

One hot afternoon in August a gorgeous young gentleman, one would say the last of his race in London, set out from the Circus end, and proceeded to stroll along the lonely expanse of Piccadilly Deserta. True to the traditions of his race, faithful even in the wilderness, he had not bated one jot or tittle of the regulation equipage; a glorious red and yellow blossom in his exquisitely cut frock coat proclaimed him a true son of the carnation; hat and boots and chin were all polished to the highest pitch; though there had not been rain for many weeks his trouser-ends were duly turned up, and the poise of the gold-headed cane was in itself a liberal education. But ah! the heavy changes since June, when the leaves glanced green in the sunlit air, and the club windows were filled, and the hansoms flashed in long processions through the streets, and girls smiled from every carriage. The young man sighed; he thought of the quiet little evenings at the Phoenix, of encounters on the Row, of the drive to Hurlingham, and many pleasant dinners in joyous company. Then he glanced up and saw a bus, half empty, slowly lumbering along the middle of the street, and in front of the "White Horse Cellars" a four-wheeler had stopped still (the driver was asleep on his seat), and in the "Badminton" the blinds were down. He half expected to see the Briar Rose trailing gracefully over the Hotel Cosmopole; certainly the Beauty, if such a thing were left in Piccadilly, was fast asleep.

Absorbed in these mournful reflections the hapless Johnny strolled on without observing that an exact duplicate of himself was advancing on the same pavement from the opposite direction; save that the inevitable carnation was salmon color, and the cane a silver-headed one, instruments of great magnifying power would have been required to discriminate between them. The two met; each raised his eyes simultaneously at the strange sight of a well-dressed man, and each adjured the same old-world deity.

"By Jove! old man, what the deuce are you doing here?"

The gentleman who had advanced from the direction of Hyde Park Corner was the first to answer.

"Well, to tell the truth, Austin, I am detained in town on—ah—legal business. But how is it you are not in Scotland?"

"Well, it's curious; but the fact is, I have legal business in town also."

"You don't say so? Great nuisance, ain't it? But these things must be seen to, or a fellow finds himself in no end of a mess, don't you know?"

"He does, by Jove! That's what I thought."

Mr. Austin relapsed into silence for a few moments.

"And where are you off to, Phillipps?"

The conversation had passed with the utmost gravity on both sides; at the joint mention of legal business, it was true, a slight twinkle had passed across their eyes, but the ordinary observer would have said the weight of ages rested on those unruffled brows.

"I really couldn't say. I thought of having a quiet dinner at Azario's. The Badminton is closed, you know, for repairs or somethin', and I can't stand the Junior Wilton. Come along with me, and let's dine together."

"By Jove! I think I will. I thought of calling on my solicitor, but I daresay he can wait."

"Ah! I should think he could. We'll have some of that Italian wine —stuff in salad-oil flasks—you know what I mean."

The pair solemnly wheeled round, and solemnly paced toward the Circus, meditating, doubtless, on many things. The dinner in the little restaurant pleased them with a grave pleasure, as did the Chianti, of which they drank a good deal too much; "quite a light wine, you know," said Phillipps, and Austin agreed with him, so they emptied a quart flask between them, and finished up with a couple of glasses apiece of Green Chartreuse. As they came out into the quiet street smoking vast cigars, the two slaves to duty and "legal business" felt a dreamy delight in all things, the street seemed full of fantasy in the dim light of the lamps, and a single star shining in the clear sky above seemed to Austin exactly the same color as Green Chartreuse. Phillipps agreed with him. "You know, old fellow," he said, "there are times when a fellow feels all sorts of strange things—you know, the sort of things they put in magazines, don't you know, and novels. By Jove, Austin, old man, I feel as if I could write a novel myself."

The pair wandered aimlessly on, not quite knowing where they were going, turning from one street to another, and discoursing in a maudlin strain. A great cloud had been slowly moving up from the south, darkening the sky, and suddenly it began to rain, at first slowly with great heavy drops, and then faster and faster in a pitiless, hissing shower; the gutters flooded over, and the furious drops danced up from the stones. The two Johnnies walked on as fast as they could, whistling and calling "Hansom!" in vain; they were really getting very wet.

"Where the dickens are we?" said Phillipps. "Confound it all, I don't know. We ought to be in Oxford Street."

They walked on a little farther, when suddenly, to their great joy, they found a dry archway, leading into a dark passage or courtyard. They took shelter silently, too thankful and too wet to say anything. Austin looked at his hat; it was a wreck; and Phillipps shook himself feebly, like a tired terrier.

"What a beastly nuisance this is," he muttered. "I only wish I could see a hansom."

Austin looked into the street; the rain was still falling in torrents; he looked up the passage, and noticed for the first time that it led to a great house, which towered grimly against the sky. It seemed all dark and gloomy, except that from some chink in a shutter a light shone out. He pointed it out to Phillipps, who stared vacantly about him, then exclaimed:

"Hang it! I know where we are now. At least, I don't exactly know, you know, but I once came by here with Wylliams, and he told me there was some club or somethin' down this passage; I don't recollect exactly what he said. Hullo! Why, there goes Wylliams. I say, Wylliams, tell us where we are!"

A gentleman had brushed past them in the darkness and was walking fast down the passage. He heard his name and turned round, looking rather annoyed.

"Well, Phillipps, what do you want? Good evening, Austin; you seem rather wet, both of you."

"I should think we were wet; got caught in the rain. Didn't you tell me once there was some club down here? I wish you'd take us in, if you're a member."

Mr. Wylliams looked steadfastly at the two forlorn young men for a moment, hesitated, and said:

"Well, gentlemen, you may come with me if you like. But I must impose a condition; that you both give me your word of honor never to mention the club, or anything that you see while you are in it, to any individual whatsoever."

"Certainly not," replied Austin; "of course we shouldn't dream of doing so, should we, Phillipps?"

"No, no; go ahead, Wylliams, we'll keep it dark enough."

The party moved slowly down the passage till they came to the house. It was very large and very old; it looked as though it might have been an embassy of the last century. Wylliams whistled, knocked twice at the door, and whistled again, and it was opened by a man in black.

"Friends of yours, Mr. Wylliams?"

Wylliams nodded and they passed on.

"Now mind," he whispered, as they paused at a door, "you are not to recognize anybody, and nobody will recognize you."

The two friends nodded, and the door was opened, and they entered a vast room, brilliantly lighted with electric lamps. Men were standing in knots, walking up and down, and smoking at little tables; it was just like any club smoking-room. Conversation was going on, but in a low murmur, and every now and then someone would stop talking, and look anxiously at a door at the other end of the room, and then turn round again. It was evident that they were waiting for someone or somebody.

Austin and Phillipps were sitting on a sofa, lost in amazement;

nearly every face was familiar to them. The flower of the Row was in that strange clubroom: several young noblemen, a young fellow who had just come into an enormous fortune, three or four fashionable artists and literary men, an eminent actor, and a well-known canon. What could it mean? They were all supposed to be scattered far and wide over the habitable globe, and yet here they were. Suddenly there came a loud knock at the door; and every man started, and those who were sitting got up. A servant appeared.

"The president is awaiting you, gentlemen," he said, and vanished.

One by one the members filed out, and Wylliams and the two guests brought up the rear. They found themselves in a room still larger than the first, but almost quite dark. The president sat at a long table and before him burned two candles, which barely lighted up his face. It was the famous Duke of Dartington, the largest landowner in England. As soon as the members had entered he said in a cold hard voice, "Gentlemen, you know our rules; the book is prepared. Whoever opens it at the black page is at the disposal of the committee and myself. We had better begin."

Someone began to read out the names in a low distinct voice, pausing after each name, and the member called came up to the table and opened at random the pages of a big folio volume that lay between the two candles. The gloomy light made it difficult to distinguish features, but Phillipps heard a groan beside him, and recognized an old friend. His face was working fearfully, the man was evidently in an agony of terror. One by one the members opened the book; as each man did so he passed out by another door.

At last there was only one left; it was Phillipps' friend. There was foam upon his lips as he passed up to the table, and his hand shook as he opened the leaves. Wylliams had passed out after whispering to the president, and had returned to his friends' side. He could hardly hold them back as the unfortunate man groaned in agony and leant against the table; he had opened the book at the black page. "Kindly come with me, Mr. D'Aubigny," said the president, and they passed out together.

"We can go now," said Wylliams. "I think the rain has gone off. Remember your promise, gentlemen. You have been at a meeting of the Lost Club. You will never see that young man again. Good night."

"It isn't *murder,* is it?" gasped Austin.

"Oh no, not at all. Mr. D'Aubigny will, I hope, live for many years; he has disappeared, merely disappeared. Good night; there's a hansom that will do for you."

The two friends went to their home in dead silence. They did not meet again for three weeks, and each thought the other looked ill and shaken. They walked drearily, with grave, averted face, down Piccadilly, each afraid to begin the recollection of the terrible club. Of a sudden Phillipps stopped as if he had been shot.

"Look there, Austin," he muttered, "look at that."

The posters of the evening papers were spread out beside the pavement, and on one of them Austin saw in large blue letters, "Mysterious disappearance of a gentleman." Austin bought a copy and turned over the leaves with shaking fingers till he found the brief paragraph—

> Mr. St. John D'Aubigny, of Stoke D'Aubigny, in Sussex, has disappeared under mysterious circumstances. Mr. D'Aubigny was staying at Strathdoon, in Scotland, and came up to London, as is stated, on business, on August 16th. It has been ascertained that he arrived safely at King's Cross, and drove to Piccadilly Circus, where he got out. It is said that he was last seen at the corner of Glass House Street, leading from Regent into Soho. Since the above date the unfortunate gentleman, who was much liked in London society, has not been heard of. Mr. D'Aubigny was to have been married in September. The police are extremely reticent.

"Good God! Austin, this is dreadful. You remember the date. Poor fellow, poor fellow!"

"Phillipps, I think I shall go home, I feel sick."

D'Aubigny was never heard of again. But the strangest part of the story remains to be told. The two friends called upon Wylliams, and charged him with being a member of the Lost Club, and an accomplice in the fate of D'Aubigny. The placid Mr. Wylliams at first stared at the two pale, earnest faces, and finally roared with laughter.

"My dear fellows, what on earth are you talking about? I never heard such a cock-and-bull story in my life. As you say, Phillipps, I once pointed out to you a house said to be a club, as we were walking through Soho; but that was a low gambling club, frequented by German waiters. I am afraid that Azario's Chianti was rather too strong for you. However, I will try to convince you of your mistake."

Wylliams forthwith summoned his man, who swore that he and his master were in Cairo during the whole of August, and offered to produce the hotel bills. Phillipps shook his head, and they went away.

Their next step was to try and find the archway where they had taken shelter, and after a good deal of trouble they succeeded. They knocked at the door of the gloomy house, whistling as Wylliams had done. They were admitted by a respectable mechanic in a white apron, who was evidently astonished at the whistle; in fact he was inclined to suspect the influence of a "drop too much." The place was a billiard table factory, and had been so (as they learnt in the neighborhood) for many years. The rooms must once have been large and magnificent, but most of them had been divided into three or four separate workshops by wooden partitions.

Phillipps sighed; he could do no more for his lost friend; but both he and Austin remained unconvinced. In justice to Mr. Wylliams, it must be stated that Lord Henry Harcourt assured Phillipps that he had seen Wylliams in Cairo about the middle of August; he thought, but could not be sure, on the 16th; and also, that the recent disappearances of some well-known men about town are patient of explanations which would exclude the agency of the Lost Club.

"Wet Straw," published in January 1953, marked the first of two *Weird Tales* appearances of stories by RICHARD MATHESON (1926–   ), one of America's most important authors and screenwriters of horror and terror. Matheson's novels include *The Incredible Shrinking Man, I Am Legend, A Stir of Echoes, What Dreams May Come* and *Hell House,* my vote for the most ghoulish haunted house story ever written. "Wet Straw" was later included in Matheson's short story collection, *Shock Waves.*

WET STRAW

by Richard Matheson

It began some months after his wife died.

He had moved into a boarding house. There he lived a sheltered life; sale of her bonds had provided money. A book a day, concerts, solitary meals, visits to the museum—these sufficed. He listened to his radio and napped and thought a good deal. Life was good enough.

One night he put down his book and undressed. He turned out the lights and opened the window. He sat down on the bed and stared a moment at the floor. His eyes ached a little. Then he lay down and put his arms behind his head. There was a cold draft from the window, so he pulled the covers over his head and closed his eyes.

It was very still. He could hear his own regular breathing. The warmth began to cover him. The heat fondled his body and soothed it. He sighed heavily and smiled.

In an instant, his eyes were open.

There was a thin breeze stroking his cheek, and he could smell something like wet straw. It was not to be mistaken.

Reaching out, he could touch the wall and feel the breeze from the window. Yet, under the covers, where there had been only warmth before, was another breeze. And a damp, chilling smell of wet straw.

He threw the covers from him and lay on the bed, breathing harshly.

Then he laughed in his mind. A dream, a nightmare. Too much reading. Bad food.

He pulled up the covers and closed his eyes. He kept his head outside the blankets and slept.

The next morning he forgot about it. He had breakfast and went to the museum. There he spent the morning. He visited all the rooms and looked at everything.

When he was about to leave, he felt a desire to go back and look at a painting he had only glanced at before.

He stopped in front of it.

It was a painting of a countryside. There was a big barn down in the valley.

He began to breathe heavily, and his fingers played on his tie. How ridiculous, he thought after a moment, that such a thing should make me nervous.

He turned away. At the door he looked back at the painting.

The barn had frightened him. Only a barn, he thought, a barn in a painting.

After dinner he returned to his room.

As soon as he opened the door he remembered the dream. He went to the bed. He drew up the blanket and the sheets and shook them.

There was no smell of wet straw. He felt like a fool.

That night, when he went to bed, he left the window closed. He turned out the lights and got in bed and pulled the covers over his head.

At first it was the same. Silent and breathless and the creeping warmth.

Then the breeze began again and he distinctly felt his hair ruffled by it. He could smell wet straw. He stared into the blackness and breathed through his mouth so he wouldn't have to smell the straw.

Somewhere in the dark, he saw a square of grayish light.

It's a window, he thought, suddenly.

He looked longer and his heart jumped as a sudden flash of light showed in the window. It was like lightning. He listened. He smelled the wet straw.

He heard it starting to rain.

He became frightened and pulled the covers off his head.

The warm room was around him. It was not raining. It was oppressively hot because the window was closed.

He stared at the ceiling and wondered why he was having this illusion.

Again he pulled up the blanket to make sure. He lay still and kept his eyes tightly closed.

The smell was in his nostrils again. The rain was beating violently on the window. He opened his eyes and watched it and made out sheets of rain in the flashes. Then rain began to beat above him, too, on a wooden roof. He was in some place with a wooden roof and wet straw.

He was in a barn.

That was why the picture had frightened him. But why frightened?

He tried to touch the window, but he couldn't reach it. The breeze blew on his hand and arm. He wanted to touch the window. Maybe, he delighted in the thought, maybe open it and stick his head out in the rain and then pull down the covers quickly to see if his hair were wet.

He began to sense himself surrounded by space. There was no feeling of confinement in the bed. He felt the mattress, yet it was as though he lay on it in an open place. The breeze blew over his entire body. And the smell was more pronounced.

He listened. He heard a squeak and then a horse whinnying. He listened a while longer.

Then he realized he couldn't feel the whole mattress:

It felt as though he were lying on a cold wooden floor from his waist down.

He reached out his hands in alarm and felt the edge of the blankets. He pulled them down.

He was covered with sweat and his pajamas stuck to his body. He got out of bed and turned on the light. A refreshing breeze came through the window when he opened it.

His legs shook as he walked and he had to grab at the dresser to keep from falling.

In the mirror he saw his face pale with fear. He held up his hand and watched it shake. His throat was dry.

He went to the bathroom and got a drink of water. Then he went to the room and looked down at his bed. Nothing there but the tangled blanket and sheets and the stain where he had perspired. He held up the blanket and the sheets. He shook them before the light and examined them minutely. There was nothing.

He took up a book and read for the rest of the night.

The next day he went to the museum again and looked at the picture.

He tried to remember if he had ever been in a barn. Had it been raining and had he stared out a window at the lightning?

He remembered.

It was on his honeymoon. They had gone for a walk and been caught in the rain and stayed in a barn until it stopped. There had been a horse down in the stall and mice running and wet straw.

But what did it mean? There was no reason to remember it now.

That night he was afraid to go to bed. He put it off. At last, when his eyes would not stay open, he lay down fully dressed and left the window closed. He didn't use a blanket.

He slept heavily and there was no dream.

Toward early morning, he woke up. It was just getting light. Without thinking, he pulled a blanket off the chair and threw it over himself.

There was no wait. He was suddenly in the barn.

There was no sound. It was not raining. There was a gray light in the window. Could it be that it was also morning in his imaginary barn?

He smiled drowsily. It was all too charming. He would have to try it in the afternoon to see if the barn were fully lighted.

He started to pull the blanket off his head, when there was a rustle by his side.

He caught his breath. His heart seemed to stop and there was a tingling in his scalp.

A soft sigh reached his ears.

Something warm and moist brushed over his hand.

With a scream, he flung off the blanket and jumped onto the floor.

He stood there staring at the bed and clutching the blanket in his hands. His heart struck with gigantic beats.

He sank down weakly on the bed. The sun was just rising.

For a week, he slept sitting up in a chair. At last, he had to have a good night's rest and lay down on the bed, fully dressed. He would never use a blanket again.

Sleep came, dreamless and black.

He didn't know what time it was when he woke up. A sob caught in his throat. *He was in the barn again.* Lightning flashed in the window and rain was pounding on the roof.

He felt around in dread, but there was no blanket anywhere. His hands slapped at the air, frenziedly.

Suddenly, he looked at the window. If he could open it, he might escape! He stretched out his hand as far as he could. Closer. Closer. He was almost there. Another inch and his fingers would touch it.

"John."

A sudden reflex made his hand plunge through the glass. He felt the rain spattering across the back of his hand and his wrist burned terribly. He jerked back his hand and stared in terror at where the voice had come from.

Something white stirred at his side and a warm hand caressed his arm.

"John," came the murmur. *"John."*

He couldn't speak. He reached around, clutching agonizingly for his blanket. But only the breeze blew over his fingers. There was a cold wooden floor under him.

He whimpered in fright. His name was spoken again.

Then the lightning flashed and he saw his wife lying by him, smiling at him.

Suddenly, the edge of the blanket was in his hand, and pulling it down, he rolled off the bed onto the floor.

Something was running across his wrist; there was a dull ache in his arm.

He stood up and put on the light. The bright glare filled the room.

He saw his arm covered with blood. He picked a piece of glass from his wrist and dropped it on the floor in horror.

On his lower arm, the prints of her fingers were red.

He tore the sheet from the bed and ran down the hall to the bathroom. He washed the blood off and poured iodine into the thick gash and bandaged it. The burning made him dizzy. Drops of cold sweat ran into his eyes.

One of the boarders came in. John told him he had cut himself accidentally. When the man saw the blood running, he ran and called a doctor on the telephone.

John sat on the edge of the bathtub and watched his blood dripping on the tiles.

The next day the cut was cleaned and bandaged.

The doctor was dubious about the explanation. John told him he did it with a knife; but there was no knife to be found, and there were thick patterns of blood all over the sheets and blanket.

He was told to stay in his room and keep his arm still.

He read most of the day and thought about how he had cut himself on a dream.

The thought of her excited him. She was still beautiful.

Memories became vivid.

They had lain in each other's arms in the straw and listened to the rain. He couldn't remember what they said.

He was not afraid she was coming back. His outlook on life was realistic. She was dead and buried.

It was some aberration of the mind. Some mental climax that had put itself off until now.

Then he looked at his wrist and saw the bandage.

It hadn't been her fault, though. She didn't ask him to crash his hand through the glass.

Perhaps he could be with her in one existence and have her money in another.

Something held him from it. It *had* been frightening. The wet straw and the darkness, the mice and the rain, the bone-stiffening chill.

He made up his mind what he would do.

That night he turned out the lights early. He got on his knees beside the bed.

He put his head under the covers. If anything went wrong he had only to pull away quickly.

He waited.

Soon he smelled the straw and heard the rain and looked for her. He called her name softly.

There was a rustling. A warm hand caressed his cheek. He started at first. Then he smiled. Her face appeared and she put her cheek against his. The perfume of her hair intoxicated him.

Words filled his mind.

John. We are always one. Promise? Never part? If one of us dies the other will wait? If I die you'll wait and I'll find a way to come to you? I'll come to you and take you with me.

And now I have gone. You made me that drink and I died. And you opened the window so the breeze would come in. And now I am back.

He began to shake.

Her voice became harsher, he could hear her teeth grinding. Her breath was faster. Her fingers touched his face. They ran through his hair and fondled his neck.

He began to moan. He asked her to let go. There was no answer. She breathed faster still. He tried to pull away. He felt the floor of his room with his feet. He tried hard to pull his head from under the blanket. But her grasp was very strong.

She began to kiss his lips. Her mouth was cold, her eyes wide open. He stared into them while her breath mingled with his.

Then she threw back her head and she was laughing and lightning was bursting through the window. Rain was thundering on the roof and the mice shrieked and the horse stamped and made the barn shake. Her fingers clenched on his neck. He pulled with all his might and gritted his teeth and wrenched from her grasp. There was a sudden pain, and he rolled across the floor.

When the landlady came in two days later to clean, he was in the same position. His arms were sprawled in the dried puddle of blood and his body was taut and cold. His head was not to be found.

DARRELL SCHWEITZER (1952-   ) is a novelist, short story writer, critic and recently coeditor of the brand-new revival of *Weird Tales*. (See Appendix III, page 582.) The first new issue of The Unique Magazine, dated Spring 1988, includes many excellent contemporary fantasy stories, the darkest and most complex of which is, in my opinion, the editor's own "The Mysteries of the Faceless King."

MYSTERIES OF THE FACELESS KING

by Darrell Schweitzer

When I was eight, my father took me deep into the forest to see the altar of the Faceless King. Voinos, my elder brother, came too; mostly because, as I was smugly certain at the time, Father didn't trust him out of his sight. Voinos was fourteen then; and he hated everyone: me, Father, Mother, the town elders, and even, I think, himself. That year, when he was fourteen, was the last time anyone was ever able to control him.

It was in the autumn, when the leaves had turned brilliant red and gold and yellow, on the morning of the Festival of the Masks, when children make masks out of those leaves and try and go into other people's houses and impersonate other children, only to receive treats when they are discovered. But the Festival of Masks is for younger children, and that year my father decided that I was older. Only fathers can know when this happens, and when they do it is the time of *going,* when fathers and sons go off together, to some private place the gods reveal, to learn together such wisdom as the gods see fit to inspire. In this way, boys become men. So I came a man at the age of eight, and Voinos at fourteen because Father did not trust him.

Going. Old Decronos, the chief priest of our town, was there by the gate, seated at a table sipping broth. He barely looked up when the three of us knelt before him and Father said softly, "Going."

The priest touched Voinos and me on the shoulder with his feather-tipped cane and waved us away. Then the guards opened the heavy log gates, and off we went.

The terraced fields above the Great River were places of mud and dead corn stalks. It was bad to be there at this time of year, I knew, because sometimes ancestors rise up out of the mud, begging to be remembered; and if you don't remember them, it can bring a curse. I wanted to get away quickly, but we walked for most of the morning through the empty fields in silence, following the river. Once we came to a calf's skull and some beads stuck on a post. It was a charm, Father explained, to make the ancestors gather *there* and not bother anyone. We walked a wide half-circle around it.

Going. By noon we were far from any path, in the unbroken twilight beneath heavy pine branches. No birds sang. No animals ran before us. The forest stood silent and expectant all around, the bright leaves of autumn now a memory among the faded blue-greens and browns and the all-pervasive grey.

Voinos complained a lot. He would insist we stop to rest, then sit down; and Father would have to drag him up by the scruff of the neck. Then he'd try to run off, but Father was too quick and his long arms would always have him. Voinos made a fist once, but Father just swatted it aside. He could have hurt Voinos. He was a big, agile, powerful man. That alone my brother respected in him.

The shadows deepened, and it seemed night already. The soft needles muffled our footsteps. The horizontal rays of the setting sun flickered between the black trunks.

We paused then, built a fire and had our supper, then sat without a word while the flames burned low, Voinos glowering, I almost too excited to be still, a little scared, expecting wonders.

After the sun had been gone for perhaps an hour, the moon rose, gleaming among the branches, like a huge penny.

Father was a bard, one of the very best. He was often called to recite in the halls of the great lords. There, in the forest before his sons, he got out his harp and began to make a story—for a bard is a *maker;* he calls up his matter out of nothing, and when he has finished, it lives.

He sat for a moment with his eyes closed, gazing into himself, strumming softly on the harp; and when he began to speak, it was with all the intensity of a bardic tale, for all that his words were less formal.

"These things came to me in a dream," he said, "and that was why I brought you here. The dream came from the gods."

"Well, what did the gods *say?*" Voinos demanded.

I gasped and looked away, shocked at the interruption; but Father merely answered.

"I dreamed of Verunnos-Kemad, the most secretive of the gods. He is known by the wind in the night, by the pattern of the leaves as they fall, by the voice of the river and the running beasts, by the multitudes of birds. All these are signs of him. I dreamed that the holy one stood here, almost where we sit, in the darkness of a night a few scant centuries after the creation of the world. His whole body shone like the pale moonlight. There was a man here too, prostrate on the ground before him. The name of the man I do not know. Nor did I see his face. It does not matter. He was but one man of many.

"In this time, so long ago, there were dragons in the land, swarming thick as starlings." Father turned to me suddenly, still strumming the harp. "Did you know about the dragons, Evad?"

"There's bones," I said, startled. "Bones in the cliff by the river road."

"Yes, one of the last of the dragons died there, and his bones remain for all to see; but these were *living* dragons, great and terrible. They hovered in black flocks, their wings like thunder. Sometimes people make offerings to them, gold, animals, even their children; and the dragons would go away for a while. But sometimes they would just burn the towns with their breath and swoop down to devour the fleeing people."

Voinos shifted about, rustling.

"You're changing the subject," he said. "What do dragons have to do with Veruna—Vero—whatever his stupid name is?"

Again I was afraid of my father's sudden anger, but as long as he was telling the story, his patience seemed limitless.

"I think the man's children had been taken by the dragons, or perhaps they were about to be. I don't know. But I saw, in my dream, the man lying there and the god bending down over him. The hand of Verunnos-Kemad glowed softly, like a paper lantern. He touched the man on the shoulder and raised him up, and placed on the man's face a mask of brilliant silver, shaped like the full Moon, mottled, with thin rays. And he gave him a silver staff and a silver-bladed sword, and said to him in terrible, relentless whispers, *You are the first. Let it begin.*

"Then he was gone, and the man stood alone in the forest darkness, until the first light of dawn touched the mask and staff, and they shone more brilliantly than the sunrise. But in the full day they were merely silver, for their power and their glory were of the night.

"This man was the Faceless King. Whoever he had been previously had ceased to exist, for he could never remove the mask, never return to being just an ordinary man. He emerged from the forest in the evening with his sword drawn, and the bravest of heroes followed him, and together they slew all the dragons, including the one who died by the river. At last they slew even the mighty Mother of Dragons in her cavern at the center of the world. Then the Faceless King parted from the heroes. He sent with them his farewell to all he had ever known, and he remained in the cavern of the Mother Dragon, among the treasures and the pillars of stone the color of blood. He sits there still, watching over the world. The wisest and the bravest know his sendings, for he is their lord."

"It's just an old story," Voinos said. "You've taken us all the way out here to tell us an old story. We could have stayed home. You could have told it any market day."

Father stiffened. I could hear barely restrained rage in his voice.

"Some of it I could tell again, as a story, for it is good to have the truth in a story. But the dream itself is a secret thing, between me, your father, and Voinos and Evad, my sons. I do not know why the Secret God sent it to me. That is a mighty and even terrible mystery. But I am sure that your lives will be shaped by it. This is the night of *going* and now I have told you all that I have to tell you."

"But—but, Father," I asked softly, as respectfully as I could, "what does it *mean?*"

Father pointed to a rise of land, a tree-lined ridge I could barely make out in the darkness. It looked like the back of a huge, sleeping dragon to me.

"There. Just beyond is a little valley. The heroes built an altar there, in secret, for the Faceless King. Sometimes he would manifest himself there and even give them gifts, rare crowns and jewels from the Mother Dragon's hoard, and he would speak to them in prophecies, for he shared the thoughts of Verunnos-Kemad, and at such times his voice was the voice of the god."

Suddenly Voinos was up and running toward the ridge.

"Where are you —?" I managed to say.

Father cursed, grabbed his staff and a burning brand from the fire, and took after him. I followed.

But as we were running the shadows of the night began to move. I thought it was black smoke at first, rushing silently between the trees, but then I saw that it was an enormous flight of birds rising from the earth. Soon the whole forest shook with the whirring of their wings.

I knew this was a sign, a miracle, for there were millions of them. The very air shuddered with their passage, yet not a single bird cried out. Pine needles and twigs rained down on us. Above, the Moon vanished, like a shiny pebble beneath a dark tide.

"Father!" I shouted.

He dropped his staff and brand, then fell to his knees, covering his face. I think he was weeping. I groped toward him, bent against the mighty wind of countless wings, hundreds of birds colliding with me. I reached out. His hand found mine and I embraced him, and so we remained, he kneeling and I standing hunched against him for what seemed like hours, until at last the night was still. The Moon reappeared. There was no wind. Not a branch rustled. I could hear my father's heart, and my own, racing.

"Father . . . ? Voinos, he —"

"Come!"

Still holding my hand, he leapt to his feet, snatched up his staff, and yanked me along as he ran. We topped the rise and looked down into a hollow, where Voinos stood in the moonlight before a roughly rectangular slab of white marble.

"What have you done?" Father shouted as we approached.

Voinos turned slowly. He spoke with open contempt.

"It's just an old rock."

He spat on the altar stone. I let out a sudden cry of "No!" and cringed at the desecration. It was then that my eyes met my brother's, and I *knew* that the sign had not been for him. He had seen no flight of birds.

Father demanded again, *"What did you do?"*

"Nothing. I was looking for gold. I wanted to see if there was any treasure left." Voinos acted as if it were a commonplace, completely ignoring Father's mounting rage.

"You didn't intend to share it."

"What matter? There's nothing *to* share. The Faceless King is dead, if there ever was any Faceless King. He'd have to be a god himself to live so long. It's just a stupid old story."

"He is but a man," Father said, intoning his words as if speaking a doom. "Some say that the mask extends his life, and he lives for many centuries, but in the end, he dies like any man. When he is dying, he summons his successor from out of the world, and someone else becomes the Faceless King. He dies in secret. No one, not his attendants, not his messengers, ever sees his face."

Voinos laughed, shockingly. "Then how do they know it's *him?*"

Even Father was stunned at that.

I merely said, "Huh?"

Voinos turned to me sharply. "Idiot, if they can't see his face, it could be just anybody." He leaned over and poked my chest viciously. "Even *you.*"

Father still held my hand. I felt him tremble.

"The one who wears the mask *is* the Faceless King. He hears every leaf that falls —"

Voinos mimicked him in sing-song mockery, "He hears every piece of dung plop in every privy in the whole wide world —"

Father let out a terrible cry, almost a scream, shoved me aside, and swung his staff, Voinos rolled out of his way and ran. The unexpended force of the stroke sent Father reeling. He slipped in mud and pine needles, and fell face down before the altar of the Faceless King.

Voinos laughed as he ran, then turned and shouted filthy names, ran again, and was gone.

Strangely, Father made no attempt to pursue him.

He sat up slowly. I crouched down by his side.

"Father . . . I . . . *saw* the Faceless King. So I know you're telling the truth."

He grabbed me with both hands and shook me so hard it frightened me.

"When?"

"When the birds . . . I saw the silver mask in the darkness, coming toward me. The eyes were open. The mouth was about to say something."

Father began to weep. I stood there, bewildered. I did not even know if I was telling the truth. I *wanted* it to be true, but my mind was in such a muddle I couldn't be sure.

But Father believed me.

"No matter where you go or how you live, my son, this night will remain with you, and you will spend all your days uncovering its mysteries. *That* is the meaning of your *going.*"

"What about . . . Voinos?"

"It's his night too. Already he is searching for the answers."

Voinos kept on running. I did not see him again for many years, although sinister rumors soon reached us of how he had gathered a band of ruffians around himself and had begun to rob travellers. By the time I was fifteen, there were more than rumors, and Voinos was widely feared. The bodies of his victims were always found mutilated — no one knew why — their faces slashed beyond recognition, or even burned until no trace of the features remained.

Mother died that year, more of grief than anything else, and Father placed *two* wooden skulls above the doorway of our house. He told everyone he had only one son now, and the chief priest— the new one, Hamilcestos, for Decronos had been murdered on a journey— came to exorcise the spirit and memory of Voinos.

But it did little good. The next day, as if to mock us, three faceless corpses were found seated in a neat row against the town's stockade. Thereafter, whenever I walked anywhere, people would turn and stare, then glance away quickly if they thought I'd noticed them. Sometimes I even overheard a whisper. "There! That's him! The brother of Voinos the madman."

People even said that Voinos came to us at night by a secret tunnel, and that we lived better than we should off of our share of his loot.

I followed my father in his profession, and he and the other bards trained me in the ways of the art. I spent long days reciting to myself, chanting all the old stories of our people. And when it came time for me to recite in the marketplace, people listened, perhaps out of respect for the stories, not the teller. But I was never summoned to the halls of the lords, either because I lacked skill, or because I was the brother of a murderer.

At seventeen, I managed to marry, a year and more later than most young men of the town. My wife was called in public merely Evad-ka, the woman of Evad, but I alone called her by the name I had given her, Rael-Hisna, the Flower of the River. She had come from the Great River, with traders on a barge from a strange place far upstream, where villages perch on cliffs above steep gorges, and the people do not worship the gentle gods of the fields and forest, but only the terrible Ragun-Temad, who commands eagles from mountaintops above the clouds.

I truly loved my Flower of the River. She was the one great joy in my life, which was otherwise often bitter. Father was growing old more rapidly than his years, weighed down by his sorrows. One winter, his voice left him, and he was reduced to playing the harp while *I* sang or recited, desperately trying to reconstruct the wonder of *his* half-remembered performances. He never saw the inside of a lord's hall again.

Gossips said the gods had cursed him for having sired Voinos, to which he replied hoarsely that such a son was curse enough, and the gods didn't have to do anything.

Then Rael-Hisna gave birth to a son, my son, and Father was glad again for the first time in a long while.

But that very day Voinos's band, now hundreds strong, seized nine barges on the river. Faceless corpses floated by our town for a week.

It was a sign. I knew that I had to go into the forest as my father had, in secret, and pray before the altar of the Faceless King, that perhaps the King or even Verunnos-Kemad might look on me and restore some order to my life. I wanted things to be better for my son. When he was grown, I would take him to that altar as I had been taken, and things would work out better at his *going*. Mine had been such a disaster.

The path seemed longer this time. Perhaps I strayed from it. I walked all night through the forest. A fog had come in and the needles were wet, so I made no sound as I went. I listened always, but heard nothing, and still I was afraid. The whole countryside was infested with bandits, with wild beasts, or worse. Toward dawn I slept seated against a tree and dreamed that hundreds of armed men stood before me, all of them wearing the silver mask of the Faceless

King, like a mirror image endlessly repeated. I cried out, in my dream, and was answered with familiar laughter. The masks came off. Each face was that of my brother. He made to speak, but the only sounds were the crackling of flames, and all those faces burned away like parchment. The rising sparks cried out fragments of words.

I fell forward, suddenly awake. I knew where I was. The familiar, dragonbacked ridge rose before me in the twilight. I ran, looking for some other sign, another flight of birds perhaps, but there was only the mist and the dank smell of the deep forest.

And there was Voinos, waiting for me. He had changed much since we had last been here together, and was now a black-bearded, barrel-chested giant nearly twice my size, who wore jewels in his hair and rings dangling from his ears, and a wildly colorful costume which seemed all bright sashes and pantaloons.

He stood leaning on a hammer, catching his breath. He had been working hard. He had broken the altar of the Faceless King to bits. Now he watched me coldly, as if I were mere prey.

"Are you . . . still looking for treasure?"

He made no reply.

I spread my hands apart from my body to show that I was not armed, all the while glancing furtively about, certain his men had arrows trained on me every step of the way.

Suddenly a morning bird began to chirp merrily, followed by a chorus of others, announcing the new day.

I stood there, facing my brother, while the sky lightened. A light spray of rain blew in my face.

At last I said, "You've changed a lot."

And with terrifying suddenness he lunged forward and grabbed the front of my jacket with a meaty hand and yanked me off my feet as if I were a rag doll.

"Yes!" he said, holding me inches from his face. His breath stank. "I've changed. I'm no longer a child and you *still* are. You always will be a child, Evad."

"Why —?"

"*Why?* I came here to put an end to an old story. *How?* No magic. I had the town watched. I *know* you, child-brother. I knew you'd come here eventually. When you set out, that was the signal."

I barely managed to gasp, "The signal for . . . what?"

"For a little homecoming." He shook me, again like a doll or a small child. "I haven't been back to my town for such a long time. My men are there even now, delivering my regards. When they are done, I'll go piss in the ashes."

I struggled against him. He only laughed. It was then that I understood that there were no hidden archers in the bushes. Voinos had only contempt for me. He was certainly not afraid.

"You're not going back, child-brother. I've spared you, just you, because you are my *dear* brother."

Suddenly he was pressing the point of a knife under my chin. He pressed harder. I felt it slicing the skin and tried not to breathe. There was a warm trickle of blood.

Then he held the knife up where I could see it. The blade was silver, the handle gold inset with jewels. The sign on it, in relief on the blade, was of the lunar-mask, the emblem of the Faceless King.

"Pretty, isn't it? I found it inside the altar. There was a secret compartment. Think of it as one last gift from the gods to our loving family. And because we love each other so much, child-brother, you are going to perform a task for me."

I thought of our family now, Father and my wife and child probably butchered by Voinos's men, and I said grimly, "Just kill me and get it over with. I'll do nothing for you."

Incredibly, he forced the knife into my hand and closed my fingers around the grip. Then he flung me to the ground, hard, and I lay stunned, while he stood astride me.

"Well? You might kill me with that." He indicated the knife. "But you can't, can you?"

"Yes," I said. "I can."

He slammed his foot down on my chest.

"I don't think so. I am not planning on it. Instead, you will help me carry out my beautiful scheme. Do you remember, dear child-brother, what we talked about when last we, ah, *enjoyed* each other's company here?"

"I . . . remember." I gasped for breath. His foot was crushing me.

"I reasoned then that if nobody has ever seen the face of the Faceless King, he could be, well, *anybody*. Remember?"

He leaned harder. There was a sharp pain as ribs cracked. I could only sob hoarsely.

"That is the point, child-brother. The knife is a token from the god. With it, you will journey very far. All men will make way for you. And, if such a person as the Faceless King really exists — you know, I have never made up my mind about that — you will return his token, *preferably in the heart.* If there is no such King, then you'll wander forever, which I think will be very funny. But if there is, well, you will use this dagger. Then the face behind the mask will be *yours.* No one will ever know, will they? Just you and me. A secret between brothers."

He let up the pressure a little and I whispered, "Why . . . ?

He shrugged. "I want to pray to you, child-brother. It's good to have family connections in high places."

"I won't," I said.

"You will. What else can you do?"

With that, he took his foot away, hefted the hammer onto his shoulder, and vanished into the forest on long, relentless strides.

It rained all day. Late in the afternoon, I approached the town. The smell of burnt wood carries very far in the rain, so I knew that everything my brother said was true. I believed, too, that he had gone out of his way to piss in the ashes. That would have been just like him.

I was utterly alone, and moreover, incomplete. The pain had not settled yet. I was like a warrior in battle who has just received a terrible wound, but so far has only felt a light blow. He has a little momentum left.

I had a little momentum left as I turned, clutching the sacred dagger Voinos had given me, and walked *away* from the town and everything I had ever known in my life. I refused to see with my own eyes that my wife and child and everyone else in my world — except Voinos! — were dead. That way there would always be the nagging doubt that I had dreamt it, and eventually the nagging would drive me mad, and in madness there would be some relief.

But the smell of the wood followed after me, and in time I stopped and sat down on a stone and just waited there, shivering, until it was almost evening and the rain ceased. Then I entered the town and saw the blackened logs and the heaps of ashy mud. An occasional corpse lay half-buried. Shadows lengthened as night came on, and I could not tell who any of the dead people were.

The place was very quiet. Here and there smoke rose. Crows cawed in the distance. Above me, the first stars began to appear.

I think I went mad then, for a little while. I screamed and wept and did a strange dance, kicking the heaps of ash and splintered wood, cursing the gods and the Faceless King and even my Father who had, after all, sired Voinos to kill and me to suffer.

And I held up the sacred dagger to the night sky. It gleamed a brilliant silver, like a moonrise. Then I threw it from me, as hard as I could. But I ran after it, and found it glowing where it had fallen. I picked it up, and suddenly the ashes all around me heaved and burst, as if the earth were boiling, and once again there was a miraculous flight of thousands upon thousands of grey and black birds buffetting me, their wings like thunder, rising to fill the sky. I lay huddled there, clutching the knife, and when I closed my eyes I saw the Faceless King clearly this time, sitting on a silver throne in the darkness behind tapestried curtains woven silver on black. His mask seemed to float in the air like a pale moon. He leaned forward, his robes wrinkling, and I was certain he was about to speak, but then the birds were gone and the vision passed.

I hated him. I swore that if I ever did find him, I *would* kill him, not because Voinos wanted me to, but because *I* wanted to.

But then I walked a little ways in a direction I somehow knew and there on the ground was my father's harp, coated with ash but whole. It seemed to me then the most precious object in the world. I sat down and placed it on my lap, weeping softly, and my rage passed as I spent hours carefully cleaning the harp and tuning its strings.

I wore the sacred dagger of the Faceless King around my neck on a cord, the blade exposed and dangling before me. Wherever I travelled, men recognized it and stood aside to let me pass. Even among the wildest mountain trails, in countryside filled with robbers, I was not molested.

I was summoned to the halls of the great lords as my father had been in the old days, but my song was not what the lords commanded. It was always the same, though the words changed like the passing waters of the Great River. There was anger in it and I sang of bloody vengeance; and then there was sorrow; and longing; and I sang of memories and my soul was purged. At the end I always sang of the Faceless King, whose ways are ever a mystery, who yet guides each one of us on the pathway of this life.

Men came to me from many lands asking to know the secrets of the Faceless King: when this or that lord would die, how a certain god must be placated, the answer to some ancient riddle. When I told them I did not know, they continued to follow me from place to place, saying, "He is testing us," or, "We are not yet worthy to know his mind." When I sang to them, they went away appeased, and yet I myself was not appeased for to me the mysteries remained mysteries, and I could find no reason for all the things that had happened.

I saw the Faceless King often in my dreams, always leaning forward in the darkness behind the curtains, about to speak but never speaking.

I thought this was because I was not worthy to know his mind.

When a youth came to me and said, "Make me your apprentice. Your singing is the most beautiful I have ever heard," I replied sadly, "You are as I once was. Remain so."

But he would not go away. He followed me for days. At last I turned to him and said, "You must choose to follow your own path, your own way, wherever it may lead you. I don't know what you want or need or will ever find. It is a mystery to me."

I just mumbled the first words that came into my mind and tried to make them sound like instruction. When I had finished, the youth touched his forehead to the ground at my feet and remained crouched down like that as I walked away from him. Later, I learned that he had founded a sect of mendicant philosophers called The Wanderers, whose symbols are the shoe and the staff, and the empty bag which remains empty because they have not yet found wisdom. Each of them takes a vow never to sleep in the same place for two nights until that bag is filled.

I came to many places I had never even known existed; and after many years reached the City of the Delta, where the Great River empties into a sea like a blue-metal shield beneath the hot sun. My fame had preceded me. People gathered by the thousands on the beach before the white-walled city. I sang for them of sorrow and longing and of the mysteries of the Faceless King. Many fell to their knees as I approached and begged to become my disciples. But I told them that my mission, or curse, or whatever it was, was for me alone; and I would not wish it on anyone else. Still the great mob of them followed me shouting into the city.

The priests summoned me; and I sang for them in the temple, before the enormous image of the god of the city, Bel-Hemad. Afterwards the mob proclaimed that the image had shifted, grinding its stone guts like an earthquake, so that the god might lean down and hear me better. Up near the ceiling, amid the shadows and the pigeons, Bel-Hemad smiled his inscrutable smile and said nothing.

"This man is possessed of an evil spirit," the chief priest said. "He drives the people to blasphemy!"

I was immediately arrested. Soldiers drove the mob from the temple, while the priests demanded of me the true meaning of my message.

I could only tell them that the Faceless King was an instrument of the secret god Verunnos-Kemad, and I in turn was an instrument of the King, even as my harp was my instrument. I knew that much. I no longer had any doubt.

But the priests were not satisfied. There was money in it, they said. Travellers would come from every land to heap gold on the altars to hear me sing.

"The Faceless King dwells amid the treasure-hoard of the Mother Dragon," I said. "What need has he of your money? I am filled with his music. What need have I?"

The priests brought the King of the city to me, an old, feeble man they had to hold up by either arm. He commanded me to explain the magic of my song, and I told him the story of my life, but that was not enough.

The King stared at me intently. He pursed his lips as if about to spit. Just then he looked like an ancient mummy, not a living man.

"Each man hears something different in your song," the King said at last, "and his soul is touched by it. Even I cannot touch a man's soul. Your song is a greater treasure than all my riches. I would possess it."

"Majesty," I said with bowed head. "You are not worthy. Nor am I."

Then the King gave me over to his torturers and they tortured me with great cunning, so that my pain would never end even after many years, but they did not let me die. And they would not take away my hands, lest I could no longer play the harp, nor my voice; nor did they dare steal the holy dagger I wore around my neck.

In the end, they put out my eyes with it.

There were many times when I fell into a delirium and dreamed that I was home, that I was still a boy in the walled town by the river, and none of this had ever happened.

Once I sat up suddenly in my bed at home, alarmed by some sudden noise in the night. My father stood there at the foot of my bed holding a lantern which was not a lantern at all, but the glowing mask of the Faceless King. He came forward to put the mask on me, but I struggled and cried out and woke with a start in utter darkness, rattling my chains.

Twenty years passed. My former life fell away like old leaves. I could no longer remember my wife's name, nor summon her face into my memory. I still knew Voinos. He was but a minor agony among many.

I saw the Faceless King every night as I slept. He was always there, leaning forward, about to speak.

At last I screamed to him, whether waking or asleep I do not know, "Let it end! Let me come to you!"

And at last he did speak, saying, "Then come to me right now."

That night ships arrived from across the sea to sack the City of the Delta. They must have taken the city by surprise. In the morning, I could hear the fighting below my window, and I could smell the smoke of burning houses. By evening there was only the smoke and an occasional cry. Then the lock on my door was being smashed, and a wild-voiced, strange-smelling barbarian burst into my cell, panting with exertion. But then I heard only shuffling. I groped about and found his shoulder level with my waist. He was kneeling before me. Gently, he pressed my harp into my hands.

My chains fell off of their own accord. The barbarian did not strike them.

"I must follow my own path," I said aloud. I remembered my conversation with the young man on the road, so many years before. "I am like a man on a swaying rope bridge above a deadly gorge. I cannot remain there. I must go either forward or back, and after so much travelling, I do not wish to go back."

The barbarian cried out something in his own language. I could only make out a few words. He was afraid. I am sure he thought me mad, and to barbarians, madness is a sure sign of the presence of the gods.

I hobbled through the city unopposed. Often someone would take me gently by the arm and guide me a little ways. Once I heard many women weeping. Often I heard masonry crashing, as if the conquerers did not intend to leave any stone atop another.

Finally I was on the beach, the sea breeze blowing in my face, driving away the smoke of the dying city. The lukewarm surf broke around my ankles.

I began to play my father's harp softly, and sing of my home for the first time in a long while. All the good memories came back. That was the greatest mystery of the Faceless King now, that I could remember a time when I had not known him, and had lived in a remote town and been happy.

Then I began to see stars in the dark sky. I thought for a moment that they were an illusion of my brain, like an itch in an amputated limb, but I went on singing, and I called on the Faceless King.

A silver glow spread across the sea and sky; and the huge mask of the Faceless King rose above the midnight waters; and thousands of black ships bobbed on the waves, their masts hung with lanterns; and these lanterns were the stars. Millions upon millions of birds soared up from between the ships, their wings like murmuring thunder, the stars flickering at their passage. Then I walked upon the water amid huge trees of utterly black stone, while the ships with their lanterns drifted among the trunks, and the birds flew in an endless, swirling mass before the Faceless King. I walked until I came to a dark place in the heart of the black stone forest, where silver-masked priests came out of a temple and challenged me. But I showed them the dagger I still wore around my neck; and they let me pass up the high, black steps of the temple, past endless rows of pillars, until, almost imperceptibly at first, the smooth floor gave way to tumbled stone and the pillars were rough fangs dripping from the ceiling and uncountable treasures lay about in heaps, glowing like coals in the darkness. I knew where I was then, that my quest had come to an end, that I had arrived by strange and devious ways at the Earth's heart, in the lair of the Mother Dragon.

I stood at the lip of an alcove, before black curtains embroidered with silver thread.

I began to sing once more, the song of the secret god; and for the only time in my life my song was completely pure, devoid of any longing or hatred or wish, as eternal as the wheel of the sky.

But the Faceless King spoke harshly from behind the curtain.

"Well, what have you come for?"

Astonished beyond all reason, I dropped the harp. It struck the ground with a resonant clang. It was as if *I* had been dropped suddenly from a great height.

"Evad," the King said. "You know for what purpose you have come here."

I could not bring myself to reply, so stricken was I with a terror that goes beyond any mere dread of danger.

"Come to me," the King said, his voice grating.

I opened the curtains. The masked King leaned forward on his throne, regarding me.

"You know the reason," he said.

I lifted the cord from around my neck and held the sacred dagger in my hand. I thought back, then, over many terrors and many years. *No,* I told myself. *It is all too insane. I will not.*

But the Faceless King spoke *with my brother's voice,* saying, "You will always be a child, Evad." And he began to laugh, and it was my brother's laugh.

It all came back to me, my fear, my hatred of Voinos, the deaths of everyone I had ever known, the laughter of Voinos in the forest where he'd smashed the altar.

And the King said in my brother's voice, *"It's good to have family connections in high places."*

Screaming, I lunged forward and grabbed the Faceless King by the front of his robe, yanking him off his throne and onto the blade of my knife. I held him in a terrible embrace while I stabbed him again and again and again.

When he was still and limp, and I felt his hot blood on my hands, I stood there trembling, not so much out of fear, but out of an appreciation of the sheer absurdity of my position. I let the knife and the body of the King drop to the cavern floor.

But the King was not quite dead. He whispered in the voice of my father.

"It is finished."

I began to sob with crazy remorse. I fell to my knees beside him. I cradled his head in my hands.

"Why?"

"Why?" he said. "Because I am weary. Because I wanted to die. When you have heard every leaf fall and known the flight of every sparrow, when the thoughts of all men living and the cries of their ghosts have merged into an endless babble for *so long,* one can only yearn for an ending. Therefore I caused you to be born, Evad. I made you as you are and Voinos as he had to be, shaping your lives, directing every step of your wanderings, all as part of my plan to bring you here. It was a long labor, but now it is done. Have I not concluded it well?"

"No," I said, feeling rising anger within myself, all the while shocked into terror at the mere fact that I *could* be angry at such a time in such a place. "You have not. What about me? I am merely left here."

"Oh yes, you," he said. His voice was now that of a stranger, very old, very tired. "I had nearly forgotten." He laughed softly, sadly. "It must have been the confusion of the moment. Forgive me."

He was silent for a moment, and I shook him in my terror. "Tell *me.*"

"You may turn from your path even now. You may go back to the village by the river and live as you always did. That much I can promise you. I will restore you to your former state."

I shook my head sadly. "It cannot be so. I would remember all these things, if only in dreams; and the memories have changed me. I am no longer that Evad who dwelt by the river. I have travelled too far and too long, and learned too much — and not enough."

And, one last time, he had my father's voice.

"It is finished," he said.

"No," I whispered into his ear. "You have not finished it well, or badly. You have not finished it at all."

Then I let his head drop to the floor. He was dead.

Indeed, it was not finished. Many things happened very quickly. I have never been able to fully account for all of them, even after many centuries of meditation.

I was blind again. I heard the priests come running, shouting in alarm. I was afraid, ridiculously, that my assassination would be discovered and I would be punished.

Quickly I groped around for the mask, found it, and put it on. Then I could see through eyes of silver.

The face of the dead man was first my father's, then my brother's, then face after face of countless strangers, the features running together, blurring, melting like wax. I stripped off the King's robes and put them on, then sat on the throne.

When the priests arrived, their masks glowing like little moons in the darkness, there was a King seated before them, and a corpse on the ground which had no face at all, merely a blank oval of flesh.

As Voinos had once remarked, *How do they know it's him?*

I leaned forward, indicating the corpse and the bloody dagger.

"Take that away," I said. "It has served its purpose."

They took the corpse but left the dagger, and it lies there still among the pebbles at my feet. I have regarded it often.

Even then I had not come to the end of my wanderings. I thought I had, but I was mistaken.

Through the mask, many things were revealed to me. I looked out into the world and I knew the flight of birds and the ambitions of kings and the words of lovers. I beheld armies in the night and grain ripening slowly in the summer sun, and I heard the songs of the leviathans in the depths of the midnight seas.

I sought my brother Voinos, and found him standing in a dank cell, his wrists chained to the wall. I manifested myself to him, and the cell was alight with the glory of the silver mask.

He started when he saw me, rattling his chains.

"So you do exist," he said. "I was never sure of that."

"Voinos —"

He let out a shriek of hysterical laughter, and dropped down limp in his chains. "That's *very funny*," he said. "You have the voice of a child I knew once. I'd always intended to throttle him, but I never got around to it. I don't know why." He banged his head against the wall, first gently, then harder, and laughed some more. There was only pain in his laughter.

"Voinos, it is I, Evad, your brother," I said, and I told him some of the things that had happened to me.

"That's the funny part," he said, sobbing gently now. "The Faceless King shaped us like a pair of clay pots. For all the good it did him. Or us. Now, as you will be glad to hear, my celebrated crimes have caught up with me. I shall die tomorrow. What a pleasure to spend the last night of my life with you, dearest brother. But then, what choice did I ever have?"

"I think you could have set your foot in another direction. You could have turned aside."

He screamed again and leapt up, straining at his chains. "You say I can *turn aside*. Well let me do it, now. Work a miracle for me and I'll be as wretchedly virtuous as you, snivelling brother —"

I saw then that even I could not bring him peace, not yet, while he still raged at the terrors within his own heart, and I left him.

I found him again later, hanging from a gibbet, black birds pecking out his eyes, and a third time in the grey dawn mists, wandering aimlessly among the trees near the ruined altar of the Faceless King. That third time I bore his poor ghost in my arms and placed him at the feet of the gods, not to be judged, but to be unmade.

All these things are as one to me, for I know the secrets of the dark forest, and of dreams, and of the grave.

For I am the Faceless King, the Blessed of Verunnos-Kemad; and I am also the hero of old, the slayer of dragons; and I am a man called Genimer who dwelt in a land far to the south and once designed a clock to measure eternity (but it did not work, for he has outlived it); and I am, further, En-Riose, the foolish one who longed for and actually believed he could achieve death by the shaping of the life of that Evad who dwelt down by the river.

I contain multitudes. En-Riose should have known that no one who has been the Faceless King ever dies, though their bodies might perish. All of them join together in the next, each newcomer changing the rest, like a new color stirred into a mixture of paints.

I am still Evad, who did not want to turn back, lest all his sufferings be for naught. So we go on — I go on — until we find the final mystery, and our empty bag is filled and we might rest.

I am Evad, who caused the eyes of En-Riose to be opened, so that he too might understand.

I am Evad, who granted to Voinos the only release he could ever have.

Somehow, I was worthy.

For the mind of Verunnos-Kemad is my mind and the splendors of the worlds are before me — as new gods awaken by the hundreds and make themselves known, and the Earth is filled up with magic, and the holy powers thunder in the night like great storms. I sit on the throne in the dark temple, yet I am everywhere, year into year, even as the signs in the heavens are slowly rewritten.

This is my path. I will not turn from it.

DOROTHY QUICK was the author of fifteen stories that appeared in *Weird Tales,* beginning with "The Horror in the Studio" in June 1935 and ending with "More Than Shadow" in July 1954, the next-to-the-last issue of the "original" run. According to *Weird Tales* historian Robert Weinberg, the elderly Ms. Quick was, in her youth, a personal friend of Mark Twain.

MORE THAN SHADOW

by Dorothy Quick

The third time it happened she was aware of its strangeness.

Up till then it hadn't mattered or seemed important, but the third time made her realize that something unusual was taking place and that there was cause for alarm.

She had just finished lunch and thought the philodendrons on either side of the mantelpiece needed watering. So, because she had gotten into the habit of saving water during the shortage, she took her glass, which was as full as when the maid had filled it, and started towards the fireplace. Halfway there the glass, for no reason which she could account, slipped from her hand.

The water spilled on the delft blue rug and rapidly began to coagulate into a shape as the glass rolled off towards the fireplace.

She watched the wet shape on the rug. "It *is* a little dog," she half whispered.

Almost as though an artist had painted it, there on the rug was the outline of a dog, a tiny dog with puffy, curly hair and, due to the way the water had absorbed and the wet and dry patches, it had a most beguiling expression. It was so real that she had to restrain herself from bending over to pick it up.

It looked exactly like a little dog waiting to be lifted into its mistress' arms. It had dimension and a definite personality. It seemed more than a shadow or a wet spot.

Just then Mona remembered that this had happened before—twice.

The first time had been at the table—here in the dining room. Her youngest daughter, aged three, had upset her glass of milk, purposely Mona suspected, knowing her offspring didn't like the bounty of the cow. She was just about to utter a reprimand when the child, Carol, had cried out, "Look, Mummy, it's a little dog."

The milk had run across the table as fluids do and settled in front of Mona's place. The shape of the damp place on the linen tablecloth was definitely that of a little dog.

The same little dog at which she was looking now, Mona thought and shuddered.

That day at the table she had laughed. It had seemed funny. Because the spilled milk had settled in the form of a little dog Carol had escaped the scolding and Mona had mopped up the milk reluctantly because the little dog shape was so cunning.

But she forgot about it almost immediately.

Three days later, a rainy Sunday afternoon it was, she was sitting in the living room with her husband, Hal; the three children, Carol, Meg and Harry, Jr. were playing nearby. Ellen, the maid, brought the tea. Mona gave the two older children a very weak version and Carol had milk in her cup. Then she handed Hal his stronger share. He started with it towards his favorite chair. The cup, which had seemed firm on its saucer, could not have been, for it bounced off, spilling the tea on the beige carpet.

For an instant there was silence. Then Carol came running over from the other side of the room. "Little dog, little dog," she exclaimed, pointing to the wet spot.

Mona stared. It was true. There was the outline of a little dog, curly haired, with an uplifted paw.

Her husband laughed, "You're right, Carol. It *is* a little dog, and it's cute too. I'd like a little dog like that around the house."

Carol clapped her hands, "Daddy, get one for Carol."

"Maybe." Hal nodded, "if we could find an attractive one like that."

The other two children were there by then, exclaiming, saying they'd like a dog too.

Hal got another cup of tea and reached his favorite chair with it safely before he delivered the pronouncement, "You can't all have dogs. If you'll just settle for a community animal—"

By the time the argument was over, the carpet had dried and Mona forgot the whole business as quickly as the children did. But now here was the dog again, and more real than ever.

Tiny, curly-haired, with a front paw elevated appealingly, a sharp, pointed nose, utterly beguiling. "It must be a poodle," Mona thought, "a very small poodle. But why does it keep happening? Is it an omen, does it mean we ought to have a dog?"

It was probably a trick of wind ruffling the rug, but it seemed as though the paw was further outthrust and the outline of the little creature quivered with eagerness.

Ellen came into the dining room. Mona called her, pointed to the spot. "What does that look like?" she asked.

The girl giggled, "Why, for all the world like a little dog, the kind the leprechauns keep. 'Tis said in Ireland the little people ride them on moonlight nights."

"Where do they go?" Mona was surprised at herself for putting the question.

"Now that we do not be asking." Ellen lapsed into the brogue she'd brought with her two years ago when she came over to visit her Aunt Mary who cooked for Mr. and Mrs. Hal Devitt. "But," she dropped her voice as though afraid of being overheard, "some say the little dogs take them over the mountain to the land of youth."

A quotation from Yeats leaped into Mona's mind.

Where nobody gets old and godly and grave
Where nobody gets old and crafty and wise
Where nobody gets old and bitter of tongue
And she is still there, busied with a dance,
Deep in the dewy shadow of a wood
Or where stars walk upon the mountainside.

The words had always appealed to Mona, ever since she had played the girl in the play the graduating class had done at school, "The Land of Heart's Desire." The lines had stuck in her mind and now they were echoing over and over, "Deep in the dewy shadows of a wood, or where stars walk upon a mountaintop."

And the little dog could take you there—over the mountaintop to the land of heart's desire where—what was it the child in the play had said? "Could make you ride upon the winds, run on the top of the dishevelled tide, and dance upon the mountains like a flame." Her mind went back to the play. There had been more. She remembered the child's speech:

You shall go with me, newly married bride
And gaze upon a merrier multitude.

Then there had been Irish names, Nuala, Ardoe the wise, Feacra and Finvarra,

And their land of Heart's Desire
Where beauty has no ebb, decay no flood,
But joy is wisdom. Time an endless song.

The little dog could take you to that!

Mona caught herself up sharply. The coincidence of the dog's outline happening three times and Ellen's old-world leprechauns with their dogs to ride had woven a spell over her—that and Yeat's magic poetry. But she mustn't be a dreamer as she had been in the part of Maire which she had acted in the play—and never forgotten. She could remember now how when she had sunk to the floor, playing dead, the child having stolen her soul away, she had felt that it would have been worth it to find that land where people were forever young, never to grow old, "to dance upon the mountains like a flame." It would have been worth losing your soul, she had thought.

Then the curtain had fallen and the child was her schoolmate, Meg, again, and she was Mona, alive and hoping Hal had liked her performance.

He had; that very night he had proposed. "I shouldn't yet. I've got three more years of college, but, after seeing you so ethereal, so beautiful, and so far away, I had to be sure of you. Will you marry me, Mona, when I can support you?"

She would, and they had been married before he had taken his place in his father's law office. They had been very happy. Their life had been full. They loved each other, had three wonderful children, she had wanted nothing. Yet why did the outline, something more than a shadow, of a dog, make her remember and long for the Land of Heart's Desire? This was nonsense. She mustn't even think of it any more. She turned to Ellen. "Get a cloth," she commanded and was ashamed at the edgy tone in her voice, "and mop it up."

"Yes ma'm," said Ellen, and then in a sharp tone of surprise, "But it's all dry—the little dog has gone."

A week after that the dog came. It was a poodle and Carol found it down by the garden gate. She and Meg came running to Mona, the little bunch of black fluff clasped tightly in Meg's arms.

Out of the chorus of exclamations and requests of "Can we keep him?" Mona gathered that the dog had been sitting by the gate, that it had greeted the children like a long-lost friend, that they already adored it. There was no sign of a collar or license tag. It hadn't been clipped, and it was adorable. The minute they put it down it capered up to Mona, turned several circles in front of her and then put up one paw. "Like the dog on the rug," Mona thought. She felt strange about the dog, but she had to admit it was captivating. When it jumped up in her arms and cuddled its head against her neck she was completely won over.

"Yes. You can keep it if no one claims it," she said, absurdly conscious of the appeal of the little creature. She was as desirous as the children to have the little dog, but common sense warned her not to let them count too much on having it. "But I'm sure that it has an owner. It's such a beautiful dog," she caressed the little head "that it must belong to someone. It's probably lost—run away maybe. They might advertise for it in the paper—"

"We don't have to read the papers," Meg suggested with practicality.

"That wouldn't be honest," Mona told them. "We will watch out. In the meantime you can play with him. Suppose you get him some milk, Harry."

Harry obliged. Mona reluctantly put the little dog down. It drank a little, then cavorted about, jumping up on the children, licking their hands. When it came to Carol it leaped into her lap and, putting its paws on her shoulders, seemed to be whispering into her ear.

"Did you ever see anything so cute?" Meg asked.

Mona was conscious of a twinge of jealousy. She had loved the feeling of the tiny head nestling close to her face. She shoved her feeling into the back of her consciousness and agreed that the little dog was cute.

So did Hal and Ellen. They all hoped that no one would claim the tiny poodle. It was so gay, such good company. It seemed to know just what their mood was and fit into it.

"I've always heard poodles were smart," Hal said after it had been with them two days, "but I swear this one is almost human."

With that the little dog climbed up his leg and licked the man's big hand as though it were saying 'thank you.' "See what I mean?" boomed Hal, patting the small head. "I certainly hope no one comes for it."

No one did.

After a week they felt safe, and as though they owned "Jet," so called for his beady, black eyes and "because he was jettisoned," Hal added, and then had to explain to the children what the word meant.

They all, except Ellen, adored the poodle. Ellen kept insisting there was something strange about him. The poodle seemed to like them all equally well. To Mona there was something specially appealing about the little dog. She actually reached the point where she tried to get him off to herself, carrying him into her room to be with her while she napped—but, whether by design or not, he always barked or made some noise that brought the children running.

Baby Carol would put up her three-year-old hands to the bed. "Yet," she would call, "Yet," her tongue not able to master the intricacies of the letter J.

Then Mona would have to lift the little thing down, and off he would go with the children scampering with all the abandon of youth —so oddly at variance with the wise look in his shoe-button eyes.

"It's that that makes me love him so," Mona thought, "that queer mixture of youth and wisdom. It's amazing what a difference a dog makes in a house."

And it really was. The children never needed to be amused now. They had Jet. If they got restless he brought his ball, dropped it in Meg or Harry's lap for them to throw. He retrieved without being taught. Even Hal was forced into the game and Mona—no matter how busy the children were there was always some time during the day when the dog cuddled up into her neck as he had done the first day he came.

Mona found herself looking forward to it almost as a ritual. "It's ridiculous," she scolded herself, "but when he's there I seem to have visions of a never-never land, Yeats' Land of Heart's Desire. I suppose because I thought of the play with all the nonsense of Ellen's when he first came and its association of ideas. But it's uncanny, really."

Finally she told Hal about it. "I think I'm going mad. I keep wishing he'd grow life-size and I could ride away on his back. I see visions in which I—sober, sedate Mona—dance upon the mountains like a flame. Do you think I'm crazy?"

Hal looked at his pretty wife. "You're anything but sedate, Mona. You know you're lovely and you're not nuts, either. There's something about that animal—you know, when he licks my hand it feels like water touching my skin. I think of the rushing waters of a bright brook with motes dancing in the sunlight, and I feel like chucking business and going fishing. Pretty silly the end of April."

"Well, you could go to Florida," Mona said seriously.

"Now don't you go encouraging me. I don't have a vacation till August! I just wanted to explain the dog's effect on me." He patted Mona's shoulder. "You see, dear, it's because the little dog is so young, so blithe and gay he releases our inhibitions. It's good for us."

Mona wasn't convinced. "The children are young, blithe and gay. They don't make me want to 'dance on the mountain like a flame.'"

Hal threw back his head and laughed. "That would be pretty difficult to do. Have you ever seen a flame dance on a mountain? These poetic imageries are all right until you break them down. Then what have you—nothing, nothing at all."

He was right of course. A flame could dance in a fireplace but on a mountain it would be, as Hal said, nothing, or a forest fire. She joined in her husband's laughter and forgot the whole business when he suggested they might go out dancing.

They hadn't done that for a long time. It would be fun indeed. "I'll go nap," she told him, "so I'll look my best."

"You always do." He kissed her as he had when they were engaged. Mona forgot everything but the moment.

The poodle was on her bed waiting for her—wagging its pom-pom tail in an utter abandon of ecstasy, cavorting up and down regardless of her blue satin bedspread. Mona wondered idly how he'd gotten up on the high bed. He was such a little thing. "Jet," she said in the manner proverbial to all dog lovers, "Good Jet" and patted the tiny head.

As she took off her dress the poodle watched her gravely. He was like a little old woman sitting on the end of the bed—or a gnome. She slipped into a wrapper, a filmy thing of lace and nylon and curled up on the bed. In two seconds flat he was beside her, nestled into the curve of her shoulder, his head close to her cheek.

For once the children didn't come and she lay there strangely content, her fingers caressing the soft wool of Jet's pompadour.

Presently she began to hear a weird music, soft and slow, unlike any she had ever heard before, a line from a song came to her— "Strange Music of the Spheres." Someone must be playing a radio, she thought, and yet no radio had ever produced music like this, yet in some odd way it seemed mixed up with the poodle's rhythmic breathing and the Yeats' play came back into her mind. *The Land of Heart's Desire, where nobody gets old.*

Then she must have fallen asleep for the poodle began to talk. "I can take you there—where everything is wondrous strange and beautiful, where running water makes music all day long, where there is no age, no pain, nothing but happiness. Will you come with me? Ride upon my back to eternal joy?"

And then incredibly the poodle was beside the bed, the size of a pony, small but big enough to carry her.

Mona knew instinctively that if she got on his back she would achieve the Land of Heart's Desire. Out of the large body the same poodle eyes looked into hers. In them was eternal youth and an age-old wisdom. But there was something else—something that filled her with horror—a cold, calculating look that was evil. She shivered and pulled her robe close.

In her ears the music swelled and the poodle's voice mingled with it. "Come, come with me to eternal joy. Just get on my back."

The music was louder. Suddenly she forgot the evil, forgot everything but the promise of eternal joy. She swung around on the bed, her legs dangling over the side. Then she was on her feet and the poodle threw back its coal black head and made a sound that was half human, half animal, but wholly triumphant, and it was the same evil she saw in the shining eyes. For the first time she was aware of the dog's sharply pointed white teeth. She had noticed the incisors when the poodle had been small, thought they were over-large. Now they looked exactly like the fangs they were. She visioned them dripping with blood—her blood—and she stopped advancing, standing stock still. Her eyes met those of the dog's, those jet-like button eyes that had given him his name.

"No," she whispered, "no, I cannot come."

"Only one step." The voice came from the poodle's throat, mingling with the music. "Only one step and it is yours—eternal youth—with me." The poodle's eyes were veiled. It lifted one foot enticingly. "Come," it insisted, and moved nearer to her.

Again she began to move towards the dog who now seemed larger than ever. "You won't get out of the door with me on your back," she said.

"There will be no doors for us now, or ever again," the dog replied. It looked at her again.

This time she saw the evil in its eyes but she didn't care. The music had her in its spell. The poodle had charmed her, too. She no longer thought it evil or that it was strange it had enlarged itself. She knew that it would bear her through the door or the wall, if necessary, to another world—to eternal joy or eternal damnation. She didn't care which as long as the music lasted.

She took another step. The poodle cavorted like a prancing horse as it had done when it was a tiny dog showing off. "Hurry," its words rang in her ears. "Hurry, get on my back so we can ride."

She put her hand on its shining topknot, the black hair that was soft as cashmere.

The music enveloped her like a mantle of lovely vibrating sound.

She put her other hand on the poodle's back that was cleanshaven, smooth as broadtail and as high as her shoulder.

Just as she was about to swing herself into place, the door opened and the children tumbled in, Baby Carol, Meg and Harry Junior.

"Mother," Meg said reproachfully, "you've got Jet in here."

She was back on her bed, the poodle lying curled against her neck, tiny as always, but looking at her with deep unfathomable eyes.

Even as she looked at it, she saw and felt the deep sigh that wracked its fragile little body.

In her ears was a whisper, "Too late." The music was gone.

"Yet, Yet." Baby Carol was pushing herself against the bed.

"I was asleep," Mona told herself, "and I dreamed, but what a dream!"

Almost in a daze she reached up for the poodle, cradled the tiny body in her two hands. "Run along, little Jet," she said.

The poodle leaned towards her and licked her cheek.

For an instant she thought she heard the music again. But it was only wishful thinking. Except for the children the room was quiet.

"Yet, Yet," Baby Carol was calling.

Mona gave the poodle to Harry Junior.

"Run along, children," she admonished, "Mother has to dress."

They left her and she got off the bed. She felt enervated. "What a dream!" she said, half aloud. "I'm actually exhausted—over a dream —no, I guess it was more than a dream. It was in the nightmare class."

She shook the memory of it off, bathing her face with cold water to get rid of it. She dressed quickly. When she reached the living room and Hal she wore her new Dior taffeta suit with the bell-like flaring skirt and the jeweled cap that perched jauntily on her golden curls.

"Mona," her husband exclaimed, "you're ravishing." He kissed her.

"What a fool I was," she thought, "to want to leave him for eternal joy—even in a dream! Why, I've got eternal joy with him! And the children. It took a nightmare to make me realize it, though."

She sighed as the poodle had sighed.

"Come along," Hal said.

"Shouldn't we tell the children goodbye?" she asked.

"I sent them off to the garden to play—and I've told Ellen we're going out. Come on, dear, tonight is entirely our own."

"I must tell you about the silliest dream I had," she began as they hailed a taxi.

"Later," he said. "Right now I want to talk about you and how lovely you are."

She never did tell him about the dream.

It was late when they reached home. "It's been a perfect evening," Mona said as Hal put his key in the front door lock.

The door swung open before he turned the key. A white-faced Ellen stood inside peering out at them anxiously.

"Is anything wrong?" Mona asked, alarmed by the look on her maid's face.

Ellen kept staring. "Did you take the baby with you?" she asked. Her voice was unsteady.

"No," Hal replied tersely. "Why?"

Ellen's lips quivered. "I so hoped you'd taken her, even though I was sure you hadn't. She's gone. She wasn't there when I called the children for supper—neither she nor the little dog. I asked Meg and Harry where she was and they said the last time they'd seen her she was playing with Jet in the far corner of the garden."

"But surely—" Mona began over Hal's, "We'd better phone the police."

"Oh, no sir." Ellen wailed, "It's no use. It's May eve, the time when the 'little people' have power. They've spirited her away. The little dog was their emissary. He came ahead to get someone from this house. I never liked the little dog. I think I knew from the first—"

"Nonsense," Hal broke in, "there was nothing wrong with the dog. There are no little people. I'll phone the police and ask the neighbors—"

"I did that," Ellen cut in. "Two of them saw Carol. They said she was laughing happily, riding on the back of a poodle dog as large as a pony."

Mona remembered what she had thought was a dream—a nightmare. When the poodle had grown big—big enough to take her to the Land of Heart's Desire. She remembered the cold, calculating look—the evil.

It had been actuality, not a dream. In one sickening moment she glimpsed another world, another dimension and knew it was more than shadow and that she would never see her child again.

F. MARION CRAWFORD (1854–1909), born in Italy of American parents, wrote more than forty romantic novels and several excellent supernatural stories, including "The Doll's Ghost," "The Screaming Skull," the nautical ghost story "The Upper Berth" and the following little-known terrifying narrative. "The Dead Smile" appeared in the Summer 1974 issue of the Leo Margulies– Sam Moskowitz *Weird Tales* revival.

THE DEAD SMILE

by F. Marion Crawford

Sir Hugh Ockram smiled as he sat by the open window of his study, in the late August afternoon; and just then a curiously yellow cloud obscured the low sun, and the clear summer light turned lurid, as if it had been suddenly poisoned and polluted by the foul vapors of a plague.

Sir Hugh's face seemed, at best, to be made of fine parchment drawn skin-tight over a wooden mask, in which two eyes were sunk out of sight, and peered from crevices under the slanting, wrinkled lids, alive and watchful like two toads in their holes, side by side and exactly alike.

Nurse Macdonald said once that when Sir Hugh smiled he saw the faces of two women in hell—two dead women he had betrayed. Nurse Macdonald was a hundred years old.

Sir Hugh's smile widened, stretching the pale lips across the discolored teeth in an expression of profound self-satisfaction, blended with the most unforgiving hatred and contempt. The hideous disease of which he was dying had touched his brain.

His son stood beside him, tall, white and delicate as an angel in a primitive picture; and though there was deep distress in his violet eyes, as he looked at his father's face, he felt the shadow of that sickening smile stealing across his own lips and parting them and drawing them against his will. It was like a bad dream, for he tried not to smile, and smiled the more.

Beside him, strangely like him in her wan, angelic beauty, with the same shadowy golden hair, the same sad violet eyes, the same luminously pale face, Evelyn Warburton rested one hand upon his arm. As she looked into her uncle's eyes, and could not turn her own away, she knew that the deathly smile was hovering on her own red lips, drawing them tightly across her little teeth—and the smile was like the shadow of death and the seal of damnation upon her pure young face.

"Of course," said Sir Hugh very slowly, and still looking out at the trees, "if you have made up your mind to be married, I can not hinder you, and I don't suppose you attach the smallest importance to my consent—"

"Father!" exclaimed Gabriel, reproachfully.

"No, I do not deceive myself," continued the old man, smiling terribly. "You will marry when I am dead, though there is a very good reason why you had better not —why you had better not," he repeated very emphatically, and he slowly turned his toad eyes upon the lovers.

"What reason?" asked Evelyn in a frightened voice.

"Never mind the reason, my dear. You will marry just as if it did not exist." There was a long pause.

"Two gone," he said, his voice lowering strangely, "and two more will be four—all together—for ever and ever, burning, burning, burning bright."

At the last words his head sank slowly back and the little glare of the toad eyes disappeared under the swollen lids; and the lurid cloud passed from the westering sun, so that the earth was green again, and the light pure. Sir Hugh had fallen asleep, as he often did in his last illness, even while speaking.

Gabriel Ockram drew Evelyn away, and from the study they went out into the dim hall, softly closing the door behind them. Each audibly drew breath, as though some sudden danger had been passed.

They laid their hands each in the other's, and their strangely-like eyes met in a long look, in which love and perfect understanding were darkened by the secret terror of an unknown thing. Their pale faces reflected each other's fear.

"It is his secret," said Evelyn at last. "He will never tell us what it is."

"If he dies with it," answered Gabriel, "let it be on his head!"

"On his head," echoed the dim hall. It was a strange echo, and some were frightened by it, for they said that if it were a real echo, it should repeat everything, and not give just a phrase here and there. Nurse Macdonald said that the great hall would never echo a prayer when an Ockram was to die, though it would give back curses ten for one.

"On his head!" it repeated, quite softly, and Evelyn started and looked round.

"It is only the echo," said Gabriel, leading her away.

They went out into the late afternoon light, and sat upon a stone seat behind the chapel. It was very still, not a breath stirred, and there was no sound near them.

"It's very lonely here," said Evelyn, taking Gabriel's hand nervously, and speaking as if she dreaded to disturb the silence. "If it were dark I should be afraid."

"Of what? Of me?" Gabriel turned to her.

"Oh no! How could I be afraid of you? But of the old Ockrams—they say they are just under our feet here in the north vault outside the chapel, all in their shrouds with no coffins, as they used to bury them."

"As they always will—as they will bury my father, and me. They say an Ockram will not lie in a coffin."

"But it cannot be true—those are fairy tales—ghost stories!" Evelyn nestled nearer to her companion, grasping his hand more tightly, as the sun began to go down.

"Of course. But there is the story of old Sir Vernon, who was beheaded for treason under James the Second. The family brought his body back from the scaffold in an iron coffin with heavy locks, and they put it in the north vault. But ever afterwards, whenever the vault was opened to bury another of the family, they found the coffin wide open and the body standing upright against the wall, the head rolled away in a corner, smiling at it."

"As Uncle Hugh smiles?" Evelyn shivered.

"Yes, I suppose so," answered Gabriel, thoughtfully. "Of course I never saw it, and the vault has not been opened for thirty years—none of us have died since then."

"And if—if Uncle Hugh dies—shall you—" Evelyn stopped, and her beautiful thin face was quite white.

"Yes. I shall see him laid there, too—with his secret, whatever it is." Gabriel sighed and pressed the girl's little hand.

"I do not like to think of it," she said unsteadily. "Oh, Gabriel, what can the secret be? He said we had better not marry—not that he forbade it—but he said it so strangely, and he smiled—ugh!" Her small white teeth chattered with fear, and she looked over her shoulder while drawing still closer to Gabriel. "And somehow, I felt it in my own face—"

"So did I," answered Gabriel in a low, nervous voice. "Nurse Macdonald—" He stopped abruptly.

"What? What did she say?"

"Oh nothing. She told me things—they would frighten you, dear. Come, it is growing chilly." He rose, but Evelyn held his hand in both of hers, still sitting and looking up into his face.

"But we shall be married, just the same—Gabriel! Say that we shall!"

"Of course, darling—of course. But while my father is so very ill, it is impossible—"

"Oh, Gabriel, Gabriel, dear! I wish we were married now!" cried Evelyn in sudden distress. "I know that something will prevent it and keep us apart."

"Nothing shall!"

"Nothing?"

"Nothing human," said Gabriel Ockram, as she drew him down to her.

And their faces, that were so strangely alike, met, and touched—and Gabriel knew that the kiss had a marvelous savor of evil, but on Evelyn's lips it was like the cool breath of a sweet and mortal fear. Neither of them understood, for they were innocent and young.

"It is as if we loved in a strange dream," she said.

"I fear the waking," he murmured.

"We shall not wake, dear—when the dream is over it will have already turned into death, so softly that we shall not know it. But until then—"

She paused, and her eyes sought his, and their faces slowly came nearer. It was as if they had thoughts in their red lips that foresaw and foreknew the deep kiss of each other.

"Until then—" she said again, very low, and her mouth was nearer to his.

"Dream—till then," murmured his breath.

2

Nurse Macdonald was a hundred years old. She slept sitting all bent together in a great old leathern armchair with wings, her feet in a bag footstool lined with sheepskin, and many warm blankets wrapped about her, even in summer.

Her face was very wrinkled, but the wrinkles were so small and fine and near together that they made shadows instead of lines. Two thin locks of hair, turning from white to a smoky yellow again, were drawn over her temples from under her starched white cap.

Now and then she woke and her eyelids were drawn up in tiny folds, like little pink silk curtains, and her queer blue eyes looked straight before her, through doors and walls and worlds to a far place beyond.

Then she slept again, and her hands lay one upon the other on the edge of the blanket; the thumbs had grown longer than the fingers with age and the joints shone in the low lamplight like polished crabapples.

It was nearly one o'clock in the night, and the summer breeze was blowing the ivy branch against the panes of the window, with a hushing caress. In the small room beyond, with the door ajar, the girl maid who took care of Nurse Macdonald was fast asleep. All was very quiet. The old woman breathed regularly, and her indrawn lips trembled each time as the breath went out, and her eyes were shut.

Outside the closed window there was a face, and violet eyes were looking steadily at the ancient sleeper, for it was like the face of Evelyn Warburton. Yet the cheeks were thinner than Evelyn's, and as white as a gleam, and the eyes stared, and the lips were not red with life; they were dead and painted with new blood.

Slowly Nurse Macdonald's wrinkled eyelids folded themselves back, and she looked straight at the face at the window to the count of ten.

"Is it time?" she asked, in her little old, faraway voice.

The face at the window changed; the eyes opened wider and wider till the white glared all round the bright violet, and the bloody lips

opened over gleaming teeth, and stretched and widened and
stretched again, and the shadowy golden hair rose and streamed
against the window in the night breeze. And in answer to Nurse
Macdonald's question came the sound that freezes the living flesh.

The low-moaning voice that rises suddenly, like the scream of
storm, from a moan to a wail, from a wail to a howl, from a howl to
the fear-shriek of the tortured dead—he who has heard, knows, and
can bear witness that the cry of the Banshee is an evil cry to hear
alone in the deep night.

When it was over and the face was gone, Nurse Macdonald shook
a little in her great chair, and still she looked at the black square of
the window, but there was nothing more there, nothing but the
night, and the whispering ivy branch. She turned her head to the
door that was ajar, and there stood the maid, in her white gown, her
teeth chattering with fright.

"It is time, child," said Nurse Macdonald. "I must go to him, for
it is the end."

She rose slowly, leaning her withered hands upon the arms of the
chair, and the girl brought her a woolen gown and a great mantle,
and her crutch-stick, and made her ready.

Often the girl looked at the window and was unjointed with fear,
and often Nurse Macdonald shook her head and said words which
the maid could not understand.

"It was like the face of Miss Evelyn," said the girl at last, trembling.

But the ancient woman looked up sharply and angrily, and her
queer blue eyes glared. She held herself by the arm of the great chair
with her left hand, and lifted up her crutch-stick to strike the maid
with all her might. But she did not.

"You are a good girl," she said, "but you are a fool. Pray for wit,
child, pray for wit—or else find service in another house than
Ockram Hall. Bring the lamp and help me under my left arm."

The crutch-stick clacked on the wooden floor, and the low heels of
the old woman's slippers clappered after, in slow triplets, as Nurse
Macdonald got toward the door.

Each step she took was a labor in itself, and by the clacking noise
the waking servants knew that she was coming long before they saw
her.

No one was sleeping now, and there were lights, and whisperings, and pale faces in the corridors near Sir Hugh's bedroom, and now someone went in, and now someone came out, but every one made way for Nurse Macdonald, who had nursed Sir Hugh's father more than eighty years ago.

The light was soft and clear in the room. There stood Gabriel Ockram by his father's bedside, and there knelt Evelyn Warburton, her hair lying like a golden shadow down her shoulders and her hands clasped nervously together. And opposite Gabriel a nurse was trying to make Sir Hugh drink. But he would not, and though his lips were parted his teeth were set. He was very, very thin and yellow now, and his eyes caught the light sideways and were as yellow coals.

"Do not torment him," said Nurse Macdonald to the woman who held the cup. "Let me speak to him, for his hour is come."

"Let her speak to him," said Gabriel, in a dull voice.

So the ancient woman leaned to the pillow and laid the feather weight of her withered hand upon Sir Hugh's yellow fingers, and she spoke to him earnestly, while only Gabriel and Evelyn were left in the room to hear.

"Hugh Ockram," she said, "this is the end of your life, and as I saw you born, and saw your father born before you, I am come to see you die. Hugh Ockram, will you tell me the truth?"

The dying man recognized the little faraway voice he had known all his life, and he very slowly turned his yellow face to Nurse Macdonald; but he said nothing. Then she spoke again.

"Hugh Ockram, you will never see the daylight again. Will you tell the truth?"

His toadlike eyes were not yet dull. They fastened themselves on her face.

"What do you want of me?" he asked and each word struck hollow upon the last. "I have no secrets. I have lived a good life."

Nurse Macdonald laughed—a tiny, cracked laugh, that made her head bob and tremble a little, as if her neck were on a steel spring. But Sir Hugh's eyes grew red, and his pale lips began to twist.

"Let me die in peace," he said, slowly.

Nurse Macdonald shook her head, and her brown, mothlike hand left his and fluttered to his forehead.

"By the mother that bore you and died of grief for the sins you did, tell me the truth!"

Sir Hugh's lips tightened on his discolored teeth.

"Not on earth," he answered, slowly.

"By the wife who bore your son and died heartbroken, tell me the truth!"

"Neither to you in life, nor to her in eternal death."

His lips writhed, as if the words were coals between them, and a great drop of sweat rolled across the parchment of his forehead. Gabriel Ockram bit his hand as he watched his father die. But Nurse Macdonald spoke a third time.

"By the woman whom you betrayed, and who waits for you this night, Hugh Ockram, tell me the truth!"

"It is too late. Let me die in peace."

The writhing lips began to smile across the set yellow teeth, and the toad eyes glowed like evil jewels in his head.

"There is time," said the ancient woman. "Tell me the name of Evelyn Warburton's father. Then I will let you die in peace."

Evelyn started back, kneeling as she was, and stared at Nurse Macdonald, and then at her uncle.

"The name of Evelyn's father?" he repeated, slowly, while the awful smile spread upon his dying face.

Now the light was growing strangely dim in the great room. As Evelyn looked, Nurse Macdonald's crooked shadow on the wall grew gigantic. Sir Hugh's breath came thick, rattling in his throat, as death crept in like a snake and choked it back. Evelyn prayed aloud, high and clear.

Then something rapped at the window, and she felt her hair rise upon her head in a cool breeze, as she looked around, in spite of herself.

And when she saw her own white face looking in at the window, and her own eyes staring at her through the glass, wide and fearful, and her own hair streaming against the pane, and her own lips dashed with blood, she rose slowly from the floor, and stood rigid for one moment, till she screamed once and fell straight back into Gabriel's arms.

The shriek that answered hers was the fear-shriek of the tormented corpse, out of which the soul cannot pass for shame of deadly sins, though the devils fight in it with corruption, each for their due share.

Sir Hugh Ockram sat upright in his deathbed, and saw and cried aloud:

"Evelyn!" His harsh voice broke and rattled in his chest, as he sank down. But still Nurse Macdonald tortured him, for there was a little life left in him still.

"You have seen the mother, as she waits for you, Hugh Ockram. Who was this girl Evelyn's father? What was his name?"

For the last time the dreadful smile came upon the twisted lips, very slowly, very surely, now. And the toad eyes glared red, and the parchment face glowed a little in the flickering light. For the last time words came.

"They know it in Hell."

Then the glowing eyes went out quickly, the yellow face turned waxen pale and a great shiver ran through the thin body as Hugh Ockram died.

But in death he still smiled, for he knew his secret and kept it still, on the other side, and he would take it with him, to lie with him forever in the north vault of the chapel where Ockrams lie uncoffined in their shrouds—all but one.

Though he was dead, he smiled, for he had kept his treasure of evil truth to the end, and there was none left to tell the name he had not spoken, but there was all the evil he had not undone left to bear fruit.

As they watched—Nurse Macdonald and Gabriel, who held Evelyn still unconscious in his arms while he looked at the father—they felt the dead smile crawling along their own lips—the ancient crone and the youth with the angel's face.

Then they shivered a little, and both looked at Evelyn as she lay with her head on his shoulder, and though she was very beautiful, the same sickening smile was twisting her young mouth, too; and it was like the foreshadowing of a great evil which they could not understand.

They carried Evelyn out and she opened her eyes, and the smile was gone. From far away in the great house the sound of weeping and crooning came up the stairs and echoed along the dismal corridors, for the women had begun to mourn the dead master, after the Irish fashion, and the hall had echoes of its own all that night, like the far-off wail of the Banshee among forest trees.

When the time was come they took Sir Hugh in his winding-sheet on a trestle bier, and bore him to the chapel and through the iron door and down the long descent to the north vault, with tapers, to lay him by his father. Two men went in first to prepare the place, and came back staggering like drunken men, and white, leaving their lights behind them.

But Gabriel Ockram was not afraid, for he knew. And he went in alone and saw that the body of Sir Vernon Ockram was leaning upright against the stone wall, and that its head lay on the ground near by with the face turned up, and the dried leathern lips smiled horribly at the dried-up corpse, while the iron coffin, lined with black velvet, stood open on the floor.

Then Gabriel took the thing in his hands for it was very light, being quite dried by the air of the vault, and those who peeped in from the door saw him lay it in the coffin again, and it rustled a little, like a bundle of reeds and sounded hollow as it touched the sides and the bottom. He placed the head upon the shoulders, and shut down the lid, which fell to, with a rusty spring that snapped.

After that they laid Sir Hugh beside his father, with the trestle bier on which they had brought him; and they went back to the chapel.

But when they saw one another's faces, master and men, they were all smiling, with the dead smile of the corpse they had left in the vault, so that they could not bear to look at one another until it had faded away.

3

Gabriel Ockram became Sir Gabriel, inheriting the baronetcy with the half-ruined fortune left by his father, and still Evelyn Warburton lived at Ockram Hall, in the south room that had been hers ever since she could remember anything. She could not go away, ever, for there were no relatives to whom she could have gone, and besides, there seemed to be no reason why she should not stay.

The world would never trouble itself to care what the Ockrams did on their Irish estates, and it was long since the Ockrams had asked anything of the world.

Sir Gabriel took his father's place at the dark old table in the dining room, and Evelyn sat opposite to him, until such time as their mourning should be over, and they might be married at last.

Their lives went on as before, since Sir Hugh had been a hopeless invalid during the last year of his life, and they had seen him but once a day for the little while, spending most of their time together in a strangely perfect companionship.

Though the late summer saddened into autumn, and autumn darkened into winter, and storm followed storm, and rain poured on rain through the short days and the long nights, yet Ockram Hall seemed less gloomy since Sir Hugh had been laid in the north vault beside his father.

At Christmastide, Evelyn decked the great hall with holly and green boughs, and huge fires blazed on every hearth. Then the tenants were all bidden to a New Year's dinner, and they ate and drank well, while Sir Gabriel sat at the head of the table. Evelyn came in when the port wine was brought, and the most respected of the tenants made a speech to propose her health.

"It is long," he said, "since there has been a Lady Ockram." Sir Gabriel shaded his eyes with his hand and looked down at the table, but a faint color came into Evelyn's transparent cheeks.

"But," said the gray-haired farmer, "it is longer still since there has been a Lady Ockram so fair as the next is to be," and he gave the health of Evelyn Warburton.

The tenants all stood up and shouted for her, and Sir Gabriel stood up likewise, beside Evelyn. And when the men gave the last and loudest cheer of all there was a voice not theirs, above them all, higher, fiercer, louder—a scream not earthly, shrieking for the Bride of Ockram Hall. And the holly and the green boughs over the great chimney piece shook and slowly waved as if a cool breeze were blowing over them.

The men turned very pale, and many of them set down their glasses, but others let them fall upon the floor, for fear. And looking into one another's faces, they were all smiling strangely, a dead smile, like dead Sir Hugh's.

One cried out words in Irish, and the fear of death was suddenly upon them all, so that they fled in panic, falling over one another like wild beasts in the burning forest, when the thick smoke runs along before the flame. Tables were overset, and drinking glasses and bottles were broken in heaps, and the dark red wine crawled like blood upon the polished floor.

Sir Gabriel and Evelyn stood alone at the head of the table before the wreck of the feast, not daring to turn and see each other for each knew that the other smiled. But his right arm held her and his left hand clasped her right as they stared before them. But for the shadows of her hair one might not have told their two faces apart.

They listened long, but the cry came not again, and the dead smile faded from their lips, while each remembered that Sir Hugh Ockram lay in the north vault, smiling in his winding-sheet, in the dark, because he had died with his secret.

So ended the tenants' New Year's dinner.

From that time on Sir Gabriel grew more and more silent, and his face grew even paler and thinner than before.

Often, without warning and without words, he would rise from his seat, as if something moved him against his will. He would go out into the rain, or the sunshine to the north side of the chapel, and sit on the stone bench, staring at the ground as if he could see through it, and through the vault below, and through the white winding-sheet in the dark, to the dead smile that would not die.

Always when he went out in that way Evelyn came out presently and sat beside him. Once, too, as in the summer, their beautiful faces came suddenly near, and their lids drooped, and their red lips were almost joined together.

But as their eyes met, they grew wide and wild, and their teeth chattered, and their hands were like hands of corpses for the terror of what was under their feet, and of what they knew but could not see.

Once, also, Evelyn found Sir Gabriel in the chapel alone, standing before the iron door that led down to the place of death, and in his hand there was the key to the door; but he had not put it into the lock.

Evelyn drew him away, shivering, for she had also been driven in waking dreams to see that terrible thing again, and to find out whether it had changed since it had lain there.

"I am going mad," said Sir Gabriel, covering his eyes with his hand as he went with her. "I see it in my sleep, I see it when I am awake—it draws me to it, day and night—and unless I see it I shall die!"

"I know," answered Evelyn, "I know. It is as if threads were spun from it, like a spider's, drawing us down to it."

She was silent for a moment, and then she started violently and grasped his arm with a man's strength, and almost screamed the words she spoke.

"But we must not go there!" she said. "We must not go!"

Sir Gabriel's eyes were half shut and he was not moved by the agony of her face.

"I shall die, unless I see it again," he said, in a quiet voice not like his own. And all that day and that evening he scarcely spoke, thinking of it, always thinking.

Evelyn Warburton went alone, on a gray winter's morning, to Nurse Macdonald's room in the tower, and sat down beside the great leathern easy chair, laying her thin white hand upon the withered fingers.

"Nurse," she said, "what was it that Uncle Hugh should have told you, that night before he died? It must have been an awful secret— and yet, though you asked him, I feel somehow that you know it, and that you know why he used to smile so dreadfully."

The old woman's head moved slowly from side to side.

"I only guess—I shall never know," she answered slowly in her cracked little voice.

"But what do you guess? Who am I? Why did you ask who my father was? You know I am Colonel Warburton's daughter, and my mother was Lady Ockram's sister, so that Gabriel and I are cousins. My father was killed in Afghanistan. What secret can there be?"

"I do not know. I can only guess."

"Guess what?" asked Evelyn imploringly, and pressing the soft withered hands, as she leaned forward. But Nurse Macdonald's wrinkled lids dropped suddenly over her queer blue eyes, and her lips shook a little with her breath, as if she were asleep.

Evelyn waited. By the fire the Irish maid was knitting fast, and the needles clicked like three or four clocks ticking against each other.

The real clock on the wall solemnly ticked alone, checking off the seconds of the woman who was a hundred years old, and had not many days left. Outside, the ivy branch beat the window in the wintry wind, as it had beaten against the glass a hundred years ago.

Then as Evelyn sat there she felt the waking of a horrible desire— a sickening wish to go down to the thing in the north vault, and to open the winding sheet, and see whether it had changed, and she held Nurse Macdonald's hands as if to keep herself in her place and fight against the appalling attraction of the evil dead.

The old woman had opened her eyes again, and she touched her cat with the end of her crutch-stick, whereupon its back went down and its tail shrunk, and it sidled back to its place on the bag footstool. But its yellow eyes looked up sideways at Evelyn, between the slits of its lids.

"What is it that you guess, nurse?" asked the young girl again.

"A bad thing—a wicked thing. But I dare not tell you, lest it might not be true, and the very thought should blast your life. For if I guess right, he meant that you should not know, and that you two should marry, and pay for his old sin with your souls."

"He used to tell us that we ought not to marry—"

"Yes—he told you that, perhaps—but it was as if a man put poisoned meat before a starving beast, and said, 'do not eat,' but never raised his hand to take the meat away.

"And if he told you that you should not marry, it was because he hoped you would; for of all men living or dead, Hugh Ockram was the falsest man that ever told a cowardly lie, and the cruelest that ever hurt a woman, the worst that ever loved sin."

"But Gabriel and I love each other," said Evelyn very sadly.

Nurse Macdonald's old eyes looked far away, at sights seen long ago, and that rose in the gray winter air amid the mists of an ancient youth.

"If you love, you can die together,' she said, very slowly. "Why should you live, if it is true? I am a hundred years old. What has life given me? The beginning is fire; the end is a heap of ashes; and between the end and the beginning lies all the pain of the world. Let me sleep, since I cannot die."

Then the old woman's eyes closed again, and her head sank a little lower upon her breast.

So Evelyn went away and left her asleep, with the cat asleep on the bag footstool; and the young girl tried to forget Nurse Macdonald's words, but she could not, for she heard them over and over again in the wind, and behind her on the stairs

And as she grew sick with fear of the frightful unknown evil to which her soul was bound, she felt a bodily something pressing her, and pushing her, and forcing her on, and from the other side she felt the threads that drew her mysteriously; and when she shut her eyes, she saw in the chapel, behind the altar, the low iron door through which she must pass to go to the thing.

Even as she lay awake at night, she drew the sheet over her face, lest she should see shadows on the wall beckoning to her; and the sound of her own warm breath made whisperings in her ears, while she held the mattress with her hands, to keep from getting up and going to the chapel.

It would have been easier if there had not been a way thither through the library, by a door which was never locked. It would be fearfully easy to take her candle and go softly through the sleeping house. And the key of the vault lay under the altar behind a stone that turned. She knew the little secret. She could go alone and see.

But when she thought of it, she felt her hair rise on her head, and first she shivered so that the bed shook, and then the horror went through her in a cold thrill that was agony again, like myriads of icy needles, boring into her nerves.

4

The old clock in Nurse Macdonald's tower struck midnight.

Downstairs Sir Gabriel sat straight up as the clock struck, for he had dreamed a fearful dream of horror, and his heart stood still, till he awoke at its stopping, and it beat again furiously with his breath, like a wild thing set free.

He pressed his hands to his temples as he sat up in bed, and his hands were icy cold, but his head was hot. The dream faded far, and in its place there came the thought that racked his life; with the thought also came the sick twisting of his lips in the dark that would have been a smile.

And far off, Evelyn Warburton dreamed that the dead smile was on her mouth, and awoke, starting with a little moan, her face in her hands, shivering.

But Sir Gabriel struck a light and got up and began to walk up and down his great room. It was midnight, and he had barely slept half an hour, and in the north of Ireland the winter nights are long.

"I shall go mad," he said to himself, holding his forehead. He knew that it was true. For weeks and months the possession of the thing had grown upon him like a disease, till he could think of nothing without thinking first of that.

And now, all at once, it outgrew his strength.

He took the candlestick in his hand, the old fashioned heavy candlestick that had always been used by the head of the house. He did not think of dressing, but went as he was in his silk night clothes and his slippers, and he opened the door.

Everything was very still in the great old house. He shut the door behind him and walked noiselessly on the carpet through the long corridor. A cool breeze blew over his shoulder, and blew the flame of his candle straight out from him.

Instinctively he stopped and looked round, but all was still, and the upright flame burned steadily. He walked on, and instantly a strong draught was behind him, almost extinguishing the light. It seemed to blow him on his way, ceasing whenever he turned, coming again when he went on—invisible, icy.

Down the great staircase to the echoing hall he went, seeing nothing but the flaring flame of the candle standing away from him over the guttering wax, while the cold wind blew over his shoulder and through his hair.

On he passed through the open door into the library, dark with old books and carved bookcases; on through the door in the shelves, with painted shelves on it, and the imitated backs of books, so that one needed to know where to find it—and it shut itself after him with a soft click. He entered the low arched passage, and, though the door was shut behind him and fitted tightly in its frame, still the cold breeze blew the flame forward as he walked.

And he was not afraid; but his face was very pale, and his eyes were wide and bright, looking before him, seeing already in the dark air the picture of the thing beyond. But in the chapel he stood still, his hand on the little turning stone tablet in the back of the stone altar.

On the tablet were engraved words: *"Clavis sepulchri Clarissimorum Dominorum De Ockram"*—"the key to the vault of the most illustrious Lords of Ockram."

Sir Gabriel paused and listened. He fancied that he heard a sound far off in the great house where all had been so still, but it did not come again. Yet he waited, at the last, and looked at the low iron door. Beyond it, down the long descent, lay his father, uncoffined, six months dead, corrupt, terrible in the enveloping, clinging shroud.

The strangely preserving air of the vault could not yet have done its work completely. But on the thing's ghastly features, with their half dried, open eyes, there would still be the frightful smile with which the man had died—the smile that haunted—

As the thought crossed Sir Gabriel's mind, he felt his lips writhing, and he struck his own mouth in wrath with the back of his hand so fiercely that a drop of blood ran down to his chin, and another, and more, falling black in the gloom upon the chapel pavement. But still his bruised lips twisted themselves.

He turned the tablet by the simple secret.

He took the great old key and set it into the lock of the iron door; and the heavy rattling noise echoed down the descent beyond like footsteps, as if a watcher had stood behind the iron and were running away within, with heavy dead feet.

Sir Gabriel saw that his candle was short. There were new ones on the altar, with long candlesticks, and he lit one, and left his own burning on the floor. As he set it down on the pavement his lip began to bleed again and another drop fell upon the stones.

He drew the iron door open and pushed it back against the chapel wall, so that it should not shut of itself, while he was within; and the horrible draught of the sepulchre came up out of the depths in his face, foul and dark.

He went in, but though the fetid air met him, yet the flame of the tall candle was blown straight from him against the wind while he walked down the easy incline with steady steps, his loose slippers slapping the pavement as he trod.

He shaded the candle with his hand, and his fingers seemed to be made of wax and blood as the light shone through them. And in spite of him the unearthly draught forced the flame forward, till it was blue over the black wick, and it seemed as if it must go out. But he went straight on, with shining eyes.

The downward passage was wide, and he could not always see the walls, by the struggling light, but he knew when he was in the place of death by the larger, drearier echo of his steps in the greater space, and by the sensation of a distant blank wall.

He stood still, almost enclosing the flame of the candle in the hollow of his hand. He could see a little, for his eyes were growing used to the gloom. Shadowy forms were outlined in the dimness, where the biers of the Ockrams stood crowded together, side by side, each with its straight, shrouded corpse, strangely preserved by the dry air, like the empty shell that the locust sheds in summer.

And a few steps before him he saw clearly the dark shape of

headless Sir Vernon's iron coffin, and he knew that nearest to it lay the thing he sought.

He was as brave as any of those dead men had been, and they were his fathers, and he knew that sooner or later he should lie there himself, beside Sir Hugh, slowly drying to a parchment shell. He closed his eyes a moment, and three great drops stood on his forehead.

Then he looked again, and by the whiteness of the winding sheet he knew his father's corpse, for all the others were brown with age; and, moreover, the flame of the candle was blown toward it.

He made four steps till he reached it, and suddenly the light burned straight and high shedding a dazzling yellow glare upon the fine linen that was all white, save over the face, and where the joined hands were laid on the breast. And at those places ugly stains had spread, darkened with outlines of the features and of the tight-clasped fingers. There was a frightful stench of drying death.

As Sir Gabriel looked down, something stirred behind him, softly at first, then more noisily, and something fell to the stone floor with a dull thud and rolled up to his feet; he started back, and saw a withered head lying almost face upward on the pavement grinning at him. He felt the cold sweat standing on his face, and his heart beat painfully.

For the first time in all his life that evil thing which men call fear was getting hold of him, checking his heartstrings as a cruel driver checks a quivering horse, clawing at his backbone with icy hands, lifting his hair with freezing breath, climbing up and gathering in his midriff with leaden weight.

Yet presently he bit his lip and bent down, holding the candle in one hand, to lift the shroud back from the head of the corpse with the other. Slowly he lifted it.

It clove to the half-dried skin of the face, and his hand shook as if someone had struck him on the elbow, but half in fear and half in anger at himself, he pulled it, so that it came away with a little ripping sound. He caught his breath as he held it, not yet throwing it back, and not yet looking.

The horror was working in him, and he felt that old Vernon Ockram was standing up in his iron coffin, headless, yet watching him with the stump of his severed neck.

While he held his breath he felt the dead smile twisting his lips. In sudden wrath at his own misery, he tossed the death-stained linen backward, and looked at last. He ground his teeth lest he should shriek aloud.

There it was, the thing that haunted him, that haunted Evelyn Warburton, that was like a blight on all that came near him.

The dead face was blotched with dark stains, and the thin gray hair was matted about the discolored forehead. The sunken lids were half open, and the candle light gleamed on something foul where the toad eyes had lived.

But yet the dead thing smiled, as it had smiled in life; the ghastly lips were parted and drawn wide and tight upon the wolfish teeth, cursing still, and still defying Hell to do its worst—defying, cursing, and always and forever smiling alone in the dark.

Sir Gabriel opened the winding sheet where the hands were, and the blackened, withered fingers were closed upon something stained and mottled. Shivering from head to foot, but fighting like a man in agony for his life he tried to take the package from the dead man's hold.

But as he pulled at it, the clawlike fingers seemed to close more tightly, and when he pulled harder the shrunken hands and arms rose from the corpse with a horrible look of life following his motion —then as he wrenched the sealed packet loose at last the hands fell back into their place still folded.

He set down the candle on the edge of the bier to break the seals from the stout paper. And kneeling on one knee, to get a better light, he read what was within, written long ago in Sir Hugh's queer hand.

He was no longer afraid.

He read how Sir Hugh had written it all down that it might perchance be a witness of evil and of his hatred; how he had loved Evelyn Warburton, his wife's sister; and how his wife had died of a broken heart with his curse upon her, and how Warburton and he had fought side by side in Afghanistan and Warburton had fallen; but Ockram had brought his comrade's wife back a full year later, and little Evelyn, her child, had been born in Ockram Hall.

And next, how he had wearied of the mother and she had died like her sister with his curse on her. And then, how Evelyn had been brought up as his niece, and how he trusted that his son Gabriel and his daughter, innocent and unknowing, might love and marry, that the souls of the women he had betrayed might suffer another anguish before eternity was out.

And last of all, he hoped that some day, when nothing could be undone, the two might find his writing and live on, not daring to tell the truth for their children's sake and the world's word, man and wife.

This he read, kneeling beside the corpse in the north vault, by the light of the altar candle; and when he had read it all, he thanked God aloud that he had found the secret in time. But when he rose to his feet and looked down at the dead face it was changed, and the smile was gone from it forever, and the jaw had fallen a little, and the tired dead lips were relaxed.

And then there was a breath behind him and close to him, not cold like that which had blown the flame of the candle as he came, but warm and human. He turned suddenly.

There she stood, all in white, with her shadowy golden hair—for she had risen from her bed and had followed him noiselessly, and had found him reading, and had herself read over his shoulder. He started violently when he saw her, for his nerves were unstrung—and then he cried out her name in the still place of death:

"Evelyn!"

"My brother!" she answered, softly and tenderly, putting out both hands to meet his.

Though ROBERT BLOCH (1917–   ) is best known for his novel *Psycho,* the basis of Alfred Hitchcock's famous film, his finest work is generally considered to be many of the sixty-seven *Weird Tales* short stories he wrote, including "Yours Truly, Jack the Ripper" (July 1943); "The Skull of the Marquis de Sade" (September 1945), filmed in 1965 as *The Skull* with Peter Cushing and Christopher Lee; "Enoch" (September 1946); "Tell Your Fortune" (May 1950); and "The Sorcerer's Apprentice" (January 1949), a grisly *conte cruelle* variation of the tale of the same name by Lucian. (See page 31.)

THE SORCERER'S APPRENTICE

by Robert Bloch

I wish you would turn off the lights. They hurt my eyes. You don't need the lights. I'll tell you anything you want to know. I'll tell you all about it, everything.

But turn off the lights.

And please don't stare at me. How can a man think, with all of you crowding around and asking questions, questions, questions—

All right, I'll be calm. I'll be very calm. I didn't mean to shout. It is not like me to lose my temper. I am a gentle man. You know I'd never hurt anyone.

Why are you laughing? There is nothing to laugh about. It was all an accident, you know that. I lost the Power.

But you don't know about the Power, do you? You don't know about Sadini and how he sold his soul to Satan for a black gift.

No, I'm not raving. That is the truth, gentlemen. I can prove it. Here, listen to me. I'm going to tell you all about it, from the very beginning. If only you'll turn off the lights—

My name is Hugo. No, just Hugo. That's all they ever called me at the Home. I lived at the Home ever since I can remember, and the Sisters were very kind to me. The other children, they would not play with me because of my back and my squint, but the Sisters were kind. They didn't call me "Crazy Hugo" and make fun of me because I couldn't recite. They didn't get me in the corner and hit me and make me cry.

No, I'm all right. You'll see. I was telling you about the Home, but it's not important. It all started after I ran away.

You see, I was getting too old, the Sisters told me. They wanted me to go with the Doctor to another place, a County place. But Fred —he was one of the boys who didn't hit me—he told me that I mustn't go with the Doctor. He said the County place was bad and the Doctor was bad. They had rooms with bars on the windows in this place and the Doctor would tie me to a table and cut out my brain. He wanted to operate on my brain, Fred said, and then I would die.

So I could see that the Sisters really thought I was crazy too, and the Doctor was coming for me the very next day. That's why I ran away, sneaking out of my room and over the wall that night.

But you're not interested in what happened after that, are you? I mean, about when I was living under the bridge and selling newspapers and in winter it was so cold—

Sadini? Yes, but that's part of it; the winter and the cold, I mean. Because it was the cold that made me faint in that alley behind the theatre, and that's how Sadini found me.

I remember the snow in the alley and how it came up and hit me in the face, the icy, icy snow just smothering me in cold, and I sank down in it forever.

Then, when I woke up, I was in this warm place inside the theatre, in the dressing-room, and there was an angel looking at me.

I thought she was an angel, anyway. Her hair was long, like golden harp strings, and I reached up to feel it and she smiled.

"Feeling better?" she asked. "Here, drink this."

She gave me something nice and warm to drink. I was lying on a couch and she held my head while I drank.

"How did I get here?" I asked. "Am I dead?"

"I thought you were when Victor carried you in. But you'll be all right now, I guess."

"Victor?"

"Victor Sadini. Don't tell me you haven't heard of the Great Sadini?"

I shook my head.

"He's a magician. He's on now. Good heavens, that reminds me, I'll have to change!" She took the cup away and stood up. "You just rest until I get back."

I smiled at her. It was very hard to talk, because everything was going round and round.

"Who are you?" I whispered.

"Isobel."

"Isobel," I said. It was a pretty name. I whispered it over and over again until I went to sleep.

I don't know how long it was until I woke up again—I mean, until I woke up and felt all right. In between times I would be sort of half-awake, and sometimes I could see and hear for a little while.

Once I saw a tall man with black hair and a mustache bending over me. He was dressed all in black, too, and he had black eyes. I thought maybe it was the Devil coming to carry me down to Hell. The Sisters used to tell us about the Devil. I was so frightened I just fainted again.

Another time I could hear voices talking, and I opened my eyes again and saw the man in black and Isobel sitting over on the side of the room. I guess they didn't know I was awake because they were talking about me.

"How much longer do you think I'm going to put up with this, Vic?" she was saying. "I am sick and tired of playing nursemaid to a lousy tramp. What's the big idea? You don't know him from Adam, anyway."

"But we can't just throw him out in the snow to die, can we?" The man in black was walking up and down, pulling on the ends of his mustache. "Be reasonable, darling. The poor kid's been starving to death, can't you tell? No identification, nothing; he's in trouble and needs help."

"Nuts to that noise! Call the wagon—there's charity hospitals, aren't there? If you expect me to spend all my time between shows cooped up with a mangy—"

I couldn't understand what she meant, what she was saying. She was so beautiful, you see. I knew she must be kind, and it was all a mistake, maybe I was too sick to hear right.

Then I fell asleep again, and when I woke up I felt better, different, and I knew it was a mistake. Because she was there, and she smiled at me again.

"How are you?" she asked. "Ready to eat something now?"

I could only stare at her and smile. She was wearing a long green cloak all covered with silver stars, and now I know she must be an angel for sure.

Then the Devil came in.

"He's conscious, Vic," said Isobel.

The Devil looked at me and grinned.

"Hi, pal! Glad to have you with us. For a day or so there, I didn't think we'd have the pleasure of your company much longer."

I just stared at him.

"What's the matter, my makeup frighten you? That's right, you don't even know who I am, do you? My name's Victor Sadini. The Great Sadini—magic act, you know."

Isobel was smiling at me, too, so I guessed it was all right. I nodded. "My name is Hugo," I whispered. "You saved my life, didn't you?"

"Skip it. Leave the talking till later. Right now, you've got to eat something and get some more rest. You've been camping here on the sofa for three days now, chum. Better get some strength, because the act closes here Wednesday and we jump to Toledo."

On Wednesday the act closed, and we jumped to Toledo. Only we didn't really jump, we took a train. Oh yes, I went along. Because I was Sadini's new assistant.

This was before I knew he was a servant of the Devil. I just thought he was a kind man who had saved my life. He sat there in the dressing-room and explained everything to me; how he grew the mustache and combed his hair that way and wore black just because that's the way stage magicians are supposed to look.

He did tricks for me; wonderful tricks with cards and coins and handkerchiefs that he pulled out of my ears and colored water he poured from my pockets. He could make things vanish too, and I was afraid of him until he told me it was all a trick.

On the last day he let me get up and stand behind the stage while he went out in front of the people and did what he called his "act" and then I saw wonderful things.

He made Isobel stretch out on a table and then he waved a wand and she floated up in the air with nothing to hold her. Then he lowered her down and she didn't fall, just smiled while all the people clapped. Then she would hand him things to do tricks with, and he would point his magic wand at them and make them vanish, or explode, or change. He made a big tree grow out of a little plant right before my eyes. And then he put Isobel into a box and some men wheeled out a huge steel blade, with teeth in it, and he said he was going to saw her in half. He tied her down, too.

I almost ran out on the stage then, to stop him, but she wasn't afraid, and the men who pulled the curtains behind the scenes were laughing too, and so I guessed it must be another trick.

But when he turned on the electric current and began to saw into the box, I stood there with the sweat popping out all over me because I could see him cutting into her. Only she smiled, even when he sawed right through her. She smiled, and she wasn't dead at all!

Then he covered her up and took the saw away and waved his magic wand and she jumped up, all in one piece again. It was the most wonderful thing I'd ever heard of, and I guess it was seeing the show that made me decide I'd have to go with him.

So after that I talked to him, about how he'd saved my life and who I was, and not having any place to go, and how I'd work for him for nothing, do anything, if only I could come along. I didn't tell him I wanted to go just so I could see Isobel, because I guessed he wouldn't like that. And I didn't think she'd like it either. She was his wife, I knew that now.

It didn't make much sense, what I told him, but he seemed to understand.

"Maybe you can make yourself useful at that," he said. "We have to have someone to look after the props, and it would save time for me. Besides, you could set them up and pack them again."

"Ixnay," said Isobel. "Utsnay." I didn't understand her, but Sadini did. Maybe it was magic talk.

"Hugo's going to be all right," he said. "I need somebody, Isobel. Somebody I can really depend on—if you know what I mean."

"Listen, you cheap ham—"

"Take it easy, Isobel." She was scowling, but when he looked at her she just sort of wilted and tried to smile.

"All right, Vic. Whatever you say. But remember, it s your headache, not mine."

"Right." Sadini came over to me. "You can come along," he said. "From now on you're my assistant."

That's how it was.

That's how it was for a long, long time. We went to Toledo, and to Detroit and Indianapolis and Chicago and Milwaukee and St. Paul—oh, a lot of places. But they were all alike to me. We would ride on a train and then Sadini and Isobel would go to a hotel and I would stay behind and watch them unload the baggage car. I would get the trunks filled with props (that's what Sadini called the things he used in his act) and hand a slip of paper to a truck driver. We would go to the theatre then, and the truck driver took the props into the alley where I'd haul them up to the dressing-room and backstage. Then I unloaded props and that's how it went.

I slept in the theatre, in the dressing-room most of the time, and I'd eat with Sadini and Isobel. Not often with Isobel, though. She liked to sleep late at the hotel, and I guess she was ashamed of me at first. I didn't blame her, the way I looked, with my clothes and my eyes and back.

Of course Sadini bought me new clothes after a while. He was good to me, Sadini was. He talked a lot about his tricks and his act, and he even talked about Isobel. I didn't understand how such a nice man could say such things about her.

Even though she didn't seem to like me, and kept away from Sadini too, I knew she was an angel. She was beautiful the way the angels were in the books the Sisters showed me. Of course, Isobel wouldn't be interested in ugly people like myself or Sadini, with his black eyes and his black mustache. I don't know why she ever married him in the first place when she could find handsome men like George Wallace.

She saw George Wallace all the time, because he had another act in the same show we traveled with. He was tall, and he had blonde hair and blue eyes, and he was a singer and dancer in the show. Isobel used to stand in the wings (that's the part on the side of the stage) when he was singing, and look at him. Sometimes they would talk together and laugh, and once when Isobel said she was going to the hotel because she had a headache, I saw her and George Wallace walk into his dressing-room.

Maybe I shouldn't have told Sadini about that, but it just came out before I could stop it. He got very angry and he asked me questions and then he told me to keep my mouth shut and my eyes open.

It was wrong for me to say yes, I know that now; but all I could think of then was that Sadini had been kind to me. So I watched Isobel and George Wallace, and one day when Sadini was downtown between shows, I saw them again in Wallace's dressing-room. It was on the balcony, and I tiptoed up to the door and looked through the keyhole. Nobody else was around, and nobody could see me blushing.

Because Isobel was kissing George Wallace and he was saying, "Come on, darling—let's not stall any longer. When the show closes, it's you and me. We'll blow out of here together, head for the coast and—"

"Quit talking like a schmoe!" Isobel sounded mad. "I'm nuts about you, Georgie-boy, but I know a good deal when I see it. Vic's a headliner; he'll be pulling in his grand a week when you're doing a single for smokers. Fun's fun, but there's no percentage in such a deal for me."

"Vic!" George Wallace made a face. "What's that phony got, anyway? A couple of trunks full of props and a mustache. Anybody can do a magic act—I could myself, if I had the stake for the gimmicks. Why, hell, you know all his routines. You and I could build our own act, baby. How's that for any angle? The Great Wallace and Company—"

"Georgie!"

She said it so fast and she moved so fast, I didn't have time to get away. Isobel walked right over to the door and yanked it open and there I was.

"What the—"

George Wallace came up behind her and when he saw me he started to reach out, but she slapped his hands down.

"Can it!" she said. "I'll handle this." Then she smiled at me, and I knew she wasn't angry. "Come on downstairs, Hugo," she said. "Let's you and I have a little talk."

I'll never forget that little talk.

We sat there in the dressing-room, just Isobel and me, all alone. And she held my hand—she had such soft, sweet hands—and looked into my eyes, and talked with her low voice that was like singing and stars and sunshine.

"So you found out," she said. "And that means I'll have to tell you the rest. I—I didn't want you to know, Hugo. Not ever. But now I'm afraid there's no other way."

I nodded. I didn't trust myself to look at her, so I just stared at the dressing-table. Sadini's wand was lying there—his long black wand with the golden tip. It glittered and shone and dazzled my eyes.

"Yes, it's true, Hugo. George Wallace and I are in love. He wants me to go away."

"B-but Sadini is such a nice man," I told her. "Even if he does look that way."

"How do you mean?"

"Well, when I first saw him, I thought he was the Devil, but now—"

She sort of caught her breath. "You thought he looked like the Devil, Hugo?"

I laughed. "Yes. You know, the Sisters, they said I wasn't very bright. And they wanted to operate on my head because I couldn't understand things. But I'm all right. You know that. I just thought Sadini might be the Devil until he told me everything was a trick. It wasn't really a magic wand and he didn't really saw you in half—"

"And you believed him!"

I looked at her now. She was sitting up straight, and her eyes were shining. "Oh, Hugo, if I'd only known! You see, I was the same way, once. When I first met him, I trusted him. And now I'm his slave. That's why I can't run away, because I'm his slave. Just as he is the slave of—the Devil."

My eyes must have bugged out, because she kept looking at me funny as she went on.

"You didn't know that, did you? You believed him when he said he just did tricks, and that he sawed me in half on the stage for an illusion, using mirrors."

"But he does use mirrors," I said. "Don't I pack them and unpack them and set them up just so?"

"That's only to fool the stagehands," she said. "If they knew he was really a sorcerer, they'd lock him up. Didn't the Sisters tell you about the Devil and selling your soul?"

"Yes, I have heard stories, but I thought—"

"You believe me, don't you, Hugo?" She took my hand again and looked right at me. "When he takes me out on the stage and raises me from the ground, that's sorcery. One word and I would fall to my death. When he saws me in half, it's real. That's why I can't run away, that's why I'm his slave."

"Then it must have been the Devil who gave him the magic wand that does the tricks."

She nodded, watching me.

I looked at the wand. It was glittering away, and her hair glittered and her eyes glittered.

"Why can't I steal the wand?" I asked.

She shook her head. "It wouldn't help. Not as long as he's alive."

"Not as long as he's alive," I repeated.

"But if he were to—oh, Hugo, you must help me! There's only one way, and it wouldn't be a sin, not when he's sold his soul to the Devil. Oh, Hugo, you must help me, you will help me—"

She kissed me.

She *kissed* me. Yes, she put her arms around my back, and her golden hair wound round and round me, and her lips were soft and her eyes were like glory, and she told me what to do, how to do it, and it wouldn't be a sin, he was sold to the Devil, no one would ever know.

So I said yes, I would do it.

She told me how.

And she made me promise never to tell anyone, no matter what happened, even if things went wrong and they asked questions of me.

I promised.

And then I waited. I waited for Sadini to come back that night. I waited until after the show, when everyone went home. Isobel left and she told Sadini to stay behind and help me pack because I was sick, and he said he would. It all worked just as she promised it would.

We started packing, and there was nobody left in the theatre but the doorman, and he was way downstairs in the room next to the alley. I went out into the hall while Sadini was packing and saw how dark and still it was. Then I came into the dressing-room again and watched Sadini putting away his props.

He hadn't touched the wand, though. It glittered and glittered, and I wanted to pick it up and feel the magic of the Power the Devil had given him.

But there was no time for that, now. Because I had to walk up behind Sadini as he bent over the trunk. I had to take the piece of iron pipe out of my pocket and raise it over his head and bring it down once, twice, three times.

There was an awful cracking sound, and then a thump, when he fell to the floor.

Now all I had to do was lift him into the trunk and—

There was another sound.

Somebody knocked on the door.

Somebody rattled the doorknob as I dragged Sadini's body over to the corner and tried to find a place to hide it. But it was no use. The knocking came again and I heard a voice calling, "Hugo—open up! I know you're there!"

So I opened the door, holding the pipe behind my back. George Wallace came in.

I guess he was drunk. Anyway, he didn't seem to notice Sadini lying on the floor at first. He just looked at me and waved his arms.

"Hugo, I gotta talk t'you." He was drunk all right, I could smell the liquor now. "She told me," he whispered. "She told me what was up. Tried to get me drunk, but I'm wise to her. I sneaked away. Gotta talk t'you before you do 'nything foolish.

"She told me. Gonna frame you, that's what. You kill Sadini, she'll tell the cops, deny everything. You're supposed t'be—well, kinda soft in the head. 'N when you spill that hooey about the Devil they'll figure you're crazy for sure, lock you up. Then she wanted us to run away, take the act. I hadda come back here, warn you before—"

Then he saw Sadini. He just sort of froze up, standing there stiff as a board with his mouth open. That made it easy for me to come up behind him and hit him with the pipe; hit him and hit him and hit him.

Because I knew he lied, he was lying about her, he couldn't have her, he couldn't run away, I wouldn't permit it. I knew what he really wanted—he wanted the wand of Power, the Devil's wand. And it was now all mine.

I walked over and took it up in my hands, felt the Power surging along my arm as I looked at the glittering tip. I was still holding it in my hand when she came in.

She must have followed him, but she was too late now. She could tell, when she saw him lying there on the floor with the back of his head laughing up like a big red mouth.

She was frozen for a moment, too, but then before I could say anything, Isobel slid to the floor. She just fainted.

I stood there, holding the wand of Power, looking down at her and feeling sorry. Sorry for Sadini, burning in Hell. Sorry for George Wallace because he had come here. Sorry for her, because all the plans had gone wrong.

Then I looked at the wand, and I got this wonderful idea. Sadini was dead, and George was dead, but she still had me. She wasn't afraid of me—she had even kissed me.

And I had the wand. That was the secret of the magic. Now, while she was still asleep, I could find out if it was true. And then when she woke up, what a surprise for her! I would tell her, "You were right, Isobel. It does work. And from now on, you and I will do the act. I have the wand and you need never be afraid again. Because I can do it. I already did it when you were asleep."

There was nothing to interfere. I carried her out to the stage. I carried the props, too. I even turned on the spotlight, because I knew where it was. It felt funny, standing there all alone in the empty theatre, bowing into the blackness.

But I was wearing Sadini's cloak, and I stood there for a moment with Isobel lying before me. With the magic wand in my hand I felt like a new person—iike Hugo the Great.

And I was Hugo the Great.

That night, in the empty theatre, I was Hugo the Great. I knew just what to do, how to do it. There were no stagehands so I didn't need to bother with the mirrors, and I had to strap her and turn on the electric current myself. The blade didn't seem to turn so fast, either, when I put it right up against the board box covering her, but I made it work.

It buzzed away and buzzed away, and then she opened her eyes and screamed, but I had her strapped down, and besides there was nothing to be afraid of. I showed her the magic wand, but she just

screamed and screamed until the buzzing drowned out her voice and
the blade came through.

The blade was red. Dripping red.

It made me sick to look at it, so I closed my eyes and waved the
magic wand of Power very quickly.

Then I looked down.

Everything was—the same.

I waved the wand again.

Still nothing happened.

Something had gone wrong.

Then I was screaming, and the doorman finally heard and ran in,
and then you came and took me away.

So, you see, it was just an accident. The wand didn't work. Maybe
the Devil took the power away when Sadini died. I don't know. All I
know is that I'm very tired.

Will you turn off the lights now, please?

I want to go to sleep . . .

Most of the stories published in the four Leo Margulies—Sam Moskowitz
Weird Tales revival issues in 1973–74 were reprints, but a few were original,
notably Edward D. Hoch's "Funeral in the Fog" (see page 316) and the
following chucklesome treasure by KATHERINE MAC LEAN (1925–   ), a Mas-
sachusetts author, and MARY KORNBLUTH (1920–   ), writer, editor and
widow of science fiction writer C. M. Kornbluth. "Chicken Soup" was
printed in the Winter 1973 issue. (For further comment, see Appendix II,
page 576.

CHICKEN SOUP

by Katherine MacLean
and Mary Kornbluth

Herbie's last morning class ended at eleven, which left him easily
time enough to take the subway and see what his grandmother was
having for lunch. You might think a grown man, a student at the
university, would be too busy to visit his grandmother, but Herbie
was a good boy. He remembered how fondly she used to kiss him,
and what wonderful things she and his mother used to cook and
serve whenever they visited together.

The minute he entered her house, half past the hour, he smelled a
fine rich smell of chicken soup. Taking a firm grip on the books
under his arm, he followed the scent through the living room to the
kitchen door.

"Grandma," he called, expecting his voice to come out louder
than it did.

He could hear her humming inside. That kitchen was a mysterious
place, for women only, full of secrets. His mother and grandmother
had never let him in there when they cooked together. He pushed
open the kitchen door anyhow, and sidled in.

His grandmother was plump and round-shouldered; she was stirring a pot and singing to herself. It was a pleasant little chant, full of
repeating sounds.

Herbie came up behind her and gave her a light hug and a kiss on the ear, but she shrugged him off and continued stirring and chanting. He saw that she was stirring the soup with a long bony chicken foot. He had seen chicken feet used to flavor soup but there was something about the way his grandmother did it. Something mediaeval. It reminded him of witches and wattled huts and peasants and the knights in Chapter 3 of his history text. The witches used to make a kind of brew that would let them fly, or something, didn't they?

The idea pleased him. He perched on a tall kitchen stool to watch. She finished the monotonous little song and dropped the chicken foot in the pot.

"What are you doing, Grandma?"

She smiled briefly. "I'm making chicken soup, the way my own grandmother made chicken soup. What's so special?" She came over and gave him a warm hug and a squeezing kiss on the cheek. "You're getting bigger every day, Herbie. Already last year you're the size of a man, and you keep getting bigger."

He didn't want to talk about that. "What were you singing, Grandma?"

She bridled, as if he had criticized her. "My grandmother used to sing when she made her chicken soup, and the soup was good. People used to come for miles, when someone was sick . . ."

"May I taste, Grandma?"

With the mixture of irritation and self-satisfaction with which artists face their critics, she dipped the ladle into the soup, and held it, steaming, for him to sip.

He sipped. Delicious and penetrating and subtly spiced, but not quite what he expected. Nothing tastes just as it did in childhood. He remembered some more from Chapter 3, Volume II of *The Rise of Western Civilization.*

"Was it a white-feathered chicken, Grandma?" He sipped, took the ladle and drank the warm soup that remained. Buttered toast flavor? These spices were subtle.

"A white capon, yes. They are more tender. All the Delaware chickens are white. Your cousin Abner is in the chicken business in Delaware."

"Did a priest let its blood on an altar?"

"Herbie, you're sick maybe?" Her voice was a croon of concern.

"It's a good koshered chicken, by a rabbi. Who knows what they do with the blood? Are you worrying it has blood in it? Don't worry, the rabbi can be trusted. Your cousin Abner—"

There was a singing in his ears, a pleasant lightness in his heart. "Grandma, it doesn't taste just right. There's something missing." He heaved *The Rise of Western Civilization* out from under his arm and opened it on his knee. "There's a recipe here . . . A copper pot, a virgin white-feathered cock, killed—ah, skip that." He skipped down the line and raised his voice. "Well-water, leeks, parsley, henbane, thorn apple, green hemp (cannabis)—"

Herbie stopped talking. His grandmother was pottering about the kitchen throwing out discarded peelings and parings. Her back was stiff, to let him know she was ignoring advice and recipes from an amateur.

He cleared his throat. "Grandma, what are those long-stemmed greens you just threw out?"

She was surprised into answering. "They grow wild in the empty lot at the corner. I put their leaves in the soup, for flavor." She picked up a fallen leaf from the floor and threw it after the stems.

Herbie had seen leaves like that. And he knew what some of the wild students did with them at the university . . . rolled and smoked them . . . but always behind locked doors.

"You pick them? Don't people see you?"

She cleaned the kitchen briskly, her back looking stubborn as outraged virtue again.

He ventured farther. "The policeman at the corner, he stops the traffic for the school children. Have you talked about picking those leaves with him?"

Her back still turned stiffly, she rinsed a pot. "I don't discuss cooking with the Irish! Is that what you learn at school, Herbie?"

"It says here in the book, use henbane, and those tall greens you put into the soup already, and thorn apple."

"Yes?" She dried her hands and came over to him. "Maybe in your book they know a little. Henbane I added already. What about this thorn apple? When do you add it?"

"It doesn't say when to add it, Grandma. What is thorn apple?"

"They don't know how to write a recipe." She went over to the copper kettle and tasted thoughtfully, "Thorn apple? In the rock garden, that green prickly plant, the one your cousin Edmund put his hand on when I sent him out to get some sweet basil. I didn't know thorn apple was good for flavor."

She shrugged. "Herbie, go pick a thorn apple."

"Yes, Grandma." He was out the door to the backyard before she finished asking.

"Be careful; your cousin Edmund pricked his thumb—"

Herbie was back already, bearing a green fruitlike object covered with broad thorns. "Here it is."

Shrugging again she pared it, diced it, and dropped it into the chicken soup, singing a bit more of the doggerel chant. He could not make out the words.

"What is that you're singing, Grandma?"

"Oh." She stopped. She even laughed. "It tells the soup to get inside you and go to heart and head, muscles and toes, you know, like a good soup should."

"Let's taste it."

"Too soon," she protested, but already was reaching for the big kitchen spoons, one for her, one for Herbie.

They both sat on kitchen stools, their feet on the rungs, watching each other's expression and sipping the hot steaming broth delicately from the edge of the spoons, so as not to burn the lips.

"Herbie, what was that recipe? Is it kosher?"

"No, Grandma," he answered dreamily, as if in childhood.

"Christian then?"

"No, Grandma."

"What then? Let me look in your book, please, Herbie."

He shook his head. "It will be hard to find the page again, Grandma!" He rose. "Let's taste the soup some more. I don't taste anything different."

"I told you we had to wait until the thorn apple cooked."

With pleasure they returned to the pot and the delicately changed aroma of the soup. Like epicures they inhaled the rich steam and dipped their spoons into the boiling broth. With their eyes meeting in the pleasure of experimentation, they each sipped the new flavor.

Whooosh.

The world spun to a blur and stopped, steady again, but had drastically changed.

They found themselves transported. They stood on the side of a mountain with their ladles still in their hands. It must have been the other side of the world, for it was nighttime there and the wind was whistling around them.

A firelit ceremony was in progress some distance up the hill, with dancing and leaping and prancing.

Herbie had a chance for only a second of delighted gazing before his grandmother covered his eyes with her hands.

"A nudist colony! Oy vey, don't look, Herbie, don't peek!"

Instantly they found themselves back in the kitchen.

"Grandma, did you see that giant goat? And the little goats? And girls . . ."

She compressed her lips. "I wouldn't remember."

He reached for the soup with his spoon. "Let's try it again. Let's go back and watch. It is research, scientific research."

She took the spoon and put it in the sink. "Research! Looking at those goyim dancing and hopping? Where are their mothers, I'd like to know?"

"But Grandma," Herbie protested, his eyes looking into memory, "how can you tell, when they aren't wearing any—"

"I can tell." Her lips shut tightly against further comment. She picked up two potholder cloths and approached the stove.

"What are you doing?" He was dismayed.

"What does it look like?" With a sigh and a grunt she carried the large pot out the back door and poured its contents into a metal bucket. "A spoiled batch you throw away. It's good for the neighbor's dog. Hot soup shouldn't go to waste. It's a skinny dog. The neighbor, him!"

Herbie leaned toward her coaxingly. "Let's try the recipe again, Grandma. This time no garlic. The books say garlic frightens away the spirits."

"Next time, more garlic, and no thorn apple at all," the plump little woman said firmly. "I should know better than to let a man help with cooking! From a history book, even." She looked at him seriously, wrinkling her forehead. "You're getting to be a big boy, Herbie. Your mother and I will find a marriage broker and find for you a nice Jewish girl. You'll like her, you'll see."

"Oh, Grandma, you're so old-fashioned!" He picked up his history book and tucked it under his arm. "I have to get back to class. It takes a half hour on the subway." He kissed her and turned to leave.

Claws clacked on the stairs to the back porch. The neighbor's dog appeared, tail wagging. At first he hesitated over the hot soup. The little old woman, tired from vain labor, sat on the kitchen stool and watched with an impartial, almost scientific expression.

Tantalized by the rich aroma, the dog lapped eagerly at the soup. Suddenly he howled, and vanished without having moved a step. Not even a bit of his tail was left.

Herbie's grandmother sighed. "I hope he's happy with those goats."

THE HAUNTED BURGLAR

by W. C. Morrow

Anthony Ross doubtless had the oddest and most complex temperament that ever assured the success of burglary as a business. This fact is mentioned in order that those who choose may employ it as an explanation of the extraordinary ideas that entered his head and gave a strangely tragic character to his career.

Though ignorant, the man had an uncommonly fine mind in certain aspects. Thus it happened that, while lacking moral perception, he cherished an artistic pride in the smooth, elegant, and finished conduct of his work. Hence a blunder on his part invariably filled him with grief and humiliation; and it was the steadily increasing recurrence of these errors that finally impelled him to make a deliberate analysis of his case.

Among the stupid acts with which he charged himself was the murder of the banker Uriah Mattson, a feeble old man whom a simple choking or a sufficient tap on the skull would have rendered helpless. Instead of that, he had choked his victim to death in the most brutal and unnecessary manner, and in doing so had used the

fingers of his left hand in a singularly sprawled and awkward fash
ion. The whole act was utterly unlike him; it appalled and horrified
him—not for the sin of taking human life, but because it was unnec
essary, dangerous, subversive of the principles of skilled burglary,
and monstrously inartistic.

A similar mishap had occurred in the case of Miss Jellison, a
wealthy spinster, merely because she was in the act of waking, which
meant an ensuing scream. In this case, as in the other, he was un
speakably shocked to discover that the fatal choking had been done
by the left hand, with sprawled and awkward fingers, and with a
savage ferocity entirely uncalled for by his peril.

In setting himself to analyze these incongruous and revolting
things he dragged forth from his memory numerous other acts, unlike those two in detail, but similar to them in spirit. Thus, in a fit of
passionate anger at the whimpering of an infant, he had flung it
brutally against the wall. Another time he was nearly discovered
through the needless torturing of a cat, whose cries set pursuers at
his heels. These and other insane, inartistic and ferocious acts he
arrayed for serious analysis.

Finally the realization burst upon him that all his aberrations of
conduct had proceeded from his left hand and arm. Search his recollection ever so diligently, he could not recall a single instance
wherein his right hand had failed to proceed on perfectly fine, sure
and artistic lines. When he made this discovery he realized that he
had brought himself face to face with a terrifying mystery; and its
horrors were increased when he reflected that while his left hand had
committed acts of stupid atrocity in the pursuit of his burglarious
enterprises, on many occasions when he was not so engaged it had
acted with a less harmful but none the less coarse, irrational and
inartistic purpose.

It was not difficult for such a man to arrive at strange conclusions.
The explanation that promptly suggested itself, and that his coolest
and shrewdest wisdom could not shake, was that his left arm was
under the dominion of a perverse and malicious spirit, that it was an
entity apart from his own spirit and that it had fastened itself upon
that part of his body to produce his ruin. It were useless, however
inviting, to speculate upon the order of mind capable of arriving at
such a conclusion; it is more to the point to narrate the terrible
happenings to which it gave rise.

About a month after the burglar's mental struggle, a strange-looking man applied for a situation at a sawmill a hundred miles away. His appearance was exceedingly distressing. Either a grievous bodily illness or fearful mental anguish had made his face wan and haggard and filled his eyes with the light of a hard desperation that gave promise of dire results. There were no marks of a vagabond on his clothing or in his manner. He did not seem to be suffering for physical necessities. He held his head aloft and walked like a man, and an understanding glance would have seen that his look of determination meant something profounder and more far-reaching than the ordinary business concerns of life.

He gave the name of Hope. His manner was so engaging, yet withal so firm and abstracted, that he secured a position without difficulty; and so faithfully did he work, and so quick was his intelligence, that in good time his request to be given the management of a saw was granted. It might have been noticed that his face thereupon wore a deeper and more haggard look, but that its rigors were softened by a light of happy expectancy. As he cultivated no friendships among the men, he had no confidants; he went his dark way alone to the end.

He seemed to take more than the pleasure of an efficient workman in observing the products of his skill. He would stealthily hug the big brown logs as they approached the saw and his eyes would blaze when the great tool went singing and roaring at its work. The foreman, mistaking this eagerness for carelessness, quietly cautioned him to beware; but when the next log was mounted for the saw the stranger appeared to slip and fall. He clasped the moving log in his arms and the next moment the insatiable teeth had severed his left arm near the shoulder and the stranger sank with a groan into the soft sawdust that filled the pit.

There was the usual commotion attending such accidents, for the faces of the workmen turn white when they see one of their number thus maimed for life. But Hope received good surgical care and in due time was able to be abroad. Then the men observed that a remarkable change had come over him. His moroseness had disappeared and in its stead was a hearty cheer of manner that amazed them. Was the losing of a precious arm a thing to make a wretched man happy? Hope was given light work in the office, and might have remained to the end of his days a competent and prosperous man; but one day he left and was never seen thereabout again.

Then Anthony Ross, the burglar, reappeared upon the scenes of his former exploits. The police were dismayed to note the arrival of a man whom all their skill had been unable to convict of terrible crimes which they were certain he had committed, and they questioned him about the loss of his arm; but he laughed them away with the fine old *sang-froid* with which they were familiar, and soon his handiwork appeared in reports of daring burglaries.

A watch of extraordinary care and minuteness was set upon him, but that availed nothing until a singular thing occurred to baffle the officers beyond measure: Ross had suddenly become wildly reckless and walked red-handed into the mouth of the law. By evidence that seemed indisputable, a burglary and atrocious murder were traced to him. Stranger than all else, he made no effort to escape, though leaving a hanging trail behind him. When the officers overhauled him, they found him in a state of utter dejection, wholly different from the lighthearted bearing that had characterized him ever since he had returned without his left arm. Neither admitting nor denying his guilt, he bore himself with the hopelessness of a man already condemned to the gallows.

Even when he was brought before a jury and placed on trial, he made no fight for his life. Although possessed of abundant means, he refused to employ an attorney, and treated with scant courtesy the one assigned him by the judge. He betrayed irritation at the slow dragging of the case as the prosecution piled up its evidence against him. His whole manner indicated that he wished the trial to end as soon as possible and hoped for a verdict of guilty.

This incomprehensible behavior placed the young and ambitious attorney on his mettle. He realized that some inexplicable mystery lay behind the matter and this sharpened his zeal to find it. He plied his client with all manner of questions and tried in all ways to secure his confidence: Ross remained sullen, morose and wholly given over to despairing resignation. The young lawyer had made a wonderful discovery, which he at first felt confident would clear the prisoner, but any mention of it to Ross would only throw him into a violent passion and cause him to tremble as with a palsy. His conduct on such occasions was terrible beyond measure. He seemed utterly beside himself, and thus his attorney had become convinced of the man's insanity. The trouble in proving it was that he dared not mention his discovery to others, and that Ross exhibited no signs of mania unless that one subject was broached.

The prosecution made out a case that looked impregnable, and this fact seemed to fill the prisoner with peace. The young lawyer for the defence had summoned a number of witnesses, but in the end he used only one. His opening statement to the jury was merely that it was a physical impossibility for the prisoner to have committed the murder—which was done by choking. Ross made a frantic attempt to stop him from putting forth that defence and from the dock wildly denounced it as a lie.

The young lawyer nevertheless proceeded with what he deemed his duty to his unwilling client. He called a photographer and had him produce a large picture of the murdered man's face and neck. He proved that the portrait was that of the person whom Ross was charged with having killed. As he approached the climax of the scene, Ross became entirely ungovernable in his frantic efforts to stop the introduction of the evidence and so it became necessary to bind and gag him and strap him to the chair.

When quiet was restored, the lawyer handed the photograph to the jury and quietly remarked:

"You may see for yourselves that the choking was done with the left hand and you have observed that my client has no such member."

He was unmistakably right. The imprint of the thumb and fingers, forced into the flesh in a singularly ferocious, sprawling and awkward manner, was shown in the photograph with absolute clearness. The prosecution, taken wholly by surprise, blustered and made attempts to assail the evidence but without success. The jury returned a verdict of not guilty.

Meanwhile the prisoner had fainted, and his gag and bonds had been removed; but he recovered at the moment when the verdict was announced. He staggered to his feet and his eyes rolled; then with a thick tongue he exclaimed:

"It was the left arm that did it! This one"—holding his right arm as high as he could reach—"never made a mistake. It was always the left one. A spirit of mischief and murder was in it. I cut it off in a sawmill, but the spirit stayed where the arm used to be and it choked this man to death. I didn't want you to acquit me. I wanted you to

hang me. I can't go through life having this thing haunting me and
spoiling my business and making a murderer of me. It tries to choke
me while I sleep. There it is! Can't you see it?" And he looked with
wide-staring eyes at his left side.

"Mr. Sheriff," gravely said the judge, "take this man before the
Commissioners of Lunacy tomorrow."

More than a century after his death, EDGAR ALLAN POE (1809–1849) still towers over other American fantasy-horror writers, with the possible exception of Nathaniel Hawthorne. *Weird Tales* reprinted fourteen Poe classics, including "The Murders in the Rue Morgue," "The Pit and the Pendulum," "The Tell-Tale Heart," "The Black Cat," "The Masque of the Red Death" and—perhaps the greatest Gothic tale ever written—"The Fall of the House of Usher." Despite editor Farnsworth Wright's reticence to publish humor in The Unique Magazine, he ran the galumphing "Never Bet the Devil Your Head" in March 1924. Though heavy-handed, at its best it is reminiscent of my friend Brother Theodore's macabre brand of ghoulish comedy. A very free film adaptation called *Toby Dammit* was made by Federico Fellini as the third and most impressive segment of the French-Italian cinematic anthology *Spirits of the Dead* (1968).

NEVER BET THE DEVIL YOUR HEAD

A TALE WITH A MORAL

by Edgar Allan Poe

"Con tal que las costumbres de un autor," says Don Thomas De Las Torres in the preface to his "Amatory Poems," *"sean puras y castas, importo muy poco que no sean igualmente severas sus obras"*—meaning, in plain English, that, provided the morals of an author are pure, personally, it signifies nothing what are the morals of his books. We presume that Don Thomas is now in Purgatory for the assertion. It would be a clever thing, too, in the way of poetical justice, to keep him there until his "Amatory Poems" get out of print, or are laid definitely upon the shelf through lack of readers. Every fiction *should* have a moral; and what is more to the purpose, the critics have discovered that every fiction *has*. Philip Melancthon, some time ago,

wrote a commentary upon the "Batrachomyomachia," and proved that the poet's object was to excite a distaste for sedition. Pierre La Seine, going a step farther, shows that the intention was to recommend to young men temperance in eating and drinking. Just so, too, Jacobus Hugo has satisfied himself that, by Euenis, Homer meant to insinuate John Calvin; by Antinöus, Martin Luther; by the Lotophagi, Protestants in general; and, by the Harpies, the Dutch. Our more modern Scholiasts are equally acute. These fellows demonstrate a hidden meaning in "The Antediluvians," a parable in "Powhatan," new views in "Cock Robin," and transcendentalism in "Hop O' My Thumb." In short, it has been shown that no man can sit down to write without a very profound design. Thus to authors in general much trouble is spared. A novelist, for example, need have no care of his moral. It is there—that is to say, it is somewhere—and the moral and the critics can take care of themselves. When the proper time arrives, all that the gentleman intended, and all that he did not intend, will be brought to light, in the *Dial,* or the *Down-Easter,* together with all that he ought to have intended, and the rest that he clearly meant to intend:—so that it will all come very straight in the end.

There is no just ground, therefore, for the charge brought against me by certain ignoramuses—that I have never written a moral tale, or, in more precise words, a tale with a moral. They are not the critics predestined to bring me out, and *develop* my morals:—that is the secret. By and by the *North American Quarterly Humdrum* will make them ashamed of their stupidity. In the meantime, by way of staying execution—by way of mitigating the accusations against me —I offer the sad history appended—a history about whose obvious moral there can be no question whatever, since he who runs may read it in the large capitals which form the title of the tale. I should have credit for this arrangement—a far wiser one than that of La Fontaine and others, who reserve the impression to be conveyed until the last moment, and thus sneak it in at the fag end of their fables.

Defuncti injuriâ ne afficiantur was a law of the twelve tables, and *De mortuis nil nisi bonum* is an excellent injunction—even if the dead in question be nothing but dead small beer. It is not my design, therefore, to vituperate my deceased friend, Toby Dammit. He was a sad dog, it is true, and a dog's death it was that he died; but he himself was not to blame for his vices. They grew out of a personal defect in his mother. She did her best in the way of flogging him while an infant—for duties to her well-regulated mind were always pleasures, and babies like tough steaks, or the modern Greek olive trees, are invariably the better for beating—but, poor woman! she had the misfortune to be left-handed, and a child flogged left-handedly had better be left unflogged. The world revolves from right to left. It will not do to whip a baby from left to right. If each blow in the proper direction drives an evil propensity out, it follows that every thump in an opposite one knocks its quota of wickedness in. I was often present at Toby's chastisements, and, even by the way in which he kicked, I could perceive that he was getting worse and worse every day. At last I saw, through the tears in my eyes, that there was no hope of the villain at all, and one day when he had been cuffed until he grew so black in the face that one might have mistaken him for a little African, and no effect had been produced beyond that of making him wriggle himself into a fit, I could stand it no longer, but went down upon my knees forthwith, and, uplifting my voice, made prophecy of his ruin.

The fact is that his precocity in vice was awful. At five months of age he used to get into such passions that he was unable to articulate. At six months, I caught him gnawing a pack of cards. At seven months he was in the constant habit of catching and kissing the female babies. At eight months he peremptorily refused to put his signature to the Temperance pledge. Thus he went on increasing in iniquity, month after month, until, at the close of the first year, he not only insisted upon wearing *moustaches,* but had contracted a propensity for cursing and swearing, and for backing his assertions by bets.

Through this latter most ungentlemanly practice, the ruin which I had predicted to Toby Dammit overtook him at last. The fashion had "grown with his growth and strengthened with his strength," so that, when he came to be a man, he could scarcely utter a sentence without interlarding it with a proposition to gamble. Not that he actually *laid* wagers—no. I will do my friend the justice to say that he would as soon have laid eggs. With him the thing was a mere formula—nothing more. His expressions on this head had no meaning attached to them whatever. They were simple if not altogether innocent expletives—imaginative phrases wherewith to round off a sentence. When he said "I'll bet you so and so," nobody ever thought of taking him up; but still I could not help thinking it my duty to put him down. The habit was an immoral one, and so I told him. It was a vulgar one —this I begged him to believe. It was discountenanced by society— here I said nothing but the truth. It was forbidden by act of Congress —here I had not the slightest intention of telling a lie. I remonstrated —but to no purpose. I demonstrated—in vain. I entreated—he smiled. I implored—he laughed. I preached—he sneered. I threatened—he swore. I kicked him—he called for the police. I pulled his nose—he blew it, and offered to bet the Devil his head that I would not venture to try that experiment again.

Poverty was another vice which the peculiar physical deficiency of Dammit's mother had entailed upon her son. He was detestably poor; and this was the reason, no doubt, that his expletive expressions about betting seldom took a pecuniary turn. I will not be bound to say that I ever heard him make use of such a figure of speech as "I'll bet you a dollar." It was usually "I'll bet you what you please," or "I'll bet you what you dare," or "I'll bet you a trifle," or else, more significantly still, *"I'll bet the Devil my head."*

This latter form seemed to please him best—perhaps because it involved the least risk; for Dammit had become excessively parsimonious. Had any one taken him up, his head was small, and thus his loss would have been small too. But these are my own reflections, and I am by no means sure that I am right in attributing them to him. At all events the phrase in question grew daily in favor, notwithstanding the gross impropriety of a man betting his brains like banknotes—but this was a point which my friend's perversity of disposition would not permit him to comprehend. In the end, he abandoned all other forms of wager and gave himself up to *"I'll bet the Devil my head,"* with a pertinacity and exclusiveness of devotion that displeased not less than it surprised me. I am always displeased by circumstances for which I cannot account. Mysteries force a man to think and so injure his health. The truth is, there was something in *the air* with which Mr. Dammit was wont to give utterance to his offensive expression—something in his *manner* of enunciation— which at first interested and afterward made me very uneasy—something which, for want of a more definite term at present, I must be permitted to call *queer;* but which Mr. Coleridge would have called mystical, Mr. Kant pantheistical, Mr. Carlyle twistical, and Mr. Emerson hyperquizzitistical. I began not to like it at all. Mr. Dammit's soul was in a perilous state. I resolved to bring all my eloquence into play to save it. I vowed to serve him as St. Patrick, in the Irish chronicle, is said to have served the toad—that is to say, "awaken him to a sense of his situation." I addressed myself to the task forthwith. Once more I betook myself to remonstrance. Again I collected my energies for a final attempt at expostulation.

When I had made an end of my lecture, Mr. Dammit indulged himself in some very equivocal behavior. For some moments he remained silent, merely looking me inquisitively in the face. But presently he threw his head to one side and elevated his eyebrows to a great extent. Then he spread out the palms of his hands and shrugged up his shoulders. Then he winked with the right eye. Then he repeated the operation with the left. Then he shut them both up very tight. Then he opened them both so very wide that I became seriously alarmed for the consequences. Then, applying his thumb to his nose, he thought proper to make an indescribable movement with the rest of his fingers. Finally, setting his arms akimbo, he condescended to reply.

I can call to mind only the heads of his discourse. He would be obliged to me if I would hold my tongue. He wished none of my advice. He despised all my insinuations. He was old enough to take care of himself. Did I still think him baby Dammit? Did I mean to say any thing against his character? Did I intend to insult him? Was I a fool? Was my maternal parent aware, in a word, of my absence from the domiciliary residence? He would put this latter question to me as to a man of veracity, and he would bind himself to abide by my reply. Once more he would demand explicitly if my mother knew that I was out. My confusion, he said, betrayed me, and he would be willing to bet the Devil his head that she did not.

Mr. Dammit did not pause for my rejoinder. Turning upon his heel he left my presence with undignified precipitation. It was well for him that he did so. My feelings had been wounded. Even my anger had been aroused. For once I would have taken him up upon his insulting wager. I would have won for the Arch-Enemy Mr. Dammit's little head—for the fact is, my mamma *was* very well aware of my merely temporary absence from home.

But *Khoda shefa midêhed*—Heaven gives relief—as the Mussulmans say when you tread upon their toes. It was in pursuance of my duty that I had been insulted, and I bore the insult like a man. It now seemed to me, however, that I had done all that could be required of me, in the case of this miserable individual, and I resolved to trouble him no longer with my counsel, but to leave him to his conscience and himself. But although I forbore to intrude with my advice, I could not bring myself to give up his society altogether. I even went so far as to humor some of his less reprehensible propensities; and there were times when I found myself lauding his wicked jokes, as epicures do mustard, with tears in my eyes:—so profoundly did it grieve me to hear his evil talk.

One fine day, having strolled out together, arm in arm, our route led us in the direction of a river. There was a bridge and we resolved to cross it. It was roofed over, by way of protection from the weather, and the archway, having but few windows, was thus very uncomfortably dark. As we entered the passage, the contrast between the external glare and the interior gloom struck heavily upon my spirits. Not so upon those of the unhappy Dammit, who offered to bet the Devil his head that I was hipped. He seemed to be in an unusual good humor. He was excessively lively—so much so that I entertained I know not what of uneasy suspicion. It is not impossible that he was affected with the transcendentals. I am not well enough versed, however, in the diagnosis of this disease to speak with decision upon the point; and unhappily there were none of my friends of the *Dial* present. I suggest the idea, nevertheless, because of a certain species of austere Merry-Andrewism which seemed to beset my poor friend and caused him to make quite a Tom-Fool of himself. Nothing would serve him but wriggling and skipping about under and over every thing that came in his way; now shouting out, and now lisping out, all manner of odd little and big words, yet preserving the gravest face in the world all the time. I really could not make up my mind whether to kick or to pity him. At length, having passed nearly across the bridge, we approached the termination of the footway, when our progress was impeded by a turnstile of some height. Through this I made my way quietly, pushing it around as usual. But this turn would not serve the turn of Mr. Dammit. He insisted upon leaping the stile and said he could cut a pigeon-wing over it in the air. Now this, conscientiously speaking, I did not think he could do. The best pigeon-winger over all kinds of style was my friend Mr. Carlyle, and as I knew *he* could not do it, I would not believe that it could be done by Toby Dammit. I therefore told him in so many words that he was a braggadocio and could not do what he said. For this I had reason to be sorry afterward—for he straightway offered to *bet the Devil his head* that he could.

I was about to reply, notwithstanding my previous resolutions, with some remonstrance against his impiety, when I heard, close at my elbow, a slight cough, which sounded very much like the ejaculation *"ahem!"* I started and looked about me in surprise. My glance at length fell into a nook of the framework of the bridge, and upon the figure of a little lame old gentleman of venerable aspect. Nothing could be more reverend than his whole appearance; for he not only had on a full suit of black, but his shirt was perfectly clean and the collar turned very neatly down over a white cravat, while his hair was parted in front like a girl's. His hands were clasped pensively together over his stomach, and his two eyes were carefully rolled up into the top of his head.

Upon observing him more closely, I perceived that he wore a black silk apron over his small-clothes; and this was a thing which I thought very odd. Before I had time to make any remark, however, upon so singular a circumstance, he interrupted me with a second *"ahem!"*

To this observation I was not immediately prepared to reply. The fact is, remarks of this laconic nature are nearly unanswerable. I have known a Quarterly Review *non-plussed* by the word *"Fudge!"* I am not ashamed to say, therefore, that I turned to Mr. Dammit for assistance.

"Dammit," said I, "what are you about? don't you hear?—the gentleman says *'ahem!'*" I looked sternly at my friend while I thus addressed him; for, to say the truth, I felt particularly puzzled, and when a man is particularly puzzled he must knit his brows and look savage, or else he is pretty sure to look like a fool.

"Dammit," observed I—although this sounded very much like an oath than which nothing was further from my thoughts—"Dammit," I suggested—"the gentleman says *'ahem!'*"

I do not attempt to defend my remark on the score of profundity; I did not think it profound myself; but I have noticed that the effect of our speeches is not always proportionate with their importance in our own eyes; and if I had shot Mr. D. through and through with a Paixhans bomb, or knocked him on the head with the "Poets and Poetry of America," he could hardly have been more discomfited than when I addressed him with those simple words: "Dammit, what are you about?—don't you hear?—the gentleman says *'ahem!'* "

"You don't say so?" gasped he at length, after turning more colors than a pirate runs up, one after the other, when chased by a man-of-war. "Are you quite sure he said *that?* Well, at all events I am in for it now, and may as well put a bold face upon the matter. Here goes, then—*ahem!*"

At this the little old gentleman seemed pleased—God only knows why. He left his station at the nook of the bridge, limped forward with a gracious air, took Dammit by the hand and shook it cordially, looking all the while straight up in his face with an air of the most unadulterated benignity which it is possible for the mind of man to imagine.

"I am quite sure you will win it, Dammit," said he, with the frankest of all smiles, "but we are obliged to have a trial, you know, for the sake of mere form."

"Ahem!" replied my friend, taking off his coat, with a deep sigh, tying a pocket handkerchief around his waist, and producing an unaccountable alteration in his countenance by twisting up his eyes and bringing down the corners of his mouth—"ahem!" And "ahem!" said he again, after a pause; and not another word more than "ahem!" did I ever know him to say after that. "Aha!" thought I, without expressing myself aloud—"this is quite a remarkable silence on the part of Toby Dammit, and is no doubt a consequence of his verbosity upon a previous occasion. One extreme induces another. I wonder if he has forgotten the many unanswerable questions which he propounded to me so fluently on the day when I gave him my last lecture? At all events, he is cured of the transcendentals."

"Ahem!" here replied Toby, just as if he had been reading my thoughts, and looking like a very old sheep in a revery.

The old gentleman now took him by the arm, and led him more into the shade of the bridge—a few paces back from the turnstile. "My good fellow," said he, "I make it a point of conscience to allow you this much run. Wait here, till I take my place by the stile, so that I may see whether you go over it handsomely, and transcendentally, and don't omit any flourishes of the pigeon-wing. A mere form, you know. I will say 'one, two, three, and away.' Mind you start at the word 'away.' " Here he took his position by the stile, paused a moment as if in profound reflection, then *looked up* and, I thought, smiled very slightly, then tightened the strings of his apron, then took a long look at Dammit, and finally gave the word as agreed upon—

One—two—three—and—away!

Punctually at the word "away," my poor friend set off in a strong gallop. The style was not very high, like Mr. Lord's—nor yet very low, like that of Mr. Lord's reviewers, but upon the whole I made sure that he would clear it. And then what if he did not?—ah, that was the question—what if he did not? "What right," said I, "had the old gentleman to make any other gentleman jump? The little old dot-and-carry-one! who is *he?* If he asks *me* to jump, I won't do it, that's flat, and I don't care who *the devil he is.*" The bridge, as I say, was arched and covered in, in a very ridiculous manner, and there was a most uncomfortable echo about it at all times—an echo which I never before so particularly observed as when I uttered the four last words of my remark.

But what I said, or what I thought, or what I heard, occupied only an instant. In less than five seconds from his starting, my poor Toby had taken the leap. I saw him run nimbly, and spring grandly from the floor of the bridge, cutting the most awful flourishes with his legs as he went up. I saw him high in the air, pigeon-winging it to admiration just over the top of the stile; and of course I thought it an unusually singular thing that he did not *continue* to go over. But the whole leap was the affair of a moment, and, before I had a chance to make any profound reflections, down came Mr. Dammit on the flat of his back, on the same side of the stile from which he had started. At the same instant I saw the old gentleman limping off at the top of his speed, having caught and wrapt up in his apron something that fell heavily into it from the darkness of the arch just over the turn-stile. At all this I was much astonished; but I had no leisure to think, for Mr. Dammit lay particularly still, and I concluded that his feelings had been hurt, and that he stood in need of my assistance. I hurried up to him and found that he had received what might be termed a serious injury. The truth is, he had been deprived of his head, which after a close search I could not find anywhere—so I determined to take him home, and send for the homoeopathists. In the meantime a thought struck me, and I threw open an adjacent window of the bridge; when the sad truth flashed upon me at once.

About five feet just above the top of the turnstile, and crossing the arch of the footpath so as to constitute a brace, there extended a flat iron bar, lying with its breadth horizontally, and forming one of a series that served to strengthen the structure throughout its extent. With the edge of this brace it appeared evident that the neck of my unfortunate friend had come precisely in contact.

He did not long survive his terrible loss. The homoeopathists did not give him little enough physic, and what little they did give him he hesitated to take. So in the end he grew worse, and at length died, a lesson to all riotous livers. I bedewed his grave with my tears, worked a *bar* sinister on his family escutcheon, and for the general expenses of his funeral sent in my very moderate bill to the transcendentalists. The scoundrels refused to pay, so I had Mr. Dammit dug up at once, and sold him for dog's meat.

H. P. LOVECRAFT (1890–1937), the author most frequently associated with *Weird Tales,* wrote forty-eight short stories for the magazine, including the memorable "The Rats in the Walls," "The Dunwich Horror," "The Colour Out of Space," "The Outsider," "The Music of Erich Zann" and "The Hound." Lovecraft also contributed at least four collaborative works to *Weird Tales,* as well as one ghost-written piece for Harry Houdini, a serialized novel *(The Case of Charles Dexter Ward)* and a condensed version of his scholarly essay "Supernatural Horror in Literature." Many of Lovecraft's stories take place in or near Providence, Rhode Island, where he spent most of his life, but "He," published in September 1926, is set in the convoluted bypaths of Greenwich Village.

HE

by H. P. Lovecraft

I saw him on a sleepless night when I was walking desperately to save my soul and my vision. My coming to New York had been a mistake; for whereas I had looked for poignant wonder and inspiration in the teeming labyrinths of ancient streets that twist endlessly from forgotten courts and squares and waterfronts to courts and squares and waterfronts equally forgotten, and in the Cyclopean modern towers and pinnacles that rise blackly Babylonian under waning moons, I had found instead only a sense of horror and oppression which threatened to master, paralyze and annihilate me.

The disillusion had been gradual. Coming for the first time upon the town, I had seen it in the sunset from a bridge, majestic above its waters, its incredible peaks and pyramids rising flowerlike and delicate from pools of violet mist to play with the flaming clouds and the first stars of evening. Then it had lighted up window by window above the shimmering tides where lanterns nodded and glided and deep horns bayed weird harmonies and had itself become a starry firmament of dream, redolent of faery music, and one with the marvels of Carcassonne and Samarcand and El Dorado and all glorious and half-fabulous cities. Shortly afterward I was taken through those antique ways so dear to my fancy—narrow, curving alleys and passages where rows of red Georgian brick blinked with small-paned dormers above pillared doorways that had looked on gilded sedans and paneled coaches—and in the first flush of realization of these long-wished things I thought I had indeed achieved such treasures as would make me in time a poet.

But success and happiness were not to be. Garish daylight showed only squalor and alienage and the noxious elephantiasis of climbing, spreading stone where the moon had hinted of loveliness and elder magic; and the throngs of people that seethed through the flumelike streets were squat, swarthy strangers with hardened faces and narrow eyes, shrewd strangers without dreams and without kinship to the scenes about them, who could never mean aught to a blue-eyed man of the old folk, with the love of fair green lanes and white New England village steeples in his heart.

So instead of the poems I had hoped for, there came only a shuddering blackness and ineffable loneliness; and I saw at last a fearful truth which no one had ever dared to breathe before—the unwhisperable secret of secrets—the fact that this city of stone and stridor is not a sentient perpetuation of Old New York as London is of Old London and Paris of Old Paris, but that it is in fact quite dead, its sprawling body imperfectly embalmed and infested with queer animate things which have nothing to do with it as it was in life. Upon making this discovery, I ceased to sleep comfortably; though something of resigned tranquillity came back as I gradually formed the habit of keeping off the streets by day and venturing abroad only at night, when darkness calls forth what little of the past still hovers wraithlike about and old white doorways remember the stalwart forms that once passed through them. With this mode of relief I even wrote a few poems and still refrained from going home to my people lest I seem to crawl back ignobly in defeat.

Then, on a sleepless night's walk, I met the man. It was in a grotesque hidden courtyard of the Greenwich section, for there in my ignorance I had settled, having heard of the place as the natural home of poets and artists. The archaic lanes and houses and unexpected bits of square and court had indeed delighted me and when I found the poets and artists to be loud-voiced pretenders whose quaintness is tinsel and whose lives are a denial of all that pure beauty which is poetry and art, I stayed on for love of these venerable things. I fancied them as they were in their prime, when Greenwich was a placid village not yet engulfed by the town; and in the hours before dawn, when all the revellers had slunk away, I used to wander alone among their cryptical windings and brood upon the curious arcana which generations must have deposited there. This kept my soul alive and gave me a few of those dreams and visions for which the poet far within me cried out.

The man came upon me at about 2 one cloudy August morning as I was threading a series of detached courtyards; now accessible only through the unlighted hallways of intervening buildings, but once forming parts of a continuous network of picturesque alleys. I had heard of them by vague rumor and realized that they could not be upon any map of today; but the fact that they were forgotten only endeared them to me, so that I had sought them with twice my usual eagerness. Now that I had found them, my eagerness was again redoubled; for something in their arrangement dimly hinted that they might be only a few of many such, with dark, dumb counterparts wedged obscurely betwixt high blank walls and deserted rear tenements, or lurking lamplessly behind archways, unbetrayed by hordes of the foreign-speaking or guarded by furtive and uncommunicative artists whose practises do not invite publicity or the light of day.

He spoke to me without invitation, noting my mood and glances as I studied certain knockered doorways above iron-railed steps, the pallid glow of traceried transoms feebly lighting my face. His own face was in shadow and he wore a wide-brimmed hat which somehow blended perfectly with the out-of-date cloak he affected; but I was subtly disquieted even before he addressed me. His form was very slight; thin almost to cadaverousness; and his voice proved phenomenally soft and hollow, though not particularly deep. He had, he said, noticed me several times at my wanderings; and inferred that I resembled him in loving the vestiges of former years. Would I not like the guidance of one long practised in these explorations and possessed of local information profoundly deeper than any which an obvious newcomer could possibly have gained?

As he spoke, I caught a glimpse of his face in the yellow beam from a solitary attic window. It was a noble, even a handsome, elderly countenance; and bore the marks of a lineage and refinement unusual for the age and place. Yet some quality about it disturbed me almost as much as its features pleased me—perhaps it was too white, or too expressionless, or too much out of keeping with the locality, to make me feel easy or comfortable. Nevertheless I followed him; for in those dreary days my quest for antique beauty and mystery was all that I had to keep my soul alive and I reckoned it a rare favor of Fate to fall in with one whose kindred seekings seemed to have penetrated so much farther than mine.

Something in the night constrained the cloaked man to silence and for a long hour he led me forward without needless words; making only the briefest of comments concerning ancient names and dates and changes and directing my progress very largely by gestures as we squeezed through interstices, tiptoed through corridors, clambered over brick walls, and once crawled on hands and knees through a low, arched passage of stone whose immense length and tortuous twistings effaced at last every hint of geographical location I had managed to preserve. The things we saw were very old and marvelous, or at least they seemed so in the few straggling rays of light by which I viewed them, and I shall never forget the tottering Ionic columns and fluted pilasters and urnheaded iron fenceposts and flaring-linteled windows and decorative fanlights that appeared to grow quainter and stranger the deeper we advanced into this inexhaustible maze of unknown antiquity.

We met no person, and as time passed the lighted windows became fewer and fewer. The streetlights we first encountered had been of oil and of the ancient lozenge pattern. Later I noticed some with candles; and at last, after traversing a horrible unlighted court where my guide had to lead with his gloved hand through total blackness to a narrow wooden gate in a high wall, we came upon a fragment of alley lit only by lanterns in front of every seventh house—unbelievably Colonial tin lanterns with conical tops and holes punched in the sides. This alley led steeply uphill—more steeply than I thought possible in this part of New York—and the upper end was blocked squarely by the ivy-clad wall of a private estate, beyond which I could see a pale cupola and the tops of trees waving against a vague lightness in the sky. In this wall was a small, low-arched gate of nail-studded black oak, which the man proceeded to unlock with a ponderous key. Leading me within, he steered a course in utter blackness over what seemed to be a gravel path and finally up a flight of stone steps to the door of the house, which he unlocked and opened for me.

We entered, and as we did so I grew faint from a reek of infinite mustiness which welled out to meet us and which must have been the fruit of unwholesome centuries of decay. My host appeared not to notice this, and in courtesy I kept silent as he piloted me up a curving stairway, across a hall and into a room whose door I heard him lock behind us. Then I saw him pull the curtains of the three small-paned windows that barely showed themselves against the lightening sky; after which he crossed to the mantel, struck flint and steel, lighted two candles of a candelabrum of twelve sconces, and made a gesture enjoining soft-toned speech.

In this feeble radiance I saw that we were in a spacious, well-furnished and paneled library dating from the first quarter of the Eighteenth Century, with splendid doorway pediments, a delightful Doric cornice and a magnificently carved overmantel with scroll-and-urn top. Above the crowded bookshelves at intervals along the walls were well-wrought family portraits; all tarnished to an enig-matical dimness and bearing an unmistakable likeness to the man who now motioned me to a chair beside the graceful Chippendale table. Before seating himself across the table from me, my host paused for a moment as if in embarrassment; then, tardily removing his gloves, wide-brimmed hat and cloak, stood theatrically revealed in full mid-Georgian costume from queued hair and neck ruffles to knee-breeches, silk hose, and the buckled shoes I had not previously noticed. Now slowly sinking into a lyre-back chair, he commenced to eye me intently.

Without his hat he took on an aspect of extreme age which was scarcely visible before and I wondered if this unperceived mark of singular longevity were not one of the sources of my disquiet. When he spoke at length, his soft, hollow and carefully muffled voice not infrequently quavered; and now and then I had great difficulty in following him as I listened with a thrill of amazement and half-disavowed alarm which grew each instant.

"You behold, Sir," my host began, "a man of very eccentrical habits, for whose costume no apology need be offered to one with your wit and inclinations. Reflecting upon better times, I have not scrupled to ascertain their ways and adopt their dress and manners; an indulgence which offends none if practised without ostentation. It hath been my good fortune to retain the rural seat of my ancestors, swallowed though it was by two towns, first Greenwich, which built up hither after 1800, then New York, which joined on near 1830.

There were many reasons for the close keeping of this place in my family and I have not been remiss in discharging such obligations. The squire who succeeded to it in 1768 studied sartain arts and made sartain discoveries, all connected with influences residing in this particular plot of ground, and eminently desarving of the strongest guarding. Some curious effects of these arts and discoveries I now purpose to show you, under the strictest secrecy; and I believe I may rely on my judgment of men enough to have no distrust of either your interest or your fidelity."

He paused, but I could only nod my head. I have said that I was alarmed, yet to my soul nothing was more deadly than the material daylight world of New York, and whether this man were a harmless eccentric or a wielder of dangerous arts I had no choice save to follow him and slake my sense of wonder on whatever he might have to offer. So I listened.

"To—my ancestor," he softly continued, "there appeared to reside some very remarkable qualities in the will of mankind; qualities having a little-suspected dominance not only over the acts of one's self and of others, but over every variety of force and substance in Nature and over many elements and dimensions deemed more universal than Nature herself. May I say that he flouted the sanctity of things as great as space and time and that he put to strange uses the rites of sartain half-breed red Indians once encamped upon this hill? These Indians showed choler when the place was built and were plaguey pestilent in asking to visit the grounds at the full of the moon. For years they stole over the wall each month when they could and by stealth performed sartain acts. Then in '68 the new squire catched them at their doings and stood still at what he saw. Thereafter he bargained with them and exchanged the free access of his grounds for the exact inwardness of what they did; larning that their grandfathers got part of their custom from red ancestors and part from an old Dutchman in the time of the States-General. And pox on him, I'm afeared the squire must have sarved them monstrous bad rum—whether or not by intent—for a week after he larnt the secret he was the only man living that knew it. You, Sir, are the first outsider to be told there is a secret, and split me if I'd have risked tampering that much with—the powers—had ye not been so hot after bygone things."

I shuddered as the man grew colloquial—and with the familiar speech of another day. He went on.

"But you must know, Sir, that what—the squire—got from those mongrel savages was but a small part of the larning he came to have. He had not been at Oxford for nothing, nor talked to no account with an ancient chymist and astrologer in Paris. He was, in fine, made sensible that all the world is but the smoke of our intellects; past the bidding of the vulgar, but by the wise to be puffed out and drawn in like any cloud of prime Virginia tobacco. What we want, we may make about us; and what we don't want, we may sweep away. I won't say that all this is wholly true in body, but 'tis sufficient true to furnish a very pretty spectacle now and then. You, I concieve, would be tickled by a better sight of sartain other years than your fancy affords you; so be pleased to hold back any fright at what I design to show. Come to the window and be quiet."

My host now took my hand to draw me to one of the two windows on the long side of the malodorous room and at the first touch of his ungloved fingers I turned cold. His flesh, though dry and firm, was of the quality of ice; and I almost shrank away from his pulling. But again I thought of the emptiness and horror of reality and boldly prepared to follow whithersoever I might be led. Once at the window, the man drew apart the yellow silk curtains and directed my stare into the blackness outside. For a moment I saw nothing save a myriad of tiny dancing lights, far, far before me. Then, as if in response to an insidious motion of my host's hand, a flash of heat-lightning played over the scene and I looked out upon a sea of luxuriant foliage—foliage unpolluted, and not the sea of roofs to be expected by any normal mind. On my right the Hudson glittered wickedly, and in the distance ahead I saw the unhealthy shimmer of a vast salt marsh constellated with nervous fireflies. The flash died, and an evil smile illumined the waxy face of the aged necromancer.

"That was before my time—before the new squire's time. Pray let us try again."

I was faint, even fainter than the hateful modernity of that accursed city had made me.

"Good God!" I whispered; "can you do that for *any time?*" And as he nodded and bared the black stumps of what had once been yellow fangs, I clutched at the curtains to prevent myself from falling. But he steadied me with that terrible, ice-cold claw and once more made his insidious gesture.

Again the lightning flashed—but this time upon a scene not wholly strange. It was Greenwich, the Greenwich that used to be, with here and there a roof or row of houses as we see it now, yet with lovely green lanes and fields and bits of grassy common. The marsh still glittered beyond, but in the farther distance I saw the steeples of what was then all of New York; Trinity and St. Paul's and the Brick Church dominating their sisters, and a faint haze of wood smoke hovering over the whole. I breathed hard, but not so much from the sight itself as from the possibilities my imagination terrifiedly conjured up.

"Can you—dare you—go far?" I spoke with awe, and I think he shared it for a second, but the evil grin returned.

"Far? What I have seen would blast ye to a mad statue of stone! Back, back—forward, *forward*—look, ye puling lackwit!"

And as he snarled the phrase under his breath he gestured anew; bringing to the sky a flash more blinding than either which had come before. For full three seconds I could glimpse that pandemoniac sight, and in those seconds I saw a vista which will ever afterward torment me in dreams. I saw the heavens verminous with strange flying things, and beneath them a hellish black city of giant stone terraces with impious pyramids flung savagely to the moon, and devil-lights burning from unnumbered windows. And swarming loathsomely on aerial galleries I saw the yellow, squint-eyed people of that city, robed horribly in orange and red, and dancing insanely to the pounding of fevered kettle-drums, the clatter of obscene crotala, and the maniacal moaning of muted horns whose ceaseless dirges rose and fell undulantly like the waves of an unhallowed ocean of bitumen.

I saw this vista, I saw, and heard as with the mind's ear the blasphemous domdaniel of cacophony which companioned it. It was the shrieking fulfilment of all the horror which that corpse-city had ever stirred in my soul, and forgetting every injunction to silence I screamed and screamed and screamed as my nerves gave way and the walls quivered about me.

Then, as the flash subsided, I saw that my host was trembling too; a look of shocking fear half-blotting from his face the serpent distortion of rage which my screams had excited. He tottered, clutched at the curtains as I had done before, and wriggled his head wildly, like a hunted animal. God knows he had cause, for as the echoes of my screaming died away there came another sound so hellishly suggestive that only numbed emotion kept me sane and conscious. It was the steady, stealthy creaking of the stairs beyond the locked door, as with the ascent of a barefoot or skin-shod horde; and at last the cautious, purposeful rattling of the brass latch that glowed in the feeble candlelight. The old man clawed and spat at me through the moldy air and barked things in his throat as he swayed with the yellow curtain he clutched

"The full moon—damn ye—ye . . . ye yelping dog—ye called 'em, and they've come for me! Moccasined feet—dead men—Gad sink ye, ye red devils, but I poisoned no rum o' yours—han't I kept your pox-rotted magic safe?—ye swilled yourselves sick, curse ye, and ye must needs blame the squire—let go, you! Unhand that latch —I've naught for ye here—"

At this point, three slow and very deliberate raps shook the panels of the door and a white foam gathered at the mouth of the frantic magician. His fright, turning to steely despair, left room for a resurgence of his rage against me; and he staggered a step toward the table on whose edge I was steadying myself. The curtains, still clutched in his right hand as his left clawed out at me, grew taut and finally crashed down from their lofty fastenings; admitting to the room a flood of that full moonlight which the brightening of the sky had presaged. In those greenish beams the candles paled and a new semblance of decay spread over the musk-reeking room with its wormy paneling, sagging floor, battered mantel, rickety furniture and ragged draperies. It spread over the old man, too, whether from the same source or because of his fear and vehemence, and I saw him shrivel and blacken as he lurched near and strove to rend me with vulturine talons. Only his eyes stayed whole, and they glared with a propulsive, dilated incandescence which grew as the face around them charred and dwindled.

The rapping was now repeated with greater insistence and this time bore a hint of metal. The black thing facing me had become only a head with eyes, impotently trying to wriggle across the sinking floor in my direction, and occasionally emitting feeble little spits of immortal malice. Now swift and splintering blows assailed the sickly panels and I saw the gleam of a tomahawk as it cleft the rending wood. I did not move, for I could not; but watched dazedly as the door fell in pieces to admit a colossal, shapeless influx of inky substance starred with shining, malevolent eyes. It poured thickly, like a flood of oil bursting a rotten bulkhead, overturned a chair as it spread, and finally flowed under the table and across the room to where the blackened head with the eyes still glared at me. Around that head it closed, totally swallowing it up, and in another moment it had begun to recede; bearing away its invisible burden without touching me, and flowing again out that black doorway down the unseen stairs, which creaked as before, though in reverse order.

Then the floor gave way at last, and I slid gaspingly down into the nighted chamber below, choking with cobwebs and half-swooning with terror. The green moon, shining through broken windows, showed me the hall door half open; and as I rose from the plaster-strewn floor and twisted myself free from the sagged ceiling, I saw sweep past it an awful torrent of blackness, with scores of baleful eyes glowing in it. It was seeking the door to the cellar, and when it found it, it vanished therein. I now felt the floor of this lower room giving as that of the upper chamber had done, and once a crashing above had been followed by the fall past the west window of something which must have been the cupola. Now liberated for the instant from the wreckage, I rushed through the hall to the front door; and finding myself unable to open it, seized a chair and broke a window, climbing frenziedly out upon the unkempt lawn where moonlight danced over yard-high grass and weeds. The wall was high, and all the gates were locked; but moving a pile of boxes in a corner I managed to gain the top and cling to the great stone urn set there.

About me in my exhaustion I could see only strange walls and windows and old gambrel roofs. The steep street of my approach was nowhere visible, and the little I did see succumbed rapidly to a mist that rolled in from the river despite the glaring moonlight. Suddenly the urn to which I clung began to tremble, as if sharing my own lethal dizziness; and in another instant my body was plunging downward to I knew not what fate.

The man who found me said that I must have crawled a long way despite my broken bones, for a trail of blood stretched off as far as he dared look. The gathering rain soon effaced this link with the scene of my ordeal and reports could state no more than that I had appeared from a place unknown, at the entrance to a little black court off Perry Street.

I never sought to return to those tenebrous labyrinths, nor would I direct any sane man thither if I could. Of who or what that ancient creature was, I have no idea; but I repeat that the city is dead and full of unsuspected horrors. Whither *he* has gone, I do not know; but I have gone home to the pure New England lanes up which fragrant sea-winds sweep at evening.

"The Brotherhood of Blood," published in May 1932, was the first of eleven *Weird Tales* bylines garnered by HUGH B. CAVE, a native of Chester, England, who now lives in Florida. A prolific contributor to pulp magazines, Cave's stylistically distinguished fiction and articles have also appeared in *Argosy, Ellery Queen's Mystery Magazine, Esquire, Good Housekeeping, The Saturday Evening Post* and many other periodicals.

THE BROTHERHOOD OF BLOOD

by Hugh B. Cave

It is midnight as I write this. Listen! Even now the doleful chimes of the Old North Church, buried in the heart of this enormous city of mine, are tolling the funereal hour.

In a little while, when the city thinks itself immune in sleep, deep-cradled in the somber hours of night—I shall go forth from here on my horrible mission of blood.

Every night it is the same. Every night the same ghoulish orgy. Every night the same mad thirst. And in a little while——

But first, while there is yet time, let me tell you of my agony. Then you will understand, and sympathize, and suffer with me.

I was twenty-six years old then. God alone knows how old I am now. The years frighten me, and I have deliberately forgotten them. But I was twenty-six when she came.

They call me an author. Perhaps I was; and yet the words which I gave to the world were not, and could not be, the true thoughts which hovered in my mind. I had studied—studied things which the average man dares not even to consider. The occult—life after death —spiritualism—call it what you will

I had written about such things, but in guarded phrases, calculated to divulge only those elementary truths which laymen should be told. My name was well known, perhaps too well known. I can see it now as it used to appear in the pages of the leading medical journals and magazines devoted to psychic investigation.

"By—Paul Munn—Authority on the Supernatural."

In those days I had few friends; none, in fact, who were in harmony with my work. One man I did know well—a medical student at Harvard University, in Cambridge. His name was Rojer Threng.

I can remember him now as he used to sit bolt upright in the huge chair in my lonely Back Bay apartment. He filled the chair with his enormous, loosely-constructed frame. His face was angular, pointed to gaunt extremes. His eyes—ah, you will have cause to consider those eyes before I have finished!—his eyes were eternally afire with a peculiar glittering life which I could never fully comprehend.

"And you can honestly sit there, spilling your mad theories to the world?" he used to accuse me in his rasping, deep-throated voice. "Good Lord, Munn, this is the Twentieth Century—a scientific era of careful thought—not the time of werewolves and vampires! You are mad!"

And yet, for all his open condemnation, he did not dare to stand erect, with his face lifted, and *deny* the things I told him. That sinister gleam of his eyes; there was no denying the thoughts lurking behind it. On the surface he was a sneering, indifferent doubter; but beneath the surface, where no man's eyes penetrated, he *knew*.

He was there in my apartment when she came. That night is vivid even now. There we sat, enveloped in a haze of gray cigarette smoke. I was bent over the desk in the corner, hammering a typewriter. He lay sprawled in the great overstuffed chair, watching me critically, intently, as if he would have liked to continue the heated argument which had passed between us during the past hour.

He had come in his usual unannounced manner, bringing with him an ancient newspaper clipping from some forgotten file in the university. Thrusting the thing into my hand, he had ordered me to read it.

That clipping was of singular interest. It was a half-hearted account of the infamous vampire horror of the little half-buried village of West Surrey. You recall it? It was known, luridly, as the "crime of eleven terrors." Eleven pitiful victims, each with the same significant blood-marks, were one after the other the prey of the unknown vampire who haunted that little village in the heart of an English moor. And then, when the eleventh victim had succumbed, Scotland Yard —with the assistance of the famous psychic investigator, Sir Edmund Friel—discovered the vampire to be the same aged, seemingly innocent old woman who had acted as *attendant nurse* to the unfortunate victims. A ghastly affair.

But Threng held the newspaper clipping up to me as a mere "trick" of journalism. He denounced it bitterly.

"What *is* a vampire, Munn?" he sneered.

I did not answer him. I saw no use in continuing a futile debate on a subject in which we had nothing in common.

"Well?" he insisted.

I swung around, facing him deliberately.

"A vampire," I said thoughtfully, choosing my words with extreme care, "is a creature of living death, dependent upon human blood for its existence. From sunset to sunrise, during the hours of darkness, it is free to pursue its horrible blood-quest. During the day it must remain within the confines of its grave—dead. and yet alive."

"And how does it appear?" he bantered. "As the usual skeletonic intruder, cowled in black, or perhaps as a mystic wraith without substance?"

"In either of two forms," I said coldly, angered by his twisted smile. "As a bat—or in its natural human substance. In either shape it leaves the grave each night and seeks blood. It obtains its blood from the throats of its victims, leaving two significant wounds in the neck from which it has drawn life. Its victims, after such a death, inherit the powers of their persecutor—and become vampires."

"Rot!" Threng exclaimed. "Utter sentimentality and imagination."

I turned back to my typewriter, ignoring him. His words were not pleasant. I would have been glad to be rid of him.

But he was persistent. He leaned forward in his chair and said critically:

"Suppose I wished to become a vampire, Munn. How could I go about it? How *does* a man obtain life after death, or life *in* death?"

"By study," I answered crisply. "By delving into thoughts which men like you sneer at. By going so deeply into such things that he becomes possessed of inhuman powers."

That ended our discussion. He could not conceive of such possibilities; and he laughed aloud at my statement. Bitterly resentful, I forced myself to continue the work before me. He, in turn, thrust a cigarette into his mouth and leaned back in his chair like a great lazy animal. And then—*she* came.

The soft knock on the door panel—so suggestive that it seemed from the world beyond—startled me. I swung about, frowning at the intrusion. Visitors at this hour of night were not the kind of guests I wished to face.

I went to the door slowly, hesitantly. My hand touched the latch nervously. Then I forced back the foolish fear that gripped me, and drew the barrier wide. And there I saw her for the first time—tall, slender, radiantly lovely as she stood in the half-light of the outer passage.

"You—are Mr. Paul Munn?" she inquired quietly.

"I am," I admitted.

"I am Margot Vernee. It is unconventional, I suppose, calling upon you at this hour; but I have come because of your reputation. You are the one man in this great city who may be able to—help me."

I would have answered her, but she caught sight, then, of Rojer Threng. Her face whitened. She stepped back very abruptly, fearful —or at least so I thought—that he might have overheard her.

"I—I am sorry," she said quickly. "I thought that you were alone, Mr. Munn. I—may I return later? Tomorrow, perhaps—when you are not occupied?"

I nodded. At that particular moment I could not find a voice to answer her; for she had inadvertently stepped directly beneath the bracket lamp in the wall, and her utter beauty fascinated me, choking the words back into my throat.

Then she went; and as I closed the door reluctantly, Rojer Threng glanced quizzically into my face and said dryly:

"Wants you to help her, eh? I didn't know you went in for that sort of thing, Munn. Better be careful!"

And he laughed. God, how I remember that laugh—and the cruel, derisive hatred that was inherent in it! But I did not answer him. In fact, his words were driven mechanically into my mind, and I hardly heard them. Returning to the typewriter, I attempted to force myself once more into the work that confronted me; but the face of that girl blurred the lines of my manuscript. She seemed to be still in the room, still standing near me. Imagination, of course; and yet, in view of what has happened since that night, I do not know.

She did not return as she had promised. All during the following day I awaited her coming—restless, nervous, unable to work. At eleven in the evening I was still pacing automatically back and forth across the floor when the doorbell rang. It was Rojer Threng who stepped over the threshold.

At first he did not mention the peculiar affair of the previous night. He took his customary place in the big chair and talked idly about medical topics of casual interest. Then, bending forward suddenly, he demanded:

"Did she return, Munn?"

"No," I said.

"I thought not," he muttered harshly. "Not after she saw me here. I—used to know her."

It was not so much the thing he said, as the complete bitterness with which he spoke, that brought me about with a jerk, confronting him.

"You—knew her?" I said slowly.

"I knew her," he scowled. "Think of the name, man. Margot Vernee. Have I never mentioned it to you?"

"No." And then I knew that he had. At least, the inflection of it was vaguely familiar.

"Her story would interest you," he shrugged. "Peculiar, Munn— very peculiar, in view of what you were telling me last night, before she came."

He looked up at me oddly. I did not realize the significance of that crafty look then, but now I know.

"The Vernee family," he said, "is as old as France."

"Yes?" I tried to mask my eagerness.

"The Château Vernee is still standing—abandoned—forty miles south of Paris. A hundred years before the Revolution it was occupied by Armand Vernee, noted for his occult research and communications with the spirit world. He was dragged from the château by the peasants of the surrounding district when he was twenty-eight years old and burned at the stake—for witchcraft."

I stared straight into Threng's angular face. If ever I noticed that unholy gleam in his strange eyes, it was at that moment. His eyes were wide open, staring, burning with a dead, phosphorescent glow. Never once did they flicker as he continued his story in that sibilant, half-hissing voice of his.

"After Armand Vernee's execution, his daughter Regine lived alone in the château. She married a young count, gave birth to a son. In her twenty-eighth year she was prostrated with a strange disease. The best physicians in the country could not cure her. She——"

"What—kind of disease?" I said very slowly.

"The symptoms," he said, sucking in his breath audibly, "baffled all those who examined her. Two small red marks at the throat, Munn—and a continual loss of blood *while she slept*. She confessed to horrible dreams. She told of a great bat which possessed her father's face, clawing at the window of her chamber every night—gaining admittance by forcing the shutters open with its claws—hovering over her."

"And—she died?"

"She died. In her twenty-eighth year."

"And then?" I shuddered.

"Her son, François Vernee Leroux, lived alone in the château. The count would not remain. The horror of her death drove him away—drove him mad. The son, François, lived—alone."

Threng looked steadily at me. At least, his *eyes* looked. The rest of his face was contorted with passion, malignant.

"François Vernee died when he was twenty-eight years of age," he said meaningly. "He, too, left a son—and *that* son died at the age of twenty-eight. Each death was the same. The same crimson marks at the throat. The same loss of blood. The same—madness."

Threng reached for a cigarette and held a match triumphantly to the end of it. His face, behind the sudden glare of that stick of wood, was horrible with exultation.

"Margot Vernee is the last of her line," he shrugged. "Every direct descendant of Armand Vernee had died in the same ghastly way, at twenty-eight years of age. *That* is why the girl came here for help, Munn. She knows the inevitable end that awaits her! She knows that she cannot escape the judgment which Armand Vernee has inflicted upon the family of Vernee!"

Rojer Threng was right. Three weeks after those significant words had passed his lips, the girl came to my apartment. She repeated, almost word for word, the very fundamental facts that Threng had disclosed to me. Other things she told me, too—but I see no need to repeat them here.

"You are the only man who knows the significance of my fate," she said to me; and her face was ghastly white as she said it. "Is there no way to avert it, Mr. Munn? Is there no alternative?"

I talked with her for an eternity. The following night, and every night for the next four weeks, she came to me. During the hours of daylight I delved frantically into research work, in an attempt to find an outlet from the dilemma which faced her. At night, alone with her, I learned bit by bit the details of her mad story, and listened to her pleas for assistance.

Then came that fatal night. She sat close to me, talking in her habitually soft, persuasive voice.

"I have formed a plan," I said quietly.

"A plan, Paul?"

"When the time comes, I shall prepare a sleeping-chamber for you with but one window. I shall seal that window with the mark of the cross. It is the only way."

She looked at me for a long while without speaking. Then she said, very slowly:

"You had better prepare the room, Paul—soon."

"You mean——" I said suddenly. But I knew what she meant.

"I shall be twenty-eight tonight—at midnight."

God forgive me that I did not keep her with me that night! I was already half in love with her. No—do not smile at that. You, too, after looking into her face continually for four long weeks—sitting close to her—listening to the soft whisper of her voice—you, too, would have loved her. I would have given my work, my reputation, my very life for her; and yet I permitted her to walk out of my apartment that night, to the horror that awaited her!

She came to me the next evening. One glance at her and I knew the terrible truth. I need not have asked the question that I did, but it came mechanically from my lips, like a dead voice.

"It—came?"

"Yes," she said quietly. "It came."

She stood before me and untied the scarf from her neck. And there, in the center of her white throat, I saw those infernal marks—two parallel slits of crimson, an eighth of an inch in length, horrible in their evil.

"It was a dream," she said, "and yet I know that it was no dream, but vivid reality. A gigantic bat with a woman's face—my mother's face—appeared suddenly at the window of my room. Its claws lifted the window. It circled over my bed as I lay there, staring at it in mute horror. Then it descended upon me, and I felt warm lips on my neck. A languid, wonderfully contented feeling came over me. I relaxed—and slept."

"And—when you awoke?" I said heavily.

"The mark of the vampire was here on my throat."

I stared at her for a very long time, without speaking. She did not move. She stood there by my desk; and a pitiful, yearning look came into her deep eyes.

Then, of a sudden, I was gripped with the helplessness of the whole evil affair. I stormed about the room, screaming my curses to the walls, my face livid with hopeless rage, my hands clawing at anything within reach of them. I tore at my face. I seized the wooden smoking-stand and broke it in my fingers, hurling the shattered pieces into a grinning, maddening picture of the Creator which hung beside the door. Then I tripped, fell, sprawled headlong—and groped again to my feet, quivering as if some tropic fever had laid its cold hands upon me.

There were tears in Margot's eyes as she came toward me and placed her hands on my arm. She would have spoken, to comfort me. I crushed her against me, holding her until she cried out in pain.

"Merciful Christ!" I cried. And the same words spurted from my lips, over and over again, until the room echoed with the intensity of them.

"You—love me, Paul?" she said softly.

"Love you!" I said hoarsely. "*Love* you! God, Margot—is there no way——"

"I love you, too," she whispered wearily. "But it is too late, Paul. The thing has visited me. I am a part of it. I——"

"I can keep you away from it!" I shouted. "I can hide you—protect you—where the thing will never find you!"

She shook her head, smiling heavily.

"It is too late, Paul."

"It is never too late!"

God! The words sounded brave enough then. Since then I have learned better. The creature that was preying on her possessed the infernal powers of life-in-death—powers which no mortal could deny. I knew it well enough, even when I made that rash promise. I had studied those things long enough to know my own limitations against them.

And yet I made the attempt. Before I left her that night, I hung the sign of the cross about her lovely throat, over the crimson stain of the vampire. I locked and sealed the windows of my apartment, breathing a prayer of supplication at each barrier as I made it secure. And then, holding her in my arms for a single unforgettable moment, I left her.

The apartment above mine was occupied by a singular fellow who had more than once called upon me to discuss my work. He, too, was a writer of sorts, and we had a meager something in common because of that. Therefore, when I climbed the stairs at a quarter to twelve that night and requested that he allow me to remain with him until morning, he was not unwilling to accede to my request, though he glanced at me most curiously as I made it.

However, he asked no questions, and I refrained from supplying any casual information to set his curiosity at rest. He would not have understood.

All that night I remained awake, listening for signs of disturbance in the rooms below me. But I heard nothing—not so much as a whisper. And when daylight came I descended the stairs with false hope in my heart.

There was no answer to my knock. I waited a moment, thinking that she might be yet asleep; then I rapped again on the panels. Then, when the silence persisted in haunting me, I fumbled frantically in my pockets for my spare key. I was afraid—terribly afraid.

And she was lying there when I stumbled into the room. Like a creature already dead she lay upon the bed, one white arm drooping to the floor. The silken comforter was thrown back. The breast of her gown was torn open. Fresh blood gleamed upon those dread marks in her throat.

I thought that she was dead. A sob choked in my throat as I dropped down beside her, peering into her colorless face. I clutched at her hand, and it was cold—stark cold. And then, unashamed of the tears that coursed down my cheeks, I lay across her still body, kissing her lips—kissing them as if it were the last time that I should ever see them.

She opened her eyes.

Her fingers tightened a little on my hand. She smiled—a pathetic, tired smile.

"It—came," she whispered. "I—knew it would."

I will not dwell longer on the death of the girl I loved. Enough to recount the simple facts.

I brought doctors to her. No less than seven expert physicians attended her and consulted among themselves about her affliction. I told them my fears; but they were men of the world, not in sympathy with what I had to tell them.

"Loss of blood," was their diagnosis—but they looked upon me as a man gone mad when I attempted to *explain* the loss of blood.

There was a transfusion. My own blood went into her veins, to keep her alive. For three nights she lived. Each of those nights I stood guard over her, never closing my eyes while darkness was upon us. And each night the thing came, clawing at the windows, slithering its horrible shape into the room where she lay. I did not know, then, how it gained admittance. Now—God help me—I know all the powers of that unholy clan. Its nocturnal creatures know no limits of space or confinement.

And this thing that preyed upon the girl I loved—I refuse to describe it. You will know *why* I make such a refusal when I have finished.

Twice I fought it, and found myself smothered by a ghastly shape of fog that left me helpless. Once I lay across her limp body with my hands covering her throat to keep the thing away from her—and I was hurled unmercifully to the floor, with an unearthly, long-dead stench of decayed flesh in my nostrils. When I regained consciousness, the wounds in her throat were newly opened, and my own wrists were marked with the ragged stripes of raking claws.

I realized, after that, that I could do nothing. The horror had gone beyond human power of prevention.

The mark of the cross which I had given her—that was worse than useless. I *knew* that it was useless. Had she worn it on that very first night of all, before the thing had claimed her for its own, it might have protected her. But now that this infernal mark was upon her throat, even the questionable strength of the cross was nullified by its evil powers. There was nothing left—nothing that could be done.

As a last resort I called upon Rojer Threng. He came. He examined her. He turned to me and said in a voice that was pregnant with unutterable malice:

"I can do nothing. If I could, I *would* not."

And so he left me—alone with the girl who lay there, pale as a ghost, upon the bed.

I knelt beside her. It was eight o'clock in the evening. Dusk was beginning to creep into the room. And she took my hand in hers, drawing me close so that she might speak to me.

"Promise me, Paul——" she whispered.

"Anything," I said.

"In two years you will be twenty-eight," she said wearily. "I shall be forced to return to you. It is not a thing that I can help; it is the curse of my family. I have no descendants—I am the last of my line. You are the one dearest to me. It is *you* to whom I must return. Promise me——"

She drew me very close to her, staring into my face with a look of supplication that made me cold, fearful.

"Promise me—that when I return—you will fight against me," she entreated. "You must wear the sign of the cross—always—Paul. No matter how much I plead with you—to remove it—promise me that you will not!"

"I would rather join you, even in such a condition," I said bitterly, "than remain here alone without you."

"No, Paul. Forget me. Promise!"

"I—promise."

"And you will wear the cross always, and never remove it?"

"I will—fight against you," I said sadly.

Then I lost control. I flung myself beside her and embraced her. For hours we lay there together in utter silence.

She died—in my arms.

It is hard to find words for the rest of this. It was hard, then, to find any reason for living. I did no work for months on end. The typewriter remained impassive upon its desk, forgotten, dusty, mocking me night after night as I paced the floor of my room.

In time I began to receive letters from editors, from prominent medical men, demanding to know why my articles had so suddenly ceased to appear in current periodicals. What could I say to them? Could I explain to them that when I sat down at the typewriter, *her* face held my fingers stiff? No; they would not have understood; they would have dubbed me a rank sentimentalist. I could not reply to their requests. I could only read their letters over and over again, in desperation, and hurl the missives to the floor, as a symbol of my defeat.

I wanted to talk. God, how I wanted to! But I had no one to listen to me. Casual acquaintances I did not dare take into my confidence. Rojer Threng did not return. Even the fellow in the rooms above me, who shared his apartment with me that night, did not come near me. He sensed that something peculiar, something beyond his scope of reason, enveloped me.

Six months passed and I began, slowly at first, to return to my regular routine. That first return to work was agony. More than one thesis I started in the proper editorial manner, only to find myself, after the first half-dozen pages, writing about *her*—*her* words, *her* thoughts. More than once I wrenched pages from the roll of the typewriter, ripped them to shreds and dashed them to the floor— only to gather them together again and read them a hundred times more, because they spoke of her.

And so a year passed. A year of my allotted time of loneliness, before she should return.

Three months more, and I was offered an instructorship at the university, to lecture on philosophy. I accepted the position. There I learned that Rojer Threng had graduated from the medical school, had hung out his private shingle, and was well along the road to medical fame. Once, by sheer accident, I encountered him in the corridors of the university. He shook my hand, spoke to me for a few minutes regarding his success, and excused himself at the first opportunity. He did not mention *her*.

Then, months later, came the night of my twenty-eighth birthday.

That night I did a strange thing. When darkness had crept into my room, I drew the great chair close to one of the windows, flung the aperture open wide, and waited. Waited—and *hoped*. I *wanted* her to come.

Yet I remembered my promise to her. Even as I lowered myself into the chair, I hung a crucifix about my throat and made the sign of the cross. Then I sat stiff, rigid, staring into the black void before me.

The hours dragged. My body became stiff, sore from lack of motion. My eyes were glued open, rimmed with black circles of anxiety. My hands clutched the arms of the chair, and never relaxed their intense grip.

I heard the distant bell of the Old North Church tolling eleven o'clock; and later—hours and hours and hours later—it struck a single note to indicate the half-hour before midnight.

Then, very suddenly, a black, bat-like shape was fluttering in the open window. It had substance, for I heard the dead impact of its great wings as they struck the ledge in front of me; and yet it had *no* substance, for I could discern the definite, unbroken shape of the window frame *through* its massive body! And I sat motionless, transfixed—staring.

The thing swooped past me. I saw it strike the floor—heard it struggling erratically between the legs of the table. Then, in front of my eyes, it dissolved into a creature of mist; and another shape took form. I saw it rise out of the floor—saw it become tall and lithe and slender. And then—then *she* stood before me, radiantly beautiful.

In that moment of amazement I forgot my danger. I lurched up from the chair and took a sudden step toward her. My arms went out. Her arms were already out; and she was standing there waiting for me to take her.

But even as I would have clasped her slender body, she fell away from me, staring in horror at the crucifix that hung from my throat. I stopped short. I spoke to her, calling her by name. But she retreated from me, circling around me until she stood before the open window. Then, with uncanny quickness, she was gone—and a great black-winged bat swirled through the opening into the outer darkness.

For an eternity I stood absolutely still, with my arms still outstretched. Then, with a dry, helpless sob, I turned away.

Need I repeat what must already be obvious? She returned. Night after night she returned to me, taking form before me with her lovely, pleading arms outstretched to enfold me. I could not bring myself to believe that this utterly lovely, supplicating figure could wish to do me harm. For that matter, I could not believe that she was dead—that she had ever died. I wanted her. God, how I wanted her! I would have given my life to take her beautiful body once more in my arms and hold her close to me.

But I remembered my promise to her. The crucifix remained about my throat. Never once did she touch it—or touch me. In fact, never once did I see her for more than a single fleeting instant. She took birth before my eyes—stood motionless while I stumbled out of the chair and groped toward her—and then the awful power of the sign of the cross thrust her back. Always the same. One maddening moment—and hours upon hours of abject, empty loneliness that followed.

I did no work. All day, every day, I waited in agony for the hour of her coming. Then one day I sat by myself and thought. I reasoned with myself. I argued my personal desires against the truths which I knew to be insurmountable.

And that night, when she stood before me, I tore the crucifix from my throat and hurled it through the open window. I took her in my arms. I embraced her; and I was glad, wonderfully glad, for the first time in more than two years.

We clung to each other. She, too, was glad. I could see it in her face, in her eyes. Her lips trembled as they pressed mine. They were warm, hot—alive.

I am not sure of all that happened. I do not want to be sure. Even as her slender body quivered in my arms, a slow stupor came over me. It was like sleep, but more—oh, so much more desirous than mere slumber. I moved back—I was forced back—to the great chair. I relaxed. Something warm and soft touched my throat. There was no pain, no agony. Life was drawn out of me.

It was daylight when I awoke. The room was empty. The sunlight streamed through the open window. Something wet and sticky lay upon my throat. I reached up, touched it, and stared at my fingers dispassionately. They were stained with blood.

I did not need to seize upon a mirror. The two telltale marks of the vampire were upon my neck. I knew it.

She came the next night. Again we lay together, deliriously happy. I had no regrets. I felt her lips at my throat . . .

Next morning I lay helpless in the big chair, unable to move. My strength had been drawn from me. I had no power to rise. Far into the day I remained in the same posture. When a knock came at my door, I could not stand up to admit the visitor. I could only turn my head listlessly and murmur: "Come in."

It was the manager of the house who entered. He scuffed toward me half apologetically and stood there, looking down at me.

"I've been 'avin' complaints, sor," he scowled, as if he did not like to deliver his message. "The chap up above yer 'as been kickin' about the noise yer makes down 'ere o' nights. It'll 'ave ter stop, sor. I don't like to be tellin' yer—but the chap says as 'ow 'e's seen yer sittin' all night long in front o'yer winder, with the winder wide open. 'E says 'e 'ears yer talkin' ter some 'un down 'ere late at night, sor."

"I'm—very ill, Mr. Robell," I said weakly. "Will you—call a doctor?"

He blinked at me. Then he must have seen that significant thing on my throat, for he bent suddenly over me and said harshly:

"My Gawd, sor. You *are* sick!"

He hurried out. Fifteen minutes later he returned with a medical man whom I did not recognize. The fellow examined me, ordered me to bed, spent a long while peering at the mark on my neck, and finally went out—perplexed and scowling. When he came back, in an hour or so, he brought a more experienced physician with him.

They did what they could for me; but they did not understand, nor did I undertake to supply them with information. They could not prevent the inevitable; that I knew. I did not want them to prevent it.

And that night, as I lay alone, *she* came as usual. Ten minutes before the luminous hands of the clock on the table beside me registered eleven o'clock, she came to my bed and leaned over me. She did not leave until daylight was but an hour distant.

The next day was my last; and that day brought a man I had never expected to see again. It brought Rojer Threng!

I can see his face even now, as he paced across the room and stood beside my bed. It was repulsive with hate, masked with terrible triumph. His lips curled over his teeth as he spoke; and his eyes—those boring, glittering, living eyes—drilled their way into my tired brain as he glared into my face.

"You wonder why I have come, Munn?"

"Why——" I replied wearily. I was already close to eternity; and having him there beside me, feeling the hideous dynamic quality of his gaunt body, drew the last tongue of life out of me.

"She has been here, eh?" he grinned evilly.

I did not answer. Even the word *she* coming from his lips, was profanity.

"I came here to tell you something, Munn," he rasped. "Something that will comfort you on the journey you are about to take. Listen——"

He lowered himself into the great chair and hunched himself close. And I was forced to listen to his savage threat, because I could not lift my hand to silence him.

"I used to love Margot Vernee, Munn," he said. "I loved her as much as you do—but in a different way. She'd have none of me. Do you understand? She would have none of me! She despised me. She *told* me that she despised me! *She!*"

His massive hands clenched and unclenched, as if they would have twisted about my throat. His eyes flamed.

"Then she loved *you! You*—with your thin, common body and hoary brain. She refused me, with all I had to offer her, and accepted you! Now do you know why I've come here?"

"You can do nothing—now," I said heavily. "It is too late. She is beyond your power."

Then he laughed. God, that laugh! It echoed and reechoed across the room, vibrating with fearful intensity. It lashed into my brain like fire—left me weak and limp upon the bed. And there I lay, staring after him as he strode out of the room.

I never saw Rojer Threng again.

I wonder if you know the meaning of death? Listen . . .

They carried me that evening to a strange place. I say *they*, but perhaps I should say *he*, for Rojer Threng was the man who ordered the change of surroundings. As for myself, I was too close to unconsciousness to offer resistance. I know only that I was lifted from my bed by four strong arms, and placed upon a stretcher, and then I was carried out of my apartment to a private car which waited at the curb below.

I bear no malice toward the two subordinates who performed this act. They were doing as they had been told to do. They were pawns of Rojer Threng's evil mind.

They made me as comfortable as possible in the rear section of the car. I heard the gears clash into place; then the leather cushion beneath me jerked abruptly, and the car droned away from the curb.

I could discern my surroundings, and I took mental note of the route we followed, though I do not know that it matters particularly. I remembered crossing the Harvard Bridge above the Charles River, with innumerable twinkling lights showing their reflections in the quiet water below. Then we followed one of the central thoroughfares, through a great square where the noise and harsh glare beat into my mind. And later—a long time later—the car came to a stop in the yards of the university.

Once again I was placed upon a stretcher. Where they took me I do not know; except that we passed through a maze of endless corridors in the heart of one of the university's many buildings. But the end of my journey lay in a small, dimly lighted room on one of the upper floors; and there I was lifted from the stretcher and placed upon a comfortable brocaded divan.

It was dusk then, and my two attendants set about making my comfort more complete. They spooned broth between my lips. They turned the light out of my eyes. They covered my prostrate body with a silken robe of some deep red color.

"Why," I murmured, "have you—brought me here?"

"It is Doctor Threng's order, sir," one of them said quietly.

"But I don't want——"

"Doctor Threng fully understands the nature of your malady, sir," the attendant replied, silencing my protest. "He has prepared this room to protect you."

I studied the room, then. Had he not spoken in such a significant tone, I should probably never have given a thought to the enclosure; but the soft inflection of his words was enough to remove my indifference.

As I have said, it was a small room. That in itself was not peculiar; but when I say that the walls were broken by only *one* window, you too will realize something sinister. The walls were low, forming a perfect square with the divan precisely in the center. No hangings, no pictures or portraits of any kind, adorned the walls themselves; they were utterly bare. I know now that they were *not* bare; but the infernal wires that extended across them were so nearly invisible that my blurred sight did not notice.

One thing I shall never forget. When the attendants left me, after preparing me for the night, one of them said deliberately, as if to console me:

"You will be guarded every moment of this night, sir. The wall facing you has been bored through with a spy-hole. Doctor Threng, in the next room asked me to inform you that he will remain at the spy-hole all night—and will allow nothing to come near you."

And then they left me alone.

I knew that she would come. It was my last night on earth, and I was positive that she would see it through by my side, to give me courage. The strange room would not keep her away. She would be able to find me, no matter where they secreted me.

I waited, lying limp on the divan with my face toward the window. The window was open. I thought then that the attendants had left it open by mistake; that they had overlooked it. I know now that it was left wide because of Rojer Threng's command.

An hour must have passed after they left me to myself. An hour of despair and emptiness for me. She did not come. I began to doubt—to be afraid. I knew that I should die soon—very soon—and I dreaded to enter the great unknown without her guidance. And so I waited and waited and waited, and never once took my eyes from the window which was my only hope of relief.

Then—it must have been nearly midnight—I heard the doleful howling of a dog somewhere down in the yard below. I knew what it meant. I struggled up, propping myself on one elbow, staring eagerly.

A moment later the faint square of moonlight which marked the window-frame was suddenly blotted out. I saw a massive, winged shape silhouetted in the opening. For an instant it hovered there, flapping its great body. Then it swooped into the room where I lay.

I saw again that uncanny transformation of spirit. The nocturnal spectre dissolved before my eyes and assumed shape again, rising into a tall, languid, divinely beautiful woman. And *she* stood there, smiling at me.

All that night she remained by my side. She talked to me in a voice that was no more than a faint whisper, comforting me for the ordeal which I must soon undergo. She told me secrets of the grave—secrets which I may not repeat here, nor ever wish to repeat. Ah, but it was a relief from the loneliness and restlessness of my heart to have her there beside me, sitting so quietly, confidently, in the depths of the divan. I no longer dreaded the fate in store for me. It meant that I should be with her always. You who love or ever have loved with an all-consuming tenderness—you will understand.

The hours passed all too quickly. I did not take account of them. I knew that she would leave when it was necessary for her to go. I knew the unfair limits that were imposed upon her very existence. Hers was a life of darkness, from sunset to sunrise. Unless she returned to the secrets of the grave before daylight crept upon us, her life would be consumed.

The hour of parting drew near. I feared to think of it. With her close to me, holding my hand, I was at peace; but I knew that without her I should lapse again into an agony of doubt and fear. If I could have died then with her near me, I think I should have been contented.

But it was not to be. She bent over to kiss me tenderly and then rose from the divan.

"I—must go back, beloved," she whispered.

"Stay a moment more," I begged. "One moment——"

"I dare not, Paul."

She turned away. I watched her as if she were taking my very soul with her. She walked very softly, slowly, to the window, I saw her look back at me, and she smiled. God, how I remember that last smile! It was meant to give me courage—to put strength into my heart.

And then she stepped to the window.

Even as she moved that last step, the horrible thing happened. A monstrous, livid streamer of white light seared across the space in front of her. It blazed in her face like a rigid snake, hurling her back. There, engraved upon the wall, hung the sign of the cross, burning like a thing possessed of life!

She staggered away from it. I saw the terror in her face as she ran to the opposite wall. Ten steps she took; and then that wall too shone livid with the cross. Two horrible wires, transformed into writhing reality by some tremendous charge of electricity, glowed before her.

She sought frantically for a means of escape. Back and forth she turned. The sign of the cross confronted her on every side, hemming her in. There *was* no escape. The room was a veritable trap—a trap designed and executed by the infernally cunning mind of Rojer Threng.

I watched her in mute madness. Back and forth she went, screaming, sobbing her helplessness. I have watched a mouse in a wire cage do the same thing, but this—this was a thousand times more terrible.

I called out to her. I attempted to rise from the divan and go to her, but weakness came over me and I fell back quivering.

She realized then that it was the end. She fought to control herself, and she walked to the divan where I lay, and knelt beside me.

She did not speak. I think she had no voice at that moment. I held her close against me, my lips pressed into her hair. Like a very small, pitiful leaf she trembled in my arms.

And then—even as I held her—the first gleam of dawn slid across the floor of that ghastly room. She raised her head and looked into my face.

"Goodbye—Paul——"

I could not answer her. Something else answered. From the spy-hole in the opposite wall of the room came a hoarse, triumphant cackle—in Rojer Threng's malignant voice.

The girl was dead—dead in my arms. And that uncouth voice from the wall, screaming its derision, brought madness to my heart.

I lunged to my feet, fighting against the torture that drove through my body. I stumbled across the room. I reached the wall—found the spy-hole with my frozen fingers—clawed at it—raged against it——

And there, fighting to reach the man who had condemned me to an eternity of horror—I died.

My story is finished. The chimes of the Old North Church have just tolled a single funereal note to usher in the hour. One o'clock . . .

It is many, many years since that fateful night when I became a creature of the blood. I do not dare to remember the number of them. Between the hours of sunrise and sunset I cling to the earth of my grave—where I refuse to stay, until I have avenged her. Then I shall write more, perhaps, pleading for your assistance that I may join her in the true death. A spike through the heart will do it . . .

From sunset until sunrise, throughout the hours of night, I am as one of you. I breathe, I drink; occasionally, as at this moment, I write—so that I may speak her name again and see it before me. I have attended social functions, mingled with people. Only one precaution must I take, and that to avoid mirrors, since my deathless body casts no reflection.

Every night—*every night*—I have visited the great house where Rojer Threng lives. No, I have not yet avenged her. The monster is too cunning, too clever. The sign of the cross is always upon him, to keep me from his throat. But sometime—*sometime*—he will forget. And then—ah, *then!*

When it is done, I shall find a way to quit this horrible brotherhood. I shall die the real death, as she did—and I shall find her.

CLARK ASHTON SMITH (1893–1961), one of the so-called "Lovecraft Circle," was a good friend of H. P. Lovecraft's and a frequent contributor to *Weird Tales* (sixty-five stories and miscellaneous verse). Smith, a native of the mining country near Auburn, California, considered himself principally an artist and poet; he chiefly wrote fiction to support his elderly parents. His gloatingly ironic "The Weird of Avoosl Wuthoqquan" appeared in the June 1932 issue of *Weird Tales*.

THE WEIRD OF AVOOSL WUTHOQQUAN

by Clark Ashton Smith

"Give, give, O magnanimous and liberal lord of the poor," cried the beggar.

Avoosl Wuthoqquan, the richest and most avaricious money-lender in all Commoriom, and, by that token, in the whole of Hyperborea, was startled from his train of revery by the sharp, eery, cicada-like voice. He eyed the supplicant with acidulous disfavor. His meditations, as he walked homeward that evening, had been splendidly replete with the shining of costly metals, with coins and ingots and gold-work and argentry, and the flaming or sparkling of many-tinted gems in rills, rivers and cascades, all flowing toward the coffers of Avoosl Wuthoqquan. Now the vision had flown; and this untimely and obstreperous voice was imploring him for alms.

"I have nothing for you." His tones were like the grating of a shut clasp.

"Only two *pazoors*, O generous one, and I will prophesy."

Avoosl Wuthoqquan gave the beggar a second glance. He had never seen so disreputable a specimen of the mendicant class in all his wayfarings through Commoriom. The man was preposterously old and his mummy-brown skin, wherever visible, was webbed with wrinkles that were like the heavy weaving of some giant jungle spider. His rags were no less fabulous; and the beard that hung down and mingled with them was hoary as the moss of a primeval juniper.

"I do not require your prophecies."

"One *pazoor* then."

"No."

The eyes of the beggar became evil and malignant in their hollow sockets, like the heads of two poisonous little pit-vipers in their holes.

"Then, O Avoosl Wuthoqquan," he hissed, "I will prophesy gratis. Harken to your weird: the godless and exceeding love which you bear to all material things and your lust therefor, shall lead you on a strange quest and bring you to a doom whereof the stars and the sun will alike be ignorant. The hidden opulence of earth shall allure you and ensnare you; and earth itself shall devour you at the last."

"Begone," said Avoosl Wuthoqquan. "The weird is more than a trifle cryptic in its earlier clauses; and the final clause is somewhat platitudinous. I do not need a beggar to tell me the common fate of mortality."

It was many moons later in that year which became known to preglacial historians as the year of the Black Tiger.

Avoosl Wuthoqquan sat in a lower chamber of his house, which was also his place of business. The room was obliquely shafted by the brief, aerial gold of the reddening sunset, which fell through a crystal window, lighting a serpentine line of irised sparks in the jewel-studded lamp that hung from copper chains and touching to fiery life the tortuous threads of silver and similor in the dark arrases. Avoosl Wuthoqquan, seated in an umber shadow beyond the aisle of light, peered with an austere and ironic mien at his client, whose swarthy face and somber mantle were gilded by the passing glory.

The man was a stranger; possibly a travelling merchant from outland realms, the usurer thought—or else an outlander of more dubious occupation. His narrow, slanting, beryl-green eyes, his bluish unkempt beard and the uncouth cut of his sad raiment were sufficient proof of his alienage in Commoriom.

"Three hundred *djals* is a large sum," said the money-lender thoughtfully. "Moreover, I do not know you. What security have you to offer?"

The visitor produced from the bosom of his garment a small bag of tiger-skin, tied at the mouth with sinew, and opening the bag with a deft movement, poured on the table before Avoosl Wuthoqquan two uncut emeralds of immense size and flawless purity. They flamed at the heart with a cold and ice-green fire as they caught the slanting sunset; and a greedy spark was kindled in the eyes of the usurer. But he spoke coolly and indifferently.

"It may be that I can loan you one hundred and fifty *djals*. Emeralds are hard to dispose of; and if you should not return to claim the gems and repay me the money, I might have reason to repent my generosity. But I will take the hazard."

"The loan I ask is a mere tithe of their value," protested the stranger. "Give me two hundred and fifty *djals* . . . there are other money-lenders in Commoriom, I am told."

"Two hundred *djals* is the most I can offer. It is true that the gems are not without value. But you may have stolen them. How am I to know? It is not my habit to ask indiscreet questions."

"Take them," said the stranger, hastily. He accepted the silver coins which Avoosl Wuthoqquan counted out, and offered no further protest. The usurer watched him with a sardonic smile as he departed and drew his own inferences. He felt sure that the jewels had been stolen, but was in no wise perturbed or disquieted by this fact. No matter whom they had belonged to, or what their history, they would form a welcome and valuable addition to the coffers of Avoosl Wuthoqquan. Even the smaller of the two emeralds would have been absurdly cheap at three hundred *djals;* but the usurer felt no apprehension that the stranger would return to claim them at any time . . . no, the man was plainly a thief, and had been glad to rid himself of the evidence of his guilt. As to the rightful ownership of the gems—that was hardly a matter to arouse the concern or the curiosity of the money-lender. They were his own property now, by virtue of the sum in silver which had been tacitly regarded by himself and the stranger as a price rather than a mere loan.

The sunset faded swiftly from the room and a brown twilight began to dull the metal broideries of the curtains and the colored eyes of the gems. Avoosl Wuthoqquan lit the fretted lamp; and then, opening a small brazen strong-box, he poured from it a flashing rill of jewels on the table beside the emeralds. There were pale and ice-clear topazes from Mhu Thulan, and gorgeous crystals of tourmaline from Tscho Vulpanomi; there were chill and furtive sapphires of the north and arctic carnelians like frozen blood and diamonds that were hearted with white stars. Red, unblinking rubies glared from the coruscating pile, chatoyants shone like the eyes of tigers, garnets and alabraundines gave their somber flames to the lamplight amid the restless hues of opals. Also, there were other emeralds, but none so large and flawless as the two that he had acquired that evening.

Avoosl Wuthoqquan sorted out the gems in gleaming rows and circles, as he had done so many times before; and he set apart all the emeralds with his new acquisitions at one end, like captains leading a file. He was well pleased with his bargain, well satisfied with his overflowing caskets. He regarded the jewels with an avaricious love, a miserly complacence; and one might have thought that his eyes were little beads of jasper, set in his leathery face as in the smoky parchment cover of some olden book of doubtful magic. Money and precious gems—these things alone, he thought, were immutable and non-volatile in a world of never-ceasing change and fugacity.

His reflections, at this point, were interrupted by a singular occurrence. Suddenly and without warning—for he had not touched or disturbed them in any manner—the two large emeralds started to roll away from their companions on the smooth, level table of black *ogga*-wood; and before the startled money-lender could put out his hand to stop them, they had vanished over the opposite edge and had fallen with a muffled rattling on the carpeted floor.

Such behavior was highly eccentric and peculiar, not to say unaccountable; but the usurer leapt to his feet with no other thought save to retrieve the jewels. He rounded the table in time to see that they had continued their mysterious rolling and were slipping through the outer door, which the stranger in departing had left slightly ajar. This door gave on a courtyard; and the courtyard, in turn, opened on the streets of Commoriom.

Avoosl Wuthoqquan was deeply alarmed, but was more concerned by the prospect of losing the emeralds than by the eeriness and mystery of their departure. He gave chase with an agility of which few would have believed him capable, and throwing open the door, he saw the fugitive emeralds gliding with an uncanny smoothness and swiftness across the rough, irregular flags of the courtyard. The twilight was deepening to a nocturnal blue; but the jewels seemed to wink derisively with a strange phosphoric luster as he followed them. Clearly visible in the gloom, they passed through the unbarred gate that gave on a principal avenue and disappeared.

It began to occur to Avoosl Wuthoqquan that the jewels were bewitched; but not even in the face of an unknown sorcery was he willing to relinquish anything for which he had paid the munificent sum of two hundred *djals.* He gained the open street with a running leap and paused only to make sure of the direction in which his emeralds had gone.

The dim avenue was almost entirely deserted, for the worthy citizens of Commoriom, at that hour, were preoccupied with the consumption of their evening meal. The jewels, gaining momentum, and skimming the ground lightly in their flight, were speeding away on the left toward the less reputable suburbs and the wild, luxuriant jungle beyond. Avoosl Wuthoqquan saw that he must redouble his pursuit if he were to overtake them.

Panting and wheezing valiantly with the unfamiliar exertion, he renewed the chase; but in spite of all his efforts, the jewels ran always at the same distance before him, with a maddening ease and eery volitation, tinkling musically at whiles on the pavement. The frantic and bewildered usurer was soon out of breath, and being compelled to slacken his speed, he feared to lose sight of the eloping gems; but strangely, thereafterward, they ran with a slowness that corresponded to his own, maintaining ever the same interval.

The money-lender grew desperate. The flight of the emeralds was leading him into an outlying quarter of Commoriom where thieves and murderers and beggars dwelt. Here he met a few passers, all of dubious character, who stared in stupefaction at the fleeing stones, but made no effort to stop them. Then the foul tenements among which he ran became smaller, with wider spaces between; and soon there were only sparse huts, where furtive lights gleamed out in the full-grown darkness, beneath the lowering frondage of high palms.

Still plainly visible and shining with a mocking phosphorescence, the jewels fled before him on the dark road. It seemed to him, however, that he was gaining upon them a little. His flabby limbs and pursy body were faint with fatigue and he was grievously winded; but he went on in renewed hope, gasping with eager avarice. A full moon, large and amber-tinted, rose beyond the jungle and began to light his way.

Commoriom was far behind him now; and there were no more huts on the lonely forest road, nor any other wayfarers. He shivered a little—either with fear or the chill night air; but he did not relax his pursuit. He was closing in on the emeralds, very gradually but surely; and he felt that he would recapture them soon. So engrossed was he in the weird chase, with his eyes on the ever-rolling gems, that he failed to perceive that he was no longer following an open highway. Somehow, somewhere, he had taken a narrow path that wound among monstrous trees whose foliage turned the moonlight to a mesh of quicksilver with heavy, fantastic raddlings of ebony. Crouching in grotesque menace, like giant retiarii, they seemed to close in upon him from all sides. But the money-lender was oblivious of their shadowy threats and heeded not the sinister strangeness and solitude of the jungle path, nor the dank odors that lingered beneath the trees like unseen pools.

Nearer and nearer he came to the fleeting gems, till they ran and flickered tantalizingly a little beyond his reach and seemed to look back at him like two greenish, glowing eyes, filled with allurement and mockery. Then as he was about to fling himself forward in a last and supreme effort to secure them, they vanished abruptly from view, as if they had been swallowed by the forest shadows that lay like sable pythons athwart the moonlit way.

Baffled and disconcerted, Avoosl Wuthoqquan paused and peered in bewilderment at the place where they had disappeared. He saw that the path ended in a cavern-mouth yawning blackly and silently before him and leading to unknown subterranean depths. It was a doubtful and suspicious-looking cavern, fanged with sharp stones and bearded with queer grasses; and Avoosl Wuthoqquan, in his cooler moments, would have hesitated a long while before entering it. But just then he was capable of no other impulse than the fervor of the chase and the prompting of avarice.

The cavern that had swallowed his emeralds in a fashion so nefarious was a steep incline running swiftly down into darkness. It was low and narrow and slippery with noisome oozings; but the money-lender was heartened as he went on by a glimpse of the glowing jewels, which seemed to float beneath him in the black air, as if to illuminate his way. The incline led to a level, winding passage, in which Avoosl Wuthoqquan began to overtake his elusive property once more; and hope flared high in his panting bosom.

The emeralds were almost within reach; then, with sleightful suddenness, they slipped from his ken beyond an abrupt angle of the passage; and following them, he paused in wonder, as if halted by an irresistible hand. He was half blinded for some moments by the pale, mysterious, bluish light that poured from the roof and walls of the huge cavern into which he had emerged; and he was more than dazzled by the multitinted splendor that flamed and glowed and glistened and sparkled at his very feet.

He stood on a narrow ledge of stone; and the whole chamber before and beneath him, almost to the level of this ledge, was filled with jewels even as a granary is filled with grain! It was as if all the rubies, opals, beryls, diamonds, amethysts, emeralds, chrysolites and sapphires of the world had been gathered together and poured into an immense pit. He thought that he saw his own emeralds, lying tranquilly and decorously in a nearer mound of the undulant mass; but there were so many others of like size and flawlessness that he could not be sure of them.

For awhile he could hardly believe the ineffable vision. Then, with a single cry of ecstasy, he leapt forward from the ledge, sinking almost to his knees in the shifting and tinkling and billowing gems. In great double handfuls, he lifted the flaming and scintillating stones and let them sift between his fingers, slowly and voluptuously, to fall with a light clash on the monstrous heap. Blinking joyously, he watched the royal lights and colors run in spreading or narrowing ripples; he saw them burn like steadfast coals and secret stars, or leap out in blazing eyes that seemed to catch fire from each other.

In his most audacious dreams the usurer had never even suspected the existence of such riches. He babbled aloud in a rhapsody of delight as he played with the numberless gems, and he failed to perceive that he was sinking deeper with every movement into the unfathomable pit. The jewels had risen above his knees, were engulfing his pudgy thighs, before his avaricious rapture was touched by any thought of peril.

Then, startled by the realization that he was sinking into his new-found wealth as into some treacherous quicksand, he sought to extricate himself and return to the safety of the ledge. He floundered helplessly; for the moving gems gave way beneath him and he made no progress but went deeper still till the bright, unstable heap had risen to his waist.

Avoosl Wuthoqquan began to feel a frantic terror amid the intolerable irony of his plight. He cried out, and as if in answer, there came a loud, unctuous, evil chuckle from the cavern behind him. Twisting his fat neck with painful effort so that he could peer over his shoulder, he saw a most peculiar entity that was crouching on a sort of shelf above the pit of jewels. The entity was wholly and outrageously unhuman, and neither did it resemble any species of animal or any known god or demon of Hyperborea. Its aspect was not such as to lessen the alarm and panic of the money-lender, for it was very large and pale and squat, with a toad-like face and a swollen, squidgy body and numerous cuttlefish limbs or appendages. It lay flat on the shelf with its chinless head and long slit-like mouth overhanging the pit and its cold, lidless eyes peering obliquely at Avoosl Wuthoqquan. The usurer was not reassured when it began to speak in a thick and loathsome voice, like the molten tallow of corpses dripping from a wizard's kettle.

"Ho! what have we here?" it said. "By the black altar of Tsathoggua, 'tis a fat money-lender, wallowing in my jewels like a lost pig in a quagmire!"

"Help me!" cried Avoosl Wuthoqquan. "See you not that I am sinking?"

The entity gave its oleaginous chuckle. "Yes, I see your predicament, of course . . . What are you doing here?"

"I came in search of my emeralds—two fine and flawless stones for which I have just paid the sum of two hundred *djals.*"

"*Your* emeralds?" said the entity. "I fear that I must contradict you. The jewels are mine. They were stolen not long ago from this cavern, in which I have been wont to gather and guard my subterranean wealth for many ages. The thief was frightened away . . . when he saw me . . : and I suffered him to go. He had taken only the two emeralds, and I knew that they would return to me—as my jewels always return—whenever I choose to call them. The thief was lean and bony and I did well to let him go; for now, in his place, there is a plump and well-fed usurer."

Avoosl Wuthoqquan, in his mounting terror, was barely able to comprehend the words or to grasp their implications. He had sunk slowly but steadily into the yielding pile; and green, yellow, red and violet gems were blinking gorgeously about his bosom and sifting with a light tinkle beneath his armpits.

"Help! help!" he wailed. "I shall be engulfed!"

Grinning sardonically and showing the cloven tip of a fat white tongue, the singular entity slid from the shelf with boneless ease; and spreading its flat body on the pool of gems, into which it hardly sank, it slithered forward to a position from which it could reach the frantic usurer with its octopus-like members. It dragged him free with a single motion of incredible celerity. Then, without pause or preamble or further comment, in a leisurely and methodical fashion, it began to devour him.

Like Clark Ashton Smith, FRANK BELKNAP LONG, JR. (1903–   ), was one of H. P. Lovecraft's closest friends; the thirty stories he wrote for *Weird Tales* sometimes showed thematic kinship to Lovecraft's tales, but "Men Who Walk Upon the Air" is a wholly original "revenant" story with a "real" protagonist, the great itinerant French poet-rogue François Villon (1431–63?). The following, Long's fourth *Weird Tales* appearance, was first published in May 1925.

MEN WHO WALK UPON THE AIR

by Frank Belknap Long, Jr.

Yellow water filled the ditches by the roadside. Yellow clouds drifted lazily through tranquil webs of darkness and obscured far, glimmering stars. Horror and misery stared out of sodden eyes and the night was filled with voices. Men with packs made vivid, grotesque gestures against the yellow sky and swore in their beards. Men ambled over stony paths and climbed hills and passed with disgust through shadowy orchards and gray deserted vineyards.

François Villon fingered his stained cowl and sighed. The thing above his head moaned and gibbered in the wind and occasionally the chains upon its poor maimed wrists and ankles clinked like jolly glasses raised to toast a well-fed abbot or a stout beneficent knight. The night wind whistled through its flapping garments as it swung pathetically to and fro and Villon pitied it.

Villon pitied all outcast shameful things. He had wasted his lean years in an orgy of pity and exaltation and song. Unfortunately he had lost his teeth and he had no hair to warm his chastened head; but still he pitied. Through the vineyards of Picardy he strolled in his splendid misery and shame and he stopped and wept when he met men who could no longer exchange happy memories, or slap unresisting backs or laugh over deliciously calculated jests. High up in the cool damp air they swung—and no one over spoke to them.

Villon wiped the corners of his shapeless, dissipated mouth and stared indignantly at the yellow sky. The feet of the thing on the gibbet swept rapidly across his world of clouds and owls and trees and made no sound under the stars. Then the chains clinked out a curt command and the gibbet held itself erect and replied with a barbaric rattle. Villon knew that on still, cold nights gibbets become restless and chafe under their heavy burdens and move about, seeking warmth and companionship. They have been known to stroll at midnight through lonely vineyards; and legends of walking gibbets were rife in Picardy. Villon coughed and shivered and suddenly he thought: "It is very cold and that poor man has no covering for his feet!"

Something fumbled nervously with the edge of his ragged cowl. He turned and stared into inconceivable blue eyes wide with horror. The eyes were mild and soft and tears had gathered in the corners of them.

"A wonderful profile," thought Villon. "Beautifully proportioned, too. And hair like fields of waving summer corn and Flora or Archipiade or Heloisa did not possess such eyes!"

While he reflected thus, she took him by the hand and dragged him ruthlessly across the road. "I have a favor of great magnitude to beg of you," she said.

Villon scowled, but he was secretly elated, and he observed how gracefully the small yellow curls clung to the nape of her neck and how buoyantly she held herself as she walked over the hard, frozen ground. He followed her indoors and watched her spread a table and make a fire. Then she turned to him. Pity and misery and terror looked together at him out of her vividly unconventional eyes.

"He is my husband and there is no one else to whom I can appeal. Of course you will get him down. I ask only that. I want you to climb up and cut him down. It will be difficult, of course, with the wind whistling about your ears and the horrible birds—" she blushed and dropped her eyes.

Villon nodded. "I understand," he said. "And as you suggest, it will be exceedingly disagreeable. But when I think of his poor frozen feet, I am prepared to sacrifice both my comfort and peace of mind!"

"And I shall give you a good dinner,' she added shyly, feeling perhaps that she owed him some inducement.

"Very well," said Villon, "I shall do it!" It had not occurred to Villon that she might invite him to dinner. Now that he thought of it, he was atrociously hungry. For three days he had tramped through the vineyards, scribbling ballads to Guenevere the mythical and Guillemette the upholstress and Jenny the hatter, and to his cronies Master Jehan Cornu and the Seigneur de Grigny, to notaries and abbesses and to Merlin, but nought to whet his appetite had he derived therefrom and he had munched disconsolately at insufficient cheese and tasted of immature wine and once he had crawled on his hands and knees to a pool by the roadside to cool his thirst with water that stank. It would be good to sit at a merry provincial board and with such a companion the time would pass right jollily.

"Sit by the fire," she commanded, "while I cook the meat. Do you like rice and sugar? And would you care for some champagne of the vintage of 1216?"

"I am not at all difficult to please," said Villon, as he slid into a chair and removed his boots.

The fire was warm and luxurious. Villon spread out his feet and warmed his great cumbersome toes by shoving them into the glowing coals and withdrawing them before the heat could painfully or seriously blister them. Then he stretched his fingers above the coals and whistled a Parisian tune.

The wife of the man on the gibbet unwrapped a dozen white loaves and heated some broth in a bronze kettle and rolled several small casks of wine into the center of the room. The table was spread with embroidered yellow linen, filigreed on the edges with designs of falcons and hydra-headed dogs wrought in gold and silver wire. Upon the gorgeous cloth she laid large wooden spoons, copper cups and knives and tiny containers replete with various seasoning: vermilion pepper, spice, oil of cloves, nutmeg.

The dinner heralded itself by enticing and glorious odors. Villon sat up, and drew into his nostrils the rich variegated smells of roast geese, fried snails and scrambled ostrich eggs. Villon displayed upon the whole an admirable restraint. Only once did he lose countenance.

A loud hissing sound arose from behind his chair and Villon shook like an aspen-leaf in an October gale. "What is that?" he demanded, considerably put out.

"Only mussels from Marseilles. I am putting them into hot water. Don't you like them?"

Villon sighed and relaxed. The fire became less hot and he permitted his toes the luxury of a longer interval of repose between the blinking coals.

He was fairly famished and when she invited him to the board, he fell to with relish. He ate furiously, immoderately and with passion. He swallowed, stuffed and crammed. He discarded spoons and knives and took between his soiled fingers great chunks of firm, white meat. His manners were deplorable, but his enthusiasm deserved commendation.

"Now," she said, when he had finished, "you must go out and cut him down. I ask only that. It is so cold that his feet will freeze!"

But Villon had forgotten the man upon the gibbet. His hostess was charming. Theoretically he had noticed it before, but he suddenly discovered that she was made of flesh and blood. And the champagne had unfortunately gone to his head.

"Perhaps you do not know that I am a poet," said Villon, holding on to his chair for support.

"I should never have guessed it!"

"But I am, really. And in Paris I am famous, in spite of—er—an unfortunate accident."

"An accident?"

"I killed a booby. But it doesn't really matter. And I'm a master of arts at the University of Paris and I belong by birth to an exceedingly aristocratic family."

"But that has nothing to do with my husband, whose feet will surely freeze if you do not go out and cut him down."

"Naturally. But it is not pleasant to go out in the cold, with the wind whistling about your ears and the birds—"

"What more do you wish?"

"Well, you might spare me one little kiss. No one would ever know. Your husband is scarcely in a position to care and a kiss is never taken seriously outside of Paris."

Villon's hostess seemed a little angry and her eyes narrowed dangerously. Villon preferred this, since he disliked both high-pitched and docile women. The quiet, angry variety pleased him.

He knew that his proposal was odious to her, but he reflected that a hopeless desire frankly expressed was better than innumerable beatings about the bush. She might refuse his request, but he would not have failed through a cowardly reticence. The thought of his courage nerved him and he released his hold upon the chair. Then he discovered that he was hopelessly drunk. He seemed so pitiful as he swung back and forth above the table with his crimson cowl rent in twain and covered with stains that his considerate and adorable hostess could not contemplate him with anger.

"If I kiss you just once," she asked, "will you go out and cut him down?"

Villon nodded dejectedly and confessed that he would do anything within reason to please her.

"Very well," she said, "you may kiss me."

Villon wondered if perchance he had fallen asleep and he tweaked his nose to assure himself that he did not dream. He had scarcely expected a victory so complete. It seemed unreasonable. Nevertheless he prepared to take advantage of the opportunity offered him. He smoothed his mustache, and endeavored to cover up the rents in his cowl. "So rapid a conquest is really very flattering," he reflected.

She stood in the center of the room and she did not move away when he came up to her and took her into his arms. "Remember," she said, "you are only to kiss me once!"

Villon nodded, and sighed. "That is a misfortune!" he said, and kissed her with delectable impudence. She made no attempt to push him away and he kissed her eyes, and her hair. Then he quailed and released her. Something horrible had taken place in the soul of the woman before him. The skin on her face had gone suddenly bloodless and her eyes did not blink at him, but simply stared. Her mouth hung agape and her shoulders rose up until her head seemed lost between them. She threw out her arms, as if warding off some unthinkable *spiritual* presence and retreated toward the corner of the room.

Villon stepped forward, and then, all at once, a sense of profound physical fatigue overwhelmed him. He stood horribly still in the center of the room and gazed at his hostess reproachfully as shriek after shriek came from between her colorless lips.

"He's at the window!" she screamed. "Don't you see him? And he's holding up his poor frozen hands and little streams of blood are running out of his eyes down his frozen cheeks! He saw you kiss me and now he's come—he's come!"

Villon turned slowly and gazed stupidly at the window. It was a small diamond-paned window set high up in the wall and Villon saw nothing but darkness and vague disturbing shadows that occasionally passed to and fro in back of the shimmering blue grass. "You are very idiotic," said Villon, "to disturb yourself over shadows!"

He knew that women often behaved unaccountably, but he could not explain the change in the woman in the corner. A moment before she had been in his arms and had not objected to his innumerable caresses; but now she lay huddled in the corner, shivering and wailing, which put quite a different complexion upon the affair. "One never knows," thought Villon, "what they will take it into their heads to think or do!"

Villon wished that he had not accepted the invitation of his erratic hostess and he cast anxious glances toward the door. The words that came from between her lips did not carry moral conviction and Villon preferred not to test her allegations in the light of reason. He preferred to ignore them, which was wise.

But he was really quaking from toe to chin and when he heard a voice without calling him loudly and urgently by name he sought to establish friendly relations with the woman in the corner. She might, conceivably, be able to intercede for him. "You know that my intentions were honorable," he said and this might have led to further talk and discussion, but someone pounded heavily upon the door.

"Don't let him in!" shrieked the woman in the corner and tears ran down her sallow face and her wide unblinking blue eyes glittered with unspeakable terror. Villon's actions failed to reassure her and when she had exhausted a repertoire of conventional emotions, she collapsed in a heap upon the floor.

Villon devoted his entire attention to the door. It was an enormous door, fashioned of stout oak and it was heavily studded with great bronze nails and it might have resisted Satan; but Villon felt that the bolt was feeble and the suspense was killing him. The door bulged inward and shook visibly and Villon resolved to seize the occasion by its tail. He stepped quickly to the door and unbolted it. A gust of wind swept into the room and whistled up the chimney.

And there in the doorway stood what Villon had feared. It had come down from the gibbet and it stood trembling with wrath and waving its blood-clotted skeleton arms against a glimmering square of yellow sky.

For a moment it wavered uncertainly in the doorway and then it raised its right foot and stepped over the sill and into the room. The chains on its wrists and ankles clanked as it advanced leeringly over the smooth floor. Its hollow eyes glittered and phosphorescently illumed a face that was eaten away at the corners. Its mouth gaped and a portion of the lower jaw had fallen away and its teeth projected through a surface layer of mottled and striated and nauseously flabby skin. Villon screamed when he saw its flaring eyes and the tiny rivulets of blood that oozed from beneath its lids and ran out of the corners of its poor mouth. He covered his eyes with his hands and endeavored to shut out the noisome sight; but the thing from the gibbet was a screeching reality and Villon was so intent upon trying to turn it into the stuff of dreams that he aided his imagination to his own hurt. He saw it imaginatively, which was imprudent. He was probably unable to seize upon any straw that might have saved him and he got to explaining the situation in a manner that was ridiculously trite. It was the champagne, he told himself and he assured himself that the best thing he could do would be to ignore the thing that had come down from the gibbet.

Perhaps that is the reason why he stood still and did nothing when the thing came up to him and breathed heavily into his pinched, frightened face. But the thing was quite blind in spite of its coruscating eyes and it somehow failed to get wind of Villon and it stood shivering and moaning and showing all of its yellow teeth and Villon was conspicuously upset.

Villon stared frowningly for a moment and thought how much the thing reminded him of the woman in the corner. Married women, thought Villon, noticeably resemble their husbands. For himself he began to wonder why he had ever desired to kiss her. He had, for no definite reason, impaired his dignity. He was so deeply moved when he thought of his humiliation that he entirely forgot the insane, hybrid creature that had stumbled into the room. He could not help feeling that the cards were against him. His several fates had played him a scurvy trick, had rubbed it in disconcertingly thick. With something like a grimace, he sat down upon the floor.

The thing went tearing past him and collided against the opposite wall. It collapsed with a terrific rattle and lay still for a few seconds, breathing heavily. Then it got awkwardly to its feet and prepared to search the room. It made a disastrous circuit of the walls, groping blindly. It could not speak, but it hissed and whistled and Villon was sorry, for in spite of his affected indifference, he strenuously objected to half-articulate vituperation. The thing was facetiously cursing him and Villon's spleen rose eloquently. He got to his feet and stepped forward and affirmed to the creature's face that while he conceded its hallucinatory nature he was ill-prepared to overlook even imaginary insults. But the thing continued to search the room and finally it stumbled upon the woman in the corner.

It bent, evidently in a state of profound agitation and its thin bony fingers fastened upon the woman's left wrist. Then it drew itself erect and started across the floor, dragging the woman brutally with it. Villon's drunken and speculative anger was succeeded by white-hot terror. But he valiantly endeavored to intercept the thing he could not subdue.

Unfortunately the initiative displayed by Villon proved curiously worthless. When he stood in the creature's path and endeavored to wave it back it simply spat at him and then it extended a long, bony arm and struck him across the face with the flat of its hand. Villon reeled back and the knowledge that he had deserved the blow sobered him. He made no further attempt to retard the creature's progress and he did not even object when the thing from the gibbet pummeled the woman from the corner until she awoke and screamed —and screamed. He did nothing when the loathsome thing released its grip upon the woman's arm and seized upon her long yellow hair. And when it dragged her out through the door into a night of clouds and owls and trees, Villon simply stared and groaned and fell back against the wall.

Later on he found his way out into the cool night, and discovered to his delight that every little wind awoke and sang. Owls were hooting on the twisted, cankerous arms of hopelessly distorted trees and the boles of the great oaks resembled men walking. The night was filled with futile whispering and men swore roundly and ambled through gray orchards and lonely vineyards.

Villon fingered his stained cowl and sighed. Above his head two gray amorphous forms swung merrily in the night wind. The wind tore through their flapping garments and they made no sound under the stars. Only the chains clanked on their poor maimed wrists and ankles and Villon noticed that one figure held the other closely.

He turned on his heels and walked in the opposite direction. "The pity of it!" he murmured. "Oh, the pity of it!"

Weird Tales reprinted three stories by the great English novelist CHARLES DICKENS (1812–70): "The Bagman's Story" from The Pickwick Papers; the powerful precognitive ghost story "The Signal-Man"; and in July 1930 the following touching bit of sentiment, "A Child's Dream of a Star."

A CHILD'S DREAM OF A STAR

by Charles Dickens

There was once a child, and he strolled about a good deal, and thought of a number of things. He had a sister, who was a child too, and his constant companion. These two used to wonder all day long. They wondered at the beauty of the flowers; they wondered at the height and blueness of the sky; they wondered at the depth of the bright water; they wondered at the goodness and the power of God who made the lovely world.

They used to say to one another, sometimes, Supposing all the children upon earth were to die, would the flowers, and the water, and the sky, be sorry? They believed they would be sorry. For, said they, the buds are the children of the flowers, and the little playful streams that gambol down the hillsides are the children of the water; and the smallest bright specks playing at hide-and-seek in the sky all night must surely be the children of the stars; and they would all be grieved to see their playmates, the children of men, no more.

There was one clear shining star that used to come out in the sky before the rest, near the church spire, above the graves. It was larger and more beautiful, they thought, than all the others, and every night they watched for it, standing hand in hand at a window. Whoever saw it first, cried out, 'I see the star!' And often they cried out both together, knowing so well when it would rise, and where. So they grew to be such friends with it, that, before lying down in their beds, they always looked out once again, to bid it good night; and when they were turning round to sleep, they used to say, 'God bless the star!'

But while she was still very young—oh, very, very young!—the sister drooped, and came to be so weak that she could no longer stand in the window at night; and then the child looked sadly out by himself, and when he saw the star, turned round and said to the patient pale face on the bed, 'I see the star!' and then a smile would come upon the face, and a little weak voice used to say, 'God bless my brother and the star!'

And so the time came all too soon when the child looked out alone, and when there was no face on the bed, and when there was a little grave among the graves, not there before; and when the star made long rays down towards him, as he saw it through his tears.

Now, these rays were so bright, and they seemed to make such a shining way from earth to Heaven, that when the child went to his solitary bed, he dreamed about the star; and dreamed that, lying where he was, he saw a train of people taken up that sparkling road by angels. And the star, opening, showed him a great world of light, where many more such angels waited to receive them.

All these angels, who were waiting, turned their beaming eyes upon the people who were carried up into the star; and some came out from the long rows in which they stood, and fell upon the people's necks, and kissed them tenderly, and went away with them down avenues of light, and were so happy in their company, that lying in his bed he wept for joy.

But there were many angels who did not go with them, and among them one he knew. The patient face that once had lain upon the bed was glorified and radiant, but his heart found out his sister among all the host.

His sister's angel lingered near the entrance of the star and said to the leader among those who had brought the people thither, 'Is my brother come?'

And he said, 'No.'

She was turning hopefully away, when the child stretched out his arms and cried, 'Oh, sister, I am here! Take me!' and then she turned her beaming eyes upon him, and it was night; and the star was shining into the room, making long rays down towards him as he saw it through his tears.

From that hour forth, the child looked out upon the star as on the home he was to go to, when his time should come; and he thought that he did not belong to the earth alone, but to the star too, because of his sister's angel gone before.

There was a baby born to be a brother to the child; and while he was so little that he never yet had spoken a word, he stretched his tiny form out on his bed, and died.

Again the child dreamed of the opened star, and of the company of angels, and the train of people, and the rows of angels with their beaming eyes all turned upon those people's faces.

Said his sister's angel to the leader, 'Is my brother come?'

And he said, 'Not that one, but another.'

As the child beheld his brother's angel in her arms, he cried, 'Oh, sister, I am here! Take me!' And she turned and smiled upon him, and the star was shining.

He grew to be a young man, and was busy at his books when an old servant came to him and said, 'Thy mother is no more. I bring her blessing on her darling son!'

Again at night he saw the star, and all that former company. Said his sister's angel to the leader, 'Is my brother come?'

And he said, 'Thy mother!'

A mighty cry of joy went forth through all the star, because the mother was reunited to her two children. And he stretched out his arms and cried, 'Oh, mother, sister, and brother, I am here! Take me!' And they answered him, 'Not yet,' and the star was shining.

He grew to be a man, whose hair was turning grey, and he was sitting in his chair by the fireside, heavy with grief, and with his face bedewed with tears, when the star opened once again.

Said his sister's angel to the leader, 'Is my brother come?'

And he said, 'Nay, but his maiden daughter.'

And the man who had been the child saw his daughter, newly lost to him, a celestial creature among those three, and he said, 'My daughter's head is on my sister's bosom, and her arm is round my mother's neck, and at her feet there is the baby of old time, and I can bear the parting from her, God be praised!'

And the star was shining.

Thus the child came to be an old man, and his once smooth face was wrinkled, and his steps were slow and feeble, and his back was bent. And one night as he lay upon his bed, his children standing round, he cried, as he had cried so long ago, 'I see the star!'

They whispered to one another, 'He is dying.'

And he said, 'I am. My age is falling from me like a garment, and I move towards the star as a child. And oh, my Father, now I thank thee that it has so often opened to receive those dear ones who await me!'

And the star was shining; and it shines upon his grave.

The final spot in my anthologies is always reserved for the selection that I consider to be the most remarkable. Without question, the late THEODORE STURGEON's (1918–85) novella "The Perfect Host" deserves the honor this time; it is one of the most unusual horror stories I have ever read. It appeared in November 1948, one of eight Sturgeon tales to run in The Unique Magazine.

THE PERFECT HOST

by Theodore Sturgeon

1

RONNIE DANIELS

I was fourteen then. I was sitting in the car waiting for Dad to come out of the hospital. Dad was in there seeing Mother. It was the day after Dad told me I had a little sister.

It was July, warm, and I suppose about four in the afternoon. It was almost time for Dad to come out. I half opened the car door and looked for him.

Someone called, "Mister! Mister!"

There was a red squirrel arcing across the thick green lawn, and a man with balloons far down the block. I looked at them. Nobody would call me Mister. Nobody ever had, yet. I was too young.

"Mister!"

It was a woman's voice, but rough; rough and nasty. It was strong, and horrible for the pleading in it. No strong thing should beg. The sun was warm and the red of the brick buildings was warm, too. The squirrel was not afraid. The grass was as green and smooth as a jellybean; Mother was all right, Dad said, and Dad felt fine. We would go to the movies, Dad and I, close together with a closeness that never happened when things were regular, meals at home, Mother up making breakfast every morning, and all that. This week it would be raids on the ice box and staying up late sometimes, because Dad forgot about bedtime and anyway wanted to talk.

"Mister!"

Her voice was like a dirty mark on a new collar. I looked up.

She was hanging out of a window on the second floor of a near ell of the hospital. Her hair was dank and stringy, her eyes had mud in them, and her teeth were beautiful. She was naked, at least to the waist. She was saying "Mister!" and she was saying it to me.

I was afraid, then. I got in the car and slammed the door.

"Mister! Mister! Mister!"

They were syllables that meant nothing. A "mis," a "ter"—sounds that rasped across the very wound they opened. I put my hands over my ears, but by then the sounds were inside my head, and my hands just seemed to keep them there. I think I sobbed. I jumped out of the car and screamed, "What? What?"

"I got to get out of here," she moaned.

I thought, why tell me? I thought, what can I do? I had heard of crazy people, but I had never seen one. Grown-up people were sensible, mostly. It was only kids who did crazy things, without caring how much sense they made. I was only fourteen.

"Mister," she said. "Go to—to . . . Let me think, now . . . Where I live. Where I live."

"Where do you live?" I asked.

"In Homeland," she said. She sank down with her forehead on the sill, slowly, as if some big slow weight were on her shoulderblades. I could see only the top of her head, the two dank feathers of her hair and the point of an elbow. Homeland was a new residential suburb.

"Where in Homeland?" It seemed to be important. To me, I mean, as much as to her.

"Twenty," she mumbled. "I have to remember it . . ." and her voice trailed off. Suddenly she stood bolt upright, looking back into the room as if something had happened there. Then she leaned far out. "Twenty sixty five," she snarled. "You hear? Twenty sixty five. That's the one."

"Ron! Ronnie!"

It was Dad, coming down the path, looking at me, looking at the woman.

"That's the one," said the woman again. There was a flurry of white behind her. She put one foot on the sill and sprang out at me. I closed my eyes. I heard her hit the pavement. When I opened my eyes they were still looking up at the window. There was a starched white nurse up there with her fingers in her mouth, all of them, and eyes as round and blank as a trout's. I looked down. I felt Dad's hand on my upper arm. "Ronnie!"

I looked down. There was blood, just a little, on the cuff of my trousers. There was nothing else.

"Dad . . ."

Dad looked all around, on the ground.

He looked up at the window and at the nurse. The nurse looked at Dad and at me, and then put her hands on the sill and leaned out and looked all around on the ground. I could see, in the sunlight, where her fingers were wet from being in her mouth. Dad looked at me and again at the nurse and I heard him draw a deep quivering breath as if he'd forgotten to breathe for a while and had only just realized it. The nurse straightened up, put her hands over her eyes and twisted back into the room.

Dad and I looked at each other. He said, "Ronnie—what was— what . . ." and then licked his lips. I was not as tall as my father, though he was not a tall man. He had thin, fine obedient hair, straight and starting high. He had blue eyes and a big nose and his mouth was quiet. He was broad and gentle and close to the ground, close to the earth. I said, "How's Mother?"

Dad gestured at the ground where something should be, and looked at me. Then he said, "We'd better go, Ron."

I got into the car. He walked around it and got in and started it, and then sat holding the wheel, looking back at where we had been standing. There was still nothing there. The red squirrel, with one cheek puffed out, came bounding and freezing across the path. I asked again how Mother was.

"She's fine. Just fine. Be out soon. And the baby. Just fine." He looked back carefully for traffic, shifted and let in the clutch. "Good as new," he said.

I looked back again. The squirrel hopped and arched and stopped, sitting on something. It sat on something so that it was perhaps ten inches off the ground, but the thing it sat on couldn't be seen. The squirrel put up its paws and popped a chestnut into them from its cheek, and put its tail along its back with the big tip curled over like a fern-frond, and began to nibble. Then I couldn't see any more.

After a time Dad said, "What happened there just as I came up?"

I said, "What happened? Nothing. There was a squirrel."

"I mean, uh, up at the window."

"Oh. I saw a nurse up there."

"Yes, the nurse." He thought for a minute. "Anything else?"

"No. What are you going to call the baby?"

He looked at me strangely. I had to ask him again about the baby's name.

"I don't know yet," he said distantly. "Any ideas?"

"No, Dad."

We rode along for quite a while without saying anything. A little frown came and went between Dad's eyes, the way it did when he was figuring something out, whether it was a definition at charades, or an income tax report, or a problem of my school algebra.

"Dad. You know Homeland pretty well, don't you?"

"I should. Our oufit agented most of those sites. Why?"

"Is there a Homeland Street, or a Homeland Avenue out there?"

"Not a one. The north and south ones are streets, and are named after trees. The east and west ones are avenues, and are named after flowers. All alphabetical. Why?"

"I just wondered. Is there a number as high as 2065?"

"Not yet, though I hope there will be some day . . . unless it's a telephone number. Why, Ron? Where did you get that number?"

"I dunno. Just thought of it. Just wondered. Where are we going to eat?"

We went to the Bluebird.

I suppose I knew then what had gotten into me when the woman jumped; but I didn't think of it, any more than a redhead goes around thinking to himself "I have red hair" or a taxi-driver says to himself "I drive a cab." I knew, that's all. I just knew. I knew the *purpose*, too, but didn't think of it, any more than a man thinks and thinks of the place where he works, when he's on his way to work in the morning.

2
BENTON DANIELS

Ronnie's not an unusual boy. Oh, maybe a little quieter than most, but it takes all kinds . . . He's good in school, but not brilliant; averages in the low eighties, good in music and English and history, weak in math, worse in science than he could be if he cared a little bit more about it.

That day when we left the hospital grounds, though, there was something unusual going on. Yes, sir. I couldn't make head nor tail of it, and I must say I still can't. Sometimes I think it's Ronnie, and sometimes I think it was something temporarily wrong with me. I'm trying to get it all straight in my mind, right from the start.

I had just seen Clee and the baby. Clee looked a little tired, but her color was wonderful. The baby looked like a baby—that is, like a little pink old man, but I told Clee she was beautiful and takes after her mother, which she will be and do, of course, when she gets some meat on her bones.

I came along the side path from the main entrance, toward where the car was parked. Ronnie was waiting for me there. I saw him as I turned toward the road, just by the north building. Ronnie was standing by the car, with one foot on the running board, and he seemed to be talking with somebody in the second-floor window. I called out to him, but he didn't hear. Or he paid no attention. I looked up, and saw someone in the window. It was a woman, with a crazy face. I remember an impression of very regular, white teeth, and scraggly hair. I don't think she had any clothes on. I was shocked, and then I was very angry. I thought, here's some poor sick person gone out of her mind, and she'll maybe mark Ronnie for life, standing up there like that and maybe saying all sorts of things.

I ran to the boy, and just as I reached him, the woman jumped. I think someone came into the room behind her.

Now, look. I distinctly heard that woman's body hit. It was a terrible sound. And I remember feeling a wave of nausea just then, but for some reason I was sure then, and I'm sure now, that it had nothing to do with the thing I saw. That kind of shock-nausea only hits a person after the shock, not before or during. I don't even know why I think of this at all. It's just something I feel sure about, that's all.

I heard her body hit. I don't know whether I followed her body down with my eyes or not. There wasn't much time for that; she didn't fall more than twenty-five, maybe twenty-eight feet. I heard the noise, and when I looked down—*there wasn't anything there!*

I don't know what I thought then. I don't know if a man does actually *think* at a time like that. I know I looked all around, looking for a hole in the ground or maybe a sheet of camouflage or something which might be covering the body. It was too hard to accept that disappearance. They say that a dog doesn't bother with his reflection in a mirror because he can't smell it, and he believes his nose rather than his eyes. Humans aren't like that, I guess. When your brain tells you one thing and your eyes another, you just don't know what to believe. I looked back up at the window, perhaps thinking I'd been mistaken, that the woman would still be up there. She was gone, all right. There was a nurse up there instead, looking down, terrified.

I turned to Ronnie and started to ask him what had happened. I stopped when I saw his face. It wasn't shocked, or surprised, or anything. Just relaxed. He asked me how his mother was.

I said she was fine. I looked at his face and marveled that it showed nothing of this horrible thing that had happened. It wasn't blank, mind you. It was just as if nothing had occurred at all, or as if the thing had been wiped clean out of his memory. I thought at the moment that that was a blessing, and, with one more glance at the window—the nurse had gone—I went to the car and got in. Ronnie sat next to me. I started the car, then looked back at the path. There was nothing there.

I suppose the reaction hit me then—that, or the thought that I had had a hallucination. If I had, I was naturally worried. If I had not, what had happened to Ronnie?

I drove off, finally. Ronnie made some casual small talk; I questioned him about the thing, carefully, but he seemed honestly to know nothing about it. I decided to let well enough alone, at least for the time being . . .

We had a quick dinner at the Bluebird, and then went home. I suppose I was poor company for the boy, because I kept finding myself mulling over the thing. We went to the Criterion, and I don't believe I heard or saw a bit of it. Then we picked up an evening paper and went home. He went to bed while I sat up with the headlines.

I found it down at the bottom of the third page. This is the item.

WOMAN DIES IN HOSPITAL LEAP

Mrs. Helmuth Stoye, of Homeland, was found yesterday afternoon under her window at Memorial Hospital, Carstairs. Dr. R. B. Knapp, head physician at the hospital, made a statement to the press in which he absolved the hospital and staff from any charges of negligence. A nurse, whose name is withheld, had just entered Mrs. Stoye's room when the woman leaped to her death. "There was no way to stop her," said Dr. Knapp. "It happened too fast."

Dr. Knapp said that Mrs. Stoye had shown no signs of depression or suicidal intent on admission to the hospital four days ago. Her specific illness was not divulged.

Mrs. Stoye, the former Grace Korshak of Ferntree, is survived by her husband, a well known printer here.

I went straight to the telephone and dialed the hospital. I heard the ringing signal once, twice, and then, before the hospital could answer, I hung up again. What could I ask them, or tell them? "I saw Mrs. Stoye jump." They'd be interested in that, all right. Then what? "She disappeared when she hit the ground." I can imagine what they'd say to that. "But my son saw it too!" And then questions from hospital officials, a psychiatrist or two . . . Ronnie being questioned, after he had mercifully forgotten about the whole thing . . . no. No; better let well enough alone.

The newspaper said Mrs. Stoye was found under her window. Whoever found her must have been able to see her.

I wonder what the nurse saw?

I went into the kitchen and heated some coffee, poured it, sweetened it, stirred it, and then left it untasted on the table while I put on my hat and got my car keys.

I had to see that nurse. First I tore out the newspaper article—I didn't want Ronnie ever to see it—and then I left the house.

3

LUCILLE HOLDER

1 have seen a lot of ugly things as a trainee and as a nurse, but they don't bother me very much. It isn't that the familiarity hardens one; it is rather that one learns the knack of channeling one's emotions around the ugly thing.

When I was a child in England I learned how to use this knack. I lived in Coventry, and though Herr Hitler's treatment of the city seems to have faded from the news and from fiction, the story is still vividly written on the memories of us who were there, and is read and reread more often than we care to say.

You can't know what this means until you know the grim happiness that the chap you've dug out of the ruins is a dead 'un, for the ones who still live horrify you so.

So—one gets accustomed to the worst. Further, one is prepared when a worse "worst" presents itself. And I suppose that it was this very preparation which found me jolly well unprepared for what happened when Mrs. Stoye jumped out of her window.

There were two things happening from the instant I opened her door. One thing was what I did, and the other thing is what I felt.

These are the things I did:

I stepped into the room, carrying a washing tray on my arm Everything seemed in order, except, of course, that Mrs. Stoye was out of bed. That didn't surprise me; she was ambulant. She was over by the window; I suppose I glanced around the room before I looked directly at her. When I saw her pajama-top lying on the bedclothes I looked at her, though. She straightened up suddenly as she heard me, barked something about "That's the one!" and jumped—dived, rather—right out. It wasn't too much of a drop, really—less than thirty feet, I'd say, but she went down head first, and I knew instantly that she hadn't a chance.

I can't remember setting down the washing tray; I saw it later on the bed. I must have spun around and set it there and rushed to the window. I looked down, quite prepared for the worst, as I've said.

But what I saw was so terribly much worse than it should have been. I mean, an ill person is a bad thing to see, and an accident case can be worse, and burn cases, I think, are worst of all. The thing is, these all get worse in one direction. One simply cannot be prepared for something which is bad in a totally unexpected, impossible way.

There was nothing down there at all. Nothing. I saw Mrs. Stoye jump out, ran to the window, it couldn't have been more than three seconds later; and there was nothing there.

But I'm saying now how I felt. I mean to say first what I did, because the two are so different, from this point on.

I looked down; there was no underbrush, no flowerbed, nothing which could have concealed her had she rolled. There were some people—a stocky man and a young boy, perhaps fourteen or fifteen —standing nearby. The man seemed to be searching the ground as I was; I don't remember what the boy was doing. Just standing there. The man looked up at me; he looked badly frightened. He spoke to the boy, who answered quietly, and then they moved off together to the road. I looked down once more, still could not see Mrs. Stoye and turned and ran to the signal-button. I rang it and then rushed out into the hall. I must have looked very distraught. I ran right into Dr. Knapp, all but knocking him over, and gasped out that Mrs. Stoye had jumped.

Dr. Knapp was terribly decent. He led me back into the room and told me to sit down. Then he went to the window, looked down and grunted. Miss Flaggon came in just then. I was crying. Dr. Knapp told her to get a stretcher and a couple of orderlies and take them outside, under this window. She asked no questions, but fled; when Dr. Knapp gives orders in that voice, people jump to it. Dr. Knapp ran out, calling to me to stay where I was until he came back. In spite of the excitement, he actually managed to make his voice gentle.

I went to the window after a moment and looked down. Two medical students were running across the lawn from the south building and the orderlies with their stretcher, still rolled, were pelting down the path. Dr. Knapp, bag in hand, was close behind them. Dr. Carstairs and Dr. Greenberg were under the window and already shunting away the few curious visitors who had appeared as if from out of the ground, the way people do after an accident anywhere. But most important of all, I saw Mrs. Stoye's body. It was lying crumpled up, directly below me, and there was no doubt of it that her neck was broken and her skull badly fractured. I went and sat down again.

Afterward Dr. Knapp questioned me closely and, I must say, very kindly. I told him nothing about the srange disappearance of the body. I expect he thought I was crying because I felt responsible for the death. He assured me that my record was in my favor, and it was perfectly understandable that I was helpless to stop Mrs. Stoye. I apparently went quite to pieces then and Dr. Knapp suggested that I take my two weeks' leave—it was due in another twenty days in any case—immediately, and rest up and forget this thing.

"Go out with the glamour boy every night while you're off," he suggested, grinning. "You'll be okay."

I thought of Mervin and what it would be like to have him saying those sweet things about how tiny I was—he used to call me Midge and Shorty and things like that, the idiot—every evening for two weeks and how nice it would be to feel small and incompetent and—well, protected for a change. I said, "Perhaps I will."

I went out to the Quarters to bathe and change. And now I had better say how I *felt* during all this . . .

I was terrified when Mrs. Stoye jumped. When I reached the window right afterward, I was exactly as excited as one might expect.

But the instant I looked down, something happened. It wasn't anything I can describe, except to say that there was a change of attitude. That doesn't seem to mean much, does it? Well, I can only say this; that from that moment I was no longer frightened nor shocked nor horrified nor anything else. I remember putting my hands up to my mouth, and I must have given a perfect picture of a terrified nurse. I was actually quite calm. I was quite cool as I ran to the bell and then out into the hall. I collapsed, I cried, I sobbed. I produced a flood of tears and streaks for my face. But during every minute of it I was completely calm.

Now I knew that was strange, but I felt no surprise at it. I knew that it could be called dishonest. I don't know how to analyze it. I am a nurse and a profound sense of duty has been drilled into me for years. I felt that it was my duty to cry, to say nothing about the disappearance of the body, to get the two weeks leave immediately and to do the other things which I have done and must do.

While I bathed, I thought. I was still calm, and I suppose I behaved calmly; it didn't matter, for there was no one to see.

Two people had seen Mrs. Stoye jump besides myself. I realized that I must see them. I didn't think about the disappearing body. I didn't feel I had to, somehow, any more than one thinks consciously of the water in the pipes and heaters as one draws a bath. The thing was there and needed no investigation. But it was necessary to see that man and the boy. What I must do when I saw them required no thought, either. That seemed all arranged, unquestionable, so evident that it needed no thought or definition.

I put away the white stockings and shoes with a feeling of relief and slipped into underthings with a bit of lace on them and sheer hose. I put on my wine rayon with the gored skirt and the matching shoes. I combed my hair out and put it up in a roll around the back, cool and out of the way. Money, keys, cigarette case, knife, lighter, compact. All ready.

I went round by the administration offices, thinking hard. A man visits the hospital with his boy—it was probably his boy—and leaves the boy outside while he goes in. He would be seeing a wife, in all probability. He'd leave the boy outside only if the woman's condition were serious or if she were immediately post-operative or post-partem. So many patients go in and out that I naturally don't remember many of them; on the other hand, I can almost always tell a new patient or visitor . . . marvelous the way the mind, unbidden, clocks and catalogs, to some degree, all that passes before it . . .

So the chances were that these people, the man and the boy, were visiting a new patient. Maternity would be as good a guess as any, to start with.

It was well after nine o'clock, the evening of Mrs. Stoye's death, and the administration offices were deserted except for Miss Kaye, the night registrar. It was not unusual for nurses to check up occasionally on patients. I nodded to Miss Kaye and went back to the files. The Maternity Admission file gave me five names for the previous two days. I got the five cards out of the Patients Alphabetical and glanced over them. Two of these new mothers had other children; a Mrs. Korff, with three sons and a daughter at home, and a Mrs Daniels, who had one son. Here: "Previous children: One. Age this date: 14 yrs. 3 months." And further down: "Father's age: 41."

It looked like a bull's eye. I remember feeling inordinately pleased with myself, as if I had assisted particularly well in an operation or had done a bang-up job of critical first aid. I copied down the address of the Daniels family and, carefully replacing all the cards, made my vacation checkout and left the building.

It seemed late to go calling, but I knew that I must. There had been a telephone number on the card, but I had ignored it. What I must do could not be done over the phone.

I found the place fairly easily, although it was a long way out in the suburbs on the other side of the town. It was a small, comfortable-looking place, set well back from the road and with wide lawns and its own garage. I stepped up on the porch and quite shamelessly looked inside.

The outer door opened directly into the living room, without a foyer. There was a plate-glass panel in the door with a sheer curtain on the inside. I could see quite clearly. The room was not too large—fireplace, wainscoting, stairway in the left corner, big easy chairs, a studio-couch—that sort of thing. There was a torn newspaper tossed on the arm of one fireside chair. Two end-table lamps were lit. There was no one in the room.

I rang the bell, waited, rang again, peering in. Soon I saw a movement on the stairs. It was the boy, thin-looking and touseled, thumping down the carpeted steps, tying the cord of a dark-red dressing gown as he came. On the landing he stopped. I could just hear him call "Dad!" He leaned over the banister, looking up and back. He called again, shrugged a shrug which turned into a stretch and, yawning, came to the door. I hid the knife in my sleeve.

"Oh!" he said, startled, as he opened the door. Unaccountably, I felt a wave of nausea. Getting a grip on myself, I stepped inside before I spoke. He stood looking at me, flushing a bit, conscious, I think, of his bare feet, for he stood on one of them, trying to curl the toes of the other one out of sight.

"Daniels . . ." I murmured.

"Yes," he said. "I'm Ronald Daniels." He glanced quickly back into the room. "Dad doesn't seem to be . . . I don't . . . I was asleep."

"I'm so sorry."

"Gosh, that's all right," he said. He was a sweet little chap, not a man yet, not a child—less and less of a child as he woke up, which he was doing slowly. He smiled. "Come in. Let me have your coat. Dad ought to be here now. Maybe he went for cigarettes or something." It was as if a switch had been thrown and a little sign had lit up within him—"Remember your manners."

Abruptly I felt the strangest compulsion—a yearning, a warming toward this lad. It was completely a sexual thing, mind you—completely. But it was as if a part of me belonged to a part of him . . . no; more the other way round. I don't know. It can't be described. And with the feeling, I suddenly knew that it was all right, it was all quite all right. I did not have to see Mr. Daniels after all. That business would be well-taken care of when the time came and not by me. Better—much better—for him to do it.

He extended his hand for my coat. "Thank you *so* much," I said, smiling, liking him—more than liking him, in this indefinable way— "but I really must go. I—if your father—" How could I say it? How could I let him know that it was different now; that everything might be spoiled if his father knew I had come here? "I mean, when your father comes back . . ."

Startlingly, he laughed. "Please don't worry," he said. "I won't tell him you were here."

I looked at his face, his round, bland face, so odd with his short slender frame. That thing like a sense of duty told me not to ask, but I violated it. "You don't know who I am, do you?"

He shook his head. "Not really. But it doesn't matter. I won't tell Dad."

"Good," I smiled, and left.

4

JENNIE BEAUFORT

You never know what you're going to run up against when you're an information operator, I mean, really, people seem to have the craziest idea of what we're there for. Like the man called up the other day and wanted to know how you spell conscientious—"Just conscientious," he says, "I know how to spell objector" and I gave him the singsong, you know, the voice with a smile, "I'm soreee! We haven't that infor*may*—shun!" and keyed him out, thinking to myself, what a shmoe. (I told Mr. Parker, he's my super, and he grinned and said it was a sign of the times; Mr. Parker's always making jokes.) And like the other man wants to know if he gets a busy signal and hangs on to the line, will the signal stop and the bell ring when the party he is calling hangs up. I want to say to him, who do you think I am, Alexander Graham Bell or something, maybe Don Ameche, instead of which I tell him "One moment, sir, and I will get that information for you?" (not that I'm asking a question, you raise your voice that way because it leaves the customer breathless) and I nudge Sue and she tells me, Sue knows everything.

Not that everything like that comes over the wire, anything is liable to happen right there in the office or in the halls to say nothing of the stage-door johnnies with hair-oil and cellophane boxes who ask all the girls if they are Operator 23, she has such a nice voice.

Like the kid that was in here yesterday, not that he was on the prowl, he was too young, though five years from now he'll be just dreamy, with his cute round face and his long legs. Mr. Parker brought him in to me and told me the kid was getting up a talk on telephones for his civics class in high school, and tells the kid to just ask Miss Beaufort anything he wants to know, and walks off rubbing his hands, which I can understand because he has made me feel good and made the kid feel good and has me doing all the work while he gets all the credit. Not that I felt good just at that particular moment, my stomach did a small flip-flop but that has nothing to do with it, it must have been the marshmallow whip I had with my lunch, I should remember to keep away from marshmallow when I have gravy-and-mashed, at least on weekdays.

Anyway this kid was cute, with his pleases and his thank you's and his little almost-bows-from-the-waist like a regular Lord Calvert. He asked me all sorts of questions and all smart too, but he never asked them right out, I mean, he would say, "Please tell me how you can find a number so *fast?*" and then listen to every word I said and squiggle something down in his notebook. I showed him the alphabeticals and the central indexes and the assonance file (and you can bet I called it by its full name to that nice youngster) where we find out that a number for Meyer, say, is listed as Maior. And he wanted to know why it was that we never give a street address to someone who has the phone number, but only the other way around, and how we found out the phone number from just the street address. So I showed him the street index and the checking index, which has the numbers all in order by exchanges with the street addresses, which is what we use to trace calls when we have to. And lots more. And finally he said he wanted to pretend he was me for a minute, to see if he understood everything. He even blushed when he said it. I told him to go ahead and got up and let him sit down. He sat there all serious and bright-eyed and said, "Now, suppose I am you and someone wants to know the number of—uh—Fred Zimmerman, who lives out at Bell Hill, but they have no street number." And I showed him how to flip out the alphabetical, and how to ask the customer which one he wants if there should be more than one Fred Zimmerman. He listened so carefully and politely and made a note in his book. Then he asked me what happens if the police or somebody has a phone number and wants the address, we'll say, out in Homeland, like Homeland 2050. I showed him the numerical index, and he whipped it out and opened it like an old hand. My, he caught on quickly. He made another note in his book . . well, it went on like that, and inside of twenty minutes I bet he could take over from me any time and not give Mr. Parker a minute's worry, which is more than I can say for some of the girls who have been working here for years, like that Patty Mawson with her blonde hair and her awful New Look.

Well, that boy picked my brains dry in short order, and he got up and for a moment I thought he was going to kiss my hand like a Frenchman or a European, but he didn't, he just thanked me as if I had given him the crown jewels or my hand in marriage and went out to do the same for Mr. Parker, and all I can say is, I wish one-tenth of the customers showed as much good house-breaking.

I'll tell you one thing, though. One of these days I'm going to win a radio quiz or have an uncle die—not Uncle Fred or Uncle Tom, but some uncle I never heard of—and get a million dollars or so, and I'm going to go out and buy a whole truckload of big heavy clocks. Then I will work one more week and trace the call of every bubblehead who calls "information" and asks what time it is, instead of dialling the time number. Then I will quit my job and take my truck and go to every one of those houses and heave a clock through whatever window to the front parlor they've left closed.

Maybe I'll need two trucks.

5

HELMUTH STOYE

Grace . . . Grace . . . *Grace!*

Oh, my darling, my gentle, my soft little bird with the husky voice. Miss Funny-Brows. Little Miss Teeth. You used to laugh such a special laugh when I made up new names for you, Coral-cache, Cadenza, Viola-voice . . . and you'll never laugh again, because I killed you.

I killed you, I killed you.

Yesterday I stopped all the clocks.

I couldn't stand it. It was wrong; it was a violation. You were dead. I drew the blinds and sat in the dark, not really believing that it had happened—how *could* it happen? You're *Grace,* you're the humming in the kitchen, the quick footfalls in the foyer as I come up the porch steps. I think for a while I believed that your coming back was the most real, the most obvious thing; in a moment, any moment, you would come in and kiss the nape of my neck; you would be smelling of vanilla and cut flowers and you'd laugh at me and together we'd fling up the blinds and let in the light. And then Tinkle struck—Tinkle, the eight-foot grandfather's clock with the *basso profundo* chime. That was when I knew what was real. It was real that you were dead, it was real . . .

I got angry at that violation, that sacrilege, that clock. What right had the clock to strike, the hands to move? How could it go on? It was wrong. I got up and stopped it. I think I spoke to it, not harshly, angry as I was; I said, "You don't know, do you, Tinkle? No one's told you yet," and I caught it by its swinging neck and held it until its ticking brain was quiet. I told all the clocks, one by one, that you were dead—the glowing Seth Thomas ship's clock, with its heavy threads and its paired syllables, and Drowsy the alarm and the cuckoo with the cleft palate who couldn't say anything but "hook-who!"

A truck roared by outside and I remember the new surge of fury because of it, and then the thought that the driver hadn't been told yet . . . and then the mad thought that the news would spread from these silent clocks, from these drawn blinds, spread like a cloud-shadow over the world, and when it touched birds, they would glide to the ground and crouch motionless, with no movement in their jewelled eyes; when it touched machines, they would slow and stop; when it touched flowers they would close themselves into little soft fists and bend to knuckle the earth; when it touched people they would finish that stride, end that sentence, slowing, softening, and would sink down and be still. There would be no noise or confusion as the world slipped into its stasis, and nothing would grow but silence. And the sun would hang on the horizon with its face thickly veiled, and there would be eternal dusk. These things would not happen as a tribute to you; nothing would grieve, for grief, God help me, is too alive a thing . . .

That was yesterday, and I was angry. I am not angry today. It was better, yesterday, the sitting in turmoil and uselessness, the useless raging up and down rooms so hollow, yet still so full of you they would not echo. It got dark, you see, and in good time the blinds were brighter than the walls around them again. I looked out, squinting through grainy eyelids, and saw a man walking by, walking easily, his hands in his pockets, and he was whistling. After that I could not be angry any more, not at the man, not at the morning. I knew only the great cruel pressure of a fact, a fact worse than the fact of emptiness or of death—the fact that nothing ever stops, that things must go on.

ᵗt was better to be angry and to lose myself in uselessness. Now I am ⁿot angry and I have no choice but to think usefully. I have lived a useful life and have built it all on useful thinking, and if I had not thought so much and so carefully Grace would be here with me now, with her voice like a large soft breeze in some springtime place, and perhaps tickling the side of my neck with feather-touches of her moving lips . . . it was my useful, questing, thirsty thought which killed her, killed her.

The accident was all of two years ago—almost two years, anyway. We had driven all the way back from Springfield without stopping and we were very tired. Grace and Mr. Share and I were squeezed into the front seat. Mr. Share was a man Grace had invented long before, even before we were married. He was a big invisible fat man who always sat by the right-hand window and always looked out to the side so that he never watched us. But since he was so fat, Grace had to press up close to me as we drove.

There was a stake-bodied truck bowling along ahead of us and in the back of it was a spry old man, or perhaps a weather-beaten young man—you couldn't tell—in blue dungarees and a red shirt. He had a yellow woolen muffler tied around his waist and the simple strip of material made all the difference between "clothes" and "costume."

Behind him, lashed to the bed of the truck just back of the cab, was a large bundle of burlap. It would have made an adequate seat for him, cushioned and out of the wind. But the man seemed to take the wind as a heady beverage and the leaping floor as a challenge. He stood with his arms away from his sides and his knees slightly flexed and rode the truck as if it were a live thing. He yielded himself to each lurch and bump, brought himself back with each recession, guarding his equilibrium with an easy virtuosity.

Grace was, I think, dozing; my shout of delighted laughter at the performance on the bounding stage before us brought her upright. She laughed with me for the laugh alone, for she had not looked through the windshield yet, and she kissed my cheek.

He saw her do it, the man on the truck, and he laughed with us. "He's *our* kind of people," Grace said. "A pixie," I agreed, and we laughed again.

The man took off an imaginary plumed hat, swung it low toward us, but very obviously toward Grace. She nodded back to him, with a slight sidewise turn of her face as it went down that symbolized a deep curtsey.

Then he held out his elbow, and the pose, the slightly raised shoulder over which he looked fondly at the air over his bent arm, showed that he had given his arm to a lady. The lady was Grace, who, of course, would be charmed to join him in the dance . . . she clapped her hands and crowed with delight, as she watched her imaginary self with the courtly, colorful figure ahead.

The man stepped with dainty dignity to the middle of the truck and bowed again, and you could all but hear the muted minuet as it began. It was a truly wonderful thing to watch, this pantomime; the man knew the ancient, stately steps to perfection, and they were unflawed by the careening surface on which they were performed. There was no mockery in the miming, but simply the fullness of good, the sheer, unspoiled sharing of a happy magic. He bowed, he took her hand, smiled back into her eyes as she pirouetted behind him. He stood back to the line waiting his turn, nodding slightly to the music; he dipped ever so little, twice, as his turn came, and stepped gracefully out to meet her, smiling again.

I don't know what made me look up. We were nearing the Speedway Viaduct and the truck ahead was just about to pass under it. High up over our heads was the great span, and as my eye followed its curve, to see the late afternoon sun on the square guard-posts which bounded the elevated road, three of the posts exploded outward, and the blunt nose of a heavy truck plowed through and over the edge, to slip and catch and slip again, finally to teeter to a precarious stop. Apparently its trailer was loaded with light steel girders; one of them slipped over the tractor's crumpled shoulder and speared down toward us.

Our companion of the minuet on the truck ahead, had finished his dance and, turned to us, was bowing low, smiling, looking up through his eyebrows at us. The girder's end took him on the back of the head. It did not take the head off; it obliterated it. The body struck flat and lay still, as still as wet paper stuck to glass. The girder bit a large piece out of the tailgate and somersaulted to the right, while I braked and swerved dangerously away from it. Fortunately there were no cars coming toward us.

There was, of course, a long, mixed-up, horrified sequence of the two truckdrivers, the one ahead and the one who came down later from the viaduct and was sick. Ambulances and bystanders and a lot of talk . . . none of it matters, really. No one ever found out who the dead man was. He had no luggage and no identification; he had been hitchhiking and he had over ninety dollars in his pocket. He might have been anybody—someone from show business, or a writer perhaps, on a haywire vacation of his own wild devising. I suppose that doesn't matter, either. What does matter is that he died while Grace was in a very close communion with what he was doing and her mind was wide open for his fantasy. Mine is, generally, I suppose; but at that particular moment, when I had seen the smash above and the descending girder, I was wide awake, on guard. I think that had a lot to do with what has happened since. I think it has everything to do with Grace's—with Grace's—.

There is no word for it. I can say this, though. Grace and I were never alone together again until the day she died. Died, died, Grace is dead.

Grace!

I can go on with my accursed useful thinking now, I suppose.

Grace was, of course, badly shaken, and I did what I could for her over the next few weeks. I tried my best to understand how it was affecting her. (That's what I mean by useful thinking—trying to understand. Trying and trying—prying and prying. Arranging, probing, finding out. Getting a glimpse, a scent of danger, rooting it out—bringing it out into the open where it can get at you.) Rest and new clothes and alcohol rubdowns; the theatre, music and music, always music, for she could lose herself in it, riding its flux, feeling and folding herself in it, following it, sometimes, with her hushed, true voice, sometimes lying open to it, letting it play its colors and touches over her.

There is always an end to patience, however. After two months, knowing her as I did, I knew that there was more here than simple shock. If I had known her less well—if I had cared less, even, it couldn't have mattered.

It began with small things. There were abstractions which were unusual in so vibrant a person. In a quiet room, her face would listen to music; sometimes I had to speak twice and then repeat what I had said. Once I came home and found supper not started, the bed not made. Those things were not important—I am not a fusspot nor an autocrat; but I was shaken when, after calling her repeatedly I found her in the guest room, sitting on the bed without lights. I had no idea she was in there; I just walked in and snapped on the light in the beginnings of panic because she seemed not to be in the house; she had not answered me. And at first it was as if she had not noticed the sudden yellow blaze from the paired lamps; she was gazing at the wall and on her face was an expression of perfect peace. She was wide awake—at least her eyes were. I called her: "Grace!"

"Hellion, darling," she said quietly. Her head turned casually toward me and she smiled—oh, those perfect teeth of hers!—and her smile was only partly for me; the rest of it was inside, with the nameless things with which she had been communing.

I sat beside her, amazed, and took her hands. I suppose I spluttered a bit, "Grace, are you all right? Why didn't you answer? The bed's not—have you been out? What's happened? Here—let me see if you have a fever."

Her eyes were awake, yes; but not awake to me, to here and now.

They were awake and open to some *elsewhere* matters . . . She acquiesced as I felt her forehead and cheeks for fever, and while I was doing it I could see the attention of those warm, pleased, living eyes shifting from the things they had been seeing, to me. It was as if they were watching a scene fade out while another was brought in on a screen, so that for a second all focussing points on the first picture were lost, and there was a search for a focussing point on the second. And then, apparently, the picture of Helmuth Stoye sitting next to her, holding one of her hands, running his right palm across her forehead and down her cheek, came into sharp, true value and she said, "Darling! You're home! What happened? Holiday or strike? You're not sick?"

I said, "Sweetheart, it's after seven."

"No!" She rose, smoothed her hair in front of the mirror. Hers was a large face and her appeal had none of the doll-qualities, the candy-and-peaches qualities of the four-color ads. Her brow and cheekbones were wide and strong, and the hinges of her jaw were well-marked, hollowed underneath. Her nostrils were flared and sensuously tilted and her shoulders too wide to be suitable for fashion plates or pinups. But clothes hung from those shoulders with the graceful majesty of royal capes and her breasts were large, high, separated and firm. Her torso was flat and strong and strength was in the smooth turn of muscles in her arms and sturdy legs. Yet for all her width and flatness and strength, for all her powerfully-set features, she was woman all through; and with clothes or without, she looked it.

She said, "I had no idea . . . after seven! Oh, darling, I'm sorry. You poor thing, and no dinner yet. Come help me," and she dashed out of the room, leaving me flapping my lips, calling, "But Grace! Wait! Tell me first what's the mat—"

And when I got to the kitchen she was whipping up a dinner, efficiently, deftly, and all my questions could wait, could be interrupted with "Hellion, honey, open these, will you?" "I don't know, b'loved; we'll dig it out after supper. Will you see if there're any French-fries in the freezer?"

And afterward she remembered that "The Pearl" was playing at the Ascot Theater, and we'd missed it when it first came to town, and this was the last night . . . we went, and the picture was fine, and we talked of nothing else that night.

I could have forgotten about that episode, I suppose. I could have forgotten about any one of them—the time she turned her gaze so strangely inward when she was whipping cream, and turned it to butter because she simply forgot to stop whipping it when it was ready; the times she had the strong, uncharacteristic urges to do and feel things which had never interested her before—to lose herself in distances from high buildings and tall hills, to swim under water for long, frightening minutes; to hear new and ever new kinds of music —saccharine foxtrots and atonal string quartets, arrangements for percussion alone and oriental modes. And foods—rattlesnake ribs, moo goo gai pan, curried salmon with green rice, *Paella* with its chicken and clams, headcheese, *canolas,* sweet-and-pungent pork; all these Grace made herself, and well.

But in food as in music, in new sensualities as in new activities, there was no basic change in Grace. These were additions only; for all the exoticism of the dishes, for example, we still had and enjoyed the things she had always made—the gingered leg of lamb, the acorn-squash filled with creamed onions, the *crepes suzettes.* She could still be lost in the architecture of Bach's "Passacaglia and Fugue" and in the raw heartbeat of the Haggard-Bauduc "Big Noise from Winnetka." Because she had this new passion for underwater swimming, she did not let it take from her enjoyment of highboard diving. Her occasional lapses from efficiency, as in the whipped-cream episode, were rare and temporary. Her sometime dreaminess, when she would forget appointments and arrangements and time itself, happened so seldom that, in all justice, they could have been forgotten, or put down, with all my vaunted understanding, to some obscure desire for privacy, for aloneness. (No human soul should be denied the privilege of solitude, for only in solitude can the mind resolve its intake with its wealth . . .)

So—she had everything she had always had, and now more. She was everything she always had been, and now more. She did everything she had always done, and now more. Then what, what on earth and in heaven, was I bothered, worried, and—and afraid of?

I know now. It was jealousy. It was—one of the jealousies.

There wasn't Another Man. That kind of poison springs from insecurity—from the knowledge that there's enough wrong with you that the chances are high that another man—any other man—could do a better job than you in some department of your woman's needs.

Besides, that kind of thing can never be done by the Other Man alone; your woman must cooperate, wilfully and consciously, or it can't happen. And Grace was incapable of that. Should the fantastic situation arise, should she want to, she would have cut me off with one clean blow and gone to the other with all her heart. Suspicion of such a thing would be unjust, weak, and psychopathic, and I had none of it.

No; it was because of the sharing we had had. My marriage was a magic one because of what we shared; because of our ability to see a red-gold leaf, exchange a glance and say never a word, for we knew so well each other's pleasure, its causes and expressions and associations. The pleasures were not the magic; the sharing was.

A poor analogy: you have a roommate who is a very dear friend, and together you have completely redecorated your room. The colors, the lighting, the concealed shelves and drapes, all are a glad communion of your separated taste. You are both proud and fond of your beautiful room . . . and one day you come home and find a new television set. Your roommate has acquired it and brought it in to surprise you. You are surprised and you are happy, too, and you enjoy the new extra pleasures of this conqueror of space and time; but slowly an ugly thing creeps into your mind. The set is a big thing, an important, dominating thing in the room and in the things for which you use the room. And it is *his*—not mine or ours, but *his*. There is his unspoken, undemanded authority in the choice of programs in the evenings; and where are the chess games, the folksinging with your guitar, the long hours of phonograph music? They are there, of course, ready for you every moment; no one has taken them away. But now the room is different. It can continue to be a happy room; only a petty mind would resent the new shared riches; but the fact that the *source* of the riches is not shared, was not planned by you both, was not discussed or agreed upon even when there was no possibility for disagreement—this changes the room and everything in it, the colors, the people, the shape and warmth.

So with my marriage. A thing had come to Grace which made us both richer . . . but I did not share that source; and damn, damn my selfishness, I could not bear it; if I could not share it, I wanted her deprived of it.

And I poked and I prodded and pried, and now look . . . *Grace is dead!*

Petalfinger, Langue-douce, *Ol' Miss Structural Shoulders . . . Tease-tears, Mother-mouth . . . Once you said, "Hellion, darling, you know how I hold you?" and I said, "Show me," and you cupped your hands together, closed tight, and raised them to your face, and opened them swiftly to peer inside, to clap them shut again, to hug them tight to your breast while you laughed with delight at the pretend-thing you had seen so closely held within that soft strong chamber . . . "Like that," you said, and I could have cried.*

So . . . there was a long period when I kept my questing to myself, which was a sin; poor possessed darling, she shared everything with me that she could, I know it now; it was I who did not share, but buttoned up my pointed studyings, my twisted, hunting, fretting jealousy within myself. What was it? What was it? Why was she different? Mine was a strange and devious melody against that reiterated choral phrase . . .

I was gentle; beginning with, "How do you feel, sweetheart? But you aren't all right; what were you thinking of? It couldn't be 'nothing' . . . you were giving more attention to it than you are to me right now!"

I was firm; beginning with, "Now look, darling; there's something here that we have to face. Please help. Now exactly why are you so interested in hearing that Hindemith sketch? You never used to be interested in music like that. It has no melody, no key, no rhythm; it's unpredictable and ugly. I'm quoting you, darling; that's what you used to say about it. And now you want to soak yourself in it. Why? Why? What has changed you? Yes—people must grow and change; I know that. But—growing so fast, so quickly, in so many different directions! Tell me now. Tell me exactly why you feel moved to hear this thing at this time."

And—I was angry, beginning with, "Grace! Why didn't you answer me? Oh, you heard me, did you? What did I say? Yes; that's right; you did . . . then why didn't you answer? Well? Not important? Not important to reply to a general remark like the one I made? You'll have to realize that it's important to me to be answered when I speak to you!"

She tried. I could see her trying. I wouldn't stop. I began to watch her every minute. I stopped waiting for openings and made them myself. I trapped her. I put on music in which I knew she would be lost and spoke softly, and when she did not answer, I would kick

over my chair with a shout and demand that she speak up. She tried
. . . Sometimes she was indignant, and demanded the peace that
should be her right. Once she got hysterical and said I was going
mad, and once I struck her.

That did it. Oh, the poor, brutalized beloved!

Now I can see it; *now!*

She never could answer me, until the one time. What could she
have said? Her "I don't know!" was the truth. Her patience went too
far, her anger not far enough and I know that her hurt was without
limits.

I struck her and she answered my questions. I was even angrier
after she had than I had been before, for I felt that she had known all
along, that until now she had withheld what she knew; and I cursed
myself for not using force earlier and more often. I did. For not
hitting *Grace* before!

I came home that night tired, for there was trouble at the shop; I
suppose I was irascible with the compositors, but that was only because I had not slept well the night before, which was because . . .
anyway, when I got home, I slammed the door, which was not usual,
and, standing there with my raincoat draped over one shoulder,
looking at the beautiful spread on the coffee table in front of the
fireplace, I demanded, "What's that for?" There were canapes and
dainty round and rolled and triangular sandwiches; a frosty bluish
beverage twinkling with effervescence in its slender pitcher; there
were stars and flowers of tiny pickles, pastes and dressings, a lovely
coral potato-chip and covered dishes full of delicate mysteries. There
were also two small and vivid bowls of cut blooms, beautifully arranged. She said, "Why, for us. Just for us two."

I said, "Good God. Is there anything the matter with sitting up to
a table and eating like a human being?" Then I went to hang up the
coat.

She had not moved when I came back; she was still standing facing the door and perhaps a quarter of her welcoming smile was
frozen on her face.

No, I said to myself, no you don't. Don't go soft, now. You have
her on the run; let's break this thing up now, all at once, all over the
place. The healing can come later. I said "Well?"

She turned to me, her eyes full of tears. "Helmuth . . ." she said
weakly. I waited. "Why did you . . . it was only a surprise A

pretty surprise for you. We haven't been together for so long . . . you've been . . ."

"You haven't been yourself since that accident," I said coldly. "I think you know why, and you won't tell me. I think you like being different. Turn off the tears, honey. They'll do you no good."

"I'm *not* different!" she wailed; and then she began to cry in earnest. "I can't stand it." she moaned, "I can't, I can't . . . Helmuth, you're losing your mind. I'm going to leave you. Leave you . . . maybe for just a while, maybe for . . ."

"You're going to *what?*" I whispered, going very close to her.

She made a supreme effort and answered, flatly, looking me in the eye, "I'm going, Helmuth; I've got to."

I think if she'd seen it coming she would have stood back; perhaps I'd have missed her. I think that if she'd expected it, she would have fled after I hit her once. Instead she stood still, unutterably shocked, unmoving, so it was easy to hit her again.

She stood watching me, her face dead, her eyes, and, increasingly, the flames of the fingermarks on her bleached cheeks, burning. In that instant I knew how she felt, what her mind was trying frantically to do. She was trying to think of a way to make this a dream, to explain it as an accident, to find some excuse for me; and the growing sting in her beaten cheeks slowly proved and reproved that it was true. I know this, because the tingling sting of my hands was proving it to me.

Finally she put one hand up to her face. She said, *"Why?"*

I said, "Because you have kept a secret from me."

She closed her eyes, swayed. I did not touch her. Still with her eyes closed, she said:

"It wants to be left alone. It feeds on vital substance, but there is always an excess . . . there is in a healthy person, anyway. It only takes a small part of that excess, not enough to matter, not enough for anyone but a jealous maniac like you to notice. It lives happily in a happy person, it lives richly in a mind rich with the experience of the senses, feeding only on what is spare and extra. And you have made me unfit, forever and ever, with your prodding and scarring, and because you have found it out it can never be left alone again, it can never be safe again, it can never be safe while you live, it can never be content, it can never leave me while I live, it can never, it can never, it can never." Her voice did not trail off—it simply stopped, without a rise or fall in pitch or volume, without any normal human aural punctuation. What she said made no sense to me; it was then that I was sure she had known all along what was wrong with her, that she had concealed it from me, that if I had beaten her sooner I'd have gotten the whole mad thing from her, that what she was doing now was to cloak the truth in cryptic histrionics. I snarled at her—I don't think it was a word—and turned my back. I heard her fall, and when I looked she was crumpled up like a castoff, empty, trodden-on white paper box.

I fought my battle between fury and tenderness that night and met the morning with the dull conclusion that Grace was possessed and that what had possessed her had gone mad . . . that I didn't know where I was, what to do; that I must save her if I could, but in any case relentlessly track down and destroy the—the—No, it hadn't a name . . . Grace was conscious, docile, and had nothing to say. She was not angry or resentful; she was nothing but—obedient. She did what she was told, and when she finished she stopped until she was told to do something else.

I called in Doc Knapp. He said that what was mostly wrong with her was outside the field of a medical doctor, but he didn't think a little regimented rest and high-powered food therapy would hurt. I let him take her to the hospital. I think I was almost glad to see her go. No, I wasn't. I couldn't be glad. How could I be glad about anything? Anyway, Knapp would have her rested and fed and quieted down and fattened up and supplied with two alcohol rubs a day until she was fit to start some sort of psychotherapy. She always liked alcohol rubs. She killed her—she died just before the second alcohol rub, on the fourth day . . . Knapp said, when he took her away, "I can't understand it, Helmuth. It's like shock, but in Grace that doesn't seem right at all. She's too strong, too alive."

Not any more she isn't.

My mind's wandering. Hold on tight, you . . . Hold . . .

Where am I? I am at home. I am sitting in the chair. I am getting up. Uh! I have fallen down. Why did I fall down? Because my leg was asleep. Why was it asleep? Because I have been sitting here all day and most of the night without moving. The doorbell is ringing. Why is the doorbell ringing? Because someone wants to come in. Who is it? Someone who comes visiting at two o' clock in the morning, I know that because I started the clocks again and Tinkle says what time it is. Who visits at two o' clock in the morning? Drunks and police and death. There is a small person's shadow on the frosted door, which I open, "Hello small person, Grace is dead." It is not a drunk it is not the police it is Death who has a child's long lashes and small hands, one to hold up a blank piece of paper for me to stare at, one to slide the knife between my ribs, feel it scrape on my breastbone . . . a drama, Enter Knife Left Center, and I fall back away from the door, my blood leaping lingering after the withdrawn blade, Grace, Grace, treasure me in your cupped hands—

6

LAWRENCE DELEHANTY

I got the call on the car radio just before half-past two. Headquarters had a phone tip of some funny-business out on Poplar Street in Homeland. The fellow who phoned was a milk-truck dispatcher on his way to work. He says he thought he saw someone at the door of this house stab the guy who came to the door, close the door and beat it.

I didn't see anyone around. There were lights on in the house—in what seemed to be the living room and in the hallway just inside the door. I could see how anyone passing by could get a look at such a thing if it had happened.

I told Sam to stay in the prowl-car and ran up the path to the house. I knocked on the door, figuring maybe there'd be prints on the bell-push. There was no answer. I tried again and finally opened the door, turning the knob by the shaft, which was long enough for me to get ahold of without touching the knob.

It had happened all right. The stiff was just inside the door. The guy was on his back, arms and legs spread out, with the happiest look on his face I ever saw. No kidding—that guy looked as if he'd just been given a million dollars. He had blood all over his front.

I took one look and went back and called Sam. He came up asking questions and stopped asking when he saw the stiff. "Go phone," I told him, "and be careful. Don't touch nothin'." While he was phoning I took a quick squint around. There was a few dirty dishes in the kitchen sink on the table, and half a bottle of some liqueur on an end table in the living room sitting right on the polished wood, where it'd sure leave a ring. I'd say this guy had been in there some time without trying to clean up any.

I inched open the drawer in the big sideboard in the dining room and all the silver was there. None of the drawers in the two bedrooms was open; it looked like a grudge-killing of some kind; there wasn't no robbery I could see.

Just as I came back down the stairs the doorbell rang. Sam came out of the front room and I waved him back. "There goes our prints on the bell," I said. "I'll get it." I pussyfooted to the door and pulled it wide open, real sudden.

"Mr. Stoye?" says a kid standing there. He's about fourteen, maybe, small for his age. He's standing out there, three o'clock in the morning, mind you, smiling real polite, just like it was afternoon and he'd come around to sell raffle tickets. I felt a retch starting in my stomach just then—don't know why. The sight of the stiff hadn't bothered me none. Maybe something I ate. I swallowed it down and said, "Who are you?"

He said, "I would like to see Mr. Stoye."

"Bub," I said, "Mr. Stoye isn't seeing anybody just now. What do you want?"

He squinted around me and saw the stiff. I guess I should've stopped him but he had me offguard. And you know, he didn't gasp or jump back or any of the things you expect anyone to do. He just straightened up, and he smiled. "Well," he says, sort of patting his jacket pocket, "I don't s'pose there's anything I can do now," and he smiles at me, real bright. "Well, good night," he says, and turns to go.

I nabbed him and spun him inside and shut the door. "What do you know about this?" I asked him.

He looked at the stiff, where I nodded, and he looked at me. The stiff didn't bother him. "Why, nothing," he said. "I don't know anything at all. Is that really Mr. Stoye?"

"You know it is."

"I think I did know, all right," he said. "Well, can I go home now? Dad doesn't know I'm out."

"I bet he doesn't. Let's see what you got in your pockets."

He didn't seem to mind. I frisked him. Inside that jacket pocket was a jump-knife—one of those Army issue paratrooper's clasp-knives with a spring; touch the button and *click!* you've got four and a half inches of razor-steel sticking out of your fist, ready for business. A lot of 'em got out in war surplus. Too many. We're always finding 'em in carcasses. I told him he'd have to stick around. He frowned a little bit and said he was worried about his father, but I didn't let that make no difference. He gave his name without any trouble. His name was Ronnie Daniels. He was a clean-cut little fellow, just as nice and polite as I ever saw.

Well, I asked him all kinds of questions. His answers just didn't make no sense. He said he couldn't recall just what it was he wanted to see Stoye about. He said he had never met Stoye and had never been out here before. He said he got the address from knowing the phone number; went right up to the telephone company and wormed it out of one of the girls there. He said he didn't remember at all where he got the number from. I looked at the number just out of curiosity; it was Homeland 2065, which didn't mean nothing to me.

After that there wasn't anything to do until the homicide squad got there. I knew the kid's old man, this Daniels, would have to get dragged into it, but that wasn't for me to do; that would be up to the detective looey. I turned the kid over to Sam. I remember Sam's face just then; it turned pale. I asked him what was the matter but he just swallowed hard and said he didn't know; maybe it was the pickles he had with his midnight munch. He took the kid into the front room and they got into a fine conversation about cops and murders. He sure seemed to be a nice, healthy, normal kid. Quiet and obedient— you know. I can't really blame Sam for what happened.

The squad arrived—two carloads, sirens and all, making so much noise I thought sure Stoye would get up and tell 'em to let him rest in peace—and in they came—photogs, print men, and the usual bunch of cocky plainclothes men. They swarmed all over. Flick was the man in charge, stocky, tough, mad at everybody all the time, especially on the night detail. Man, how he hated killers that worked at night and dragged him away from his pinochle!

I told the whole story to him and his little book. "His name's Tommy," I said, "and he says he lives at—"

"His name's Ronnie," says Sam, from behind me.

"Hey," I says. "I thought I told you to stay with him."

"I had to go powder my nose," says Sam. "My stomach done a flip-flop a while back that had me worried. It's okay. Brown was dusting in the room there when I went out. And besides, that's a nice little kid. He wouldn't—"

"Brown!" Flick roared.

Brown came out of the living room. "Yeah, Chief."

"You done in the front room?"

"Yeah; everything I could think of. No prints except Stoye's, except on the phone. I guess they'd be Sam's."

"The kid's all right?"

"Was when I left," said Brown, and went back into the living room. Flick and me and Sam went into the front room.

The kid was gone.

Sam turned pale. "Ronnie!" he bellows. "Hey, you, Ronnie!"

No answer.

"You hadda go powder your big fat nose," says Flick to Sammy. Sam looked bad. The soft seats in a radio car feel awful good to a harness bull, and I think Sam decided right then that he'd be doing his job on foot for quite a while.

It was easy to see what had happened. Sammy left the room, and then Brown got finished and went out, and in those few seconds he was alone, the kid had stepped through the short hall into the kitchen and out the side door. Sam looked even worse when I suddenly noticed that the ten-inch ham slicer was gone from the knife rack; that was one of the first things I looked at after I saw Stoye had been stabbed. You always look for the kitchen knives in a home stabbing.

Flick turned to Sam and opened his mouth, and in that moment, believe me, I was glad I was me and not him even if Sam has got the most whistleable wife I ever saw. I thought fast. "Flick." I said, "I know where that kid's going. He was all worried about what his old man would think. Here—I got his address in my book."

"Okay," snapped Flick. "Get down there right away. I'll call what's-his-name—Daniels—from here and tell him to wait for the kid and hold him if he shows up before you do. Get down there, now, and hurry. Keep your eyes peeled on the way; you might see him on the street. Look out for that knife. Kelly, get a general alarm out for that kid soon's I'm off the phone. Or send it from your car." He turned back to me, thumbed at Sam. "Take him with you," he says, "I want him out of my sight. And if his hot damned nose gets shiny again, see he don't use your summons-book."

We ran out and piled into the car and took off. We didn't go straight to Daniels' address. Sam hoped we would see the kid on the way; I think he had some idea of a heroic hand-to-hand grapple with the kid in which maybe he'd get a little bit stabbed in line of duty, which might quiet Flick down some. So we cut back and forth between Myrtle Avenue and Varick; the kid could've taken a trolley on one or a bus on the other. We found out soon enough that he'd done neither; he'd found a cab; and I'd like to know who it was drove that hack. He must've been a jet pilot.

It was real dark on Daniels' street. The nearest streetlight was a couple hundred feet away, and there was a big maple tree in Daniels' yard that cast thick black shadow all over the front of the house. I missed the number in the dark and pulled over to the curb; I knew it must be somewhere around here.

Me and Sam got out and Sam went up on the nearest porch to see the house number; Daniels was two doors away. That's how it was we happened to be far to the left of the house when the killer rang Daniels' bell.

We both saw it, Sam and me, that small dark shadow up against Daniels' front door. The door had a glass panel and there was some sort of a night-light on inside, so all we saw was the dark blob waiting there, ringing on the bell. I guess Daniels was awake after Flick's phone call.

I grabbed Sam's arm and he shook me free. He had his gun out. I said, "What are you gonna do?" He was all hopped up, I guess.

He wanted to make an arrest or something. He wanted to be The Man here. He didn't want to go back on a beat. He said, "You know how Stoye was killed. Just like that."

That made sense, but I said, "Sam! You're not going to shoot a kid!"

"Just wing him, if it looks—"

Just then the door opened. There wasn't much light. I saw Daniels, a stocky, balding man with a very mild face, peering out. I saw an arm come up from that small shadowy blob. Then Sam fired, twice. There was a shrill scream, and the clatter of a knife on the porch. I heard Ronnie yell, "Dad! Dad!" Then Sam and I were pounding over to the house. Daniels was frozen there, staring down onto the porch and the porch steps.

At the foot of the steps, the kid was huddled. He was unconscious. The ham slicer gleamed wickedly on the steps near his hand.

I called out, "Mr. Daniels! We're the police. Better get back inside." And together Sam and I lifted up the kid. He didn't weigh much. Going inside, Sam tripped over his big flat feet and I swore at him.

We put the kid down on the couch. I didn't see any blood. Daniels was dithering around like an old lady. I pushed him into a chair and told him to stay there and try to take it easy. Sam went to phone Flick. I started going over the kid.

There was no blood.

There were no holes in him, either; not a nick, not a graze. I stood back and scratched my head.

Daniels said, "What's wrong with him? What happened?"

Inside, I heard Sam at the phone. "Yeah, we got 'im. It was the kid all right. Tried to stab his old man. I winged him. Huh? I don't know. We're looking him over now. Yeah."

"Take it easy," I said again to Daniels. He looked rough. "Stay right there."

I went to the door, which was standing open. Over by the porch rail I saw something shining green and steel-blue. I started over to it, tripped on something yielding, and went flat on my face. Sam came running out. "What's the—*uh!*" and he came sailing out and landed on top of me. He's a big boy. I said, "My goodness, Sam, that was careless of you," or words to that effect, and some other things amounting to maybe Flick had the right idea about him.

"Damn it, Delehanty," he says, "I tripped on something. What are you doing sprawled out here, anyway?"

"I was looking for—" and I picked it up, the green and steel-blue thing. It was a Finnish sheath-knife, long and pointed, double razor-edges, scrollwork up near the hilt. Blood, still a bit tacky, in the scrollwork.

"Where'd that come from?" grunted Sam, and took it. "Hey! Flick just told me the medic says Stoye was stabbed with a two-edged knife. You don't suppose—"

"I don't suppose nothin'," I said, getting up. "On your feet, Sam. Flick finds us like this, he'll think we're playing mumblety-peg . . . tell you what, Sam; I took a jump-knife off the kid out there, and it only had a single edge. And that ham slicer has only a single edge." I went down the steps and picked it up. Sam pointed out that the kid had never had a chance to use the ham slicer.

I shrugged that off. Flick was paid the most for thinking—let him do most of the thinking. I went to the side of the door and looked at the bell-push to get an idea as to how it might take prints, and then went inside. Sam came straight in and tripped again.

"Pick up ya feet!"

Sam had fallen to his knees this time. He growled something and, swinging around, went to feeling around the porch floor with his hands. "Now it's patty-cake," I said. "For pete's sake, Sam—"

Inside Daniels was on the floor by the couch, rubbing the kid's hands, saying, real scared like, "Ronnie! Ronnie!"

"Delehanty!"

Half across the room, I turned. Sam was still on his knees just outside the door and his face was something to see. "Delehanty, just come here, will you?"

There was something in his voice that left no room for a wisecrack. I went right to him. He motioned me down beside him, took my wrist and pushed my hand downward.

It touched something, but—*there was nothing there!*

We looked at each other, and I wish I could write down what that look said.

I touched it again, felt it. It was like cloth, then like flesh, yielding, then bony.

"It's the Invisible Man!" breathed Sam, bug-eyed.

"Stop talking nonsense," I said thickly. "And besides, it's a woman. Look here."

"I'll take your word for it," said Sam, backing away. "Anyhow, I'm a married man."

Cars came, screaming as usual. "Here's Flick."

Flick and his mob came streaming up the steps. "What's going on here? Where's the killer?"

Sam stood in front of the doorway, holding his hands out like he was unsnarling traffic. He was shaking. "Walk over this side," he said, "or you'll step on her."

"What are you gibbering about? Step on who?"

Sam flapped his hands and pointed at the floor. Flick and Brown and the others all looked down, then up again. I don't know what got into me. I just couldn't help it. I said, "He found a ladybug and he don't want you to step on it."

Flick got so mad, so quick, he didn't even swear. He made a sort of bubbling noise and pushed past Sam into the house. Sam looked at me and said, "My pal."

Before he could kill me I said, "He'll find out soon enough." That stopped Sam; he thought it over and then began to grin. Flick really had something in store for him.

We went inside. The medic was working over the boy, who was still unconscious. Flick was demanding, "Well? Well? What's the matter with him?"

"Not a thing I can find out, not without a fluoroscope and some blood tests. Shock, maybe."

"Shot?" gasped Daniels.

"Definitely not," said the M. O.

Flick said, very, very quietly, "Sam told me over the phone that he had shot the boy. What about this, Delehanty? Can you talk sense, or is Sam contagious?"

I told him what we had seen from the side of the house. I told him that we couldn't be sure who it was that rang the bell, but that we saw whoever it was raise a knife to strike and then Sam fired and then we ran up and found the kid lying at the bottom of the steps. We heard a knife fall.

"Did you hear him fall down the steps?"

"No," said Sam.

"Shut up, you," said Flick, not looking at him. "Well, Delehanty?"

"I don't think so," I said, thinking hard. "It all happened so fast."

"It was a girl."

"What was a girl? Who said that?"

Daniels shuffled forward. "I answered the door. A girl was there. She had a knife. A long one, pointed. I think it was double-edged."

"Here it is," said Sam brightly.

Flick raised his eyes to heaven, moved his lips silently, and took the knife.

"That's it," said Daniels. "Then there was a gunshot, and she screamed and fell."

"She did, huh? Where is she?"

"I—I don't know," said Daniels in puzzlement.

"She's still there," said Sam smugly. I thought, oh-oh. This is it.

"Thank you, Sam," said Flick icily. "Would you be good enough to point her out to me?"

Sam nodded. "There. Right there," and he pointed.

"See her, lying there in the doorway," I piped up.

Flick looked at Sam, and he looked at me. "Are you guys trying to —*uk!*" His eyes bulged, and his jaw went slack.

Everyone in the room froze. There, in plain sight on the porch, lay the body of a girl. She was quite a pretty girl, small and dark. She had a bullet hole on each side of her neck, a little one here and a great big one over here.

7

THEODORE STURGEON

I don't much care for the way this story's going.

You want to write a story, see, and you sit down in front of the mill, wait until that certain feeling comes to you, hold off a second longer just to be quite sure that you know exactly what you want to do, take a deep breath, and get up and make a pot of coffee.

This sort of thing is likely to go for days, until you are out of coffee and can't get more until you can pay for same, which you can do by writing a story and selling it; or until you get tired of messing around and sit down and write a yarn purely by means of knowing how to do it and applying the knowledge

But this story's different. It's coming out as if it were being dictated to me and I'm not used to that. It's a haywire sort of yarn; I have no excuses for it and can think of no reasons for such a plot having unfolded itself to me. It isn't that I can't finish it up; far from it—all the plot factors tie themselves neatly together at the end and this with no effort on my part at all.

This can be demonstrated; it's the last chapter that bothers me. You see, I didn't write it. Either someone's playing a practical joke on me, or— No. I prefer to believe someone's playing a practical joke on me. Otherwise, this thing is just too horrible.

But about that demonstration: here's what happened:

Flick never quite recovered from the shock of seeing that sudden corpse. The careful services of the doctor were not required to show that the young lady was dead and Flick recovered himself enough to start asking questions.

It was Daniels who belatedly identified her as the nurse he had seen at the hospital the day Mrs. Stoye killed herself. The nurse's name was Lucille Holder; she had come from England as a girl; she had a flawless record abroad and in this country. The head doctor told the police, on later investigation, that he had always been amazed at the tremendous amount of work Miss Holder could turn out and had felt that inevitably some sort of a breakdown must come. She went all to pieces on Mrs. Stoye's death and he sent her on an immediate vacation.

Her movements were not difficult to trace after she left the administrative office, where she ascertained Mr. Daniels' address. She went first to his house and the only conclusion the police could come to was that she had done so on purpose to kill him. But he was not there: he, it seems, had been trying to find her at the hospital at the time! So she left. The following night she went out to Stoye's, rang the bell and killed him.

Ronnie followed her, apparently filled with the same unaccountable impulse, and was late. Miss Holder went then to Daniels' house and tried to kill him, but was shot by the policeman, just as Ronnie, late again, arrived.

Ronnie lay in a coma for eight weeks. The diagnosis was atypical brain-fever, which served as well as anything else. He remembered little, and that confused. He did, however, vouch for the nurse's visit to his home the night of Mrs. Stoye's death. He could not explain why he had kept it a secret from his father, nor why he had had the impulse to kill Mr. Stoye (he admitted this impulse freely and without any horror) nor how he had happened to think of finding Stoye's address through the information operator at the telephone company. He simply said that he wanted to get it without asking any traceable questions. He also admitted that when he found that Mr. Stoye had already been killed, he felt that he must secure another weapon and go and kill his father. He says he remembers thinking of it without any emotion whatsoever at the time, though he was appalled at the thought after he came out of the coma. "It's all like a story I read a

long time ago," he said. "I don't remember doing these things at all;
I remember seeing them done."

When the policemen shot Miss Holder, Ronnie felt nothing; the
lights went out and he knew nothing until eight weeks later.

These things remained unexplained to the participants:

Mrs. Stoye's disappearing body. The witnesses were the two Daniels
and Miss Holder. Miss Holder could not report it; Ronnie did not
remember it; Mr. Daniels kept his own counsel.

Lucille Holder's disappearing body. Daniels said nothing about
this either, and for the rest of his life tried to forget it. The members
of the homicide detail and the two prowl-car men tried to forget it,
too. It was not entered in the records of the case. It seemed to have
no bearing and all concerned were happy to erase it as much as
possible. If they spoke of it at all, it was in terms of mass hypnosis—
which was reasonably accurate, at that . . .

Lucille Holder's motive in killing Mr. Stoye and in trying to kill
Mr. Daniels. This could only be guessed at; it was simple to put it
down to the result of a nervous breakdown after overwork.

Mrs. Stoye's suicide. This, too, was attributed to a mounting
mental depression and was forgotten as quickly as possible.

And two other items must be mentioned. The radio patrolman
Sam was called on the carpet by Detective Lieutenant Flick for ineffi-
ciency in letting the boy Ronnie go. He was not punished, oddly
enough. He barely mentioned the corpse of Lucille Holder and that
there were witnesses to the fact that *apparently* the Lieutenant had
not seen it, though he had stepped right over it on the way into
Daniels' house. Flick swore that he was being framed, but let Sam
alone thereafter.

The other item has to do with Miss Jennie Beaufort, an operator in
the Information Office of the telephone company. Miss Beaufort won
a prize on a radio quiz—a car, a plane, two stoves, a fur coat, a
diamond ring, a set of SwingFree Shoulder pads and a 38-day South
American cruise. She quit her job the following day, took the cruise,
enjoyed it mightily, learned on her return that income tax was due
on the valuation of all her prizes, sold enough to pay the tax and was
so frightened at the money it took that she went back to work at her
old job.

So, you see, these tangled deaths, these mad actions, were all explained, forgotten, rationalized—made to fit familiar patterns, as were Charles Fort's strange lights and shapes in the night, as were the Flying Discs, the disappearance of Lord Bathhurst, the teleportation of Kaspar Hauser and the disappearance of the crew of the *Mary Celeste.*

I leave it to the reader to explain the following chapter. I found it by and in my typewriter yesterday afternoon (I'd been writing this story all the previous night). Physically, it was the most extraordinary looking manuscript I have ever seen. In the first place the paper bails had apparently been released most of the time and letters ran into each other and lines crossed and recrossed each other with wild abandon. In the second place there were very few capital letters; I was reminded of Don Marquis's heroic archy the cockroach, who used to write long effusions while Mr. Marquis was asleep, by jumping from one key to the other. But archy was not heavy enough to operate the shift key and so he eschewed the upper-case characters. In the third place, the spelling was indescribable. It was a mixture of phonetics and something like Speedwriting, or ABC shorthand. It begins this way:

> i mm a thngg wch livz n fantsy whr tru fantsy z fond n th mynz v mn.

I couldn't possibly inflict it all on you in its original form. It took me the better part of two hours just to get the pages in order—they weren't numbered, of course. After I plowed through it myself, I undertook a free translation. I have rewritten it twice since, finding more rhythm, more fluidity, each time, as I became familiar with the extraordinary idiom in which it was written. I think that as it now stands it closely follows the intent and mood of the original. The punctuation is entirely mine; I regard punctuation as inflection in print and have treated this accordingly, as if it were read aloud.

I must say this: there are three other people who could conceivably have had access to this machine while I was asleep. They are Jeff and Les and Mary. I know for a fact that Jeff, who is an artist, was busy the entire time with a nonobjective painting of unusual vividness and detail; I know how he works, and I know what the picture looked like when I quit writing for the night, and what it looked like when I woke up, and believe me, he must have been painting like mad the entire time—he and no one else. As for Les, he works in the advertising department of a book publisher and obviously has not the literary command indicated by this manuscript. And Mary—I am lucky enough to be able to say that Mary is very fond of me, and would be the last person in the world to present me with such a nasty jolt as is innate in this final chapter. Here it is; and please forgive me for this lengthy but necessary introduction to it, and for my intrusion; this sort of thing is strictly against the rules

8

" "

I am a Thing which lives in fantasy, where true fantasy lives in the minds of men.

What fumbling is this, what clumsiness, what pain . . . I who never was a weight, who never turned, coerced, nor pressed a person, never ordered, never forced—I who live with laughter, die with weeping, rise and hope and cheer with man's achievements, yet with failure and despair go numb and cold and silent and unnoticeable—what have I to do with agony?

Know me, mankind, know me now and let me be.

Know the worst. I feed on you. I eat and breathe no substance but a precious ether. No, not souls (but where a soul is strong and clean I live my best.) I take this guarded essence where I can and thrive on it; and when I choose a host I am imprisoned, for I may not leave him while he lives, and when he dies I must locate another to inhabit. And I have . . . powers.

But know this too: The thing that I take is the essence of joy—and in joy is created an excess of that which I need. I drink in your reservoir, yes; but when there is drought and the level is low and your needs are increased and the water turns bitter with flavors of worry, and anger, and fear, then I shrink and I soften, and lose all my hunger; and then if you grieve, if your spirit is broken, if you should forget all the pleasure and glory and wonder of being a man —then I die. . . .

Such a death is not death as you know it. It is more an encysting, a waiting unmoving within a soul's winter, to wake with the spring of the heart. But where people grieve over years, or let fear share their souls with me, then I must wait for the walls of my prison to crumble.

Then, after the death of my host I go drifting, seeking another. That is my Search, and in it, for me, is the ultimate cold. No human can know such a thing, for death, for a human, is kinder.

I am and I am not a parasite. I feed on your substance; yet what living thing in the world does not feed on the substance of others? And I take only excess—take only that which you radiate gaily when you feel joy.

When you feel otherwise, then I must wait, or must sleep, or must die. Where is the evil in being a parasite, when I take only a product which you never need? I demand only sustenance; that is the right of all living things. I ask in addition a thing which is simple enough—I ask to be left to myself, to encyst or to flower or sleep or be joyful, without any devilish probing.

I do not know how old I am; I do not know if there are others like me. I do not know how many hosts I have inhabited, or whether I was born or hatched, or whether, like a human, I must one day truly die. I shall, no doubt; I am alive, and nothing lives forever. I know my years are thousands, and my hosts have been in scores of hundreds. I have no interest in statistics.

Yet you must know me . . . I think my origins were like a plant's —an accidental seed of sensuality perhaps. My infancy was passed in dreams, in sightless stirrings when the stimulation merited, and blacknesses between. I think that when my hosts passed on, my knotted insubstantial cyst just drifted like a petal on a roiling stream, it bumped and nuzzled and at last slipped in when chance presented hosts which qualified.

To qualify, in those uncaring phases, men had but to show an openness and nothing more. And when I gained experience and consciousness increased, and realization came to me, and I was grown and had ability to choose, I gained as well the power of rejection. And after that I was no longer bound to sickly children, open to me through their thirst for colors, senses, odors, vivid to them through unsaid convictions that the end was near. I became increasingly meticulous in choosing; I became an expert in detecting signs of whimsy-richness in its earliest potential. I have powers . . .

You have powers too, you human ones. You can change the color of a life by vicious striking at a stranger-child. You can give away a thing you treasure, making memories which later might compose a symphony. You can do a thousand thousand things you never do; you never try; there is no reason to depart from paths you have established. When, however, circumstances force you into it, you do the "superhuman." Once my host was Annabelle, a woman on a farm. (She loved the birds!) In a blizzard she was lost; she was old and had a crippled knee, and could not find the road, and could not last the night. She stumbled on a post which stood erect and lonesome on the prairie, and, without a conscious thought of bravery, or what mankind might say of her, she put a hand upon the weathered wood, and in the blowing snow and bitter cold, she walked around the post—around, around, in spite of age and pain and growing numbness, walked around the post until the sun came up in blowing grey, then growing cold. They found her and they saved her, when in truth she saved herself. There was about her such a cloud of pure achievement, such a joy at having cheated wind and cold! (I fed that day; I still possess the energies she radiated!) . . . I have powers; all have powers, when we're forced to use them. I have powers, you have too, which you have never cataloged.

I have powers—now I use them!

I have no host. Such bitterness and agony as I have just experienced I never want again. My Search this time will be a thorough one and for it, now, I make my sacrifice. I am unknown; but with this script, these purposely hypnotic words, *I shall be known!* I sacrifice my privacy, my yearning for the pleasant weightless dark where I have dwelt. I challenge mankind's probing, for through these bright words and burnished continuities, I shall locate a host who will defend me!

I had a man—he had me, possibly—who would have fought for me. And after him I dwelt within a woman's mind—the richest and most magical of all. The man was one of those who, on maturing, never lost the colorful ability to wonder like a child. And one day, miming, imitating a precise and dainty minuet in joyful incongruity (he danced alone upon the bouncing platform of a truck) a falling girder struck him and he died. I had no warning and no way to make a Search; I flung myself into the mind of one who was nearby in close communion with my dead host's whimsy.

Grace had a mind that was magic throughout Never in thousands of years have I seen such a shimmering jewel; never in thousands of pages in words found in thousands of languages could such a trove be described. All that she saw was transmuted in sibilant subtleties; all that she heard was in breathtaking colors and shapes. What she touched, what she said, what she saw, what she felt, what she thought—these were all blended in joy.

She was the pinnacle; she was the source of the heady exuberant food which in flavor eclipsed my most radiant memories. She, like the blizzard of Annabelle—she was the suitable circumstance, bringing about the release of the powers I held all untried.

I stirred in her mind. I found I could reach out and touch certain sources of hunger—sights that she never had seen and sensations she never had turned to, things which should surely delight such a sensitive soul.

I found to my joy that with care I controlled them, the hungers for things I remembered in hosts less responsive. I practiced this skill as she broadened her life, and I led her to music and poems and thoughts which she never, perhaps, could have found by herself. She had every reason for happiness with all these riches, and I—oh, I gloried in bringing things to her, as many a gifted composer has brought a new music to some virtuoso.

But her husband was Stoye.

Stoye was a devil. He hated me for what I was before he could define it. His mind was quite as rich as hers, but something curbed it. Growing with her was impossible; he sensed with rare perception that a Thing had come to her, and since that Thing was not of him, he hated it. It mattered not to him that she was better for it. Brutally he turned away from sharing what I brought into his home. And she —I could not take her from him. How I tried! Poor treasure-trove, she was at last a battleground between that questing creature and myself. He hounded me through her, and I struck back by taking her to rare enchantments in which he could not share.

He was the first—the very first—of all the humans I have known, to recognize and to seek me out. This recognition was intolerable; all my life I have avoided it and lived in warm and secret joyfulness. He goaded me until I evidenced myself; I never realized I could make a human speak, but Grace spoke for me when she said that "It wants only to be let alone." She might as well have died right then and there for all the sustenance I got from her thereafter. I knew that she would kill herself; between us, her and me, there was a madness caught from Stoye.

Stoye put her, numb and docile, in the hospital. I started to encyst, for Grace's well was dry to me. I found a likely subject in the nurse, who seemed as sensitive as Grace (but lacked that fine capacity for whimsy) and I poised myself to make the change. While waiting, then, I thought of Stoye—and realized that, with Grace's death, he would not rest until he found me and destroyed me, either by attacking all my hosts, or if he learned the way of it, by closing minds against me by his printed propaganda. He had to be destroyed.

Grace killed herself; her one blind foolishness, her love for Stoye, and all her stupid thoughts that she had lost it, made her do it. I might have stopped her; but why should I, when I needed a release from all her bitterness? Believe me, it was just as strong as all her joys had been . . . before she leaped she tried to warn him, tried to send some crazy message to him through a youngster standing down below. My connection with her was not close just then; I am not sure; she still was set on death as an escape but wished her husband to be watchful and protect himself. And then she leaped.

And then it came—that awful amputation.

I could not know that Ronnie was so strong a host, potentially— that so well suited to me was he that, as I flashed upward to the nurse, to take possession, I was torn apart!

I have no substance; yet I am an entity, with limits and with boundaries. These were ruptured; while my greater part found room within the nurse's mind, a fragment nestled into Ronnie's.

At first I felt a transcendental pain and dizziness; and then I did the things I could to be protected. I hid the crumpled body with a forced hypnotic wave (this is no subtle mystery; a thousand men can do it) to keep the wave of terror all confused with curiosity, for terror undiluted quite inhibits my possession of a host.

I settled into Lucille Holder's mind and tested the controls which Stoye had forced me to develop. Lucille was far less strong than Grace had been and forcing her was easy. I was wounded, I was maddened and at last I drank, with purpose and a new dark joy, the thing called hate.

Stoye had to die. The man called Daniels, Ronnie's father, saw Grace leap and was a witness. Possibly he might become too curious, with his son possessed, and be another probing devil. He must die. Ronnie had a part of me, and I did not think he could release it while he lived. So he must die.

To test my new controls, I sent the nurse at first to do the minor task. The elder Daniels was not there; and when I found myself confronted with that other part of me, I nearly died of yearning. And I realized, in that closeness, that the boy could be controlled as well, and that he could destroy his father quite at my convenience, while Lucille could kill him later. Satisfied, I went away.

I spent that night and all next day securing my controls and practicing. And late the night that followed I killed Stoye, and two strange things happened.

One was when Stoye died; I felt a wave of powerful protectiveness about him as he fled his body, and I sensed again the fullest, richest magic that was Grace. I was terrified of it; I had never known before that humans could outlive their carcasses . . .

The other thing was the arrival of Ronnie, apparently moved by the part of me carried within him. Yet since he possessed but a fragment, his effort was late and his motive was weak, and I feared that he might make a botch of the killing of Daniels, I therefore sent Lucille to do it; Ronnie, again weak and tardy, followed my orders.

The gunshot, the bullet which shattered the neck of the nurse, were quite unexpected. I was flung unprepared into cold, in my nakedness, cold indescribable, cold beyond bearing. Yet I was glad; for the fraction of me that was Ronnie's came streaming toward me as I was exploded away from the nurse. The wrench it gave Ronnie must have been dreadful; when I settle into a host all my roots go down deep.

I hid Lucille's body and searched all the minds in the house for a suitable host. Ronnie was perfect, unconscious and closed. Daniels was fretful; I can't abide fear. I fought back the cold, drew inward, contracted, and formed, at long last, a new cyst. I let Lucille's body be seen and ignoring the others—their whimsy was flat as their oversized feet—I withdrew.

And I have been thinking.

Some things were important that now cannot matter. I am different because of the searchings of Stoye—I blame him for all that has happened, and that is a thing which can no longer matter. I know how to hate now and how to make murder; the taste of these things is still bitter, but so is the taste of good stout when first taken and stout has a taste worth acquiring. Like Grace, I still have all my earlier qualities—the sun on a mountain or watching the curve of the wing of a gull (through a host) certainly has all the zest for me that it has ever had. Now I have more, though; and that is a thing which can matter very much, indeed.

I have been selfish. It never occurred to me, back in the days of the man who did minuets joyfully, that I might do something *for* him whom I choose as a host. Grace taught me that, purely by feeding me richly through her experiences, purely by being a subject for my schooled suggestions. There may have been many who carried me, who were susceptible to my control. I could not know without trying, and I never tried this command until Grace took me in. And since then I hunger, I thirst for the richness and beauty and shifting and changing of colors and sounds which she brought me, and never again will rest and be fed and be happy to have just enough to sustain me.

I drift, now, encysted, but testing my powers when never before had I thought of them. I find I am mobile; also to certain degrees, I can move things—this writing machine, for example, though it is slow and laborious. I find I can whisper to humans and fit some strange thoughts and ideas to each other.

I have looked for a host for a weary, cold while, and my energies seem to be dwindling. I still have enough, though, to search for a time, and soon now I'll have what I need.

I'll find, soon, a person, a man or a woman, or even a sensitive child. This one will be mine and I'll lead him to wonders of sense and of music and heady adventure. I think I am learning to savor the tartness of terror, the bloody salt flavor of killing with purpose. My host will exist in a series of colorful pageants and move in a world of emotional riches, all of my carefullest choosing.

And for this I sacrifice that which I guarded—my passion for quiet and secret enjoyments. I say to you, Know me! Suspect me! for by your suspicion you open yourself to my coming. And when some great mural is painted by someone who never did passable work in his life before that, suspect me. And when in a prison some cringing psychotic says, over and over, "A voice said to do it!" suspect me. Whenever you walk in the street and feel a strange spasm of nausea, suspect me indeed; for then I am injured and what you have seen is a part-host like Ronnie; and know that that person must die—and can kill if I will it, and might kill in ways which afford me enjoyment.

I am so cold . . .

I write this because in my search for a host who is perfect, I find that one segment of humans is almost entirely open. These are the readers and tellers of tales of the dark and of terror and madness. The one who has written these chapters would serve as a host—but I fear he would turn on me, feed on my memories, use me for piddling profit in plying his trade. Besides, he's a bit superficial for one of my tastes. I know his intentions, however, and what he will do with this script. I know he is frightened because of the way this long tale has unfolded. I know, too, that nothing will keep him from seeing it printed. When it is read, though, by thousands of like-minded people all over the world and he hears of the music and murder created by someone who fell to me only through reading it, then he will curse and will wish he were dead, and wish he had torn this to pieces.

The early days of *Weird Tales* were difficult ones, both financially and in terms of editorial direction. After a dozen issues, the magazine's initial incarnation came to an end with the April 1924 number: Vol. 3, No. 4. There was no Volume 4, No. 1, but the next issue, dated May-June-July 1924 (Vol. 4, No. 2) was a mammoth three-in-one Anniversary Issue, a 192-page bargain at half-a-dollar a copy.

Perhaps the best statement ever published of the *Weird Tales* editorial policy appeared in that giant issue. "Why *Weird Tales?*", though unsigned, is reliably attributed to Otis Adelbert Kline, a frequent contributor to the magazine who performed key editorial duties in the preparation of the 1924 Anniversary Issue. In addition to the reprinting below, "Why *Weird Tales?*" reappeared in the magazine's March 1934 issue and in Robert Weinberg's history *The Weird Tales Story* (Fax Collector's Editions, Inc., 1977).

WHY WEIRD TALES

Attributed to Otis Adelbert Kline

Up to the day the first issue of *Weird Tales* was placed on the stands, stories of the sort you read between these covers each month were taboo in the publishing world. Each magazine had its fixed policy. Some catered to mixed classes of readers, most specialized in certain types of stories, but all agreed in excluding the genuinely weird stories. The greatest weird story and one of the greatest short stories ever written, *The Murders in the Rue Morgue,* would not have stood the ghost of a show in any modern editorial office previous to the launching of *Weird Tales.* Had Edgar Allan Poe produced that masterpiece in this generation he would have searched in vain for a publisher before the advent of this magazine.

And so every issue of this magazine fulfills its mission, printing the kind of stories you like to read—stories which you have no opportunity of reading in other periodicals because of their orthodox editorial policies.

We make no pretension of publishing, or even trying to publish, a magazine that will please everybody. What we have done, and will continue to do, is to gather around us an ever-increasing body of readers who appreciate the weird, the bizarre, the unusual—who recognize true art in fiction.

The writing of the common run of stories today has, unfortunately for American literature, taken on the character of an exact science. Such stories are entirely mechanical, conforming to fixed rules. A good analogy might be found in the music of the electric piano. It is technically perfect, mechanically true, but lacking in expression. As is the case with any art when mechanics is permitted to dominate, the soul of the story is crushed—suffocated beneath a weight of technique. True art—the expression of the soul—is lacking.

The types of stories we have published and will continue to publish may be placed under two classifications. The first of these is the story of psychic phenomena or the occult story. These stories are written from three viewpoints: The viewpoint of the spiritualist who believes that such phenomena are produced by spirits of the departed; the scientist, who believes they are either the result of fraud, or may be explained by known, little-known or perhaps unknown phases of natural law; and the neutral investigator, who simply records the facts, lets them speak for themselves and holds no brief for either side.

The second classification might be termed "highly imaginative stories." These are stories of advancement in the sciences and the arts to which the generation of the writer who creates them has not attained. All writers of such stories are prophets, and in the years to come, many of these prophecies will come true.

There are a few people who sniff at such stories. They delude themselves with the statement that they are too practical to read such stuff. We can not please such readers, nor do we aim to do so. A man for whom this generation has found no equal in his particular field of investigation, none other than the illustrious Huxley, wrote a suitable answer for them long ago. He said: "Those who refuse to go beyond fact rarely get as far as fact."

Writers of highly imaginative fiction have, in times past, drawn back the veil of centuries, allowing their readers to look at the wonders of the present. True, these visions were often distorted, as by a mirror with a curved surface, but just as truly were they actual reflections of the present. It is the mission of *Weird Tales* to find present-day writers who have this faculty, so that our readers may glimpse the future—may be vouchsafed visions of the wonders that are to come.

Looking back over the vast sea of literature that has been produced since man began to record his thoughts, we find two types predominating—two types that have lived up to the present and will live on into the future: the weird story and the highly imaginative story. The greatest writers of history have been at their best when producing such stories: Homer, Shakespeare, Milton, Dante, Irving, Hawthorne, Poe, Verne, Dickens, Maeterlinck, Doyle, Wells and scores of other lesser lights. Their weird and highly imaginative stories will live forever.

Shakespeare gave forceful expression to the creed of writers of the weird and highly imaginative when he wrote the oft-quoted saying: "There are more things in Heaven and Earth, Horatio, than are dreamt of in your philosophy."

The writer of the highly imaginative story intuitively knows of the existence of these things and endeavors to search them out. He has an unquenchable thirst for knowledge. He is at once the scientist, the philosopher and the poet. He evolves fancies from known facts and new and startling facts are in turn evolved from the fancies. For him, in truth, as for no other less gifted, "Stone walls do not a prison make." His ship of imagination will carry him the four thousand miles to the center of the earth, *Twenty Thousand Leagues Under the Sea,* on a journey to another planet millions of miles distant, or on a trip through the universe, measured only in millions of light-years, with equal facility. Material obstacles can not stay his progress. He laughs at those two bogies which have plagued mankind from time immemorial, time and space: things without beginning and without end, which man is vainly trying to measure; things that have neither length, breadth nor thickness, yet to which men would ascribe definite limits.

To the imaginative writer the upper reaches of the ether, the outer limits of the galactic ring, the great void that gapes beyond and the infinity of universes that may, for all we know, lie still further on, are as accessible as his own garden. He flies to them in the ship of his imagination in less time than it takes a bee to flit from one flower to another on the same spike of a delphinium.

Some of the stories now being published in *Weird Tales* will live forever. Men in the progressive ages to come will wonder how it was possible that writers of the crude and uncivilized age known as the Twentieth Century could have had foreknowledge of the things that will have, by that time, come to pass. They will marvel, as they marvel even now at the writings of Poe and Verne.

It has always been the human desire to experience new emotions and sensations without actual danger. A tale of horror is told for its own sake and becomes an end in itself. It is appreciated most by those who are secure from peril.

Using the term in a wide sense, horror stories probably began with the magnificent story of the *Writing on the Wall at Belshazzar's Feast.* Following this were the *Book of Job,* the legends of the *Deluge* and the *Tower of Babel* and *Saul's Visit to the Woman of Endor.* Byron once said the latter was the best ghost story ever written.

The ancient Hebrews used the element of fear in their writings to spur their heroes to superhuman power or to instill a moral truth. The sun stands still in the heavens that Joshua may prevail over his enemies.

The beginning of the English novel during the middle of the Eighteenth Century brought to light Fielding, Smollett, Sterne and several others. Since this time terror has never ceased to be used as a motive in fiction. This period marked the end of the Gothic romance whose primary appeal was to women readers. Situations fraught with terror are frequent in *Jane Eyre.* The Brontes, however, never used the supernatural element to increase tension.* Theirs are the terrors of actual life. Wilkie Collins wove elaborate plots of hair-raising events. Bram Stoker, Richard Marsh and Sax Rohmer do likewise. Conan Doyle realized that darkness and loneliness place us at the mercy of terror and he worked artfully on our fear of the unknown. The works of Rider Haggard combine strangeness, wonder, mystery and horror, as do those of Verne, Hichens, Blackwood, Conrad and others.

Charles Brockden Brown was the first American novelist to introduce supernatural occurrences and then trace them to natural causes. Like Mrs. Radcliffe, he was at the mercy of a conscience which forbade him to introduce spectres in which he himself did not

---

* Kline here overlooks *Wuthering Heights.* —M.K.

believe. Brown was deeply interested in morbid psychology and he took delight in tracing the working of the brain in times of emotional stress. His best works are *Edgar Huntly, Wieland* and *Ormond.*

The group of "Strange Stories by a Nervous Gentleman" in *Tales of a Traveller* proves that Washington Irving was well versed in ghostly lore. He was wont to summon ghosts and spirits at will but could not refrain from receiving them in a jocose, irreverent mood. However, in the *Adventure of the German Student* he strikes a note of real horror.

Hawthorne was not a man of morose and gloomy temper. An irresistible impulse drove him toward the somber and gloomy. In his notebook he says: "I used to think that I could imagine all the passions, all the feelings and states of the heart and mind, but how little did I know! Indeed, we are but shadows, we are not endowed with real life, but all that seems most real about us is but the thinnest shadow of a dream—till the heart be touched."

The weird story of *The Hollow of the Three Hills,* the gloomy legend of *Ethan Brand* and the ghostly *White Old Maid* are typical of Hawthorne's mastery of the bizarre. His introduction of witches into *The Scarlet Letter* and of mesmerism into *The Blithedale Romance* shows that he was preoccupied with the terrors of magic and of the invisible world.

Hawthorne was concerned with mournful reflections, not frightful events. The mystery of death, not its terror, fascinated him. He never startled you with physical horror, save possibly in *The House of the Seven Gables.* With grim and bitter irony Hawthorne mocks and taunts the dead body of Judge Jaffery Pyncheon until the ghostly pageantry of the dead Pyncheons—including at last Judge Jaffery himself with the fatal crimson stain on his neckcloth—fades away with the coming of daylight.

Edgar Allan Poe was penetrating the trackless regions of terror while Hawthorne was toying with spectral forms and "dark ideas." Where Hawthorne would have shrunk back, repelled and disgusted, Poe, wildly exhilarated by the anticipation of a new and excruciating thrill, forced his way onward. Both Poe and Hawthorne were fascinated by the thought of death. The hemlock and cypress overshadowed Poe night and day and he describes death accompanied by its direct physical and mental agonies. Hawthorne wrote with finished perfection, unerringly choosing the right word; Poe experimented with language, painfully acquiring a studied form of expression which was remarkably effective at times. In his *Masque of the Red Death* we are forcibly impressed with the skillful arrangement of words, the alternation of long and short sentences, the use of repetition and the deliberate choice of epithets.

But enough of Poe. His works are immortal and stand today as the most widely read of any American author. The publishers of *Weird Tales* hope they will be instrumental in discovering or uncovering some American writer who will leave to posterity what Poe and Hawthorne have bequeathed to the present generation. Perhaps in the last year we have been instrumental in furnishing an outlet to writers whose works would not find a ready market in the usual channels. The reception accorded us has been cordial and we feel that we will survive. We dislike to predict the future of the horror story. We believe its powers are not yet exhausted. The advance of science proves this. It will lead us into unexplored labyrinths of terror and the human desire to experience new emotions will always be with us.

Doctor Frank Crane says: "What I write is my tombstone." And again—"As for me, let my bones and flesh be burned and the ashes dropped in the moving waters, and if my name shall live at all, let it be found among books, the only garden of forget-me-nots, the only human device for perpetuating this personality."

So *Weird Tales* has endeavored from its inception and will endeavor in the future to find and publish those stories that will make their writers immortal. It will play its humble but necessary part in perpetuating those personalities that are worthy to be crowned as immortals.

MISCELLANEOUS NOTES

"THE HOUSE OF ECSTASY" (pp. 3–11)

This tale appeared in the April 1938 issue of *Weird Tales*. Though its pulpish exploitation of "the powers of hypnosis" seems naïve today, it is still a clever attempt to involve the actual reader as the tale's protagonist. To augment the effect and make its bizarre events seem timely, Ralph Milne Farley's third paragraph originally read, "To begin with, where were you at eight o'clock on that warm evening of August 4, 1937?" To preserve the author's intent, I deleted that long-gone year in favor of the phrase "last summer."

It is interesting to compare "The House of Ecstasy" with Theodore Sturgeon's "The Perfect Host," found on page 521, which employs quite different methods to achieve a similar effect.

"THE SORCERER'S APPRENTICE" (pp. 31–32)

It seems to me that this simple plot is essentially a cautionary tale warning against hubris, that overweening pride that made Prometheus challenge the gods. In Lucian's story, the sorcerer merely quits his untrustworthy disciple in disgust, but in the Goëthe adaptation, the apprentice is forcibly ejected from the wizard's domain—which virtually reshapes the myth into a whimsical variation on the expulsion of humanity from the Garden of Eden.

"THE LEGEND OF ST. JULIAN THE HOSPITALLER" (pp. 179–203)

In spite of its title and climactic "miracle," this tale appears to be a humanist's jaundiced view of the beatific process, inasmuch as it is obtained only through elaborate bloodshed and the suffering of the innocent. Though one *Weird Tales* author, E. Hoffmann Price, says that editor Farnsworth Wright tried "to avoid any pointed offense against sincere religious conviction," Price also states that Wright "admired the iconoclastic approach." After waiting six trepidatious months, Wright ran Price's then-daring dialogue between Christ and Satan, "The Stranger in Kurdistan," in July 1925 and reprinted it in December 1929, during which time the Flaubert piece appeared (in April 1928), as well as Leonid Andreyeff's staggeringly unorthodox redaction of the New Testament tale of "Lazarus" (in March 1927). Also compare Val Lewton's "The Bagheeta" (July 1930), found on page 292.

"SEED" (pp. 212–26)

When I read the climactic revelation of "Seed," it instantly reminded me of the final moments of Roger Corman's film *The Little Shop of Horrors,* the ending of which was also utilized in the Off-Broadway musical of the same name, though not in the recent motion picture of that show. While it is conceivable that Charles Griffith, screenwriter of the Corman movie, may have read Snow's story, which ran in *Weird Tales* fourteen years before the original *Little Shop of Horrors* was shot (in two days!), it is equally possible that Snow was familiar with "The Seeds of Death" by David H. Keller, M.D., a horror story with a very similar plot gimmick to "Seed." The Keller story appeared in *Weird Tales* in June/July 1931.

"THE DAMP MAN" (pp. 332–66)

This strange Allison V. Harding chiller—published in July 1947 during Dorothy McIlwraith's editorship—was immediately followed in September 1947 by a sequel, "The Damp Man Returns." The second tale's lively plot tells a great deal more about the titular antagonist; this unfortunately vitiates much of the original story's eeriness, but at least the melodramatic *ex machina* resolution "dries out" the Damp Man for good—or so it seems. But two years later, *Weird Tales'* May 1949 cover story was titled "The Damp Man Again." In it, the heroic reporter George Pelgrim sifts through the deceased villain's papers and reads about his pathetic, violent early life. "The Damp Man Again" is an odd, essentially static composition that yet rewards the patient reader with sensitive and compassionate character exploration—and a twist ending that suggests that if the author had lived, she might have continued the saga of Lother Remsdorf, Jr.

"CHICKEN SOUP" (pp. 445–50)

Coauthor Katherine MacLean says that "Chicken Soup" was partly written to boost Mary Kornbluth's spirits shortly after the death of her writer-husband, science fiction author C. M. Kornbluth, but editorial trepidation that the story might be construed as anti-Semitic delayed its acceptance; it finally appeared in the Winter 1973 revival issue of *Weird Tales.*

How anything in "Chicken Soup" can be construed as the least bit anti-Semitic is puzzling. This amused, amusing, affectionate portrait of an old-school matriarch would be equally valid if Grandma were Italian, Pennsylvania Dutch or Japanese. The only passage that may require explanation is the question Herbie asks, "Did a priest let its blood on an altar?" Grandma is understandably shocked: the laws of kosher cooking decree that slaughtered animals must be killed as humanely as possible and as for blood, it is as strictly forbidden to be ingested as pig flesh. Presumably Herbie is an apostatic member of the younger generation, but once Grandma and his mother consult the marriage broker, he probably won't stand much chance against tradition . . . but would *you* want *your* grandson to dance naked with the goats?

RECOMMENDATIONS FOR FURTHER READING

Anthologies by Marvin Kaye

It has been persuasively claimed that *Weird Tales* is the magazine more frequently consulted by anthologists than any other American periodical. In my own earlier collections, I certainly utilized this source. The stories I used and the issues they come from are listed below.

Ghosts: a Treasury of Chilling Tales Old & New (Doubleday, 1981), contains three *Weird Tales* stories:

• "Legal Rites," a comical western ghost story by Isaac Asimov and Frederik Pohl, was published in the September 1950 issue (Vol. 42, No. 6), with Pohl employing a pen name, James MacCreigh.

• "The Old Nurse's Story," a chilling tale of a child ghost by Elizabeth Gaskell, was the Weird Tales Reprint in the October 1927 issue (Vol. 10, No. 4).

• "The Tale of the German Student," a gruesome horror story by Washington Irving, was published as the February 1927 (Vol. 9, No. 2) Weird Tales Reprint, but appeared under an alternate title, "The Lady of the Velvet Collar."

Masterpieces of Terror and the Supernatural: A Treasury of Spellbinding Stories Old & New (Doubleday, 1985), includes nine *Weird Tales* selections:

• "Dracula's Guest," the posthumous prologue to the famous vampire novel by Bram Stoker, was the Weird Tales Reprint for December 1927 (Vol. 10, No. 6).

• "His Unconquerable Enemy," the Weird Tales Reprint for August 1929 (Vol. 14, No. 2), is a hideous tale of dismemberment, insanity and revenge.

• "Lazarus," a bleak nihilistic variant of the Biblical story, was the Weird Tales Reprint for March 1927 (Vol. 9, No. 3); its author's name was accorded an odd transliterative spelling: Leonid Andreyeff.

• "The Music of Erich Zann" by H. P. Lovecraft, a tale of cosmic terror that reads like a newly discovered manuscript by Edgar Allan Poe, first appeared in May 1925 (Vol. 5, No. 5) and again, as the *Weird Tales* Reprint, in November 1934 (Vol. 24, No. 5).

• "Night and Silence" by Grand Guignol writer Maurice Level (the pseudonym, according to the Library of Congress, of Jeanne Mareteux-Level) was published in February 1932 (Vol. 19, No. 2).

• "The Night Wire" by H. F. Arnold, first appeared in September 1926 (Vol. 8, No. 3) as a back-of-the-magazine filler. Editor Farnsworth Wright later admitted he underestimated its power and should have made it the cover story. One of the most popular stories ever to appear in *Weird Tales,* "The Night Wire" was reprinted in January 1933 (Vol. 21, No. 1).

• "The Professor's Teddy Bear," one of Theodore Sturgeon's most justly famous horror stories, was printed in March 1948 (Vol. 40, No. 3).

• "The Vengeance of Nitocris," the first published tale of Tennessee Williams, is, according to the author, the true tale of an Egyptian queen's revenge on those subjects who murdered her royal brother. Williams was sixteen when he made the sale; the story, bylined Thomas Lanier Williams, ran in August 1928 (Vol. 12, No. 2).

• "When the Clock Strikes," a bizarre retelling by Tanith Lee of the Cinderella myth, appeared in the first of Lin Carter's four Zebra Books *Weird Tales* editions: Spring 1981 (Vol. 48, No. 1).

Devils and Demons: A Treasury of Fiendish Tales Old & New (Doubleday, 1987), contains eight *Weird Tales* choices:

• "The Burial of the Rats," a long suspense narrative by Bram Stoker, was the Weird Tales Reprint for September 1928 (Vol. 12, No. 3).

• "The Devilish Rat," a black comedy by Edward Page Mitchell (but erroneously attributed to "Albert Page Mitchell"), was in the last issue of the four Leo Margulies/Sam Moskowitz *Weird Tales* revivals: Spring 1974 (Vol. 47, No. 4).

• "Enoch" is a grisly short story by—and one of the personal favorites of—Robert Bloch, author of *Psycho.* It first appeared in *Weird Tales* in September 1946 (Vol. 39, No. 7).

• "The Graveyard Rats" marked the debut of one of *Weird Tales'* finest authors, Henry Kuttner; the nightmarish short story was published in March 1936 (Vol. 27, No. 3).

• "The Hound" is the third tale that H. P. Lovecraft sold to *Weird Tales,* a gory effort that first appeared in February 1924 (Vol. 3, No. 2) and was reprinted in September 1929 (Vol. 14, No. 3).

• "The Imitation Demon" was published in the final issue of the original run of the magazine: September 1954 (Vol. 46, No. 4). It is a clever deal-with-the-devil tale by Robert Kuttner.

• "Markheim," sometimes called a five-finger exercise for *Dr. Jekyll and Mr. Hyde,* is the only Robert Louis Stevenson story to appear in the periodical. It was the Weird Tales Reprint for April 1927 (Vol. 9, No. 4).

OTHER ANTHOLOGIES

Avid collectors regularly "scare up" original issues of *Weird Tales* in second-hand book shops, via mail order and on the dealer tables at fantasy and science fiction conventions throughout the world. Since single copies are pricey and become more so for older issues, a more economical alternative is to purchase other anthologies that include selections from America's weirdest magazine. Though most of the latter are also out of print, they are generally easier to find by way of used-book suppliers:

Great Tales of Terror and the Supernatural (Modern Library, 1944), edited by Herbert Wise and Phyllis Fraser, has many treasures, notably two of H. P. Lovecraft's best stories, "The Rats in the Walls" and "The Dunwich Horror."

Not at Night, a once popular British series, was mostly culled from the U.K. editions of *Weird Tales.*

Weird Tales (Pyramid Books, 1964), edited by Leo Margulies, has the following contents: "A Question of Etiquette" (September 1942) by Robert Bloch; "The Body-masters" (February 1935) by Frank Belknap Long; "The Drifting Snow" (February 1939) by August Derleth; "The Man Who Returned" (February 1934) by Edmond Hamilton; "Pigeons from Hell" (May 1938; reprinted November 1951) by Robert E. Howard; "The Sea-witch" (December 1937; reprinted July 1953) by Nictzin Dyalhis; "Spider Mansion" (September 1942) by Fritz Leiber; "The Strange High House in the Mist" (October 1931) by H. P. Lovecraft.

Worlds of Weird (Pyramid Books, 1965), edited by Leo Margulies, includes the following stories: "Giants in the Sky" (August 1939) by Frank Belknap Long; "He That Hath Wings" (July 1938) by Edmond Hamilton; "Mother of Toads" (July 1938) by Clark Ashton Smith; "Roads" (January 1938) by Seabury Quinn; "The Sapphire Goddess" (February 1934) by Nictzin Dyalhis; "The Thing in the Cellar" (March 1932) by David H. Keller, M.D.; "The Valley of the Worm" (February 1934) by Robert E. Howard.

Weird Tales (Spearman, 1976), edited by British anthologist Peter Haining, has, in addition to an introduction and a selection of ongoing features such as reader letters and the column, "Weirdisms," the following stories from the 1930s through 1950s: "Bang! You're Dead!" (September 1944) by Ray Bradbury; "The Beasts of Barsac" (July 1942) by Robert Bloch; "Beyond the Phoenix" (October 1938) by Henry Kuttner; "Beyond the Wall of Sleep" (March 1938) by H. P. Lovecraft; "Black Hound of Death" (November 1936) by Robert E. Howard; "The Black Monk" (October 1938) by G. G. Pendarves; "Cellmate" (January 1947) by Theodore Sturgeon; "Displaced Person" (September 1948) by Eric Frank Russell; "The Familiars" (January 1947) by H. P. Lovecraft; "From the Vasty Deep" (July 1949) by H. Russell Wakefield; "Frozen Beauty" (February 1938) by Seabury Quinn; "The Garden of Adompha" (April 1938) by Clark Ashton Smith; "Heart of Atlantan" (September 1940) by Nictzin Dyalhis; "The Little Red Owl" (July 1951) by Margaret St. Clair; "The Man Who Returned" (February 1934) by Edmond Hamilton; "Ooze" by Anthony M. Rud (Haining's contents page assigns this to the January 1952 issue, but this was a Weird Tales Reprint; "Ooze" is an often-anthologized tale that originally appeared in March 1923, Vol. 1, No. 1, of *Weird Tales);* "The Passing of a God" (December 1938) by Henry S. Whitehead; "The Phantom Slayer" (January 1942) by Fritz Leiber; "Roman Remains" (March 1948) by Algernon Blackwood; "The Shot Tower Ghost" (September 1949) by Mary Elizabeth Counselman; "The Shuttered House" (April 1937) by August Derleth; "Take the Z-Train" (March 1950) by Allison V

Harding; "The Valley Was Still" (August 1939) by Manly Wade Wellman.

Weird Tales: Thirty-Two Unearthed Treasures, edited by Robert Weinberg, published by Outlet Books in early 1988 with the following contents: "A Square of Canvas" (April 1923; reprinted January 1952; reprinted Summer 1983) by Anthony M. Rud; "The Automatic Pistol" (May 1940) by Fritz Leiber; "Black Barter" (September 1943) by Robert Bloch; "The Black Stone Statue" (December 1937) by Mary Elizabeth Counselman; "Call Not Their Names" (March 1954) by Everil Worrell; "Carnaby's Fish" (July 1945) by Carl Jacobi; "The Case of Charles Dexter Ward" (a novel that originally ran in abridged form as a two-part serial in May and July 1941) by H. P. Lovecraft; "The Chain" (April 1928) by H. Warner Munn; "Charon" (January 1935) by Laurence J. Cahill; "Come and Go Mad" (July 1949) by Fredric Brown; "Dust of Gods" (August 1934) by C. L. Moore; "Evolution Island" (March 1927) by Edmond Hamilton; "Far Below" (June/July 1939) by Robert Barbour Johnson; "The Green Parrot" (July 1952) by Joseph Payne Brennan; "The Hairy Ones Shall Dance" (three-part serial in January, February and March 1938) bylined Gans T. Field, but attributed by Robert Weinberg to Manly Wade Wellman; "The Isle of Torturers" (March 1933) by Clark Ashton Smith; "Legal Rites" (September 1950) by Isaac Asimov and "James MacCreigh" (Frederik Pohl); "Let's Play 'Poison'" (November 1946) by Ray Bradbury; "The Loved Dead" (May/June/July 1924) by C. M. Eddy, Jr.; "Masquerade" (May 1942) by Henry Kuttner; "The Parasitic Hand" (November 1926; reprinted August 1934) by R. Anthony; "The Peeper" (March 1944) by Frank Belknap Long; "The Professor's Teddy Bear" (March 1948) by Theodore Sturgeon; "The Room of Shadows" (May 1936) by Arthur J. Burks; "Satan's Stepson" (September 1931) by Seabury Quinn; "The Shadow Kingdom" (August 1929) by Robert E. Howard; "The Shut Room" (April 1930) by Henry S. Whitehead; "Slaughter House" (July 1953) by Richard Matheson; "Something from Out There" (January 1951) by August Derleth; "The Wand of Doom" (October 1932) by Jack Williamson; "When the Green Star Waned" (April 1925; reprinted January 1929) by Nictzin Dyalhis; "The Will of Claude Ashur" (July 1947) by C. Hall Thompson.

FOR THE COMPLETIST

The Collector's Index to Weird Tales (Bowling Green State University Popular Press, 1985), by Sheldon Jaffery and Fred Cook, is an indispensable reference for the aficionado. It has, in addition to a preface, introduction, illustrations and useful appendices, an index to the contents of all but the two recent "California numbers," an issue by issue listing from March 1923 to Summer 1983; a listing of all stories arranged alphabetically by author; an index of all poets and verse that have appeared in The Unique Magazine and an alphabetical list of cover artists, including the issue and story illustrated.

The Weird Tales Story (Fax Collector's Editions, Inc., 1977), written and edited by Robert Weinberg, is a lavishly illustrated history and appreciation of the periodical and includes fascinating memorabilia by many *Weird Tales* contributors, including Robert Bloch, Edmond Hamilton, Robert Barbour Johnson, Frank Belknap Long, H. Warner Munn, E. Hoffmann Price and others.

AND STILL THEY COME . . .

Weird Tales—The Magazine That Never Dies has returned once more! The newest version, designed to represent the magazine that *Weird Tales* would be today if the editorial run had never ceased, boasts an excellent editorial staff consisting of George Scithers, four-time Hugo winner and former editor of *Amazing Stories* and *Isaac Asimov's Science Fiction Magazine;* author-critic-essayist Darrell Schweitzer and author-critic John Gregory Betancourt. The first issue, dated Spring 1988, represents Vol. 50, No. 1 and carries the cover banner "Sixty-fifth Anniversary Issue!" The popular author Gene Wolfe is featured within with no fewer than six tales and is ably backed up with short stories by Ramsey Campbell, Lloyd Arthur Eshbach, Felix C. Gotschalk, T. E. D. Klein, Tanith Lee, Darrell Schweitzer ("The Mysteries of the Faceless King", included in the present volume), Keith Taylor, F. Paul Wilson and Chet Williamson. The second issue features stories by Tanith Lee, Morgan Llywelyn, Brian Lamley, Nancy Springer and others.

To subscribe to the latest incarnation of *Weird Tales,* write for information to Terminus Publishing Co , Inc. P.O. Box 13418, Philadelphia, PA 19101.